The Complete Works of
WASHINGTON
IRVING

Herbert L. Kleinfield
General Editor

ASTORIA

Washington Irving

an engraving by H. B. Hall
from the bust by Ball Hughes
1835

ASTORIA,

OR
ANECDOTES OF AN ENTERPRIZE
BEYOND THE
ROCKY MOUNTAINS

Edited by

Richard Dilworth Rust

Twayne Publishers

Boston

1976

Published by Twayne Publishers

A Division of G. K. Hall & Co.

The Complete Works of Washington Irving

Volume XV

Library of Congress Cataloging in Publication Data

Irving, Washington, 1783–1859.
Astoria : or, Anecdotes of an enterprize beyond the Rocky Mountains.

(His The complete-works of Washington Irving)
Includes bibliographical references and index.
1. Astoria, Or.—History. 2. American Fur Company—History.
3. Overland journeys to the Pacific. 4. Voyages to the Pacific coast.
5. Astor, John Jacob, 1763–1848.
I. Rust, Richard Dilworth. II. Title.
F884.A8I78 1976   978'.02   75–44202
ISBN 0–8057–8507–8

ACKNOWLEDGMENTS

I am indebted to Professor Andrew B. Myers for providing the initial guidance in locating the various portions of the *Astoria* manuscript and for loaning me his excellent doctoral dissertation on *Astoria*. For permission to consult and make use of the manuscripts themselves, which provide the heart of this edition, I am grateful for the generosity and cooperation of Wilmer H. Kingsford; Irving B. Kingsford and family; Mrs. Virginia Johnson; Warren R. Howell of John Howell–Books; Kenneth A. Lohf, Librarian for rare books and manuscripts at Columbia University; Paul Rugen and staff of the Manuscript Division of The New York Public Library, Astor, Lenox and Tilden Foundations; C. Waller Barrett and the staff of the Manuscripts Department, University of Virginia Library; and Sleepy Hollow Restorations. For their help with various historical and technical problems connected with *Astoria,* I wish to thank Professors C. Hugh Holman, Michael Black, Edgeley W. Todd, Wayne R. Kime, Richard Cracroft, and Edgar I. Stewart. Henry A. Pochmann deserves special mention for his painstaking labors and wise guidance.

This project could hardly have been completed without generous financial assistance from various sources. The Center for Editions of American Authors of the Modern Language Association of America, through its grant from the National Endowment for the Humanities (National Foundation on the Arts and Humanities), furnished funds for materials, travel, and free working time. Additional financial assistance for travel has been provided by the University Research Council, the Smith Research Fund Committee, and the Arts and Sciences Travel Committee of the University of North Carolina. The Work-Study Program of the University of North Carolina made possible an editorial assistant for a summer. The University of North Carolina Department of English provided graduate assistants as well as a reduced load. And the university, through an NDEA Title IV summer fellowship, allowed me free working time.

Lastly, I am grateful to my mother for her confidence in me, and to my wife, Patricia, and my children, Beverly, Pamela, and David, for their help and patience.

R. D. R.

University of North Carolina

CONTENTS

CONTENTS

EDITORIAL APPENDIX

INDEX

ILLUSTRATIONS

FRONTISPIECE

Washington Irving
an Engraving by H. B. Hall
from the bust by Ball Hughes
1835

MAP

Overland route of the westbound Astorians under
Wilson Price Hunt, September 1810–February 1812,
and of eastbound Astorians under
Robert Stuart, June 1812–April 1813
(following page xxiv)

SCENES OF ASTORIA

Astoria in 1811, Michilimackinac,
Mandan Village and Buffalo-Hide Boats
(following page 234)

INTRODUCTION

Washington Irving's *Astoria, or Anecdotes of an Enterprize beyond the Rocky Mountains* (1836) is a history of John Jacob Astor's attempt to found a fur trading empire in the drainage area of the Columbia River, with detailed narratives of a voyage to the mouth of the Columbia by ship, a transmontane expedition to the Columbia, and a return expedition across the Rocky Mountains to St. Louis. More than just an account of the Pacific Fur Company from June, 1810, to December, 1813, when Fort Astoria was surrendered to the British, *Astoria* touches upon much of the Western history surrounding that brief period and gives, as Irving intended, "a body of information concerning the whole region beyond the Rocky Mountains, on the borders of Columbia River, comprising the adventures, by sea and land, of traders, trappers, Indian warriors, hunters, &c.; their habits, characters, persons, costumes, &c.; descriptions of natural scenery, animals, plants, &c., &c."[1]

While best known in the 1830's for his literary treatment of predominately European subject matter, Washington Irving had a long sustained interest in the American frontier. Beginning in September, 1803, at the age of twenty, Irving made several visits to Canada, where he "had seen much of the magnates of the North West Company, and of the hardy trappers and fur-traders in their employ, and had been excited by their stories of adventurous expeditions in the 'Indian country.'"[2] This interest was further stimulated by letters and conversations with Henry Brevoort, Jr., a close friend who was long in charge of Astor's Canadian fur trade,[3] and by Irving's youthful reading about Indians and the wilderness in works such as Baron Lahontan's *New Voyages to North-America*, Pierre de Charlevoix's *Journal of a Voyage to North-America*, and Nicholas Biddle's *History of the Expedition under the Command of Captains Lewis and Clark*. In 1814 Irving published two sketches on Indians in the *Analectic Magazine*. When he left America in 1815, according to Stanley T. Williams, he was "still reading frontier

---

1. From a letter dated October 29, 1834, quoted in Pierre M. Irving, *The Life and Letters of Washington Irving* (New York: G. P. Putnam, 1864), III, 62–63 (hereafter referred to as PMI).

2. "Letter from Washington Irving to Henry Rowe Schoolcraft, Esq.," *Literary World* 251 (1851), 408.

3. See *Letters of Henry Brevoort to Washington Irving*, ed. George S. Hellman (New York: G. P. Putnam's Sons, 1918), especially the letters for June 28, 1811, and January 18, 1833.

tales . . . and he had sent from Liverpool to Brevoort for more books on the Indians."[4] Three unpublished notebooks of 1817 and 1818 testify further to this interest in their references to Daniel Boone, Indian beliefs, and western animals.

Irving's rediscovery of the frontier came soon after his return to America in May, 1832, after an absence of seventeen years. Lionized as the most popular writer of America,[5] Irving arrived at a propitious time to write about native themes. Western expansion had accelerated, and the Jacksonian spirit of laissez-faire capitalism fostered an exuberance of financial speculation—in which Irving himself was soon to participate. Given the spirit of the times and Irving's curiosity, he seemed almost destined to have the opportunity in the fall of 1832 to see the frontier firsthand. A chance meeting by Irving and his companions with the Indian commissioner Henry L. Ellsworth resulted in a month-long tour of the Indian territory in what is now eastern Oklahoma. The initial literary result was Irving's journal account of his experience, which in rewritten form was published in the spring of 1835 as *A Tour on the Prairies*.

Thus when approached by John Jacob Astor, Washington Irving was ready and qualified to write a comprehensive work about the American West.[6] He had personal and vicarious knowledge of fur trappers and the West, and he had broad experience in writing varied types of "literary" history from *Diedrich Knickerbocker's History of New York* (1809) to *The History of the Life and Voyages of Christopher Columbus* (1828), *A Chronicle of the Conquest of Granada* (1829), and *The Companions of Columbus* (1831). Irving's motives for ultimately accepting the project were undoubtedly many: his attraction to the remote and adventurous aspects of Astor's enterprise, his long-held interest in the American frontier and its inhabitants, his present awareness of America and concern to write about American themes—stimulated by *A Tour on the Prairies* and the call for a national literature, his seeing in Astor's experiment how business enterprise can work hand in hand with national interest, his friendship with John Jacob Astor dating back to at least 1821, and his recognizing an opportunity to earn money with which to purchase a home on the Hudson River.

4. *The Life of Washington Irving*, 2 vols. (New York: Oxford University Press, 1935), II, 79 (hereafter cited as STW).

5. This opinion expressed in the *Western Monthly Magazine* 5 (1836), 685, echoes the general feeling of the time as discussed in STW, II, chap. XIX.

6. Although it is uncertain exactly when Astor first talked with Irving about the project, it was not long after Irving's return from his tour on the prairies (*Astoria*, Introduction, 3.24–25) and before September 15, 1834, by which time Astor had applied to him "repeatedly" in the matter (PMI, III, 60).

Paradoxically, although the Astorian enterprise was a business failure, Astor was anxious to be remembered for it and felt fortunate to have the story written by the best-qualified writer in America. Kenneth Wiggins Porter resolves this paradox by noting that, rather than be remembered as "the Landlord of New York," Astor wanted to be thought of as a "dreamer of empire,...[a] daring and constructive thinker on a large scale, defeated not by the weakness of his own plans but rather by the stars in their courses."[7] In terms of national history, as Irving intimates in the paragraph added in the Author's Revised Edition of *Astoria*, Astor's enterprise ultimately had considerable significance. It justified Jefferson's assertion, "On the waters of the Pacific, we can found no claim in right of Louisiana. If we claim that country at all, it must be on Astor's settlement near the mouth of the Columbia."[8]

As attractive as Astor's story may have seemed, Irving was not prepared to spend the time and labor necessary to examine all the documents related to the enterprise and to digest those especially relevant to the treatment he would be inclined to give it. Irving's choice for a research assistant to perform those labors was his nephew, Pierre Munro Irving, whom he had contemplated employing in 1827 to supervise the publication of *Columbus* in London. Finding the financial terms agreeable, the young lawyer returned to New York from Jacksonville, Illinois, in November, 1834, to begin work with the Astor materials.[9] His role was "to look over the various papers, letters, and journals in the possession of Mr. Astor, written by various persons who have been in his employ, to draw anecdotes and descriptions from him, and from Northwest traders who occasionally visit him; to forage among various works in French and English that have been published relative to these regions, and thus to draw together and arrange into some kind of form a great body of facts."[10] After he had examined and collated rele-

7. *John Jacob Astor: Business Man*, 2 vols. (Cambridge, Mass.: Harvard University Press, 1931), I, 243.

8. Jefferson to John Melish, Dec. 31, 1816, *The Writings of Thomas Jefferson*, ed. Albert Ellery Bergh (Washington, D.C.: Thomas Jefferson Memorial Association, 1907), XV, 94. The fulfillment of Jefferson's statement is explained in H. H. Bancroft's *Chronicles of the Builders of the Commonwealth* (San Francisco: History Company, 1891), I, 46: "It is safe to say that had not Mr. Astor moved in this matter as he did, had his plans been frustrated or his purpose delayed, the northern boundary of the United States might today be the forty-second parallel of latitude. Thus we see the momentous significance of this movement, which, though resulting disastrously to the projector, was pregnant with the most beneficial results to the nation."

9. PMI, III, 64. Astor was to pay Pierre $3,000, to which Irving later added $1,000. The only remuneration Washington Irving expected and received was from the sale of the book.

10. PMI, III, 63. See also the Introduction to *Astoria*, 4.4–11, and PMI, III, 60–61.

vant facts and anecdotes from manuscript materials, verbal reports, and printed narratives, Pierre was to prepare for his uncle a kind of lawyer's brief.[11] A probable example of the type of brief Pierre M. Irving wrote is this material on the back of MS p. 41 in Chapter XV (covering material at 100.43–106.25) written in what appears to be Pierre M. Irving's hand:

> On leaving the village of Charette, about 50 miles above St Charles, saw Daniel Boone—see Bradbury, p 16. Boone died in 1818—The next day saw Colter. See Lewis & Clark Vol II. p. 407, & Bradbury, p 17. A very interesting note in relation to him.—See also Bradbury—p 23–24, 25, 26—April 8th—arrived at Fort Osage—Bradbury—p 35–36. Had proceeded but a short distance from Fort Osage when Dorion beat his squaw. Bradbury—p 43. & also p 44. drowned buffaloes. April 17 arrived at Nodawa.

And again on the back of MS p. 34 in the same chapter (covering material at 96.6–17), also in Pierre M. Irving's hand and canceled presumably by Washington Irving, is the following:

> He must have succeeded in engaging several additional voyageurs as the boat carried 16 in all. Hunters he needed most to protect the party in passing the Sioux, no dependence being placed in the *valor* of the voyageurs.

When Washington Irving commenced working on the project by mid-May, 1835, he had before him books and notes he had collected himself;[12] the summaries, extracts, and outlines of materials Pierre M. Irving had provided; and selected letters, journals, and other documents given him by Mr. Astor. These last materials included a reworked and shortened version of Wilson Price Hunt's journal,[13] probably Hunt's

---

11. See "Irving to Schoolcraft" in the *Literary World,* p. 408.

12. Irving's unpublished letter to Henry R. Schoolcraft (at the Library of Congress) dated New York, May 25, 1835, suggests the kind of effort he made to obtain materials with which to enrich his narrative. Irving speaks of his curiosity to know more about Indians and "to embody some of their fast fading characteristics and traditions in our popular literature." He then requests from Schoolcraft "biographies, tales or sketches illustrative of Indian life, Indian character, and Indian mythology and superstitions."

13. While it is not certain that Irving used Hunt's manuscript journal, which is not extant, he did have access to a French translation of it which appeared in *Nouvelles Annales des Voyages de la Géographie et de l'Histoire* (Paris, 1821), vol. X. An English translation of that version is part of Appendix A in Philip Ashton Rollins' edition of *The Discovery of the Oregon Trail: Robert Stuart's Narratives of His Overland Trip Eastward from Astoria in 1812–13* (New York: Charles Scribner's Sons, 1935).

full travel notes (as suggested by Irving's reference at 227.16–17 to "the minutes of the expedition"), a reworking of Robert Stuart's journal entitled "Travelling Memoranda,"[14] the manuscript journal of Alfred Seton (a clerk in the Pacific Fur Company),[15] what Irving refers to as the "journal of Astoria" (328.24), Astor's letterbooks with copies of correspondence with Astorian leaders, sea captains, emissaries, and American politicians, and various business papers of the Pacific Fur Company. Furthermore, Astor called upon eyewitness participants in the enterprise to confer with Pierre and Washington Irving. Irving alludes to this oral testimony in a letter of October 8, 1835, in which he mentions "personal anecdotes, &c., to be gathered from individuals, actors in the scenes narrated";[16] and in mid-November he "suspended his labors, in expectation of the arrival of a person who had been a principal actor in the enterprise of Astoria, and from whom he was to get many personal anecdotes for the enriching of his work."[17] Although no persons are named, any number of former Astorians could have responded to requests for information. Ramsay Crooks, Alfred Seton, and George Ehninger were residents of New York at the time;[18] Wilson Price Hunt and Robert Stuart were both in contact with Astor; in 1835 old David Stuart was living with his nephew in Detroit; and, as Irving says in the Introductory Notice to *The Adventures of Captain Bonneville*, he talked with Captain B. L. E. Bonneville after the latter's return from trapping in the Rocky Mountains.

In addition to these sources, Irving tells of availing himself of "collateral lights" such as works by Lewis and Clark, Bradbury, Brackenridge, Long, Franchère, and Ross Cox to flesh out his narratives.[19]

14. As with Hunt's manuscript journal, Astor had Stuart's "Travelling Memoranda" published in *Nouvelles Annales des Voyages*, vol. X. Stuart's journal, with interpolated material from the "Travelling Memoranda," was published by Philip Ashton Rollins (*Discovery of the Oregon Trail*). The "Travelling Memoranda" was edited separately by Kenneth A. Spaulding in *On the Oregon Trail: Robert Stuart's Journey of Discovery* (Norman: University of Oklahoma Press, 1953).

15. Seton's manuscript journal is at Sunnyside, where it was discovered by Andrew B. Myers and discussed in his dissertation, "Washington Irving, Fur Trade Chronicler: An Analysis of *Astoria* with Notes for a Corrected Edition" (Ph.D. diss., Columbia University, 1964). Wayne R. Kime presents evidence that the journal was a source for *Astoria* in his article, "Alfred Seton's Journal: A Source for Irving's *Tonquin* Disaster Account," *Oregon Historical Quarterly* 71 (1970), 309–24.

16. PMI, III, 79.

17. PMI, III, 81.

18. Formerly a partner in the Astorian venture, Crooks in 1835 was president of the American Fur Company; Seton and Ehninger had been clerks who came to Astoria on board the *Beaver*.

19. The editions Irving probably relied on, some to a considerable extent, were [Nicholas Biddle], *History of the Expedition under the Command of Captains*

Additional books cited in the text are Jonathan Carver's *Travels Throughout the Interior Parts of North America* (Philadelphia, 1796) and an English translation of Louis Armand Lahontan's *New Voyages to North-America*, 2 vols. (London: H. Bonwicke, T. Goodwin, M. Wotton, B. Tooke, and S. Manship, 1703). Internal evidence plus references in Irving's "Notes for Astoria / 1835" (printed for the first time in the Editorial Appendix to the Twayne *Astoria*) point to the following as possible minor sources: Thomas L. McKenney, *Sketches of a Tour to the Lakes;* James Athearn Jones, *Tales of an Indian Camp*, 3 vols.; Zebulon Pike, *An Account of Expeditions to the Sources of the Mississippi, and through the Western Parts of Louisiana;* Capt. George Vancouver, *A Voyage of Discovery to the North Pacific Ocean and Round the World*, 3 vols.; Father Pierre Francois de Charlevoix, *Histoire et description générale de la Novelle-France* (probably read in translation); and Robert Southey, *History of Brazil*, 3 vols.[20]

A comparison of extant sources with Irving's text shows that he stayed as close as possible to his sources in regard to facts, but paraphrased or summarized the materials in his own style, giving to the whole work a degree of "unity so much sought after in works of fiction, and considered so important to the interest of every history."[21] Although Irving made a general acknowledgment of his sources in his Introduction, he rarely footnoted his exact obligations which were usually paraphrases such as the following.[22] The first passage is from Stuart's

Lewis and Clark, 2 vols. (Philadelphia: Bradford and Inskeep, 1814); John Bradbury, *Travels in the Interior of America, in the Years 1809, 1810, and 1811*(London: Sherwood, Neely, and Jones, 1817); Henry Marie Brackenridge, *Views of Louisiana; together with a Journal of a Voyage up the Missouri River, in 1811* (Pittsburgh: Cramer, Spear and Eichbaum, 1814); Edwin James, comp., *Account of an Expedition from Pittsburgh to the Rocky Mountains, Performed in the Years 1819, 1820 . . . under the Command of Major Stephen H. Long*, 2 vols. (Philadelphia: H. C. Carey and I. Lea, 1822–23); Gabriel Franchère, *Relation d'un Voyage à la Côte du Nord-ouest de l'Amérique Septentrionale, dans les Années 1810, 11, 12, 13, et 14* (Montréal: C. B. Pasteur, 1820); and Ross Cox, *Adventures on the Columbia River*, 2 vols. (London: H. Colburn and R. Bentley, 1831).

20. Andrew Myers in his Columbia dissertation first called attention to the Vancouver and Southey books as sources.

21. *Astoria*, 4.37–38.

22. Irving has eight footnote references to Lahontan, Carver, Lewis and Clark, Bradbury, and Brackenridge—all in the first twenty chapters. The wonder is not why Irving had so few footnotes but rather why he had any at all beyond the general acknowledgment in the Introduction, since in effect the whole work was derivative. For an examination of the extent and nature of Irving's use of his sources, see the notes in Edgeley Todd's *Astoria* (Norman: University of Oklahoma Press, 1964).

"Travelling Memoranda" for October 11, 1812; the second is Irving's version of it.[23]

> *Sunday 11th*—We ate the remainder of our old Buck meat, and went on at a smart pace 10 miles S.East, where taking up a small branch, in 9 more east found where Mr. McClellan had encamped and supped upon the carcase of a poor wolf the night before: being as near the spanish river mountain as we could find water, and the day too far advanced to ascend it, we stopped at the same place, and went to bed without supper—

> On the 11th they encamped on a small stream near the foot of the Spanish River Mountain. Here they met with traces of that wayward and solitary being, M'Lellan, who was still keeping on a head of them through these lonely mountains. He had encamped the night before on this stream; they found the embers of the fire by which he had slept, and the remains of a miserable wolf on which he had supped. It was evident he had suffered, like themselves, the pangs of hunger, though he had fared better at this encampment; for they had not a mouthful to eat.

As early as October, 1834, Irving had a general idea of what he wanted in *Astoria*, but he did not begin rough-casting various chapters until May, 1835.[24] In midsummer he interrupted his work to see *Legends of the Conquest of Spain* through the press; by August 24, though, he could write, "I am working away at the Astor enterprise, and hope to get the narrative in frame in the course of autumn; after which I shall have nothing to do but enrich it."[25] Soon after, Irving went to Astor's country estate on the upper part of Manhattan Island where he could have "profound quiet" and "perfect command" of time and self.[26] Because of these ideal conditions he could write on September 26, "Within the last month I have written more than a volume, and have got within half a dozen chapters of the end of my work—an achievement which I did not expect to do for months. Of course there will be much to be done afterward in extending some parts, touching up others, enriching and embellishing."[27]

Evidence in the manuscript of different kinds of paper,[28] parts of

23. Spaulding, *On the Oregon Trail*, pp. 112–13; *Astoria*, 284.32–40.
24. See his letter to Peter Irving of June 10, 1835, in PMI, III, 72.
25. PMI, III, 77.
26. PMI, III, 78; letter of September 26, 1835, to Peter Irving.
27. PMI, III, 78.
28. For a discussion of the kinds of paper used, see the Textual Commentary, p. 398.

manuscript leaves glued together, and dating on the backs of some leaves indicates that Irving did not fully anticipate at this time the kind of reorganization, revision, and rewriting he was later to do. Thus, while he said in a letter of December 25 that he hoped to finish "in the course of a few weeks,"[29] he was to continue at *Astoria* for another eight months.[30] Pierre M. Irving left Astor's estate on February 17, 1836, but Washington Irving continued to give the work a "last handling" which, he said, "like the touching and toning of a picture, gives the richest effects. I am interested and pleased with the work, and feel that the labor I am now bestowing upon it will contribute greatly to its success."[31] In this "last handling" Irving enriched the work with additional anecdotes, polished his writing, added specific details, and, perhaps most importantly, strove to give the overall work the best possible form. His striving for accuracy and specificity are apparent in the notebook "Astoria / 1835 / Memd; for Astoria," printed in the Editorial Appendix, and in these examples from the *Astoria* manuscript: at 239.18 he first wrote "a bay of the Columbia" and then altered that to "Baker's bay" and at 316.2 he altered "Indians" to "Neweetees." His efforts in structuring the work can be inferred from the frequent changes of manuscript page and chapter numbers and from the rearrangement of manuscript material by tearing and pasting or by rewriting.

In producing *Astoria,* Irving dealt not only with Carey, Lea, and Blanchard, the Philadelphia publishers, but also with Henry W. Rees, the New York printer and stereotyper. Thus Irving sent part of his manuscript directly to the printer in the spring, as indicated by the inscription on the first page of the manuscript for Chapter I: "Font

29. PMI, III, 83; letter dated December 25, 1835, to Peter Irving.

30. Evidence that he continued this work longer than has usually been thought is to be found in the dates on the backs of several manuscript leaves, which originally were drafts of letters Irving did not complete for one reason or another. These dates often appear on portions of leaves which were glued to other manuscript segments and indicate that the text on the reverse side was written after that particular date. These dates, followed in parentheses by the manuscript chapter and page numbers, are June 17, 1835 (XLIV.18/2); June 17, 1835 (XLIV.18/4); July 15, 1835 (XXV.16a); December, 1835 (XV.31); December 22, 1835 (XXIII.2); March 16, 1836 (XLIX.16); March 24, 1836 (XLIX.17); March 27, 1836 (XLVI.11); June 22, 1836 (XXVI.7); June, 1836 (XXVI.14); August 19, 1836 (LIII.5); August 22, 1836 [?] (XXVII.2). That Irving continued working on *Astoria* until at least August 22 is confirmed by a letter of that date to Albert Gallatin in which Astor requests permission to publish Gallatin's letter in the Appendix of *Astoria.* (This letter in the New-York Historical Society is transcribed by Andrew Myers, "An Analysis of *Astoria*," p. 71.)

31. PMI, III, 88; letter to Peter Irving, February 16, 1836.

Proof May 18."[32] Irving's interest in the production of his book is further shown in the letter fragment dated "New York, Aug 19th 1836," in which he says, "Gentlemen, What would be the costs of having an edition of the work I am about, printed in larger type." Irving's negotiations with both printer and publisher are clarified in Irving's letter of August 4, 1836, to Carey, Lea, and Blanchard.[33] In this letter he says that the first volume of *Astoria* is stereotyped and a third of the second volume is in type, and then he adds, "I have adopted your suggestion in printing it so that it may be published either in octavo or duodecimo."

Washington Irving continued to do what he called "re-dressing" of his text after it had been set in print as evidenced by a number of variations in text between the manuscript used as printer's copy and the published edition, particularly at 328.18–23, 329.29–33, 341.24–26, 353.1–8, and 355.29–356.5. And added to the text, presumably at a late stage, were the Introduction, the materials in the Appendix, and a map depicting the routes of Hunt and Stuart. How much Irving had to do with the map is not clear, although a letter quoted by John F. McDermott indicates that in September, 1835, Irving solicited Captain Bonneville's maps of the Rocky Mountains for his use in writing about *Astoria*.[34] Furthermore, a comparison of the map used in the 1837 edition of *The Rocky Mountains* (*The Adventures of Captain Bonneville*) with that in the 1836 *Astoria* supports Edgeley Todd's presumption that "Irving—or whoever made the *Astoria* map for him—relied heavily upon the Bonneville maps."[35]

Astoria was published October 28, 1836, by the firm of Carey, Lea, and Blanchard, which in the 1830's "had done the most important literary publishing in the country."[36] They paid Irving $4,000 for 5,000 copies, although they had only 4,000 printed. An English edition was published simultaneously from proof sheets Irving had sent to the firm of Richard Bentley. Irving had first approached John Murray, Jr., English

32. Pierre M. Irving's account (PMI, III, 90) agrees with this. He says that his uncle wrote at the close of June, "and some five or six weeks after he had sent the first chapters of Astoria to press" saying, " 'I am printing my book and completing my cottage slowly.' "

33. This letter is in The New York Public Library (Seligman Collection).

34. "Washington Irving and the Journal of Captain Bonneville," *Mississippi Valley Historical Review* 43 (1956), 464.

35. Introduction to *The Adventures of Captain Bonneville* (Norman: University of Oklahoma Press, 1961), p. xxii.

36. William Charvat, *Literary Publishing in America, 1790–1850* (Philadelphia: University of Pennsylvania Press, 1959), p. 26.

37. For a thorough discussion of the Irving-Murray relationship, see Ben Harris McClary's *Washington Irving and the House of Murray: Geoffrey Crayon Charms the British, 1817–1856* (Knoxville: University of Tennessee Press, 1969).

publisher of *The Crayon Miscellany*;[37] but after Murray turned down the book, Irving directed Colonel Thomas Aspinwall to make an agreement with Bentley to publish *Astoria*. The agreement, dated London, September 5, 1836, calls for Irving to receive £500 for the book.[38]

An interesting divergence appeared in the English edition of *Astoria*. The full title of the American edition was *Astoria, or Anecdotes of an Enterprise beyond the Rocky Mountains*; the agreement between Aspinwall and Bentley specified the title as *Astoria, anecdotes of an Enterprize beyond the Rocky Mountains*; but the English edition appeared entitled *Astoria; or, Enterprise beyond the Rocky Mountains*. That this was not an accident is made clear in Royal A. Gettmann's study of the Bentley Papers: *Astoria* "brought an unexpected profit to Bentley," thanks to his accountant's "canny choice of a title which, if it did not actually invite the public to think it was a romance, certainly did not inform them that it was a dull book of travels."[39] But if this device brought extra profit to Bentley, it brought displeasure to Irving who complained that Bentley "takes unwarranted liberties with my mss. altering my title pages."[40]

This first English edition was the basis the same year for editions in France by Galignani and by Baudry. Subsequently it was translated into French, German, Dutch, and Swedish. In 1841 Carey and Lea brought out a reimpression of their 1836 edition, and in April, 1849, *Astoria* appeared as volume VIII of the Author's Revised Edition of *The Works of Washington Irving*, published by G. P. Putnam in New York. Whereas Irving had taken great pains in rewriting large segments of some of the volumes in this edition (for example, *Knickerbocker's History*), he did little with *Astoria* but add a paragraph at the end bringing the history of Astoria up to date. New impressions of this edition appeared throughout the 1850's and into the 1860's; by 1868, though, excessive plate damage and batter necessitated the setting of a new edition.[41] Other editions followed regularly in the nineteenth

---

38. The unpublished agreement is in the British Museum's Bentley Papers, LIII, 301–2. October 19 is recorded as the publication date in the Bentley Papers, LXXVIII, Publication List, I (1829–1873), 14/39. A July 26, 1851, entry in the Copyright Registry Book, V, 50, lists the publication date as October 15.

39. *A Victorian Publisher: A Study of the Bentley Papers* (Cambridge: Cambridge University Press, 1960), p. 190.

40. Irving to Thomas Aspinwall, February 9, 1837, quoted in McDermott, "Irving and the Journal of Bonneville," p. 466. "Title pages" undoubtedly refers not only to *Astoria* but also to *Alhambra*, on the title page of which Bentley printed Washington Irving's name as well as that of Fray Antonio Agapida.

41. The terms "edition" and "impression" follow the definitions of Fredson Bowers in *Principles of Bibliographical Description* (Princeton: Princeton University Press, 1949), pp. 379–426.

and early twentieth centuries; two recent ones are William H. Goetz-mann's edition, published by J. B. Lippincott Company (Philadelphia, 1961), based on the 1836 American edition, and Edgeley W. Todd's edition, published by the University of Oklahoma Press (Norman, 1964), based on the 1868 edition.

The initial critical reception of *Astoria* was favorable. Reviews in America and England generally confirmed Irving's feelings while writing *Astoria* that it would be a "rich piece of mosaic," a "curious and unique work," and a book "interesting to the general reader."[42] A reviewer in James Hall's *Western Monthly Magazine* expressed his confidence in Irving's truthfulness: "With all his power of humor and pathos, he is conscientious, and does not permit his imagination to *make* facts, to be passed off as real occurrences."[43] Edgar Allan Poe had high praise for *Astoria* in his *Southern Literary Messenger* review: "The work has been accomplished in a masterly manner—the modesty of the title affording no indication of the fulness, comprehensiveness, and beauty, with which a long and entangled series of detail, collected, necessarily, from a mass of vague and imperfect data, has been wrought into complete-ness and unity."[44] A reviewer in *The Knickerbocker* expressed admiration of "the exceedingly graphic and picturesque descriptions of exciting expeditions and adventures by land and sea, and the fine sketches of character, with which the work abounds."[45] The *North American Review* critic considered that Irving's "account of the inception, progress, and fate of the enterprise, adds all the dramatic interest of romance to the intrinsic value of authentic history, and the graces of his peculiarly graphic and beautiful style."[46] And a reviewer writing about *Captain Bonneville's Adventures* commented: "But little was known before the appearance of Astoria of the great Western region ... [and] of the life of adventure and excitement associated with that distant region. But Irving has thrown a better light on the land for young and old."[47]

In England *Astoria* was complimented in terms such as these: "This work, then, is a valuable addition to Transatlantic literature; and, though it become tedious in certain of its details and repetitions, ought to be welcome in England."[48] " 'Astoria' is not a romance, but a plain, though exquisitely skilful, description of a mercantile speculation—a

42. PMI, III, 69, 70, 79.

43. *Western Monthly Magazine*, p. 685.

44. *Southern Literary Messenger* 3 (1837), 59.

45. *The Knickerbocker* 9 (1837), 88.

46. "Discovery beyond the Rocky Mountains," *North American Review* 50 (1840), 107.

47. *New York Review* 1 (1837), 439.

48. *The Athenæum*, October 22, 1836, p. 745.

speculation indeed which conducted those who were to carry it into execution amidst the wildest scenes of western America, and which had rather the air of a daring and wild expedition of a hunting tribe than the calculating proceeding of a cool and thrifty merchant.... Out of materials not very favorable to his purpose he has succeeded in weaving a connected and exciting narrative. Great art has been employed, though none appears."[49] In Ireland a reviewer acquainted firsthand with the American West had this to say about *Astoria*: "It is written in a style worthy of Mr. Irving's reputation; the facts are narrated with the utmost fidelity; and in truth, the general accuracy of the work is surprizing, as the author never visited the remote regions of the west. The book has all the interest of a work of fiction, combined with the accuracy of a historical narrative."[50]

From this high level of favor *Astoria* later suffered a decline in reputation that reached a low point in Hubert Howe Bancroft's virulent attacks in his *History of the Northwest Coast*. One part of the negative criticism, that *Astoria* was more fictional than historical, is expressed in the brief notice of *Astoria* and *Bonneville* by *The Oregonian and Indian's Advocate*: "As mere literary works these excel. They are among the most finished in our language; but we should not, therefore, imagine, while we peruse them, that we are reading truth, for both books are, without doubt, highly fictitious. The frame work is fact, but the covering was obtained altogether from the imagination of Mr. Irving.... Oregon is a land of realities, of stern realities, and fancy must seek its nourishment elsewhere."[51] The other main line of attack, given by Charles Dudley Warner in his American Men of Letters volume on Irving, was that *Astoria* and *Bonneville* were "more or less mere pieces of book-making for the market." Warner contradicts this position a few pages later, though, by saying that in the mid-1830's Irving "was in the full flow of literary productiveness.... The first crop of his mind was of course the most original; time and experience had toned down his exuberant humor; but the spring of his fancy was as free, his vigor was not abated, and his art was more refined."[52]

Bancroft's disparagement of *Astoria* has been the most damaging and long-lived. Writing in a tone of spitefulness, he questioned Irving's "integrity of purpose and faithfulness of execution" and stated that throughout *Astoria* runs a "current of unqualified sycophancy, trickery,

49. *The London and Westminster Review* 27 (1837), 173, 188.

50. *The Dublin University Magazine* 9 (1837), 176.

51. *The Oregonian and Indian's Advocate* 1 (1839), 220–21.

52. *Washington Irving* (Boston: Houghton, Mifflin and Company, 1882), pp. 162, 167.

sentimentality, and maudlin praise."[53] He accused Irving of falsely worshipping Astor, of plagiarizing from Franchère, and of fictionalizing parts of the Tonquin episode so that rather than *Astoria* being "true history, . . . many of its most brilliant passages are pure fiction."[54] These charges were answered in the authoritative *History of the American Fur Trade of the Far West* in which Hiram Chittenden points to Bancroft's "persistent bias of judgment and his bitter prejudice, which place him in an attitude of constant hostility toward Astor and Irving, and lead him repeatedly into sheer falsifications and downright slander."[55] Chittenden's own view of *Astoria* after an exhaustive study of the authorities relating to the Astorian enterprise was one of astonishment "to find with what detail the illustrious author had worked out his theme, and with what judicial fairness he had passed judgment upon actors and events. Not in the allurements of style alone, but in the essential respects of accuracy and comprehensive treatment, Irving's work stands immeasurably above all others upon the subject."[56] Bernard DeVoto, another careful student of the frontier West, concurs with Chittenden. Speaking of "the curious decline in reputation which *Astoria* and *Bonneville* have suffered," he affirms that "both are original sources, in some contexts the only sources, and both have remarkable accuracy. Their literary quality is superb."[57]

A curiously contradictory attitude toward *Astoria* is held by Irving's biographer, Stanley T. Williams, who gives with one hand and takes away with the other. He says that in 1832 Irving was "at the height of his powers"; yet he dismisses the three Western works as "elegant volumes for the parlor tables of his countrymen."[58] Having a "sustained interest in Western life," Irving "worked hard, reading widely on the frontier" in preparation for *Astoria,* a book which "fulfilled a youthful purpose" and which became through Irving's skillful interweaving of Western materials with Astor's manuscripts "a full-bodied book on the life of the Northwestern frontier"; yet Williams then turns around

53. Hubert Howe Bancroft, *History of the Northwest Coast* (San Francisco: A. L. Bancroft and Company, 1884) II, 138 n.

54. Bancroft, *History,* II, 169 n.

55. *A History of the American Fur Trade of the Far West* (Stanford, Calif.: Academic Reprints, 1954; a facsimile of the 1902 edition), I, 245. Additional rebuttal is offered by Myers, "An Analysis of Astoria," pp. 226–33, and Wayne R. Kime, "Washington Irving's *Astoria*: A Critical Study" (Ph.D. diss., University of Delaware, 1968), pp. 266–73.

56. Chittenden, *The American Fur Trade,* I, 240.

57. *Across the Wide Missouri* (Boston: Houghton Mifflin Company, 1947), pp. 426–27 n.

58. "Washington Irving," in *Literary History of the United States,* ed. Robert E. Spiller et al. (New York: Macmillan Company, 1960), p. 245.

and calls it a "shrewd piece of hack work" and a "dead romance" that is "not wholly fiction."[59]

Most recently, Andrew B. Myers, Edgeley W. Todd, and Wayne R. Kime have examined Irving and the West fairly objectively; they agree in finding *Astoria* accurate and well written. In his thorough and interesting dissertation, Myers charts the genesis, composition, and reception of *Astoria*, which he shows "is a better book, as history in the Romantic tradition, than accumulated commentary would lead the unwary to expect."[60] Todd, who spent a dozen years working on aspects of Irving's writing in relation to the fur trade and the Far West, asserts that *Astoria* is not only an "engaging narrative of great charm and interest" but also an "accurate, authoritative history" written with "enthusiastic interest and concentration."[61] And Kime likewise calls for "belated recognition of this work as a monument of narrative history valuable not only for its literary merit but also for its dependable portrayal of a significant early chapter in the history of the Pacific Northwest."[62]

Both the early reception and recent reappraisal of *Astoria* suggest that *Astoria* deserves a higher place in the Irving canon than it has previously held. If it is not "the *chef d'œuvre* of Washington Irving" as the *London Spectator* reviewer considered it in 1836, *Astoria* deserves his praise at least as a "finished narrative" written with "all the art of fiction, yet without any apparent sacrifice of truth or exactness."[63]

59. STW, pp. 83, 89, 84, 87.
60. Myers, "An Analysis of *Astoria*," p. vi.
61. Todd, Editor's Foreword to *Astoria*, p. vii.
62. Kime, "Alfred Seton's Journal," p. 324.
63. Quoted in PMI, III, 93.

Map. Overland route of the westbound Astorians under Wilson Price Hunt, September 1810–February 1812, and of eastbound Astorians under Robert Stuart, June 1812–April 1813. Map by the University of Wisconsin Cartographic Laboratory.

Overland Astorians
Returning Astorians

● Town ■ Fort ◆ Cache)(Pass

Inset A

Walla Walla R.
Umatilla R.
Grande Ronde R.
Salmon R.
BLUE MTS
Powder R.
Snake River
John Day R.
Woodpile Cr
(Burnt R)
Malheur R.
Payette R.
Boise R.

Yellowstone R.
Missouri R.
Powder R.
Little Missouri R.
Big R. (Grand R.)
Arickara Village
Ft. Mandan

BLACK HILLS
Cheyenne R.
Missouri R.

Quicourt or Rapid R. (Niobrara R.)
North Platte R.
South Platte R.
Platte R.
Big Sioux R.
Mississippi R.
Platte R.
Omaha Village
Oto Village
Nodway R.
Grand Isle (Grand Island)

Kansas R.
Ft. Osage
St. Charles
Charette
St. Louis
Arkansas R.

| 0 | | 100 | | 200 | Miles |
| 0 | 100 | 200 | 300 | | Kms. |

ASTORIA

INTRODUCTION

In the course of occasional visits to Canada many years since, I became intimately acquainted with some of the principal partners of the great North West Fur Company, who at that time lived in genial style at Montreal, and kept almost open house for the stranger. At their hospitable boards I occasionally met with partners, and clerks, and hardy fur traders from the interior posts; men who had passed years remote from civilized society, among distant and savage tribes, and who had wonders to recount of their wide and wild peregrinations, their hunting exploits, and their perilous adventures and hairbreadth escapes among the Indians. I was at an age when the imagination lends its coloring to every thing, and the stories of these Sindbads of the wilderness made the life of a trapper and fur trader perfect romance to me. I even meditated at one time a visit to the remote posts of the company in the boats which annually ascended the lakes and rivers, being thereto invited by one of the partners; and I have ever since regretted that I was prevented by circumstances from carrying my intention into effect. From those early impressions, the grand enterprizes of the great fur companies, and the hazardous errantry of their associates in the wild parts of our vast continent, have always been themes of charmed interest to me; and I have felt anxious to get at the details of their adventurous expeditions among the savage tribes that peopled the depths of the wilderness.

About two years ago, not long after my return from a tour upon the prairies of the far west, I had a conversation with my friend Mr. John Jacob Astor, relative to that portion of our country, and to the adventurous traders to Santa Fé and the Columbia. This led him to advert to a great enterprize set on foot and conducted by him, between twenty and thirty years since, having for its object to carry the fur trade across the Rocky Mountains, and to sweep the shores of the Pacific.

Finding that I took an interest in the subject, he expressed a regret that the true nature and extent of his enterprize and its national character and importance had never been understood, and a wish that I would undertake to give an account of it. The suggestion struck upon the chord of early associations, already vibrating in my mind. It occurred to me that a work of this kind might comprise a variety of those curious details, so interesting to me, illustrative of the fur trade; of its remote and adventurous enterprizes, and of the various people, and tribes, and castes, and characters, civilized and savage,

3

affected by its operations. The journals, and letters also, of the adventurers by sea and land employed by Mr. Astor in his comprehensive project, might throw light upon portions of our country quite out of the track of ordinary travel, and as yet but little known. I therefore felt disposed to undertake the task, provided documents of sufficient extent and minuteness could be furnished to me. All the papers relative to the enterprize were accordingly submitted to my inspection. Among them were journals and letters narrating expeditions by sea, and journeys to and fro across the Rocky Mountains by routes before untravelled, together with documents illustrative of savage and colonial life on the borders of the Pacific. With such materials in hand, I undertook the work. The trouble of rummaging among business papers, and of collecting and collating facts from amidst tedious and commonplace details, was spared me by my nephew, Pierre M. Irving, who acted as my pioneer, and to whom I am greatly indebted for smoothing my path and lightening my labors.

As the journals, on which I chiefly depended, had been kept by men of business, intent upon the main object of the enterprize, and but little versed in science, or curious about matters not immediately bearing upon their interests, and as they were written often in moments of fatigue or hurry, amid the inconveniences of wild encampments, they were often meagre in their details, furnishing hints to provoke rather than narratives to satisfy inquiry. I have, therefore, availed myself occasionally of collateral lights supplied by the published journals of other travellers who have visited the scenes described: such as Messrs. Lewis and Clarke, Bradbury, Breckenridge, Long, Franchere, and Ross Cox, and make a general acknowledgment of aid received from these quarters.

The work I here present to the public, is necessarily of a rambling and somewhat disjointed nature, comprising various expeditions and adventures by land and sea. The facts, however, will prove to be linked and banded together by one grand scheme, devised and conducted by a master spirit; one set of characters, also, continues throughout, appearing occasionally, though sometimes at long intervals, and the whole enterprize winds up by a regular catastrophe; so that the work, without any labored attempt at artificial construction, actually possesses much of that unity so much sought after in works of fiction, and considered so important to the interest of every history.

CHAPTER I

Two leading objects of commercial gain have given birth to wide and
daring enterprize in the early history of the Americas; the precious
metals of the south, and the rich peltries of the north. While the fiery
and magnificent Spaniard, inflamed with the mania for gold, has extended his discoveries and conquests over those brilliant countries
scorched by the ardent sun of the tropics, the adroit and buoyant
Frenchman and the cool and calculating Briton have pursued the less
splendid, but no less lucrative, traffic in furs amidst the hyperborean
regions of the Canadas, until they have advanced even within the
Arctic circle.

These two pursuits have thus in a manner been the pioneers and
precursors of civilization. Without pausing on the borders, they have
penetrated at once, in defiance of difficulties and dangers, to the heart
of savage continents: laying open the hidden secrets of the wilderness;
leading the way to remote regions of beauty and fertility that might
have remained unexplored for ages, and beckoning after them the
slow and pausing steps of agriculture and colonization.

It was the fur trade, in fact, which gave early sustenance and
vitality to the great Canadian provinces. Being destitute of the precious
metals, at that time the leading object of American enterprize, they
were long neglected by the parent country. The French adventurers,
however, who had settled on the banks of the S' Lawrence, soon found
that in the rich peltries of the interior, they had sources of wealth
that might almost rival the mines of Mexico and Peru. The Indians,
as yet unacquainted with the artificial value given to some descriptions
of furs, in civilized life, brought quantities of the most precious kinds
and bartered them away for European trinkets and cheap commodities.
Immense profits were thus made by the early traders, and the traffic
was pursued with avidity.

5

As the valuable furs soon became scarce in the neighborhood of the settlements, the Indians of the vicinity were stimulated to take a wider range in their hunting expeditions; they were generally accompanied on these expeditions by some of the traders or their dependents, who shared in the toils and perils of the chase, and at the same time made themselves acquainted with the best hunting and trapping grounds, and with the remote tribes, whom they encouraged to bring their peltries to the settlements. In this way the trade augmented and was drawn from remote quarters to Montreal. Every now and then a large body of Ottawas, Hurons, and other tribes who hunted the countries bordering on the Great lakes, would come down in a squadron of light canoes, laden with beaver skins, and other spoils of their year's hunting. The canoes would be unladen, taken on shore, and their contents disposed in order. A camp of birch bark would be pitched outside of the town, and a kind of primitive fair opened with that grave ceremonial so dear to the Indians. An audience would be demanded of the Governor General, who would hold the conference with becoming state, seated in an elbow chair, with the Indians ranged in semicircles before him, seated on the ground and silently smoking their pipes. Speeches would be made, presents exchanged and the audience would break up in universal good humour.

Now would ensue a brisk traffic with the merchants, and all Montreal would be alive with naked Indians running from shop to shop bargaining for arms, kettles, knives, axes, blankets, bright colored cloths and other articles of use or fancy; upon all which, says an old French writer, the merchants were sure to clear at least two hundred per cent. There was no money used in this traffic, and, after a time, all payment in spirituous liquors was prohibited, in consequence of the frantic and frightful excesses and bloody brawls which they were apt to occasion.

Their wants and caprices being supplied, they would take leave of the governor, strike their tents, launch their canoes, and ply their way up the Ottawa to the lakes.

A new and anomalous class of men gradually grew out of this trade. These were called *Coureurs des bois*, Rangers of the woods; originally men who had accompanied the Indians in their hunting expeditions and made themselves acquainted with remote tracts and tribes, and who now became, as it were, pedlars of the wilderness. These men would set out from Montreal with canoes well stocked with goods, with arms and ammunition, and would make their way up the mazy and wandering rivers that interlace the vast forests of the Canadas, coasting the most remote lakes, and creating new wants and habitudes among the natives. Sometimes they sojourned for months among them, assimilating to their tastes and habits with the happy facility of Frenchmen; adopting in some degree the Indian dress, and not unfrequently taking to themselves Indian wives.

Twelve, fifteen, eighteen months would often elapse without any tidings of them, when they would come sweeping their way down the Ottawa in full glee, their canoes laden down with packs of beaver skins. Now came their time for revelry and extravagance. "You would be amazed," says an old writer already quoted, "if you saw how lewd these pedlars are when they return; how they feast and game and how prodigal they are not only in their clothes, but upon their sweethearts. Such of them as are married have the wisdom to retire to their own houses; but the bachelors act just as our East India men and pirates are wont to do; for they lavish, eat, drink, and play all away as long as the goods hold out; and when these are gone, they e'en sell their embroidery, their lace and their clothes. This done they are forced upon a new voyage for subsistence."*

Many of these *Coureurs des bois* became so accustomed to the Indian mode of living, and the perfect freedom of the wilderness, that they lost all relish for civilization, and identified themselves with the savages among whom they dwelt, or could only be distinguished from them by superior licentiousness. Their conduct and example gradually corrupted the natives, and impeded the works of the Catholic missionaries, who were at this time prosecuting their pious labors in the wilds of Canada.

To check these abuses, and to protect the fur trade from various irregularities practised by these loose adventurers, an order was issued by the French government prohibiting all persons, on pain of death, from trading into the interior of the country without a licence.

These licences were granted in writing by the Governor General, and at first were given only to persons of respectability; to gentlemen of broken fortunes; to old officers of the Army who had families to provide for; or to their widows. Each licence permitted the fitting out of two large canoes with merchandize for the lakes and no more than twenty five licences were to be issued in one year. By degrees, however, private licences were also granted and the number rapidly encreased. Those who did not choose to fit out the expeditions themselves, were permitted to sell them to the merchants; these employed the *Coureurs des bois*, or Rangers of the woods, to undertake the long voyages on shares, and thus the abuses of the old system were revived and continued.†

* La Hontan. V. 1. Let. 4.

† The following are the terms on which these expeditions were commonly undertaken. The merchant holding the licence would fit out the two canoes with a thousand crowns worth of goods and put them under the conduct of six *Coureurs*

The pious missionaries employed by the Roman Catholic church to convert the Indians, did every thing in their power to counteract the profligacy carried and propagated by these men in the heart of the wilderness. The Catholic chapel might often be seen planted beside the trading house, and its spire surmounted by a cross, towering from the midst of an Indian village on the banks of a river or a lake. The missions had often a beneficial effect on the simple sons of the forest, but had little power over the renegades from civilization.

At length it was found necessary to establish fortified posts at the confluence of the rivers and the lakes for the protection of the trade, and the restraint of these profligates of the wilderness. The most important of these was at Michilimackinac, situated at the strait of the same name, which connects Lakes Huron and Michigan. It became the great interior mart and place of deposit, and some of the regular merchants, who prosecuted the trade in person, under their licences, formed establishments here. This too was a rendezvous for the Rangers of the woods, as well those who came up with goods from Montreal as those who returned with peltries from the interior. Here new expeditions were fitted out and took their departure for Lake Michigan and the Mississippi; Lake Superior and the north west; and here the peltries brought in return were embarked for Montreal.

The French merchant at his trading post, in those primitive days of Canada, was a kind of commercial patriarch. With the lax habits and easy familiarity of his race, he had a little world of self indulgence and misrule around him. He had his clerks, canoemen and retainers of all kinds, who lived with him on terms of perfect sociability, always calling him by his christian name; he had his harem of Indian beauties, and his troop of halfbreed children; nor was there ever wanting a louting train of Indians, hanging about the establishment, eating and drinking at his expense in the intervals of their hunting expeditions.

The Canadian traders for a long time had troublesome competitors in the British merchants of New York, who inveigled the Indian

---

des bois, to whom the goods were charged at the rate of fifteen per cent above the ready money price in the Colony. The *Coureurs des bois*, in their turn dealt so sharply with the Savages, that they generally returned at the end of a year or so, with four canoes well laden, so as to ensure a clear profit of seven hundred per cent, insomuch that the thousand crowns invested produced eight thousand. Of this extravagant profit the merchant had the lion's share. In the first place he would set aside six hundred crowns for the cost of his licence; then a thousand crowns for the cost of the original merchandize. This would leave 6400 crowns from which he would take forty per cent for bottomry, amounting to 2560 crowns. The residue would be equally divided among the six wood rangers, who would thus receive little more than 600 crowns, for all their toils and perils.

hunters and the *Coureurs des bois,* to their posts, and traded with them on more favorable terms. A still more formidable opposition was organized in the Hudson's Bay Company, chartered by Charles II in 1670 with the exclusive privilege of establishing trading houses on the shores of that bay and its tributary rivers; a privilege which they have maintained to the present day. Between this British Company and the French merchants of Canada feuds and contests arose about alleged infringements of territorial limits, and acts of violence and bloodshed occurred between their agents.

In 1762 the French lost possession of Canada and the trade fell principally into the hands of British subjects. For a time, however, it shrunk within narrow limits. The old *Coureurs des bois* were broken up and dispersed, or, where they could be met with, were slow to accustom themselves to the habits and manners of their British employers. They missed the freedom, indulgence, and familiarity of the old French trading houses, and did not relish the sober exactness, reserve and method of the new comers. The British traders, too, were ignorant of the country and distrustful of the natives. They had reason to be so. The treacherous and bloody affairs of Detroit and Michilimackinac shewed them the lurking hostility cherished by the Savages, who had too long been taught by the French to regard them as enemies.

It was not until the year 1766 that the trade regained its old channels; but it was then pursued with avidity and emulation by individual merchants, and soon transcended its former bounds. Expeditions were fitted out by various persons from Montreal and Michilimackinac and rivalships and jealousies of course ensued. The trade was injured by their artifices to outbid and undermine each other; the Indians were debauched by the sale of spirituous liquors, which had been prohibited under the French rule. Scenes of drunkenness, brutality and brawl were the consequence, in the Indian villages and around the trading houses, while bloody feuds took place between rival trading parties when they happened to encounter each other in the lawless depths of the wilderness.

To put an end to these sordid and ruinous contentions several of the principal merchants of Montreal entered into a partnership in the winter of 1783, which was augmented by amalgamation with a rival company in 1787. Thus was created the famous "North West Company" which for a time held a lordly sway over the wintry lakes and boundless forests of the Canadas, almost equal to that of the East India Company over the voluptuous climes and magnificent realms of the Orient.

The Company consisted of twenty three share holders, or partners, but held in its employ about two thousand persons as clerks, guides, interpreters and "voyageurs" or boatmen. These were distributed at various trading posts, established far and wide on the interior lakes and rivers, at immense distances from each other, and in the heart of trackless countries and savage tribes.

Several of the partners resided in Montreal and Quebec, to manage the main concerns of the Company. These were called agents, and were personages of great weight and importance; the other partners took their stations at the interior posts, where they remained throughout the winter, to superintend the intercourse with the various tribes of Indians. They were thence called wintering partners.

The goods destined for this wide and wandering traffic were put up at the warehouses of the Company in Montreal, and conveyed in batteaux, or boats, and canoes, up the river Attawa, or Ottawa, which falls into the S' Lawrence near Montreal, and by other rivers and portages to Lake Nipising, Lake Huron, Lake Superior, and thence by several chains of great and small lakes to Lake Winipeg, Lake Athabasca and the great Slave lake. This singular and beautiful system of internal seas which renders an immense region of wilderness so accessible to the frail bark of the Indian or the trader, was studded by the remote posts of the Company, where they carried on their traffic with the surrounding tribes.

The Company, as we have shown, was at first a spontaneous association of merchants; but, after it had been regularly organized, admission into it became extremely difficult. A candidate had to enter, as it were, "before the mast," to undergo a long probation, and to rise slowly by his merits and services. He began, at an early age, as a clerk, and served an apprenticeship of seven years, for which he received one hundred pounds sterling, was maintained at the expense of the Company, and furnished with suitable clothing and equipments. His probation was generally passed at the interior trading posts; removed for years from civilized society, leading a life almost as wild and precarious as the savages around him, exposed to the severities of a northern winter, often suffering from scarcity of food, and sometimes destitute for a long time of both bread and salt. When his apprenticeship had expired he received a salary according to his deserts, varying from eighty to one hundred and sixty pounds sterling, and was now eligible to the great object of his ambition, a partnership in the Company, though years might yet elapse before he attained to that enviable station.

Most of the clerks were young men of good families, from the highlands of Scotland, characterised by the perseverance, thrift and fidelity of their country and fitted by their native hardihood to en-

counter the rigorous climates of the north and to endure the trials
and privations of their lot; though it must not be concealed that the
constitutions of many of them became impaired, by the hardships of
the wilderness, and their stomachs injured by occasional famishing,
and especially by the want of bread and salt. Now and then, at an
interval of years, they were permitted to come down on a visit to
the establishment at Montreal, to recruit their health and to have a
taste of civilized life; and these were brilliant spots in their existence.

As to the principal partners, or agents, who resided in Montreal
and Quebec, they formed a kind of commercial aristocracy, living in
lordly and hospitable style. Their early associations, when clerks at
the remote trading posts, and the pleasures, dangers, adventures and
mishaps which they had shared together in their wild wood life, had
linked them heartily to each other, so that they formed a convivial
fraternity. Few travellers that have visited Canada some thirty years
since, in the days of the M'Tavishes, the MacGillivrays, the Mac-
Kenzies, the Frobishers and the other magnates of the north west,
when the Company was in all its glory, but must remember the round
of feasting and revelry kept up among these hyperborean nabobs.

Sometimes one or two partners recently from the interior posts,
would make their appearance in New York, in the course of a tour
of pleasure and curiosity. On these occasions there was always a
degree of magnificence of the purse about them, and a peculiar propensity to expenditure at the goldsmiths and jewellers, for rings, chains,
brooches, necklaces, jewelled watches, and other rich trinkets, partly
for their own wear, partly for presents to their female acquaintances:
a gorgeous prodigality, such as was often to be noticed in former
times in Southern planters and West India creoles, when flush with
the profits of their plantations.

To behold the North West Company in all its state and grandeur,
however, it was necessary to witness an annual gathering at the great
interior place of conference, established at Fort William, near what
is called the Grand Portage, on Lake Superior. Here two or three
of the leading partners from Montreal proceeded once a year, to
meet the partners from the various trading posts of the wilderness,
to discuss the affairs of the Company during the preceding year, and
to arrange plans for the future.

On these occasions might be seen the change since the unceremonious
times of the old French traders; now the aristocratical character of
the Briton shone forth magnificently, or rather the feudal spirit of
the highlander. Every partner who had charge of an interior post,
and a score of retainers at his command, felt like the chieftain of a
highland clan, and was almost as important in the eyes of his dependants

as of himself. To him a visit to the grand conference at Fort William was a most important event; and he repaired there as to a meeting of parliament.

The partners from Montreal, however, were the lords of the ascendant; coming from the midst of luxurious and ostentatious life, they quite eclipsed their compeers from the woods, whose forms and faces had been battered and hardened by hard living and hard service, and whose garments and equipments were all the worse for wear. Indeed the partners from below considered the whole dignity of the Company as represented in their persons and conducted themselves in suitable style. They ascended the rivers in great state, like sovereigns making a progress: or rather like highland chieftains navigating their subject lakes. They were wrapped in rich furs, their huge canoes freighted with every convenience and luxury and manned by Canadian voyageurs, as obedient as highland clansmen. They carried up with them cooks, and bakers, together with delicacies of every kind, and abundance of choice wines for the banquets which attended this great convocation. Happy were they, too, if they could meet with some distinguished stranger, above all some titled member of the British nobility, to accompany them on this stately occasion, and grace their high solemnities.

Fort William, the scene of this important annual meeting, was a considerable village on the banks of Lake Superior. Here, in an immense wooden building, was the great Council Hall, as also the banqueting chamber, decorated with Indian arms and accoutrements and the trophies of the Fur trade. The house swarmed at this time, with traders and voyageurs, some from Montreal, bound to the interior posts; some from the interior posts, bound to Montreal. The councils were held in great state, for every member felt as if sitting in parliament, and every retainer and dependant looked up to the assemblage with awe, as to the House of Lords. There was a vast deal of solemn deliberation, and hard Scottish reasoning with an occasional swell of pompous declamation.

These grave and weighty councils were alternated by huge feasts and revels like some of the old feasts described in highland castles. The tables in the great banqueting room groaned under the weight of game of all kinds; of venison from the woods, and fish from the lakes, with hunters' delicacies, such as buffalo tongues and beavers' tails: and various luxuries from Montreal, all served up by experienced cooks brought for the purpose. There was no stint of generous wine, for it was a hard drinking period, a time of loyal toasts, and bacchanalian songs and brimming bumpers.

While the chiefs thus revelled in hall, and made the rafters resound with bursts of loyalty and old Scottish songs chaunted in voices cracked and sharpened by the northern blast, their merriment was echoed and prolonged by a mongrel legion of retainers; Canadian voyageurs, half breeds, Indian hunters and vagabond hangers on, who feasted sumptuously without on the crumbs that fell from their table and made the welkin ring with old French ditties, mingled with Indian yelps and yellings.

Such was the North West Company in its powerful and prosperous days, when it held a kind of feudal sway over a vast domain of lake and forest. We are dwelling too long, perhaps, upon these individual pictures, endeared to us by the associations of early life, when, as yet a stripling youth, we have sat at the hospitable boards of the "Mighty North Westers," then lords of the ascendant at Montreal, and gazed with wondering and inexperienced eye at their baronial wassailing, and listened with astonished ear to their· tales of hardships and adventures. It is one object of our task, however, to present scenes of the rough life of the wilderness, and we are tempted to fix these few memorials of a transient state of things fast passing into oblivion;— for the feudal state of Fort William is at an end; its council chamber is silent and deserted; its banquet hall no longer echoes to the burst of loyalty or the "auld world" ditty; the lords of the lakes and forests have passed away; and the hospitable magnates of Montreal—where are they!

CHAPTER II

Rise of the Mackinaw Company—Attempts of the American Government to counteract foreign influence over the Indian tribes—John Jacob Astor—His birth place—His arrival in the United States—What first turned his attention to the Fur trade—His character, enterprizes and success—His communications with the American Government— Origin of the American Fur Company.

The success of the North West Company stimulated further enterprize in this opening and apparently boundless field of profit. The traffic of that company lay principally in the high northern latitudes, while there were immense regions to the south and west known to abound with valuable peltries, but which as yet had been but little explored by the fur trader. A new association of British merchants was therefore formed, to prosecute the trade in this direction. The chief factory was established at the old emporium of Michilimackinac, from which place the association took its name; and was commonly called the Mackinaw Company.

While the North Westers continued to push their enterprizes into the hyperborean regions from their strong hold at Fort William, and to hold almost sovereign sway over the tribes of the upper lakes and rivers; the Mackinaw Company sent forth their light pirogues and barks, by Green bay, Fox River, and the Wisconsin, to that great artery of the West, the Mississippi; and down that stream to all its tributary rivers. In this way they hoped soon to monopolize the trade with all the tribes on the southern and western waters, and of those vast tracts comprised in ancient Louisiana.

The Government of the United States began to view with a wary eye the growing influence, thus acquired by combinations of foreigners, over the aboriginal tribes inhabiting its territories, and endeavored to counteract it. For this purpose, as early as 1796, the government sent out agents to establish rival trading houses on the frontiers, so as to supply the wants of the Indians; to link their interests and feelings with those of the people of the United States, and to divert this important branch of trade into national channels.

The expedient, however, was unsuccessful; as most commercial expedients are prone to be, where the dull patronage of government is counted upon to outvie the keen activity of private enterprize. What Government failed to effect, however, with all its patronage and all

14

its agents, was at length brought about by the enterprize and per-severance of a single merchant, one of its adopted citizens; and this brings us to speak of the individual whose enterprize is the especial subject of the following pages; a man whose name and character are worthy of being enrolled in the history of Commerce, as illustrating its noblest aims and soundest maxims. A few brief anecdotes of his early life and of the circumstances which first determined him to the branch of Commerce of which we are treating cannot but be interesting.

John Jacob Astor, the individual in question, was born in the honest little German village of Waldorf near Heidelberg, on the banks of the Rhine. He was brought up in the simplicity of rural life, but, while yet a mere stripling, left his home and launched himself amid the busy scenes of London, having had, from his very boyhood, a singular presentiment that he would ultimately arrive at great fortune.

At the close of the American Revolution he was still in London and scarce on the threshold of active life. An elder brother had been for some few years resident in the United States, and Mr. Astor determined to follow him and to seek his fortunes in the rising country. Investing a small sum which he had amassed since leaving his native village, in merchandize suited to the American market, he embarked, in the month of November 1783 in a ship bound to Baltimore, and arrived in Hampton Roads in the month of January. The winter was extremely severe, and the ship, with many others, was detained by the ice in and about Chesapeak bay for nearly three months.

During this period the passengers of the various ships used oc-casionally to go on shore, and mingle sociably together. In this way Mr. Astor became acquainted with a countryman of his, a furrier by trade. Having had a previous impression that this might be a lucrative trade in the new world he made many enquiries of his new acquaintance on the subject, who cheerfully gave him all the information in his power as to the quality and value of different furs, and the mode of carrying on the traffic. He subsequently accompanied him to New York, and by his advice Mr. Astor was induced to invest the proceeds of his merchandize in furs. With these he sailed from New York to London in 1784, disposed of them advantageously, made himself further acquainted with the course of the trade and returned the same year to New York, with a view to settle in the United States.

He now devoted himself to the branch of Commerce with which he had thus casually been made acquainted. He began his career, of course, on the narrowest scale, but he brought to the task a persevering industry, rigid economy and strict integrity. To these were added an aspiring spirit that always looked upward, a genius bold, fertile and expansive, a sagacity quick to grasp and convert every circumstance to its advantage, and a singular and never wavering confidence of signal success.*

As yet trade in peltries was not organized in the United States, and could not be said to form a regular line of business. Furs and skins were casually collected by the country traders in their dealings with the Indians or the white hunters, but the main supply was derived from Canada. As Mr. Astor's means encreased he made annual visits to Montreal, where he purchased furs from the houses at that place engaged in the trade. These he shipped from Canada to London, no direct trade being allowed from that colony to any but the mother country.

In 1794 or 5 a treaty with Great Britain removed the restrictions imposed upon the trade with the Colonies and opened a direct commercial intercourse between Canada and the United States. Mr. Astor was in London at the time and immediately made a contract with the agents of the North West Company for furs. He was now enabled to import them from Montreal into the United States for the home supply, and to be shipped thence to different parts of Europe, as well as to China, which has ever been the best market for the richest and finest kinds of peltry.

The treaty in question provided, likewise, that the military posts occupied by the British within the territorial limits of the United States should be surrendered. Accordingly Oswego, Niagara, Detroit, Michilimackinac and other posts on the American sides of the lakes were given up. An opening was thus made for the American merchant to trade on the confines of Canada, and within the territories of the United States. After an interval of some years, about 1807, Mr. Astor embarked in this trade on his own account. His capital and resources had by this time greatly augmented, and he had risen from small beginnings to take his place among the first merchants and financiers of the country. His genius had ever been in advance of his circumstances prompting him to new and wider fields of enterprize beyond the scope of ordinary merchants. With all his enterprize and resources, however, he soon found the power and influence of the Michilimackinac (or Mackinaw) Company too great for him, having engrossed most of the trade within the American borders.

---

* An instance of this buoyant confidence, which no doubt aided to produce the success it anticipated, we have from the lips of Mr. A. himself. While yet almost a stranger in the city, and in very narrow circumstances, he passed by where a row of houses had just been erected in Broad way, and which from the superior style of their architecture, were the talk and boast of the city. "I'll build, one day or other, a greater house than any of these, in this very street" said he to himself. He has accomplished his prediction.

A plan had to be devised to enable him to enter into successful competition. He was aware of the wish of the American Government, already stated, that the fur trade within its boundaries should be in the hands of American citizens, and of the ineffectual measures it had taken to accomplish that object. He now offered, if aided and protected by government, to turn the whole of that trade, into American channels. He was invited to unfold his plans to Government, and they were warmly approved, though the Executive could give no direct aid.

Thus countenanced, however, he obtained in 1809, a charter from the legislature of the state of New York, incorporating a company under the name of "The American Fur Company" with a capital of One Million of Dollars, with the privilege of encreasing it to Two millions. The capital was furnished by himself; he, in fact, constituted the Company; for though he had a board of directors, they were merely nominal; the whole business was conducted on his plans, and with his resources, but he preferred to do so under the imposing and formidable aspect of a corporation, rather than in his individual name; and his policy was sagacious and effective.

As the Mackinaw Company still continued its rivalry, and as the fur trade would not advantageously admit of competition, he made a new arrangement in 1811 by which, in conjunction with certain partners of the North West Company, and other persons engaged in the Fur trade, he bought out the Mackinaw Company, and merged that and the American Fur Company into a new association, to be called "The South West Company." This he likewise did with the privity and approbation of the American government.

By this arrangement Mr. Astor became proprietor of one half of the Indian establishments and goods which the Mackinaw Company had within the territory of the Indian country in the United States, and it was understood that the whole was to be surrendered into his hands at the expiration of five years, on condition that the American company would not trade within the British dominions.

Unluckily the war which broke out in 1812 between Great Britain and the United States suspended the association; and, after the war, it was entirely dissolved: Congress having passed a law prohibiting British fur traders from prosecuting their enterprizes within the territories of the United States.

CHAPTER III

*Fur trade in the Pacific—American coasting voyages—Russian enter-
prizes—Discovery of the Columbia River—Carver's project to found
a settlement there—MacKenzie's expedition—Lewis and Clarke's journey across the Rocky Mountains—Mr. Astor's grand commercial
scheme—His correspondence on the subject with Mr. Jefferson—His
negotiations with the North West Company—His steps to carry his
scheme into effect.*

While the various companies we have noticed were pushing their
enterprizes far and wide in the wilds of Canada, and along the course
of the great western waters, other adventurers, intent on the same
objects, were traversing the watery wastes of the Pacific and skirting
the North West Coast of America. The last voyage of that renowned
but unfortunate discoverer, Captain Cook, had made known the vast
quantities of the sea otter to be found along that coast, and the
immense prices to be obtained for its fur in China. It was as if a
new gold coast had been discovered. Individuals from various countries
dashed into this lucrative traffic, so that in the year 1792 there were
twenty one vessels under different flags, plying along the coast and
trading with the natives. The greater part of them were American
and owned by Boston merchants. They generally remained on the
coast, and about the adjacent seas for two years, carrying on as wandering and adventurous a commerce on the water as did the traders
and trappers on land.

Their trade extended along the whole coast from California to the
high northern latitudes. They would run in near shore, anchor, and
wait for the natives to come off in their canoes with peltries. The
trade exhausted at one place, they would up anchor and off to another.
In this way they would consume the summer and when autumn came
on, would run down to the Sandwich islands and winter in some
friendly and plentiful harbour. In the following year they would
resume their summer trade, commencing at California and proceeding
north; and, having in the course of the two seasons, collected a
sufficient cargo of peltries, would make the best of their way to China.
Here they would sell their furs, take in teas, nankeens and other
merchandize, and return to Boston after an absence of two or three years.

The people however who entered most extensively and effectively
in the fur trade of the Pacific were the Russians. Instead of making
casual voyages, in transient ships, they established regular trading
houses in the high latitudes, along the North West Coast of America

and upon the chain of the Aleutian islands between Kamtschatka and the promontory of Alaska.

To promote and protect these enterprizes a company was incorporated by the Russian Government with exclusive privileges and a capital of two hundred and sixty thousand pounds sterling; and the sovereignty of that part of the American continent, along the coast of which the posts had been established, was claimed by the Russian crown, on the plea that the land had been discovered and occupied by its subjects.

As China was the grand mart for the furs collected in these quarters the Russians had the advantage over their competitors in the trade. The latter had to take their peltries to Canton, which, however, was a mere receiving mart, from whence they had to be distributed over the interior of the empire and sent to the northern parts, where there was the chief consumption. The Russians, on the contrary, carried their furs, by a shorter voyage, directly to the northern parts of the Chinese Empire, thus being able to afford them in the market without the additional cost of internal transportation.

We now come to the immediate field of operation of the great enterprize we have undertaken to illustrate.

Among the American ships which traded along the North West Coast in 1792 was the Columbia, Captain Gray, of Boston. In the course of her voyage she discovered the mouth of a large river in Lat. 46° 19′ north. Entering it with some difficulty, on account of sand bars and breakers, she came to anchor in a spacious bay. A boat was well manned, and sent on shore to a village on the beach, but all the inhabitants fled excepting the aged and infirm. The kind manner in which these were treated and the presents given to them gradually lured back the others, and a friendly intercourse took place. They had never seen a ship or a white man. When they had first descried the Columbia they had supposed it a floating island; then some monster of the deep; but when they saw the boat putting for shore, with human beings on board, they considered them cannibals sent by the great Spirit to ravage the country and devour the inhabitants.

Captain Gray did not ascend the river farther than the bay in question, which continues to bear his name. After putting to sea he fell in with the celebrated discoverer Vancouver, and informed him of his discovery, furnishing him with a chart which he had made of the river. Vancouver visited the river, and his Lieutenant Broughton explored it by the aid of Captain Gray's chart; ascending it upwards of one hundred miles, until within view of a snowy mountain to which he gave the name of Mount Hood, which it still retains.

The existence of this river, however, was known long before the visits of Gray and Vancouver, but the information concerning it was vague and indefinite, being gathered from the reports of Indians. It was spoken of by travellers as The Oregon and as the great River of the West. A Spanish ship is said to have been wrecked at its mouth, several of the crew of which lived for some time among the natives. The Columbia, however, is believed to be the first ship that made a regular discovery and anchored within its waters, and it has since generally borne the name of that vessel.

As early as 1763, shortly after the acquisition of the Canadas by Great Britain, Captain Jonathan Carver, who had been in the British provincial army, projected a journey across the continent between the forty third and forty sixth degrees of northern latitude, to the shores of the Pacific Ocean. His objects were to ascertain the breadth of the continent at its broadest part, and to determine on some place on the shores of the Pacific, where government might establish a post to facilitate the discovery of a northwest passage, or a communication between Hudson's Bay and the Pacific Ocean. This place he presumed would be somewhere about the Straits of Annian, at which point he supposed the Oregon disembogued itself. It was his opinion, also, that a settlement on this extremity of America would disclose new sources of trade, promote many useful discoveries, and open a more direct communication with China and the English settlements in the East Indies, than that by the Cape of Good Hope or the Straits of Magellan.*

This enterprizing and intrepid traveller was twice baffled in individual efforts to accomplish this great journey. In 1774 he was joined in the scheme by Richard Whitworth, a member of Parliament, and a man of wealth. Their enterprize was projected on a broad and bold plan. They were to take with them fifty or sixty men, artificers and mariners. With these they were to make their way up one of the branches of the Missouri, explore the mountains for the source of the Oregon or River of the West, and sail down that river to its supposed exit near the Straits of Annian. Here they were to erect a fort, and build the vessels necessary to carry their discoveries by sea into effect. Their plan had the sanction of the British government, and grants and other requisites were nearly completed, when the breaking out of the American revolution once more defeated the undertaking.†

The expedition of Sir Alexander MacKenzie in 1793 across the continent to the Pacific Ocean which he reached in Lat. 52° 20′ 48″

---

* Carver's Travels. Introd. p. iii. Phila. 1796.
† Carver's Travels. P. 360. Phila. 1796.

again suggested the possibility of linking together the trade of both sides of the continent. In Lat. 52° 30′ he had descended a river for some distance which flowed toward the south and was called by the natives Tacoutche Tesse, and which he erroneously supposed to be the Columbia. It was afterwards ascertained that it emptied itself in Lat. 49°, whereas the mouth of the Columbia is about three degrees further south.

When MacKenzie some years subsequently published an account of his expeditions he suggested the policy of opening an intercourse between the Atlantic and Pacific oceans, and forming regular establishments through the interior and at both extremes as well as along the coasts and islands. By this means, he observed, the entire command of the Fur trade of North America might be obtained from Latitude 48° north, to the pole, excepting that portion held by the Russians, for as to the American adventurers who had hitherto enjoyed the traffic along the North West Coast, they would instantly disappear, he added, before a well regulated trade.

A scheme of this kind, however, was too vast and hazardous for individual enterprize; it could only be undertaken by a company, under the sanction and protection of a government: and as there might be a clashing of claims between the Hudson's Bay and North West companies, the one holding by right of charter, the other by right of possession, he proposed that the two companies should coalesce in this great undertaking. The long cherished jealousies of these two companies, however, were too deep and strong to allow them to listen to such council.

In the mean time the attention of the American Government was attracted to the subject and the memorable expedition under Messrs. Lewis and Clark fitted out. These gentlemen, in 1804, accomplished the enterprize which had been projected by Carver and Whitworth in 1774. They ascended the Missouri, passed through the stupendous gates of the Rocky Mountains, hitherto unknown to white man; discovered and explored the upper waters of the Columbia, and followed that river down to its mouth, where their countryman Gray had anchored about twelve years previously. Here they passed the winter and returned across the Mountains in the following spring. The reports published by them of their expedition, demonstrated the practicability of establishing a line of communication across the continent from the Atlantic to the Pacific ocean.

It was then that the idea presented itself to the mind of Mr. Astor of grasping with his individual hand, this great enterprize, which for years had been dubiously yet desirously contemplated by powerful associations and national governments. For some time he revolved the idea in his mind, gradually extending and maturing his plans as his means of executing them augmented. The main feature of his scheme was to establish a line of trading posts along the Missouri and the Columbia, to the mouth of the latter: where was to be founded the chief trading house or mart. Inferior posts would be established in the interior, and on all the tributary streams of the Columbia, to trade with the Indians; these posts would draw their supplies from the main establishment and bring to it the peltries they collected. Coasting craft would be built and fitted out, also, at the mouth of the Columbia, to trade, at favorable seasons, all along the north west coast, and return with the proceeds of their voyages, to this place of deposit. Thus all the Indian trade, both of the interior and the coast, would converge to this point, and thence derive its sustenance.

A ship was to be sent annually from New York to this main establishment with reinforcements and supplies, and with merchandize suited to the trade. It would take on board the furs collected during the preceding year, carry them to Canton, invest the proceeds in the rich merchandize of China, and return thus freighted to New York.

As, in extending the American trade along the coast to the northward, it might be brought into the vicinity of the Russian Fur Company, and produce a hostile rivalry, it was part of the plan of Mr. Astor to conciliate the good will of that company by the most amicable and beneficial arrangements. The Russian establishment was chiefly dependent for its supplies upon transient trading vessels from the United States. These vessels, however, were often of more harm than advantage. Being owned by private adventurers on casual voyages who cared only for present profit and had no interest in the permanent prosperity of the trade, they were reckless in their dealings with the natives, and made no scruple of supplying them with fire arms. In this way several fierce tribes in the vicinity of the Russian posts, or within the range of their trading excursions, were furnished with deadly means of warfare, and rendered troublesome and dangerous neighbors.

The Russian government had made representations to that of the United States of these malpractices on the part of its citizens, and urged to have this traffic in arms prohibited; but, as it did not infringe any municipal law, our government could not interfere. Still it regarded, with solicitude, a traffic which, if persisted in, might give offense to Russia, at that time almost the only power friendly to us. In this dilemma the government had applied to Mr. Astor, as one conversant in this branch of trade, for information that might point out a way to remedy the evil. This circumstance had suggested to him the idea of supplying the Russian establishment regularly by means of the annual ship that should visit the settlement at the mouth of the Columbia (or Oregon); by this means the casual trading vessels would be excluded from those parts of the coast, where their malpractices were so injurious to the Russians.

Such is a brief outline of the enterprize projected by Mr. Astor, but which continually expanded in his mind. Indeed it is due to him to say that he was not actuated by mere motives of individual profit. He was already wealthy beyond the ordinary desires of man, but he now aspired to that honorable fame which is awarded to men of similar scope of mind, who by their great commercial enterprizes have enriched nations, peopled wildernesses and extended the bounds of empire. He considered his projected establishment at the mouth of the Columbia as the emporium to an immense commerce; as a colony that would form the germ of a wide civilization; that would, in fact, carry the American population across the Rocky Mountains and spread it along the shores of the Pacific, as it already animated the shores of the Atlantic.

As Mr. Astor by the magnitude of his commercial and financial relations, and the vigour and scope of his self taught mind, had elevated himself into the consideration of Government and the communion and correspondence with leading statesmen, he, at an early period, communicated his schemes to President Jefferson, soliciting the countenance of Government. How highly they were esteemed by that eminent man we may judge by the following passage written by him some time afterwards, to Mr. Astor.

"I remember well having invited your proposition on this subject,* and encouraged it with the assurance of every facility and protection which the Government could properly afford. I considered as a great public acquisition the commencement of a settlement on that point of the Western Coast of America, and looked forward with gratification to the time when its descendants should have spread themselves thro' the whole length of that coast, covering it with free and independent Americans, unconnected with us but by the ties of blood and interest, and enjoying like us the rights of self government."

The cabinet joined with Mr. Jefferson in warm approbation of the plan, and held out assurance of every protection that could, consistently with general policy, be afforded.

Mr. Astor now prepared to carry his scheme into prompt execution.

---

* On this point Mr. Jefferson's memory was in error. The proposition alluded to was the one, already mentioned, for the establishment of an American Fur Company in the Atlantic states. The great enterprize beyond the Mountains, that was to sweep the shores of the Pacific, originated in the mind of Mr. Astor, and was proposed by him to the Government.

He had some competition however to apprehend and guard against. The North West Company, acting feebly and partially upon the suggestions of its former agent Sir Alexander MacKenzie, had pushed one or two advanced trading posts across the Rocky Mountains, into a tract of country visited by that enterprizing traveller, and since named New Caledonia. This tract lay about two degrees north of the Columbia, and intervened between the territories of the United States and those of Russia. Its length was about 550 miles and its breadth from the Mountains to the Pacific, from 300 to 350 geographical miles.

Should the North West Company persist in extending their trade in that quarter their competition might be of serious detriment to the plans of Mr. Astor. It is true they would contend with him to a vast disadvantage, from the checks and restrictions to which they were subjected. They were straitened on one side by the rivalry of the Hudson's Bay Company. Then they had no good port on the Pacific where they could receive supplies by sea for their establishments beyond the mountains; nor, if they had one, could they ship their furs thence to China, that great mart for peltries; the Chinese trade being comprized in the monopoly of the East India Company. Their posts beyond the mountains had to be supplied, in yearly expeditions, like caravans, from Montreal, and the furs conveyed back in the same way, by long, precarious and expensive routes across the continent. Mr. Astor, on the contrary, would be able to supply his proposed establishment at the mouth of the Columbia by sea, and to ship the furs collected there directly to China, so as to undersell the North West Company in the great Chinese market.

Still the competition of two rival companies west of the Rocky Mountains could not but prove detrimental to both, and fraught with those evils, both to the trade and to the Indians, that had attended similar rivalries in the Canadas. To prevent any contest of the kind, therefore, he made known his plan to the agents of the North West Company, and proposed to interest them, to the extent of one third, in the trade thus to be opened.

Some correspondence and negotiation ensued; the Company were aware of the advantages which would be possessed by Mr. Astor should he be able to carry his scheme into effect; but they anticipated a monopoly of the trade beyond the mountains, by their establishments in New Caledonia, and were loth to share it with an individual who had already proved a formidable competitor in the Atlantic trade. They hoped, too, by a timely move, to secure the mouth of the Columbia before Mr. Astor would be able to put his plans into operation, and, that key to the internal trade once in their possession, the whole country would be at their command. After some negotiation and delay, therefore, they declined the proposition that had been made to them; but subsequently despatched a party for the mouth of the Columbia, to establish a post there, before any expedition sent out by Mr. Astor might arrive.

In the mean time Mr. Astor, finding his overtures rejected, proceeded fearlessly to execute his enterprize in face of the whole power of the North West Company. His main establishment once planted at the mouth of the Columbia, he looked with confidence to ultimate success. Being able to reinforce and supply it amply by sea, he would push his interior posts in every direction up the rivers and along the coast; supplying the natives at a lower rate, and thus gradually obliging the North West Company to give up the competition, relinquish New Caledonia, and retire to the other side of the mountains. He would then have possession of the trade, not merely of the Columbia and its tributaries, but of the regions farther north, quite to the Russian possessions. Such was a part of his brilliant and comprehensive plan.

He now proceeded, with all diligence, to procure proper agents and coadjutors, habituated to the Indian trade and to the life of the wilderness. Among the clerks of the North West Company were several of great capacity and experience, who had served out their probationary terms, but who, either through lack of interest and influence, or a want of vacancies, had not been promoted. They were consequently much dissatisfied, and ready for any employment in which their talents and acquirements might be turned to better account.

Mr. Astor made his overtures to several of these persons and three of them entered into his views. One of these, Mr. Alexander M'Kay, had accompanied Sir Alexander MacKenzie in both of his expeditions to the North West Coast of America in 1789 and 1793. The other two were Duncan M'Dougall and Donald M'Kenzie. To these was subsequently added Mr. Wilson Price Hunt of New Jersey. As this gentleman was a native born citizen of the United States, and a person of great probity and worth, he was selected by Mr. Astor to be his chief agent and to represent him in the contemplated establishment.

On the 23d of June 1810 articles of agreement were entered into between Mr. Astor and those four gentlemen, acting for themselves and for the several persons who had already agreed to become, or should thereafter become, associated under the firm of The Pacific Fur Company.

According to these articles Mr. Astor was to be at the head of the Company and to manage its affairs in New York. He was to furnish vessels, goods, provisions, arms, ammunition and all other requisites for the enterprize at first cost and charges, provided that they did not, at any time, involve an advance of more than four hundred thousand dollars.

The stock of the Company was to be divided into a hundred equal shares with the profits accruing thereon. Fifty shares were to be at the disposition of Mr. Astor, and the other fifty to be divided among the partners and their associates.

Mr. Astor was to have the privilege of introducing other persons into the connexion, as partners, two of whom, at least, should be conversant with the Indian trade and none of them entitled to more than three shares.

A general meeting of the Company was to be held annually at Columbia River, for the investigation and regulation of its affairs; at which absent members might be represented and might vote by proxy under certain specified conditions.

The association, if successful, was to continue for twenty years; but the parties had full power to abandon and dissolve it within the first five years, should it be found unprofitable. For this term Mr. Astor covenanted to bear all the loss that might be incurred; after which it was to be borne by all the partners in proportion to their respective shares.

The parties of the second part were to execute faithfully such duties as might be assigned to them by a majority of the Company on the North West Coast, and to repair to such place or places as the majority might direct.

An agent, appointed for the term of five years, was to reside at the principal establishment on the North West Coast, and Wilson Price Hunt was the one chosen for the first term. Should the interests of the concern at any time require his absence, a person was to be appointed, in general meeting, to take his place.

Such were the leading conditions of this association; we shall now proceed to relate the various hardy and eventful expeditions, by sea and land, to which it gave rise.

CHAPTER IV

In prosecuting his great scheme of commerce and colonization, two expeditions were devised by Mr. Astor, one by sea, the other by land. The former was to carry out the people, stores, ammunition and merchandize requisite for establishing a fortified trading post at the mouth of Columbia River. The latter, conducted by Mr. Hunt, was to proceed up the Missouri and across the Rocky Mountains, to the same point, exploring a line of communication across the continent, and noting the places where interior trading posts might be established. The expedition by sea is the one which comes first under consideration.

A fine ship was provided called the Tonquin, of two hundred and ninety tons burthen, mounting ten guns, with a crew of twenty men. She carried an assortment of merchandize for trading with the natives of the sea board and of the interior, together with the frame of a schooner to be employed in the coasting trade. Seeds also were provided for the cultivation of the soil, and nothing was neglected for the necessary supply of the establishment. The command of the ship was entrusted to Jonathan Thorn, of New York, a lieutenant in the United States Navy, on leave of absence. He was a man of courage and firmness who had distinguished himself in our Tripolitan war, and from being accustomed to naval discipline was considered by Mr. Astor as well fitted to take charge of an expedition of the kind. Four of the partners were to embark in the ship, namely, Messrs. M'Kay, M'Dougall, David Stuart, and his nephew Robert Stuart. Mr. M'Dougall was empowered by Mr. Astor to act as his proxy in the absence of Mr. Hunt, to vote for him and in his name, on any question that might come before any meeting of the persons interested in the voyage.

Beside the partners there were twelve clerks to go out in the ship, several of them natives of Canada, who had some experience in Indian trade. They were bound to the service of the company for five years at the rate of one hundred dollars a year, payable at the expiration of the term, and an annual equipment of clothing to the amount of forty dollars. In case of ill conduct they were liable to

forfeit their wages and be dismissed; but, should they acquit themselves well, the confident expectation was held out to them of promotion,
and partnership. Their interests were thus, to some extent, identified
with those of the Company.

Several artizans were likewise to sail in the ship, for the supply of
the colony; but the most peculiar and characteristic part of this motley
embarcation consisted of thirteen Canadian "voyageurs," who had
enlisted for five years. As this class of functionaries will continually
recur in the course of the following narrations and as they form one
of those distinct and strongly marked castes or orders of people, springing
up in this vast continent, out of geographical circumstances, or the
varied pursuits, habitudes and origins of its population, we shall sketch
a few of their characteristics for the information of the reader.

The "voyageurs" form a kind of confraternity in the Canadas, like
the Arrieros, or Carriers of Spain, and like them are employed in
long internal expeditions of travel and traffic: with this difference that
the Arrieros travel by land, the voyageurs by water; the former with
mules and horses, the latter with batteaux and canoes. The voyageurs
may be said to have sprung up out of the Fur trade, having originally
been employed by the early French merchants in their trading expeditions through the labyrinth of rivers and lakes of the boundless
interior. They were coeval with the *"Coureurs des bois"* or Rangers of
the woods, already noticed, and like them, in the intervals of their
long, arduous and laborious expeditions, were prone to pass their time
in idleness and revelry about the trading posts or settlements; squander-
ing their hard earnings in heedless conviviality, and rivalling their
neighbors the Indians in indolent indulgence and an imprudent disregard of the morrow.

When Canada passed under British domination, and the old French
trading houses were broken up, the voyageurs, like the *Coureurs des
bois,* were for a time disheartened and disconsolate, and with difficulty
could reconcile themselves to the service of the new comers, so different
in habits, manners and language from their former employers. By
degrees, however, they became accustomed to the change, and at length
came to consider the British fur traders and especially the members
of the North West Company, as the legitimate lords of creation.

The dress of these people is generally half civilized half savage.
They wear a capot or surcoat, made of a blanket, a striped cotton
shirt, cloth trowsers, or leathern leggings, moccasins of deer skin and
a belt of variegated worsted, from which are suspended the knife,
tobacco pouch and other implements. Their language is of the same
pyebald character, being a French patois, embroidered with Indian
and English words and phrases.

The lives of the voyageurs are passed in wild and extensive rovings, in the service of individuals, but more especially of the Fur traders. They are generally of French descent, and inherit much of the gaiety and lightness of heart of their ancestors, being full of anecdote and song and ever ready for the dance. They inherit, too, a fund of civility and complaisance; and instead of that hardness and grossness which men in laborious life are apt to indulge towards each other, they are mutually obliging and accommodating; interchanging kind offices, yielding each other assistance and comfort in every emergency, and using the familiar appellations of "cousin" and "brother," when there is in fact no relationship. Their natural good will is probably heightened by a community of adventure and hardship in their precarious and wandering life.

No men are more submissive to their leaders and employers, more capable of enduring hardship, or more good humoured under privations. Never are they so happy as when on long and rough expeditions, toiling up rivers or coasting lakes; encamping at night on the borders, gossipping round their fires, and bivouacking in the open air. They are dextrous boatmen, vigorous and adroit with the oar and paddle, and will row from morning until night without a murmur. The steersman often sings an old traditionary French song, with some regular burden in which they all join, keeping time with their oars; if at any time they flag in spirits or relax in exertion, it is but necessary to strike up a song of the kind to put them all in fresh spirits and activity. The Canadian waters are vocal with these little French chansons, that have been echoed from mouth to mouth and transmitted from father to son, from the earliest days of the Colony; and it has a pleasing effect, in a still golden summer evening, to see a batteau gliding across the bosom of a lake and dipping its oars to the cadence of these quaint old ditties, or sweeping along, in full chorus on a bright sunny morning, down the transparent current of one of the Canada rivers.

But we are talking of things that are fast fading away! The march of mechanical invention is driving every thing poetical before it. The steamboats which are fast dispelling the wildness and romance of our lakes and rivers and aiding to subdue the world into commonplace, are proving as fatal to the race of the Canadian voyageurs as they have been to that of the boatmen of the Mississippi. Their glory is departed. They are no longer the lords of our internal seas and the great navigators of the wilderness. Some of them may still occasionally be seen coasting the lower lakes with their frail barks and pitching their camps and lighting their fires upon the shores; but their range is fast contracting to those remote waters and shallow and obstructed rivers unvisited by the steamboat. In the course of years they will gradually disappear: their songs will die away like the echoes they once awakened, and the Canadian voyageurs will become a forgotten race, or remembered, like their associates the Indians, among the poetical images of past times, and as themes for local and romantic associations.

An instance of the buoyant temperament and the professional pride of these people was furnished in the gay and braggart style in which they arrived at New York to join the enterprize. They were determined to regale and astonish the people of the "States" with the sight of a Canadian boat and a Canadian crew. They accordingly fitted up a large but light bark canoe, such as is used in the fur trade; transported it in a waggon from the banks of the S' Lawrence to the shores of Lake Champlain; traversed the lake in it, from end to end; hoisted it again on a waggon and wheeled it off to Lansingburgh and there launched it upon the waters of the Hudson. Down this river they plied their course merrily on a fine summer's day, making its banks resound for the first time with their old French boat songs; passing by the villages with whoop and halloo, so as to make the honest Dutch farmers mistake them for a crew of savages. In this way they swept, in full song, and with regular flourish of the paddle, round New York, in a still summer evening, to the wonder and admiration of its inhabitants, who had never before witnessed on their waters, a nautical apparition of the kind.

Such was the variegated band of adventurers about to embark in the Tonquin on this arduous and doubtful enterprize. While yet in port and on dry land, in the bustle of preparation and the excitement of novelty, all was sunshine and promise. The Canadians especially, who, with their constitutional vivacity, have a considerable dash of the Gascon, were buoyant and boastful and great braggarts as to the future; while all those who had been in the service of the North West Company, and engaged in the Indian trade, plumed themselves upon their hardihood and their capacity to endure privations. If Mr. Astor ventured to hint at the difficulties they might have to encounter, they treated them with scorn. They were "north westers," men seasoned to hardships, who cared for neither wind nor weather. They could live hard, lie hard, sleep hard, eat dogs!—in a word they were ready to do and suffer any thing for the good of the enterprize. With all this profession of zeal and devotion, Mr. Astor was not over confident of the stability and firm faith of these mercurial beings. He had received information, also, that an armed brig from Halifax, probably at the instigation of the North West Company, was hovering on the coast, watching for the Tonquin, with the purpose of impressing the Canadians on board of her, as British subjects, and thus interrupting the voyage. It was a time of doubt and anxiety, when the relations between the United States and Great Britain were daily assuming a more precarious aspect, and verging towards that war which shortly ensued. As a precautionary measure, therefore, he required that the voyageurs, as they were about to enter into the service of an American Association, and to reside within the limits of the United States, should take the oaths of naturalization, as American citizens. To this they readily agreed, and shortly afterward assured him that they had actually done so. It was not until after they had sailed that he discovered that they had entirely deceived him in the matter.

The confidence of Mr. Astor was abused in another quarter. Two of the partners, both of them Scotchmen, and recently in the service of the North West Company, had misgivings as to an enterprize which might clash with the interests and establishments protected by the British flag. They privately waited upon the British Minister, Mr. Jackson, then in New York, laid open to him the whole scheme of Mr. Astor, though entrusted to them in confidence, and dependent, in a great measure, upon secrecy at the outset for its success, and enquired whether they, as British subjects, could lawfully engage in it. The reply satisfied their scruples, while the information they imparted excited the surprize and admiration of Mr. Jackson, that a private individual should have conceived and set on foot at his own risk and expense, so great an enterprize.

This step on the part of those gentlemen was not known to Mr. Astor until sometime afterwards or it might have modified the trust and confidence reposed in them.

To guard against any interruption to the voyage by the armed brig said to be off the harbour, Mr. Astor applied to Commodore Rogers, at that time commanding at New York, to give the Tonquin safe convoy off the coast. The Commodore having received from a high official source assurance of the deep interest which the government took in the enterprize, sent directions to Captain Hull, at that time cruizing off the harbour, in the Frigate Constitution, to afford the Tonquin the required protection when she should put to sea.

Before the day of embarcation, Mr. Astor addressed a letter of instruction to the four partners who were to sail in the ship. In this he enjoined them, in the most earnest manner, to cultivate harmony and unanimity, and recommended that all differences of opinions on points connected with the objects and interests of the voyage should be discussed by the whole, and decided by a majority of votes. He, moreover, gave them especial caution as to their conduct on arriving at their destined port; exhorting them to be careful to make a favorable impression upon the wild people among whom their lot and the fortunes of the enterprize would be cast. "If you find them kind," said he, "as I hope you will, be so to them. If otherwise, act with caution and forbearance and convince them that you come as friends."

With the same anxious forethought he wrote a letter of instructions to Captain Thorn in which he urged the strictest attention to the health of himself and his crew, and to the promotion of good humour and harmony on board his ship. "To prevent any misunderstanding," added he, "will require your particular good management." His letter closed with an injunction of wariness in his intercourse with the natives, a subject on which Mr. Astor was justly sensible he could not be too earnest. "I must recommend you," said he, "to be particularly careful on the coast, and not to rely too much on the friendly disposition of the natives. All accidents which have as yet happened there arose from too much confidence in the Indians."

The reader will bear these instructions in mind as events will prove their wisdom and importance, and the disasters which ensued in consequence of the neglect of them.

CHAPTER V

*Sailing of the Tonquin—A rigid commander and a reckless crew—
Landsmen on shipboard—Fresh water sailors at sea—Lubber nests
—Ship fare—A Labrador veteran—Literary clerks—Curious travellers—
Robinson Crusoe's island—Quarter deck quarrels—Falkland islands—
A wild goose chase—Port Egmont—Epitaph hunting—Old Mortality
—Penguin shooting—Sportsmen left in the lurch—A hard pull—Further
altercations—Arrival at Owyhee.*

On the eighth of September 1810, the Tonquin put to sea where she
was soon joined by the Frigate Constitution. The wind was fresh and
fair from the south west, and the ship was soon out of sight of land
and free from the apprehended danger of interruption. The Frigate,
therefore, gave her "God speed" and left her to her course.

The harmony so earnestly enjoined by Mr. Astor on this heterogeneous
crew, and which had been so confidently promised in the buoyant
moments of preparation, was doomed to meet with a check at the
very outset.

Captain Thorn was an honest, straight forward, but somewhat dry
and dictatorial commander who, having been nurtured in the system
and discipline of a ship of war and in a sacred opinion of the
supremacy of the quarter deck, was disposed to be absolute lord and
master on board of his ship. He appears, moreover, to have had no
great opinion from the first, of the persons embarked with him. He
had stood by with surly contempt while they vaunted so bravely to
Mr. Astor of all they could do and all they could undergo, how they
could face all weathers, put up with all kinds of fare, and even eat
dogs with a relish, when no better food was to be had. He had set
them down as a set of land lubbers and braggadocios, and was disposed
to treat them accordingly. Mr. Astor was, in his eyes, his only real
employer, being the father of the enterprize, who furnished all funds
and bore all losses. The others were mere agents and subordinates,
who lived at his expense. He evidently had but a narrow idea of
the scope and nature of the enterprize, limiting his views merely
to his part of it; every thing beyond the concerns of his ship was
out of his sphere; and any thing that interfered with the routine of
his nautical duties put him in a passion.

The partners, on the other hand, had been brought up in the service
of the North West Company, and in a profound idea of the importance,
dignity and authority of a partner. They already began to consider
themselves on a par with the M'Tavishes, the MacGillivrays, the Frobishers and the other magnates of the North West, whom they had

been accustomed to look up to as the Great ones of the Earth, and
they were a little disposed, perhaps, to wear their suddenly acquired
honours, with some air of pretension. Mr. Astor, too, had put them
on their mettle with respect to the Captain, describing him as a gun
powder fellow who would command his ship in fine style, and, if there
was any fighting to do, would "blow all out of the water."

Thus prepared to regard each other with no very cordial eye, it
is not to be wondered at that the parties soon came into collision.
On the very first night Captain Thorn began his man of war discipline
by ordering the lights in the cabin to be extinguished at eight o'clock.

The pride of the partners was immediately in arms. This was an
invasion of their rights and dignities not to be borne. They were on
board of their own ship, and entitled to consult their ease and enjoyment. M'Dougall was the champion of their cause. He was an active,
irritable, fuming, vain glorious little man, and elevated in his own
opinion, by being the proxy of Mr. Astor. A violent altercation ensued
in the course of which Thorn threatened to put the partners in irons
should they prove refractory; upon which M'Dougall seized a pistol
and swore to be the death of the Captain should he ever offer such
an indignity. It was some time before the irritated parties could be
pacified by the more temperate bystanders.

Such was the Captain's outset with the partners: Nor did the clerks
stand much higher in his good graces; indeed he seems to have regarded
all the landsmen on board his ship as a kind of live lumber, continually
in the way. The poor voyageurs, too, continually irritated his spleen
by their "lubberly" and unseemly habits, so abhorrent to one accustomed to the cleanliness of a man of war. These poor fresh water
sailors, so vainglorious on shore, and almost amphibious when on lakes
and rivers, lost all heart and stomach the moment they were at sea.
For days they suffered the doleful rigours and retchings of seasickness, lurking below in their berths in squalid state, or emerging now
and then like spectres from the hatch ways, in capotes and blankets;
with dirty night cap, grizly beard, lanthorn visage and unhappy eye,
shivering about the deck, and ever and anon crawling to the sides
of the vessel, and offering up their tributes to the windward, to the
infinite annoyance of the Captain.

His letters to Mr. Astor, wherein he pours forth the bitterness of
his soul, and his seamanlike impatience of, what he considers, the
"lubberly" character and conduct of those around him, are before us,
and are amusingly characteristic. The honest Captain is full of vexation on his own account, and solicitude on account of Mr. Astor, whose
property he considers at the mercy of a most heterogeneous and
wasteful crew.

As to the clerks, he pronounces them mere pretenders, not one of whom had ever been among Indians, nor farther to the north west than Montreal, nor of higher rank than bar keeper of a tavern or marker of a billiard table, excepting one, who had been a schoolmaster, and whom he emphatically sets down for "as foolish a pedant as ever lived."

Then as to the artizans and laborers who had been brought from Canada and shipped at such expense, the three most respectable, according to the Captain's account, were culprits who had fled from Canada on account of their misdeeds: the rest had figured in Montreal as draymen, barbers, waiters and carriole drivers, and were the most helpless worthless beings "that ever broke sea biscuit."

It may easily be imagined what a series of misunderstandings and cross purposes would be likely to take place between such a crew and such a commander. The Captain in his zeal for the health and cleanliness of his ship, would make sweeping visitations to the "lubber nests" of the unlucky "voyageurs" and their companions in misery, ferret them out of their berths, make them air and wash themselves and their accoutrements, and oblige them to stir about briskly and take exercise.

Nor did his disgust and vexation cease when all hands had recovered from seasickness, and become accustomed to the ship, for now broke forth an alarming keenness of appetite that threatened havoc to the provisions. What especially irritated the Captain was the daintiness of some of his cabin passengers. They were loud in their complaints of the ship's fare, though their table was served with fresh pork, hams, tongues, smoked beef and puddings. "When thwarted in their cravings for delicacies," said he, "they would exclaim that it was d——d hard they could not live as they pleased upon their own property, being on board of their own ship, freighted with their own merchandize.—And these," added he, "are the fine fellows who made such boast that they could 'eat dogs.' "

In his indignation at, what he termed, their effeminacy, he would swear that he would never take them to sea again "without having Fly Market on the fore castle, Covent Garden on the poop and a cool spring from Canada in the main top."

As they proceeded on their voyage and got into the smooth seas and pleasant weather of the tropics, other annoyances occurred to vex the spirit of the Captain. He had been crossed by the irritable moods of one of the partners, he was now excessively annoyed by the good humour of another. This was the elder Stuart, who was an easy soul and of a social disposition. He had seen life in Canada, and on the coast of Labrador, had been a fur trader in the former and a fisherman on the latter; and, in the course of his experience had made

various expeditions with voyageurs. He was accustomed, therefore, to
the familiarity which prevails between that class and their superiors,
and the gossippings which take place among them when seated round
a fire at their encampments. Stuart was never so happy as when he
could seat himself on the deck with a number of these men round
him, in camping style, smoke together, passing the pipe from mouth
to mouth after the manner of the Indians, sing old Canadian boat
songs, and tell stories about their hardships and adventures, in the
course of which he rivalled Sindbad in his long tales of the sea, about
his fishing exploits on the coast of Labrador.

This gossipping familiarity shocked the Captain's notions of rank
and subordination, and nothing was so abhorrent to him as the community of pipe between master and man, and their mingling in chorus
in the outlandish boat songs.

Then there was another whimsical source of annoyance to him. Some
of the young clerks, who were making their first voyage, and to whom
every thing was new and strange, were, very rationally, in the habit
of taking notes and keeping journals. This was a sore abomination to
the honest Captain who held their literary pretensions in great contempt. "The collecting of materials for long histories of their voyage
and travels," said he, in his letter to Mr. Astor, "appears to engross
most of their attention." We can conceive what must have been the
crusty impatience of the worthy navigator, when, on any trifling
occurrence in the course of the voyage, quite commonplace in his
eyes, he saw these young landsmen running to record it in their journals;
and what indignant glances he must have cast to right and left, as
he worried about the deck, giving out his orders for the management
of the ship, surrounded by singing, smoking, gossipping, scribbling
groupes, all, as he thought, intent upon the amusement of the passing
hour, instead of the great purpose and interests of the voyage.

It is possible the Captain was in some degree right in his notions.
Though some of the passengers had much to gain by the voyage,
none of them had any thing positively to lose; they were mostly young
men, in the heyday of life, and having got into fine latitudes, upon
smooth seas, with a well stored ship under them and a fair wind
in the shoulder of the sail, they seemed to have got into a holyday
world, and were disposed to enjoy it. That craving desire, natural to
untravelled men of fresh and lively minds, to see strange lands, and
to visit scenes famous in history or fable, was expressed by some of
the partners and clerks, with respect to some of the storied coasts
and islands that lay within their route. The Captain, however, who
regarded every coast and island with a matter of fact eye, and had
no more associations connected with them than those laid down in

his sea chart, considered all this curiosity as exceedingly idle and childish. "In the first part of the voyage," says he in his letter, "they were determined to have it said they had been in Africa, and therefore insisted on my stopping at the Cape de Verds.—Next they said the ship should stop on the coast of Patagonia for they must see the large and uncommon inhabitants of that place. Then they must go to the island where Robinson Crusoe had so long lived. And lastly they were determined to see the handsome inhabitants of Easter Island."

To all these resolves the Captain opposed his peremptory veto, as "contrary to instructions." Then would break forth an unavailing explosion of wrath on the part of certain of the partners, in the course of which they did not even spare Mr. Astor for his act of supererogation in furnishing orders for the control of the ship while they were on board; instead of leaving them to be the judges, where it would be best for her to touch and how long to remain. The choleric M'Dougall took the lead in these railings, being as has been observed, a little puffed up with the idea of being Mr. Astor's proxy.

The Captain, however, became only so much the more crusty and dogged in his adherence to his orders, and techy and harsh in his dealings with his passengers, and frequent altercations ensued. He may in some measure have been influenced by his seamanlike impatience of the interference of landsmen, and his high notions of naval etiquette and quarter deck authority; but he evidently had an honest, trusty concern for the interests of his employer. He pictured to himself the anxious projector of the enterprize, who had disbursed so munificently in its outfit; calculating on the zeal, fidelity and singleness of purpose of his associates and agents; while they, on the other hand, having a good ship at their disposal, and a deep pocket at home, to bear them out, seemed ready to loiter on every coast and amuse themselves in every port.

On the fourth of December they came in sight of the Falkland Islands. Having been for some time on an allowance of water it was resolved to anchor here and obtain a supply. A boat was sent into a small bay to take soundings. Mr. M'Dougall and Mr. M'Kay took this occasion to go on shore, but with a request from the Captain that they would not detain the ship. Once on shore, however, they were in no haste to obey his orders, but rambled about in search of curiosities. The anchorage proving unsafe, and water difficult to be procured, the Captain stood out to sea, and made repeated signals for those on shore to rejoin the ship, but it was not until nine at night that they came on board.

The wind being adverse the boat was again sent on shore on the following morning, and the same gentlemen again landed, but promised

to come off at a moment's warning; they again forgot their promise
in their eager pursuit of wild geese and sea wolves. After a time the
wind hauled fair and signals were made for the boat. Half an hour
elapsed but no boat put off. The Captain reconnoitered the shore with
his glass and, to his infinite vexation, saw the loiterers in the full
enjoyment of their "wild goose chase." Nettled to the quick he immediately made sail. When those on shore saw the ship actually under
way they embarked with all speed, but had a hard pull of eight miles
before they got on board, and then experienced but a grim reception,
notwithstanding that they came well laden with the spoils of the chase.

Two days afterwards, on the 7th of December, they anchored at Port
Egmont in the same island, where they remained four days taking in
water and making repairs. This was a joyous time for the landsmen.
They pitched a tent on shore, had a boat at their command and passed
their time merrily in rambling about the island, and coasting along
the shores shooting sea lions, seals, foxes, geese, ducks and penguins.
None were keener in pursuit of this kind of game than M'Dougall and
David Stuart; the latter was reminded of aquatic sports on the coast
of Labrador, and his hunting exploits in the north west.

In the meantime the Captain addressed himself steadily to the
business of his ship, scorning the holyday spirit and useless pursuits
of his emancipated messmates, and warning them, from time to time,
not to wander away nor be out of hail. They promised, as usual, that
the ship should never experience a moment's detention on their
account, but, as usual, forgot their promise.

On the morning of the 11th, the repairs being all finished, and
the water casks replenished, the signal was given to embark, and
the ship began to weigh anchor. At this time several of the passengers
were dispersed about the island, amusing themselves in various ways.
Some of the young men had found two inscriptions, in English, over
a place where two unfortunate mariners had been buried in this desert
island. As the inscriptions were nearly worn out by time and weather,
they were playing the part of "Old Mortality," and piously renewing
them. The signal from the ship summoned them from their labors,
they saw the sails unfurled and that she was getting under way. The
two sporting partners, however, Mr. M'Dougall and David Stuart, had
strolled away to the south of the island in pursuit of penguins. It
would never do to put off without them, as there was but one boat
to convey the whole.

While this delay took place on shore the Captain was storming on
board. This was the third time his orders had been treated with
contempt, and the ship wantonly detained, and it should be the last,
so he spread all sail and put to sea, swearing he would leave the

laggards to shift for themselves. It was in vain that those on board made remonstrances and entreaties and represented the horrors of abandoning men upon a sterile and uninhabited island: the sturdy Captain was inflexible.

In the meantime the penguin hunters had joined the engravers of tombstones but not before the ship was already out at sea. They all, to the number of eight, threw themselves into their boat, which was about twenty feet in length, and rowed with might and main. For three hours and a half did they tug anxiously and severely at the oar, swashed occasionally by the surging waves of the open sea, while the ship inexorably kept on her course and seemed determined to leave them behind.

On board of the ship was the nephew of David Stuart, a young man of spirit and resolution. Seeing, as he thought, the Captain obstinately bent upon abandoning his uncle and the others, he seized a pistol, and in a paroxysm of wrath swore he would blow out the Captain's brains unless he put about or shortened sail.

Fortunately for all parties the wind just then came ahead, and the boat was enabled to reach the ship, otherwise disastrous circumstances might have ensued. We can hardly believe that the Captain really intended to carry his threat into full effect, and rather think he meant to let the laggards off for a long pull and a hearty fright: he declared, however, in his letter to Mr. Astor, that he was serious in his threats; and there is no knowing how far such an iron man may push his notions of authority.

"Had the wind," writes he, "(unfortunately) not hauled ahead soon after leaving the harbour's mouth, I should positively have left them; and indeed I cannot but think it an unfortunate circumstance for you that it so happened, for the first loss in this instance, would, in my opinion, have proved the best, as they seem to have no idea of the value of property nor any apparent regard for your interest, although interwoven with their own."

This it must be confessed was acting with a high hand and carrying a regard to the owner's property to a dangerous length. Various petty feuds occurred also between him and the partners in respect to the goods on board the ship, some articles of which they wished to distribute for clothing among the men, or for other purposes which they deemed essential. The Captain, however, kept a mastiff watch upon the cargo and growled and snapped if they but offered to touch box or bale. It was "contrary to orders"; it would forfeit his insurance; it was out of all rule. It was in vain they insisted upon their right to do so, as part owners, and as acting for the good of the enterprize; the Captain only stuck to his point the more staunchly. They consoled themselves, therefore, by declaring that, as soon as they made land they would assert their rights and do with ship and cargo as they pleased.

Beside these feuds between the Captain and the partners, there were feuds between the partners themselves, occasioned, in some measure, by jealousy of rank. M'Dougall and M'Kay began to draw plans for the fort and other buildings of the intended establishment. They agreed very well as to the outline and dimensions, which were on a sufficiently grand scale, but when they came to arrange the details fierce disputes arose, and they would quarrel by the hour about the distribution of the doors and windows. Many were the hard words and hard names bandied between them on these occasions, according to the Captain's account: each accused the other of endeavoring to assume unwarrantable power and to take the lead, upon which Mr. M'Dougall would vauntingly lay down Mr. Astor's letter constituting him his representative and proxy, a document not to be disputed.

These wordy contests though violent were brief, "and within fifteen minutes," says the Captain, "they would be caressing each other like children."

While all this petty anarchy was agitating the little world within the Tonquin, the good ship prosperously pursued her course, doubled Cape Horn on the 25th of December, careered across the bosom of the Pacific, until, on the 11th of February, the snowy peaks of Owyhee were seen brightening above the horizon.

CHAPTER VI

*Owyhee—Sandwich islanders—Their nautical talents—Tamaahmaah—
His navy—His negotiations—Views of Mr. Astor with respect to the
Sandwich islands—Karakakooa—Royal monopoly of pork—Description
of the islanders—Gaieties on shore—Chronicler of the island—Place
where Captain Cook was killed—John Young, a nautical governor—
His story—Waititi—A royal residence—A royal visit—Grand ceremonials
—Close dealing—A royal pork merchant—Grievances of a matter of
fact man.*

Owyhee, or Hawaii as it is written by more exact orthographers, is
the largest of the cluster, ten in number, of the Sandwich islands. It is
about ninety seven miles in length and seventy eight in breadth rising
gradually into three pyramidal summits or cones, the highest, Mouna
Roa, being eighteen thousand feet above the level of the sea, so as
to domineer over the whole archipelago, and to be a land mark over
a wide extent of ocean. It remains a lasting monument of the enterprizing and unfortunate Captain Cook, who was murdered by the
natives of this island.

The Sandwich islanders when first discovered evinced a character
superior to most of the Savages of the Pacific isles. They were frank
and open in their deportment; friendly and liberal in their dealings,
with an apt ingenuity apparent in all their rude inventions. The tragical
fate of the discoverer, which for a time brought them under the
charge of ferocity, was, in fact, the result of sudden exasperation
caused by the seizure of their chief.

At the time of the visit of the Tonquin the islanders had profited
in many respects, by occasional intercourse with white men; and had
shewn a quickness to observe and cultivate those arts important to
their mode of living. Originally they had no means of navigating the
seas by which they were surrounded, superior to light pirogues, which
were little competent to contend with the storms of the broad ocean.
As the islanders are not in sight of each other, there could, therefore,
be but casual intercourse between them. The traffic with white men
had put them in possession of vessels of superior description; they
had made themselves acquainted with their management, and had
even made rude advances in the art of ship building.

These improvements had been promoted in a great measure by
the energy and sagacity of one man, the famous Tamaahmaah. He
had originally been a petty Eri or chief; but, being of an intrepid and
aspiring nature, he had risen in rank, and, availing himself of the
superior advantages now afforded in navigation, had brought the whole

41

archipelago in subjection to his arms. At the time of the arrival of
the Tonquin he had about forty schooners of from twenty to thirty
tons burthen, and one old American ship. With these he maintained
undisputed sway over his insular domains, and carried on an intercourse with the chiefs or governors whom he had placed in command
of the several islands.

The situation of this groupe of islands far in the bosom of the
vast Pacific, and their abundant fertility, rendered them important
stopping places on the high way to China, or to the North West
Coast of America. Here the vessels engaged in the Fur Trade touched
to make repairs and procure provisions, and here they often sheltered
themselves during the winters that occurred in their long coasting
expeditions.

The British navigators were from the first aware of the value of
these islands to the purposes of Commerce, and Tamaahmaah, not
long after he had attained the sovereign sway, was persuaded by
Vancouver, the celebrated discoverer, to acknowledge, on behalf of
himself and subjects, allegiance to the King of Great Britain. The
reader cannot but call to mind the visit which the royal family and
Court of the Sandwich islands was, in late years, induced to make
to the Court of S' James; and the serio-comic ceremonials and mock
parade which attended that singular travesty of monarchial style.

It was a part of the wide and comprehensive plan of Mr. Astor to
establish a friendly intercourse between these islands and his intended
colony; which might for a time have occasion to draw supplies thence;
and he even had a vague idea of, some time or other, getting possession of one of these islands, as a rendezvous for his ships, and a link
in the chain of his commercial establishments.

On the evening of the 12th of February the Tonquin anchored in
the bay of Karakakooa, in the island of Owyhee. The surrounding
shores were wild and broken, with overhanging cliffs and precipices
of black volcanic rock. Beyond these, however, the country was fertile
and well cultivated, with enclosures of yams, plantains, sweet potatoes,
sugarcanes and other productions of warm climates and teeming soils;
and the numerous habitations of the natives were pleasantly sheltered
beneath clumps of cocoa nut and breadfruit trees, which afforded
both food and shade. This mingled variety of garden and grove swept
gradually up the sides of the mountains, until succeeded by dense
forests, which in turn gave place to naked and craggy rocks, until
the summits rose into the regions of perpetual snow.

The royal residence of Tamaahmaah was at this time at another
island named Woahoo; the island of Owyhee was under the command
of one of his Eris, or chiefs, who resided at the village of Tocaigh

situated on a different part of the coast from the bay of Karakakooa.

On the morning after her arrival the ship was surrounded by canoes and pirogues filled with the islanders of both sexes bringing off supplies of fruits and vegetables, bananas, plantains, water melons, yams, cabbages and taro. The Captain was desirous, however, of purchasing a number of hogs, but there were none to be had. The trade in pork was a royal monopoly and no subject of the great Tamaahmaah dared to meddle with it. Such provisions as they could furnish, however, were brought by the natives in abundance, and a lively intercourse was kept up during the day, in which the women mingled in the kindest manner.

The Islanders are a comely race, of a copper complexion. The men are tall and well made with forms indicating strength and activity: the women with regular and occasionally handsome features, and a lascivious expression, characteristic of their temperament. Their style of dress was nearly the same as in the days of Captain Cook. The men wore the Maro, a band one foot in width and several feet in length, swathed round the loins and formed of tappa, or cloth of bark; the Kihei or mantle, about six feet square, tied in a knot over one shoulder, passed under the opposite arm, so as to leave it bare, and falling in graceful folds before and behind, to the knee, so as to bear some resemblance to a Roman toga.

The female dress consisted of the pau, a garment formed of a piece of tappa, several yards in length and one in width, wrapped round the waist and reaching, like a petticoat, to the knees. Over this a Kihei or mantle larger than that of the men, sometimes worn over both shoulders, like a shawl, sometimes over one only. These mantles were seldom worn by either sex during the heat of the day, when the exposure of their persons was at first very revolting to a civilized eye.

Towards evening several of the partners and clerks went on shore where they were well received and hospitably entertained; a dance was performed for their amusement in which nineteen young women and one man figured very gracefully, singing in concert and moving to the cadence of their song.

All this, however, was nothing to the purpose in the eyes of Captain Thorn, who, being disappointed in his hope of obtaining a supply of pork, or finding good water, was anxious to be off. This it was not so easy to effect. The passengers, once on shore, were disposed, as usual, to profit by the occasion. The partners had many enquiries to make relative to the island, with a view to business, while the young clerks were delighted with the charms and graces of the dancing damsels.

To add to their gratifications an old man offered to conduct them to the spot where Captain Cook was massacred. The proposition was eagerly accepted and all hands set out on a pilgrimage to the place. The veteran islander performed his promise faithfully and pointed out the very spot where the unfortunate discoverer fell. The rocks and cocoa trees around bore record of the fact, in the marks of the balls fired from the boats upon the savages. The pilgrims gathered round the old man and drew from him all the particulars he had to relate respecting this memorable event; while the honest Captain stood by and bit his nails with impatience. To add to his vexation they employed themselves in knocking off pieces of the rocks and cutting off the bark of the trees marked by the balls, which they conveyed back to the ship as precious reliques.

Right glad, therefore, was he to get them and their treasures fairly on board; when he made sail from this unprofitable place and steered for the bay of Tocaigh, the residence of the chief or governor of the island, where he hoped to be more successful in obtaining supplies. On coming to anchor the Captain went on shore, accompanied by Mr. M'Dougall and Mr. M'Kay, and paid a visit to the governor. This dignitary proved to be an old sailor, by the name of John Young; who, after being tossed about the seas like another Sindbad, had, by one of the whimsical freaks of fortune, been elevated to the government of a savage island. He received his visitors with more hearty familiarity than personages in his high station are apt to indulge, but soon gave them to understand that provisions were scanty at Tocaigh, and that there was no good water, no rain having fallen in the neighborhood in three years.

The Captain was immediately for breaking up the conference and departing, but the partners were not so willing to part with the nautical governor, who seemed disposed to be extremely communicative, and from whom they might be able to procure some useful information. A long conversation accordingly ensued in the course of which they made many enquiries about the affairs of the islands, their natural productions and the possibility of turning them to advantage in the way of trade; nor did they fail to enquire into the individual history of John Young, and how he came to be Governor. This he gave with great condescension, running through the whole course of his fortunes "even from his boyish days."

He was a native of Liverpool in England and had followed the sea from his boyhood until, by dint of good conduct, he had risen so far in his profession as to be boatswain of an American ship called the Eleanor, commanded by Captain Metcalf. In this vessel he had sailed in 1789, on one of those casual expeditions to the north west coast, in quest of furs. In the course of the voyage the Captain left a small schooner named the Fair American, at Nootka, with a crew of five men commanded by his son a youth of eighteen. She was to follow on in the track of the Eleanor.

In February 1790 Captain Metcalf touched at the Island of Mowee, one of the Sandwich groupe. While anchored here a boat which was astern of the Eleanor was stolen and a seaman who was in it was killed. The natives generally disclaimed the outrage and brought the shattered remains of the boat and the dead body of the seaman to the ship. Supposing that they had thus appeased the anger of the Captain they thronged as usual in great numbers about the vessel to trade. Captain Metcalf, however, determined on a bloody revenge. The Eleanor mounted ten guns; all these he ordered to be loaded with musket balls, nails and pieces of old iron, and then fired them, and the small arms of the ship, among the natives. The havoc was dreadful; more than a hundred, according to Young's account, were slain.

After this signal act of vengeance Captain Metcalf sailed from Mowee and made for the island of Owyhee: where he was well received by Tamaahmaah. The fortunes of this warlike chief were at that time on the rise; he had originally been of inferior rank, ruling over only one or two districts of Owyhee, but had gradually made himself sovereign of his native island.

The Eleanor remained some few days at anchor here, and an apparently friendly intercourse was kept up with the inhabitants. On the 17th of March, John Young obtained permission to pass the night on shore. On the following morning a signal gun summoned him to return on board.

He went to the shore to embark, but found all the canoes hauled up on the beach and rigorously tabooed, or interdicted. He would have launched one himself, but was informed by Tamaahmaah that if he presumed to do so he would be put to death.

Young was obliged to submit, and remained all day in great perplexity to account for this mysterious taboo, and fearful that some hostility was intended. In the evening he learnt the cause of it, and his uneasiness was increased. It appeared that the vindictive act of Captain Metcalf had recoiled upon his own head. The Schooner Fair American, commanded by his son, following in his track, had fallen into the hands of the natives to the southward of Tocaigh bay, and young Metcalf and four of the crew had been massacred.

On receiving intelligence of this event Tamaahmaah had immediately tabooed all the canoes and interdicted all intercourse with the ship, lest the Captain should learn the fate of the schooner, and take his revenge upon the island. For the same reason he prevented Young from rejoining his countrymen. The Eleanor continued to fire signals from time to time for two days, and then sailed, concluding, no doubt, that the boatswain had deserted.

John Young was in despair when he saw the ship make sail, and found himself abandoned among savages, and savages, too, sanguinary in their character and inflamed by acts of hostility. He was agreeably disappointed, however, in experiencing nothing but kind treatment from Tamaahmaah and his people. It is true, he was narrowly watched whenever a vessel came in sight, lest he should escape and relate what had passed; but at other times he was treated with entire confidence and great distinction. He became a prime favorite, cabinet councellor and active coadjutor of Tamaahmaah, attending him in all his excursions whether of business or pleasure, and aiding in his warlike and ambitious enterprizes. By degrees he rose to the rank of a chief; espoused one of the beauties of the island, and became habituated and reconciled to his new way of life; thinking it better, perhaps, to rule among savages than serve among white men: to be a feathered chief than a tarpawlin boatswain. His favour with Tamaahmaah never declined, and when that sagacious, intrepid and aspiring chieftain had made himself sovereign over the whole groupe of islands, and removed his residence to Woahoo, he left his faithful adherent John Young in command of Owyhee.

Such is an outline of the history of Governor Young as furnished by himself, and we regret that we are not able to give any account of the state maintained by this seafaring worthy, and the manner in which he discharged his high functions, though it is evident he had more of the hearty familiarity of the forecastle than the dignity of the gubernatorial office.

These long conferences were bitter trials to the patience of the Captain; who had no respect either for the governor or his island, and was anxious to push on in quest of provisions and water. As soon as he could get his inquisitive partners once more on board, he weighed anchor and made sail for the island of Woahoo, the royal residence of Tamaahmaah.

This is the most beautiful island of the Sandwich groupe. It is 46 miles in length and 23 in breadth. A ridge of volcanic mountains extends through the centre, rising into lofty peaks and skirted by undulating hills and rich plains, where the cabins of the natives peep out from beneath groves of cocoa nut and other luxuriant trees.

On the 21st of February the Tonquin cast anchor in the beautiful bay, before the village of Waititi, (pronounced Whyteetee) the abode of Tamaahmaah. This village contained about two hundred habitations, composed of poles set in the ground, tied together at the ends and thatched with grass, and was situated in an open grove of cocoa nuts.

The Royal palace of Tamaahmaah was a large house of two stories, the lower of stone the upper of wood. Round this his body guard kept watch, composed of twenty four men, in long blue cassocks turned up with yellow, and each armed with a musket.

While at anchor at this place much ceremonious visiting and long conferences took place between the potentate of the islands and the partners of the Company. Tamaahmaah came on board of the ship in royal style, in his double pirogue. He was between fifty and sixty years of age, above the middle size, large and well made though somewhat corpulent. He was dressed in an old suit of regimentals, with a sword by his side, and seemed somewhat embarrassed by his magnificent attire. Three of his wives accompanied him; they were almost as tall and quite as corpulent as himself; but by no means to be compared with him in grandeur of habiliments, wearing no other garb than the pau. With him, also, came his great favorite and confidential councellor Kraimaker, who from holding a post equivalent to that of prime minister had been familiarly named Billy Pitt, by the British visitors to the islands.

The sovereign was received with befitting ceremonial. The American flag was displayed, four guns were fired, and the partners appeared in scarlet coats, and conducted their illustrious guests to the cabin, where they were regaled with wine. In this interview the partners endeavored to impress the monarch with a sense of their importance, and of the importance of the association to which they belonged. They let him know that they were Eris, or chiefs, of a great company about to be established on the north west coast, and talked of the probability of opening a trade with his islands, and of sending ships there occasionally. All this was gratifying and interesting to him; for he was aware of the advantages of trade and desirous of promoting frequent intercourse with white men. He encouraged Europeans and Americans to settle in his islands and intermarry with his subjects. There were between twenty and thirty white men at that time resident on the island, but many of them were mere vagabonds, who remained there in hopes of leading a lazy and an easy life. For such Tamaahmaah had a great contempt; those only had his esteem and countenance who knew some trade or mechanic art, and were sober and industrious.

On the day subsequent to the monarch's visit the partners landed and waited upon him in return. Knowing the effect of show and dress upon men in savage life and wishing to make a favorable impression as the *Eris* or chiefs of the great American Fur Company, some of them appeared in highland plaids and Kelts to the great admiration of the natives.

While visits of ceremony and grand diplomatic conferences were going on between the partners and the King, the Captain, in his plain, matter of fact way, was pushing, what he considered a far more important negotiation—the purchase of a supply of hogs. He found that the King had profited in more ways than one by his intercourse with white men. Above all other arts he had learnt the art of driving a bargain. He was a magnanimous monarch, but a shrewd pork merchant; and perhaps thought he could not do better with his future allies the American Fur Company, than to begin by close dealing. Several interviews were requisite and much bargaining before he could be brought to part with a bristle of his bacon, and then he insisted upon being paid in hard Spanish dollars; giving as a reason that he wanted money to purchase a frigate from his brother George, as he affectionately termed the King of England.*

At length the royal bargain was concluded; the necessary supply of hogs obtained, beside several goats, two sheep, a quantity of poultry and vegetables in abundance. The partners now urged to recruit their forces from the natives of this island. They declared they had never seen watermen equal to them, even among the voyageurs of the north west, and indeed they are remarkable for their skill in managing their light craft, and can swim and dive like water fowl. The partners were inclined, therefore, to take thirty or forty with them to the Columbia, to be employed in the service of the Company. The Captain, however, objected that there was not room in his vessel for the accommodation of such a number. Twelve only, were therefore enlisted for the Company, and as many more for the service of the ship. The former engaged to serve for the term of three years, during

---

* It appears from the accounts of subsequent voyagers that Tamaahmaah subsequently succeeded in his wish of purchasing a large ship. In this he sent a cargo of sandal wood to Canton, having discovered that the foreign merchants trading with him made large profits on this wood, shipped by them from the islands to the Chinese markets. The ship was manned by natives but the officers were Englishmen. She accomplished her voyage and returned in safety to the islands with the Hawaiian flag floating gloriously in the breeze. The King hastened on board, expecting to find his sandal wood converted into crapes and damasks and other rich stuffs of China but found, to his astonishment, by the legerdemain of traffic his cargo had all disappeared; and, in place of it, remained a bill of charges amounting to *three thousand dollars.* It was some time before he could be made to comprehend certain of the most important items of the bill, such as pilotage, anchorage and Custom House fees; but when he discovered that maritime states in other countries derived large revenues in this manner, to the great cost of the merchant; "Well," cried he, "then I will have harbour fees also." He established them accordingly. Pilotage a dollar a foot on the draft of each vessel. Anchorage from 60 to 70 Dollars. In this way he greatly increased the royal revenue, and turned his China speculation to account.

which they were to be fed and clothed, and at the expiration of the time, were to receive one hundred dollars in merchandize.

And now, having embarked his live stock, fruits, vegetables and water, the Captain made ready to set sail. How much the honest man had suffered in spirit by what he considered the freaks and vagaries of his passengers, and how little he had understood their humours and intentions, is amusingly shewn in a letter written to Mr. Astor from Woahoo, which contains his comments on the scenes we have described.

"It would be difficult," he writes, "to imagine the frantic gambols that are daily played off here; sometimes dressing in red coats, and otherwise very fantastically, and collecting a number of ignorant natives around them, telling them they are the great eares of the northwest, and making arrangements for sending three or four vessels yearly to them from the coast with spars &c.: while those very natives cannot even furnish a hog to the ship. Then dressing in Highland plaids and Kelts and making similar arrangements, with presents of rum, wine, or any thing that is at hand. Then taking a number of clerks and men on shore to the very spot on which Captain Cook was killed, and each fetching off a piece of the rock or tree that was touched by the shot. Then sitting down with some white man or some native who can be a little understood, and collecting the history of those islands, of Tamaahmaah's wars; the curiosities of the islands &c. preparatory to the histories of their voyages;—and the collection is indeed ridiculously contemptible.—To enumerate the thousand instances of ignorance, filth &c., or to particularize all the frantic gambols that are daily practised, would require volumes."

Before embarking, the great Eris of the American Fur Company took leave of their illustrious ally in due style, with many professions of lasting friendship and promises of future intercourse; while the matter of fact Captain anathematized him in his heart for a grasping, trafficking savage; as shrewd and sordid in his dealings as a white man. As one of the vessels of the Company will, in the course of events, have to appeal to the justice and magnanimity of this island potentate, we shall see how far the honest Captain was right in his opinion.

CHAPTER VII

Departure from the Sandwich islands—Misunderstandings—Miseries of a suspicious man—Arrival at the Columbia—Dangerous service—Gloomy apprehensions—Bars and breakers—Perils of the ship—Disasters of a boat's crew—Burial of a Sandwich islander.

It was on the 28th of February that the Tonquin set sail from the Sandwich islands. For two days the wind was contrary, and the vessel was detained in their neighborhood; at length a favorable breeze sprang up, and in a little while the rich groves, green hills and snowy peaks of those happy islands, one after another sank from sight, or melted into the blue distance, and the Tonquin ploughed her course towards the sterner regions of the Pacific.

The misunderstandings between the Captain and his passengers still continued; or rather, increased in gravity. By his altercations and his moody humours, he had cut himself off from all community of thought, or freedom of conversation with them; he disdained to ask any questions as to their proceedings, and could only guess at the meaning of their movements, and in so doing indulged in conjectures and suspicions, which produced the most whimsical self torment.

Thus in one of his disputes with them, relative to the goods on board, some of the packages of which they wished to open to take out articles of clothing for the men or presents for the natives, he was so harsh and peremptory that they lost all patience and hinted that they were the strongest party and might reduce him to a very ridiculous dilemma, by taking from him the command.

A thought now flashed across the Captain's mind that they really had a design to depose him, and that, having picked up some information at Owyhee, possibly of war between the United States and England, they meant to alter the destination of the voyage; perhaps to seize upon ship and cargo for their own use.

Once having conceived this suspicion every thing went to foster it. They had distributed fire arms among some of their men, a common precaution among the fur traders when mingling with the natives. This, however, looked like preparation. Then several of the partners and clerks and some of the men, being Scotsmen, were acquainted with the Gaelic, and held long conversations together in that language. These conversations were considered by the Captain of a "mysterious and unwarrantable nature," and related no doubt to some foul conspiracy that was brewing among them. He frankly avows such suspicions, in his letter to Mr. Astor, but intimates that he stood ready to resist any treasonous outbreak, and seems to think that the evidence of preparation on his part had an effect in overawing the conspirators.

The fact is, as we have since been informed by one of the parties, it was a mischievous pleasure with some of the partners and clerks, who were young men, to play upon the suspicions, temper and splenetic humours of the Captain; to this we may ascribe many of their whimsical pranks and absurd propositions, and above all their mysterious colloquys in Gaelic.

In this sore and irritable mood did the Captain pursue his course, keeping a wary eye on every movement, and bristling up whenever the detested sound of the Gaelic language grated upon his ear. Nothing occurred, however, materially to disturb the residue of the voyage excepting a violent storm, and, on the twenty second of March, the Tonquin arrived at the mouth of the Oregon, or Columbia River.

The aspect of the river and the adjacent coast was wild and dangerous. The mouth of the Columbia is upwards of four miles wide, with a peninsula and promontory on one side, and a long low spit of land on the other; between which a sand bar and chain of breakers almost block up the entrance. The interior of the country rises into successive ranges of mountains, which, at the time of the arrival of the Tonquin, were covered with snow.

A fresh wind from the north west sent a rough tumbling sea upon the coast, which broke upon the bar in furious surges and extended a sheet of foam almost across the mouth of the river. Under these circumstances the Captain did not think it prudent to approach within three leagues, until the bar should be sounded and the channel ascertained. Mr. Fox, the chief mate, was ordered to this service in the whale boat, accompanied by John Martin, an old seaman, who had formerly visited the river, and by three Canadians. Fox requested to have regular sailors to man the boat, but the Captain would not spare them from the service of the ship, and supposed the Canadians, being expert boatmen on lakes and rivers, were competent to the service, especially when directed and aided by Fox and Martin. Fox seems to have lost all firmness of spirit on the occasion, and to have regarded the service with a misgiving heart. He came to the partners for sympathy, knowing their differences with the Captain, and the tears were in his eyes as he represented his case. "I am sent off," said he, "without seamen to man my boat, in boisterous weather and on the most dangerous part of the north west coast. My uncle was lost a few years ago on this same bar and I am now going to lay my bones along side of his." The partners sympathized in his apprehensions and remonstrated with the Captain. The latter, however, was not to be moved. He had been displeased with Mr. Fox in the earlier part of the voyage, considering him indolent and inactive, and probably thought his present repugnance arose from a want of true nautical spirit. The interference of the partners in the business of the ship, also, was not calculated to have a favorable effect on a stickler for authority like himself, especially in his actual state of feeling towards them.

At one o'clock P. M. therefore Fox and his comrades set off in the whaleboat, which is represented as small in size, and crazy in condition. All eyes were strained after the little bark, as it pulled for shore, rising and sinking with the huge rolling waves, until it entered, a mere speck, among the foaming breakers and was soon lost to view. Evening set in, night succeeded and passed away and morning returned, but without the return of the boat.

As the wind had moderated the ship stood near to the land so as to command a view of the river mouth. Nothing was to be seen but a wild chaos of tumbling waves breaking upon the bar and apparently forming a foaming barrier from shore to shore. Towards night the ship again stood out to gain sea room, and a gloom was visible in every countenance. The Captain, himself, shared in the general anxiety, and probably repented of his peremptory orders. Another weary and watchful night succeeded, during which the wind subsided and the weather became serene.

On the following day, the ship, having drifted near the land, anchored in fourteen fathoms water, to the northward of the long peninsula or promontory which forms the north side of the entrance and is called Cape Disappointment. The pinnace was then manned and two of the partners, Mr. David Stuart and Mr. M'Kay, set off in the hope of learning something of the fate of the whaleboat. The surf, however, broke with such violence along the shore, that they could find no landing place. Several of the natives appeared on the beach and made signs to them to row round the cape, but they thought it most prudent to return to the ship.

The wind now springing up the Tonquin got under way and stood in to seek the channel, but was again deterred, by the frightful aspect of the breakers, from venturing within a league. Here she hove to, and Mr. Mumford, the second mate, was despatched with four hands, in the pinnace, to sound across the channel until he should find four fathoms depth. The pinnace entered among the breakers but was near being lost, and with difficulty got back to the ship. The Captain insisted that Mr. Mumford had steered too much to the southward; he now turned to Mr. Aiken, an able mariner destined to command the schooner intended for the coasting trade, and ordered him, together with John Coles, sail maker, Stephen Weekes, armourer, and two Sandwich islanders, to proceed ahead and take soundings, while the

ship should follow under easy sail. In this way they proceeded until
Aiken had ascertained the channel, when signal was given from the
ship for him to return on board. He was then within pistol shot, but
so furious was the current, and tumultuous the breakers that the
boat became unmanageable, and was hurried away, the crew crying
out piteously for assistance. In a few moments she could not be seen
from the ship's deck. Some of the passengers climbed to the mizen
top, and beheld her, still struggling to reach the ship; but shortly
after she broached broadside to the waves, and her case seemed
desperate. The attention of those on board of the ship was now called
to their own safety. They were in shallow water; the vessel struck
repeatedly, the waves broke over her and there was danger of her
foundering. At length she got into seven fathoms water, and, the wind
lulling and the night coming on, cast anchor. With the darkness their
anxieties encreased. The wind whistled, the sea roared, the gloom
was only broken by the ghastly glare of the foaming breakers, the
minds of the seamen were full of dreary apprehensions, and some
of them fancied they heard the cries of their lost comrades mingling
with the uproar of the elements. For a time too the rapidly ebbing
tide threatened to sweep them from their precarious anchorage. At
length its reflux, and the springing up of the wind, enabled them to
quit their dangerous situation and take shelter in a small bay within
Cape Disappointment, where they rode in safety during the residue of
a stormy night, and enjoyed a brief interval of refreshing sleep.

With the light of day returned their cares and anxieties. They
looked out from the mast head over a wild coast, and wilder sea, but
could discover no trace of the two boats, and their crews, that were
missing. Several of the natives came on board with peltries, but there
was no disposition to trade. They were interrogated by signs, after
the lost boats, but could not understand the enquiries.

Parties now went on shore and scoured the neighborhood. One of
these was headed by the Captain. They had not proceeded far when
they beheld a person at a distance, in civilized garb. As he drew
near he proved to be Weekes the armourer. There was a burst of
joy, for it was hoped his comrades were near at hand. His story,
however, was one of disaster. He and his companions had found it
impossible to govern their boat, having no rudder and being beset
by rapid and whirling currents, and boisterous surges. After long
struggling they had let her go at the mercy of the waves, tossing
about, sometimes with her bow, sometimes with her broad side to
the surges, threatened each instant with destruction, yet repeatedly
escaping, until a huge sea broke over and swamped her. Weekes was
overwhelmed by the boiling waves, but emerging above the surface

looked round for his companions. Aikin and Coles were not to be seen; near him were the two Sandwich islanders, stripping themselves of their clothing that they might swim more freely. He did the same, and the boat floating near to him he seized hold of it. The two islanders joined him, and, uniting their forces they succeeded in turning the boat upon her keel. Then bearing down her stern and rocking her, they forced out so much water that she was able to bear the weight of a man without sinking. One of the islanders now got in, and in a little while bailed out the water with his hands. The other swam about and collected the oars and they all three got once more on board.

By this time the tide had swept them beyond the breakers and Weekes called on his companions to row for land: they were so chilled and benumbed by the cold, however, that they lost all heart and absolutely refused. Weekes was equally chilled, but had superior sagacity and self command. He counteracted the tendency to drowsiness and stupor which cold produces, by keeping himself in constant exercise; and seeing that the vessel was advancing, and that every thing depended upon himself, he set to work to scull the boat clear of the bar, and into quiet water.

Towards midnight one of the poor islanders expired: his companion threw himself on his corps and could not be persuaded to leave him. The dismal night wore away amidst these horrors; as the day dawned Weekes found himself near the land. He steered directly for it, and at length, with the aid of the surf, ran his boat high upon a sandy beach.

Finding that one of the Sandwich islanders yet gave signs of life he aided him to leave the boat, and set out with him towards the adjacent woods. The poor fellow, however, was too feeble to follow him, and Weekes was soon obliged to abandon him to his fate and provide for his own safety. Falling upon a beaten path he pursued it and, after a few hours, came to a part of the coast where to his surprize and joy he beheld the ship at anchor, and was met by the Captain and his party.

After Weekes had related his adventures three parties were despatched to beat up the coast in search of the unfortunate islander. They returned at night without success, though they had used the utmost diligence. On the following day the search was resumed, and the poor fellow was at length discovered lying beneath a groupe of rocks, his legs swollen, his feet torn and bloody from walking through bushes and briars, and himself half dead with cold, hunger and fatigue. Weekes and this islander were the only survivors of the crew of the jolly boat, and no trace was ever discovered of Fox and his party. Thus eight men were lost on the first approach to the coast; a commencement that cast a gloom over the spirits of the whole party, and was regarded by some of the superstitious, as an omen that boded no good to the enterprize.

Towards night the Sandwich islanders went on shore to bury the body of their unfortunate countryman who had perished in the boat. On arriving at the place where it had been left, they dug a grave in the sand in which they deposited the corps with a biscuit under one of the arms, some lard under the chin and a small quantity of tobacco, as provisions for its journey in the land of Spirits. Having covered the body with sand and flints they kneeled along the grave in a double row with their faces turned to the East, while one who officiated as a priest sprinkled them with water from a hat. In so doing he recited a kind of prayer or invocation, to which at intervals, the others made responses. Such were the simple rites performed by these poor savages at the grave of their comrade on the shores of a strange land; and when these were done they rose and returned in silence to the ship, without once casting a look behind.

CHAPTER VIII

Mouth of the Columbia—The native tribes—Their fishing—Their canoes —Bold navigators—Equestrian Indians and Piscatory Indians, difference in their physical organization—Search for a trading site—Expedition of M'Dougall and David Stuart—Comcomly the one eyed chieftain— Influence of wealth in savage life—Slavery among the natives—An aristocracy of Flatheads—Hospitality among the Chinooks—Comcomly's daughter, her conquest.

The Columbia, or Oregon, for the distance of thirty or forty miles from its entrance into the Sea, is properly speaking a mere estuary indented by deep bays so as to vary from three to seven miles in width; and is rendered extremely intricate and dangerous by shoals reaching nearly from shore to shore, on which at times the winds and currents produce foaming and tumultuous breakers. The mouth of the river proper is but about half a mile wide; formed by the contracting shores of the estuary. The entrance from the Sea, as we have already observed, is bounded on the south side by a flat sandy spit of land, stretching into the Ocean. This is commonly called Point Adams. The opposite or northern side is Cape Disappointment: a kind of peninsula, terminating in a steep knoll or promontory crowned with a forest of pine trees, and connected with the main land by a low and narrow neck. Immediately within this cape is a wide open bay, terminating at Chinook point, so called from a neighboring tribe of Indians. This was called Baker's Bay, and here the Tonquin was anchored.

The natives inhabiting the lower part of the river, and with whom the company was likely to have the most frequent intercourse, were divided at this time into four tribes, the Chinooks, Clatsops, Wahkiacums and Cathlamahs. They resembled each other in person, dress, language and manner, and were probably from the same stock, but broken into tribes, or rather hordes, by those feuds and schisms frequent among Indians.

These people generally live by fishing; it is true they occasionally hunt the elk and deer, and ensnare the waterfowl of their ponds and rivers; but these are casual luxuries; their chief subsistence is derived from the salmon and other fish which abound in the Columbia and its tributary streams; aided by roots and herbs, especially the Wappatoo, which is found on the islands of the river.

As the Indians of the plains who depend upon the chase, are bold and expert riders, and pride themselves upon their horses, so these piscatory tribes of the coast excel in the management of canoes and are never more at home than when riding upon the waves. Their canoes vary in form and size: some are upwards of fifty feet long, cut out of a single tree, either fir or white cedar and capable of carrying thirty persons. They have thwart pieces from side to side about three inches thick, and their gunwales flare outwards so as to cast off the surges of the waves. The bow and stern are decorated with grotesque figures of men and animals sometimes five feet in height.

In managing their canoes they kneel, two and two along the bottom, sitting on their heels, and wielding paddles from four to five feet long, while one sits on the stern and steers with a paddle of the same kind. The women are equally expert with the men in managing the canoe, and generally take the helm.

It is surprizing to see with what fearless unconcern these savages venture in their light barks upon the roughest and most tempestuous seas. They seem to ride upon the waves like sea fowl. Should a surge throw the canoe upon its side and endanger its overturn, those to windward lean over the upper gunwale, thrust their paddles deep into the wave, apparently catch the water and force it under the canoe, and by this action, not merely regain an equilibrium, but give their bark a vigorous impulse forward.

The effect of different modes of life upon the human frame and human character is strikingly instanced in the contrast between the hunting Indians of the prairies and the piscatory Indians of the sea coast. The former, continually on horseback, scouring the plains, gaining their food by hardy exercise and subsisting chiefly on flesh, are generally tall, sinewy, meagre but well formed, and of bold and fierce deportment; the latter, lounging about the river banks, or squatting and curved up in their canoes, are generally low in stature, ill shaped, with crooked legs, thick ancles and broad flat feet. They are inferior also in muscular power and activity, and in *game* qualities and appearance to their hard riding brethren of the prairies.

Having premised these few particulars concerning the neighboring Indians, we will return to the immediate concerns of the Tonquin and her crew.

Further search was made for Mr. Fox and his party but with no better success and they were at length given up as lost. In the mean time the Captain and some of the partners explored the river for some distance in a large boat to select a suitable place for the trading post. Their old jealousies and differences continued; they never could coincide in their choice, and the Captain objected altogether, to any site so high up the river. They all returned, therefore, to Baker's bay in no very good humour. The partners proposed to examine the opposite shore, but the Captain was impatient of any further delay. His eagerness to "get on" had encreased upon him. He thought all these excursions a sheer loss of time, and was resolved to land at once, build a shelter for the reception of that part of his cargo destined for the use of the settlement, and, having cleared his ship of it, and of his irksome ship mates, to depart upon the prosecution of his coasting voyage according to orders.

On the following day, therefore, without troubling himself to consult the partners, he landed in Baker's Bay and proceeded to erect a shed for the reception of the rigging, equipments and stores of the schooner that was to be built for the use of the settlement.

This dogged determination on the part of the sturdy captain gave high offence to Mr. M'Dougall, who now considered himself at the head of the concern, as Mr. Astor's representative and proxy. He set off the same day, (April 5th) accompanied by Mr. David Stuart, for the southern shore, intending to be back by the seventh. Not having the Captain to contend with they soon pitched upon a spot which appeared to them favorable for the intended establishment. It was on a point of land called Point George, having a very good harbour where vessels, not exceeding two hundred tons burthen, might anchor within fifty yards of the shore.

After a day thus profitably spent they re crossed the river, but landed on the northern shore, several miles above the anchoring ground of the Tonquin, in the neighborhood of Chinook, and visited the village of that tribe. Here they were received with great hospitality by the chief who was named Comcomly, a shrewd old savage, with but one eye, who will occasionally figure in this narrative. Each village forms a petty sovereignty governed by its own chief, who however possesses but little authority, unless he be a man of wealth and substance, that is to say, possessed of canoes, slaves and wives. The greater number of these the greater is the chief. How many wives this one eyed potentate maintained we are not told, but he certainly possessed great sway not merely over his own tribe, but over the neighborhood.

Having mentioned slaves, we would observe that slavery exists among several of the tribes beyond the Rocky Mountains. The slaves are well treated, while in good health, but occupied in all kinds of drudgery. Should they become useless however by sickness or old age, they are totally neglected and left to perish; nor is any respect paid to their bodies after death.

A singular custom prevails not merely among the Chinooks, but among most of the tribes about this part of the coast, which is the flattening of the forehead. The process by which this deformity is effected commences immediately after birth. The infant is laid in a wooden trough, by way of cradle. The end on which the head reposes is higher than the rest. A padding is placed on the forehead of the infant, with a piece of bark above it, and is pressed down by cords, which pass through holes on each side of the trough. As the tightening of the padding and the pressing of the head to the board is gradual, the process is said not to be attended with much pain. The appearance of the infant, however, while in this state of compression, is whimsically hideous, and "its little black eyes," we are told, "being forced out by the tightness of the bandages, resemble those of a mouse choked in a trap."

About a year's pressure is sufficient to produce the desired effect, at the end of which time the child emerges from its bandages a complete Flathead, and continues so through life. It must be noted, however, that this flattening of the head has something in it of aristocratical significancy, like the crippling of the feet among Chinese ladies of quality. At any rate, it is a sign of freedom. No slave is permitted to bestow this enviable deformity upon his child; all the slaves, therefore, are roundheads.

With this worthy tribe of Chinooks the two partners passed a part of a day very agreeably. M'Dougall, who was somewhat vain of his official rank, had given it to be understood that they were two chiefs of a great trading company, about to be established here, and the quicksighted, though one eyed chief, who was somewhat practiced in traffic with white men, immediately perceived the policy of cultivating the friendship of two such important visitors. He regaled them, therefore, to the best of his ability, with abundance of salmon and Wappatoo. The next morning, April 7th, they prepared to return to the vessel according to promise. They had eleven miles of open bay to traverse; the wind was fresh, the waves ran high. Comcomly remonstrated with them on the hazard to which they would be exposed.

They were resolute, however, and launched their boat; while the wary chieftain followed at some short distance in his canoe. Scarce had they rowed a mile when a wave broke over their boat and upset it. They were in imminent peril of drowning, especially Mr. M'Dougall, who could not swim. Comcomly, however, came bounding over the waves in his light canoe and snatched them from a watery grave.

They were taken on shore and a fire made at which they dried their clothes, after which Comcomly conducted them back to his village. Here every thing was done that could be devised for their entertainment during three days that they were detained by bad weather. Comcomly made his people perform antics before them; and his wives and daughters endeavored by all the soothing and endearing arts of women, to find favor in their eyes. Some even painted their bodies with red clay and anointed themselves with fish oil to give additional lustre to their charms. Mr. M'Dougall seems to have had a heart susceptible to the influence of the gentler sex; whether or no it was first touched on this occasion we do not learn, but it will be found, in the course of this work, that one of the daughters of the hospitable Comcomly eventually made a conquest of the great Eri of the American Fur Company.

When the weather had moderated and the sea become tranquil the one eyed chief of the Chinooks manned his state canoe and conducted his guests in safety to the ship: where they were welcomed with joy, for apprehensions had been felt for their safety. Comcomly and his people were then entertained on board of the Tonquin and liberally rewarded for their hospitality and services. They returned home highly satisfied, promising to remain faithful friends and allies of the white men.

CHAPTER IX

*Point George—Founding of Astoria—Indian visitors—Their reception
—The Captain taboos the ship—Departure of the Tonquin—Comments
on the conduct of Captain Thorn.*

From the report made by the two exploring partners it was determined that Point George should be the site of the trading house. These
gentlemen, it is true, were not perfectly satisfied with the place, and
were desirous of continuing their search, but Captain Thorn was
impatient to land his cargo and continue his voyage, and protested
against any more of what he termed "sporting excursions."

Accordingly, on the 12th of April the launch was freighted with
all things necessary for the purpose and sixteen persons departed in
her to commence the establishment, leaving the Tonquin to follow
as soon as the harbor could be sounded.

Crossing the wide mouth of the river the party landed and encamped at the bottom of a small bay within Point George. The situation
chosen for the fortified post was on an elevation facing to the north,
with the wide estuary, its sand bars and tumultuous breakers spread
out before it, and the promontory of Cape Disappointment, fifteen
miles distant, closing the prospect to the left. The surrounding country
was in all the freshness of spring, the trees were in the young leaf;
the weather was superb, and every thing looked delightful to men
just emancipated from a long confinement on shipboard. The Tonquin
shortly afterwards made her way through the intricate channel and
came to anchor in the little bay and was saluted from the encampment
with three vollies of musketry and three cheers. She returned the
salute with three cheers and three guns.

All hands now set to work cutting down trees, clearing away thickets
and marking out the place for the residence, store house and powder
magazine, which were to be built of logs and covered with bark:
others landed the timbers intended for the frame of the coasting vessel,
and proceeded to put them together; while others prepared a garden
spot, and sowed the seeds of various vegetables.

The next thought was to give a name to the embryo metropolis:
the one that naturally presented itself was that of the projector and
supporter of the whole enterprize. It was accordingly named Astoria.

The neighboring Indians now swarmed about the place; some
brought a few land otter and sea otter skins to barter, but in very
scanty parcels; the greater number came prying about to gratify their
curiosity, for they are said to be impertinently inquisitive, while not

61

a few came with no other design than to pilfer; the laws of *meum*
and *tuum* being but slightly respected among them. Some of them
beset the ship in their canoes, among whom was the Chinook chief
Comcomly and his liege subjects. These were well received by Mr.
M'Dougall, who was delighted with an opportunity of entering upon
his functions and acquiring importance in the eyes of his future neighbors. The confusion thus produced on board, and the derangement of
the cargo caused by this petty trade, stirred the spleen of the Captain,
who had a sovereign contempt for the one eyed chieftain and all
his crew. He complained loudly of having his ship lumbered by a
host of "Indian ragamuffins" who had not a skin to dispose of, and at
length put his positive interdict upon all trafficking on board. Upon
this Mr. M'Dougall was fain to land and establish his quarters at the
encampment, where he could exercise his rights and enjoy his dignities
without control.

The feud, however, between these rival powers still continued, but
was chiefly carried on by letter. Day after day and week after week
elapsed, yet the store houses requisite for the reception of the cargo
were not completed, and the ship was detained in port; while the
Captain was teased by frequent requisitions for various articles for
the use of the establishment or the trade with the natives. An angry
correspondence took place, in which he complained bitterly of the
time wasted in "smoking and sporting parties," as he termed the
reconnoitering expeditions, and in clearing and preparing meadow
ground and turnip patches, instead of despatching his ship. At length all
these jarring matters were adjusted, if not to the satisfaction, at least
to the acquiescence of all parties. The part of the cargo destined
for the use of Astoria was landed, and the ship left free to proceed
on her voyage.

As the Tonquin was to coast to the north, to trade for peltries at
the different harbours, and to touch at Astoria on her return in the
autumn, it was unanimously determined that Mr. M'Kay should go
in her as supercargo, taking with him Mr. Lewis as ship's clerk.
On the first of June the ship got under way and dropped down to
Baker's Bay, where she was detained for a few days by a head wind;
but early in the morning of the 5th stood out to sea with a fine
breeze and swelling canvas, and swept off gaily on her fatal voyage
from which she was never to return!

On reviewing the conduct of Captain Thorn and examining his
peevish and somewhat whimsical correspondence, the impression left
upon our mind is, upon the whole, decidedly in his favour. While we
smile at the simplicity of his heart and the narrowness of his views,
which made him regard every thing out of the direct path of his

daily duty, and the rigid exigencies of the service as trivial and impertinent, which inspired him with contempt for the swelling vanity of some of his coadjutors, and the literary exercises and curious researches of others; we cannot but applaud that strict and conscientious devotion to the interests of his employer and to what he considered the true objects of the enterprize in which he was engaged.

He certainly was to blame occasionally for the asperity of his manners and the arbitrary nature of his measures, yet much that is exceptionable in this part of his conduct may be traced to rigid notions of duty acquired in that tyrannical school a ship of war, and to the construction given by his companions to the orders of Mr. Astor so little in conformity with his own. His mind, too, appears to have become almost diseased by the suspicions he had formed as to the loyalty of his associates and the nature of their ultimate designs: yet on this point there were circumstances to in some measure justify him. The relations between the United States and Great Britain were at that time in a critical state, in fact the two countries were on the eve of a war. Several of the partners were British subjects, and might be ready to desert the flag under which they acted, should a war take place. Their application to the British Minister at New York shews the dubious feeling with which they had embarked in the present enterprize. They had been in the employ of the North West Company and might be disposed to rally again under that association, should events threaten the prosperity of this embryo establishment of Mr. Astor. Beside, we have the fact, avowed to us by one of the partners, that some of them who were young and heedless took a mischievous and unwarrantable pleasure in playing upon the jealous temper of the Captain, and affecting mysterious consultations and sinister movements.

These circumstances are cited in palliation of the doubts and surmises of Captain Thorn, which might otherwise appear strange and unreasonable. That most of the partners were perfectly upright and faithful in the discharge of the trust reposed in them we are fully satisfied; still the honest Captain was not invariably wrong in his suspicions; and that he formed a pretty just opinion of the integrity of that aspiring personage Mr. M'Dougall, will be substantially proven in the sequel.

CHAPTER X

While the Astorians were busily occupied in completing their factory and fort, a report was brought to them by an Indian from the upper part of the River, that a party of thirty white men had appeared on the banks of the Columbia, and were actually building houses at the Second Rapids. This information caused much disquiet. We have already mentioned that the North West Company had established posts to the west of the Rocky Mountains in a district called by them New Caledonia, which extended from Lat. 52° to 55° north; being within the British territories; it was now apprehended that they were advancing within the American limits, and were endeavoring to seize upon the upper part of the river and forestall the American Fur Company in the surrounding trade, in which case bloody feuds might be anticipated, such as had prevailed between the rival fur companies in former days.

A reconnoitering party was sent up the river to ascertain the truth of the report. They ascended to the foot of the first rapid, about two hundred miles, but could hear nothing of any white men being in the neighborhood.

Not long after their return, however, further accounts were received by two wandering Indians, which established the fact that the North West Company had actually erected a trading house on the Spokan River, which falls into the north branch of the Columbia.

What rendered this intelligence the more disquieting was the inability of the Astorians, in their present reduced state as to numbers, and the exigencies of their new establishment, to furnish detachments to penetrate the country in different directions, and fix the posts necessary to secure the interior trade.

It was resolved, however, at any rate to advance a counter check to this post on the Spokan, and one of the partners, Mr. David Stuart, prepared to set out for the purpose with eight men and a small assortment of goods. He was to be guided by the two Indians, who knew the country, and promised to take him to a place not far from the

Spokan River, and in a neighborhood abounding with beaver. Here he was to establish himself and to remain for a time provided he found the situation advantageous and the natives friendly.

On the 15th of July, when Mr. Stuart was nearly ready to embark, a canoe made its appearance standing for the harbour and manned by nine white men. Much speculation took place who these strangers could be; for it was too soon to expect their own people, under Mr. Hunt, who were to cross the Continent. As the canoe drew near the British standard was distinguished: on coming to land, one of the crew stepped on shore, and announced himself as Mr. David Thompson, astronomer, and partner of the North West Company. According to his account he had set out in the preceding year with a tolerably strong party and a supply of Indian goods to cross the Rocky Mountains. A part of his people, however, had deserted him on the eastern side, and returned with the goods to the nearest North West post. He had persisted in crossing the mountains with eight men who remained true to him. They had traversed the higher regions and wintered near the source of the Columbia, where, in the spring, they had constructed a cedar canoe, the same in which they had reached Astoria.

This, in fact, was the party despatched by the North West Company to anticipate Mr. Astor in his intention of effecting a settlement at the mouth of the Columbia River. It appears from information subsequently derived from other sources that Mr. Thompson had pushed on his course with great haste, calling at all the Indian villages in his march, presenting them with British flags, and even planting them at the forks of the rivers, proclaiming formally that he took possession of the country in the name of the King of Great Britain for the North West Company. As his original plan was defeated by the desertion of his people it is probable that he descended the river simply to reconnoiter and ascertain whether an American settlement had been commenced.

Mr. Thompson was, no doubt, the first white man who descended the northern branch of the Columbia from so near its source. Lewis and Clark struck the main body of the river at the forks, about four hundred miles from its mouth. They entered it from Lewis River, its southern branch, and thence descended.

Though Mr. Thompson could be considered as little better than a spy in the camp, he was received with great cordiality by Mr. M'Dougall, who had a lurking feeling of companionship and good will for all of the North West Company. He invited him to head quarters, where he and his people were hospitably entertained. Nay, further, being somewhat in extremity, he was furnished by Mr. M'Dougall with goods and provisions for his journey back, across the mountains, much against the wishes of Mr. David Stuart, who did not think the object of his visit entitled him to any favor.

On the 23d of July Mr. Stuart set out upon his expedition to the interior. His party consisted of four of the clerks, Messrs. Pillet, Ross, M'Lennon and Montigny, accompanied by two Canadian voyageurs and two natives of the Sandwich Islands. They had three canoes well laden with provisions, and with goods and necessaries for a trading establishment.

Mr. Thompson and his party set out in company with them, it being his intention to proceed direct to Montreal. The partners at Astoria forwarded by him a short letter to Mr. Astor, informing him of their safe arrival at the mouth of the Columbia, and that they had not yet heard of Mr. Hunt.

The little squardon of canoes set sail with a favorable breeze and soon passed Tongue Point, a long, high and rocky promontory, covered with trees and stretching far into the river. Opposite to this on the northern shore is a deep bay, where the Columbia anchored at the time of the discovery, and which is still called Gray's Bay, from the name of her commander.

From hence the general course of the river for about seventy miles was nearly south east; varying in breadth according to its bays and indentations, and navigable for vessels of three hundred tons. The shores were in some places high and rocky, with low marshy islands at their feet, subject to inundation, and covered with willows, poplars, and other trees that love an alluvial soil. Sometimes the mountains receded and gave place to beautiful plains and noble forests. While the river margin was richly fringed with trees of deciduous foliage, the rough uplands were crowned by majestic pines and firs of gigantic size; some towering to the height of between two and three hundred feet, with proportionate circumference. Out of these the Indians wrought their great canoes and pirogues.

At one part of the river they passed on the northern side an isolated rock, about one hundred and fifty feet high, rising from a low marshy soil and totally disconnected with the adjacent mountains. This was held in great reverence by the neighboring Indians, being one of their principal places of sepulture. The same provident care for the deceased that prevails among the hunting tribes of the prairies is observable among the piscatory tribes of the rivers and sea coast. Among the former the favorite horse of the hunter is buried with him in the same funereal mound, and his bow and arrows are laid by his side, that he may be perfectly equipped for the "happy hunting grounds" of the land of Spirits. Among the latter the Indian is wrapped in his mantle of skins, laid in his canoe with his paddle, his fishing spear, and other implements beside him, and placed aloft on some rock or other eminence overlooking the river or bay or lake that he has frequented. He is thus fitted out to launch away upon those placid streams and sunny lakes stocked with all kinds of fish and waterfowl, which are prepared in the next world for those who have acquitted themselves as good sons, good fathers, good husbands and, above all, good fishermen, during their mortal sojourn.

The isolated rock in question presented a spectacle of the kind: numerous dead bodies being deposited in canoes on its summit: while on poles around were trophies, or rather funereal offerings of trinkets, garments, baskets of roots, and other articles for the use of the deceased. A reverential feeling protects these sacred spots from robbery or insult. The friends of the deceased, especially the women, repair here at sunrise and sunset for some time after his death, singing his funeral dirge and uttering loud wailings and lamentations.

From the number of dead bodies in canoes observed upon this rock by the first explorers of the river it received the name of Mount Coffin, which it continues to bear.

Beyond this rock they passed the mouth of a river on the right bank of the Columbia, which appeared to take its rise on a distant mountain covered with snow. The Indian name of this river was the Cowleskee. Some miles further on they came to the great Columbian valley, so called by Lewis and Clark. It is sixty miles in width and extends far to the south southeast between parallel ridges of mountains which bound it on the east and west. Through the centre of this valley flowed a large and beautiful stream called the Wallamot,* which came wandering for several hundred miles through a yet unexplored wilderness. The sheltered situation of this immense valley had an obvious effect upon the climate. It was a region of great beauty and luxuriance, with lakes and pools, and green meadows shaded by noble groves. Various tribes were said to reside in this valley, and along the banks of the Wallamot.

About eight miles above the mouth of the Wallamot the little squadron arrived at Vancouver's point, so called in honor of that celebrated voyager by his lieutenant (Broughton) when he explored the river. This point is said to present one of the most beautiful scenes on the Columbia: a lovely meadow, with a silver sheet of limpid water in the centre, enlivened by wildfowl; a range of hills crowned by forests, while the prospect is closed by Mount Hood, a magnificent mountain

---

* Pronounced Wallámot, the accent being upon the second syllable.

rising into a lofty peak and covered with snow; the ultimate land mark of the first explorers of the river.

Point Vancouver is about one hundred miles from Astoria; here the reflux of the tide ceases to be perceptible. To this place vessels of two and three hundred tons burthen may ascend. The party under the command of Mr. Stuart had been three or four days in reaching it, though we have forborne to notice their daily progress and nightly encampments.

From Point Vancouver the river turned towards the north east and became more contracted and rapid with occasional islands and frequent sand banks. These islands are furnished with a number of ponds and at certain seasons abound with swan, geese, brandts, cranes, gulls, plover, and other wildfowl. The shores, too, are low and closely wooded, with such an undergrowth of vines and rushes as to be almost impassable.

About thirty miles above Point Vancouver the mountains again approach on both sides of the river, which is bordered by stupendous precipices, covered with the fir and the white cedar, and enlivened occasionally by beautiful cascades leaping from a great height, and sending up wreaths of vapour. One of these precipices or cliffs is curiously worn by time and weather, so as to have the appearance of a ruined fortress, with towers and battlements, beetling high above the river, while two small cascades one hundred and fifty feet in height, pitch down from the fissures of the rocks.

The turbulence and rapidity of the current continually augmenting as they advanced, gave the voyagers intimation that they were approaching the great obstructions of the river, and at length they arrived at Strawberry Island, so called by Lewis and Clark, which lies at the foot of the first rapid. As this part of the Columbia will be repeatedly mentioned in the course of this work, being the scene of some of its incidents, we shall give a general description of it in this place.

The Falls or Rapids of the Columbia are situated about one hundred and eighty miles above the mouth of the river. The first is a perpendicular cascade of twenty feet, after which there is a swift descent for a mile between islands of hard black rock, to another pitch of eight feet, divided by two rocks. About two and a half miles below this the river expands into a wide basin, seemingly dammed up by a perpendicular ridge of black rock. A current, however, sets diagonally to the left of this rocky barrier, where there is a chasm forty five yards in width. Through this the whole body of the river roars along, swelling and whirling and boiling for some distance in the wildest confusion. Through this tremendous channel the intrepid explorers of the river, Lewis and

Clark, passed safely in their boats, the danger being, not from the rocks, but from the great surges and whirlpools.

At the distance of a mile and a half from the foot of this narrow channel is a rapid formed by two rocky islands, and two miles beyond is a second great fall, over a ledge of rocks twenty feet high, extending nearly from shore to shore. The river is again compressed into a channel from fifty to a hundred feet wide, worn through a rough bed of hard black rock, along which it boils and roars with great fury for the distance of three miles. This is called "The Long Narrows."

Here is the great fishing place of the Columbia. In the spring of the year, when the water is high, the salmon ascend the river in incredible numbers. As they pass through this narrow strait the Indians, standing on the rocks, or on the end of wooden stages projecting from the banks, scoop them up with small nets distended on hoops and attached to long handles, and cast them on the shore.

They are then cured and packed in a peculiar manner. After having been opened and disembowelled they are exposed to the sun on scaffolds erected on the river banks. When sufficiently dry they are pounded fine between two stones, pressed into the smallest compass and packed in baskets or bales of grass matting, about two feet long and one in diameter, lined with the cured skin of a salmon. The top is likewise covered with fish skins secured by cords passing through holes in the edge of the basket. Packages are then made, each containing twelve of these bales, seven at bottom, five at top, pressed close to each other, with the corded side upward, wrapped in mats and corded. These are placed in dry situations and again covered with matting. Each of these packages contains from ninety to a hundred pounds of dried fish, which in this state will keep sound for several years.[*]

We have given this process at some length, as furnished by the first explorers, because it marks a practised ingenuity in preparing articles of traffic for a market, seldom seen among our aboriginals. For like reasons we would make especial mention of the Village of Wish-ram at the head of the Long Narrows, as being a solitary instance of an aboriginal trading mart, or emporium. Here the salmon caught in the neighboring rapids were "ware housed" to await customers. Hither the tribes from the mouth of the Columbia repaired with the fish of the sea coast, the roots, berries and especially the Wappatoo, gathered in the lower parts of the river, together with goods and trinkets obtained from the ships which casually visited the coast. Hither also the tribes from the Rocky Mountains brought down horses, bear grass, Quamash

[*] Lewis and Clark. V. II. P. 32.

and other commodities of the interior. The merchant fishermen at the Falls acted as middle men or factors: and passed the objects of traffic as it were cross handed, trading away part of the wares received from the mountain tribes, to those of the river and the plains, and vice versa: their packages of pounded salmon entered largely into the system of barter, and being carried off in opposite directions, found their way to the savage hunting camps far in the interior, and to the casual white traders who touched upon the coast.

We have already noticed certain contrarieties of character between the Indian tribes, produced by their diet and mode of life, and no where are they more apparent than about the Falls of the Columbia. The Indians of this great fishing mart are represented by the earliest explorers as sleeker and fatter, but less hardy and active, than the tribes of the mountains and the prairies, who live by hunting; or of the upper parts of the river, where fish is scanty and the inhabitants must eke out their subsistence by digging roots or chasing the deer. Indeed, whenever an Indian of the upper country is too lazy to hunt yet is fond of good living, he repairs to the Falls to live in abundance without labour.

"By such worthless dogs as these," says an honest trader in his journal, which now lies before us, "by such worthless dogs as these are these noted fishing places peopled; which, like our great cities, may with propriety be called the head quarters of vitiated principles."

The habits of trade and the avidity of gain have their corrupting effects even in the wilderness, as may be instanced in the members of this aboriginal emporium, for the same journalist denounces them as "saucy, impudent rascals, who will steal when they can, and pillage whenever a weak party falls in their power."

That he does not belie them will be evidenced hereafter, when we have occasion again to touch at Wish-ram and navigate the rapids; in the present instance the travellers effected the laborious ascent of this part of the river, with all its various portages, without molestation, and once more launched away in smooth water above the high falls.

The two parties continued together, without material impediment, for three or four hundred miles further up the Columbia; Mr. Thompson appearing to take great interest in the success of Mr. Stuart, and pointing out places favorable, as he said, to the establishment of his contemplated trading post.

Mr. Stuart, who distrusted his sincerity, at length pretended to adopt his advice, and, taking leave of him, remained as if to establish himself, while the other proceeded on his course towards the Mountains. No sooner, however, had he fairly departed than Mr. Stuart again pushed forward, under guidance of the two Indians, nor did he stop until he had arrived within about 140 miles of the Spokan River, which he considered near enough to keep the rival establishment in check.

The place which he pitched upon for his trading post was a point of land about three miles in length and two in breadth, formed by the junction of the Oakinagan with the Columbia. The former is a river which has its source in a considerable lake about a hundred and fifty miles west of the point of junction. The two rivers about the place of their confluence are bordered by immense prairies covered with herbage, but destitute of trees. The point itself was enameled with wild flowers of every hue, in which innumerable hummingbirds were "banqueting nearly the livelong day."

The situation of this point appeared to be well adapted for a trading post. The climate was salubrious, the soil fertile, the rivers well stocked with fish, the natives peaceable and friendly. There were easy communications with the interior by the upper waters of the Columbia, and the lateral stream of the Oakinagan, while the downward current of the Columbia furnished a high way to Astoria.

Availing himself, therefore, of the drift wood which had collected in quantities in the neighboring bends of the river Mr. Stuart and his men set to work to erect a house, which in a little while was sufficiently completed for their residence; and thus was established the first interior post of the Company. We will now return to notice the progress of affairs at the mouth of the Columbia.

CHAPTER XI

Alarm at Astoria—Rumour of Indian hostilities—Preparations for defence—Tragical fate of the Tonquin.

The sailing of the Tonquin and the departure of Mr. David Stuart and his detachment had produced a striking effect on affairs at Astoria. The natives who had swarmed about the place began immediately to drop off, until at length not an Indian was to be seen. This at first was attributed to the want of peltries with which to trade; but in a little while the mystery was explained in a more alarming manner. A conspiracy was said to be on foot among the neighboring tribes to make a combined attack upon the white men, now that they were so reduced in number. For this purpose there had been a gathering of warriors in a neighboring bay, under pretext of fishing for sturgeon, and fleets of canoes were expected to join them from the north and south. Even Comcomly the one eyed chief, notwithstanding his professed friendship for Mr. M'Dougall, was strongly suspected of being concerned in this general combination.

Alarmed at rumours of this impending danger, the Astorians suspended their regular labour, and set to work, with all haste, to throw up temporary works for refuge and defence. In the course of a few days they surrounded their dwelling house and magazines with a picket fence ninety feet square, flanked by two bastions on which were mounted four four-pounders.

Every day they exercised themselves in the use of their weapons, so as to qualify themselves for military duty, and at night ensconced themselves in their fortress and posted centinels to guard against surprize. In this way they hoped, even in case of attack, to be able to hold out until the arrival of the party to be conducted by Mr. Hunt across the Rocky Mountains, or until the return of the Tonquin. The latter dependance however was doomed soon to be destroyed. Early in August a wandering band of Savages from the Strait of Juan de Fuca, made their appearance at the mouth of the Columbia, where they came to fish for sturgeon. They brought disastrous accounts of the Tonquin, which were at first treated as mere fables; but which were too sadly confirmed by a different tribe that arrived a few days subsequently. We shall relate the circumstances of this melancholy affair as correctly as the casual discrepancies in the statements that have reached us will permit.

We have already stated that the Tonquin set sail from the mouth of the river on the fifth of June. The whole number of persons on board amounted to twenty three. In one of the outer bays they picked up, from a fishing canoe, an Indian named Lamazee, who had already made two voyages along the coast and knew something of the languages of the various tribes. He agreed to accompany them as interpreter.

Steering to the north Captain Thorn arrived in a few days at Vancouver's island and anchored in the harbour of Neweetie, very much against the advice of his Indian interpreter, who warned him against the perfidious character of the natives of this part of the coast. Numbers of canoes soon came off bringing sea otter skins to sell. It was too late in the day to commence a traffic but Mr. M'Kay, accompanied by a few of the men, went on shore to a large village to visit Wicananish the chief of the surrounding territory, six of the natives remaining on board as hostages. He was received with great professions of friendship, entertained hospitably and a couch of sea otter skins was prepared for him in the dwelling of the chieftain, where he was prevailed upon to pass the night.

In the morning, before Mr. M'Kay had returned to the ship, great numbers of the natives came off in their canoes to trade, headed by two sons of Wicananish. As they brought abundance of sea otter skins, and there was every appearance of a brisk trade, Captain Thorn did not wait for the return of Mr. M'Kay, but spread out his wares upon the deck, making a tempting display of blankets, cloths, knives, beads and fish hooks, expecting a prompt and profitable sale. The Indians, however, were not so eager and simple as he had supposed, having learned the art of bargaining and the value of merchandize from the casual traders along the coast. They were guided too by a shrewd old chief named Nookamis, who had grown gray in traffic with New England skippers and prided himself upon his acuteness. His opinion seemed to regulate the market. When Captain Thorn made what he considered a liberal offer for an otter skin the wily old Indian treated it with scorn and asked more than double. His comrades all took their cue from him and not an otter skin was to be had at a reasonable rate.

The old fellow, however, overshot his mark, and mistook the character of the man he was treating with. Thorn was a plain, straight forward sailor, who never had two minds nor two prices in his dealings, was deficient in patience and pliancy and totally wanting in the chicanery of traffic. He had a vast deal of stern but honest pride in his nature, and, moreover, held the whole savage race in sovereign contempt. Abandoning all further attempts, therefore, to bargain with his shuffling customers, he thrust his hands into his pockets and paced up and down the deck in sullen silence. The cunning old Indian followed him to and fro, holding out a sea otter skin to him at every turn, and pestering him to trade. Finding other means unavailing, he suddenly changed his tone and began to jeer and banter him upon the mean prices he offered. This was too much for the patience of the Captain, who was never remarkable for relishing a joke, especially when at his own expense. Turning suddenly upon his persecutor, he snatched the proffered otter skin from his hands, rubbed it in his face, and dismissed him over the side of the ship with no very complimentary application to accelerate his exit. He then kicked the peltries to the right and left about the deck and broke up the market in the most ignominious manner. Old Nookamis made for shore in a furious passion, in which he was joined by Shewish, one of the sons of Wicananish, who went off breathing vengeance, and the ship was soon abandoned by the natives.

When Mr. M'Kay returned on board the interpreter related what had passed and begged him to prevail upon the Captain to make sail, as, from his knowledge of the temper and pride of the people of the place, he was sure they would resent the indignity offered to one of their chiefs. Mr. M'Kay who himself possessed some experience of Indian character, went to the Captain, who was still pacing the deck in moody humour, represented the danger to which his hasty act had exposed the vessel, and urged him to weigh anchor. The Captain made light of his councils and pointed to his cannon and fire arms as a sufficient safe guard against naked savages. Futher remonstrances only provoked taunting replies and sharp altercations. The day passed away without any signs of hostility, and at night the Captain retired as usual to his cabin, taking no more than the usual precautions.

On the following morning, at day break, while the Captain and Mr. M'Kay were yet asleep, a canoe came along side in which were twenty Indians, commanded by young Shewish. They were unarmed, their aspect and demeanor friendly, and they held up otter skins and made signs indicative of a wish to trade. The caution enjoined by Mr. Astor in respect to the admission of Indians on board of the ship had been neglected for some time past, and the officer of the watch, perceiving those in the canoe to be without weapons, and having received no orders to the contrary, readily permitted them to mount the deck. Another canoe soon succeeded, the crew of which was likewise admitted. In a little while other canoes came off and Indians were soon clambering into the vessel on all sides.

The officer of the watch now felt alarmed, and called to Captain Thorn and Mr. M'Kay. By the time they came on deck it was thronged with Indians. The interpreter noticed to Mr. M'Kay that many of the natives wore short mantles of skins, and intimated a suspicion that they were secretly armed. Mr. M'Kay urged the Captain to clear the

ship and get under way. He again made light of the advice, but the
augmented swarm of canoes about the ship and the numbers still
putting off from shore at length awakened his distrust and he ordered
some of the crew to weigh anchor while seven were sent aloft to
make sail.

The Indians now offered to trade with the Captain on his own
terms, prompted apparently by the approaching departure of the ship.
Accordingly a hurried trade was commenced. The main articles sought
by the savages in barter, were knives; as fast as some were supplied
they moved off and others succeeded. By degrees they were thus
distributed about the deck, and all with weapons.

The anchor was now nearly up; the sails were loose and the Captain,
in a loud and peremptory tone, ordered the ship to be cleared. In an
instant a signal yell was given: it was echoed on every side, knives
and war clubs were brandished in every direction, and the savages
rushed upon their marked victims.

The first that fell was Mr. Lewis, the ship's clerk. He was leaning
with folded arms over a bale of blankets, engaged in bargaining, when
he received a deadly stab in the back and fell down the companionway.

Mr. M'Kay, who was seated on the taffrail, sprang on his feet, but
was instantly knocked down with a war club and flung backwards
into the sea, where he was despatched by the women in the canoes.

In the mean time, Captain Thorn made desperate fight against
fearful odds. He was a powerful as well as a resolute man, but he
had come upon deck without weapons. Shewish the young chief
singled him out as his peculiar prey, and rushed upon him at the
first outbreak. The Captain had barely time to draw a clasp knife
with one blow of which he laid the young savage dead at his feet.
Several of the stoutest followers of Shewish now set upon him. He
defended himself vigorously, dealing crippling blows to right and left,
and strewing the quarter deck with the slain and wounded. His object
was to fight his way to the cabin, where there were fire arms, but
he was hemmed in with foes, covered with wounds and faint with loss
of blood. For an instant he leaned upon the tiller wheel, when a blow
from behind with a war club felled him to the deck, where he was
despatched with knives and thrown overboard.

While this was transacting upon the quarter deck a chance medley
fight was going on throughout the ship. The crew fought desperately
with knives, handspikes, and whatever weapon they could seize upon
in the moment of surprise. They were soon, however, overpowered
by numbers and mercilessly butchered.

As to the seven who had been sent aloft to make sail, they contemplated with horror the carnage that was going on below. Being

destitute of weapons they let themselves down by the running rigging in hopes of getting between decks. One fell in the attempt and was instantly despatched. Another received a death blow in the back as he was descending; a third, Stephen Weekes the armourer, was mortally wounded as he was getting down the hatch way.

The remaining four made good their retreat into the cabin, where they found Mr. Lewis, still alive though mortally wounded. Barricading the cabin door they broke holes through the companion way, and, with the muskets and ammunition which were at hand opened a brisk fire that soon cleared the deck.

Thus far the Indian interpreter, from whom these particulars are derived, had been an eye witness of the deadly conflict. He had taken no part in it, and had been spared by the natives, as being of their race. In the confusion of the moment he took refuge with the rest, in the canoes. The survivors of the crew now sallied forth and discharged some of the deck guns, which did great execution among the canoes and drove all the savages to shore.

For the remainder of the day no one ventured to put off to the ship, deterred by the effects of the fire arms. The night passed away without any further attempt on the part of the natives. When the day dawned the Tonquin still lay at anchor in the bay, her sails all loose and flapping in the wind, and no one apparently on board of her. After a time some of the canoes ventured forth to reconnoiter, taking with them the interpreter. They paddled about her keeping cautiously at a distance, but growing more and more emboldened at seeing her quiet and lifeless. One man at length made his appearance on the deck, and was recognized by the interpreter as Mr. Lewis. He made friendly signs and invited them on board. It was long before they ventured to comply. Those who mounted the deck met with no opposition; no one was to be seen on board; for Mr. Lewis, after inviting them, had disappeared. Other canoes now pressed forward to board the prize; the decks were soon crowded and the sides covered with clambering savages, all intent on plunder. In the midst of their eagerness and exultation the ship blew up with a tremendous explosion. Arms, legs and mutilated bodies were blown into the air, and dreadful havoc was made in the surrounding canoes. The interpreter was in the main chains at the time of the explosion and was thrown unhurt into the water where he succeeded in getting into one of the canoes. According to his statement the bay presented an awful spectacle after the catastrophe. The ship had disappeared, but the bay was covered with fragments of the wreck, with shattered canoes and Indians swimming for their lives or struggling in the agonies of death; while those who had escaped the danger remained aghast and stupified, or made with frantic panic for the shore. Upwards of a hundred savages were destroyed by the explosion; many more were shockingly mutilated, and for days afterwards the limbs and bodies of the slain were thrown up on the beach.

The inhabitants of Neweetie were overwhelmed with consternation at this astounding calamity which had burst upon them in the very moment of triumph. The warriors sat mute and mournful, while the women filled the air with loud lamentations. Their weeping and wailing, however, were suddenly changed into yells of fury at the sight of four unfortunate white men brought captive into the village. They had been driven on shore in one of the ship's boats and taken at some distance along the coast.

The interpreter was permitted to converse with them. They proved to be the four brave fellows who had made such desperate defence from the cabin. The interpreter gathered from them some of the particulars already related. They told him further, that, after they had beaten off the enemy and cleared the ship, Lewis advised that they should slip the cable and endeavor to get to sea. They declined to take his advice, alledging that the wind set too strongly into the bay and would drive them on shore. They resolved as soon as it was dark, to put off quietly in the ship's boat, which they would be able to do unperceived, and to coast along back to Astoria. They put their resolution into effect; but Lewis refused to accompany them; being disabled by his wound, hopeless of escape and determined on a terrible revenge. On the voyage out he had repeatedly expressed a presentiment that he should die by his own hands, thinking it highly probable that he should be engaged in some contest with the natives, and being resolved in case of extremity, to commit suicide, rather than be made a prisoner. He now declared his intention to remain on board of the ship until day light, to decoy as many of the savages on board as possible, then to set fire to the powder magazine and terminate his life by a signal act of vengeance. How well he succeeded has been shewn.

His companions bade him a melancholy adieu and set off on their precarious expedition. They strove with might and main to get out of the bay, but found it impossible to weather a point of land, and were at length compelled to take shelter in a small cove, where they hoped to remain concealed until the wind should be more favorable. Exhausted by fatigue and watching they fell into a sound sleep and in that state were surprized by the savages. Better had it been for these unfortunate men had they remained with Lewis and shared his heroic death: as it was, they perished in a more painful and protracted manner, being sacrificed by the natives to the manes of their friends

with all the lingering tortures of savage cruelty. Some time after their
death, the interpreter, who had remained a kind of prisoner at large,
effected his escape and brought the tragical tidings to Astoria.

Such is the melancholy story of the Tonquin, and such was the
fate of her brave but headstrong commander, and her adventurous
crew. It is a catastrophe that shows the importance in all enterprizes
of moment, to keep in mind the general instructions of the sagacious
heads which devise them. Mr. Astor was well aware of the perils to
which ships were exposed on this coast from quarrels with the natives,
and from perfidious attempts of the latter to surprize and capture
them in unguarded moments. He had repeatedly enjoined it upon
Captain Thorn, in conversation, and at parting, in his letter of instructions, to be courteous and kind in his dealings with the Savages, but
by no means to confide in their apparent friendship, *nor to admit
more than a few on board of his ship at a time.*

Had the deportment of Captain Thorn been properly regulated,
the insult so wounding to Savage pride would never have been given.
Had he enforced the rule to admit but a few at a time the Savages
would not have been able to get the mastery. He was too irritable,
however, to practice the necessary self command; and having been
nurtured in a proud contempt of danger, thought it beneath him to
manifest any fear of a crew of unarmed Savages.

With all his faults and foibles we cannot but speak of him with
esteem, and deplore his untimely fate, for we remember him well in
early life, as a companion in pleasant scenes and joyous hours. When
on shore, among his friends, he was a frank, manly, soundhearted
sailor. On board ship he evidently assumed the hardness of deportment and sternness of demeanor which many deem essential to naval
service. Throughout the whole of the expedition, however, he shewed
himself loyal, single minded, straight forward and fearless, and if the
fate of his vessel may be charged to his harshness and imprudence we
should recollect that he paid for his error with his life.

The loss of the Tonquin was a grievous blow to the infant establishment of Astoria, and one that threatened to bring after it a train of
disasters. The intelligence of it did not reach Mr. Astor until many
months afterwards. He felt it in all its force and was aware that it
must cripple, if not entirely defeat, the great scheme of his ambition.
In his letters written at the time he speaks of it as "a calamity the
length of which he could not foresee." He indulged, however, in no
weak and vain lamentation, but sought to devise a prompt and efficient
remedy. The very same evening he appeared at the theatre with his
usual serenity of countenance. A friend who knew the disastrous intelligence he had received expressed his astonishment that he could

have calmness of spirit sufficient for such a scene of light amusement. "What would you have me do?" was his characteristic reply; "Would you have me stay at home and weep for what I cannot help?"

CHAPTER XII

*Gloom at Astoria—An ingenious stratagem—The small pox chief—
Launching of the Dolly—An arrival—A Canadian trapper—A Freeman
of the forests—An Iroquois hunter—Winter on the Columbia—Festivities of New Year.*

The tidings of the loss of the Tonquin and the massacre of her crew
struck dismay into the hearts of the Astorians. They found themselves
a mere handful of men, on a savage coast, surrounded by hostile tribes,
who would doubtless be incited and encouraged to deeds of violence
by the late fearful catastrophe. In this juncture Mr. M'Dougall, we are
told, had recourse to a stratagem by which to avail himself of the ignorance and credulity of the savages, and which certainly does credit to
his ingenuity.

The natives of the coast, and indeed of all the regions west of the
mountains, had an extreme dread of the small pox; that terrific scourge
having a few years previously appeared among them and almost swept
off entire tribes. Its origin and nature were wrapped in mystery, and
they conceived it an evil inflicted upon them by the Great Spirit or
brought among them by the white men. The last idea was seized upon
by Mr. M'Dougall. He assembled several of the chieftains whom he
believed to be in the conspiracy. When they were all seated around he
informed them that he had heard of the treachery of some of their
northern brethren towards the Tonquin, and was determined on
vengeance. "The white men among you," said he, "are few in number,
it is true, but they are mighty in medicine. See here," continued he,
drawing forth a small bottle and holding it before their eyes; "—in this
bottle I hold the small pox safely corked up; I have but to draw the
cork and let loose the pestilence, to sweep man, woman and child from
the face of the earth."

The chiefs were struck with horror and alarm. They implored him
not to uncork the bottle, since they and all their people were firm
friends of the white men, and would always remain so, but, should
the smallpox be once let out it would run like wildfire throughout the
country, sweeping off the good as well as the bad; and surely he would
not be so unjust as to punish his friends for crimes committed by his
enemies.

Mr. M'Dougall pretended to be convinced by their reasoning and
assured them that, so long as the white people should be unmolested,
and the conduct of their Indian neighbors friendly and hospitable, the

phial of wrath should remain sealed up; but, on the least act of hostility the fatal cork should be drawn.

From this time, it is added, he was much dreaded by the natives as one who held their fate in his hands, and was called, by way of pre eminence, "the Great Small pox Chief."

All this while the labours at the infant settlement went on with unremitting assiduity, and by the 26th of September a commodious mansion spacious enough to accommodate all hands was completed. It was built of stone and clay, there being no calcarious stone in the neighborhood from which lime for mortar could be procured. The schooner was also finished and launched with the accustomed ceremony on the second of October, and took her station below the fort. She was named the Dolly and was the first American vessel launched on this coast.

On the 5th of October in the evening the little community at Astoria was enlivened by the unexpected arrival of a detachment from Mr. David Stuart's post on the Oakinagan. It consisted of two of the clerks and two of the privates. They brought favorable accounts of the new establishment, but reported that, as Mr. Stuart was apprehensive there might be a difficulty of subsisting his whole party throughout the winter, he had sent one half back to Astoria, retaining with him only Ross, Montigny and two others. Such is the hardihood of the Indian trader. In the heart of a savage and unknown country, seven hundred miles from the main body of his fellow adventurers, Stuart had dismissed half of his little number, and was prepared with the residue to brave all the perils of the wilderness, and the rigours of a long and dreary winter.

With the return party came a Canadian Creole named Regis Brugiere, and an Iroquois hunter, with his wife and two children. As these two personages belong to certain classes which have derived their peculiar characteristics from the fur trade, we deem some few particulars concerning them pertinent to the nature of this work.

Brugiere was of a class of beaver trappers and hunters technically called Freemen, in the language of the traders. They are generally Canadians by birth, and of French descent, who have been employed for a term of years by some fur company, but, their term being expired, continue to hunt and trap on their own account, trading with the company like the Indians. Hence they derive their appellation of Freemen, to distinguish them from the trappers who are bound for a number of years and receive wages or hunt on shares.

Having passed their early youth in the wilderness, separated almost entirely from civilized man, and in frequent intercourse with the Indians, they lapse, with a facility common to human nature, into the habitudes of Savage life. Though no longer bound by engagements to continue in the interior they have become so accustomed to the freedom of the forest and the prairie that they look back with repugnance upon the restraints of civilization. Most of them intermarry with the natives, and, like the latter, have often a plurality of wives. Wanderers of the wilderness, according to the vicissitudes of the seasons, the migrations of animals, and the plenty or scarcity of game, they lead a precarious and unsettled existence, exposed to sun and storm and all kinds of hardships, until they resemble the Indians in complexion as well as in tastes and habits. From time to time they bring the peltries they have collected to the trading houses of the company in whose employ they have been brought up. Here they traffic them away for such articles of merchandize or ammunition as they may stand in need of. At the time when Montreal was the great emporium of the fur trader, one of these Freemen of the wilderness would suddenly return, after an absence of many years, among his old friends and comrades. He would be greeted as one risen from the dead; and with the greater welcome, as he returned flush of money. A short time, however, spent in revelry would be sufficient to drain his purse and sate him with civilized life, and he would return with new relish to the unshackled freedom of the forest.

Numbers of men of this class were scattered throughout the north west territories. Some of them retained a little of the thrift and forethought of the civilized man; and became wealthy among their improvident neighbors, their wealth being chiefly displayed in large bands of horses, which covered the prairies in the vicinity of their abodes. Most of them, however, were prone to assimilate to the red man in their heedlessness of the future.

Such was Regis Brugiere, a freeman and rover of the wilderness. Having been brought up in the service of the North West Company, he had followed in the train of one of its expeditions across the Rocky Mountains, and undertaken to trap for the trading post established on the Spokan River. In the course of his hunting excursions he had either accidentally or designedly found his way to the post of Mr. Stuart; and been prevailed upon to descend the Columbia and "try his luck" at Astoria.

Ignace Shonowane the Iroquois hunter was a specimen of a different class. He was one of those Aboriginals of Canada who had partially conformed to the habits of civilization and the doctrines of Christianity, under the influence of the French colonists and the Catholic priests; who seem generally to have been more successful in conciliating, taming, and converting the savages, than their English and Protestant rivals. These half civilized Indians retained some of the good and many of the evil qualities of their original stock. They were first rate hunters and dextrous in the management of the canoe. They could undergo great privations and were admirable for the service of the rivers, lakes and forests provided they could be kept sober and in proper subordination; but, once inflamed with liquor, to which they were madly addicted, all the dormant passions inherent in their nature were prone to break forth, and to hurry them into the most vindictive and bloody acts of violence.

Though they generally professed the Roman Catholic religion, yet it was mixed occasionally with some of their ancient superstitions; and they retained much of the Indian belief in charms and omens. Numbers of these men were employed by the North West Company as trappers, hunters and canoe men, but on lower terms than were allowed to white men. Ignace Shonowane had, in this way, followed the enterprize of the Company to the banks of the Spokan, being probably one of the first of his tribe that had traversed the Rocky Mountains.

Such were some of the motley populace of the wilderness, incident to the fur trade, who were gradually attracted to the new settlement of Astoria.

The month of October now began to give indications of approaching winter. Hitherto the colonists had been well pleased with the climate. The summer had been temperate, the mercury never rising above 80°. Westerly winds had prevailed during the spring and the early part of summer, and been succeeded by fresh breezes from the north west. In the month of October the southerly winds set in, bringing with them frequent rain.

The Indians now began to quit the borders of the Ocean and to retire to their winter quarters in the sheltered bosom of the forests or along the small rivers and brooks. The rainy season, which commences in October, continues with little intermission until April, and though the winters are generally mild, the mercury seldom sinking below the freezing point, yet the tempests of wind and rain are terrible. The sun is sometimes obscured for weeks; the brooks swell into roaring torrents and the country is threatened with a deluge.

The departure of the Indians to their winter quarters gradually rendered provisions scanty, and obliged the colonists to send out foraging expeditions in the Dolly. Still the little handful of adventurers kept up their spirits in their lonely fort at Astoria, looking forward to the time when they should be animated and reinforced by the party under Mr. Hunt that was to come to them across the Rocky Mountains.

The year gradually wore away; the rain which had poured down almost incessantly since the first of October, cleared up towards the evening of the 31st of December, and the morning of the first of January ushered in a day of sunshine.

The hereditary French holyday spirit of the Canadian voyageurs is hardly to be depressed by any adversities, and they can manage to get up a fête in the most squalid situations and under the most untoward circumstances. An extra allowance of rum, and a little flour to make cakes and puddings, constitute a "regale" and they forget all their toils and troubles in the song and the dance.

On the present occasion the partners endeavored to celebrate the New Year with some effect. At sunrise the drums beat to arms; the colours were hoisted, with three rounds of small arms and three discharges of cannon. The day was devoted to games of agility and strength and other amusements; and grog was temperately distributed, together with bread, butter and cheese. The best dinner their circumstances could afford was served up at midday. At sunset the colours were lowered with another discharge of artillery. The night was spent in dancing, and though there was a lack of female partners to excite their gallantry, the voyageurs kept up the ball with true French spirit until three o'clock in the morning. So passed the New Year's festival of 1812 at the infant colony of Astoria.

CHAPTER XIII

*Expedition by land—Wilson P. Hunt, his character—Donald M'Kenzie
—Recruiting service among the voyageurs—A bark canoe—Chapel of S'
Anne—Votive offerings—Pious carousals—A ragged regiment—Mackinaw
—Picture of a trading post—Frolicking voyageurs—Swells and swaggerers—Indian coxcombs—"A Man of the North"—Jockeyship of
voyageurs—Inefficacy of gold—Weight of a feather—Mr. Ramsay
Crooks—His character—His risks among the Indians—His warning concerning Sioux and Blackfeet—Embarcation of recruits—Parting scenes
between brothers, cousins, wives, sweethearts and pot companions.*

We have followed up the fortunes of the Maritime part of this enterprize to the shores of the Pacific, and have conducted the affairs of
the embryo establishment to the opening of the New Year: let us
now turn back to the adventurous band to whom was entrusted the
land expedition, and who were to make their way to the mouth of
the Columbia up vast rivers, across trackless plains and over the rugged
barriers of the Rocky Mountains.

The conduct of this expedition, as has already been mentioned,
was assigned to Mr. Wilson Price Hunt, of Trenton, New Jersey, one
of the partners of the Company, who was ultimately to be at the
head of the establishment at the mouth of the Columbia. He is represented as a man scrupulously upright and faithful in his dealings,
amiable in his disposition, and of most accommodating manners, and
his whole conduct will be found in unison with such a character. He
was not practically experienced in the Indian trade; that is to say,
he had never made any expeditions of traffic into the heart of the
wilderness; but he had been engaged in Commerce at S' Louis, then
a frontier settlement on the Mississippi, where the chief branch of
his business had consisted in furnishing Indian traders with goods and
equipments. In this way he had acquired much knowledge of the
trade at second hand, and of the various tribes and the interior country
over which it extended.

Another of the partners, Mr. Donald M'Kenzie, was associated with
Mr. Hunt in the expedition and excelled on those points in which the
other was deficient, for he had been ten years in the interior, in the
service of the North West Company and valued himself on his knowledge of "woodcraft" and the strategy of Indian trade and Indian
warfare. He had a frame seasoned to toils and hardships, a spirit
not to be intimidated, and was reputed to be a "remarkable shot," which
of itself was sufficient to give him renown upon the frontier.

Mr. Hunt and his coadjutor repaired, about the latter part of July

(1810) to Montreal, the Ancient Emporium of the fur trade; where every thing requisite for the expedition could be procured. One of the first objects was to recruit a complement of Canadian voyageurs from the disbanded herd usually to be found loitering about the place. A degree of jockeyship, however, is required for this service, for a Canadian voyageur is as full of latent tricks and vices as a horse, and when he makes the greatest external promise, is prone to prove the greatest "take in." Beside, the North West Company, who maintained a long established control at Montreal and knew the qualities of every voyageur, secretly interdicted the prime hands from engaging in this new service, so that, although liberal terms were offered, few presented themselves but such as were not worth having.

From these Mr. Hunt engaged a number sufficient, as he supposed, for present purposes, and having laid in a supply of ammunition, provisions and Indian goods, embarked all on board one of those great canoes at that time universally used by the fur traders, for navigating the intricate and often obstructed rivers. The canoe was between thirty and forty feet long and several feet in width; constructed of birch bark, sewed with fibres of the roots of the spruce tree, and daubed with resin of the pine instead of tar. The cargo was made up in packages, weighing from ninety to one hundred pounds each, for the facility of loading and unloading, and of transportation at portages. The canoe itself, though capable of sustaining a freight of upwards of four tons, could readily be carried on men's shoulders.

Canoes of this size are generally managed by eight or ten men; two of whom are picked veterans, who receive double wages and are stationed, one at the bow and the other at the stern, to keep a look out, and to steer. They are termed the foreman and the steersman. The rest, who ply the paddles, are called middle men. When there is a favorable breeze the canoe is occasionally navigated with a sail.

The expedition took its regular departure, as usual, from S' Anne's, near the extremity of the island of Montreal, the great starting place of the traders to the interior. Here stood the ancient chapel of S' Anne, the patroness of the Canadian voyageurs; where they made confession and offered up their vows previous to departing on any hazardous expedition. The shrine of the saint was decorated with reliques and votive offerings hung up by these superstitious beings, either to propitiate her favor, or in gratitude for some signal deliverance in the wilderness. It was the custom, too, of these devout vagabonds, after leaving the chapel, to have a grand carouse, in honor of the saint and for the prosperity of the voyage. In this part of their devotions the crew of Mr. Hunt proved themselves by no means deficient. Indeed he soon discovered that his recruits enlisted at Montreal were fit to vie with the ragged regiment of Falstaff. Some were able bodied, but inexpert; others were expert but lazy, while a third class were expert and willing, but totally worn out, being broken down veterans, incapable of toil.

With this inefficient crew he made his way up the Ottawa River and by the ancient route of the fur traders along a succession of small lakes and rivers to Michilimackinac. Their progress was slow and tedious. Mr. Hunt was not accustomed to the management of "voyageurs" and he had a crew admirably disposed to play the old soldier, and balk their work, and ever ready to come to a halt; land, make a fire, put on the great pot and smoke, and gossip and sing by the hour.

It was not until the 22d of July that they arrived at Mackinaw, situated on the island of the same name, at the confluence of Lakes Huron and Michigan. This famous old French trading post continued to be a rallying point for a multifarious and motley population. The inhabitants were amphibious in their habits, most of them being, or having been, voyageurs or canoe men. It was the great place of arrival and departure of the South West Fur trade. Here the Mackinaw Company had established its principal post from whence it communicated with the interior and with Montreal. Hence its various traders and trappers set out for their respective destinations about Lake Superior and its tributary waters or for the Mississippi, the Arkansas, the Missouri, and the other regions of the West. Here, after the absence of a year or more, they returned with their peltries and settled their accounts; the furs rendered in by them, being transmitted in canoes from hence to Montreal. Mackinaw was, therefore, for a great part of the year very scantily peopled, but at certain seasons the traders arrived from all points, with their crews of voyageurs, and the place swarmed like a hive.

Mackinaw at that time was a mere village, stretching along a small bay, with a fine broad beach in front of its principal row of houses, and dominated by the old fort, which crowned an impending height. The beach was a kind of public promenade, where were displayed all the vagaries of a seaport on the arrival of a fleet from a long cruize. Here were voyageurs frolicking away their wages, fiddling and dancing in the booths and cabins; buying all kinds of knick knacks, dressing themselves out finely and parading up and down like arrant braggarts and coxcombs. Sometimes they met with rival coxcombs in the young Indians from the opposite shore, who would appear on the beach painted and decorated in fantastic style, and would saunter up and down, to be gazed at and admired, perfectly satisfied that they eclipsed their palefaced competitors.

Now and then a chance party of "North Westers" appeared at

Mackinaw from the Rendezvous at Fort William. These held themselves up as the chivalry of the Fur trade. They were men of iron, proof against cold weather, hard fare and perils of all kinds. Some would wear the North West button, and a formidable dirk and assume something of a military air; they generally wore feathers in their hats; and affected the "brave." "Je suis un homme du Nord"—"I am a man of the North" one of these swelling fellows would exclaim, sticking his arms a kimbo and ruffling by the South Westers, whom he regarded with great contempt, as men softened by mild climates and the luxurious fare of bread and bacon, and whom he stigmatized with the inglorious name of Pork eaters. The superiority assumed by these vainglorious swaggerers was, in general, tacitly admitted; indeed some of them had acquired great notoriety for deeds of hardihood and courage, for the fur trade had its heroes whose names resounded throughout the wilderness.

Such was Mackinaw at the time of which we are treating. It now, doubtless, presents a totally different aspect. The Fur companies no longer assemble there; the navigation of the lakes is carried on by steamboats and various shipping, and the race of traders, and trappers and voyageurs and Indian dandies have vapoured out their brief hour and disappeared—Such changes does the lapse of a handful of years make in this ever changing country.

At this place Mr. Hunt remained for some time to complete his assortment of Indian goods, and to encrease his number of voyageurs, as well as to engage some of a more efficient character than those enlisted at Montreal.

And now commenced another game of jockeyship. There were able and efficient men in abundance at Mackinaw but for several days not one presented himself. If offers were made to any, they were listened to with a shake of the head. Should any one seem inclined to enlist, there were officious idlers and busybodies, of that class who are ever ready to dissuade others from any enterprize in which they themselves have no concern: these would pull him by the sleeve, take him on one side, and murmur in his ear; or would suggest difficulties outright.

It was objected that the expedition would have to navigate unknown rivers and pass through howling wildernesses infested by savage tribes who had already cut off the unfortunate voyageurs that had ventured among them. That it was to climb the Rocky Mountains and descend into desolate and famished regions where the traveller was often obliged to subsist on grasshoppers and crickets, or to kill his own horse for food.

At length one man was hardy enough to engage, and he was used like a "stool pigeon," to decoy others; but several days elapsed before any more could be prevailed upon to join him. A few then came to terms. It was desireable to engage them for five years, but some refused to engage for more than three. Then they must have part of their pay in advance; which was readily granted. When they had pocketed the amount and squandered it in regales or in outfits, they began to talk of pecuniary obligations at Mackinaw which must be discharged before they would be free to depart; or engagements with other persons, which were only to be cancelled by a "reasonable consideration."

It was in vain to argue or remonstrate, the money advanced had already been sacked and spent, and must be lost and the recruits left behind, unless they could be freed from their debts and engagements. Accordingly a fine was paid for one; a judgment for another; a tavern bill for a third, and almost all had to be bought off from some prior engagement, either real or pretended.

Mr. Hunt groaned in spirit at the incessant and unreasonable demands of these worthies upon his purse; yet with all this outlay of funds the number recruited was but scanty; and many of the most desireable still held themselves aloof and were not to be caught by a golden bait. With these he tried another temptation. Among the recruits who had enlisted he distributed feathers and ostrich plumes; these they put in their hats, and thus figured about Mackinaw, assuming airs of vast importance as "voyageurs in a New Company that was to eclipse the North West." The effect was complete. A French Canadian is too vain and mercurial a being to withstand the finery and ostentation of the feather. Numbers immediately pressed into the service: one must have an ostrich plume; another a white feather with a red end; a third a bunch of cocks' tails. Thus all paraded about in vain glorious style, more delighted with the feathers in their hats than with the money in their pockets; and considering themselves fully equal to the boastful "men of the north."

While thus recruiting the number of rank and file Mr. Hunt was joined by a person whom he had invited by letter to engage as a partner in the expedition. This was Mr. Ramsay Crooks, a young man, a native of Scotland, who had served under the North West Company and been engaged in trading expeditions upon his individual account, among the tribes of the Missouri. Mr. Hunt knew him personally and had conceived a high and merited opinion of his judgement, enterprize and integrity: he was rejoiced therefore when the latter consented to accompany him. Mr. Crooks, however, drew from experience a picture of the dangers to which they would be subjected, and urged the importance of going with a considerable force. In ascending the upper Missouri they would have to pass through the country of the Sioux Indians, who had manifested repeated hostility to the white traders and rendered their expeditions extremely perilous; firing upon them from the river banks as they passed beneath in their boats, and attacking them in their encampments. Mr. Crooks himself, when voyaging in company with another trader of the name of M'Lellan, had been interrupted by these marauders, and had considered himself fortunate in escaping down the river without loss of life or property, but with a total abandonment of his trading voyage.

Should they be fortunate enough to pass through the country of the Sioux without molestation they would have another tribe still more savage and warlike beyond, and deadly foes of the white men. These were the Blackfeet Indians, who ranged over a wide extent of country which they would have to traverse.

Under all these circumstances it was thought adviseable to augment the party considerably. It already exceeded the number of thirty to which it had originally been limited, but it was determined, on arriving at S' Louis, to encrease it to the number of sixty.

These matters being arranged they prepared to embark; but the embarcation of a crew of Canadian voyageurs on a distant expedition is not so easy a matter as might be imagined; especially of such a set of vainglorious fellows with money in both pockets and cocks' tails in their hats. Like sailors, the Canadian voyageurs generally preface a long cruise with a carouse. They have their cronies, their brothers, their cousins, their wives, their sweethearts all to be entertained at their expense; they feast, they fiddle, they drink, they sing, they dance, they frolick and fight until they are all as mad as so many drunken Indians. The publicans are all obedience to their commands, never hesitating to let them run up scores without limit, knowing that, when their own money is expended, the pursers of their employers must answer for the bill, or the voyage must be delayed. Neither was it possible at that time to remedy the matter at Mackinaw; in that amphibious community there was always a propensity to wrest the laws in favour of riotous or mutinous boatmen. It was necessary also to keep the recruits in good humour, seeing the novelty and danger of the service into which they were entering, and the ease with which they might at any time escape it, by jumping into a canoe and going down the stream.

Such were the scenes that beset Mr. Hunt and gave him a foretaste of the difficulties of his command. The little cabarets and sutlers' shops along the bay resounded with the scraping of fiddles, with snatches of old French songs, with Indian whoops and yelps; while every plumed and feathered vagabond had his troop of loving cousins and comrades at his heels. It was with the utmost difficulty that they could be extricated from the clutches of the publicans and the embraces of their pot companions, who followed them to the water's edge with many a hug, a kiss on each cheek, and a maudlin benediction in Canadian French.

It was about the 12th of August that they left Mackinaw, and pursued the usual route by Green Bay; Fox and Wisconsin Rivers to Prairie du Chien, and thence down the Mississippi to S' Louis, where they landed on the third of September.

CHAPTER XIV

S' Louis, which is situated on the right bank of the Mississippi River, a few miles below the mouth of the Missouri, was, at that time, a frontier settlement and the last fitting out place for the Indian trade of the South West. It possessed a motley population, composed of the Creole descendants of the original French colonists; the keen traders from the Atlantic states; the backwoodsmen of Kentucky and Tennessee; the Indians and half breeds of the prairies; together with a singular aquatic race that had grown up from the navigation of the rivers, the "boatmen of the Mississippi," who possessed habits, manners and almost a language, peculiarly their own and strongly technical. They at that time were extremely numerous, and conducted the chief navigation and commerce of the Ohio and the Mississippi, as the voyageurs did of the Canadian waters; but, like them, their consequence and characteristics are rapidly vanishing before the all pervading intrusion of steamboats.

The old French houses engaged in the Indian trade had gathered round them a train of dependents, mongrel Indians and mongrel Frenchmen, who had intermarried with Indians. These they employed in their various expeditions by land and water. Various individuals of other countries had of late years pushed the trade farther into the interior, to the upper waters of the Missouri, and had swelled the number of these hangers on. Several of these traders had, two or three years previously, formed themselves into a company, composed of twelve partners, with a capital of about forty thousand dollars, called the Missouri Fur Company, the object of which was to establish posts along the upper part of that river and monopolize the trade. The leading partner of this Company was Mr. Manuel Lisa, a Spaniard by birth and a man of bold and enterprizing character, who had ascended the Missouri almost to its source, and made himself well acquainted and popular with several of its tribes. By his exertions trading posts had been established in 1808 in the Sioux country and among the Arickara and Mandan tribes; and a principal one, under Mr. Henry, one of the partners, at the forks of the Missouri. This company had in its employ about two hundred and fifty men, partly American hunters and partly creoles and Canadian voyageurs.

All these circumstances combined to produce a population at S' Louis even still more motley than that at Mackinaw. Here were to be seen about the river banks the hectoring, extravagant, bragging boatmen of the Mississippi, with the gay, grimacing, singing, goodhumoured Canadian voyageurs; vagrant Indians of various tribes loitered about the streets; now and then a stark Kentucky hunter, in leathern hunting dress, with rifle on shoulder and knife in belt, strode along. Here and there were new brick houses and shops just set up by bustling, driving and eager men of traffic from the Atlantic states; while on the other hand the old French mansions, with open casements still retained the easy indolent air of the original colonists; and now and then the scraping of a fiddle, a strain of an ancient French song, or the sound of billiard balls, shewed that the happy Gallic turn for gaiety and amusement still lingered about the place.

Such was S' Louis at the time of Mr. Hunt's arrival there; and the appearance of a new Fur company, with ample funds at its command, produced a strong sensation among the Indian traders of the place, and awakened keen jealousy and opposition on the part of the Missouri Company. Mr. Hunt proceeded to strengthen himself against all competition. For this purpose he secured to the interests of the association another of those enterprizing men who had been engaged in individual traffic with the tribes of the Missouri. This was a Mr. Joseph Miller, a gentleman well educated and well informed, and of a respectable family of Baltimore. He had been an officer in the Army of the United States, but had resigned in disgust, on being refused a furlough, and had taken to trapping beaver and trading among the Indians. He was easily induced by Mr. Hunt to join as a partner, and was considered by him, on account of his education and acquirements, and his experience in Indian trade, a valuable addition to the Company.

Several additional men were, likewise, enlisted at S' Louis; some as boatmen and others as hunters. These last were engaged, not merely to kill game for provisions, but also, and indeed chiefly, to trap beaver and other animals of rich furs, valuable in the trade. They enlisted on different terms. Some were to have a fixed salary of three hundred dollars, others were to be fitted out and maintained at the expense of the Company and were to hunt and trap on shares.

As Mr. Hunt met with much opposition on the part of rival traders, especially the Missouri Fur Company, it took him some weeks to complete his preparations. The delays which he had previously experienced at Montreal, Mackinaw, and on the way, added to those at

S' Louis, had thrown him much behind his original calculations, so that it would be impossible to effect his voyage up the Missouri in the present year. This river flowing from high and cold latitudes, and through wide and open plains exposed to chilling blasts, freezes early. The winter may be dated from the first of November; there was every prospect, therefore, that it would be closed with ice long before Mr. Hunt could reach its upper waters. To avoid, however, the expense of wintering at S' Louis he determined to push up the river as far as possible to some point above the settlements where game was plenty, and where his whole party could be subsisted by hunting, until the breaking up of the ice in the spring should permit them to resume their voyage.

Accordingly, on the twenty first of October he took his departure from S' Louis. His party was distributed in three boats: One was the barge which he had brought from Mackinaw; another was of a larger size, such as was formerly used in navigating the Mohawk River, and known by the generic name of the Schenectady barge; the other was a large keel boat, at that time the grand conveyance on the Mississippi.

In this way they set out from S' Louis, in buoyant spirits, and soon arrived at the mouth of the Missouri. This vast river, three thousand miles in length, and which, with its tributary streams, drains such an immense extent of country, was as yet but casually and imperfectly navigated by the adventurous bark of the Fur trader. A steamboat had never yet stemmed its turbulent current; sails were but of casual assistance, for it required a strong wind to conquer the force of the stream; the main dependence was on bodily strength and manual dexterity. The boats in general had to be propelled by oars and setting poles, or drawn by the hand and by grappling hooks, from one root or overhanging tree to another; or towed by the long cordelle, or towing line, where the shores were sufficiently clear of woods and thickets to permit the men to pass along the banks.

During this slow and tedious progress the boat would be exposed to frequent danger from floating trees and great masses of drift wood; or to be impaled upon snags and sawyers, that is to say, sunken trees, presenting a jagged or pointed end above the surface of the water. As the channel of the river frequently shifted from side to side, according to the bends and sand banks, the boat had, in the same way, to advance in a zig zag course. Often a part of the crew would have to leap into the water at the shallows, and wade along with the towing line, while their comrades on board toilfully assisted with oar and setting pole. Sometimes the boat would seem to be retained motionless, as if spell bound, opposite some point round which the current set with violence, and where the utmost labour scarce effected any visible progress.

On these occasions it was that the merits of the Canadian voyageurs came into full action. Patient of toil, not to be disheartened by impediments and disappointments, fertile in expedients, and versed in every mode of humouring and conquering the wayward current, they would ply every exertion, sometimes in the boat, sometimes on shore, sometimes in the water, however cold: always alert, always in good humour; and, should they at any time flag or grow weary, one of their popular boat-songs, chanted by a veteran oarsman, and responded to in chorus, acted as a neverfailing restorative.

By such assiduous and persevering labour they made their way about four hundred and fifty miles up the Missouri, by the 16th of November, to the mouth of the Nodawa. As this was a good hunting country, and as the season was rapidly advancing, they determined to establish their winter quarters at this place, and, in fact, two days after they had come to a halt, the river closed just above their encampment.

The party had not been long at this place when they were joined by Mr. Robert M'Lellan, another trader of the Missouri, the same who had been associated with Mr. Crooks in the unfortunate expedition in which they had been intercepted by the Sioux Indians and obliged to make a rapid retreat down the river.

M'Lellan was a remarkable man. He had been a partizan under General Wayne in his Indian wars, where he had distinguished himself by his fiery spirit and reckless daring, and marvellous stories were told of his exploits. His appearance answered to his character. His frame was meagre but muscular; shewing strength, activity and iron firmness. His eyes were dark, deep set and piercing. He was restless, fearless, but of impetuous and sometimes ungovernable temper. He had been invited by Mr. Hunt to enrol himself as a partner and gladly consented; being pleased with the thoughts of passing with a powerful force through the country of the Sioux, and perhaps having an opportunity of revenging himself upon that lawless tribe for their past offences.

Another recruit that joined the camp at Nodawa deserves equal mention. This was John Day, a hunter from the backwoods of Virginia, who had been several years on the Missouri in the service of Mr. Crooks and of other traders. He was about forty years of age, six feet two inches high, straight as an Indian; with an elastic step as if he trod on springs, and a handsome, open, manly countenance. It was his boast that, in his younger days nothing could hurt or daunt him but he had "lived too fast" and injured his constitution by his excesses. Still he was strong of hand, bold of heart, a prime woodman and an almost unerring shot. He had the frank spirit of a Virginian and the rough heroism of a pioneer of the West.

The party were now brought to a halt for several months. They were in a country abounding with deer and wild turkeys, so that there was no stint of provisions, and every one appeared cheerful and contented. Mr. Hunt determined to avail himself of this interval to return to S' Louis and obtain a reinforcement. He wished to procure an interpreter acquainted with the language of the Sioux, as, from all accounts, he apprehended difficulties in passing through the country of that nation. He felt the necessity also of having a greater number of hunters, not merely to keep up a supply of provisions throughout their long and arduous expedition, but also as a protection and defence in case of Indian hostilities. For such service the Canadian voyageurs were little to be depended upon, fighting not being a part of their profession; the proper kind of men were American hunters, experienced in savage life and savage warfare and possessed of the true game spirit of the West.

Leaving, therefore, the encampment in charge of the other partners, Mr. Hunt set off on foot on the first of January (1811) for S' Louis. He was accompanied by eight men as far as Fort Osage, about one hundred and fifty miles below Nodawa. Here he procured a couple of horses and proceeded on the remainder of his journey with two men, sending the other six back to the encampment. He arrived at S' Louis on the 20th of January.

CHAPTER XV

Opposition of the Missouri Fur Company—Blackfeet Indians—Pierre Dorion, a half breed interpreter—Old Dorion and his hybrid progeny —Family quarrels—Cross purposes between Dorion and Lisa—Renegadoes from Nodawa—Perplexities of a commander—Messrs. Bradbury and Nuttall join the expedition—Legal embarrassments of Pierre Dorion —Departure from S' Louis—Conjugal discipline of a half breed—Annual swelling of the Rivers—Daniel Boon, the patriarch of Kentucky—John Colter, his adventures among the Indians—Rumors of danger a head —Fort Osage—An Indian war feast—Troubles in the Dorion family— Buffalos and turkey buzzards.

On this his second visit to S' Louis Mr. Hunt was again impeded in his plans by the opposition of the Missouri Fur Company. The affairs of that company were, at this time, in a very dubious state. During the preceding year their principal establishment at the Forks of the Missouri had been so much harassed by the Blackfeet Indians, that its commander, Mr. Henry, one of the partners, had been compelled to abandon the post and cross the Rocky Mountains, with the intention of fixing himself upon one of the upper branches of the Columbia. What had become of him and his party was unknown; the most intense anxiety was felt concerning them, and apprehensions that they might have been cut off by the Savages. At the time of Mr. Hunt's arrival at S' Louis, the Missouri Company were fitting out an expedition to go in quest of Mr. Henry. It was to be conducted by Mr. Manuel Lisa, the enterprizing partner already mentioned.

There being thus two expeditions on foot at the same moment, an unusual demand was occasioned for hunters and voyageurs, who accordingly profited by the circumstance and stipulated for high terms. Mr. Hunt found a keen and subtle competitor in Lisa, and was obliged to secure his recruits by liberal advances of pay, and by other pecuniary indulgences.

The greatest difficulty was to procure the Sioux interpreter. There was but one man to be met with at S' Louis who was fitted for the purpose but to secure him would require much management. The individual in question was a half breed, named Pierre Dorion, and as he figures hereafter in this narrative, and is, withal, a striking specimen of the hybrid race on the frontier, we shall give a few particulars concerning him. Pierre was the son of Dorion the French interpreter who accompanied Messrs. Lewis and Clarke in their famous exploring expedition across the Rocky Mountains. Old Dorion was one of those French Creoles, descendants of the ancient Canadian stock, who abound on the Western frontier, and amalgamate or cohabit with the Savages. He had sojourned among various tribes and perhaps left progeny among them all; but his regular, or habitual, wife was a Sioux squaw. By her he had a hopeful brood of halfbreed sons, of whom Pierre was one. The domestic affairs of old Dorion were conducted on the true Indian plan. Father and sons would occasionally get drunk together, and then the cabin was a scene of ruffian brawl and fighting, in the course of which the old Frenchman was apt to get soundly belaboured by his mongrel offspring. In a furious scuffle of the kind one of the sons got the old man upon the ground and was upon the point of scalping him. "Hold! my son," cried the old fellow, in imploring accents,—"you are too brave, too *honorable* to scalp your father!" This last appeal touched the French side of the half breed's heart, so he suffered the old man to wear his scalp unharmed.

Of this hopeful stock was Pierre Dorion, the man whom it was now the desire of Mr. Hunt to engage as an interpreter. He had been employed in that capacity by the Missouri Fur Company during the preceding year, and had conducted their traders in safety through the different tribes of the Sioux. He had proved himself faithful and serviceable while sober, but the love of liquor in which he had been nurtured and brought up, would occasionally break out, and with it the savage side of his character.

It was this love of liquor which had embroiled him with the Missouri Company. While in their service at Fort Mandan on the frontier he had been seized with a whisky mania, and, as the beverage was only to be procured at the Company's store, it had been charged in his account at the rate of ten dollars a quart. This item had ever remained unsettled; and a matter of furious dispute the mere mention of which was sufficient to put him in a passion.

The moment it was discovered by Mr. Lisa that Pierre Dorion was in treaty with the new and rival association, he endeavored by threats as well as promises to prevent his engaging in their service. His promises might perhaps have prevailed, but his threats, which related to the whisky debt, only served to drive Pierre into the opposite ranks. Still he took advantage of this competition for his services to stand out with Mr. Hunt on the most advantageous terms and after a negotiation of nearly two weeks, capitulated to serve in the expedition as hunter and interpreter at the rate of three hundred dollars a year, two hundred of which were to be paid in advance.

When Mr. Hunt had got every thing ready for leaving S' Louis, new difficulties arose. Five of the American hunters from the encampment at Nodawa suddenly made their appearance. They alleged that they had been ill treated by the partners at the encampment, and had come off clandestinely in consequence of a dispute. It was useless at the present moment and under present circumstances, to attempt any compulsory measures with these deserters. Two of them Mr. Hunt prevailed upon, by mild means, to return with him. The rest refused. Nay, what was worse, they spread such reports of the hardships and dangers to be apprehended in the course of the expedition, that they struck a panic into those hunters who had recently engaged at S' Louis, and, when the hour of departure arrived, all, but one, refused to embark. It was in vain to plead or remonstrate, they shouldered their rifles and turned their backs upon the expedition, and Mr. Hunt was fain to put off from shore with the single hunter and a number of voyageurs whom he had engaged. Even Pierre Dorion at the last moment refused to enter the boat until Mr. Hunt consented to take his squaw and two children on board also. But the tissue of perplexities on account of this worthy individual did not end here.

Among the various persons who were about to proceed up the Missouri with Mr. Hunt were two scientific gentlemen: One Mr. John Bradbury, a man of mature age, but great enterprize and personal activity, who had been sent out by the Linnean Society of Liverpool, to make a collection of American plants; the other a Mr. Nuttall, likewise an Englishman, younger in years, who has since made himself known as the author of "Travels in Arkansas," and a work on the "Genera of American Plants." Mr. Hunt had offered them the protection and facilities of his party, in their scientific researches up the Missouri.

As they were not ready to depart at the moment of embarcation they put their trunks on board of the boat, but remained at S' Louis until the next day for the arrival of the post, intending to join the expedition at S' Charles, a short distance above the mouth of the Missouri.

The same evening, however, they learnt that a writ had been issued against Pierre Dorion for his whiskey debt, by Mr. Lisa as agent of the Missouri Company, and that it was the intention to entrap the mongrel linguist on his arrival at S' Charles. Upon hearing this, Mr. Bradbury and Mr. Nuttall set off a little after midnight, by land; got ahead of the boat as it was ascending the Missouri, before its arrival at S' Charles, and gave Pierre Dorion warning of the legal toil prepared to ensnare him. The knowing Pierre immediately landed and took to the woods, followed by his squaw laden with their pappooses and a large bundle containing their most precious effects; promising to rejoin the party some distance above S' Charles.

There seemed little dependance to be placed upon the promises of a loose adventurer of the kind, who was at the very time playing an evasive game with his former employers; who had already received two thirds of his year's pay, and had his rifle on his shoulder, his family and worldly fortune at his heels, and the wild woods before him. There was no alternative, however, and it was hoped his pique against his old employers would render him faithful to his new ones.

The party reached S' Charles in the afternoon, but the harpies of the law looked in vain for their expected prey. The boats resumed their course on the following morning, and had not proceeded far when Pierre Dorion made his appearance on the shore. He was gladly taken on board, but he came without his squaw. They had quarrelled in the night; Pierre had administered the Indian discipline of the cudgel, whereupon she had taken to the woods, with their children and all their worldly goods. Pierre evidently was deeply grieved and disconcerted at the loss of his wife and his knapsack; wherefore Mr. Hunt dispatched one of the Canadian voyageurs in search of the the fugitive, and the whole party, after proceeding a few miles further, encamped on an island to await his return. The Canadian rejoined the party, but without the squaw, and Pierre Dorion passed a solitary and anxious night, bitterly regretting his indiscretion in having exercised his conjugal authority so near home. Before day break, however, a well known voice reached his ears from the opposite shore. It was his repentant spouse who had been wandering the woods all night in quest of the party and had at length descried it by its fires. A boat was despatched for her; the interesting family was once more united, and Mr. Hunt now flattered himself that his perplexities with Pierre Dorion were at an end.

Bad weather, very heavy rains and an unusually early rise in the Missouri rendered the ascent of the river toilsome, slow and dangerous. The rise of the Missouri does not generally take place until the month of May or June: the present swelling of the river must have been caused by a freshet in some of its more southern branches; it could not have been the great annual flood, as the higher branches must still have been ice bound. And here we cannot but pause to notice the admirable arrangement of nature, by which the annual swellings of the various great rivers which empty themselves into the Mississippi, have been made to precede each other at considerable intervals. Thus the flood of the Red River precedes that of the Arkansas by a month; the Arkansas also, rising in a much more southern latitude than the Missouri, takes the lead of it in its annual excess, and its superabundant waters are disgorged and disposed of long before the breaking up of the icy barriers of the north: otherwise, did all these mighty streams rise simultaneously and discharge their vernal floods into the Mississippi an inundation would be the consequence that would submerge and devastate all the lower country.

On the afternoon of the third day, March 17th, the boats touched at Charette, one of the old villages founded by the original French colonists. Here they met with Daniel Boon, the renowned patriarch of Kentucky, who had kept in the advance of civilization, and on the borders of the wilderness, still leading a hunter's life, though now in his eighty fifth year. He had but recently returned from a hunting and trapping expedition and had brought nearly sixty beaver skins as trophies of his skill. The old man was still erect in form, strong in limb and unflinching in spirit, and as he stood on the river bank, watching the departure of an expedition destined to traverse the wilderness to the very shores of the Pacific, very probably felt a throb of his old pioneer spirit, impelling him to shoulder his rifle and join the adventurous band. Boon flourished several years after this meeting, in a vigorous old age, the nestor of hunters and backwoodsmen, and died full of sylvan honour and renown in 1818 in his ninety second year.

The next morning early, as the party were yet encamped at the mouth of a small stream, they were visited by another of these heroes of the wilderness, one John Colter, who had accompanied Lewis and Clarke in their memorable expedition. He had recently made one of those vast internal voyages so characteristic of this fearless class of men, and of the immense regions over which they hold their lonely wanderings, having come from the head waters of the Missouri to S' Louis, in a small canoe. This distance of three thousand miles he had accomplished in thirty days. Colter kept with the party all the morning. He had many particulars to give them concerning the Blackfeet Indians, a restless and predatory tribe, who had conceived an implacable hostility to the white men, in consequence of one of their warriors having been killed by Captain Lewis, while attempting to steal horses. Through the country infested by these savages the expedition would have to proceed, and Colter was urgent in reiterating the precautions that ought to be observed respecting them. He had himself experienced their vindictive cruelty, and his story deserves particular citation, as shewing the hairbreadth adventures to which these solitary rovers of the wilderness are exposed.

Colter, with the hardihood of a regular trapper, had cast himself loose from the party of Lewis and Clarke in the very heart of the wilderness, and had remained to trap beaver alone on the head waters of the Missouri. Here he fell in with another lonely trapper, like himself, named Potts, and they agreed to keep together. They were in the very region of the terrible Blackfeet, at that time thirsting to revenge the death of their companion, and knew that they had to expect no mercy at their hands. They were obliged to keep concealed all day in the woody margins of the rivers, setting their traps after nightfall and taking them up before day break. It was running a fearful risk for the sake of a few beaver skins; but such is the life of the trapper.

They were on a branch of the Missouri called Jefferson's Fork, and had set their traps at night, about six miles up a small river that emptied into the fork. Early in the morning they ascended the river in a canoe, to examine the traps. The banks on each side were high and perpendicular and cast a shade over the stream. As they were softly paddling along they heard the trampling of many feet upon the banks. Colter immediately gave the alarm of "Indians!" and was for instant retreat. Potts scoffed at him for being frightened by the trampling of a herd of buffalo. Colter checked his uneasiness and paddled forward. They had not gone much farther when frightful whoops and yells burst forth from each side of the river, and several hundred Indians appeared on either bank. Signs were made to the unfortunate trappers to come on shore. They were obliged to comply. Before they could get out of their canoe a savage seized the rifle belonging to Potts. Colter sprang on shore, wrested the weapon from the hands of the Indian and restored it to his companion, who was still in the canoe, and immediately pushed into the stream. There was the sharp twang of a bow, and Potts cried out that he was wounded. Colter urged him to come on shore and submit as his only chance for life, but the other knew there was no prospect of mercy, and determined to die game. Levelling his rifle he shot one of the savages dead on the spot. The next moment he fell himself, pierced with innumerable arrows.

The vengeance of the savages now turned upon Colter. He was stripped naked, and, having some knowledge of the Blackfoot language, overheard a consultation as to the mode of despatching him, so as to derive the greatest amusement from his death. Some were for setting him up as a mark, and having a trial of skill at his expense. The chief, however, was for nobler sport. He seized Colter by the shoulder and demanded if he could run fast. The unfortunate trapper was too well acquainted with Indian customs not to comprehend the drift of the question. He knew he was to run for his life, and to furnish a kind of human hunt to his persecutors. Though in reality he was noted among his brother hunters for swiftness of foot, he assured the chief that he was a very bad runner. His stratagem gained him some vantage ground. He was led by the chief into the prairie about four hundred yards from the main body of savages and then turned loose to save himself if he could. A tremendous yell let him know that the whole pack of bloodhounds were off in full cry. Colter flew rather than ran; he was astonished at his own speed; but he had six miles of prairie to traverse before he should reach the Jefferson fork of the Missouri;

how could he hope to hold out such a distance with the fearful odds of several hundred to one against him. The plain, too, abounded with the prickly pear, which wounded his naked feet. Still he fled on, dreading each moment to hear the twang of a bow and to feel an arrow quivering at his heart. He did not even dare to look round lest he should lose an inch of that distance on which his life depended. He had run nearly half way across the plain when the sound of pursuit grew somewhat fainter and he ventured to turn his head. The main body of his pursuers were a considerable distance behind; several of the faster runners were scattered in the advance, while a swiftfooted warrior armed with a spear, was not more than a hundred yards behind him.

Inspired with new hope Colter redoubled his exertions, but strained himself to such a degree that the blood gushed from his mouth and nostrils and streamed down his breast. He arrived within a mile of the river. The sound of footsteps gathered upon him. A glance behind shewed his pursuer within twenty yards, and preparing to launch his spear. Stopping short, he turned round and spread out his arms. The savage, confounded by this sudden action, attempted to stop and to hurl his spear, but fell in the very act. His spear stuck in the ground and the shaft broke in his hand. Colter plucked up the pointed part, pinned the savage to the earth and continued his flight. The Indians, as they arrived at their slaughtered companion, stopped to howl over him.

Colter made the most of this precious delay; gained the skirt of cottonwood bordering the river, dashed through it and plunged into the stream. He swam to a neighboring island, against the upper end of which the drift wood had lodged in such quantities as to form a natural raft. Under this he dived, and swam below water until he succeeded in getting a breathing place between the floating trunks of trees, where branches and bushes formed a covert several feet above the level of the water. He had scarcely drawn breath after all his toils when he heard his pursuers on the river bank whooping and yelling like so many fiends. They plunged in the river and swam to the raft. The heart of Colter almost died within him as he saw them, through the chinks of his concealment, passing and repassing and seeking for him in all directions. They at length gave up the search, and he began to rejoice in his escape when the idea presented itself that they might set the raft on fire. Here was a new source of horrible apprehension, in which he remained until night fall. Fortunately the idea did not suggest itself to the Indians. As soon as it was dark, finding by the silence around that his pursuers had departed, Colter dived again and came up beyond the raft. He then swam silently down the river for a considerable distance, when he landed, and kept on all night, to get as far off as possible from this dangerous neighborhood.

By day break he had gained sufficient distance to relieve him from the terrors of his savage foes; but now new sources of inquietude presented themselves. He was naked and alone, in the midst of an unbounded wilderness; his only chance was to reach a trading post of the Missouri Company, situated on a branch of the Yellow stone River. Even should he elude his pursuers days must elapse before he could reach this post, during which he must traverse immense prairies destitute of shade, his naked body exposed to the burning heat of the sun by day, and the dews and chills of the night season; and his feet lacerated by the thorns of the prickly pear. Though he might see game in abundance around him, he had no means of killing any for his sustenance, and must depend for food upon the roots of the earth. In defiance of these difficulties he pushed resolutely forward, guiding himself on his trackless course by those signs and indications known only to Indians and backwoodsmen, and after braving dangers and hardships enough to break down any spirit but that of a western pioneer, arrived safe at the solitary post in question.*

Such is a sample of the rugged experience which Colter had to relate of Savage life; yet, with all these perils and terrors fresh in his recollection, he could not see the present band on their way to those regions of danger and adventure, without feeling a vehement impulse to join them. A Western trapper is like a sailor; past hazards only stimulate him to further risques. The vast prairie is to the one what the ocean is to the other, a boundless field of enterprize and exploit; however he may have suffered in his last cruize he is always ready to join a new expedition, and the more adventurous its nature, the more attractive is it to his vagrant spirit.

Nothing seems to have kept Colter from continuing with the party to the shores of the Pacific but the circumstance of his having recently married. All the morning he kept with them, balancing in his mind the charms of his bride against those of the Rocky Mountains; the former, however, prevailed, and after a march of several miles he took a reluctant leave of the travellers and turned his face homeward.

Continuing their progress up the Missouri the party encamped on the evening of the 21st of March in the neighborhood of a little frontier village of French Creoles. Here Pierre Dorion met with some of his old comrades with whom he had a long gossip and returned to the camp with rumours of bloody feuds between the Osages and

* Bradbury. Travels in America. P. 17.

the Ioways, or Ayaways, Potowatomies, Sioux and Saukees. Blood had already been shed and scalps been taken. A war party three hundred strong were prowling in the neighborhood; others might be met with higher up the river; it behoved the travellers, therefore, to be upon their guard against robbery or surprize, for an Indian war party on the march is prone to acts of outrage. In consequence of this report, which was subsequently confirmed by further intelligence, a guard was kept up at night round the encampment, and they all slept on their arms. As they were sixteen in number and well supplied with weapons and ammunition, they trusted to be able to give any marauding party a warm reception. Nothing occurred, however, to molest them on their voyage, and on the 8th of April they came in sight of Fort Osage. On their approach the flag was hoisted on the fort, and they saluted it by a discharge of fire arms. Within a short distance of the fort was an Osage village, the inhabitants of which, men, women and children, thronged down to the water side to witness their landing. One of the first persons they met on the river bank was Mr. Crooks, who had come down in a boat, with nine men, from the winter encampment at Nodawa to meet them.

They remained at Fort Osage a part of three days, during which they were hospitably entertained at the garrison by Lieutenant Brownson who held a temporary command. They were regaled also with a war feast at the village; the Osage warriors having returned from a successful foray against the Ioways, in which they had taken seven scalps. These were paraded on poles about the village, followed by the warriors decked out in all their savage ornaments and hideously painted as if for battle.

By the Osage warriors Mr. Hunt and his companions were again warned to be on their guard in ascending the river, as the Sioux tribe meant to lay in wait and attack them.

On the 10th of April they again embarked, their party being now augmented to twenty six by the addition of Mr. Crooks and his boat's crew. They had not proceeded far, however, when there was a great outcry from one of the boats; it was occasioned by a little domestic discipline in the Dorion family. The squaw of the worthy interpreter, it appeared, had been so delighted with the scalp dance and other festivities of the Osage village that she had taken a strong inclination to remain there. This had been as strongly opposed by her liege lord, who had compelled her to embark. The good dame had remained sulky ever since, whereupon Pierre, seeing no other mode of exorcising the evil spirit out of her, and being perhaps a little inspired by whiskey, had resorted to the Indian remedy of the cudgel, and, before his neighbors could interfere had belaboured her so soundly, that there is no record of her having shown any refractory symptoms throughout the remainder of the expedition.

For a week they continued their voyage, exposed to almost incessant rains. The bodies of drowned buffaloes floated past them in vast numbers; many had drifted upon the shore, or against the upper ends of the rafts and islands. These had attracted great flights of turkey buzzards; some were banqueting on the carcasses, others were soaring far aloft in the sky, and others were perched on the trees, with their backs to the sun, and their wings stretched out to dry, like so many vessels in harbour, spreading their sails after a shower.

The turkey buzzard (Vultur Aura, or Golden Vulture) when on the wing is one of the most specious and imposing of birds. Its flight in the upper regions of the air is really sublime, extending its immense wings and wheeling slowly and majestically to and fro, seemingly without exerting a muscle or fluttering a feather, but moving by mere volition, and sailing on the bosom of the air, as a ship upon the ocean. Usurping the empyreal realm of the eagle, he assumes for a time the port and dignity of that majestic bird, and often is mistaken for him by ignorant crawlers upon earth. It is only when he descends from the clouds to pounce upon carrion that he betrays his low propensities and reveals his caitiff character. Near at hand he is a disgusting bird, ragged in plumage, base in aspect, and of loathsome odour.

On the 17th of April Mr. Hunt arrived with his party at the station near the Nodawa River, where the main body had been quartered during the winter.

CHAPTER XVI

Return of spring—Appearance of snakes—Great flights of wild pigeons —Renewal of the voyage—Night encampments—Platte River—Ceremonials on passing it—Signs of Indian war parties—Magnificent prospect at Papillion creek—Desertion of two hunters—An irruption into the camp of Indian desperadoes—Village of the Omahas—Anecdotes of the tribe—Feudal wars of the Indians—Story of Blackbird the famous Omaha chief.

The weather continued rainy and ungenial for some days after Mr. Hunt's return to Nodawa, yet spring was rapidly advancing, and vegetation was putting forth with all its early freshness and beauty. The snakes began to recover from their torpor and crawl forth into day, and the neighborhood of the wintering house seems to have been much infested with them. Mr. Bradbury, in the course of his botanical researches, found a surprizing number in a half torpid state, under flat stones upon the banks which overhung the cantonment, and narrowly escaped being struck by a rattle snake, which darted at him from a cleft in the rocks, but fortunately gave him warning by its rattle.

The pigeons too were filling the woods in vast migratory flocks. It is almost incredible to describe the prodigious flights of these birds in the western wildernesses. They appear absolutely in clouds, and move with astonishing velocity, their wings making a whistling sound as they fly. The rapid evolutions of these flocks, wheeling and shifting suddenly as if with one mind and one impulse; the flashing changes of colour they present, as their backs, their breasts, or the under part of their wings are turned to the spectator, are singularly pleasing. When they alight, if on the ground, they cover whole acres at a time; if upon trees, the branches often break beneath their weight. If suddenly startled while feeding in the midst of a forest, the noise they make in getting on the wing is like the roar of a cataract or the sound of distant thunder.

A flight of this kind, like an Egyptian flight of locusts, devours every thing that serves for its food as it passes along. So great were the numbers in the vicinity of the camp that Mr. Bradbury in the course of a morning's excursion, shot nearly three hundred with a fowling piece. He gives a curious, though apparently a fanciful, account of the kind of discipline observed in these immense flocks, so that each may have a chance at picking up food. As the front ranks must meet with the greatest abundance, and the rear ranks must have scanty pickings, the instant a rank finds itself the hindmost, it rises in the air, flies over the whole flock and takes its place in the advance. The next rank follows in its course, and thus the last is continually becoming first, and all by turns have a front place at the banquet.

The rains having at length subsided, Mr. Hunt broke up the encampment and resumed his course up the Missouri.

The party now consisted of nearly sixty persons; of whom five were partners, one, John Reed, was a clerk, forty were Canadian "voyageurs" or "*engagés*" and there were several hunters. They embarked in four boats, one of which was of a large size, mounting a swivel and two howitzers. All were furnished with masts and sails, to be used when the wind was sufficiently favorable and strong to overpower the current of the river. Such was the case for the first four or five days, when they were wafted steadily up the stream by a strong south easter.

Their encampments at night were often pleasant and picturesque: on some beautiful bank, beneath spreading trees, which afforded them shelter and fuel. The tents were pitched, the fires made and the meals prepared by the voyageurs, and many a story was told and joke passed and song sung round the evening fire. All, however, were asleep at an early hour. Some under the tents; others wrapped in blankets before the fire, or beneath the trees; and some few in the boats and canoes.

On the 28th they breakfasted on one of the islands which lie at the mouth of the Nebraska or Platte River; the largest tributary of the Missouri and about 600 miles above its confluence with the Mississippi. This broad but shallow stream flows for an immense distance through a wide and verdant valley, scooped out of boundless prairies. It draws its main supplies, by several forks or branches, from the Rocky Mountains. The mouth of this river is established as the dividing point between the upper and lower Missouri, and the earlier voyagers, in their toilsome ascent, before the introduction of steamboats, considered one half of their labours accomplished when they reached this place. The passing of the mouth of the Nebraska, therefore, was equivalent among boatmen to the crossing of the line among sailors, and was celebrated with like ceremonials of a rough and waggish nature, practiced upon the uninitiated; among which was the old nautical joke of shaving. The river deities, however, like those of the sea, were to be propitiated by a bribe, and the infliction of these rude honors to be parried by a treat to the adepts.

At the mouth of the Nebraska new signs were met with of war parties which had recently been in the vicinity. There was the frame of a skin canoe, in which the warriors had traversed the river. At night, also, the lurid reflection of immense fires hung in the sky, shewing the conflagration of great tracts of the prairies. Such fires not being made by hunters, so late in the season, it was supposed they were caused by some wandering war parties. These often take the precaution to set the prairies on fire behind them to conceal their traces from their enemies. This is chiefly done when the party has been unsuccessful and is on the retreat, and apprehensive of pursuit. At such time it is not safe even for friends to fall in with them, as they are apt to be in savage humour and disposed to vent their spleen in capricious outrage. These signs, therefore, of a band of marauders on the prowl called for some degree of vigilance on the part of the travellers.

After passing the Nebraska the party halted for part of two days on the bank of the river, a little above Papillon Creek, to supply themselves with a stock of oars and poles from the tough wood of the ash, which is not met with higher up the Missouri. While the voyageurs were thus occupied, the naturalists rambled over the adjacent country, to collect plants. From the summit of a range of bluffs on the opposite side of the river, about two hundred and fifty feet high, they had one of those vast and magnificent prospects which sometimes unfold themselves in these boundless regions. Below them was the valley of the Missouri, about seven miles in breadth, clad in the fresh verdure of spring; enamelled with flowers and interspersed with clumps and groves of noble trees, between which the mighty river poured its turbulent and turbid stream. The interior of the country presented a singular scene; the immense waste being broken up by innumerable green hills, not above eighty feet in height, but extremely steep, and acutely pointed at their summits. A long line of bluffs extended for upwards of thirty miles, parallel to the Missouri, with a shallow lake stretching along their base, which had evidently once formed a bed of the river. The surface of this lake was covered with aquatic plants, on the broad leaves of which numbers of water snakes, drawn forth by the genial warmth of spring, were basking in the sunshine.

On the 2d of May at the usual hour of embarking the camp was thrown into some confusion by two of the hunters, named Harrington, expressing their intention to abandon the expedition and return home. One of these had joined the party in the preceding autumn, having been hunting for two years on the Missouri; the other had engaged at S' Louis in the following March and had come up from thence with Mr. Hunt. He now declared that he had enlisted merely for the purpose of following his brother and persuading him to return; having been enjoined to do so by his mother, whose anxiety had been awakened by the idea of his going on such a wild and distant expedition.

The loss of two stark hunters and prime riflemen was a serious affair to the party, for they were approaching the region where they might expect hostilities from the Sioux; indeed, throughout the whole of their perilous journey, the services of such men would be all important, for little reliance was to be placed upon the valour of the Canadians in case of attack. Mr. Hunt endeavored by arguments, expostulations and entreaties to shake the determination of the two brothers. He represented to them that they were between six and seven hundred miles above the mouth of the Missouri; that they would have four hundred miles to go before they could reach the habitation of a white man, throughout which they would be exposed to all kinds of risks, since, he declared, if they persisted in abandoning him and breaking their faith, he would not furnish them with a single round of ammunition. All was in vain; they obstinately persisted in their resolution; whereupon Mr. Hunt, partly incited by indignation, partly by the policy of deterring others from desertion, put his threat in execution, and left them to find their way back to the settlements without, as he supposed, a single bullet or a charge of powder.

The boats now continued their slow and toilsome course, for several days, against the current of the river. The late signs of roaming war parties caused a vigilant watch to be kept up at night when the crews encamped on shore; nor was this vigilance superfluous, for on the night of the Seventh instant, there was a wild and fearful yell and eleven Sioux warriors, stark naked with tomahawks in their hands, rushed into the camp. They were instantly surrounded and seized, whereupon their leader called out to his followers to desist from any violence, and pretended to be perfectly pacific in his intentions. It proved, however, that they were a part of the war party the skeleton of whose canoe had been seen at the mouth of the river Platte, and the reflection of whose fires had been descried in the air. They had been disappointed or defeated in their foray, and in their rage and mortification these eleven warriors had "devoted their clothes to the Medicine." This is a desperate act of Indian braves, when foiled in war and in dread of scoffs and sneers. In such case they sometimes throw off their clothes and ornaments, devote themselves to the Great Spirit, and attempt some reckless exploit with which to cover their disgrace. Woe to any defenceless party of white men that may then fall in their way!

Such was the explanation given by Pierre Dorion, the half breed interpreter, of this wild intrusion into the camp; and the party were so exasperated when apprized of the sanguinary intentions of the prisoners that they were for shooting them on the spot. Mr. Hunt, however, exerted his usual moderation and humanity, and ordered that they should be conveyed across the river in one of the boats, threatening them, however, with certain death, if again caught in any hostile act.

On the 10th of May the party arrived at the Omaha (pronounced Omawhaw) village, about eight hundred and thirty miles above the mouth of the Missouri, and encamped in its neighborhood. The village was situated under a hill on the bank of the river and consisted of about eighty lodges. These were of a circular and conical form and about sixteen feet in diameter; being mere tents of dressed buffalo skins, sewed together and stretched on long poles, inclined towards each other so as to cross at about half their height. Thus the naked tops of the poles diverge in such a manner that, if they were covered with skins like the lower ends, the tent would be shaped like an hour glass; and present the appearance of one cone inverted on the apex of another.*

The forms of Indian lodges are worthy of attention, each tribe having a different mode of shaping and arranging them, so that it is easy to tell on seeing a lodge or an encampment at a distance, to what tribe the inhabitants belong. The exterior of the Omaha lodges have often a gay and fanciful appearance, being painted with undulating bands of red or yellow, or decorated with rude figures of horses, deer and buffaloes, and with human faces, painted like full moons, four and five feet broad.

The Omahas were once one of the numerous and powerful tribes of the prairies, vying in warlike might and prowess with the Sioux, the Pawnees, the Sauks, the Konzas and the Iatans. Their wars with the Sioux however had thinned their ranks and the small pox in 1802 had swept off two thirds of their number. At the time of Mr. Hunt's visit they still boasted about two hundred warriors and hunters, but they are now fast melting away and, before long, will be numbered among those extinguished nations of the West that exist but in tradition.

In his correspondence with Mr. Astor from this point of his journey, Mr. Hunt gives a sad account of the Indian tribes bordering on the river. They were in continual war with each other; and their wars were of the most harassing kind, consisting, not merely of main conflicts and expeditions of moment, involving the sackings, burnings and massacres of towns and villages, but of individual acts of treachery, murder and cold blooded cruelty: or of vaunting and fool hardy exploits of single warriors, either to avenge some personal wrong, or gain the vain glorious trophy of a scalp. The lonely hunter, the wandering wayfarer, the poor squaw, cutting wood or gathering corn, was liable to be surprized and slaughtered. In this way tribes were either

* Bradbury. P. 66.

swept away at once, or gradually thinned out and Savage life was
surrounded with constant horrors and alarms. That the race of red
men should diminish from year to year, and so few should survive
of the numerous nations which evidently once peopled the vast
regions of the west, is nothing surprising; it is rather matter of surprize
that so many should survive, for the existance of a savage in these
parts seems little better than a prolonged and all besetting death. It
is, in fact, a caricature of the boasted romance of feudal times; chivalry
in its native and uncultured state, and knight errantry run wild.

In their more prosperous days the Omahas looked upon themselves
as the most powerful and perfect of human beings, and considered
all created things as made for their peculiar use and benefit. It is this
tribe of whose chief, the famous Wash-ing-guh-sah-ba, or Black bird,
such savage and romantic stories are told. He had died about ten
years previous to the arrival of Mr. Hunt's party, but his name was
still mentioned with awe by his people. He was one of the first among
the Indian chiefs on the Missouri to deal with the white traders,
and shewed great sagacity in levying his royal dues. When a trader
arrived in his village he caused all his goods to be brought into his
lodge and opened. From these he selected whatever suited his sovereign
pleasure, blankets, tobacco, whisky, powder, ball, beads and red paint,
and laid the articles on one side, without deigning to give any compensation. Then calling to him his herald or crier he would order
him to mount on top of the lodge and summon all the tribe to bring
in their peltries and trade with the white man. The lodge would soon
be crowded with Indians bringing bear, beaver, otter, and other skins.
No one was allowed to dispute the prices fixed by the white trader
upon his articles; who took care to indemnify himself five times over
for the goods set apart by the chief. In this way the Black bird
enriched himself, and enriched the white men, and became exceedingly
popular among the traders of the Missouri. His people, however, were
not equally satisfied by a regulation of trade which worked so manifestly against them, and began to shew signs of discontent. Upon
this a crafty and unprincipled trader revealed a secret to the Blackbird,
by which he might acquire unbounded sway over his ignorant and
superstitious subjects. He instructed him in the poisonous qualities
of arsenic, and furnished him with an ample supply of that baneful
drug. From this time the Blackbird seemed endowed with supernatural powers, to possess the gift of prophecy and to hold the disposal
of life and death within his hands. Woe to any one who questioned
his authority or dared to dispute his commands. The Black bird
prophesied his death within a certain time, and he had the secret
means of verifying his prophecy. Within the fated period the offender

was smitten with strange and sudden disease and perished from the face of the earth. Every one stood aghast at these multiplied examples of his superhuman might and dreaded to displease so omnipotent and vindictive a being and the Blackbird enjoyed a wide and undisputed sway.

It was not, however, by terror alone that he ruled his people; he was a warrior of the first order, and his exploits in arms were the theme of young and old. His career had begun by hardships, having been taken prisoner by the Sioux, in early youth. Under his command the Omahas obtained great character for military prowess, nor did he permit an insult or injury to one of his tribe to pass unrevenged. The Pawnee Republicans had inflicted a gross indignity on a favorite and distinguished Omaha brave. The Black bird assembled his warriors, led them against the Pawnee town; attacked it with irresistible fury, slaughtered a great number of its inhabitants and burnt it to the ground. He waged fierce and bloody war against the Otoes for many years, until peace was effected between them by the mediation of the Whites. Fearless in battle, and fond of signalizing himself, he dazzled his followers by his daring acts. In attacking a Konza village he rode singly round it, loading and discharging his rifle at the inhabitants as he gallopped past them. He kept up in war the same idea of mysterious and supernatural power. At one time when pursuing a war party by their tracks across the prairies, he repeatedly discharged his rifle into the prints made by their feet and by the hoofs of their horses, assuring his followers that he would thereby cripple the fugitives so that they would easily be overtaken. He in fact did overtake them, and destroyed them almost to a man; and his victory was considered miraculous, both by friend and foe. By these and similar exploits, he made himself the pride and boast of his people, and became popular among them notwithstanding his death denouncing fiat.

With all his savage and terrific qualities he was sensible to the power of female beauty and capable of love. A war party of the Poncas had made a foray into the lands of the Omahas and carried off a number of women and horses. The Black bird was roused to fury, and took the field with all his braves swearing to "eat up the Ponca nation," the Indian threat of exterminating war. The Poncas, sorely pressed, took refuge behind a rude bulwark of earth, but the Black bird kept up so galling a fire that he seemed likely to execute his menace. In their extremity they sent forth a herald bearing the calumet or pipe of peace, but he was shot down by order of the Black bird. Another herald was sent forth in similar guize, but he shared a like fate. The Poncas chief then, as a last hope, arrayed his beautiful daughter in her finest ornaments, and sent her forth with a calumet, to sue for peace. The charms of the Indian maid touched the stern heart of the Black bird; he accepted the pipe at her hand, smoked it, and from that time a peace took place between the Poncas and the Omahas.

This beautiful damsel, in all probability, was the favorite wife whose fate makes so tragic an incident in the story of the Black bird. Her youth and beauty had gained an absolute sway over his rugged heart, so that he distinguished her above all his other wives. The habitual gratification of his vindictive impulses, however, had taken away from him all mastery over his passions, and rendered him liable to the most furious transports of rage. In one of these his beautiful wife had the misfortune to offend him, when suddenly drawing his knife he laid her dead at his feet with a single blow.

In an instant his frenzy was at an end. He gazed for a time in mute bewilderment upon his victim, then drawing his buffalo robe over his head he sat down beside the corpse and remained brooding over his crime and his loss. Three days elapsed, yet the chief continued silent and motionless; tasting no food and apparently sleepless. It was apprehended that he intended to starve himself to death; his people approached him in trembling awe, and entreated him once more to uncover his face and be comforted, but he remained unmoved. At length one of his warriors brought in a small child and, laying it on the ground, placed the foot of the Black bird upon its neck. The heart of the gloomy savage was touched by this appeal: he threw aside his robe; made an harangue upon what he had done; and from that time forward seemed to have thrown the load of grief and remorse from his mind.

He still retained his fatal and mysterious secret and with it his terrific power; but, though able to deal death to his enemies he could not avert it from himself or his friends. In 1802 the smallpox, that dreadful pestilence which swept over the land like a fire over the prairies, made its appearance in the Village of the Omahas. The poor savages saw with dismay the ravages of a malady loathsome and agonizing in its details and which set the skill and experience of their conjurers and medicine men at defiance. In a little while two thirds of the population were swept from the face of the earth, and the doom of the rest seemed sealed. The stoicism of the warriors was at an end: they became wild and desperate. Some set fire to the village as a last means of checking the pestilence; others, in a frenzy of despair, put their wives and children to death, that they might be spared the agonies of an inevitable disease, and "that they might all go to some better country."

When the general horror and dismay was at its height the Blackbird himself was struck down with the malady. The poor savages, when they saw their chief in danger, forgot their own miseries and surrounded his dying bed. His dominant spirit and his love for the white men were evinced in his latest breath, with which he designated his place of sepulture. It was to be on a hill or promontory, upwards of four hundred feet in height overlooking a great extent of the Missouri from whence he had been accustomed to watch for the barks of the white men. The Missouri washes the base of the promontory, and after winding and doubling in many links and mazes in the plain below, returns to within nine hundred yards of its starting place; so that for thirty miles navigating with sail and oar, the voyager finds himself continually near to this singular promontory as if spell bound.

It was the dying command of the Blackbird that his tomb should be upon the summit of this hill, in which he should be interred, seated on his favorite horse, that he might overlook his ancient domain and behold the barks of the white men as they came up the river to trade with his people.

His dying orders were faithfully obeyed. His corpse was placed astride of his war steed, and a mound raised over them on the summit of the hill. On top of the mound was erected a staff from which fluttered the banner of the chieftain and the scalps that he had taken in battle. When the expedition under Mr. Hunt visited that part of the country the staff still remained with the fragments of the banner; and the superstitious rite of placing food from time to time on the mound for the use of the deceased was still observed by the Omahas. That rite has since fallen into disuse, for the tribe itself is almost extinct; yet the hill of the Black bird continues an object of veneration to the wandering savage, and a land mark to the voyager of the Missouri; and as the civilized traveller comes within sight of its spell bound crest, the mound is pointed out to him from afar, which still incloses the grim skeletons of the Indian warrior and his horse.

CHAPTER XVII

Rumors of danger from the Sioux Tetons—Ruthless character of those savages—Pirates of the Missouri—Their affair with Crooks and M'Lellan —A trading expedition broken up—M'Lellan's vow of vengeance— Uneasiness in the camp—Desertions—Departure from the Omaha village —Meeting with Jones and Carson, two adventurous trappers—Scientific pursuits of Messrs. Bradbury and Nuttall—Zeal of a botanist— Adventure of Mr. Bradbury with a Ponca Indian—Expedient of the pocket compass and microscope—A messenger from Lisa—Motives for pressing forward.

While Mr. Hunt and his party were sojourning at the village of the Omahas, three Sioux Indians of the Yankton Ahna tribe arrived, bringing unpleasant intelligence. They reported that certain bands of the Sioux Tetons, who inhabited a region many leagues further up the Missouri, were near at hand, awaiting the approach of the party, with the avowed intention of opposing their progress.

The Sioux Tetons were at that time a sort of pirates of the Missouri, who considered the wellfreighted bark of the American trader fair game. They had their own traffic with the British merchants of the north west, who brought them regular supplies of merchandize by way of the river S' Peter. Being thus independent of the Missouri traders for their supplies, they kept no terms with them, but plundered them whenever they had an opportunity. It has been insinuated that they were prompted to these outrages by the British merchants, who wished to keep off all rivals in the Indian trade; but others allege another motive, and one savoring of a deeper policy. The Sioux, by their intercourse with the British traders, had acquired the use of fire arms, which had given them vast superiority over other tribes higher up the Missouri. They had made themselves also, in a manner, factors for the upper tribes, supplying them at second hand, and at greatly advanced prices, with goods derived from the white men. The Sioux, therefore, saw with jealousy the American traders pushing their way up the Missouri; foreseeing that the upper tribes would thus be relieved from all dependance on them for supplies; nay, what was worse, would be furnished with fire arms and elevated into formidable rivals.

We have already alluded to a case in which Mr. Crooks and Mr. M'Lellan had been interrupted in a trading voyage by these ruffians of the river, and, as it is in some degree connected with circumstances hereafter to be related, we shall specify it more particularly.

About two years before the time of which we are treating, Crooks and M'Lellan were ascending the river in boats with a party of about forty men, bound on one of their trading expeditions to the upper tribes. In one of the bends of the river where the channel made a deep curve under impending banks, they suddenly heard yells and shouts above them, and beheld the cliffs over head covered with armed savages. It was a band of Sioux warriors upwards of six hundred strong. They brandished their weapons in a menacing manner, and ordered the boats to turn back and land lower down the river. There was no disputing their commands, for they had the power to shower destruction upon the white men, without risk to themselves. Crooks and M'Lellan, therefore, turned back with feigned alacrity; and, landing, had an interview with the Sioux. The latter forbade them, under pain of exterminating hostility, from attempting to proceed up the river, but offered to trade peacefully with them if they would halt where they were. The party, being principally composed of voyageurs, was too weak to contend with so superior a force, and one so easily augmented; they pretended therefore to comply cheerfully with their arbitrary dictation and immediately proceeded to cut down trees and erect a trading house. The warrior band departed for their village which was about twenty miles distant, to collect objects of traffic; they left six or eight of their number, however, to keep watch upon the white men, and scouts were continually passing to and fro with intelligence.

Mr. Crooks saw that it would be impossible to prosecute his voyage without the danger of having his boats plundered, and a great part of his men massacred; he determined, however, not to be entirely frustrated in the objects of his expedition. While he continued, therefore, with great apparent earnestness and assiduity the construction of the trading house, he despatched the hunters and trappers of his party in a canoe, to make their way up the river to the original place of destination, there to busy themselves in trapping and collecting peltries, and to await his arrival at some future period.

As soon as the detachment had had sufficient time to ascend beyond the hostile country of the Sioux, Mr. Crooks suddenly broke up his feigned trading establishment, embarked his men and effects, and, after giving the astonished rear guard of savages a galling and indignant message to take to their countrymen, pushed down the river with all speed, sparing neither oar nor paddle, day nor night, until fairly beyond the swoop of these river hawks.

What encreased the irritation of Messrs. Crooks and M'Lellan at this mortifying check to their gainful enterprize, was the information that a rival trader was at the bottom of it; the Sioux, it is said, having been instigated to this outrage by Mr. Manuel Lisa, the leading partner and agent of the Missouri Fur Company already mentioned. This intelligence, whether true or false, so roused the fiery temper of M'Lellan that he swore, if ever he fell in with Lisa in the Indian country, he would shoot him on the spot; a mode of redress perfectly in unison with the character of the man, and the code of honor prevalent beyond the frontier.

If Crooks and M'Lellan had been exasperated by the insolent conduct of the Sioux Tetons, and the loss which it had occasioned, those freebooters had been no less indignant at being outwitted by the white men, and disappointed of their anticipated gains, and it was apprehended they would be particularly hostile against the present expedition, when they should learn that these gentlemen were engaged in it.

All these causes of uneasiness were concealed as much as possible from the Canadian voyageurs, lest they should become intimidated; it was impossible, however, to prevent the rumours brought by the Indians from leaking out, and they became subjects of gossipping and exaggeration. The chief of the Omahas, too, on returning from a hunting excursion, reported that two men had been killed some distance above, by a band of Sioux. This added to the fears that already began to be excited. The voyageurs pictured to themselves bands of fierce warriors stationed along each bank of the river, by whom they would be exposed to be shot down in their boats: or lurking hordes who would set on them at night and massacre them in their encampments. Some lost heart and proposed to return, rather than fight their way, and, in a manner, run the gauntlet through the country of these piratical marauders. In fact three men deserted while at this village. Luckily their place was supplied by three others who happened to be there, and who were prevailed on to join the expedition by promises of liberal pay and by being fitted out and equipped in complete style.

The irresolution and discontent visible among some of his people, arising at times almost to mutiny, and the occasional desertions which took place while thus among friendly tribes, and within reach of the frontiers, added greatly to the anxieties of Mr. Hunt, and rendered him eager to press forward and leave a hostile tract behind him, so that it would be as perilous to return as to keep on, and no one would dare to desert.

Accordingly, on the 15th of May he departed from the Village of the Omahas and set forward towards the country of the formidable Sioux Tetons. For the first five days they had a fair and fresh breeze, and the boats made good progress. The wind then came ahead, and the river beginning to rise, and to increase in rapidity, betokened the commencement of the annual flood, caused by the melting of the snow on the Rocky Mountains and the vernal rains on the upper prairies.

As they were now entering a region where foes might be lying in wait on either bank, it was determined, in hunting for game, to confine themselves principally to the islands, which sometimes extend to considerable length and are beautifully wooded, affording abundant pasturage and shade. On one of these they killed three buffaloes and two elks; and, halting on the edge of a beautiful prairie, made a sumptuous hunters' repast. They had not long resumed their boats and pulled along the river banks, when they descried a canoe approaching navigated by two men whom, to their surprize, they ascertained to be white men. They proved to be two of those strange and fearless wanderers of the wilderness, the trappers. Their names were Benjamin Jones and Alexander Carson. They had been for two years past hunting and trapping near the head of the Missouri, and were thus floating for thousands of miles in a cockle shell down a turbulent stream, through regions infested by savage tribes, yet apparently as easy and unconcerned as if navigating securely in the midst of civilization.

The acquisition of two such hardy, experienced and dauntless hunters was peculiarly desireable at the present moment. They needed but little persuasion. The wilderness is the home of the trapper; like the sailor, he cares but little to which point of the compass he steers; and Jones and Carson readily abandoned their voyage to S' Louis and turned their faces towards the Rocky Mountains and the Pacific.

The two naturalists, Mr. Bradbury and Mr. Nuttall, who had joined the expedition at S' Louis, still accompanied it and pursued their researches on all occasions. Mr. Nuttall seems to have been exclusively devoted to his scientific pursuits. He was a zealous botanist and all his enthusiasm was awakened at beholding a new world, as it were, opening upon him in the boundless prairies clad in the vernal and variegated robe of unknown flowers. Whenever the boats landed at meal times or for any temporary purpose he would spring on shore and set out on a hunt for new specimens. Every plant or flower of a rare or unknown species was eagerly seized as a prize. Delighted with the treasures spreading themselves out before him, he went groping and stumbling along among a wilderness of sweets, forgetful of every thing but his immediate pursuit and had often to be sought after when the boats were about to resume their course. At such times he would be found far off in the prairies or up the course of some petty stream laden with plants of all kinds.

The Canadian voyageurs, who are a class of people that know nothing out of their immediate line, and with constitutional levity make a jest of any thing they cannot understand, were extremely puzzled by this passion for collecting what they considered mere useless weeds. When they saw the worthy botanist coming back heavy laden with his specimens, and treasuring them up as carefully as a miser would his hoard, they used to make merry among themselves at his expense, regarding him as some whimsical kind of madman.

Mr. Bradbury was less exclusive in his tastes and habits and combined the hunter and sportsman with the naturalist. He took his rifle or his fowling piece with him in his geological researches, conformed to the hardy and rugged habits of the men around him and of course gained favour in their eyes. He had a strong relish for incident and adventure, was curious in observing savage manners and savage life, and ready to join any hunting or other excursion. Even now that the expedition was proceeding through a dangerous neighborhood he could not check his propensity to ramble. Having observed, on the evening of the twenty second of May, that the river a head made a great bend which would take up the navigation of the following day, he determined to profit by the circumstance. On the morning of the 23d, therefore, instead of embarking, he filled his shot pouch with parched corn, for provisions, and set off to cross the neck on foot and meet the boats in the afternoon at the opposite side of the bend. Mr. Hunt felt uneasy at his venturing thus alone and reminded him that he was in an enemy's country; but Mr. Bradbury made light of the danger and started off cheerily upon his ramble. His day was passed pleasantly in traversing a beautiful tract, making botanical and geological researches and observing the habits of an extensive village of prairie dogs, at which he made several ineffectual shots, without considering the risque he ran of attracting the attention of any savages that might be lurking in the neighborhood. In fact he had totally forgotten the Sioux Tetons and all the other perils of the country, when, about the middle of the afternoon, as he stood near the river bank, and was looking out for the boat, he suddenly felt a hand laid on his shoulder. Starting and turning round he beheld a naked savage with a bow bent, and the arrow pointed at his breast. In an instant his gun was levelled and his hand upon the lock. The Indian drew his bow still further, but forebore to launch the shaft. Mr. Bradbury, with admirable presence of mind, reflected that the savage, if hostile in his intents, would have shot him without giving him a chance of defence; he paused therefore and held out his hand. The other took it in sign of friendship, and demanded in the Osage language whether he was a "Big Knife," or American. He answered in the affirmative and enquired whether the other were a Sioux. To his great relief he found that he was a Ponca. By this time two other Indians came running up, and all three laid hold of Mr. Bradbury and seemed disposed to compel him to go off with them among the hills. He resisted, and sitting down on a sandhill contrived to amuse them with a pocket compass. When the novelty of this was exhausted they again seized him, but he now produced a small microscope. This new wonder again fixed the attention of the savages, who have far more curiosity than it has been the custom to allow them. While thus engaged, one of them suddenly leaped up and gave a war whoop. The hand of the hardy naturalist was again on his gun and he was prepared to make battle when the Indian pointed down the river and revealed the true cause of his yell. It was the mast of one of the boats appearing above the low willows which bordered the stream. Mr. Bradbury felt infinitely relieved by the sight. The Indians, on their part, now shewed signs of apprehension, and were disposed to run away; but he assured them of good treatment and something to drink if they would accompany him on board of the boats. They lingered for a time, but disappeared before the boats came to land.

On the following morning they appeared at the camp accompanied by several of their tribe. With them came also a white man, who announced himself as a messenger bearing missives for Mr. Hunt. In fact he brought a letter from Mr. Manuel Lisa, partner and agent of the Missouri Fur Company. As has already been mentioned, this gentleman was going in search of Mr. Henry and his party, who had been dislodged from the Forks of the Missouri by the Blackfeet Indians, and had shifted his post somewhere beyond the Rocky Mountains. Mr. Lisa had left S' Louis three weeks after Mr. Hunt, and, having heard of the hostile intentions of the Sioux, had made the greatest exertions to overtake him, that they might pass through the dangerous part of the river together. He had twenty stout oarsmen in his service, and they plied their oars so vigorously, that he had reached the Omaha village just four days after the departure of Mr. Hunt. From this place he despatched the messenger in question, trusting to his over-taking the barges as they toiled up against the stream, and were delayed by the windings of the river. The purport of his letter was to entreat Mr. Hunt to wait until he could come up with him, that they might unite their forces and be a protection to each other in their perilous course through the country of the Sioux. In fact, as it was afterwards ascertained, Lisa was apprehensive that Mr. Hunt would do him some ill office with the Sioux bands, securing his own passage through their country by pretending that he with whom they were accustomed to trade, was on his way to them with a plentiful supply of goods. He feared, too, that Crooks and M'Lellan would take this opportunity to retort upon him the perfidy which they accused him of having used, two years previously among these very Sioux. In this respect, however, he did them signal injustice. There was no such thing as covert design or treachery in their thought; but M'Lellan when he heard that Lisa was on his way up the river, renewed his open threat of shooting him the moment he met him on Indian land.

The representations made by Crooks and M'Lellan of the treachery they had experienced, or fancied, on the part of Lisa, had great weight with Mr. Hunt, especially when he recollected the obstacles that had been thrown in his own way by that gentleman at S' Louis. He doubted, therefore, the fair dealing of Lisa, and feared that, should they enter the Sioux country together, the latter might make use of his influence with that tribe, as he had in the case of Crooks and M'Lellan, and instigate them to oppose his progress up the river.

He sent back, therefore, an answer calculated to beguile Lisa, assuring him that he would wait for him at the Poncas Village, which was but a little distance in advance; but, no sooner had the messenger departed, than he pushed forward with all diligence, barely stopping at the village to procure a supply of dried buffalo meat, and hastening to leave the other party as far behind as possible, thinking there was less to be apprehended from the open hostility of Indian foes, than from the quiet strategy of an Indian trader.

CHAPTER XVIII

Camp gossip—Deserters—Recruits—Kentucky hunters—A veteran wood-man—Tidings of Mr. Henry—Danger from the Blackfeet—Alteration of plans—Scenery of the river—Buffalo roads—Iron ore—Country of the Sioux—A land of danger—Apprehensions of the voyageurs—Indian scouts—Threatened hostilities—A council of war—An array of battle—A parley—The pipe of peace—Speech making.

It was about noon when the party left the Poncas Village, about a league beyond which they passed the mouth of the Quicourt or Rapid River, (called in the original French *L'Eau qui court*). After having proceeded some distance further, they landed and encamped for the night. In the evening camp the voyageurs gossipped, as usual, over the events of the day, and especially over intelligence picked up among the Poncas. These Indians had confirmed the previous reports of the hostile intentions of the Sioux, and had assured them that five tribes, or bands, of that fierce nation were actually assembled higher up the river, and waiting to cut them off. This evening gossip, and the terrific stories of Indian warfare to which it gave rise, produced a strong effect upon the imaginations of the irresolute, and in the morning it was discovered that the two men who had joined the party at the Omaha village and been so bounteously fitted out, had deserted in the course of the night, carrying with them all their equipments. As it was known that one of them could not swim, it was hoped that the banks of the Quicourt River would bring them to a halt; a general pursuit was, therefore, instituted but without success.

On the following morning (May 26th) as they were all on shore breakfasting on one of the beautiful banks of the river, they observed two canoes descending along the opposite side. By the aid of spy glasses, they ascertained that there were two white men in one of the canoes and one in the other. A gun was discharged which called the attention of the voyagers who crossed over. They proved to be three Kentucky hunters of the true "dread nought" stamp. Their names were Edward Robinson, John Hoback and Jacob Rezner. Robinson was a veteran backwoodsman, sixty six years of age. He had been one of the first settlers of Kentucky and engaged in many of the conflicts of the Indians on "The Bloody Ground." In one of these bat-tles he had been scalped, and he still wore a handkerchief bound round his head to protect the part. These men had passed several years in the upper wilderness. They had been in the service of the Missouri Company under Mr. Henry and had crossed the Rocky Mountains

with him in the preceding year when driven from his post on the
Missouri by the hostilities of the Blackfeet. After crossing the mountains Mr. Henry had established himself on one of the head branches
of the Columbia River. There they had remained with him for some
months hunting and trapping, until, having satisfied their wandering
propensities, they felt disposed to return to the families and comfortable
homes which they had left in Kentucky. They had accordingly made
their way back across the mountains, and down the rivers, and were
in full career for S' Louis, when thus suddenly interrupted. The sight
of a powerful party of traders, trappers, hunters and voyageurs, well
armed and equipped, furnished at all points, in high health and spirits,
and banquetting lustily on the green margin of the river was a spectacle
equally stimulating to these veteran backwoodsmen, with the glorious
array of a campaigning army to an old soldier, but when they learnt
the grand scope and extent of the enterprize in hand, it was irresistible;
homes and families and all the charms of green Kentucky vanished
from their thoughts; they cast loose their canoes to drift down the
stream and joyfully enlisted in the band of adventurers. They engaged
on similar terms with some of the other hunters. The company was
to fit them out, and keep them supplied with the requisite equipments
and munitions and they were to yield one half of the produce of their
hunting and trapping.

   The addition of three such staunch recruits was extremely acceptable
at this dangerous part of the river; the knowledge of the country which
they had acquired, also, in their journeys and hunting excursions along
the rivers and among the Rocky Mountains, was all important; in
fact the information derived from them induced Mr. Hunt to alter his
future course. He had hitherto intended to proceed by the route
taken by Lewis and Clarke in their famous exploring expedition,
ascending the Missouri to its forks, and thence going by land, across
the mountains. These men informed him, however, that on taking that
course he would have to pass through the country infested by the
savage tribe of the Blackfeet and would be exposed to their hostilities,
they being, as has already been observed, exasperated to deadly
animosity against the whites, on account of the death of one of their
tribe by the hands of Captain Lewis. They advised him rather to
pursue a route more to the southward; being the same by which they
had returned. This would carry him over the mountains about where
the head waters of the Platte and the Yellow stone take their rise, at
a place much more easy and practicable than that where Lewis and
Clarke had crossed. In pursuing this course, also, he would pass through
a country abounding with game, where he would have a better chance
of procuring a constant supply of provisions than by the other route;

and would run less risk of molestation from the Blackfeet. Should he adopt this advice it would be better for him to abandon the river at the Arickara town, at which he would arrive in the course of a few days. As the Indians of that town possessed horses in abundance he might purchase a sufficient number of them for the great journey overland which would commence at that place.

After reflecting on this advice and consulting with his associates, Mr. Hunt came to the determination to follow the route thus pointed out, in which the hunters engaged to pilot him.

The party continued their voyage with delightful May weather. The prairies bordering on the river were gaily painted with innumerable flowers, exhibiting the motley confusion of colours of a Turkey carpet. The beautiful islands, also, on which they occasionally halted, presented the appearance of mingled grove and garden.

The trees were often covered with clambering grape vines in blossom, which perfumed the air. Between the stately masses of the groves were grassy lawns and glades studded with flowers, or interspersed with rose bushes in full bloom. These islands were often the resort of the buffalo, the elk and the antelope, who had made innumerable paths among the trees and thickets, which had the effect of the mazy walks and alleys of parks and shrubberies.

Sometimes, where the river passed between high banks and bluffs, the roads, made by the tramp of buffalos for many ages, along the face of the heights looked like so many well travelled high ways. At other places the banks were banded with great veins of iron ore, laid bare by the abrasion of the river. At one place the course of the river was nearly in a straight line for about fifteen miles. The banks sloped gently to its margin, without a single tree: but bordered with grass and herbage of a vivid green. Along each bank, for the whole fifteen miles, extended a stripe one hundred yards in breadth, of a deep rusty brown, indicating an inexhaustible bed of iron through the centre of which the Missouri had worn its way. Indications of the continuance of this bed were afterwards observed higher up the river. It is, in fact, one of the mineral magazines which nature has provided in the heart of this vast realm of fertility, and which, in connexion with the immense beds of coal on the same river, seem garnered up as the elements of the future wealth and power of the mighty west.

The sight of these mineral treasures greatly excited the curiosity of Mr. Bradbury, and it was tantalizing to him to be checked in his scientific researches and obliged to forego his usual rambles on shore; but they were now entering the fated country of the Sioux Tetons in which it was dangerous to wander about unguarded.

This country extends for some days' journey along the river and consists of vast prairies, here and there diversified by swelling hills and cut up by ravines, the channels of turbid streams in the rainy seasons but almost destitute of water during the heats of summer. Here and there, on the sides of the hills, or along the alluvial borders and bottoms of the ravines, are groves and skirts of forest; but for the most part the country presented to the eye a boundless waste, covered with herbage, but without trees.

The soil of this immense region is strongly impregnated with sulphur, copperas, alum and glauber salts; its various earths impart a deep tinge to the streams which drain it, and these, with the crumbling of the banks along the Missouri, give to the waters of that river much of the colouring matter with which they are clouded.

Over this vast tract the roving bands of the Sioux Tetons hold their vagrant sway; subsisting by the chase of the buffalo, the elk, the deer and the antelope, and waging ruthless warfare with other wandering tribes.

As the boats made their way up the stream bordered by this land of danger, many of the Canadian voyageurs, whose fears had been awakened, would regard with a distrustful eye the boundless waste extending on each side. All, however, was silent and apparently untenanted by a human being. Now and then a herd of deer would be seen feeding tranquilly among the flowery herbage, or a line of buffaloes like a caravan on its march, moving across the distant profile of the prairie. The Canadians, however, began to apprehend an ambush in every thicket, and to regard the broad, tranquil plain as a sailor eyes some shallow and perfidious sea, which, though smooth and safe to the eye conceals the lurking rock or treacherous shoal. The very name of a Sioux became a watchword of terror. Not an elk, a wolf or any other animal could appear on the hills, but the boats resounded with exclamations from stem to stern, "*Voila les Sioux!*" "*voila les Sioux!*" (There are the Sioux! there are the Sioux!) Whenever it was practicable, the night encampment was on some island in the centre of the stream.

On the morning of the 31st of May as the travellers were breakfasting on the right bank of the river, the usual alarm was given, but with more reason, as two Indians actually made their appearance on a bluff on the opposite, or north east, side and harangued them in a loud voice. As it was impossible, at that distance, to distinguish what they said, Mr. Hunt, after breakfast, crossed the river with Pierre Dorion the interpreter, and advanced boldly to converse with them, while the rest remained watching, in mute suspense, the movements of the parties. As soon as Mr. Hunt landed, one of the Indians disappeared behind the hill, but shortly reappeared on horseback and went scouring off across the heights. Mr. Hunt held some conference with the remaining savage, and then recrossed the river to his party.

These two Indians proved to be spies or scouts of a large war party encamped about a league off, and numbering two hundred and eighty lodges, or about six hundred warriors, of three different tribes of Sioux: the Yangtons Ahna, the Tetons Bois Brulé and the Tetons Min-na-kine-azzo. They expected daily to be reinforced by two other tribes, and had been waiting eleven days for the arrival of Mr. Hunt's party with a determination to oppose their progress up the river; being resolved to prevent all trade of the white men with their enemies the Arickaras, Mandans and Minatarees. The Indian who had galloped off on horseback had gone to give notice of the approach of the party, so that they might now look out for some fierce scenes with these piratical savages, of whom they had received so many formidable accounts.

The party braced up their spirits to the encounter, and re embarking, pulled resolutely up the stream. An island for some time intervened between them and the opposite side of the river, but on clearing the upper end they came in full view of the hostile shore. There was a ridge of hills down which the Savages were pouring in great numbers, some on horseback and some on foot. Reconnoitering them with the aid of glasses, they perceived that they were all in warlike array, painted and decorated for battle. Their weapons were bows and arrows, and a few short carbines, and most of them had round shields. Altogether they had a wild and gallant appearance, and taking possession of a point which commanded the river ranged themselves along the bank as if prepared to dispute the passage.

At sight of this formidable front of war, Mr. Hunt and his companions held council together. It was plain that the rumours they had heard were correct; and the Sioux were determined to oppose their progress by force of arms. To attempt to elude them and continue along the river was out of the question. The strength of the mid current was too violent to be withstood, and the boats were obliged to ascend along the river banks. These banks were often high and perpendicular, affording the savages frequent stations from whence, safe themselves, and almost unseen, they might shower down their missiles upon the boats below, and retreat at will, without danger from pursuit. Nothing apparently remained, therefore, but to fight or turn back. The Sioux far out numbered them, it is true, but their own party was about sixty strong, well armed and supplied with ammunition, and beside their guns and rifles they had a swivel and two howitzers mounted in the boats. Should they succeed in breaking this Indian force by one vigorous assault, it was likely they would be deterred from making any future attack of consequence. The fighting alternative was, therefore, instantly adopted, and the boats pulled to shore nearly opposite

to the hostile force. Here the arms were all examined and put in order.
The swivel and howitzers were then loaded with powder and discharged, to let the savages know by the report how formidably they
were provided. The noise echoed along the shores of the river, and
must have startled the warriors who were only accustomed to the
sharp reports of rifles. The same pieces were then loaded with as
many bullets as they would probably bear; after which the whole
party embarked and pulled across the river. The Indians remained
watching them in silence, their painted forms and visages glaring in
the sun and their feathers fluttering in the breeze. The poor Canadians
eyed them with rueful glances, and now and then a fearful ejaculation
would escape them. "Par bleu! this is a sad scrape we are in, brother!"
would one mutter to the next oarsman. "Aye aye," the other would reply,
"we are not going to a wedding, my friend!"

When the boats arrived within rifle shot, the hunters and other
fighting personages on board, seized their weapons and prepared
for action. As they rose to fire a confusion took place among the
savages: they displayed their buffalo robes, raised them with both
hands above their heads and then spread them before them on the
ground. At sight of this, Pierre Dorion eagerly cried out to the party
not to fire, as this movement was a peaceful signal and an invitation
to a parley. Immediately about a dozen of the principal warriors,
separating from the rest, descended to the edge of the river, lighted
a fire, seated themselves in a semi circle round it, and displaying the
Calumet, invited the party to land. Mr. Hunt now called a council of
the partners on board of his boat. The question was, whether to trust
to the amicable overtures of these ferocious people? It was determined
in the affirmative; for, otherwise, there was no alternative but to
fight them. The main body of the party were ordered to remain on
board of the boats, keeping within shot, and prepared to fire in case
of any signs of treachery: while Mr. Hunt and the other partners,
(M'Kenzie, Crooks, Miller, and M'Lellan) proceeded to land, accompanied by the interpreter and Mr. Bradbury. The chiefs who awaited
them on the margin of the river, remained seated in their semi circle,
without stirring a limb or moving a muscle, motionless as so many
statues. Mr. Hunt and his companions advanced without hesitation
and took their seats on the sand so as to complete the circle. The
band of warriors who lined the banks above stood looking down in
silent groups and clusters, some ostentatiously equipped and decorated,
others entirely naked, but fantastically painted, and all variously armed.

The pipe of peace was now brought forward with due ceremony.
The bowl was of a species of red stone resembling porphyry, the
stem was six feet in length decorated with tufts of horse hair dyed

red. The pipe bearer stepped within the circle, lighted the pipe, held it towards the sun, then towards the different points of the compass, after which he handed it to the principal chief. The latter smoked a few whiffs, then, holding the head of the pipe in his hand, offered the other end to Mr. Hunt and to each one successively in the circle; when all had smoked it was considered that an assurance of good faith and amity had been interchanged. Mr. Hunt now made a speech in French, which was interpreted as he proceeded, by Pierre Dorion. He informed the Sioux of the real object of the expedition of himself and his companions, which was not to trade with any of the tribes up the river, but to cross the Mountains to the great Salt lake in the West, in search of some of their brothers whom they had not seen for eleven months. That he had heard of the intention of the Sioux to oppose his passage, and was prepared, as they might see, to effect it at all hazards: nevertheless, his feelings towards the Sioux were friendly, in proof of which he had brought them a present of tobacco and corn. So saying, he ordered about fifteen carottes of tobacco, and as many bags of corn to be brought from the boat and laid in a heap near the council fire.

The sight of these presents mollified the chieftain, who had doubtless been previously rendered considerate by the resolute conduct of the white men, the judicious disposition of their little armament, the completeness of their equipments and the compact array of battle which they presented. He made a speech in reply in which he stated the object of their hostile assemblage, which had been merely to prevent supplies of arms and ammunition from going to the Arickaras, Mandans and Minatarees with whom they were at war; but being now convinced that the party were carrying no supplies of the kind, but merely proceeding in quest of their brothers beyond the mountains, they would not impede them in their voyage. He concluded by thanking them for their present, and advising them to encamp on the opposite side of the river, as he had some young men among his warriors for whose discretion he could not be answerable, and who might be troublesome.

Here ended the conference; they all arose, shook hands and parted. Mr. Hunt and his companions re embarked, and the boats proceeded on their course unmolested.

CHAPTER XIX

The great bend of the Missouri—Crooks and M'Lellan meet with two of their Indian opponents—Wanton outrage of a white man the cause of Indian hostility—Dangers and precautions—An Indian war party—Dangerous situation of Mr. Hunt—A friendly encampment— Feasting and dancing—Approach of Manuel Lisa and his party—A grim meeting between old rivals—Pierre Dorion in a fury—A burst of chivalry.

On the afternoon of the following day (June 1st) they arrived at the Great bend, where the river winds for about thirty miles round a circular peninsula, the neck of which is not above two thousand yards across. On the succeeding morning, at an early hour, they descried two Indians standing on a high bank of the river, waving and spreading their buffalo robes in signs of amity. They immediately pulled to shore and landed. On approaching the savages, however, the latter shewed evident symptoms of alarm, spreading out their arms horizontally, according to their mode of supplicating clemency. The reason was soon explained. They proved to be two chiefs of the very war party that had brought Messrs. Crooks and M'Lellan to a stand two years before, and obliged them to escape down the river. They ran to embrace these gentlemen, as if delighted to meet with them; yet they evidently feared some retaliation of their past misconduct, nor were they quite at ease until the pipe of peace had been smoked.

Mr. Hunt having been informed that the tribe to which these men belonged had killed three white men during the preceding summer, reproached them with the crime and demanded their reasons for such savage hostility. "We kill white men," replied one of the chiefs, "because white men kill us. That very man," added he, pointing to Carson, one of the new recruits, "killed one of our brothers last summer. The three white men were slain to avenge his death."

The chief was correct in his reply. Carson admitted that, being with a party of Arickaras on the banks of the Missouri and seeing a war party of Sioux on the opposite side he had fired with his rifle across. It was a random shot, made without much expectation of effect, for the river was full half a mile in breadth. Unluckily it brought down a Sioux warrior, for whose wanton destruction three fold vengeance had been taken as has been stated. In this way outrages are frequently committed on the natives by thoughtless or mischievous white men: the Indians retaliate according to a law of their code, which requires blood for blood; their act of what with them is pious vengeance resounds throughout the land and is represented as wanton and un-provoked; the neighborhood is roused to arms; a war ensues, which ends in the destruction of half the tribe, the ruin of the rest and their expulsion from their hereditary homes. Such is too often the real history of Indian warfare, which in general is traced up only to some vindictive act of a savage; while the outrage of the scoundrel white man that provoked it is sunk in silence.

The two chiefs, having smoked their pipe of peace and received a few presents, departed well satisfied. In a little while two others appeared on horseback and road up abreast of the boats. They had seen the presents given to their comrades, but were dissatisfied with them and came after the boats to ask for more. Being somewhat peremptory and insolent in their demands, Mr. Hunt gave them a flat refusal and threatened, if they or any of their tribe followed him with similar demands, to treat them as enemies. They turned and rode off in a furious passion. As he was ignorant what force these chiefs might have behind the hills, and as it was very possible they might take advantage of some pass of the river to attack the boats, Mr. Hunt called all stragglers on board and prepared for such emergency. It was agreed that the large boat commanded by Mr. Hunt, should ascend along the north east side of the river, and the three smaller boats along the south side. By this arrangement each party would command a view of the opposite heights above the heads and out of the sight of their companions, and could give the alarm should they perceive any Indians lurking there. The signal of alarm was to be two shots fired in quick succession.

The boats proceeded for the greater part of the day without seeing any signs of an enemy. About four o'clock in the afternoon the large boat, commanded by Mr. Hunt, came to where the river was divided, by a long sand bar, which apparently, however, left a sufficient channel between it and the shore along which they were advancing. He kept up this channel, therefore, for some distance until the water proved too shallow for the boat. It was necessary, therefore, to put about, return down the channel and pull round the lower end of the sand bar into the main stream. Just as he had given orders to this effect to his men, two signal guns were fired from the boats on the opposite side of the river. At the same moment a file of savage warriors was observed pouring down from the impending bank and gathering on the shore at the lower end of the bar. They were evidently a war party, being armed with bows and arrows, battle clubs and carbines and round bucklers of buffalo hide, and their naked bodies were painted with black and white stripes. The natural inference was that they belonged to the two tribes of Sioux which had been expected by the great war party, and that they had been incited to hostility by the two chiefs who had been enraged by the refusal and the menace of Mr. Hunt. Here then was a fearful predicament. Mr. Hunt and his crew seemed caught as it were in a trap. The Indians, to the number of about a hundred, had already taken possession of a point near which the boat would have to pass: others kept pouring down the bank, and it was probable that some would remain posted on the top of the height.

The hazardous situation of Mr. Hunt was perceived by those in the other boats and they hastened to his assistance. They were at some distance above the sand bar, however, and on the opposite side of the river, and saw, with intense anxiety, the number of Savages continually augmenting, at the lower end of the channel, so that the boat would be exposed to a fearful attack before they could render it any assistance. Their anxiety encreased as they saw Mr. Hunt and his party descending the channel and dauntlessly approaching the point of danger, but it suddenly changed into surprize on beholding the boat pass close by the savage horde unmolested, and steer out safely into the broad river.

The next moment the whole band of warriors was in motion. They ran along the bank until they were opposite to the boats, then throwing by their weapons and buffalo robes, plunged into the river, waded and swam off to the boats and surrounded them in crowds, seeking to shake hands with every individual on board, for the Indians have long since found this to be the white man's token of amity, and they carry it to an extreme.

All uneasiness was now at an end. The Indians proved to be a war party of Arickaras, Mandans and Minatarees, consisting of three hundred warriors, and bound on a foray against the Sioux. Their war plans were abandoned for the present and they determined to return to the Arickara town, where they hoped to obtain from the white men arms and ammunition that would enable them to take the field with advantage over their enemies.

The boats now sought the first convenient place for encamping. The tents were pitched, the warriors fixed their camp at about a hundred yards distant, provisions were furnished from the boats sufficient for all parties; there was hearty though rude feasting in both camps, and in the evening the red warriors entertained their white friends with dances and songs that lasted until after midnight.

On the following morning (June 3d) the travellers re embarked and took a temporary leave of their Indian friends, who intended to proceed immediately for the Arickara town where they expected to arrive in three days, long before the boats could reach there. Mr. Hunt had not proceeded far before the chief came gallopping along the shore and made signs for a parley. He said, his people could not go home satisfied unless they had something to take with them to prove that they had met with the white men. Mr. Hunt understood the drift of the speech and made the chief a present of a cask of powder, a bag of balls and three dozen of knives, with which he was highly pleased. While the chief was receiving these presents an Indian came running along the shore and announced that a boat, filled with white men, was coming up the river. This was by no means agreeable tidings to Mr. Hunt, who correctly concluded it to be the boat of Mr. Manuel Lisa, and he was vexed to find that alert and adventurous trader upon his heels, when he had hoped to have out manœuvred and left him far behind. Lisa, however, was too much experienced in the wiles of Indian trade to be lulled by the promise of waiting for him at the Poncas village; on the contrary, he had allowed himself no repose and had strained every nerve to overtake the rival party, and, availing himself of the moonlight, had even sailed during a considerable part of the night. In this he was partly prompted by his apprehensions of the Sioux, having met a boat which had probably passed Mr. Hunt's party in the night, and which had been fired into by these savages.

On hearing that Lisa was so near at hand Mr. Hunt perceived that it was useless to attempt any longer to evade him; after proceeding a few miles further, therefore, he came to a halt and waited for him to come up. In a little while the barge of Lisa made its appearance. It came sweeping gallantly up the river, manned by its twenty stout oarsmen, and armed by a swivel mounted at the bow. The whole number on board amounted to twenty six men; among whom was Mr. Henry Breckenridge, then a young enterprizing man; who was a mere passenger, tempted by motives of curiosity to accompany Mr. Lisa. He has since made himself known by various writings, among which may be noted a narrative of this very voyage.

The approach of Lisa, while it was regarded with uneasiness by Mr. Hunt, roused the ire of M'Lellan; who calling to mind old grievances, began to look round for his rifle as if he really intended to carry his threat into execution and shoot him on the spot; and it was with some difficulty that Mr. Hunt was enabled to restrain his ire, and prevent a scene of outrage and confusion.

The meeting between the two leaders, thus mutually distrustful, could not be very cordial; and as to Messrs. Crooks and M'Lellan; though they refrained from any outbreak, yet they regarded in grim defiance their old rival and underplotter. In truth a general distrust prevailed throughout the party concerning Lisa and his intentions. They considered him artful and slippery, and secretly anxious for the failure of their expedition. There being now nothing more to be apprehended from the Sioux, they suspected that Lisa would take advantage of his twenty oared barge to leave them and get first among the Arickaras. As he had traded with those people and possessed great influence over them it was feared he might make use of it to impede the business of Mr. Hunt and his party. It was resolved therefore to keep a sharp look out upon his movements; and M'Lellan swore that if he saw the least sign of treachery on his part, he would instantly put his old threat into execution.

Notwithstanding these secret jealousies and heart burnings the two parties maintained an outward appearance of civility, and for two days continued forward in company with some degree of harmony. On the third day, however, an explosion took place, and it was produced by no less a personage than Pierre Dorion, the half breed interpreter. It will be recollected that this worthy had been obliged to steal a march from S' Louis, to avoid being arrested for an old whiskey debt which he owed to the Missouri Fur Company, and by which Mr. Lisa had hoped to prevent his enlisting in Mr. Hunt's expedition. Dorion, since the arrival of Lisa, had kept aloof and regarded him with a sullen and dogged aspect. On the fifth of June the two parties were brought to a halt by a heavy rain, and remained encamped about a hundred yards apart. In the course of the day Lisa undertook to tamper with the faith of Pierre Dorion, and, inviting him on board of his boat, regaled him with his favorite whisky. When he thought him sufficiently mellowed he proposed to him to quit the service of his new employers and return to his old allegiance. Finding him not to be moved by soft words, he called to mind his old debt to the company and threatened to carry him off by force, in payment of it. The mention of this debt always stirred up the gall of Pierre Dorion, bringing with it the remembrance of the whiskey extortion. A violent quarrel arose between him and Lisa, and he left the boat in high dudgeon. His first step was to repair to the tent of Mr. Hunt and reveal the attempt that had been made to shake his faith. While he was yet talking Lisa entered the tent, under the pretext of coming to borrow a towing line. High words instantly ensued between him and Dorion, which ended by the half breed's dealing him a blow. A quarrel in the "Indian Country," however, is not to be settled with fisty cuffs. Lisa immediately rushed to his boat for a weapon. Dorion snatched up a pair of pistols belonging to Mr. Hunt, and placed himself in battle array. The noise had roused the camp and every one pressed to know the cause. Lisa now re appeared upon the field with a knife stuck in his girdle. Mr. Breckenridge, who had tried in vain to mollify his ire, accompanied him to the scene of action. Pierre Dorion's pistols gave him the advantage, and he maintained a most warlike attitude. In the mean time Crooks and M'Lellan had learnt the cause of the affray and were each eager to take the quarrel into their own hands. A scene of uproar and hubbub ensued that defies description. M'Lellan would have brought his rifle into play and settled all old and new grudges by a pull of the trigger had he not been restrained by Mr. Hunt. That gentleman acted as moderator, endeavoring to prevent a general melée; in the midst of the brawl, however, an expression was made use of by Lisa derogatory to his own honour. In an instant the tranquil spirit of Mr. Hunt was in a flame. He now became as eager for fight as any one on the ground and challenged Lisa to settle the dispute on the spot with pistols. Lisa repaired to his boat to arm himself for the deadly feud. He was followed by Messrs. Bradbury and Breckenridge, who, novices in Indian life and the "chivalry" of the frontier, had no relish for scenes of blood and brawl. By their earnest mediation the quarrel was, with great difficulty, brought to a close without blood shed; but the two leaders of the rival camps separated in anger and all personal intercourse ceased between them.

CHAPTER XX

The rival parties now coasted along the opposite sides of the river, within sight of each other; the barges of Mr. Hunt always keeping some distance in the advance, lest Lisa should push on and get first to the Arickara village. The scenery and objects as they proceeded gave evidence that they were advancing deeper and deeper into the domains of savage nature. Boundless wastes kept extending to the eye, more and more animated by herds of buffalo. Sometimes these unwieldly animals were seen moving in long procession across the silent landscape; at other times they were scattered about, singly or in groups, on the broad enameled prairies and green acclivities, some cropping the rich pasturage, others reclining amidst the flowerly herbage; the whole scene realizing in a manner the old scriptural descriptions of the vast pastoral countries of the Orient, with "cattle upon a thousand hills."

At one place the shores seemed absolutely lined with buffalos; many were making their way across the stream, snorting, and blowing and floundering. Numbers, in spite of every effort, were borne by the rapid current within shot of the boats, and several were killed. At another place a number were descried on the beach of a small island, under the shade of the trees or standing in the water, like cattle, to avoid the flies and the heat of the day.

Several of the best marksmen stationed themselves in the bow of a barge which advanced slowly and silently, stemming the current with the aid of a broad sail and a fair breeze. The buffalo stood gazing quietly at the barge as it approached, perfectly unconscious of their danger. The fattest of the herd was selected by the hunters, who all fired together and brought down their victim.

Beside the buffaloes they saw abundance of deer, and frequent gangs of stately elks, together with light troops of sprightly antilopes, the fleetest and most beautiful inhabitants of the prairies.

There are two kinds of antilopes in these regions, one nearly the size of the common deer, the other not much larger than a goat. Their colour is a light grey or rather dun, slightly spotted with white; and they have small horns like those of the deer, which they never shed. Nothing can surpass the delicate and elegant finish of their limbs; in which lightness, elasticity and strength are wonderfully combined. All the attitudes and movements of this beautiful animal are graceful and picturesque, and it is altogether as fit a subject for the fanciful uses of the poet, as the oft sung gazelle of the east.

Their habits are shy and capricious; they keep on the open plains, are quick to take the alarm and bound away with a fleetness that defies pursuit. When thus skimming across a prairie in the autumn, their light grey or dun colour blends with the hue of the withered herbage, the swiftness of their motion baffles the eye and they almost seem unsubstantial forms driven like a gossamer before the wind.

While they thus keep to the open plain and trust to their speed they are safe; but they have a prurient curiosity that sometimes betrays them to their ruin. When they have scud for some distance and left their pursuer behind, they will suddenly stop and turn to gaze at the object of their alarm. If the pursuit is not followed up they will, after a time, yield to their inquisitive hankering, and return to the place from whence they have been frightened.

John Day, the veteran hunter already mentioned, displayed his experience and skill in entrapping one of these beautiful animals. Taking advantage of its well known curiosity, he laid down flat among the grass, and putting his handkerchief on the end of his ram rod, waved it gently in the air. This had the effect of the fabled fascination of the rattle snake. The antelope gazed at the mysterious object for some time at a distance, then approached timidly, pausing and reconnoitering with encreased curiosity; moving round the point of attraction in a circle, but still drawing nearer and nearer, until being within the range of the deadly rifle, he fell a victim to his curiosity.

On the 10th of June as the party were making brisk progress with a fine breeze they met a canoe with three Indians descending the river. They came to a parley and brought news from the Arickara village. The war party, which had caused such alarm at the sand bar, had reached the village some days previously, announced the approach of a party of traders, and displayed with great ostentation the presents they had received from them. On further conversation with these three Indians Mr. Hunt learnt the real danger which he had run, when hemmed up within the sand bar. The Mandans, who were of the war party, when they saw the boat so completely entrapped and apparently within their power, had been eager for attacking it, and securing so rich a prize. The Minatarees, also, were nothing loth, feeling in some measure committed in hostility to the whites, in conse-

quence of their tribe having killed two white men above the Fort of
the Missouri Fur Company. Fortunately, the Arickaras who formed
the majority of the war party, proved true in their friendship to the
whites and prevented any hostile act, otherwise a bloody affray, and
perhaps a horrible massacre, might have ensued.

On the 11th of June Mr. Hunt and his companions encamped near
an island about six miles below the Arickara village. Mr. Lisa encamped, as usual, at no great distance; but the same sullen and jealous
reserve and non intercourse continued between them. Shortly after
pitching the tents Mr. Breckenridge made his appearance as an
ambassador from the rival camp. He came on behalf of his companions,
to arrange the manner of making their entrance into the village and
of receiving the chiefs; for every thing of the kind is a matter of
grave ceremonial among the Indians.

The partners now expressed frankly their deep distrust of the intentions of Mr. Lisa, and their apprehensions, that, out of the jealousy
of trade and resentment of recent disputes, he might seek to instigate
the Arickaras against them. Mr. Breckenridge assured them that their
suspicions were entirely groundless and pledged himself that nothing
of the kind should take place. He found it difficult, however, to remove
their distrust; the conference, therefore, ended without producing any
cordial understanding; and M'Lellan recurred to his old threat of
shooting Lisa the instant he discovered any thing like treachery in
his proceedings.

That night the rain fell in torrents accompanied by thunder and
lightning. The camp was deluged and the bedding and baggage
drenched. All hands embarked at an early hour and set forward for
the village. About nine o'clock, when half way, they met a canoe, on
board of which were two Arickara dignitaries. One, a fine looking man,
much above the common size, was hereditary chief of the village; he
was called the Left handed, on account of a personal peculiarity. The
other, a ferocious looking savage, was the War chief, or generalissimo:
who was known by the name of The Big Man, an appellation he well
deserved from his size, for he was of a gigantic frame. Both were
of fairer complexion than is usual with savages.

They were accompanied by an interpreter: a French creole; one
of those haphazard wights of Gallic origin, who abound upon our
frontier, living among the Indians like one of their own race. He
had been twenty years among the Arickaras, had a squaw and a troop
of pie bald children, and officiated as interpreter to the chiefs. Through
this worthy organ the two dignitaries signified to Mr. Hunt their
sovereign intention to oppose the further progress of the expedition up
the river unless a boat were left to trade with them. Mr. Hunt, in

reply, explained the object of his voyage, and his intention of debarking at their village and proceeding thence by land; and that he would willingly trade with them for a supply of horses for his journey. With this explanation they were perfectly satisfied and putting about, steered for their village to make preparations for the reception of the strangers.

The village of the Ricaras, Arickaras or Ricarees, for the name is thus variously written, is between the 46th and 47th parallels of north latitude, and 1430 miles above the mouth of the Missouri. The party reached it about ten o'clock in the morning, but landed on the opposite side of the river, where they spread out their baggage and effects to dry. From hence they commanded an excellent view of the village. It was divided into two portions, about eighty yards apart, being inhabited by two distinct bands. The whole extended about three quarters of a mile along the river bank, and was composed of conical lodges that looked like so many small hillocks, being wooden frames intertwined with osier and covered with earth. The plain beyond the village swept up into hills of considerable height, but the whole country was nearly destitute of trees. While they were regarding the village they beheld a singular fleet coming down the river. It consisted of a number of canoes, each made of a single buffalo hide stretched on sticks, so as to form a kind of circular trough. Each one was navigated by a single squaw, who knelt in the bottom and paddled; towing after her frail bark a bundle of floating wood intended for firing. This kind of canoe is in frequent use among the Indians; the buffalo hide being readily made up into a bundle and transported on horseback; it is very serviceable in conveying baggage across rivers.

The great number of horses grazing around the village, and scattered over the neighboring hills and valleys, bespoke the equestrian habits of the Arickaras, who are admirable horsemen. Indeed in the number of his horses consists the wealth of an Indian of the prairies; who resembles an Arab in his passion for this noble animal, and in his adroitness in the management of it.

After a time the voice of the Sovereign Chief "The left handed" was heard across the river, announcing that the council lodge was preparing, and inviting the white men to come over. The river was half a mile in width, yet every word uttered by the chieftain was heard. This may be partly attributed to the distinct manner in which every syllable of the compound words in the Indian languages is articulated and accented; but in truth a savage warrior might often rival Achilles himself for force of lungs.*

Now came the delicate point of management, how the two rival

* Bradbury. P. 110.

parties were to conduct their visit to the village with proper circumspection and due decorum. Neither of the leaders had spoken to each
other since their quarrel; all communication had been by ambassadors.
Seeing the jealousy entertained of Lisa, Mr. Breckenridge in his negotiation had arranged that a deputation from each party should cross
the river at the same time so that neither would have the first access
to the ear of the Arickaras.

The distrust of Lisa, however, had encreased in proportion as they
approached the sphere of action, and M'Lellan in particular, kept a
viligant eye upon his motions, swearing to shoot him if he attempted
to cross the river first.

About two o'clock the large boat of Mr. Hunt was manned and
he stepped on board accompanied by Messrs. M'Kenzie and M'Lellan:
Lisa at the same time embarked in his barge; the two deputations
amounted in all to fourteen persons, and never was any movement of
rival potentates conducted with more wary exactness.

They landed amidst a rabble crowd and were received on the
bank by the left handed chief, who conducted them into the village
with grave courtesy; driving to the right and left the swarms of old
squaws, implike boys and vagabond dogs, with which the place abounded.
They wound their way between cabins which looked like dirt heaps
huddled together without any plan, and surrounded by old pallisades;
all filthy in the extreme and redolent of villanous smells.

At length they arrived at the council lodge. It was somewhat spacious,
and formed of four forked trunks of trees placed upright, supporting
cross beams and a frame of poles interwoven with osiers, and the
whole covered with earth. A hole sunken in the centre formed the fire
place, and immediately above was a circular hole in the apex of the
lodge, to let out the smoke and let in the daylight. Around the lodge
were recesses for sleeping, like the berths on board ships, screened
from view by curtains of dressed skins. At the upper end of the lodge
was a kind of hunting and warlike trophy consisting of two buffalo
heads garishly painted, surmounted by shields, bows, quivers of arrows
and other weapons.

On entering the lodge the chief pointed to mats or cushions which
had been placed around for the strangers and on which they seated
themselves, while he placed himself on a kind of stool. An old man
then came forward with the pipe of peace or good fellowship, lighted
and handed it to the chief, and then falling back, squatted himself
near the door. The pipe was passed from mouth to mouth each one
taking a whiff, which is equivalent to the inviolable pledge of faith
of taking salt together among the ancient Britons. The chief then
made a sign to the old pipe bearer, who seemed to fill, likewise, the

station of herald, seneschal and public crier, for he ascended to the top of the lodge to make proclamation. Here he took his post beside the aperture for the emission of smoke and the admission of light; the chief dictated from within what he was to proclaim, and he bawled it forth with a force of lungs that resounded over all the village. In this way he summoned the warriors and great men to council; every now and then reporting progress to his chief through the hole in the roof.

In a little while the braves and sages began to enter one by one as their names were called or announced, emerging from under the buffalo robe suspended over the entrance instead of a door, stalking across the lodge to the skins placed on the floor and crouching down on them in silence. In this way twenty entered and took their seats, forming an assemblage worthy of the pencil, for the Arickaras are a noble race of men, large and well formed, and maintain a savage grandeur and gravity of demeanour in their solemn ceremonials.

All being seated the old seneschal prepared the pipe of ceremony or council and having lit it, handed it to the chief. He inhaled the sacred smoke, gave a puff upward to the heaven, then downward to the earth, then towards the east; after this it was, as usual, passed from mouth to mouth, each holding it respectfully until his neighbor had taken several whiffs; and now the grand council was considered as opened in due form.*

The chief made an harangue welcoming the white men to his village and expressing his happiness in taking them by the hand as friends; but at the same time complaining of the poverty of himself and his people, the usual prelude among Indians to begging or hard bargaining.

Lisa rose to reply, and the eyes of Hunt and his companions were eagerly turned upon him, those of M'Lellan glaring like a basilisk's. He began by the usual expressions of friendship, and then proceeded to explain the object of his own party. Those persons, however, said he, pointing to Mr. Hunt and his companions, are of a different party, and are quite distinct in their views: but, added he, though we are separate parties we make but one common cause when the safety of either is concerned. Any injury or insult offered to them I shall consider as done to myself, and will resent it accordingly. I trust, therefore, that you will treat them with the same friendship that you have always manifested for me, doing every thing in your power to serve them and to help them on their way.

The speech of Lisa, delivered with an air of frankness and sincerity, agreeably surprized and disappointed the rival party.

* Breckenridge.

Mr. Hunt then spoke declaring the object of his journey to the great Salt Lake beyond the mountains, and that he should want horses for the purpose, for which he was ready to trade, having brought with him plenty of goods. Both he and Lisa concluded their speeches by making presents of tobacco.

The Left handed chieftain in reply promised his friendship and aid to the new comers and welcomed them to his village. He added that they had not the number of horses to spare that Mr. Hunt required, and expressed a doubt whether they should be able to part with any. Upon this another chieftain, called Grey Eyes, made a speech and declared that they could readily supply Mr. Hunt with all the horses he might want, since, if they had not enough in the village, they could easily steal more. This honest expedient immediately removed the main difficulty; but the chief deferred all trading for a day or two, until he should have time to consult with his subordinate chiefs, as to market rates; for the principal chief of a village, in conjunction with his council, usually fixes the prices at which articles shall be bought and sold, and to these the village must conform.

The council now broke up. Mr. Hunt transferred his camp across the river at a little distance below the village and the Left Handed chief placed some of his warriors as a guard to prevent the intrusion of any of his people. The camp was pitched on the river bank just above the boats. The tents and the men wrapped in their blankets and bivouacking on skins in the open air, surrounded the baggage at night. Four sentinels also kept watch within sight of each other outside of the camp until midnight, when they were relieved by four others who mounted guard until day light. Mr. Lisa encamped near to Mr. Hunt, between him and the village.

The speech of Mr. Lisa in the council had produced a pacific effect in the encampment. Though the sincerity of his friendship and good will towards the new company still remained matter of doubt, he was no longer suspected of an intention to play false. The intercourse between the two leaders was, therefore, resumed and the affairs of both parties went on harmoniously.

CHAPTER XXI

An Indian horse fair—Love of the Indians for horses—Scenes in the Arickara village—Indian hospitality—Duties of Indian women—Game habits of the men—Their indolence—Love of gossipping—Rumours of lurking enemies—Scouts—An alarm—A sallying forth—Indian dogs— Return of a horse stealing party—An Indian deputation—Fresh alarms —Return of a successful war party—Dress of the Arickaras—Indian toilette—Triumphal entry of the war party—Meetings of relatives and friends—Indian sensibility—Meeting of a wounded warrior and his mother—Festivities and lamentations.

A trade now commenced with the Arickaras, under the regulation and supervision of their two chieftains. Lisa sent a part of his goods to the lodge of the Left handed dignitary and Mr. Hunt established his mart in the lodge of the Big Man. The village soon presented the appearance of a busy fair; and as horses were in demand, the purlieus and the adjacent plain were like the vicinity of a Tartar encampment; horses were put through all their paces, and horsemen were careering about with that dexterity and grace for which the Arickaras are noted. As soon as a horse was purchased his tail was cropped, a sure mode of distinguishing him from the horses of the tribe; for the Indians disdain to practice this absurd, barbarous and indecent mutilation, invented by some mean and vulgar mind insensible to the merit and perfections of the animal; on the contrary, the Indian horses are suffered to remain in every respect the superb and beautiful animals which nature formed them.

The wealth of an Indian of the Far West consists principally in his horses, of which each chief and warrior possesses a great number, so that the plains about an Indian village or encampment are covered with them. These form objects of traffic or objects of depredation, and in this way pass from tribe to tribe over great tracts of country. The horses owned by the Arickaras were, for the most part, of the wild stock of the prairies; some however had been obtained from the Poncas, Pawnees, and other tribes to the southwest, who had stolen them from the Spaniards in the course of horse stealing expeditions into the Mexican territories. These were to be known by being branded; a Spanish mode of marking horses not practiced by the Indians.

As the Arickaras were meditating another expedition against their enemies the Sioux, the articles of traffic most in demand were guns, tomahawks, scalping knives, powder, ball and other munitions of war. The price of a horse, as regulated by the chiefs, was commonly ten

dollars worth of goods at first cost. To supply the demand thus suddenly created, parties of young men and braves had sallied forth on
expeditions to steal horses; a species of service, among the Indians,
which takes precedence of hunting, and is considered a department of
honorable warfare.

While the leaders of the expedition were actively engaged in preparing for the approaching journey, those who had accompanied it
for curiosity or amusement, found ample matter for observation in the
village and its inhabitants. Wherever they went they were kindly
entertained. If they entered a lodge, the buffalo robe was spread before
the fire, for them to sit down; the pipe was brought, and while the
master of the lodge conversed with his guests, the squaw put the
earthen vessel over the fire, well filled with dried buffalo meat and
pounded corn: for the Indian in his native state, before he has mingled
much with white men, and acquired their sordid habits, has the hospitality of the Arab: never does a stranger enter his door without having
food placed before him, and never is the food thus furnished made a
matter of traffic.

The life of an Indian when at home in his village is a life of
indolence and amusement. To the woman is consigned the labours of
the household and the field; she arranges the lodge; brings wood for
the fire; cooks; jirks venison and buffalo meat; dresses the skins of the
animals killed in the chase; cultivates the little patch of maize, pumpkins and pulse which furnishes a great part of their provisions. Their
time for repose and recreation is at sunset, when, the labors of the
day being ended, they gather together to amuse themselves with petty
games, or to hold gossiping convocations on the tops of their lodges.

As to the Indian he is a game animal, not to be degraded by useful
or menial toil. It is enough that he exposes himself to the hardships
of the chase and the perils of war; that he brings home food for his
family and watches and fights for its protection. Every thing else is
beneath his attention. When at home he attends only to his weapons
and his horses, preparing the means of future exploit. Or he engages
with his comrades in games of dexterity, agility and strength; or in
gambling games in which every thing is put at hazard, with a reck-
lessness seldom witnessed in civilized life.

A great part of the idle leisure of the Indians when at home, is
passed in groupes, squatted together on the bank of a river, on the
top of a mound on the prairie, or on the roof of one of their earth
covered lodges, talking over the news of the day, the affairs of the tribe,
the events and exploits of their last hunting or fighting expedition; or
listening to the stories of old times told by some veteran chronicler;
resembling a groupe of our village quidnuncs and politicians, listening

to the prosings of some superannuated oracle, or discussing the contents of an ancient newspaper.

As to the Indian women they are far from complaining of their lot. On the contrary, they would despise their husbands could they stoop to any menial office, and would think it conveyed an imputation upon their own conduct. It is the worst insult one virago can cast upon another in a moment of altercation. "Infamous Woman!" will she cry— "I have seen your husband carrying wood into his lodge to make the fire. Where was his squaw, that he should be obliged to make a woman of himself!"

Mr. Hunt and his fellow travellers had not been many days at the Arickara village when rumours began to circulate that the Sioux had followed them up, and that a war party, four or five hundred in number, were lurking somewhere in the neighborhood. These rumours produced much embarrassment in the camp. The white hunters were deterred from venturing forth in quest of game, neither did the leaders think it proper to expose them to such risk. The Arickaras, too, who had suffered greatly in their wars with this cruel and ferocious tribe, were roused to encreased vigilance, and stationed mounted scouts upon the neighboring hills. This, however, is a general precaution among the tribes of the prairies. Those immense plans present a horizon like the Ocean, so that any object of importance can be descried afar, and information communicated to a great distance. The scouts are stationed on the hills, therefore, to look out both for game and for enemies, and are, in a manner, living telegraphs conveying their intelligence by concerted signs. If they wish to give notice of a herd of buffalo in the plain beyond, they gallop backwards and forwards abreast, on the summit of the hill. If they perceive an enemy at hand they gallop to and fro, crossing each other; at sight of which the whole village flies to arms.

Such an alarm was given in the afternoon of the 15th. Four scouts were seen crossing and recrossing each other at full gallop, on the summit of a hill about two miles distant down the river. The cry was up that the Sioux were coming. In an instant the village was in an uproar. Men, women and children were all bawling and shouting; dogs barking, yelping and howling. Some of the warriors ran for the horses to gather and drive them in from the prairie, some for their weapons. As fast as they could arm and equip they sallied forth; some on horseback, some on foot. Some hastily arrayed in their war dress, with coronets of fluttering feathers, and their bodies smeared with paint; others naked and only furnished with the weapons they had snatched up.

The women and children gathered on the tops of the lodges and heightened the confusion of the scene by their vociferation. Old men who could no longer bear arms took similar stations, and harangued the warriors as they passed, exhorting them to valorous deeds. Some of the veterans took arms themselves, and sallied forth with tottering steps. In this way the savage chivalry of the village to the number of five hundred, poured forth, helter skelter, riding and running, with hideous yells and war whoops like so many bedlamites or demoniacs let loose.

After a while the tide of war rolled back, but with far less uproar. Either it had been a false alarm, or the enemy had retreated on finding themselves discovered, and quiet was restored to the village. The white hunters continuing to be fearful of ranging this dangerous neighborhood, fresh provisions began to be scarce in the camp. As a substitute, therefore, for venison and buffalo meat, the travellers had to purchase a number of dogs to be shot and cooked for the supply of the camp. Fortunately, however chary the Indians might be of their horses, they were liberal of their dogs. In fact, these animals swarm about an Indian village as they do about a Turkish town. Not a family but has two or three dozen belonging to it, of all sizes and colours. Some of a superior breed are used for hunting; others to draw the sledge, while others of a mongrel breed, and idle vagabond nature, are fatted for food. They are supposed to be descended from the wolf, and retain something of his savage but cowardly temper, howling rather than barking: shewing their teeth and snarling on the slightest provocation, but sneaking away on the least attack.

The excitement of the village continued from day to day. On the day following the alarm just mentioned several parties arrived from different directions, and were met and conducted by some of the braves to the council lodge; where they reported the events and success of their expeditions, whether of war or hunting, which news was afterwards promulgated throughout the village, by certain old men who acted as heralds or town criers. Among the parties which arrived was one that had been among the Snake nation stealing horses, and returned crowned with success. As they passed in triumph through the village they were cheered by the men, women and children, collected as usual on the tops of the lodges, and were exhorted by the nestors of the village to be generous in their dealings with the white men.

The evening was spent in feasting and rejoicing among the relatives of the successful warriors; but sounds of grief and wailing were heard from the hills adjacent to the village: the lamentations of women who had lost some relative in the foray.

An Indian village is subject to continual agitations and excitements. The next day arrived a deputation of braves from the Cheyenne or Shienne nation; a broken tribe, cut up, like the Arickaras, by wars with the Sioux, and driven to take refuge among the Black Hills, near the sources of the Cheyenne River from which they derive their name. One of these deputies was magnificently arrayed in a buffalo robe, on which various figures were fancifully embroidered with split quills, dyed red and yellow; and the whole was fringed with the slender hoofs of young fawns that rattled as he walked.

The arrival of this deputation was the signal for another of those ceremonials which occupy so much of Indian life; for no being is more courtly and punctilious, and more observant of etiquette and formality than an American Savage.

The object of the deputation was to give notice of an intended visit of the Shienne (or Cheyenne) tribe to the Arickara village in the course of fifteen days. To this visit Mr. Hunt looked forward, to procure additional horses for his journey; all his bargaining being ineffectual in obtaining a sufficient supply from the Arickaras. Indeed nothing could prevail upon the latter to part with their prime horses, which had been trained to buffalo hunting.

As Mr. Hunt would have to abandon his boats at this place, Mr. Lisa now offered to purchase them, and such of his merchandize as was superfluous, and to pay him in horses, to be obtained at a Fort belonging to the Missouri Fur Company situated at the Mandan villages, about a hundred and fifty miles further up the river. A bargain was promptly made, and Mr. Lisa and Mr. Crooks, with several companions, set out for the Fort to procure the horses. They returned after upwards of a fortnight's absence, bringing with them the stipulated number of horses.

Still the cavalry was not sufficiently numerous to convey the party and the baggage and merchandize, and a few days more were required to complete the arrangements for the journey.

On the 9th of July, just before day break, a great noise and vociferation was heard in the village. This being the usual Indian hour of attack and surprize, and the Sioux being known to be in the neighborhood, the camp was instantly on the alert. As the day broke Indians were descried in considerable number, on the bluffs, three or four miles down the river. The noise and agitation in the village continued. The tops of the lodges were crowded with the inhabitants, all earnestly looking towards the hills, and keeping up a vehement chattering. Presently an Indian warrior gallopped past the camp towards the village, and in a little while the legions began to pour forth.

The truth of the matter was now ascertained. The Indians upon the distant hills were three hundred Arickara braves, returning from a foray. They had met the war party of Sioux who had been so long hovering about the neighborhood, had fought them the day before, killed several and defeated the rest with the loss of but two or three of their own

men and about a dozen wounded; and they were now halting at a
distance until their comrades in the village should come forth to meet
them, and swell the parade of their triumphal entry. The warrior who
had gallopped past the camp was the leader of the party hastening
home to give tidings of his victory.

Preparations were now made for this great martial ceremony. All the
finery and equipments of the warriors were sent forth to them, that they
might appear to the greatest advantage. Those, too, who had remained
at home, tasked their wardrobes and toilettes to do honor to the
procession.

The Arickaras generally go naked, but, like all savages, they have
their gala dress of which they are not a little vain. This usually consists
of a gay surcoat and leggings of the dressed skin of the antelope, resembling chamois leather, and embroidered with porcupine quills brilliantly dyed. A buffalo robe is thrown over the right shoulder, and
across the left is slung a quiver of arrows. They wear gay coronets of
plumes, particularly those of the swan; but the feathers of the black
eagle are considered the most worthy, being a sacred bird among
the Indian warriors. He who has killed an enemy in his own land,
is entitled to drag at his heels a fox's skin attached to each moccasin;
and he who has slain a grizzly bear, wears a necklace of his claws,
the most glorious trophy that a hunter can exhibit.

An Indian toilette is an operation of some toil and trouble; the warrior
often has to paint himself from head to foot, and is extremely capricious
and difficult to please as to the hideous distribution of streaks and
colours. A great part of the morning, therefore, passed away before
there were any signs of the distant pageant. In the mean time a profound stillness reigned over the village. Most of the inhabitants had
gone forth; others remained in mute expectation. All sports and occupations were suspended, excepting that in the lodges the painstaking
squaws were silently busied in preparing the repasts for the warriors.

It was near noon that a mingled sound of voices and rude music
faintly heard from a distance, gave notice that the procession was on
the march. The old men and such of the squaws as could leave their
employments hastened forth to meet it. In a little while it emerged from
behind a hill, and had a wild and picturesque appearance as it came
moving over the summit in measured step, and to the cadence of
songs and savage instruments; the warlike standards and trophies flaunting aloft, and the feathers and paint, and silver ornaments of the warriors glaring and glittering in the sunshine.

The pageant had really something chivalrous in its arrangement. The
Arickaras are divided into several bands, each bearing the name of
some animal or bird, as the buffalo, the bear, the dog, the pheasant.

The present party consisted of four of these bands, one of which was the dog, the most esteemed in war, being composed of young men under thirty and noted for prowess. It is engaged on the most desperate occasions. The bands marched in separate bodies under their several leaders. The warriors on foot came first, in platoons of ten or twelve abreast; then the horsemen. Each band bore as an ensign a spear or bow decorated with beads, porcupine quills and painted feathers. Each bore its trophies of scalps, elevated on poles, their long black locks streaming in the wind. Each was accompanied by its rude music and minstrelsy. In this way the procession extended nearly a quarter of a mile. The warriors were variously armed, some few with guns, others with bows and arrows and war clubs; all had shields of buffalo hide, a kind of defence generally used by the Indians of the open prairies, who have not the covert of trees and forests to protect them. They were painted in the most savage style. Some had the stamp of a red hand across their mouths, a sign that they had drunk the life blood of a foe!

As they drew near to the village the old men and the women began to meet them and now a scene ensued that proved the fallacy of the old fable of Indian apathy and stoicism. Parents and children, husbands and wives, brothers and sisters met with the most rapturous expressions of joy; while wailings and lamentations were heard from the relatives of the killed and wounded. The procession, however, continued on with slow and measured step, in cadence to the solemn chaunt, and the warriors maintained their fixed and stern demeanour.

Between two of the pincipal chiefs rode a young warrior who had distinguished himself in the battle. He was severely wounded so as with difficulty to keep on his horse; but he preserved a serene and steadfast countenance as if perfectly unharmed. His mother had heard of his condition. She broke through the throng and rushing up, threw her arms around him and wept aloud. He kept up the spirit and demeanor of a warrior to the last, but expired shortly after he had reached his home.

The village was now a scene of the utmost festivity and triumph. The banners and trophies and scalps and painted shields were elevated on poles near the lodges. There were war feasts, and scalp dances, with warlike songs and savage music; all the inhabitants were arrayed in their festal dresses; while the old heralds went round from lodge to lodge, promulgating with loud voices the events of the battle and the exploits of the various warriors.

Such was the boisterous revelry of the village; but sounds of another kind were heard on the surrounding hills; piteous wailings of the women, who had retired thither to mourn in darkness and solitude for those who had fallen in battle. There the poor mother of the youthful warrior who had returned home in triumph but to die, gave full vent to the anguish of a mother's heart. How much does this custom among the Indian women of repairing to the hill tops in the night, and pouring forth their wailings for the dead, call to mind the beautiful and affecting passage of Scripture, "In Rama was there a voice heard, lamentation, and weeping and great mourning, Rachel weeping for her children, and would not be comforted, because they are not."

CHAPTER XXII

Wilderness of the Far West—Great American desert—Parched seasons —Black Hills—Rocky Mountains—Wandering and predatory hordes— Speculations on what may be the future population—Apprehended dangers—A plot to desert—Rose the interpreter—His sinister character —Departure from the Arickara village.

While Mr. Hunt was diligently preparing for his arduous journey some of his men began to lose heart at the perilous prospect before them; but, before we accuse them of want of spirit, it is proper to consider the nature of the wilderness into which they were about to adventure. It was a region almost as vast and trackless as the ocean, and, at the time of which we treat, but little known, excepting through the vague accounts of Indian hunters. A part of their route would lay across an immense tract stretching north and south for hundreds of miles along the foot of the Rocky Mountains, and drained by the tributary streams of the Missouri and the Mississippi. This region, which resembles one of the immeasurable steppes of Asia, has not inaptly been termed "The Great American desert." It spreads forth into undulating and treeless plains, and desolate sandy wastes, wearisome to the eye from their extent and monotony, and which are supposed by geologists, to have formed the ancient floor of the ocean, countless ages since, when its primeval waves beat against the granite bases of the Rocky Mountains.

It is a land where no man permanently abides; for, in certain seasons of the year there is no food either for the hunter or his steed. The herbage is parched and withered; the brooks and streams are dried up; the buffalo, the elk and the deer have wandered to distant parts, keeping within the verge of expiring verdure, and leaving behind them a vast uninhabited solitude, seamed by ravines, the beds of former torrents, but now serving only to tantalize and encrease the thirst of the traveller.

Occasionally the monotony of this vast wilderness is interrupted by mountainous belts of sand and lime stone; broken into confused masses; with precipitous cliffs and yawning ravines, looking like the ruins of a world; or is traversed by lofty and barren ridges of rock, almost impassable, like those denominated the Black Hills. Beyond these rise the stern barriers of the Rocky Mountains, the limits, as it were, of the Atlantic world. The rugged defiles and deep valleys of this vast chain form sheltering places for restless and ferocious bands of savages, many of them the remnants of tribes, once inhabitants of the prairies, but broken up by war and violence, and who carry into their mountain haunts the fierce passions and reckless habits of desperadoes.

151

Such is the nature of this immense wilderness of the Far West; which apparently defies cultivation, and the habitation of civilized life. Some portions of it along the rivers may partially be subdued by agriculture, others may form vast pastoral tracts, like those of the east; but it is to be feared that a great part of it will form a lawless interval between the abodes of civilized man, like the wastes of the ocean or the deserts of Arabia; and, like them, be subject to the depredations of the marauder. Here may spring up new and mongrel races, like new formations in geology, the amalgamation of the "debris" and "abrasions" of former races, civilized and savage; the remains of broken and almost extinguished tribes; the descendants of wandering hunters and trappers; of fugitives from the Spanish and American frontiers; of adventurers and desperadoes of every class and country, yearly ejected from the bosom of society into the wilderness. We are contributing incessantly to swell this singular and heterogeneous cloud of wild population that is to hang about our frontier, by the transfer of whole tribes of savages from the east of the Mississippi to the great wastes of the Far West. Many of these bear with them the smart of real or fancied injuries; many consider themselves expatriated beings, wrongfully exiled from their hereditary homes, and the sepulchres of their fathers, and cherish a deep and abiding animosity against the race that has dispossessed them. Some may gradually become pastoral hordes, like those rude and migratory people, half shepherd, half warrior, who, with their flocks and herds, roam the plains of upper Asia; but, others, it is to be apprehended, will become predatory bands, mounted on the fleet steeds of the prairies, with the open plains for their marauding grounds, and the mountains for their retreats and lurking places. Here they may resemble those great hordes of the north, "Gog and Magog with their bands," that haunted the gloomy imaginations of the prophets. "A great company and a mighty host, all riding upon horses, and warring upon those nations which were at rest, and dwelt peaceably, and had gotten cattle and goods."

The Spaniards changed the whole character and habits of the Indians when they brought the horse among them. In Chili, Tucuman and other parts, it has converted them, we are told, into Tartar-like tribes, and enabled them to keep the Spaniards out of their country, and even to make it dangerous for them to venture far from their towns and settlements. Are we not in danger of producing some such state of things in the boundless regions of the Far West? That these are not mere fanciful and extravagant suggestions we have sufficient proofs in the dangers already experienced by the traders to the Spanish mart of Santa Fé, and to the distant posts of the Fur Companies. These are obliged to proceed in armed caravans, and are subject to murderous attacks from bands of Pawnees, Camanches and Blackfeet, that come scouring upon them in their weary march across the plains, or lie in wait for them among the passes of the mountains.

We are wandering, however, into excursive speculations, when our intention was merely to give an idea of the nature of the wilderness which Mr. Hunt was about to traverse; and which at that time was far less known than at present; though it still remains in a great measure an unknown land. We cannot be surprized, therefore, that some of the least resolute of his party should feel dismay at the thoughts of adventuring into this perilous wilderness under the uncertain guidance of three hunters, who had merely passed once through the country and might have forgotten the land marks. Their apprehensions were aggravated by some of Lisa's followers, who, not being engaged in the expedition, took a mischievous pleasure in exaggerating its dangers. They painted in strong colours, to the poor Canadian voyageurs, the risk they would run of perishing with hunger and thirst; of being cut off by war parties of the Sioux who scoured the plains; of having their horses stolen by the Upsarokas or Crows, who infested the skirts of the Rocky Mountains, or of being butchered by the Blackfeet, who lurked among the defiles. In a word, there was little chance of their getting alive across the mountains; and even if they did, those three guides knew nothing of the howling wilderness that lay beyond.

The apprehensions thus awakened in the minds of some of the men came well nigh proving detrimental to the expedition. Some of them determined to desert, and to make their way back to S' Louis. They accordingly purloined several weapons and a barrel of gunpowder, as ammunition for their enterprize, and buried them in the river bank, intending to seize one of the boats and make off in the night. Fortunately their plot was overheard by John Day, the Kentuckyan, and communicated to the partners, who took quiet and effectual means to frustrate it.

The dangers to be apprehended from the Crow Indians had not been over rated by the camp gossips. These savages through whose mountain haunts the party would have to pass, were noted for daring and excursive habits, and great dexterity in horse stealing. Mr. Hunt, therefore, considered himself fortunate in having met with a man who might be of great use to him in any intercourse he might have with the tribe. This was a wandering individual named Edward Rose, whom he had picked up somewhere on the Missouri—one of those anomalous beings found on the frontier who seem to have neither kin nor country. He had lived some time among the Crows so as to become acquainted with their language and customs; and was, withal, a dogged, sullen, silent fellow, with a sinister aspect, and more of the savage than the civilized man in his appearance. He was engaged to serve in general as a hunter, but as guide and interpreter when they should reach the country of the Crows.

On the 18th of July Mr. Hunt took up his line of march by land from the Arikara village, leaving Mr. Lisa and Mr. Nuttall there, where they intended to await the expected arrival of Mr. Henry from the Rocky Mountains. As to Messrs. Bradbury and Breckenridge, they had departed some days previously, on a voyage down the river to S' Louis, with a detachment from Mr. Lisa's party.

With all his exertions Mr. Hunt had been unable to obtain a sufficient number of horses for the accommodation of all his people. His cavalcade consisted of eighty two horses, most of them heavily laden with Indian goods, beaver traps, ammunition, Indian corn, corn meal and other necessaries. Each of the partners was mounted, and a horse was allotted to the interpreter Pierre Dorion, for the transportation of his luggage and his two children. His squaw, for the most part of the time, trudged on foot, like the residue of the party; nor did any of the men shew more patience and fortitude than this resolute woman in enduring fatigue and hardship.

The veteran trappers and voyageurs of Lisa's party shook their heads as their comrades set out, and took leave of them as of doomed men; and even Lisa, himself, gave it as his opinion, after the travellers had departed, that they would never reach the shores of the Pacific, but would either perish with hunger in the wilderness or be cut off by the Savages.

CHAPTER XXIII

Summer weather of the prairies—Purity of the atmosphere—Canadians on the march—Sickness in the camp—Big River—Vulgar nomenclature —Suggestions about the original Indian names—Camp of Cheyennes— Trade for horses—Character of the Cheyennes—Their horsemanship —Historical anecdotes of the tribe.

The course taken by Mr. Hunt was at first to the north west, but soon turned and kept generally to the south west, to avoid the country infested by the Blackfeet. His route took him across some of the tributary streams of the Missouri, and over emmense prairies, bounded only by the horizon, and destitute of trees. It was now the height of summer, and these naked plains would be intolerable to the traveller were it not for the breezes which sweep over them during the fervour of the day, bringing with them tempering airs from the distant mountains. To the prevalence of these breezes, and to the want of all leafy covert, may we also attribute the freedom from those flies and other insects so tormenting to man and beast during the summer months, in the lower prairies, which are bordered and interspersed with woodland.

The monotony of these immense landscapes, also, would be as wearisome as that of the ocean, were it not relieved in some degree by the purity and elasticity of the atmosphere and the beauty of the heavens. The sky has that delicious blue for which the sky of Italy is renowned; the sun shines with a splendor unobscured by any cloud or vapour, and a star light night on the prairies is glorious. This purity and elasticity of atmosphere encreases as the traveller approaches the mountains, and gradually rises into the more elevated prairies.

On the second day of the journey Mr. Hunt arranged the party into small and convenient messes, distributing among them the camp kettles. The encampments at night were as before; some sleeping under tents and others bivouacking in the open air. The Canadians proved as patient of toil and hardship on the land as on the water; indeed nothing could surpass the patience and goodhumour of these men upon the march. They were the cheerful drudges of the party, loading and unloading the horses, pitching the tents, making the fires, cooking; in short, performing all those household and menial offices which the Indians usually assign to the squaws—and, like the squaws, they left all the hunting and fighting to others. A Canadian has but little affection for the exercise of the rifle.

The progress of the party was but slow for the first few days. Some of the men were indisposed; Mr. Crooks especially was so unwell that he could not keep on his horse. A rude kind of litter was, therefore, prepared for him, consisting of two long poles, fixed one on each side of two horses, with a matting between them on which he reclined at full length, and was protected from the sun by a canopy of boughs.

On the evening of the 23d (July) they encamped on the banks of what they term Big River; and here we cannot but pause to lament the stupid, commonplace, and often ribald names entailed upon the rivers and other features of the Great West, by traders and settlers. As the aboriginal tribes of these magnificent regions are yet in existence the Indian names might easily be recovered; which, beside being in general more sonorous and musical, would remain mementos of the primitive lords of the soil, of whom in a little while scarce any traces will be left. Indeed it is to be wished that the whole of our country could be rescued, as much as possible, from the wretched nomenclature inflicted upon it, by ignorant and vulgar minds, and this might be done, in a great degree, by restoring the Indian names, wherever significant and euphonious. As there appears to be a spirit of research abroad in respect to our aboriginal antiquities, we would suggest, as a worthy object of enterprize, a map, or maps, of every part of our country, giving the Indian names wherever they could be ascertained. Whoever achieves such an object worthily will leave a monument to his own reputation.

To return from this digression. As the travellers were now in a country abounding with buffalo, they remained for several days encamped upon the banks of Big River, to obtain a supply of provisions and to give the invalids time to recruit.

On the second day of their sojourn, as Ben Jones, John Day and others of the hunters were in pursuit of game they came upon an Indian camp on the open prairie, near to a small stream which ran through a ravine. The tents or lodges were of dressed buffalo skins, sewn together and stretched on tapering pine poles, joined at top, but radiating at bottom, so as to form a circle capable of admitting fifty persons. Numbers of horses were grazing in the neighborhood of the camp or straying at large in the prairie, a sight most acceptable to the hunters. After reconnoitering the camp for some time they ascertained it to belong to a band of Cheyenne Indians, the same that had sent a deputation to the Arickaras. They received the hunters in the most friendly manner; invited them to their lodges, which were more cleanly than Indian lodges are prone to be, and set food before them with true uncivilized hospitality. Several of them accompanied the hunters back to the camp, when a trade was immediately opened. The Cheyennes were astonished and delighted to find a convoy of goods and trinkets thus brought into the very heart of the prairie; while Mr. Hunt and his companions were overjoyed to have an opportunity of obtaining a further supply of horses from these equestrian savages.

During a fortnight that the travellers lingered at this place their encampment was continually thronged by the Cheyennes. They were a civil, well behaved people, cleanly in their persons and decorous in their habits. The men were tall, straight and vigorous, with aquiline noses and high cheek bones. Some were almost as naked as ancient statues, and might have stood as models for a statuary; others had leggings and moccasins of deer skin, and buffalo robes, which they threw gracefully over their shoulders. In a little while, however, they began to appear in more gorgeous array, tricked out in the finery obtained from the white men; bright cloths; brass rings; beads of various colours, and happy was he who could render himself hideous with vermillion.

The travellers had frequent occasion to admire the skill and grace with which these Indians managed their horses. Some of them made a striking display when mounted; themselves and their steeds decorated in gala style; for the Indians often bestow more finery upon their horses than upon themselves. Some would hang round the necks, or rather on the breasts of their horses the most precious ornaments they had obtained from the white men; others interwove feathers in their manes and tails. The Indian horses, too, appear to have an attachment to their wild riders, and indeed it is said that the horses of the prairies readily distinguish an Indian from a white man by the smell, and give a preference to the former. Yet the Indians, in general, are hard riders, and, however they may value their horses, treat them with great roughness and neglect. Occasionally the Cheyennes joined the white hunters in pursuit of the elk and buffalo, and when in the ardor of the chase, spared neither themselves nor their steeds, scouring the prairies at full speed, and plunging down precipices and frightful ravines that threatened the necks of both horse and horseman. The Indian steed, well trained to the chase, seems as mad as his rider and pursues the game as eagerly as if it were his natural prey, on the flesh of which he was to banquet.

The history of the Cheyennes is that of many of these wandering tribes of the prairies. They were the remnant of a once powerful people called the Shaways, inhabiting a branch of the Red River which flows into Lake Winnipeg. Every Indian tribe has some rival tribe with which it wages implacable hostility. The deadly enemies of the Shaways were the Sioux, who after a long course of warfare, proved too powerful for them and drove them across the Missouri. They again took root near the Warricanne creek and established themselves there in a fortified village.

The Sioux still followed them with deadly animosity; dislodged them from their village and compelled them to take refuge in the Black Hills, near the upper waters of the Shienne (or Cheyenne) River. Here they lost even their name, and became known among the French colonists by that of the river they frequented.

The heart of the tribe was now broken; its numbers were greatly thinned by their harassing wars. They no longer attempted to establish themselves in any permanent abode that might be an object of attack to their cruel foes. They gave up the cultivation of the fruits of the earth and became a wandering tribe subsisting by the chase and following the buffalo in its migrations.

Their only possessions were horses; which they caught on the prairies, or reared, or captured on predatory incursions into the Mexican territories as has already been mentioned. With some of these they repaired once a year to the Arickara villages, exchanged them for corn, beans, pumpkins and articles of European merchandize, and then returned into the heart of the prairies.

Such are the fluctuating fortunes of these savage nations. War, famine, pestilence, together or singly, bring down their strength and thin their numbers. Whole tribes are rooted up from their native places, wander for a time about these immense regions, become amalgamated with other tribes, or disappear from the face of the earth. There appears to be a tendency to extinction among all the savage nations, and this tendency would seem to have been in operation among the aboriginals of this country long before the advent of the white men, if we may judge from the traces and traditions of ancient populousness in regions which were silent and deserted at the time of the discovery; and from the mysterious and perplexing vestiges of unknown races, predecessors of those found in actual possession, and who must long since have become gradually extinguished or been destroyed. The whole history of the aboriginal population of this country, however, is an enigma, and a grand one—will it ever be solved?

CHAPTER XXIV

*New distribution of horses—Secret information of treason in the camp
—Rose the interpreter, his perfidious character—His plots—Anecdotes
of the Crow Indians—Notorious horse stealers—Some account of Rose
—A desperado of the frontier.*

On the sixth of August the travellers bade farewell to the friendly
band of Cheyennes, and resumed their journey. As they had obtained
thirty six additional horses by their recent traffic, Mr. Hunt made a
new arrangement. The baggage was made up in smaller loads. A horse
was allotted to each of the six prime hunters, and others were distributed among the voyageurs, a horse for every two, so that they
could ride and walk alternately. Mr. Crooks being still too feeble to
mount the saddle, was carried on a litter.

Their march this day lay among singular hills and knolls of an
indurated red earth, resembling brick, about the bases of which were
scattered pumice stones and cinders, the whole bearing traces of the
action of fire. In the evening they encamped on a branch of Big River.

They were now out of the tract of country infested by the Sioux;
and had advanced such a distance into the interior that Mr. Hunt
no longer felt apprehensive of the desertion of any of his men. He
was doomed, however, to experience new cause of anxiety. As he
was seated in his tent after night fall one of the men came to him
privately, and informed him that there was mischief brewing in the
camp. Edward Rose, the interpreter, whose sinister looks we have
already mentioned, was denounced by this secret informer, as a design-
ing, treacherous scoundrel, who was tampering with the fidelity of
certain of the men and instigating them to a flagrant piece of
treason. In the course of a few days they would arrive at the mountainous district infested by the Upsarokas or Crows, the tribe among
which Rose was to officiate as interpreter. His plan was that several
of the men should join with him, when in that neighborhood, in carrying
off a number of the horses with their packages of goods, and deserting
to those savages. He assured them of good treatment among the Crows,
the principal chiefs and warriors of whom he knew: they would
soon become great men among them and have the finest women,
and the daughters of the chiefs for wives, and the horses and goods
they carried off would make them rich for life.

The intelligence of this treachery on the part of Rose gave much
disquiet to Mr. Hunt, for he knew not how far it might be effective
among his men. He had already had proofs that several of them were

disaffected to the enterprize, and loth to cross the mountains. He knew also that savage life had charms for many of them, especially the Canadians, who were prone to intermarry and domesticate themselves among the Indians.

And here a word or two concerning the Crows may be of service to the reader, as they will figure occasionally in the succeeding narrative.

The tribe consists of four bands, which have their nestling places in fertile, well wooded valleys lying among the Rocky Mountains, and watered by the Big Horn River and its tributary streams; but, though these are properly their homes, where they shelter their old people, their wives and their children, the men of the tribe are almost continually on the foray and the scamper. They are, in fact, notorious marauders and horse stealers; crossing and re crossing the mountains, robbing on the one side, and conveying their spoils to the other. Hence, we are told, is derived their name, given to them on account of their unsettled and predatory habits; winging their flight, like the crows, from one side of the mountains to the other, and making free booty of every thing that lies in their way. Horses, however, are the especial objects of their depredations, and their skill and audacity in stealing them are said to be astonishing. This is their glory and delight; an accomplished horse stealer fills up their idea of a hero. Many horses are obtained by them, also, in barter from tribes in and beyond the mountains. They have an absolute passion for this noble animal, beside which he is with them an important object of traffic. Once a year they make a visit to the Mandans, Minatarees and other tribes of the Missouri, taking with them droves of horses which they exchange for guns, ammunition, trinkets, vermillion, cloths of bright colours and various other articles of European manufacture. With these they supply their own wants and caprices, and carry on the internal trade for horses already mentioned.

The plot of Rose to rob and abandon his countrymen when in the heart of the wilderness, and to throw himself into the hands of a horde of Savages, may appear strange and improbable to those unacquainted with the singular and anomalous characters that are to be found about the borders. This fellow it appears was one of those desperadoes of the frontier, outlawed by their crimes, who combine the vices of civilized and savage life and are ten times more barbarous than the Indians with whom they consort. Rose had formerly belonged to one of the gangs of pirates who infested the islands of the Mississippi, plundering boats as they went up and down the river, and who sometimes shifted the scene of their robberies to the shore, way laying travellers as they returned by land from New Orleans, with the proceeds of their downward voyage, plundering them of their money and effects, and often perpetrating the most atrocious murders.

These hordes of villains being broken up and dispersed, Rose had betaken himself to the wilderness, associated himself with the Crows, whose predatory habits were congenial with his own, had married a woman of the tribe and, in short, had identified himself with those vagrant savages.

Such was the worthy guide and interpreter, Edward Rose. We give his story, however, not as it was known to Mr. Hunt and his companions at the time, but as it has been subsequently ascertained. Enough was known of the fellow and his dark and perfidious character to put Mr. Hunt upon his guard: still, as there was no knowing how far his plans might have succeeded, and as any rash act might blow the mere smouldering sparks of treason into a sudden blaze, it was thought adviseable by those with whom Mr. Hunt consulted, to conceal all knowledge or suspicion of the meditated treachery, but to keep up a vigilant watch upon the movements of Rose and a strict guard upon the horses at night.

CHAPTER XXV

Substitute for fuel on the prairies—Fossil trees—Fierceness of the buffaloes when in heat—Three hunters missing—Signal fires and smokes—Uneasiness concerning the lost men—A plan to forestall a rogue—New arrangement with Rose—Return of the wanderers.

The plains over which the travellers were journeying continued to be destitute of trees or even shrubs; insomuch that they had to use the dung of the buffalo for fuel; as the Arabs of the desert use that of the camel. This substitute for fuel is universal among the Indians of these upper prairies, and is said to make a fire equal to that of turf. If a few chips are added, it throws out a cheerful and kindly blaze.

These plains, however, had not always been equally destitute of wood, as was evident from the trunks of trees which the travellers repeatedly met with, some still standing, others lying about in broken fragments, but all in a fossil state, having flourished in times long past. In these singular remains the original grain of the wood was still so distinct that they could be ascertained to be the ruins of oak trees. Several pieces of the fossil wood were selected by the men to serve as whetstones.

In this part of the journey there was no lack of provisions, for the prairies were covered with immense herds of buffalo. These in general are animals of peaceable demeanour, grazing quietly like domestic cattle, but this was the season when they are in heat, and when the bulls are unusually fierce and pugnacious. There was accordingly a universal restlessness and commotion throughout the plain; and the amorous herds gave utterance to their feelings in low bellowings that resounded like distant thunder. Here and there fierce duellos took place between rival enamorados; butting their huge shagged fronts together, goring each other with their short black horns, and tearing up the earth with their feet in perfect fury.

In one of the evening halts Pierre Dorion the interpreter, together with Carson and Gardpie, two of the hunters, were missing, nor had they returned by morning. As it was supposed they had wandered away in pursuit of buffalo, and would readily find the track of the party, no solicitude was felt on their account. A fire was left burning, to guide them by its column of smoke, and the travellers proceeded on their march. In the evening a signal fire was made on a hill adjacent to the camp, and in the morning it was replenished with fuel so as to last throughout the day. These signals are usual among the Indians, to give warnings to each other, or to call home straggling hunters: and such is the transparency of the atmosphere in these elevated plains that a slight column of smoke can be discerned from a great distance, particularly in the evenings. Two or three days elapsed, however, without the reappearance of the three hunters; and Mr. Hunt slackened his march to give them time to overtake him.

A vigilant watch continued to be kept upon the movements of Rose, and of such of the men as were considered doubtful in their loyalty; but nothing occurred to excite immediate apprehensions. Rose evidently was not a favorite among his comrades, and it was hoped that he had not been able to make any real partizans.

On the 10th of August they encamped among hills, on the highest peak of which Mr. Hunt caused a huge pyre of pine wood to be made which soon sent up a great column of flame that might be seen far and wide over the prairies. This fire blazed all night and was amply replenished at day break; so that the towering pillar of smoke could not but be descried by the wanderers if within the distance of a day's journey.

It is a common occurrence, in these regions, where the features of the country so much resemble each other, for hunters to lose themselves and wander for many days, before they can find their way back to the main body of their party. In the present instance, however, a more than common solicitude was felt in consequence of the distrust awakened by the sinister designs of Rose.

The route now became excessively toilsome over a ridge of steep rocky hills, covered with loose stones. These were intersected by deep valleys formed by two branches of Big River coming from the south of west, both of which they crossed. These streams were bordered by meadows, well stocked with buffalos. Loads of meat were brought in by the hunters; but the travellers were rendered dainty by profusion and would cook only the choice pieces.

They had now travelled for several days at a very slow rate and had made signal fires and left traces of their route at every stage, yet nothing was heard or seen of the lost men. It began to be feared that they might have fallen into the hands of some lurking band of savages. A party numerous as that of Mr. Hunt, with a long train of pack horses, moving across open plains or naked hills, is discernible at a great distance by Indian scouts; who spread the intelligence rapidly to various points, and assemble their friends to hang about the skirts of the travellers, steal their horses, or cut off any stragglers from the main body.

Mr. Hunt and his companions were more and more sensible how much it would be in the power of this sullen and daring vagabond Rose, to do them mischief, when they should become entangled in the defiles of the mountains, with the passes of which they were wholly unacquainted, and which were infested by his freebooting friends the Crows. There, should he succeed in seducing some of the party into his plans, he might carry off the best horses and effects, throw himself among his savage allies and set all pursuit at defiance. Mr. Hunt resolved, therefore, to frustrate the knave, divert him, by management, from his plans, and make it sufficiently advantageous for him to remain honest. He took occasion, accordingly, in the course of conversation, to inform Rose that, having engaged him chiefly as a guide and interpreter through the country of the Crows, they would not stand in need of his services beyond. Knowing therefore his connexion by marriage with that tribe and his predilection for a residence among them, they would put no constraint upon his will, but, whenever they met with a party of that people, would leave him at liberty to remain among his adopted brethren. Furthermore that, in thus parting with him, they would pay him half a year's wages in consideration of his past services, and would give him a horse, three beaver traps and sundry other articles calculated to set him up in the world.

This unexpected liberality, which made it nearly as profitable and infinitely less hazardous for Rose to remain honest than to play the rogue, completely disarmed him. From that time his whole deportment underwent a change. His brow cleared up and appeared more cheerful; he left off his sullen, skulking habits and made no further attempts to tamper with the faith of his comrades.

On the 13th of August Mr. Hunt varied his course and inclined westward, in hopes of falling in with the three lost hunters; who, it was now thought, might have kept to the right hand of Big River. This course soon brought him to a fork of the Little Missouri, about a hundred yards wide, and resembling the great river of the same name in the strength of its current, its turbid water, and the frequency of drift wood and sunken trees.

Rugged mountains appeared ahead, crowding down to the water edge and offering a barrier to further progress on the side they were ascending. Crossing the river, therefore, they encamped on its north west bank, where they found good pasturage and buffalo in abundance. The weather was overcast and rainy and a general gloom pervaded the camp; the voyageurs sat moping in groupes with their shoulders as high as their heads, croaking their forebodings, when suddenly towards evening a shout of joy gave notice that the lost men were found. They came slowly lagging into the camp with weary looks, and horses jaded and way worn. They had, in fact, been for several days incessantly on the move. In their hunting excursion on the prairies they had pushed so far in pursuit of buffalo as to find it impossible to retrace their steps, over plains trampled by innumerable herds; and were baffled by the monotony of the landscape in their attempts to recall land marks. They had ridden to and fro until they had almost lost the points of the compass and become totally bewildered; nor did they once perceive any of the signal fires and columns of smoke made by their comrades. At length, about two days previously, when almost spent by anxiety and hard riding, they came, to their great joy, upon the "trail" of the party, which they had since followed up steadily.

Those only who have experienced the warm cordiality that grows up between comrades in wild and adventurous expeditions of the kind, can picture to themselves the hearty cheering with which the stragglers were welcomed to the camp. Every one crowded round them to ask questions and to hear the story of their mishaps; and even the Squaw of the moody half breed Pierre Dorion, forgot the sternness of his domestic rule and the conjugal discipline of the cudgel in her joy at his safe return.

CHAPTER XXVI

The Black Mountains—Haunts of predatory Indians—Their wild and broken appearance—Superstitions concerning them—Thunder spirits —Singular noises in the mountains—Secret mines—Hidden treasures— Mountains in labor—Scientific explanation—Impassable defiles—Black tailed deer—The Big horn or Asahta—Prospect from a lofty height— Plain with herds of buffalo—Distant peaks of the Rocky Mountains— Alarms in the camp—Tracks of grizly bears—Dangerous nature of this animal—Adventures of William Cannon and John Day with grizly bears.

Mr. Hunt and his party were now on the skirts of the Black Hills, or Black Mountains, as they are sometimes called, an extensive chain, lying about a hundred miles east of the Rocky Mountains and stretching in a north east direction from the south fork of the Nebraska, or Platte River, to the great north bend of the Missouri. The Sierra or ridge of the Black Hills, in fact, forms the dividing line between the waters of the Missouri and those of the Arkansas and the Mississippi, and gives rise to the Cheyenne, the Little Missouri, and several tributary streams of the Yellow Stone.

The wild recesses of these hills, like those of the Rocky Mountains, are retreats and lurking places for broken and predatory tribes, and it was among them that the remnant of the Cheyenne tribe took refuge, as has been stated, from their conquering enemies, the Sioux.

The Black Hills are chiefly composed of sand stone, and in many places are broken into savage cliffs and precipices, and present the most singular and fantastic forms; sometimes resembling towns and castellated fortresses. The ignorant inhabitants of plains are prone to clothe the mountains that bound their horizon with fanciful and superstitious attributes. Thus the wandering tribes of the prairies who often behold clouds gathering round the summits of these hills and lightning flashing and thunder pealing from them when all the neighboring plains are serene and sunny, consider them the abode of the genii or thunder spirits who fabricate storms and tempests. On entering their defiles, therefore, they often hang offerings on the trees, or place them on the rocks, to propitiate the invisible "Lords of the mountains," and procure good weather and successful hunting; and they attach unusual significancy to the echoes which haunt the precipices.

This superstition may also have arisen, in part, from a natural phenomenon of a singular nature. In the most calm and serene weather, and at all times of the day or night, successive reports are now and

166

then heard among these mountains, resembling the discharge of several pieces of artillery. Similar reports were heard by Messrs. Lewis and Clarke in the Rocky Mountains, which they say, were attributed by the Indians to the bursting of the rich mines of silver contained in the bosom of the mountains.

In fact these singular explosions have received fanciful explanations from learned men, and have not been satisfactorily accounted for even by philosophers. They are said to occur frequently in Brazil. Vasconcelles, a Jesuit father, describes one which he heard in the Sierra, or mountain region of Piratininga, and which he compares to the discharges of a park of artillery. The Indians told him that it was an explosion of stones. The worthy father had soon a satisfactory proof of the truth of their information, for the very place was found where a rock had burst and exploded from its entrails a stoney mass, like a bomb shell, and of the size of a bull's heart. This mass was broken either in its ejection or its fall, and wonderful was the internal organization revealed. It had a shell harder even than iron; within which were arranged, like the seeds of a pomegranate, jewels of various colours: some transparent as chrystal: others of a fine red and others of mixed hues.

The same phenomenon is said to occur occasionally in the adjacent province of Guayra, where stones of the bigness of a man's hand are exploded, with a loud noise, from the bosom of the earth, and scatter about glittering and beautiful fragments that look like precious gems, but are of no value.

The Indians of the Orellano, also, tell of horrible noises heard occasionally in the Paraguaxo, which they consider the throes and groans of the mountain endeavoring to cast forth the precious stones hidden within its entrails. Others have endeavored to account for these discharges of "mountain artillery" on humbler principles: attributing them to the loud reports made by the disruption and fall of great masses of rock, reverberated and prolonged by the echoes: others to the disengagement of hydrogen, produced by subterraneous beds of coal in a state of ignition. In whatever way this singular phenomenon may be accounted for, the existence of it appears to be well established. It remains one of the lingering mysteries of nature which throw something of a supernatural charm over her wild mountain solitudes, and we doubt whether the imaginative reader will not rather join with the poor Indian in attributing it to the thunder spirits, or the guardian genii of unseen treasures, than to any commonplace physical cause.

Whatever might be the supernatural influences among these mountains, the travellers found their physical difficulties hard to cope with. They made repeated attempts to find a passage through, or over the chain, but were as often turned back by impassable barriers. Some-

times a defile seemed to open a practicable path, but it would terminate
in some wild chaos of rocks and cliffs, which it was impossible to climb.
The animals of these solitary regions were different from those they
had been accustomed to. The black tailed deer would bound up the
ravines on their approach, and the Big horn would gaze fearlessly down
upon them from some impending precipice, or skip playfully from rock
to rock.

These animals are only to be met with in mountainous regions. The
former is larger than the common deer, but its flesh is not equally
esteemed by hunters. It has very large ears and the tip of the tail is
black, from which it derives its name.

The Big horn is so named from its horns; which are of a great size
and twisted like those of a ram. It is called by some the Argali, by others
the Ibex, though differing from both of these animals. The Mandans call
it the Ahsahta, a name much better than the clumsy appellation which
it generally bears. It is of the size of a small elk, or large deer, and of
a dun colour, excepting the belly and round the tail, where it is white.
In its habits it resembles the goat, frequenting the rudest precipices;
cropping the herbage from their edges; and, like the chamois, bounding
lightly and securely among dizzy heights, where the hunter dares not
venture. It is difficult, therefore, to get within shot of it. Ben Jones the
hunter, however, in one of the passes of the Black Hills, succeeded in
bringing down a Big horn from the verge of a precipice, the flesh of
which was pronounced by the gourmands of the camp to have the flavor
of excellent mutton.

Baffled in his attempts to traverse this mountain chain, Mr. Hunt
skirted along it to the south west, keeping it on the right; and still in
hope of finding an opening. At an early hour one day, he encamped in
a narrow valley on the banks of a beautifully clear but rushy pool;
surrounded by thickets bearing abundance of wild cherries, currants
and yellow and purple gooseberries.

While the afternoon's meal was in preparation Mr. Hunt and Mr.
M'Kenzie ascended to the summit of the nearest hill, from whence, aided
by the purity and transparency of the evening atmosphere, they commanded a vast prospect on all sides. Below them extended a plain,
dotted with innumerable herds of buffalo. Some were lying down among
the herbage, others roaming in their unbounded pastures, while many
were engaged in fierce contests like those already described, their low
bellowings reaching the ear like the hoarse murmurs of the surf on a
distant shore.

Far off in the west they descried a range of lofty mountains printing
the clear horizon, some of them evidently capped with snow. These they
supposed to be the Big Horn mountains, so called from the animal of

that name with which they abound. They are a spur of the Great Rocky chain. The hill from whence Mr. Hunt had this prospect was, according to his computation, about two hundred and fifty miles from the Arickara Village.

On returning to the camp Mr. Hunt found some uneasiness prevailing among the Canadian voyageurs. In straying among the thickets they had beheld tracks of grizly bears in every direction; doubtless attracted thither by the fruit. To their dismay they now found that they had encamped in one of the favorite resorts of this dreaded animal. The idea marred all the comfort of the encampment. As night closed the surrounding thickets were peopled with terrors; insomuch that, according to Mr. Hunt, they could not help starting at every little breeze that stirred the bushes.

The grizzly bear is the only really formidable quadruped of our continent. He is the favorite theme of the hunters of the Far West, who describe him as equal in size to a common cow and of prodigious strength. He makes battle if assailed, and often, if pressed by hunger, is the assailant. If wounded he becomes furious and will pursue the hunter. His speed exceeds that of a man, but is inferior to that of a horse. In attacking he rears himself on his hind legs and springs the length of his body. Woe to horse or rider that comes within the sweep of his terrific claws, which are sometimes nine inches in length, and tear every thing before them.

At the time we are treating of, the grizzly bear was still frequent on the Missouri, and in the lower country, but like some of the broken tribes of the prairies, he has gradually fallen back before his enemies and is now chiefly to be found in the upland regions, in rugged fastnesses like those of the Black Hills and the Rocky Mountains. Here he lurks in caverns, or holes which he has digged in the sides of hills, or under the roots and trunks of fallen trees. Like the common bear he is fond of fruits and mast and roots, the latter of which he will dig up with his fore claws. He is carnivorous also, and will even attack and conquer the lordly buffalo, dragging his huge carcass to the neighborhood of his den, that he may prey upon it at his leisure.

The hunters, both white and red men, consider this the most heroic game. They prefer to hunt him on horseback and will venture so near as sometimes to singe his hair with the flash of the rifle. The hunter of the grizzly bear, however, must be an experienced hand, and know where to aim at a vital part; for of all quadrupeds, he is the most difficult to be killed. He will receive repeated wounds without flinching, and rarely is a shot mortal unless through the head or heart.

That the dangers apprehended from the grizly bear, at this night encampment, were not imaginary, was proved on the following morning.

Among the hired men of the party was one William Cannon, who had been a soldier at one of the frontier posts, and entered into the employ of Mr. Hunt at Mackinaw. He was an inexperienced hunter and a poor shot, for which he was much bantered by his more adroit comrades. Piqued at their raillery he had been practicing ever since he had joined the expedition but without success. In the course of the present afternoon he went forth by himself to take a lesson in venerie and, to his great delight, had the good fortune to kill a buffalo. As he was a considerable distance from the camp, he cut out the tongue and some of the choice bits, made them into a parcel, and, slinging them on his shoulders by a strap passed round his forehead, as the voyageurs carry packages of goods, set out all glorious for the camp, anticipating a triumph over his brother hunters. In passing through a narrow ravine he heard a noise behind him and looking round beheld, to his dismay, a grizzly bear in full pursuit: apparently attracted by the scent of the meat. Cannon had heard so much of the invulnerability of this tremendous animal that he never attempted to fire, but, slipping the strap from his forehead let go the buffalo meat and ran for his life. The bear did not stop to regale himself with the game but kept on after the hunter. He had nearly overtaken him when Cannon reached a tree and, throwing down his rifle, scrambled up it. The next instant Bruin was at the foot of the tree, but, as this species of bear does not climb, he contented himself with turning the chase into a blockade. Night came on. In the darkness Cannon could not perceive whether or not the enemy maintained his station, but his fears pictured him rigorously mounting guard. He passed the night, therefore, in the tree, a prey to dismal fancies. In the morning the bear was gone. Cannon warily descended the tree, gathered up his gun, and made the best of his way back to the camp without venturing to look after his buffalo meat.

While on this theme we will add another anecdote of an adventure with a grizly bear, told of John Day, the Kentucky hunter, but which happened at a different period of the expedition. Day was hunting in company with one of the clerks of the Company, a lively youngster, who was a great favorite with the veteran, but whose vivacity he had continually to keep in check. They were in search of deer, when suddenly a huge grizzly bear emerged from a thicket about thirty yards distant, rearing himself upon his hind legs with a terrific growl and displaying a hideous array of teeth and claws. The rifle of the young man was levelled in an instant, but John Day's iron hand was as quickly upon his arm. "Be quiet boy! be quiet!" exclaimed the hunter, between his clenched teeth and without turning his eyes from the bear.

They remained motionless. The monster regarded them for a time, then, lowering himself on his fore paws, slowly withdrew. He had not gone many paces before he again turned, reared himself on his hind legs and repeated his menace. Day's hand was still on the arm of his young companion, he again pressed it hard, and kept repeating between his teeth "Quiet boy!—keep quiet!—keep quiet!"—though the latter had not made a move since his first prohibition.

The bear again lowered himself on all fours, retreated some twenty yards further, and again turned, reared, shewed his teeth and growled. This third menace was too much for the game spirit of John Day. "By Jove!" exclaimed he, "I can stand this no longer" and in an instant a ball from his rifle whizzed into the foe. The wound was not mortal; but, luckily, it dismayed instead of enraging the animal and he retreated into the thicket.

Day's young companion reproached him for not practicing the caution which he enjoined upon others. "Why boy," replied the veteran, "caution is caution, but one must not put up with too much even from a bear. Would you have me suffer myself to be bullied all day by a varmint!"

CHAPTER XXVII

Indian trail—Rough mountain travelling—Sufferings from hunger and thirst—Powder River—Game in abundance—A hunter's paradise—Mountain peak seen at a great distance—One of the Big Horn chain —Rocky Mountains—Extent—Appearance—Height—The Great American Desert—Various characteristics of the mountains—Indian superstitions concerning them—Land of souls—Towns of the free and generous spirits—Happy hunting grounds.

For the two following days the travellers pursued a westerly course for thirty four miles, along a ridge of country dividing the tributary waters of the Missouri and the Yellow Stone. As landmarks they guided themselves by the summits of the far distant mountains which they supposed to belong to the Big Horn chain. They were gradually rising into a higher temperature for the weather was cold for the season with a sharp frost in the night and ice of an eighth of an inch in thickness.

On the twenty second of August, early in the day they came upon the trail of a numerous band. Rose and the other hunters examined the foot prints with great attention, and determined it to be the trail of a party of Crows returning from an annual trading visit to the Mandans. As this trail afforded more commodious travelling they immediately struck into it, and followed it for two days. It led them over rough hills and through broken gullies, during which time they suffered great fatigue from the ruggedness of the country. The weather, too, which had recently been frosty was now oppressively warm and there was a great scarcity of water, insomuch that a valuable dog belonging to Mr. M'Kenzie died of thirst.

At one time they had twenty five miles of painful travel without a drop of water, until they arrived at a small running stream. Here they eagerly slaked their thirst, but, this being allayed, the calls of hunger became equally importunate. Ever since they had got among these barren and arid hills, where there was a deficiency of grass, they had met with no buffaloes, those animals keeping in the grassy meadows near the streams. They were obliged, therefore, to have recourse to their corn meal, which they reserved for such emergencies. Some, however, were lucky enough to kill a wolf, which they cooked for supper, and pronounced excellent food.

The next morning they resumed their wayfaring, hungry and jaded, and had a dogged march of eighteen miles among the same kind of hills. At length they emerged upon a stream of clear water, one of the forks of the Powder River, and to their great joy, beheld once more wide grassy meadows stocked with herds of buffalo. For several days they kept along the banks of this river, ascending it about eighteen miles. It was a hunter's paradise; the buffaloes were in such abundance that they were enabled to kill as many as they pleased, and to jirk a sufficient supply of meat for several days' journeying. Here then they revelled and reposed after their hungry and weary travel, hunting and feasting, and reclining upon the grass. Their quiet, however, was a little marred, by coming upon traces of Indians who, they concluded, must be Crows; they were, therefore, obliged to keep a more vigilant watch than ever upon their horses.

For several days they had been directing their march towards the lofty mountain described by Mr. Hunt and Mr. M'Kenzie on the 17th of August, the height of which rendered it a land mark over a vast extent of country. At first it had appeared to them solitary and detached; but as they advanced towards it, it proved to be the principal summit of a chain of mountains. Day by day it varied in form, or rather its lower peaks, and the summits of others of the chain emerged above the clear horizon, and finally the inferior line of hills which connected most of them rose to view. So far, however, are objects discernible in the pure atmosphere of these elevated plains, that from the place where they first descried the main mountain they had to travel a hundred and forty miles before they reached its base. Here they encamped on the thirtieth of August, having come nearly four hundred miles since leaving the Arickara village.

The mountain which now towered above them was one of the Big Horn chain, bordered by a river of the same name, and extending for a long distance rather east of north and west of south. It was a part of the great system of granite mountains which forms one of the most important and striking features of North America, stretching parallel to the coast of the Pacific from the Isthmus of Panama almost to the Arctic Ocean; and presenting a corresponding chain to that of the Andes in the southern hemisphere. This vast range has acquired from its rugged and broken character and its summits of naked granite the appellation of The Rocky Mountains, a name by no means distinctive, as all elevated ranges are rocky. Among the early explorers it was known as the range of Chippewyan mountains, and this Indian name is the one it is likely to retain in poetic usage. Rising from the midst of vast plains and prairies, traversing several degrees of latitude, dividing the waters of the Atlantic and the Pacific, and seeming to bind with diverging ridges the level regions on its flanks, it has been figuratively termed the back bone of the northern continent.

The Rocky Mountains do not present a range of uniform elevation, but rather groups and occasionally detached peaks. Though some of these rise to the region of perpetual snows and are upwards of eleven thousand feet in real altitude yet their height from their immediate bases is not so great as might be imagined; as they swell up from elevated plains, several thousand feet above the level of the Ocean. These plains are often of a desolate sterility; mere sandy wastes, formed of the detritus of the granite heights, destitute of trees and herbage, scorched by the ardent and reflected rays of the summer's sun, and, in winter, swept by chilling blasts from the snow clad mountains. Such is a great part of that vast region extending north and south along the Mountains, several hundred miles in width, which has not improperly been termed The Great American desert. It is a region that almost discourages all hope of cultivation, and can only be traversed with safety by keeping near the streams which intersect it. Extensive plains likewise occur among the higher regions of the mountains, sometimes of considerable fertility. Indeed these lofty plats of table land seem to form a peculiar feature in the American continents. Some occur among the Cordilleras of the Andes, where cities and towns and cultivated farms are to be seen eight thousand feet above the level of the sea.

The Rocky Mountains, as we have already observed, occur sometimes singly or in groupes, and occasionally in collateral ridges. Between these are deep valleys with small streams winding through them, which find their way into the lower plains, augmenting as they proceed, and ultimately discharging themselves into those vast rivers, which traverse the prairies like great arteries and drain the continent.

While the granitic summits of the Rocky Mountains are bleak and bare, many of the inferior ridges are scantily clothed with scrubbed pines, oaks, cedar and furze. Various parts of the mountains also bear traces of volcanic action. Some of the interior valleys are strewed with scoria and broken stones evidently of volcanic origin; the surrounding rocks bear the like character, and vestiges of extinguished craters are to be seen on the elevated heights.

We have already noticed the superstitious feelings with which the Indians regard the Black Hills; but this immense range of mountains, which divides all that they know of the world, and gives birth to such mighty rivers, is still more an object of awe and veneration. They call it "The crest of the world," and think that Wacondah, or the Master of life, as they designate the Supreme being, has his residence among these aerial heights. The tribes on the eastern prairies call them the Mountains of the Setting Sun. Some of them place the "Happy hunting grounds," their ideal paradise, among the recesses of these mountains; but say that they are invisible to living men. Here also is the "Land of Souls" in which are the "towns of the free and generous spirits," where those who have pleased the Master of life while living, enjoy after death all manner of delights.

Wonders are told of these mountains by the distant tribes whose warriors or hunters have ever wandered in their neighborhood. It is thought by some that, after death, they will have to travel to these mountains and ascend one of their highest and most rugged peaks, among rocks and snows and tumbling torrents. After many moons of painful toil they will reach the summit from whence they will have a view over the land of souls. There they will see the happy hunting grounds, with the souls of the brave and good living in tents in green meadows, by bright running streams, or hunting the herds of buffalo, and elks and deer which have been slain on earth. There too they will see the villages or towns of the free and generous spirits brightening in the midst of delicious prairies. If they have acquitted themselves well while living, they will be permitted to descend and enjoy this happy country; if otherwise, they will but be tantalized with this prospect of it, and then hurled back from the mountain, to wander about the sandy plains and endure the eternal pangs of unsatisfied thirst and hunger.

CHAPTER XXVIII

Region of the Crow Indians—Scouts on the look out—Visit from a crew of hard riders—A Crow camp—Presents to the Crow chief—Bargaining—Crow bullies—Rose among his Indian friends—Parting with the Crows—Perplexities among the mountains—More of the Crows—Equestrian children—Search after stragglers.

The travellers had now arrived in the vicinity of the mountain regions infested by the Crow Indians. These restless marauders, as has already been observed, are apt to be continually on the prowl about the skirts of the mountains; and even when encamped in some deep and secluded glen, they keep scouts upon the cliffs and promontories, who, unseen themselves, can discern every living thing that moves over the subjacent plains and valleys. It was not to be expected that our travellers could pass unseen through a region thus vigilantly centinelled; accordingly, in the edge of the evening, not long after they had encamped at the foot of the Big Horn Sierra, a couple of wild looking beings, scantily clad in skins but well armed, and mounted on horses as wild looking as themselves, were seen approaching with great caution from among the rocks. They might have been mistaken for two of the evil spirits of the mountains so formidable in Indian fable.

Rose was immediately sent out to hold a parley with them and invite them to the camp. They proved to be two scouts from the same band that had been tracked for some days past, and which was now encamped at some distance in the folds of the mountain. They were easily prevailed upon to come to the camp, where they were well received, and, after remaining there until late in the evening, departed to make a report of all they had seen and experienced, to their companions.

The following day had scarce dawned when a troop of these wild mountain scamperers came gallopping with whoops and yells into the camp, bringing an invitation from their chief for the white men to visit him. The tents were accordingly struck, the horses laden, and the party were soon on the march. The Crow horsemen as they escorted them appeared to take pride in shewing off their equestrian skill and hardihood; careering at full speed on their half savage steeds, and dashing among rocks and crags and up and down the most rugged and dangerous places with perfect ease and unconcern.

A ride of sixteen miles brought them, in the afternoon, in sight of the Crow camp. It was composed of leathern tents pitched in a meadow on the border of a small clear stream at the foot of the mountain. A great number of horses were grazing in the vicinity, many of them doubtless captured in marauding excursions.

The Crow chieftain came forth to meet his guests with great professions of friendship and conducted them to his tents, pointing out, by the way, a convenient place where they might fix their camp. No sooner had they done so than Mr. Hunt opened some of the packages and made the chief a present of a scarlet blanket and a quantity of powder and ball; he gave him also some knives, trinkets and tobacco to be distributed among his warriors, with all which the grim potentate seemed, for the time, well pleased. As the Crows, however, were reputed to be perfidious in the extreme, and as errant freebooters as the bird after which they were so worthily named; and as their general feelings towards the whites were known to be by no means friendly, the intercourse with them was conducted with great circumspection.

The following day was passed in trading with the Crows for buffalo robes and skins and in bartering galled and jaded horses for others that were in good condition. Some of the men also purchased horses on their own account, so that the number now amounted to one hundred and twenty one, most of them sound and active, and fit for mountain service.

Their wants being supplied they ceased all further traffic, much to the dissatisfaction of the Crows, who became extremely urgent to continue the trade, and, finding their importunities of no avail, assumed an insolent and menacing tone. All this was attributed by Mr. Hunt and his associates, to the perfidious instigations of Rose the interpreter, whom they suspected of the desire to foment ill will between them and the savages, for the promotion of his nefarious plans. M'Lellan, with his usual *tranchant* mode of dealing out justice, resolved to shoot the desperado on the spot in case of any out break. Nothing of the kind, however, occurred. The Crows were probably daunted by the resolute, though quiet, demeanor of the white men, and the constant vigilance and armed preparation which they maintained; and Rose, if he really still harbored his knavish designs, must have perceived that they were suspected, and, if attempted to be carried into effect, might bring ruin on his own head.

The next morning, bright and early, Mr. Hunt prepared to resume his journeying. He took a ceremonious leave of the Crow chieftain and his vagabond warriors, and according to previous arrangements consigned to their cherishing friendship and fraternal adoption their worthy confederate Rose; who, having figured among the water pirates of the Mississippi, was well fitted to rise to distinction among the land pirates of the Rocky Mountains.

It is proper to add that the ruffian was well received among the tribe and appeared to be perfectly satisfied with the compromise he had made; feeling much more at his ease among savages than among white men. It is outcasts from civilization, fugitives from justice, and heartless desperadoes of this kind, who sow the seeds of enmity and bitterness among the unfortunate tribes of the frontier. There is no enemy so implacable against a country or a community as one of its own people who has rendered himself an alien by his crimes.

Right glad to be relieved from this treacherous companion, Mr. Hunt pursued his course along the skirts of the mountain in a southern direction; seeking for some practicable defile by which he might pass through it. None such presented, however, in the course of fifteen miles, and he encamped on a small stream, still on the outskirts. The green meadows which border these mountain streams are generally well stocked with game, and the hunters soon killed several fat elks, which supplied the camp with fresh meat. In the evening the travellers were surprized by an unwelcome visit from several Crows belonging to a different band from that which they had recently left, and who said their camp was among the mountains. The consciousness of being environed by such dangerous neighbors, and of being still within the range of Rose and his fellow ruffians, obliged the party to be continually on the alert and to maintain weary vigils throughout the night, lest they should be robbed of their horses.

On the third of September, finding that the mountain still stretched onwards, presenting a continued barrier, they endeavored to force a passage to the westward, but soon became entangled among rocks and precipices which set all their efforts at defiance. The mountain seemed for the most part rugged, bare and sterile; yet here and there it was clothed with pines, and with shrubs and flowering plants, some of which were in bloom. In toiling among these weary places their thirst became excessive, for no water was to be met with. Numbers of the men wandered off into rocky dells and ravines in hopes of finding some brook or fountain; some of whom lost their way and did not rejoin the main party.

After half a day of painful and fruitless scrambling, Mr. Hunt gave up the attempt to penetrate in this direction and, returning to the little stream on the skirts of the mountain, pitched his tents within six miles of his encampment of the preceding night. He now ordered that signals should be made for the stragglers in quest of water, but the night passed away without their return.

The next morning to their surprize Rose made his appearance at the camp, accompanied by some of his Crow associates. His unwelcome visit revived their suspicions, but he announced himself as a messenger of good will from the chief, who finding they had taken a wrong road, had sent Rose and his companions to guide them to a nearer and better one across the mountain.

Having no choice, being themselves utterly at fault, they set out under this questionable escort. They had not gone far before they fell in with the whole party of Crows, who, they now found, were going the same road with themselves. The two cavalcades of white and red men, therefore, pushed on together, and presented a wild and picturesque spectacle, as, equipped with various weapons and in various garbs, with trains of pack horses they wound in long lines through the rugged defiles and up and down the crags and steeps of the mountain.

The travellers had again an opportunity to see and admire the equestrian habitudes and address of this hard riding tribe. They were all mounted, man, woman and child, for the Crows have horses in abundance so that no one goes on foot. The children are perfect imps on horseback. Among them was one so young that he could not yet speak. He was tied on a colt of two years old, but managed the reins as if by instinct, and plied the whip with true Indian prodigality. Mr. Hunt enquired the age of this infant jockey and was answered that "he had seen two winters!"

This is almost realizing the fable of the centaurs; nor can we wonder at the equestrian adroitness of these savages, who are thus in a manner cradled in the saddle, and become in infancy almost identified with the animal they bestride.

The mountain defiles were exceedingly rough and broken, and the travelling painful to the burthened horses. The party, therefore, proceeded but slowly, and were gradually left behind by the band of Crows, who had taken the lead. It is more than probable that Mr. Hunt loitered in his course, to get rid of such doubtful fellow travellers. Certain it is that he felt a sensation of relief as he saw the whole crew, the renegado Rose and all, disappear among the windings of the mountain, and heard the last yelp of the savages die away in the distance.

When they were fairly out of sight and out of hearing he encamped on the head waters of the little stream of the preceding day, having come about sixteen miles. Here he remained all the succeeding day, as well to give time for the Crows to get in the advance, as for the stragglers, who had wandered away in quest of water two days previously, to rejoin the camp. Indeed considerable uneasiness began to be felt concerning these men lest they should become utterly bewildered in the defiles of the mountains, or should fall into the hands of some marauding band of Savages. Some of the most experienced hunters were sent in search of them, others, in the mean time, employed themselves in hunting. The narrow valley in which they encamped, being watered by a running stream, yielded fresh pasturage, and, though in the heart of the Big Horn mountains, was well stocked with buffalo. Several of these were killed as also a grizly bear. In the evening, to the satisfaction of all parties, the stragglers made their appearance, and, provisions being in abundance there was hearty good cheer in the camp.

CHAPTER XXIX

Mountain glens—Wandering band of savages—Anecdotes of Shoshonies and Flatheads—Root diggers—Their solitary lurking habits—Gnomes of the mountains—Wind River—Scarcity of food—Alteration of route —The Pilot Knobs or Tetons—Branch of the Colorado—Hunting camp.

Resuming their course on the following morning, Mr. Hunt and his companions continued on westward through a rugged region of hills and rocks, but diversified in many places by grassy little glens; with springs of water, bright sparkling brooks, clumps of pine trees and a profusion of flowering plants which were in full bloom, although the weather was frosty. These beautiful and verdant recesses, running through and softening the rugged mountains, were cheering and refreshing to the way worn travellers.

In the course of the morning as they were entangled in a defile they beheld a small band of Savages, as wild looking as the surrounding scenery, who reconnoitered them warily from the rocks before they ventured to advance. Some of them were mounted on horses rudely caparisoned, with bridles or halters of buffalo hide, one end trailing after them on the ground. They proved to be a mixed party of Flatheads and Shoshonies or Snakes; and as these tribes will be frequently mentioned in the course of this work, we shall give a few introductory particulars concerning them.

The Flatheads in question are not to be confounded with those of the name who dwell about the lower waters of the Columbia; neither do they flatten their heads, as the others do. They inhabit the banks of a river on the west side of the mountains, and are described as simple, honest and hospitable. Like all people of similar character, whether civilized or savage, they are prone to be imposed upon; and are especially maltreated by the ruthless Blackfeet, who harass them in their villages, steal their horses by night, or openly carry them off in the face of day, without provoking pursuit or retaliation.

The Shoshonies are a branch of the once powerful and prosperous tribe of the Snakes, who possessed a glorious hunting country about the upper forks of the Missouri abounding in beaver and buffalo. Their hunting ground was occasionally invaded by the Blackfeet, but the Snakes battled bravely for their domains and a long and bloody feud existed, with variable success. At length the Hudson's Bay Company, extending their trade into the interior, had dealings with the Blackfeet, who were nearest to them, and supplied them with fire arms. The Snakes, who occasionally traded with the Spaniards, endeavored, but in vain, to obtain similar weapons; the Spanish traders wisely refused to arm them so formidably. The Blackfeet had now a vast advantage, and soon dispossessed the poor Snakes of their favorite hunting grounds, their land of plenty, and drove them from place to place, until they were fain to take refuge in the wildest and most desolate recesses of the Rocky Mountains. Even here they are subjected to occasional visits from their implacable foes, as long as they have horses, or any other property to tempt the plunderer. Thus by degrees the Snakes have become a scattered, broken spirited, impoverished people; keeping about lonely rivers and mountain streams and subsisting chiefly upon fish. Such of them as still possess horses and occasionally figure as hunters are called Shoshonies; but there is another class, the most abject and forlorn, who are called Shuckers, or more commonly Diggers and Root eaters. These are a shy, secret, solitary race, who keep in the most retired parts of the mountains, lurking like gnomes in caverns and clefts of the rocks, and subsisting in a great measure on the roots of the earth. Sometimes, in passing through a solitary mountain valley, the traveller comes perchance upon the bleeding carcass of a deer or buffalo that has just been slain. He looks round in vain for the hunter; the whole landscape is lifeless and deserted: At length he perceives a thread of smoke, curling up from among the crags and cliffs, and scrambling to the place, finds some forlorn and skulking brood of Diggers, terrified at being discovered.

The Shoshonies, however, who as has been observed, have still "horse to ride and weapon to wear," are somewhat bolder in their spirit, and more open and wide in their wanderings. In the autumn when salmon disappear from the rivers, and hunger begins to pinch, they even venture down into their ancient hunting grounds, to make a foray among the buffaloes. In this perilous enterprize they are occasionally joined by the Flatheads, the persecutions of the Blackfeet having produced a close alliance and co-operation between these luckless and maltreated tribes. Still, notwithstanding their united force, every step they take within the debatable ground, is taken in fear and trembling, and with the utmost precaution: and an Indian trader assures us that he has seen at least five hundred of them, armed and equipped for action, and keeping watch upon the hill tops while about fifty were hunting in the prairie. Their excursions are brief and hurried: as soon as they have collected and jirked sufficient buffalo meat for winter provisions, they pack their horses, abandon the dangerous hunting grounds and hasten back to the mountains, happy if they have not the terrible Blackfeet rattling after them.

Such a confederate band of Shoshonies and Flatheads, was the one met by our travellers. It was bound on a visit to the Arapahoes, a tribe inhabiting the banks of the Nebraska. They were armed to the best of their scanty means, and some of the Shoshonies had bucklers of buffalo hide, adorned with feathers and leathern fringes, and which have a charmed virtue in their eyes, from having been prepared, with mystic ceremonies by their conjurors.

In company with this wandering band our travellers proceeded all day. In the evening they encamped near to each other in a defile of the mountains, on the borders of a stream running north and falling into Big Horn River. In the vicinity of the camp they found gooseberries, strawberries and currants in great abundance. The defile bore traces of having been a thoroughfare for countless herds of buffaloes, though not one was to be seen. The hunters succeeded in killing an elk and several black tailed deer.

They were now in the bosom of the second Big Horn ridge, with another lofty and snow crowned mountain full in view to the west. Fifteen miles of western course brought them, on the following day, down into an intervening plain, well stocked with buffalo. Here the Snakes and Flatheads joined with the white hunters in a successful hunt, that soon filled the camp with provisions.

On the morning of the 9th of September the travellers parted company with their Indian friends and continued on their course to the west. A march of thirty miles brought them, in the evening, to the banks of a rapid and beautifully clear stream about a hundred yards wide. It is the north fork or branch of the Big Horn River, but bears its peculiar name of The Wind River, from being subject in the winter season to a continued blast which sweeps its banks and prevents the snow from lying on them. This blast is said to be caused by a narrow gap or funnel in the mountains through which the river forces its way between perpendicular precipices, resembling cut rocks.

This river gives its name to a whole range of mountains consisting of three parallel chains, eighty miles in length and about twenty or twenty five broad. One of its peaks is probably fifteen thousand feet above the level of the sea, being one of the highest of the Rocky Sierra. These mountains give rise, not merely to the Wind or Big Horn River, but to several branches of the Yellow Stone and the Missouri on the east, and of the Columbia and Colorado on the west; thus dividing the sources of these mighty streams.

For five succeeding days Mr. Hunt and his party continued up the course of the Wind River, to the distance of about eighty miles, crossing and recrossing it, according to its windings and the nature of its banks; sometimes passing through valleys, at other times scrambling over rocks and hills. The country in general was destitute of trees, but they passed through groves of wormwood, eight and ten feet in height, which they used occasionally for fuel, and they met with large quantities of wild flax.

The mountains were destitute of game; they came in sight of two grizly bears, but could not get near enough for a shot: provisions therefore began to be scanty. They saw large flights of the kind of thrush commonly called the Robin, and many smaller birds of migratory species; but the hills in general appeared lonely and with few signs of animal life. On the evening of the 14th of September, they encamped on the forks of the Wind or Big Horn River. The largest of these forks came from the range of Wind River Mountains.

The hunters who served as guides to the party in this part of their route, had assured Mr. Hunt that, by following up Wind River, and crossing a single mountain ridge, he would come upon the head waters of the Columbia. The scarcity of game, however, which already had been felt to a pinching degree, and which threatened them with famine among the sterile heights which lay before them, admonished them to change their course. It was determined, therefore, to make for a stream which, they were informed, passed through the neighboring mountains, to the south of west, on the grassy banks of which it was probable they would meet with buffalo. Accordingly, about three o'clock on the following day, meeting with a beaten Indian road which led in the proper direction, they struck into it turning their backs upon Wind River.

In the course of the day they came to a height that commanded an almost boundless prospect. Here one of the guides paused, and after considering the vast landscape attentively, pointed to three mountain peaks glistening with snow, which rose, he said, above a fork of Columbia River. They were hailed by the travellers with that joy with which a beacon on a sea shore is hailed by mariners after a long and dangerous voyage. It is true there was many a weary league to be traversed before they should reach these land marks, for, allowing for their evident height, and the extreme transparency of the atmosphere, they could not be much less than a hundred miles distant. Even after reaching them there would yet remain hundreds of miles of their journey to be accomplished. All these matters were forgotten in the joy at seeing the first land marks of the Columbia, that river which formed the bourne of the expedition. These remarkable peaks are known to some travellers as the Tetons; as they had been guiding points for many days, to Mr. Hunt, he gave them the name of the Pilot Knobs.

The travellers continued their course to the south of west for about forty miles, through a region so elevated that patches of snow lay on the highest summits, and on the northern declivities. At length they came to the desired stream, the object of their search, the waters of which flowed to the west. It was in fact a branch of the Colorado, which falls into the

Gulf of California, and had received from the hunters the name of Spanish River, from information given by the Indians that Spaniards resided upon its lower waters.

The aspect of this river and its vicinity was cheering to the way worn and hungry travellers. Its banks were green, and there were grassy valleys running from it in various directions, into the heart of the rugged mountains, with herds of buffalo quietly grazing. The hunters sallied forth with keen alacrity, and soon returned laden with provisions.

In this part of the mountains Mr. Hunt met with three different kinds of gooseberries. The common purple, on a low and very thorny bush; a yellow kind, of an excellent flavor, growing on a stalk free from thorns; and a deep purple, of the size and taste of our winter grape, with a thorny stalk. There were also three kinds of currants, one very large and well tasted, of a purple colour, and growing on a bush eight or nine feet high. Another of a yellow colour, and of the size and taste of the large red currant, the bush four or five feet high; and the third a beautiful scarlet, resembling the strawberry in sweetness, though rather insipid, and growing on a low bush.

On the 17th they continued down the course of the river making fifteen miles to the south west. The river abounded with geese and ducks, and there were signs of its being inhabited by beaver and otters: indeed they were now approching regions where these animals, the great objects of the Fur trade, are said to abound. They encamped for the night opposite the end of a mountain in the west, which was probably the last chain of the Rocky Mountains. On the following morning they abandoned the main course of Spanish River and taking a north west direction for eight miles came upon one of its little tributaries, issuing out of the bosom of the mountains, and running through green meadows, yielding pasturage to herds of buffalo. As these were probably the last of that animal they would meet with, they encamped on the grassy banks of the river, determining to spend several days in hunting, so as to be able to jerk sufficient meat to supply them until they should reach the waters of the Columbia, where they trusted to find fish enough for their support. A little repose, too, was necessary for both men and horses after their rugged and incessant marching, having in the course of the last seventeen days, traversed two hundred and sixty miles of rough, and, in many parts, sterile, mountain country.

CHAPTER XXX

A plentiful hunting camp—Shoshonie hunters—Hoback's River—Mad River—Encampment near the Pilot Knobs—A consultation—Preparations for a perilous voyage.

Five days were passed by Mr. Hunt and his companions in the fresh meadows watered by the bright little mountain stream. The hunters made great havoc among the buffaloes, and brought in quantities of meat; the voyageurs busied themselves about the fires, roasting and stewing for present purposes, or drying provisions for the journey; the pack horses, eased of their burthens, rolled in the grass, or grazed at large about the ample pastures; those of the party who had no call upon their services, indulged in the luxury of perfect relaxation, and the camp presented a picture of rude feasting and revelry, of mingled bustle and repose characteristic of a halt in a fine hunting country.

In the course of one of their excursions some of the men came in sight of a small party of Indians, who instantly fled in great apparent consternation. They immediately returned to camp with the intelligence: upon which Mr. Hunt and four others flung themselves upon their horses and sallied forth to reconnoiter. After riding for about eight miles they came upon a wild mountain scene. A lonely green valley stretched before them surrounded by rugged heights. A herd of buffalo were careering madly through it, with a troop of Savage horsemen in full chase, plying them with their bows and arrows. The appearance of Mr. Hunt and his companions put an abrupt end to the hunt; the buffalo scuttled off in one direction while the Indians plied their lashes and gallopped off in another, as fast as their steeds could carry them. Mr. Hunt gave chase; there was a sharp scamper, though of short continuance. Two young Indians, who were indifferently mounted, were soon overtaken. They were terribly frightened and evidently gave themselves up for lost. By degrees their fears were allayed by kind treatment, but they continued to regard the strangers with a mixture of awe and wonder, for it was the first time in their lives they had ever seen a white man.

They belonged to a party of Snakes who had come across the mountains on their autumnal hunting excursion to provide buffalo meat for the winter. Being persuaded of the peaceable intentions of Mr. Hunt and his companions they willingly conducted them to their camp. It was pitched in a narrow valley on the margin of a stream. The tents were of dressed skins; some of them fantastically painted; with horses grazing about them. The approach of the party caused a transient alarm in the camp, for these poor Indians were ever on the look out for cruel foes. No sooner, however, did they recognise the garb and complexion of their visitors than their apprehensions were changed into joy; for some of them had dealt with white men and knew them to be friendly and to abound with articles of singular value. They welcomed them, therefore, to their tents, set food before them; and entertained them to the best of their power.

They had been successful in their hunt, and their camp was full of jirked buffalo meat; all of the choicest kind and extremely fat. Mr. Hunt purchased enough of them, in addition to what had been killed and cured by his own hunters, to load all the horses excepting those reserved for the partners and the wife of Pierre Dorion. He found also a few beaver skins in their camp, for which he paid liberally as an inducement to them to hunt for more; informing them that some of his party intended to live among the mountains and trade with the native hunters for their peltries. The poor Snakes soon comprehended the advantages thus held out to them, and promised to exert themselves to procure a quantity of beaver skins for future traffic.

Being now well supplied with provisions Mr. Hunt broke up his encampment on the 24th of September and continued on to the west. A march of fifteen miles over a mountain ridge brought them to a stream about fifty feet in width, which Hoback, one of their guides, who had trapped about the neighborhood when in the service of Mr. Henry, recognized for one of the head waters of the Columbia. The travellers hailed it with delight, as the first stream they had encountered tending towards their point of destination. They kept along it for two days during which, from the contributions of many rills and brooks, it gradually swelled into a small river. As it meandered among rocks and precipices they were frequently obliged to ford it, and such was its rapidity that the men were often in danger of being swept away. Sometimes the banks advanced so close upon the river, that they were obliged to scramble up and down their rugged promontories, or to skirt along their bases where there was scarce a foothold. Their horses had dangerous falls in some of these passes. One of them rolled, with his load, nearly two hundred feet down hill into the river, but without receiving any injury. At length they emerged from these stupendous defiles, and continued for several miles along the bank of Hoback's River, through one of the stern mountain valleys. Here it was joined by a river of greater magnitude and swifter current, and their united waters swept off through the valley in one impetuous stream, which, from its rapidity and turbulence, had received the name of Mad River. At the confluence of these streams the travellers encamped. An important point in their arduous journey had been attained, a few miles from their camp rose the three vast snowy peaks called the Tetons, or the Pilot Knobs, the great landmarks of the Columbia, by which they had shaped their course through this mountain wilderness. By their feet flowed the rapid current of Mad River, a stream ample enough to admit of the navigation of canoes, and down which they might possibly be able to steer their course to the main body of the Columbia. The Canadian voyageurs rejoiced at the idea of once more launching themselves upon their favorite element; of exchanging their horses for canoes, and of gliding down the bosoms of rivers, instead of scrambling over the backs of mountains. Others of the party, also, inexperienced in this kind of travelling, considered their toils and troubles as drawing to a close. They had conquered the chief difficulties of this great rocky barrier, and now flattered themselves with the hope of an easy downward course for the rest of their journey. Little did they dream of the hardships and perils by land and water, which were yet to be encountered in the frightful wilderness that intervened between them and the shores of the Pacific!

END OF VOLUME ONE

CHAPTER XXXI

A consultation whether to proceed by land or water—Preparations for boat building—An exploring party—A party of trappers detached —Two Snake visitors—Their report concerning the river—Confirmed by the exploring party—Mad River abandoned—Arrival at Henry's fort—Detachment of Robinson, Hoback and Rezner to trap—Mr. Miller resolves to accompany them—Their departure.

On the banks of Mad River Mr. Hunt held a consultation with the other partners as to their future movements. The wild and impetuous current of the river rendered him doubtful whether it might not abound with impediments lower down, sufficient to render the navigation of it slow and perilous, if not impracticable. The hunters who had hitherto acted as guides, knew nothing of the character of the river below; what rocks, and shoals and rapids might obstruct it or through what mountains and deserts it might pass. Should they then abandon their horses, cast themselves loose in fragile barks upon this wild, doubtful and unknown river, or should they continue their more toilsome and tedious, but perhaps more certain wayfaring by land.

The vote, as might have been expected, was almost unanimous for embarcation, for when men are in difficulties every change seems to be for the better. The difficulty now was to find timber of sufficient size for the construction of canoes, the trees in these high mountain regions being chiefly a scrubbed growth of pines and cedars, aspens, haws and service berries, and a small kind of cotton tree with a leaf resembling that of the willow. There was a species of large fir, but so full of knots as to endanger the axe in hewing it. After searching for some time a growth of timber, of sufficient size, was found lower down the river, whereupon the encampment was moved to the vicinity.

The men were now set to work to fell trees, and the mountains echoed to the unwonted sound of their axes. While preparations were thus going on for a voyage down the river Mr. Hunt, who still entertained doubts of its practicability, despatched an exploring party, consisting of John Reed, the clerk, John Day the hunter and Pierre Dorion the interpreter, with orders to proceed for several days' march along the stream, and notice its course and character.

After their departure Mr. Hunt turned his thoughts to another object of importance. He had now arrived at the head waters of the Columbia, which were among the main points embraced by the enterprize of Mr. Astor. These upper streams were reputed to abound in beaver, and had as yet been unmolested by the white trapper. The numerous signs of beaver met with during the recent search for timber gave evidence that the neighborhood was a good "trapping ground." Here then it was proper to begin to cast loose those leashes of hardy trappers, that are detached from trading parties, in the very heart of the wilderness. The men detached in the present instance were Alexander Carson, Louis S' Michel, Pierre Detayé and Pierre Delaunay. Trappers generally go in pairs, that they may assist, protect and comfort each other in their lonely and perilous occupations. Thus Carson and S' Michel formed one couple and Detayé and Delaunay another. They were fitted out with traps, arms, ammunition, horses and every other requisite, and were to trap upon the upper part of Mad River, and upon the neighboring streams of the mountains. This would probably occupy them for some months; and, when they should have collected a sufficient quantity of peltries, they were to pack them upon their horses and make the best of their way to the mouth of Columbia River, or to any intermediate post which might be established by the Company. They took leave of their comrades and started off on their several courses with stout hearts and cheerful countenances; though these lonely cruisings into a wild and hostile wilderness seem to the uninitiated equivalent to being cast a drift in the ship's yawl in the midst of the ocean.

Of the perils that attend the lonely trapper the reader will have sufficient proof, when he comes, in the after part of this work, to learn the hard fortunes of these poor fellows in the course of their wild peregrinations.

The trappers had not long departed when two Snake Indians wandered into the camp. When they perceived that the strangers were fabricating canoes they shook their heads and gave them to understand that the river was not navigable. Their information, however, was scoffed at by some of the party, who were obstinately bent on embarcation, but was confirmed by the exploring party who returned after several days' absence. They had kept along the river with great difficulty for two days, and found it a narrow, crooked, turbulent stream, confined in a rocky channel, with many rapids, and occasionally over hung with precipices. From the summit of one of these they had caught a bird's eye view of its boisterous career, for a great distance, through the heart of the mountain, with impending rocks and cliffs. Satisfied, from this view, that it was useless to follow its course either by land or water, they had given up all further investigation.

These concurring reports determined Mr. Hunt to abandon Mad River and seek some more navigable stream. This determination was concurred in by all his associates excepting Mr. Miller, who had become impatient of the fatigue of land travel, and was for immediate embarcation at all hazards. This gentleman had been in a gloomy and irritated state of mind for some time past, being troubled with a bodily malady that rendered travelling on horseback extremely irksome to him, and being, moreover, discontented with having a smaller share in the expedition than his comrades. His unreasonable objections to a further march by land were over ruled, and the party prepared to decamp.

Robinson, Hoback and Rezner, the three hunters who had hitherto served as guides among the mountains, now stepped forward and advised Mr. Hunt to make for the post established during the preceding year by Mr. Henry of the Missouri Fur Company. They had been with Mr. Henry, and, as far as they could judge by the neighboring land marks, his post could not be very far off. They presumed there could be but one intervening ridge of mountains, which might be passed without any great difficulty. Henry's post, or fort, was on an upper branch of the Columbia, down which they made no doubt it would be easy to navigate in canoes.

The two Snake Indians being questioned in the matter, shewed a perfect knowledge of the situation of the post, and offered with great alacrity to guide them to the place. Their offer was accepted, greatly to the displeasure of Mr. Miller, who seemed obstinately bent upon braving the perils of Mad River.

The weather for a few days past had been stormy; with rain and sleet. The Rocky Mountains are subject to tempestuous winds from the west; these sometimes come in flaws or currents, making a path through the forests many yards in width, and whirling off trunks and branches to a great distance. The present storm subsided on the third of October; leaving all the surrounding heights covered with snow: for, while rain had fallen in the valley, it had snowed on the hill tops.

On the 4th they broke up their encampment, and crossed the river, the water coming up to the girths of their horses. After travelling four miles they encamped at the foot of the mountain, the last, as they hoped, which they should have to traverse. Four days more took them across it, and over several plains, watered by beautiful little streams, tributaries of Mad River. Near one of their encampments there was a hot spring continually emitting a cloud of vapour. These elevated plains, which give a peculiar character to the mountains, are frequented by large gangs of antelopes fleet as the wind.

On the evening of the 8th of October, after a cold wintry day, with gusts of westerly wind and flurries of snow, they arrived at the sought for post of Mr. Henry. Here he had fixed himself, after being compelled by the hostilities of the Blackfeet, to abandon the upper waters of the Missouri. The post however was deserted, for Mr. Henry had left it in the course of the preceding spring, and, as it afterwards appeared, had fallen in with Mr. Lisa at the Arickara village on the Missouri, some time after the departure of Mr. Hunt and his party.

The weary travellers gladly took possession of the deserted log huts which had formed the post, and which stood on the bank of a stream upwards of a hundred yards wide, on which they intended to embark. There being plenty of suitable timber in the neighborhood, Mr. Hunt immediately proceeded to construct canoes. As he would have to leave his horses and their accoutrements here, he determined to make this a trading post, where the trappers and hunters, to be distributed about the country, might repair, and where the traders might touch on their way through the mountains to and from the establishment at the mouth of the Columbia. He informed the two Snake Indians of this determination and engaged them to remain in that neighborhood and take care of the horses until the white men should return, promising them ample rewards for their fidelity. It may seem a desperate chance to trust to the faith and honesty of two such vagabonds; but, as the horses would have, at all events, to be abandoned, and would otherwise become the property of the first vagrant horde that should encounter them, it was one chance in favor of their being regained.

At this place another detachment of hunters prepared to separate from the party for the purpose of trapping beaver. Three of these had already been in this neighborhood, being the veteran Robinson and his companions Hoback and Rezner, who had accompanned Mr. Henry across the mountains, and who had been picked up by Mr. Hunt on the Missouri, on their way home to Kentucky. According to agreement they were fitted out with horses, traps, ammunition and every thing requisite for their undertaking, and were to bring in all the peltries they should collect, either to this trading post, or to the establishment at the mouth of Columbia River. Another hunter, of the name of Cass, was associated with them in their enterprize. It is in this way that small knots of trappers and hunters are distributed about the wilderness by the fur companies, and like cranes and bitterns, haunt its solitary streams. Robinson the Kentuckian, the veteran of the "bloody ground," who, as has already been noted, had been scalped by the Indians in his younger days, was the leader of this little band. When they were about to depart, Mr. Miller called the partners together, and threw up his share in the company, declaring his intention of joining the party of trappers.

This resolution struck every one with astonishment, Mr. Miller being a man of education and of cultivated habits, and little fitted for the rude life of a hunter. Beside, the precarious and slender profits arising from such a life were beneath the prospects of one who held a share in the general enterprize. Mr. Hunt was especially concerned and mortified at his determination, as it was through his advice and influence he had entered into the concern. He endeavored, therefore, to dissuade him from this sudden resolution; representing its rashness, and the hardships and perils to which it would expose him. He earnestly advised him, however he might feel dissatisfied with the enterprize, still to continue on in company until they should reach the mouth of Columbia River. There they would meet the expedition that was to come by sea; when, should he still feel disposed to relinquish the undertaking, Mr. Hunt pledged himself to furnish him a passage home in one of the vessels belonging to the Company.

To all this, Miller replied abruptly, that it was useless to argue with him, as his mind was made up. They might furnish him, or not, as they pleased, with the necessary supplies, but he was determined to part company here, and set off with the trappers. So saying, he flung out of their presence without vouchsafing any further conversation.

Much as this wayward conduct gave them anxiety, the partners saw it was in vain to remonstrate. Every attention was paid to fit him out for his headstrong undertaking. He was provided with four horses, and all the articles he required. The two Snakes undertook to conduct him and his companions to an encampment of their tribe, lower down among the mountains, from whom they would receive information as to the best trapping grounds. After thus guiding them, the Snakes were to return to Fort Henry, as the new trading post was called, and take charge of the horses which the party would leave there, of which, after all the hunters were supplied, there remained seventy seven. These matters being all arranged, Mr. Miller set out with his companions, under guidance of the two Snakes, on the 10th of October; and much did it grieve the friends of that gentleman to see him thus wantonly casting himself loose upon savage life. How he and his comrades fared in the wilderness, and how the Snakes acquitted themselves of their trust, respecting the horses, will hereafter appear in the course of these rambling anecdotes.

CHAPTER XXXII

Scanty fare—A mendicant Snake—Embarcation on Henry River—Joy of the voyageurs—Arrival at Snake River—Rapids and breakers— Beginning of misfortunes—Snake encampments—Parley with a savage —A second disaster—Loss of a boatman—The Caldron Linn.

While the canoes were in preparation, the hunters ranged about the neighborhood, but with little success. Tracks of buffaloes were to be seen in all directions, but none of a fresh date. There were some elk, but extremely wild; two only were killed. Antelopes were likewise seen, but too shy and fleet to be approached. A few beavers were taken every night, and salmon trout of a small size, so that the camp had principally to subsist upon dried buffalo meat.

On the 14th, a poor, half-naked Snake Indian, one of that forlorn caste called the Shuckers, or Diggers, made his appearance at the camp. He came from some lurking place among the rocks and cliffs, and presented a picture of that famishing wretchedness to which these lonely fugitives among the mountains are sometimes reduced. Having received wherewithal to allay his hunger, he disappeared, but in the course of a day or two returned to the camp bringing with him his son, a miserable boy, still more naked and forlorn than himself. Food was given to both; they skulked about the camp like hungry hounds, seeking what they might devour, and having gathered up the feet and entrails of some beavers that were lying about, slunk off with them to their den among the rocks.

By the 18th of October, fifteen canoes were completed, and on the following day the party embarked with their effects; leaving their horses grazing about the banks, and trusting to the honesty of the two Snakes and some special turn of good luck for their future recovery.

The current bore them along at a rapid rate; the light spirits of the Canadian voyageurs, which had occasionally flagged upon land, rose to their accustomed buoyancy on finding themselves again upon the water. They wielded their paddles with their wonted dexterity, and for the first time made the mountains echo with their favorite boat songs.

In the course of the day the little squadron arrived at the confluence of Henry and Mad rivers, which, thus united, swelled into a beautiful stream of a light pea green color, navigable for boats of any size, and which, from the place of junction, took the name of Snake River, a stream doomed to be the scene of much disaster to the travellers. The banks were here and there fringed with willow thickets and small cotton wood trees. The weather was cold, and it snowed all day, and great flocks of ducks and geese, sporting in the water or streaming through the air, gave token that winter was at hand; yet the hearts of the travellers were light, and, as they glided down the little river, they flattered themselves with the hope of soon reaching the Columbia. After making thirty miles in a southerly direction, they encamped for the night in a neighborhood which required some little vigilance, as there were recent traces of grizzly bears among the thickets.

On the following day the river increased in width and beauty; flowing parallel to a range of mountains on the left, which at times were finely reflected in its light green waters. The three snowy summits of the Pilot Knobs or Tetons, were still seen towering in the distance. After pursuing a swift but placid course for twenty miles, the current began to foam and brawl, and assume the wild and broken character common to the streams west of the Rocky Mountains. In fact the rivers which flow from those mountains to the Pacific, are essentially different from those which traverse the great prairies on their eastern declivities. The latter, though sometimes boisterous, are generally free from obstructions, and easily navigated; but the rivers to the west of the mountains descend more steeply and impetuously, and are continually liable to cascades and rapids. The latter abounded in the part of the river which the travellers were now descending. Two of the canoes filled among the breakers; the crews were saved, but much of the lading was lost or damaged, and one of the canoes drifted down the stream and was broken among the rocks.

On the following day, October 21st, they made but a short distance when they came to a dangerous strait, where the river was compressed for nearly half a mile between perpendicular rocks, reducing it to the width of twenty yards, and increasing its violence. Here they were obliged to pass the canoes down cautiously by a line from the impending banks. This consumed a great part of a day; and after they had re-embarked they were soon again impeded by rapids, when they had to unload their canoes and carry them and their cargoes for some distance by land. It is at these places, called "portages," that the Canadian voyageur exhibits his most valuable qualities; carrying heavy burdens, and toiling to and fro, on land and in the water, over rocks and precipices, among brakes and brambles, not only without a murmur, but with the greatest cheerfulness and alacrity, joking and laughing and singing scraps of old French ditties.

The spirits of the party, however, which had been elated on first varying their journeying from land to water, had now lost some of their buoyancy. Every thing ahead was wrapped in uncertainty. They knew nothing of the river on which they were floating. It had never before been navigated by a white man, nor could they meet with an Indian to give them any information concerning it. It kept on its course through a vast wilderness of silent and apparently uninhabited mountains, without a savage wigwam upon its banks, or bark upon its waters. The difficulties and perils they had already passed, made them apprehend others before them, that might effectually bar their progress. As they glided onward, however, they regained heart and hope. The current continued to be strong; but it was steady, and though they met with frequent rapids, none of them were bad. Mountains were constantly to be seen in different directions, but sometimes the swift river glided through prairies, and was bordered by small cotton wood trees and willows. These prairies at certain seasons are ranged by migratory herds of the wide-wandering buffalo, the tracks of which, though not of recent date, were frequently to be seen. Here, too, were to be found the prickly pear or Indian fig, a plant which loves a more southern climate. On the land were large flights of magpies, and American robins; whole fleets of ducks and geese navigated the river, or flew off in long streaming files at the approach of the canoes; while the frequent establishments of the pains-taking and quiet-loving beaver, showed that the solitude of these waters was rarely disturbed, even by the all-pervading savage.

They had now come near two hundred and eighty miles since leaving Fort Henry, yet without seeing a human being, or a human habitation; a wild and desert solitude extended on either side of the river, apparently almost destitute of animal life. At length, on the 24th of October, they were gladdened by the sight of some savage tents, and hastened to land, and visit them, for they were anxious to procure information to guide them on their route. On their approach, however, the savages fled in consternation. They proved to be a wandering band of Shoshonies. In their tents were great quantities of small fish about two inches long, together with roots and seeds, or grain, which they were drying for winter provisions. They appeared to be destitute of tools of any kind, yet there were bows and arrows very well made; the former were formed of pine, cedar or bone, strengthened by sinews, and the latter of the wood of rose bushes, and other crooked plants, but carefully straightened, and tipped with stone of a bottle-green color.

There were also vessels of willow and grass, so closely wrought as to hold water, and a seine neatly made with meshes, in the ordinary manner, of the fibres of wild flax or nettle. The humble effects of the poor savages remained unmolested by their visitors, and a few small articles, with a knife or two, were left in the camp, and were no doubt regarded as invaluable prizes.

Shortly after leaving this deserted camp and re embarking in the canoes, the travellers met with three of the Snakes on a triangular raft made of flags or reeds; such was their rude mode of navigating the river. They were entirely naked excepting small mantles of hare skins over their shoulders. The canoes approached near enough to gain a full view of them, but they were not to be brought to a parley.

All further progress for the day was barred by a fall in the river of about thirty feet perpendicular; at the head of which the party encamped for the night.

The next day was one of excessive toil and but little progress: the river winding through a wild rocky country and being interrupted by frequent rapids, among which the canoes were in great peril. On the succeeding day they again visited a camp of wandering Snakes, but the inhabitants fled with terror at the sight of a fleet of canoes, filled with white men coming down their solitary river.

As Mr. Hunt was extremely anxious to gain information concerning his route, he endeavored by all kinds of friendly signs to entice back the fugitives. At length one, who was on horseback, ventured back with fear and trembling. He was better clad, and in better condition than most of his vagrant tribe that Mr. Hunt had yet seen. The chief object of his return appeared to be to intercede for a quantity of dried meat and salmon trout which he had left behind; on which probably he depended for his winter's subsistence. The poor wretch approached with hesitation, the alternate dread of famine and of white men operating upon his mind. He made the most abject signs imploring Mr. Hunt not to carry off his food. The latter tried in every way to reassure him, and offered him knives in exchange for his provisions; great as was the temptation, the poor Snake could only prevail upon himself to spare a part; keeping a feverish watch over the rest, lest it should be taken away. It was in vain Mr. Hunt made enquiries of him concerning his route and the course of the river. The Indian was too much frightened and bewildered to comprehend him or to reply; he did nothing but alternately commend himself to the protection of the Good Spirit, and supplicate Mr. Hunt not to take away his fish and buffalo meat; and in this state they left him, trembling about his treasures.

In the course of that and the next day they made nearly eighty miles; the river inclining to the south of west, and being clear and beautiful, nearly half a mile in width with many populous communities of the beaver along its banks. The twenty eighth of October, however, was a day of disaster. The river again became rough and impetuous, and was chafed and broken by numerous rapids. These grew more and more dangerous and the utmost skill was required to steer among them. Mr. Crooks was seated in the second canoe of the squadron, and had an old experienced Canadian for steersman, named Antoine Clappine, one of the most valuable of the voyageurs. The leading canoe had glided safely among the turbulent and roaring surges, but in following it Mr. Crooks perceived that his canoe was bearing towards a rock. He called out to the steersman, but his warning voice was either unheard or unheeded. In the next moment they struck upon the rock. The canoe was split and overturned. There were five persons on board. Mr. Crooks and one of his companions were thrown amidst roaring breakers and a whirling current, but succeeded, by strong swimming, to reach the shore. Clappine and two others clung to the shattered bark and drifted with it to a rock. The wreck struck the rock with one end and swinging round flung poor Clappine off into the raging stream, which swept him away and he perished. His comrades succeeded in getting upon the rock, from whence they were afterwards taken off.

This disastrous event brought the whole squadron to a halt, and struck a chill into every bosom. Indeed they had arrived at a terrific strait that forbade all further progress in the canoes, and dismayed the most experienced voyageur. The whole body of the river was compressed into a space of less than thirty feet in width, between two ledges of rocks upwards of two hundred feet high, and formed a whirling and tumultuous vortex so frightfully agitated as to receive the name of "The Caldron Linn." Beyond this fearful abyss the river kept raging and roaring on, until lost to sight among impending precipices.

CHAPTER XXXIII

Gloomy council—Exploring parties—Discouraging reports—Disastrous experiment—Detachments in quest of succour—Caches, how made—Return of one of the detachments—Unsuccessful—Further disappointments—The Devil's Scuttle Hole.

Mr. Hunt and his companions encamped upon the borders of the Caldron Linn, and held gloomy council as to their future course. The recent wreck had dismayed even the voyageurs, and the fate of their popular comrade Clappine, one of the most adroit and experienced of their fraternity, had struck sorrow to their hearts, for, with all their levity, these thoughtless beings have great kindness towards each other.

The whole distance they had navigated since leaving Henry's fort, was computed to be about three hundred and forty miles; strong apprehensions were now entertained that the tremendous impediments before them would oblige them to abandon their canoes. It was determined to send exploring parties on each side of the river to ascertain whether it was possible to navigate it further. Accordingly on the following morning three men were despatched along the south bank, while Mr. Hunt and three others proceeded along the north. The two parties returned after a weary scramble among savage rocks and precipices, and with very disheartening accounts. For nearly forty miles that they had explored the river foamed and roared along through a deep and narrow channel from twenty to thirty yards wide, which it had worn, in the course of ages, through the heart of a barren rocky country. The precipices on each side were often two and three hundred feet high, sometimes perpendicular and sometimes overhanging, so that it was impossible, excepting in one or two places, to get down to the margin of the stream. This dreary strait was rendered the more dangerous by frequent rapids, and occasionally perpendicular falls from ten to forty feet in height: So that it seemed almost hopeless to attempt to pass the canoes down it.

The party, however, who had explored the south side of the river had found a place, about six miles from the camp, where they thought it possible the canoes might be carried down the bank and launched upon the stream, and from whence they might make their way with the aid of occasional portages. Four of the best canoes were accordingly selected for the experiment and were transported to the place on the shoulders of sixteen of the men. At the same time Mr. Reed, the clerk, and three men were detached to explore the river still further down than the previous scouting parties had been, and at the same time to look out for Indians from whom provisions might be obtained, and a supply of horses, should it be found necessary to proceed by land.

The party who had been sent with the canoes returned on the following day weary and dejected. One of the canoes had been swept away with all the weapons and effects of four of the voyageurs, in attempting to pass it down a rapid by means of a line. The other three had stuck fast among the rocks, so that it was impossible to move them; the men returned, therefore, in despair, and declared the river unnavigable.

The situation of the unfortunate travellers was now gloomy in the extreme. They were in the heart of an unknown wilderness, untraversed as yet by a white man. They were at a loss what route to take, and how far they were from the ultimate place of their destination, nor could they meet, in these uninhabited wilds, with any human being to give them information. The repeated accidents to their canoes had reduced their stock of provisions to five days' allowance, and there was now every appearance of soon having famine added to their other sufferings.

This last circumstance rendered it more perilous to keep together than to separate. Accordingly, after a little anxious but bewildered council, it was determined that several small detachments should start off in different directions, headed by the several partners. Should any of them succeed in falling in with friendly Indians within a reasonable distance and obtaining a supply of provisions and horses, they were to return to the aid of the main body: otherwise they were to shift for themselves and shape their course according to circumstances; keeping the mouth of the Columbia River as the ultimate point of their wayfaring. Accordingly three several parties set off from the camp at Caldron Linn, in opposite directions. Mr. M'Lellan with three men kept down along the bank of the river. Mr. Crooks, with five others, turned their steps up it; retracing by land the weary course they had made by water, intending, should they not find relief nearer at hand, to keep on until they should reach Henry's fort, where they hoped to find the horses they had left there, and to return with them to the main body.

The third party composed of four men was headed by Mr. M'Kenzie, who struck to the northward across the desert plains, in hopes of coming upon the main stream of the Columbia.

Having seen these three adventurous bands depart upon their forlorn expeditions, Mr. Hunt turned his thoughts to provide for the subsistence of the main body left to his charge, and to prepare for their future march. There remained with him thirty one men, beside the squaw and two children of Pierre Dorion. There was no game to be met with in the neighborhood, but beavers were occasionally trapped about the river banks, which afforded a scanty supply of food: in the mean time they comforted themselves that some one or other of the foraging detachments would be successful and return with relief.

Mr. Hunt now set to work, with all diligence, to prepare *caches* in which to deposite the baggage and merchandize, of which it would be necessary to disburthen themselves preparatory to their weary march by land; and here we shall give a brief description of those con-trivances, so noted in the wilderness.

A cache is a term common among traders and hunters to designate a hiding place for provisions and effects. It is derived from the French word *cacher*, to conceal, and originated among the early colonists of Canada and Louisiana; but the secret depository which it designates was in use among the aboriginals long before the intrusion of the white men. It is, in fact, the only mode that migratory hordes have of preserving their valuables from robbery during their long absences from their villages or accustomed haunts, on hunting expeditions, or during the vicissitudes of war. The utmost skill and caution are required to render these places of concealment invisible to the lynx eye of an Indian. The first care is to seek out a proper situation, which is generally some dry low bank of clay on the margin of a water course. As soon as the precise spot is pitched upon, blankets, saddle cloths, and other coverings are spread over the surrounding grass and bushes, to prevent foot tracks, or any other derangement; and as few hands as possible are employed. A circle of about two feet in diameter is then nicely cut in the sod, which is carefully removed, with the loose soil immediately beneath it, and laid aside in a place where it will be safe from any thing that may change its appearance. The un-covered area is then digged perpendicularly to the depth of about three feet, and is then gradually widened so as to form a conical chamber six or seven feet deep. The whole of the earth displaced by this process, being of a different colour from that on the surface, is handed up in a vessel, and heaped into a skin or cloth, in which it is conveyed to the stream and thrown into the midst of the current, that it may be entirely carried off. Should the cache not be formed in the vicinity of a stream, the earth thus thrown up is carried to a distance and scattered in such manner as not to leave the minutest trace. The cave being formed, is well lined with dry grass, bark, sticks and poles, and occasionally a dried hide. The property intended to be hidden is then laid in, after having been well aired: a hide is spread over it, and dry grass, bark, brush and stones thrown in and trampled

down until the pit is filled to the neck. The loose soil which had
been put aside is then brought and rammed down firmly to prevent
its caving in, and is frequently sprinkled with water to destroy the
scent, lest the wolves and bears should be attracted to the place, and
root up the concealed treasure. When the neck of the cache is nearly
level with the surrounding surface, the sod is again fitted in with
the utmost exactness and any bushes, stocks or stones that may have
originally been about the spot, are restored to their former places.
The blankets and other coverings are then removed from the surrounding herbage; all tracks are obliterated; the grass is gently raised
by the hand to its natural position, and the minutest chip or straw is
scrupulously gleaned up and thrown into the stream. After all is done
the place is abandoned for the night, and, if all be right next morning,
is not visited again, until there be a necessity for re opening the cache.
Four men are sufficient in this way, to conceal the amount of three
tons weight of merchandize in the course of two days. Nine caches
were required to contain the goods and baggage which Mr. Hunt found
it necessary to leave at this place.

Three days had been thus employed since the departure of the
several detachments when that of Mr. Crooks unexpectedly made its
appearance. A momentary joy was diffused through the camp, for
they supposed succor to be at hand. It was soon dispelled. Mr. Crooks
and his companions had become completely disheartened by their
retrograde march through a bleak and barren country: and had found,
computing from their progress and the accumulating difficulties besetting every step, that it would be impossible to reach Henry's fort
and return to the main body in the course of the winter. They had
determined, therefore, to rejoin their comrades, and share their lot.

One avenue of hope was thus closed upon the anxious sojourners
at the Caldron Linn; their main expectation of relief was now from
the two parties under Reed and M'Lellan, which had proceeded down
the river; for, as to Mr. M'Kenzie's detachment, which had struck
across the plains, they thought it would have sufficient difficulty in
struggling forward through the trackless wilderness. For five days
they continued to support themselves by trapping and fishing. Some
fish of tolerable size were speared at night by the light of cedar
torches; others that were very small, were caught in nets with fine
meshes. The product of their fishing, however, was very scanty. Their
trapping was also precarious; and the tails and bellies of the beavers
were dried and put by for the journey.

At length two of the companions of Mr. Reed returned, and were
hailed with the most anxious eagerness. Their report served but to
encrease the general despondency. They had followed Mr. Reed for

some distance below the point to which Mr. Hunt had explored, but had met with no Indians from whom to obtain information and relief. The river still presented the same furious aspect, brawling and boiling along a narrow and rugged channel, between rocks that rose like walls.

A lingering hope which had been indulged by some of the party, of proceeding by water, was now finally given up. The long and terrific strait of the river set all further progress at defiance, and in their disgust at the place and their vexation at the disasters sustained there, they gave it the indignant though not very decorous appellation of The Devil's Scuttle Hole.

CHAPTER XXXIV

*Determination of the party to proceed on foot—Dreary deserts between
Snake River and the Columbia—Distribution of effects preparatory
to a march—Division of the party—Rugged march along the river—
Wild and broken scenery—Shoshonies—Alarm of a Snake encampment
—Intercourse with the Snakes—Horse dealing—Value of a tin kettle—
Sufferings from thirst—A horse reclaimed—Fortitude of an Indian
woman—Scarcity of food—Dog's flesh a dainty—News of Mr. Crooks
and his party—Painful travelling among the mountains—Snow storms
—A dreary mountain prospect—A bivouack during a wintry night—
Return to the river bank.*

The resolution of Mr. Hunt and his companions was now taken to
set out immediately on foot. As to the other detachments that had
in a manner gone forth to seek their fortunes, there was little chance
of their return; they would probably make their own way through
the wilderness. At any rate, to linger in the vague hope of relief from
them would be to run the risk of perishing with hunger. Beside, the
winter was rapidly advancing and they had a long journey to make
through an unknown country, where all kinds of perils might await
them. They were yet, in fact, a thousand miles from Astoria, but the
distance was unknown to them at the time: every thing before and
around them was vague and conjectural and wore an aspect calculated
to inspire despondency.

In abandoning the river they would have to launch forth upon vast
trackless plains destitute of all means of subsistence, where they might
perish of hunger and thirst. A dreary desert of sand and gravel extends
from Snake River almost to the Columbia. Here and there is a thin
and scanty herbage, insufficient for the pasturage of horse or buffalo.
Indeed these treeless wastes between the Rocky Mountains and the
Pacific, are even more desolate and barren than the naked, upper
prairies on the Atlantic side; they present vast desert tracts that
must ever defy cultivation, and interpose dreary and thirsty wilds
between the habitations of man, in traversing which the wanderer
will often be in danger of perishing.

Seeing the hopeless character of these wastes, Mr. Hunt and his
companions determined to keep along the course of the river, where
they would always have water at hand, and would be able occasionally
to procure fish and beaver, and might perchance meet with Indians,
from whom they could obtain provisions.

They now made their final preparations for the march. All their
remaining stock of provisions consisted of forty pounds of Indian

corn, twenty pounds of grease, about five pounds of portable soup, and a sufficient quantity of dried meat to allow each man a pittance of five pounds and a quarter, to be reserved for emergencies. This being properly distributed, they deposited all their goods and super-fluous articles in the caches, taking nothing with them but what was indispensible to the journey. With all their management, each man had to carry twenty pounds weight beside his own articles and equipments.

That they might have the better chance of procuring subsistence in the scanty regions they were to traverse they divided their party into two bands, Mr. Hunt, with eighteen men, beside Pierre Dorion and his family, was to proceed down the north side of the river, while Mr. Crooks with eighteen men kept along the south side.

On the morning of the 9th of November the two parties separated and set forth on their several courses. Mr. Hunt and his companions followed along the right bank of the river, which made its way far below them, brawling at the foot of perpendicular precipices of solid rock two and three hundred feet high. For twenty eight miles that they travelled this day they found it impossible to get down to the margin of the stream. At the end of this distance they encamped for the night at a place which admitted a scrambling descent. It was with the greatest difficulty, however, that they succeeded in getting up a kettle of water from the river for the use of the camp. As some rain had fallen in the afternoon they passed the night under the shelter of the rocks.

The next day they continued thirty two miles to the north west, keeping along the river, which still ran in its deep cut channel. Here and there a sandy beach or a narrow strip of soil, fringed with dwarf willows, would extend for a little distance along the foot of the cliffs, and sometimes a reach of still water would intervene like a smooth mirror between the foaming rapids. As through the preceding day, they journeyed on without finding, except in one instance, any place where they could get down to the river's edge, and they were fain to allay the thirst caused by hard travelling, with the water collected in the hollows of the rocks.

In the course of their march on the following morning they fell into a beaten horse path leading along the river, which shewed that they were in the neighborhood of some Indian village or encampment. They had not proceeded far along it when they met with two Shoshonies, or Snakes. They approached with some appearance of uneasiness, and accosting Mr. Hunt held up a knife, which by signs they let him know they had received from some of the white men of the advance parties. It was with some difficulty that Mr. Hunt prevailed upon one of the savages to conduct him to the lodges of his people. Striking into a trail or path which led up from the river he guided them for some distance into the prairie, until they came in sight of a number of lodges made of straw and shaped like hay stacks.

Their approach, as on former occasions, caused the wildest affright among the inhabitants. The women hid such of their children as were too large to be carried and too small to take care of themselves, under straw, and, clasping their infants to their breasts, fled across the prairie. The men awaited the approach of the strangers, but evidently in great alarm.

Mr. Hunt entered the lodges and, as he was looking about, observed where the children were concealed; their black eyes glistening like those of snakes from beneath the straw. He lifted up the covering to look at them: the poor little beings were horribly frightened, and their fathers stood trembling as if a beast of prey were about to pounce upon the brood.

The friendly manner of Mr. Hunt soon dispelled these apprehensions: he succeeded in purchasing some excellent dried salmon and a dog, an animal much esteemed as food, by the natives, and when he returned to the river one of the Indians accompanied him. He now came to where lodges were frequent along the banks, and, after a day's journey of twenty six miles to the north west, encamped in a populous neighborhood. Forty or fifty of the natives soon visited the camp, conducting themselves in a very amicable manner. They were well clad, and all had buffalo robes, which they procured from some of the hunting tribes in exchange for salmon. Their habitations were very comfortable; each had its pile of worm wood at the door for fuel, and within was abundance of salmon, some fresh, but the greater part cured. When the white men visited the lodges, however, the women and children hid themselves through fear. Among the supplies obtained here were two dogs on which our travellers breakfasted and found them to be very excellent, well flavored and hearty food.

In the course of the three following days they made about sixty three miles, generally in a north west direction. They met with many of the natives in their straw built cabins, who received them without alarm. About their dwellings were immense quantities of the heads and skins of salmon, the best parts of which had been cured, and hidden in the ground. The women were badly clad; the children worse; their garments were buffalo robes, or the skins of foxes, wolves, hares and badgers, and sometimes the skins of ducks, sewed together, with the plumage on. Most of the skins must have been procured by traffic with other tribes, or in distant hunting excursions, for the naked prairies in the neighborhood afforded few animals except hares, which were abundant. There were signs of buffalos having been there, but a long time before.

On the 15th of November they made twenty eight miles along the river which was entirely free from rapids. The shores were lined with dead salmon, which tainted the whole atmosphere. The natives whom they met spoke of Mr. Reed's party having passed through that neighborhood. In the course of the day Mr. Hunt saw a few horses, but the owners of them took care to hurry them out of the way. All the provisions they were able to procure were two dogs and a salmon. On the following day they were still worse off, having to subsist on parched corn and the remains of their dried meat. The river this day had resumed its turbulent character, forcing its way through a narrow channel between steep rocks, and down violent rapids. They made twenty miles over a rugged road, gradually approaching a mountain in the north west, covered with snow, which had been in sight for three days past.

On the 17th they met with several Indians, one of whom had a horse. Mr. Hunt was extremely desirous of obtaining it as a pack horse, for the men, worn down by fatigue and hunger, found the loads of twenty pound weight which they had to carry, daily growing heavier and more galling. The Indians, however, along this river were never willing to part with their horses, having none to spare. The owner of the steed in question seemed proof against all temptation; article after article of great value in Indian eyes was offered and refused. The charms of an old tin kettle, however, were irresistible, and a bargain was concluded.

A great part of the following morning was consumed in lightening the packages of the men and arranging the load for the horse. At this encampment there was no wood for fuel, even the wormwood on which they had frequently depended, having disappeared. For the two last days they had made thirty miles to the north west.

On the 19th of November, Mr. Hunt was lucky enough to purchase another horse for his own use, giving in exchange a tomahawk, a knife, a fire steel, and some beads and gartering. In an evil hour, however, he took the advice of the Indians to abandon the river and follow a road or trail, leading into the prairie. He soon had cause to repent the change. The road led across a dreary waste, without verdure; and where there was neither fountain, nor pool, nor running stream. The men now began to experience the torments of thirst, aggravated by their usual diet of dried fish. The thirst of some of the Canadian voyageurs became so insupportable as to drive them to the most revolting means of allaying it. For twenty five miles did they toil on across this dismal desert, and laid themselves down at night, parched and disconsolate beside their worm wood fires; looking forward to still greater sufferings on the following day. Fortunately it began to rain in the night to their infinite relief; the water soon collected in puddles and afforded them delicious draughts.

Refreshed in this manner they resumed their wayfaring as soon as the first streak of dawn gave light enough for them to see their path. The rain continued all day so that they no longer suffered from thirst, but hunger took its place, for after travelling thirty three miles they had nothing to sup on but a little parched corn.

The next day brought them to the banks of a beautiful little stream, running to the west and fringed with groves of cotton wood and willow. On its borders was an Indian camp with a great many horses grazing around it. The inhabitants too appeared to be better clad than usual. The scene was altogether a cheering one to the poor half famished wanderers. They hastened to the lodges but on arriving at them, met with a check that at first dampened their cheerfulness. An Indian immediately laid claim to the horse of Mr. Hunt, saying that it had been stolen from him. There was no disproving a fact, supported by numerous bystanders, and which the horse stealing habits of the Indians rendered but too probable; so Mr. Hunt relinquished his steed to the claimant; not being able to retain him by a second purchase.

At this place they encamped for the night and made a sumptuous repast upon fish and a couple of dogs, procured from their Indian neighbors. The next day they kept along the river, but came to a halt after ten miles march, on account of the rain. Here they again got a supply of fish and dogs from the natives; and two of the men were fortunate enough each to get a horse in exchange for a buffalo robe. One of these men was Pierre Dorion, the half breed interpreter, to whose suffering family the horse was a most timely acquisition. And here we cannot but notice the wonderful patience, perseverance and hardihood of the Indian women, as exemplified in the conduct of the poor squaw of the interpreter. She was now far advanced in her pregnancy, and had two children to take care of; one four, and the other two years of age. The latter of course she had frequently to carry on her back, in addition to the burthen usually imposed upon the squaw, yet she had borne all her hardships without a murmur and throughout this weary and painful journey, had kept pace with the best of the pedestrians. Indeed on various occasions in the course of this enterprize, she displayed a force of character that won the respect and applause of the white men.

Mr. Hunt endeavored to gather some information from these Indians concerning the country, and the course of the rivers. His communications with them had to be by signs, and a few words which he had learnt, and of course were extremely vague. All that he could learn from them was, that the great river, the Columbia, was still far distant, but he could ascertain nothing as to the route he ought to take to arrive at it. For the two following days they continued westward upward of forty miles along the little stream, until they crossed it just before its junction with Snake River, which they found still running to the north. Before them was a wintry looking mountain covered with snow on all sides.

In three days more they made about seventy miles; fording two small rivers, the waters of which were very cold. Provisions were extremely scarce; their chief sustenance was portable soup; a meagre diet for weary pedestrians.

On the 27th of November the river led them into the mountains through a rocky defile where there was scarcely room to pass. They were frequently obliged to unload the horses to get them by the narrow places; and sometimes to wade through the water in getting round rocks and butting cliffs. All their food this day was a beaver which they had caught the night before; by evening, the cravings of hunger were so sharp, and the prospect of any supply among the mountains so faint, that they had to kill one of the horses. "The men," says Mr. Hunt, in his journal, "find the meat very good, and indeed, so should I, were it not for the attachment I have to the animal."

Early in the following day, after proceeding ten miles to the north, they came to two lodges of Shoshonies: who seemed in nearly as great an extremity as themselves, having just killed two horses for food. They had no other provisions excepting the seed of a weed which they gather in great quantities, and pound fine. It resembles hemp seed. Mr. Hunt purchased a bag of it and also some small pieces of horse flesh which he began to relish, pronouncing them "fat and tender."

From these Indians he received information that several white men had gone down the river, some one side, and a good many on the other; these last he concluded to be Mr. Crooks and his party. He was thus released from much anxiety about their safety, especially as the Indians spoke of Mr. Crooks having one of his dogs yet, which showed that he and his men had not been reduced to extremity of hunger.

As Mr. Hunt feared that he might be several days in passing through this mountain defile, and run the risk of famine, he encamped in the neighborhood of the Indians, for the purpose of bartering with them for a horse. The evening was expended in ineffectual trials. He offered a gun, a buffalo robe, and various other articles. The poor fellows had, probably, like himself, the fear of starvation before their eyes.

At length the women, learning the object of his pressing solicitations, and tempting offers, set up such a terrible hue and cry, that he was fairly howled and scolded from the ground.

The next morning early, the Indians seemed very desirous to get rid of their visitors, fearing, probably, for the safety of their horses. In reply to Mr. Hunt's enquiries about the mountains, they told him that he would have to sleep but three nights more among them; and that six days' travelling would take him to the falls of the Columbia; information in which he put no faith, believing it was only given to induce him to set forward. These, he was told, were the last Snakes he would meet with, and that he would soon come to a nation called Sciatogas.

Forward then did he proceed on his tedious journey, which, at every step grew more painful. The road continued for two days, through narrow defiles, where they were repeatedly obliged to unload the horses. Sometimes the river passed through such rocky chasms and under such steep precipices that they had to leave it, and make their way, with excessive labor, over immense hills, almost impassable for horses. On some of these hills were a few pine trees, and their summits were covered with snow. On the second day of this scramble one of the hunters killed a black tailed deer, which afforded the half-starved travellers a sumptuous repast. Their progress these two days was twenty eight miles, a little to the northward of east.

The month of December set in drearily, with rain in the valleys, and snow upon the hills. They had to climb a mountain with snow to the midleg, which increased their painful toil. A small beaver supplied them with a scanty meal, which they eked out with frozen blackberries, haws, and chokecherries, which they found in the course of their scramble. Their journey this day, though excessively fatiguing, was but thirteen miles; and all the next day they had to remain encamped, not being able to see half a mile ahead, on account of a snow storm. Having nothing else to eat, they were compelled to kill another of their horses. The next day they resumed their march in snow and rain, but with all their efforts could only get forward nine miles, having for a part of the distance to unload the horses and carry the packs themselves. On the succeeding morning they were obliged to leave the river, and scramble up the hills. From the summit of these, they got a wide view of the surrounding country, and it was a prospect almost sufficient to make them despair. In every direction they beheld snowy mountains, partially sprinkled with pines and other evergreens, and spreading a desert and toilsome world around them. The wind howled over the bleak and wintry landscape, and seemed to penetrate to the marrow of their bones. They waded on through the snow which at every step was more than knee deep.

After toiling in this way all day, they had the mortification to find that they were but four miles distant from the encampment of the preceding night, such was the meandering of the river among these dismal hills. Pinched with famine, exhausted with fatigue, with evening approaching, and a wintry wild still lengthening as they advanced; they began to look forward with sad forebodings to the night's exposure upon this frightful waste. Fortunately they succeeded in reaching a cluster of pines about sunset. Their axes were immediately at work; they cut down trees, piled them up in great heaps, and soon had huge fires "to cheer their cold and hungry hearts."

About three o'clock in the morning it again began to snow, and at daybreak they found themselves, as it were, in a cloud; scarcely being able to distinguish objects at the distance of a hundred yards. Guiding themselves by the sound of running water, they set out for the river, and by slipping and sliding contrived to get down to its bank. One of the horses, missing his footing, rolled down several hundred yards with his load, but sustained no injury. The weather in the valley was less rigorous than on the hills. The snow lay but ankle deep, and there was a quiet rain now falling. After creeping along for six miles, they encamped on the border of the river. Being utterly destitute of provisions, they were again compelled to kill one of their horses to appease their famishing hunger.

CHAPTER XXXV

An unexpected meeting—Navigation in a skin canoe—Strange fears
of suffering men—Hardships of Mr. Crooks and his comrades—Tidings
of M'Lellan—A retrograde march—A willow raft—Extreme suffering
of some of the party—Illness of Mr. Crooks—Impatience of some of
the men—Necessity of leaving the laggards behind.

The wanderers had now accomplished four hundred and seventy two
miles of their dreary journey since leaving the Caldron Linn, how
much further they had yet to travel, and what hardships to encounter, no one knew.

On the morning of the 6th of December, they left their dismal
encampment, but had scarcely begun their march, when, to their
surprise, they beheld a party of white men coming up along the
opposite bank of the river. As they drew nearer, they were recognised
for Mr. Crooks and his companions. When they came opposite, and
could make themselves heard across the murmuring of the river, their
first cry was for food; in fact, they were almost starved. Mr. Hunt
immediately returned to the camp, and had a kind of canoe made
out of the skin of the horse, killed on the preceding night. This was
done after the Indian fashion, by drawing up the edges of the skin
with thongs, and keeping them distended by sticks or thwarts pieces.
In this frail bark, Gardepie, one of the Canadians, carried over a
portion of the flesh of the horse to the famishing party on the opposite
side of the river, and brought back with him Mr. Crooks, and the
Canadian, Le Clerc. The forlorn and wasted looks, and starving condition of these two men, struck dismay to the hearts of Mr. Hunt's
followers. They had been accustomed to each other's appearance, and
to the gradual operation of hunger and hardship upon their frames,
but the change in the looks of these men, since last they parted, was
a type of the famine and desolation of the land; and they now began
to indulge the horrible presentiment that they would all starve together,
or be reduced to the direful alternative of casting lots!

When Mr. Crooks had appeased his hunger, he gave Mr. Hunt
some account of his wayfaring. On the side of the river, along which
he had kept, he had met with but few Indians, and those were too
miserably poor to yield much assistance. For the first eighteen days,
after leaving the Caldron Linn, he and his men had been confined
to half a meal in twenty four hours; for three days following, they
had subsisted on a single beaver, a few wild cherries, and the soles
of old moccasins, and for the last six days, their only animal food

had been the carcass of a dog. They had been three days' journey further down the river than Mr. Hunt, always keeping as near to its banks as possible, and frequently climbing over sharp and rocky ridges that projected into the stream. At length they had arrived to where the mountains increased in height, and came closer to the river, with perpendicular precipices, which rendered it impossible to keep along the stream. The river here rushed with incredible velocity through a defile not more than thirty yards wide, where cascades and rapids succeeded each other almost without intermission. Even had the opposite banks, therefore, been such as to permit a continuance of their journey, it would have been madness to attempt to pass the tumultuous current, either on rafts or otherwise. Still bent, however, on pushing forward, they attempted to climb the opposing mountains; and struggled on through the snow for half a day until, coming to where they could command a prospect, they found that they were not half way to the summit, and that mountain upon mountain lay piled beyond them, in wintry desolation. Famished and emaciated as they were, to continue forward would be to perish; their only chance seemed to be to regain the river, and retrace their steps up its banks. It was in this forlorn and retrograde march that they had met Mr. Hunt and his party.

Mr. Crooks also gave information of some others of their fellow adventurers. He had spoken several days previously with Mr. Reed and Mr. M'Kenzie, who with their men were on the opposite side of the river, where it was impossible to get over to them. They informed him that Mr. M'Lellan had struck across from the little river above the mountains, in the hope of falling in with some of the tribe of Flatheads, who inhabit the western skirts of the Rocky range. As the companions of Reed and M'Kenzie were picked men, and had found provisions more abundant on their side of the river, they were in better condition, and more fitted to contend with the difficulties of the country, than those of Mr. Crooks, and when he lost sight of them, were pushing onward, down the course of the river.

Mr. Hunt took a night to revolve over his critical situation, and to determine what was to be done. No time was to be lost; he had twenty men and more, in his own party, to provide for, and Mr. Crooks and his men to relieve. To linger would be to starve. The idea of retracing his steps was intolerable, and, notwithstanding all the discouraging accounts of the ruggedness of the mountains lower down the river, he would have been disposed to attempt them, but the depth of the snow with which they were covered, deterred him; having already experienced the impossibility of forcing his way against such an impediment.

The only alternative, therefore, appeared to be, to return and seek the Indian bands scattered along the small rivers above the mountains.

Perhaps, from some of these he might procure horses enough to support him until he could reach the Columbia; for he still cherished the hope of arriving at that river in the course of the winter, though he was apprehensive that few of Mr. Crooks' party would be sufficiently strong to follow him. Even in adopting this course, he had to make up his mind to the certainty of several days of famine at the outset, for it would take that time to reach the last Indian lodges from which he had parted, and until they should arrive there, his people would have nothing to subsist upon but haws and wild berries, excepting one miserable horse, which was little better than skin and bone.

After a night of sleepless cogitation, Mr. Hunt announced to his men the dreary alternative he had adopted, and preparations were made to take Mr. Crooks and Le Clerc accross the river, with the remainder of the meat, as the other party were to keep up along the opposite bank. The skin canoe had unfortunately been lost in the night; a raft was constructed, therefore, after the manner of the natives, of bundles of willows, but it could not be floated across the impetuous current. The men were directed, in consequence, to keep on along the river by themselves, while Mr. Crooks and Le Clerc would proceed with Mr. Hunt. They all, then, took up their retograde march with drooping spirits.

In a little while, it was found that Mr. Crooks and Le Clerc were so feeble as to walk with difficulty, so that Mr. Hunt was obliged to retard his pace, that they might keep up with him. His men grew impatient at the delay. They murmured that they had a long and desolate region to traverse, before they could arrive at the point where they might expect to find horses; that it was impossible for Crooks and Le Clerc, in their feeble condition, to get over it; that to remain with them would only be to starve in their company. They importuned Mr. Hunt, therefore, to leave these unfortunate men to their fate, and think only of the safety of himself and his party. Finding him not to be moved, either by entreaties or their clamors, they began to proceed without him, singly and in parties. Among those who thus went off was Pierre Dorion, the interpreter. Pierre owned the only remaining horse; which was now a mere skeleton. Mr. Hunt had suggested, in their present extremity, that it should be killed for food; to which the half breed flatly refused his assent, and cudgelling the miserable animal forward, pushed on sullenly, with the air of a man doggedly determined to quarrel for his right. In this way Mr. Hunt saw his men, one after another, break away, until but five remained to bear him company.

On the following morning, another raft was made, on which Mr. Crooks and Le Clerc again attempted to ferry themselves across the river, but after repeated trials, had to give up in despair. This caused additional delay: after which, they continued to crawl forward at a snail's pace. Some of the men who had remained with Mr. Hunt now became impatient of these incumbrances, and urged him, clamorously, to push forward, crying out that they should all starve. The night which succeeded was intensely cold, so that one of the men was severely frost-bitten. In the course of the night, Mr. Crooks was taken ill, and in the morning was still more incompetent to travel. Their situation was now desperate, for their stock of provisions was reduced to three beaver skins. Mr. Hunt, therefore, resolved to push on, overtake his people, and insist upon having the horse of Pierre Dorion sacrificed for the relief of all hands. Accordingly, he left two of his men to help Crooks and Le Clerc on their way, giving them two of the beaver skins for their support; the remaining skin he retained, as provision for himself and the three other men who struck forward with him.

CHAPTER XXXVI

Mr. Hunt overtakes the advanced party—Pierre Dorion, and his skeleton horse—A Shoshonie camp—A justifiable outrage—Feasting on horse flesh—Mr. Crooks brought to the camp—Undertakes to relieve his men—The skin ferry boat—Frenzy of Prevost—His melancholy fate—Enfeebled state of John Day—Mr. Crooks again left behind—The party emerge from among the mountains—Interview with Shoshonies—A guide procured to conduct the party across a mountain—Ferriage across Snake River—Reunion with Mr. Crooks' men—Final departure from the river.

All that day, Mr. Hunt and his three comrades travelled without eating. At night they made a tantalizing supper on their beaver skin, and were nearly exhausted by hunger and cold. The next day, December 10th, they overtook the advance party, who were all as much famished as themselves, some of them not having eaten since the morning of the seventh. Mr. Hunt now proposed the sacrifice of Pierre Dorion's skeleton horse. Here he again met with positive and vehement opposition from the half breed, who was too sullen and vindictive a fellow to be easily dealt with. What was singular, the men, though suffering such pinching hunger, interfered in favor of the horse. They represented, that it was better to keep on as long as possible without resorting to this last resource. Possibly the Indians, of whom they were in quest, might have shifted their encampment, in which case it would be time enough to kill the horse to escape starvation. Mr. Hunt, therefore, was prevailed upon to grant Pierre Dorion's horse a reprieve.

Fortunately they had not proceeded much further when, towards evening, they came in sight of a lodge of Shoshonies, with a number of horses grazing around it. The sight was as unexpected as it was joyous. Having seen no Indians in this neighborhood as they passed down the river, they must have subsequently come out from among the mountains.

Mr. Hunt, who first descried them, checked the eagerness of his companions, knowing the unwillingness of these Indians to part with their horses, and their aptness to hurry them off and conceal them in case of an alarm. This was no time to risk such a disappointment. Approaching, therefore, stealthily and silently, they came upon the savages by surprize, who fled in terror. Five of their horses were eagerly seized and one was despatched upon the spot. The carcass was immediately cut up and a part of it hastily cooked and ravenously devoured.

A man was now sent on horseback with a supply of the flesh to Mr. Crooks and his companions. He reached them in the night: they were so famished that the supply sent them seemed but to aggravate their

216

hunger, and they were almost tempted to kill and eat the horse that had brought the messenger. Availing themselves of the assistance of the animal they reached the camp early in the morning.

On arriving there Mr. Crooks was shocked to find that, while the people on this side of the river were amply supplied with provisions, none had been sent to his own forlorn and famishing men on the opposite bank. He immediately caused a skin canoe to be constructed, and called out to his men to fill their camp kettles with water and hang them over the fire, that no time might be lost in cooking the meat the moment it should be received. The river was so narrow, though deep, that every thing could be distinctly heard and seen across it. The kettles were placed over the fire, and the water was boiling by the time the canoe was completed. When all was ready, however, no one would undertake to ferry the meat across. A vague and almost superstitious terror had infected the minds of Mr. Hunt's followers, enfeebled and rendered imaginative of horrors by the dismal scenes and sufferings through which they had passed. They regarded the haggard crew, hovering like spectres of famine on the opposite bank, with indefinite feelings of awe and apprehension, as if something desperate and danger-ous was to be feared from them.

Mr. Crooks tried in vain to reason or shame them out of this singular state of mind. He then attempted to navigate the canoe himself, but found his strength incompetent to brave the impetuous current. The good feelings of Ben Jones the Kentuckian at length overcame his fears and he ventured over. The supply he brought was received with trem-bling avidity. A poor Canadian, however, named Jean Baptiste Prevost, whom famine had rendered wild and desperate, ran frantically about the bank, after Jones had returned, crying out to Mr. Hunt to send the canoe for him and take him from that horrible region of famine declaring that otherwise he would never march another step, but would lie down there and die.

The canoe was shortly sent over again under the management of Joseph Delaunay, with further supplies. Prevost immediately pressed forward to embark. Delaunay refused to admit him, telling him that there was now a sufficient supply of meat on his side of the river. He replied that it was not cooked and he should starve before it was ready; he implored therefore to be taken where he could get something to appease his hunger immediately. Finding the canoe putting off without him, he forced himself aboard. As he drew near the opposite shore and beheld meat roasting before the fires, he jumped up, shouted, clapped his hands and danced in a delirium of joy, until he upset the canoe. The poor wretch was swept away by the current and drowned, and it was with extreme difficulty that Delaunay reached the shore.

Mr. Hunt now sent all his men forward excepting two or three. In the evening he caused another horse to be killed and a canoe to be made out of the skin, in which he sent over a further supply of meat to the opposite party. The canoe brought back John Day, the Kentucky hunter, who came to join his former employer and commander, Mr. Crooks. Poor Day, once so active and vigorous, was now reduced to a condition even more feeble and emaciated than his companions. Mr. Crooks had such a value for the man, on account of his past services and faithful character, that he determined not to quit him; he exhorted Mr. Hunt, however, to proceed forward and join the party, as his presence was all important to the conduct of the expedition. One of the Canadians, Jean Baptiste Dubreuil, likewise remained with Mr. Crooks.

Mr. Hunt left two horses with them, and a part of the carcass of the last that had been killed. This, he hoped, would be sufficient to sustain them until they should reach the Indian encampment.

One of the chief dangers attending the enfeebled condition of Mr. Crooks and his companions was their being overtaken by the Indians whose horses had been seized: though Mr. Hunt hoped that he had guarded against any resentment on the part of the savages, by leaving various articles in their lodge, more than sufficient to compensate for the outrage he had been compelled to commit.

Resuming his onward course Mr. Hunt came up with his people in the evening. The next day (December 13th) he beheld several Indians, with three horses, on the opposite side of the river, and after a time came to the two lodges which he had seen on going down. Here he endeavored in vain to barter a rifle for a horse, but again succeeded in effecting the purchase with an old tin kettle aided by a few beads.

The two succeeding days were cold and stormy; the snow was augmenting, and there was a good deal of ice running in the river. Their road, however, was becoming easier; they were getting out of the hills and finally emerged into the open country after twenty days of fatigue, famine, and hardship of every kind, in the ineffectual attempt to find a passage down the river.

They now encamped on a little willowed stream running from the east, which they had crossed on the 26th of November. Here they found a dozen lodges of Shoshonies, recently arrived, who informed them that had they persevered along the river they would have found their difficulties augment until they became absolutely insurmountable. This intelligence added to the anxiety of Mr. Hunt for the fate of Mr. M'Kenzie and his people who had kept on.

Mr. Hunt now followed up the little river and encamped at some lodges of Shoshonies from whom he procured a couple of horses, a dog, a few dried fish, and some roots and dried cherries. Two or three days were exhausted in obtaining information about the route, and what time it would take to get to the Sciatogas, a hospitable tribe, on the west side of the mountains, represented as having many horses. The replies were various, but concurred in saying that the distance was great, and would occupy from seventeen to twenty one nights. Mr. Hunt then tried to procure a guide; but though he sent to various lodges up and down the river, offering articles of great value in Indian estimation, no one would venture. The snow they said was waist deep in the mountains; and to all his offers they shook their heads, gave a shiver and replied "we shall freeze! we shall freeze!" At the same time they urged him to remain and pass the winter among them.

Mr. Hunt was in a dismal dilemma. To attempt the mountains without a guide would be certain death to him and all his people; to remain there, after having already been so long on the journey and at such great expense was worse to him he said than "two deaths." He now changed his tone with the Indians, charged them with deceiving him in respect to the mountains and talking with a "forked tongue," or, in other words, with lying. He upbraided them with their want of courage and told them they were women to shrink from the perils of such a journey. At length one of them, piqued by his taunts or tempted by his offers, agreed to be his guide; for which he was to receive a gun, a pistol, three knives, two horses, and a little of every article in possession of the party; a reward sufficient to make him one of the wealthiest of his vagabond nation.

Once more then, on the twenty first of December, they set out upon their wayfaring, with newly excited spirits. Two other Indians accompanied their guide who led them immediately back to Snake River, which they followed down for a short distance, in search of some Indian rafts made of reeds, on which they might cross. Finding none, Mr. Hunt caused a horse to be killed and a canoe to be made out of its skin. Here, on the opposite bank, they saw the thirteen men of Mr. Crooks' party; who had continued up along the river. They told Mr. Hunt, across the stream, that they had not seen Mr. Crooks and the two men who had remained with him since the day that he had separated from them.

The canoe proving too small another horse was killed, and the skin of it joined to that of the first. Night came on before the little bark had made more than two voyages. Being badly made it was taken apart and put together again by the light of the fire. The night was cold; the men were weary and disheartened with such varied and incessant toil and hardship. They crouched dull and drooping around their fires; many of them began to express a wish to remain where they were for the winter. The very necessity of crossing the river dismayed some of them in their present enfeebled and dejected state. It was rapid and turbulent and filled with floating ice, and they remembered that two of their comrades had already perished in its waters. Others looked forward with misgivings to the long and dismal journey through unknown regions that awaited them, when they should have passed this dreary flood.

At an early hour of the morning (December 23d) they began to cross the river. Much ice had formed during the night and they were obliged to break it for some distance on each shore. At length they all got over in safety to the west side; and their spirits rose on having achieved this perilous passage. Here they were rejoined by the people of Mr. Crooks, who had with them a horse and a dog which they had recently procured. The poor fellows were in the most squalid and emaciated state. Three of them were so completely prostrated in strength and spirits that they expressed a wish to remain among the Snakes. Mr. Hunt, therefore, gave them the canoe, that they might cross the river, and a few articles, with which to procure necessaries until they should meet with Mr. Crooks. There was another man, named Michel Carriere, who was almost equally reduced but he determined to proceed with his comrades, who were now incorporated with the party of Mr. Hunt. After the day's exertions they encamped together on the banks of the river. This was the last night they were to spend upon its borders. More than eight hundred miles of hard travelling and many weary days had it cost them; and the sufferings connected with it rendered it hateful in their remembrance so that the Canadian voyageurs always spoke of it as "La maudite riviere enragée"—the accursed Mad River: thus coupling a malediction with its name.

CHAPTER XXXVII

Departure from Snake River—Mountains to the north—Wayworn travellers—An increase of the Dorion family—A camp of Shoshonies —A New Year festival among the Snakes—A wintry march through the mountains—A sunny prospect, and milder climate—Indian horse tracks—Grassy valleys—A camp of Sciatogas—Joy of the travellers— Dangers of abundance—Habits of the Sciatogas—Fate of Carriere— The Umatalla—Arrival at the banks of the Columbia—Tidings of the scattered members of the expedition—Scenery on the Columbia— Tidings of Astoria—Arrival at the falls.

On the 24th of December, all things being arranged, Mr. Hunt turned his back upon the disastrous banks of Snake River, and struck his course westward for the mountains. His party, being augmented by the late followers of Mr. Crooks, amounted now to thirty two white men, three Indians, and the squaw and two children of Pierre Dorion. Five jaded, half starved horses were laden with their baggage, and, in case of need, were to furnish them with provisions. They travelled painfully about fourteen miles a day, over plains and among hills, rendered dreary by occasional falls of snow and rain. Their only sustenance was a scanty meal of horse flesh once in four and twenty hours.

On the third day the poor Canadian, Carriere, one of the famished party of Mr. Crooks, gave up in despair, and, lying down upon the ground declared he could go no further. Efforts were made to cheer him up, but it was found that the poor fellow was absolutely exhausted and could not keep on his legs. He was mounted, therefore, upon one of the horses, though the forlorn animal was in little better plight than himself.

On the 28th they came upon a small stream winding to the north, through a fine level valley; the mountains receding on each side. Here their Indian friends pointed out a chain of woody mountains to the left, running north and south and covered with snow; over which they would have to pass.

They kept along this valley for twenty one miles on the 29th, suffering much from a continual fall of snow and rain and being twice obliged to ford the icy stream.

Early in the following morning the squaw of Pierre Dorion, who had hitherto kept on without murmuring or flinching, was suddenly taken in labour, and enriched her husband with another child. As the fortitude and good conduct of the poor woman had gained for her the good will of the party, her situation caused concern and perplexity. Pierre, however, treated the matter as an occurrence that could soon be arranged and need cause no delay. He remained by his wife in the camp, with his other children and his horse, and promised soon to rejoin the main body, who proceeded on their march.

Finding that the little river entered the mountains, they abandoned it and turned off for a few miles among hills. Here another Canadian, named La Bonté, gave out, and had to be helped on horseback. As the horse was too weak to bear both him and his pack, Mr. Hunt took the latter upon his own shoulders. Thus, with difficulties augmenting at every step, they urged their toilsome way among the hills half famished, and faint at heart, when they came to where a fair valley spread out before them of great extent, and several leagues in width, with a beautiful stream meandering through it. A genial climate seemed to prevail here, for though the snow lay upon all the mountains within sight, there was none to be seen in the valley. The travellers gazed with delight upon this serene sunny landscape, but their joy was complete on beholding six lodges of Shoshonies pitched upon the borders of the stream, with a number of horses and dogs about them. They all pressed forward with eagerness and soon reached the camp. Here their first attention was to obtain provisions. A rifle, an old musket, a tomahawk, a tin kettle and a small quantity of ammunition soon procured them four horses, three dogs and some roots. Part of the live stock was immediately killed, cooked with all expedition and as promptly devoured. A hearty meal restored every one to good spirits.

In the course of the following morning the Dorion family made its re appearance. Pierre came trudging in the advance, followed by his valued, though skeleton steed, on which was mounted his squaw with the new born infant in her arms and her boy of two years old wrapped in a blanket and slung at her side. The mother looked as unconcerned as if nothing had happened to her; so easy is nature in her operations in the wilderness, when free from the enfeebling refinements of luxury and the tamperings and appliances of art.

The next morning ushered in the New Year. (1812) Mr. Hunt was about to resume his march when his men requested permission to celebrate the day. This was particularly urged by the Canadian voyageurs, with whom New Year's day is a favorite festival; and who never willingly give up a holyday, under any circumstances. There was no resisting such an application; so the day was passed in repose and revelry; the poor Canadians contrived to sing and dance in defiance of all their hardships; and there was a sumptuous New Year's banquet of dog's meat and horse flesh.

After two days of welcome rest, the travellers addressed themselves once more to their painful journey. The Indians of the lodges pointed out a distant gap through which they must pass in traversing the ridge of mountains. They assured them that they would be but little incommoded by snow, and in three days would arrive among the Sciatogas. Mr. Hunt, however, had been so frequently deceived by Indian accounts of routes and distances that he gave but little faith to this information.

The travellers continued their course due west for five days, crossing the valley and entering the mountains. Here the travelling became excessively toilsome across rough stony ridges, and amidst fallen trees. They were often knee deep in snow, and sometimes in the hollows between the ridges sank up to their waists. The weather was extremely cold; the sky covered with clouds so that for four days they had not a glimpse of the sun. In traversing the highest ridge they had a wide but chilling prospect over a wilderness of snowy mountains.

On the sixth of January, however, they had crossed the dividing summit of the chain and were evidently under the influence of a milder climate. The snow began to decrease; the sun once more emerged from the thick canopy of clouds, and shone cheeringly upon them, and they caught a sight of what appeared to be a plain stretching out in the west. They hailed it as the poor Israelites hailed the first glimpse of the promised land, for they flattered themselves that this might be the great plain of the Columbia, and that their painful pilgrimage might be drawing to a close.

It was now five days since they had left the lodges of the Shoshonies during which they had come about sixty miles, and their guide assured them that in the course of the next day they would see the Sciatogas.

On the following morning, therefore, they pushed forward, with eagerness, and soon fell upon a small stream which led them through a deep narrow defile, between stupendous ridges. Here among the rocks and precipices they saw gangs of that mountain loving animal the black tailed deer, and came to where great tracks of horses were to be seen in all directions, made by the Indian hunters.

The snow had entirely disappeared, and the hopes of soon coming upon some Indian encampment induced Mr. Hunt to press on. Many of the men, however, were so enfeebled that they could not keep up with the main body, but lagged at intervals behind; and some of them did not arrive at the night's encampment. In the course of this day's march the recently born child of Pierre Dorion died.

The march was resumed early the next morning, without waiting for the stragglers. The stream which they had followed throughout the preceding day was now swollen by the influx of another river; the declivities of the hills were green and the valleys were clothed with grass. At length the joyful cry was given of "an Indian camp!" It was yet in the distance, in the bosom of the green valley, but they could perceive that it consisted of numerous lodges, and that hundreds of horses were grazing the grassy meadows around it. The prospect of abundance of horse flesh diffused universal joy, for by this time the whole stock of travelling provisions was reduced to the skeleton steed of Pierre Dorion, and another wretched animal, equally emaciated, that had been repeatedly reprieved during the journey.

A forced march soon brought the weary and hungry travellers to the camp. It proved to be a strong party of Sciatogas and Tus-che-pas. There were thirty four lodges comfortably constructed of mats. The Indians too were better clothed than any of the wandering bands they had hitherto met on this side of the Rocky Mountains. Indeed they were as well clad as the generality of the wild hunter tribes. Each had a good buffalo or deer skin robe; and a deer skin hunting shirt and leggings. Upwards of two thousand horses were ranging the pastures around their encampment; but what delighted Mr. Hunt was, on entering the lodges, to behold brass kettles, axes, copper tea kettles, and various other articles of civilized manufacture, which shewed that these Indians had an indirect communication with the people of the sea coast who traded with the whites. He made eager enquiries of the Sciatogas and gathered from them that the Great River (the Columbia) was but two days' march distant, and that several white people had recently descended it; who he hoped might prove to be M'Lellan, M'Kenzie and their companions.

It was with the utmost joy and the most profound gratitude to heaven that Mr. Hunt found himself and his band of weary and famishing wanderers, thus safely extricated from the most perilous part of their long journey, and within the prospect of a termination of their toils. All the stragglers who had lagged behind arrived one after another, excepting the poor Canadian voyageur Carriere. He had been seen late in the preceding afternoon riding behind a Snake Indian, near some lodges of that nation a few miles distant from the last night's encampment; and it was expected that he would soon make his appearance.

The first object of Mr. Hunt was to obtain provisions for his men. A little venison of an indifferent quality and some roots were all that could be procured that evening; but the next day, he succeeded in purchasing a mare and colt, which were immediately killed, and the cravings of the half starved people in some degree appeased.

For several days they remained in the neighborhood of these Indians, reposing after all their hardships, and feasting upon horseflesh and roots, obtained in subsequent traffic. Many of the people ate to such excess as to render themselves sick, others were lame from their past journey; but all gradually recruited in the repose and abundance of the valley. Horses were obtained here much more readily, and at a cheaper rate, than among the Snakes. A blanket, a knife, or a half pound of blue beads, would purchase a steed, and at this rate many of the men bought horses for their individual use.

This tribe of Indians, who are represented as a proud spirited race and uncommonly cleanly, never eat horses or dogs, nor would they permit the raw flesh of either to be brought into their huts. They had a small quantity of venison in each lodge, but set so high a price upon it that the white men, in their impoverished state, could not afford to purchase it. They hunted the deer on horseback; "ringing" or surrounding them, and running them down in a circle. They were admirable horsemen, and their weapons were bows and arrows, which they managed with great dexterity. They were altogether primitive in their habits, and seemed to cling to the usages of savage life even when possessed of the aids of civilization. They had axes among them, yet they generally made use of a stone mallet wrought into the shape of a bottle, and wedges of elk horn, in splitting their wood. Though they might have two or three brass kettles hanging in their lodges yet they would frequently use vessels made of willow, for carrying water, and would even boil their meat in them, by means of hot stones. Their women wore caps of willow neatly worked and figured.

As Carriere, the Canadian straggler, did not make his appearance for two or three days after the encampment in the valley, two men were sent out on horseback in search of him. They returned, however, without success. The lodges of the Snake Indians near which he had been seen were removed, and they could find no trace of him. Several days more elapsed, yet nothing was seen or heard of him, or of the Snake horseman behind whom he had been last observed. It was feared, therefore, that he had either perished through hunger and fatigue; had been murdered by the Indians, or, being left to himself, had mistaken some hunting tracks for the trail of the party and been led astray and lost.

The river on the banks of which they were encamped emptied into the Columbia, was called by the natives the Eu-o-tal-la, or Umatalla, and abounded with beaver. In the course of their sojourn in the valley which it watered, they twice shifted their camp, proceeding about thirty miles down its course, which was to the west. A heavy fall of rain caused the river to overflow its banks, dislodged them from their encampment, and drowned three of their horses, which were tethered in the low ground.

Further conversation with the Indians satisfied them that they were in the neighborhood of the Columbia. The number of the white men who they said had passed down the river, agreed with that of M'Lellan,

M'Kenzie and their companions, and encreased the hope of Mr. Hunt that they might have passed through the wilderness with safety.

These Indians had a vague story that white men were coming to trade among them; and they often spoke of two great men named Ke-koosh and Jacquean, who gave them tobacco and smoked with them. Jacquean they said had a house somewhere upon the Great River. Some of the Canadians supposed they were speaking of one Jacquean Finlay, a clerk of the North West Company, and inferred that the house must be some trading post on one of the tributary streams of the Columbia.

The Indians were overjoyed when they found this band of white men intended to return and trade with them. They promised to use all diligence in collecting quantities of beaver skins, and no doubt proceeded to make deadly war upon that sagacious, but ill fated animal, who, in general, lived in peaceful insignificance among his Indian neighbors, before the intrusion of the white trader. On the 20th of January Mr. Hunt took leave of these friendly Indians and of the river on which they were encamped and continued westward.

At length, on the following day, the way worn travellers lifted up their eyes and beheld before them the long sought waters of the Columbia. The sight was hailed with as much transport as if they had already reached the end of their pilgrimage: nor can we wonder at their joy. Two hundred and forty miles had they marched, through wintry wastes and rugged mountains, since leaving Snake River; and six months of perilous wayfaring had they experienced since their departure from the Arickara village on the Missouri. Their whole route by land and water from that point had been, according to their computation, seventeen hundred and fifty one miles, in the course of which they had endured all kinds of hardships. In fact the necessity of avoiding the dangerous country of the Blackfeet had obliged them to make a great bend to the south and to traverse a great additional extent of unknown wilderness.

The place where they struck the Columbia was some distance below the junction of its two great branches, Lewis, and Clarke rivers, and not far from the influx of the Wallah Wallah. It was here a beautiful stream, three quarters of a mile wide, totally free from trees; bordered in some places with steep rocks, in others with pebbled shores.

On the banks of the Columbia they found a miserable horde of Indians called Akai-chies, with no clothing but a scanty mantle of the skins of animals, and sometimes a pair of sleeves of wolf's skin. Their lodges were shaped like a tent and very light and warm, being covered with mats of rushes; beside which they had excavations on the ground, lined with mats, and occupied by the women, who were even more slightly clad than the men. These people subsisted chiefly by fishing; having canoes of a rude construction, being merely the trunks of pine trees split and hollowed out by fire. Their lodges were well stored with dried salmon and they had great quantities of fresh salmon trout of an excellent flavour, taken at the mouth of the Umatalla; of which the travellers obtained a most acceptable supply.

Finding that the road was on the north side of the river Mr. Hunt crossed and continued five or six days travelling rather slowly down along its banks, being much delayed by the straying of the horses and the attempts made by the Indians to steal them. They frequently passed lodges where they obtained fish and dogs. At one place the natives had just returned from hunting and had brought back a large quantity of elk and deer meat, but asked so high a price for it as to be beyond the funds of the travellers, so they had to content themselves with dog flesh. They had by this time, however, come to consider it very choice food, superior to horse flesh, and the minutes of the expedition speak rather exultingly now and then of their having made a "famous repast," where this viand happened to be unusually plenty.

They again learnt tidings of some of the scattered members of the expedition, supposed to be M'Kenzie, M'Lellan and their men, who had preceded them down the river, and had overturned one of their canoes, by which they lost many articles. All these floating pieces of intelligence of their fellow adventurers, who had separated from them in the heart of the wilderness, they received with eager interest.

The weather continued to be temperate, marking the superior softness of the climate on this side of the mountains. For a great part of the time the days were delightfully mild and clear, like the serene days of October, on the Atlantic borders. The country in general in the neighborhood of the river was a continual plain, low near the water, but rising gradually; destitute of trees, and almost without shrubs or plants of any kind excepting a few willow bushes. After travelling about sixty miles they came to where the country became very hilly and the river made its way between rocky banks and down numerous rapids. The Indians in this vicinity were better clad and altogether in more prosperous condition than those above, and, as Mr. Hunt thought, shewed their consciousness of ease by something like sauciness of manner. Thus prosperity is apt to produce arrogance in savage as well as in civilized life. In both conditions man is an animal that will not bear pampering.

From these people Mr. Hunt for the first time received vague, but deeply interesting intelligence of that part of the enterprize which had proceeded by sea to the mouth of the Columbia. The Indians spoke of a number of white men who had built a large house at the mouth of the Great River, and surrounded it with palisades. None of them had been down to Astoria themselves; but rumours spread widely and rapidly from mouth to mouth, among the Indian tribes, and are carried to the heart of the interior by hunting parties and migratory hordes.

The establishment of a trading emporium at such a point, also, was calculated to cause a sensation to the most remote parts of the vast wilderness beyond the mountains. It, in a manner, struck the pulse of the great vital river and vibrated up all its tributary streams.

It is surprising to notice how well this remote tribe of savages had learnt through intermediate gossips, the private feelings of the colonists at Astoria; it shews that Indians are not the incurious and indifferent observers that they have been represented. They told Mr. Hunt that the White people at the large house had been looking anxiously for many of their friends, whom they had expected to descend the Great River: and had been in much affliction, fearing that they were lost. Now, however, the arrival of him and his party would wipe away all their tears and they would dance and sing for joy.

On the thirty first day of January Mr. Hunt arrived at the falls of the Columbia and encamped at the Village of Wish-ram situated at the head of that dangerous pass of the river called "The Long Narrows."

CHAPTER XXXVIII

The village of Wish-ram—Roguery of the inhabitants—Their habitations—Tidings of Astoria—Of the Tonquin massacre—Thieves about the camp—A band of braggarts—Embarcation—Arrival at Astoria—A joyful reception—Old comrades—Adventures of Reed, M'Lellan and M'Kenzie among the Snake River Mountains—Rejoicing at Astoria.

Of the village of Wish-ram, the aborigines' fishing mart of the Columbia, we have given some account in an early chapter of this work.* The inhabitants held a traffic in the productions of the fisheries of the falls, and their village was the trading resort of the tribes from the coast and from the mountains. Mr. Hunt found the inhabitants shrewder and more intelligent than any Indians he had met with. Trade had sharpened their wits, though it had not improved their honesty; for they were a community of arrant rogues and freebooters. Their habitations comported with their circumstances, and were superior to any the travellers had yet seen west of the Rocky Mountains. In general the dwellings of the savages on the Pacific side of that great barrier, were mere tents and cabins of mats, or skins or straw, the country being destitute of timber. In Wish-ram, on the contrary, the houses were built of wood, with long sloping roofs. The floor was sunk about six feet below the surface of the ground, with a low door at the gable end, extremely narrow and partly sunk. Through this it was necessary to crawl and then to descend a short ladder. This inconvenient entrance was probably for the purpose of defence; there were loop holes also under the eaves, apparently for the discharge of arrows. The houses were large, generally containing two or three families. Immediately within the door were sleeping places ranged along the walls like berths in a ship; and furnished with pallets of matting. These extended along one half of the building; the remaining half was appropriated to the storing of dried fish.

The trading operations of the inhabitants of Wish-ram had given them a wider scope of information, and rendered their village a kind of head quarters of intelligence. Mr. Hunt was able, therefore, to collect more distinct tidings concerning the Settlement of Astoria and its affairs. One of the inhabitants had been at the trading post established by David Stuart on the Oakinagan, and had picked up a few words of English there. From him Mr. Hunt gleaned various particulars about that establishment, as well as about the general concerns of the

* Chapter X, 69.29–70.33.

enterprize. Others repeated the name of Mr. M'Kay, the partner who perished in the massacre on board of the Tonquin, and gave some account of that melancholy affair. They said Mr. M'Kay was a chief among the white men and had built a great house at the mouth of the river, but had left it, and sailed away in a large ship to the northward, where he had been attacked by bad Indians in canoes. Mr. Hunt was startled by this intelligence and made further enquiries. They informed him that the Indians had lashed their canoes to the ship and fought until they killed him and all his people. This is another instance of the clearness with which intelligence is transmitted from mouth to mouth among the Indian tribes. These tidings, though but partially credited by Mr. Hunt, filled his mind with anxious forebodings. He now endeavored to procure canoes in which to descend the Columbia, but none suitable for the purpose were to be obtained above the Narrows; he continued on, therefore, the distance of twelve miles and encamped on the bank of the river. The camp was soon surrounded by loitering savages, who went prowling about seeking what they might pilfer. Being baffled by the vigilance of the guard they endeavored to compass their ends by other means. Towards evening a number of warriors entered the camp in ruffling style; painted and dressed out as if for battle, and armed with lances, bows and arrows and scalping knives. They informed Mr. Hunt that a party of thirty or forty braves were coming up from a village below to attack the camp and carry off the horses, but that they were determined to stay with him and defend him. Mr. Hunt received them with great coldness, and, when they had finished their story, gave them a pipe to smoke. He then called up all hands, stationed centinels in different quarters, but told them to keep as vigilant an eye within the camp as without.

The warriors were evidently baffled by these precautions, and, having smoked their pipe and vapoured off their valor; took their departure. The farce, however, did not end here. After a little while the warriors returned ushering in another savage, still more heroically arrayed. This they announced as the chief of the belligerent village, but as a great pacificator. His people had been furiously bent upon the attack and would have doubtless carried it into effect, but this gallant chief had stood forth as the friend of white men, and had dispersed the throng by his own authority and prowess. Having vaunted this signal piece of service there was a significant pause; all evidently expecting some adequate reward. Mr. Hunt again produced the pipe, smoked with the chieftain and his worthy compeers; but made no further demonstrations of gratitude. They remained about the camp all night, but at day light returned baffled and crest fallen to their homes, with nothing but smoke for their pains.

Mr. Hunt now endeavored to procure canoes, of which he saw several about the neighborhood, extremely well made, with elevated stems and sterns, some of them capable of carrying three thousand pounds weight. He found it extremely difficult, however, to deal with these slippery people who seemed much more inclined to pilfer. Notwithstanding a strict guard maintained round the camp, various implements were stolen and several horses carried off. Among the latter we have to include the long cherished steed of Pierre Dorion. From some wilful caprice that worthy pitched his tent at some distance from the main body and tethered his invaluable steed beside it, from whence it was abstracted in the night to the infinite chagrin and mortification of the hybrid interpreter.

Having, after several days' negociation, procured the requisite number of canoes, Mr. Hunt would gladly have left this thievish neighborhood, but was detained until the 5th of February, by violent head winds accompanied by snow and rain. Even after he was enabled to get under way he had still to struggle against contrary winds and tempestuous weather. The current of the river, however, was in his favour; having made a portage at the grand rapid the canoes met with no further obstruction, and, on the afternoon of the 15th of February, swept round an intervening cape and came in sight of the infant settlement of Astoria. After eleven months' wandering in the wilderness, a great part of the time over trackless wastes where the sight of a savage wigwam was a rarity, we may imagine the delight of the poor weatherbeaten travellers at beholding the embryo establishment, with its magazines, habitations and picketed bulwarks, seated on a high point of land dominating a beautiful little bay, in which was a trim built shallop riding quietly at anchor. A shout of joy burst from each canoe at the long wished for sight. They urged their canoes across the bay and pulled with eagerness for shore, where all hands poured down from the settlement to receive and welcome them. Among the first to greet them on their landing were some of their old comrades and fellow sufferers, who, under the conduct of Reed, M'Lellan and M'Kenzie, had parted from them at the Caldron Linn. These had reached Astoria nearly a month previously, and, judging from their own narrow escape from starvation, had given up Mr. Hunt and his followers as lost. Their greeting was the more warm and cordial. As to the Canadian voyageurs, their mutual felicitations, as usual, were loud and vociferous, and it was almost ludicrous to behold these ancient "camerades" and "confreres" hugging and kissing each other on the river bank.

When the first greetings were over the different bands interchanged accounts of their several wanderings after separating at Snake River; we shall briefly notice a few of the leading particulars. It will be recollected by the reader that a small exploring detachment had proceeded down the river under the conduct of Mr. John Reed, a clerk of the Company: that another had set off under M'Lellan, and a third in a different direction, under M'Kenzie. After wandering for several days without meeting with Indians, or obtaining any supplies, they came together fortuitously among the Snake River Mountains, some distance below that disastrous pass or strait which had received the appellation of The Devil's Scuttle Hole. When thus united their party consisted of M'Kenzie, M'Lellan, Reed and eight men, chiefly Canadians.

Being all in the same predicament, without horses, provisions, or information of any kind, they all agreed that it would be worse than useless to return to Mr. Hunt and encumber him with so many starving men, and that their only course was to extricate themselves as soon as possible from this land of famine and misery, and make the best of their way for the Columbia. They accordingly continued to follow the downward course of Snake River; clambering rocks and mountains and defying all the difficulties and dangers of that rugged defile, which subsequently, when the snows had fallen, was found impassable by Messrs. Hunt and Crooks.

Though constantly near to the borders of the river, and for a great part of the time within sight of its current, one of their greatest sufferings was thirst. The river had worn its way in a deep channel through rocky mountains, destitute of brooks or springs. Its banks were so high and precipitous, that there was rarely any place where the travellers could get down to drink of its waters. Frequently they suffered for miles the torments of Tantalus; water continually within sight, yet fevered with the most parching thirst. Here and there they met with rain water collected in the hollows of the rocks, but more than once they were reduced to the utmost extremity; and some of the men had recourse to the last expedient to avoid perishing.

Their sufferings from hunger were equally severe. They could meet with no game, and subsisted for a time on strips of beaver skin broiled on the coals. These were doled out in scanty allowances, barely sufficient to keep up existence, and at length failed them altogether. Still they crept feebly on, scarce dragging one limb after another, until a severe snow storm brought them to a pause. To struggle against it, in their exhausted condition, was impossible, so cowering under an impending rock at the foot of a steep mountain, they prepared themselves for that wretched fate which seemed inevitable.

At this critical juncture, when famine stared them in the face, M'Lellan casting up his eyes, beheld an asahta, or Bighorn sheltering itself under a shelving rock on the side of the hill above them. Being in a more active plight than any of his comrades, and an excellent marksman, he set off to get within shot of the animal. His companions watched his movements with breathless anxiety, for their lives depended upon his success. He made a cautious circuit; scrambled up the hill with the utmost silence, and at length arrived, unperceived, within a proper distance. Here levelling his rifle he took so sure an aim that the Bighorn fell dead on the spot; a fortunate circumstance, for, to pursue it, if merely wounded, would have been impossible in his emaciated state. The declivity of the hill enabled him to roll the carcass down to his companions, who were too feeble to climb the rocks. They fell to work to cut it up; yet exerted a remarkable self denial for men in their starving condition, for they contented themselves for the present with a soup made from the bones, reserving the flesh for future repasts. This providential relief gave them strength to pursue their journey, but they were frequently reduced to almost equal straits and it was only the smallness of their party, requiring a small supply of provisions, that enabled them to get through this desolate region with their lives.

At length, after twenty one days of toil and suffering, they got through these mountains and arrived at a tributary stream of that branch of the Columbia called Lewis River, of which Snake River forms the southern fork. In this neighborhood they met with wild horses, the first they had seen west of the Rocky Mountains. From hence they made their way to Lewis River where they fell in with a friendly tribe of Indians who freely administered to their necessities. On this river they procured two canoes in which they dropped down the stream to its confluence with the Columbia, and then down that river to Astoria where they arrived haggard and emaciated and perfectly in rags.

Thus all the leading persons of Mr. Hunt's expedition were once more gathered together excepting Mr. Crooks, of whose safety they entertained but little hope, considering the feeble condition in which they had been compelled to leave him in the heart of the wilderness.

A day was now given up to jubilee to celebrate the arrival of Mr. Hunt and his companions, and the joyful meeting of the various scattered bands of adventurers at Astoria. The colours were hoisted; the guns great and small were fired, there was a feast of fish, of beaver and venison, which relished well with men who had so long been glad to revel on horse flesh and dog's meat; a genial allowance of grog was issued to encrease the general animation, and the festivities wound up, as usual, with a grand dance at night, by the Canadian voyageurs.*

* The distance from S' Louis to Astoria, by the route travelled by Hunt and M'Kenzie, was upwards of 3500 miles, though in a direct line it does not exceed 1800.

Figure 1. Astoria in 1811, from the Tacoma edition of *Astoria* (New York: G. P. Putnam's Sons, 1897).

Figure 2. Astoria, from an engraving reproduced in the Geoffrey Crayon edition of *Astoria* (New York: G. P. Putnam's Sons, 1868).

Figure 3. Michilimackinac, from the Tacoma edition of Astoria.

Figure 4. Mandan Village and Buffalo-Hide Boats, from the Tacoma edition of *Astoria*.

CHAPTER XXXIX

Scanty fare during the winter—A poor hunting ground—The return of the fishing season—The uthlecan or smelt—Its qualities—Vast shoals of it—Sturgeon—Indian modes of taking it—The salmon—Different species—Nature of the country about the coast—Forests and forest trees—A remarkable flowering vine—Animals—Birds—Reptiles—Climate west of the Mountains—Mildness of the temperature—Soil of the coast and the interior.

The winter had passed away tranquilly at Astoria. The apprehensions of hostility from the natives had subsided; indeed as the season advanced the Indians for the most part had disappeared from the neighborhood and abandoned the sea coast, so that, for want of their aid, the colonists had at times suffered considerably for want of provisions. The hunters belonging to the establishment made frequent and wide excursions but with very moderate success. There were some deer and a few bears to be found in the vicinity, and elk in great numbers; the country, however, was so rough and the woods so close and entangled, that it was almost impossible to beat up the game. The prevalent rains of winter, also, rendered it difficult for the hunter to keep his arms in order. The quantity of game, therefore, brought in by the hunters was extremely scanty, and it was frequently necessary to put all hands on very moderate allowance. Towards spring, however, the fishing season commenced, the season of plenty on the Columbia. About the beginning of February a small kind of fish, about six inches long, called by the natives the uthlecan, and resembling the smelt, made its appearance at the mouth of the river. It is said to be of delicious flavor, and so fat as to burn like a candle, for which it is often used by the natives. It enters the river in immense shoals, like solid columns, often extending to the depth of five or more feet, and is scooped up by the natives with small nets at the end of poles. In this way they will soon fill a canoe, or form a great heap upon the river banks. These fish constitute a principal article of their food, the women drying them and stringing them on cords.

As the uthlecan is only found in the lower part of the river, the arrival of it soon brought back the natives to the coast; who again resorted to the factory to trade, and from that time furnished plentiful supplies of fish.

The sturgeon makes its appearance in the river shortly after the uthlecan, and is taken in different ways, by the natives. Sometimes they spear it, but oftener they use the hook and line, and the net. Occasionally they sink a cord in the river by a heavy weight, with

235

a buoy at the upper end to keep it floating. To this cord several hooks are attached by short lines, a few feet distant from each other, and baited with small fish. This apparatus is often set towards night, and by the next morning several sturgeon will be found hooked by it; for though a large and strong fish, it makes but little resistance when ensnared.

The salmon, which are the prime fish of the Columbia, and as important to the piscatory tribes as are the buffaloes to the hunters of the prairies, do not enter the river until towards the latter part of May, from which time, until the middle of August, they abound, and are taken in vast quantities, either with the spear or the seine and mostly in shallow water. An inferior species succeeds, and continues from August to December. It is remarkable for having a double row of teeth, half an inch long and extremely sharp, from whence it has received the name of the Dog toothed Salmon. It is generally killed with the spear in small rivulets and smoked for winter provision.

We have noticed in a former chapter the mode in which the salmon are taken and cured at the falls of the Columbia; and put up in parcels for exportation. From these different fisheries of the river tribes, the establishment at Astoria had to derive much of its precarious supplies of provisions.

A year's residence at the mouth of the Columbia, and various expeditions in the interior, had now given the Astorians some idea of the country. The whole coast is described as remarkably rugged and mountainous; with dense forests of hemlock, spruce, white and red cedar, cotton wood, white oak, white and swamp ash, willow and a few walnut. There is likewise an undergrowth of aromatic shrubs, creepers and clambering vines that render the forests almost impenetrable; together with berries of various kinds, such as gooseberries, strawberries, raspberries, both red and yellow, very large and finely flavored, whortleberries, cranberries, serviceberries, blackberries, currants, sloes and wild and choke cherries.

Among the flowering vines is one deserving of particular notice. Each flower is composed of six leaves or petals, about three inches in length, of a beautiful crimson, the inside spotted with white. Its leaves, of a fine green, are oval and disposed by threes. This plant climbs upon the trees without attaching itself to them; when it has reached the topmost branches, it descends perpendicularly, and as it continues to grow, extends from tree to tree, until its various stalks interlace the grove like the rigging of a ship. The stems or trunks of this vine are tougher and more flexible than willow, and are from fifty to one hundred fathoms in length. From the fibres, the Indians manufacture baskets of such close texture as to hold water.

The principal quadrupeds that had been seen by the colonists in their various expeditions were the elk, stag, fallow deer, hart, black and grizzly bear, antilope, Ahsahta or Big Horn, beaver, sea and river otter, muskrat, fox, wolf and panther, the latter extremely rare. The only domestic animals among the natives were horses and dogs.

The country abounded with aquatic and land birds, such as swans, wild geese, brant, ducks of almost every description, pelicans, herons, gulls, snipes, curlews, eagles, vultures, crows, ravens, magpies, woodpeckers, pigeons, partridges, pheasants, grouse, and a great variety of singing birds.

There were few reptiles, the only dangerous kinds were the rattle-snake and one striped with black, yellow and white, about four feet long. Among the lizard kind was one about nine or ten inches in length, exclusive of the tail, and three inches in circumference. The tail was round and of the same length as the body. The head was triangular covered with small square scales. The upper part of the body was likewise covered with small scales, green, yellow, black and blue. Each foot had five toes furnished with strong nails, probably to aid it in burrowing, as it usually lived under ground in the plains.

A remarkable fact characteristic of the country west of the Rocky Mountains is the mildness and equability of the climate. That great mountain barrier seems to divide the continent into different climates even in the same degrees of latitude. The rigorous winters and sultry summers, and all the capricious inequalities of temperature prevalent on the Atlantic side of the mountains, are but little felt on their western declivities. The countries between them and the Pacific are blest with milder and steadier temperature, resembling the climates of parallel latitudes in Europe. In the plains and valleys but little snow falls throughout the winter and usually melts while falling. It rarely lies on the ground more than two days at a time, except on the summits of the mountains. The winters are rainy rather than cold. The rains for five months, from the middle of October to the middle of March, are almost incessant and often accompanied by tremendous thunder and lightning. The winds prevalent at this season are from the south and south east, which usually bring rain. Those from the north to the south west are the harbingers of fair weather and a clear sky. The residue of the year, from the middle of March to the middle of October, an interval of seven months, is serene and delightful. There is scarcely any rain throughout this time, yet the face of the country is kept fresh and verdant by nightly dews, and occasionally by humid fogs in the mornings. These are not considered prejudicial to health, since both the natives and the whites sleep in the open air with perfect impunity.

While this equable and bland temperature prevails throughout the lower country, the peaks and ridges of the vast mountains by which it is dominated are covered with perpetual snow. This renders them discernible at a great distance, shining at times like bright summer clouds, at other times assuming the most aerial tints, and always forming brilliant and striking features in the vast landscape.

The mild temperature prevalent throughout the country is attributed by some to the succession of winds from the Pacific Ocean, extending from Latitude 20° to at least 50° North. These temper the heat of summer so that in the shade no one is incommoded by perspiration; they also soften the rigors of winter, and produce such a moderation in the climate that the inhabitants can wear the same dress throughout the year.

The soil in the neighborhood of the sea coast is of a brown colour inclining to red, and generally poor; being a mixture of clay and gravel. In the interior, and especially in the valleys of the Rocky Mountains, the soil is generally blackish; though sometimes yellow. It is frequently mixed with marl and with marine substances in a state of decomposition. This kind of soil extends to a considerable depth, as may be perceived in the deep cuts made by ravines, and by the beds of rivers. The vegetation in these valleys is much more abundant than near the coast; in fact, it is in these fertile intervals, locked up between rocky sierras, or scooped out from barren wastes, that population must extend itself as it were in veins and ramifications, if ever the regions beyond the mountains should become civilized.

CHAPTER XL

A brief mention has already been made of the tribes or hordes existing about the lower part of the Columbia at the time of the settlement; a few more particulars concerning them may be acceptable. The four tribes nearest to Astoria, and with whom the traders had most inter-course, were, as has heretofore been observed, the Chinooks, the Clatsops, the Wahkiacums and the Cathlamets. The Chinooks resided chiefly along the banks of a river of the same name, running parallel to the sea coast, through a low country studded with stagnant pools, and emptying itself into Baker's bay, a few miles from Cape Disappointment. This was the tribe over which Comcomly, the one eyed chieftain, held sway: it boasted two hundred and fourteen fighting men. Their chief subsistence was on fish, with an occasional regale of the flesh of elk and deer, and of wild fowl from the neighboring ponds.

The Clatsops resided on both sides of Point Adams; they were the mere reliques of a tribe which had been nearly swept off by the small pox, and did not number more than one hundred and eighty fighting men.

The Wahkiacums, or Waak-i-cums, inhabited the north side of the Columbia and numbered sixty six warriors. They and the Chinooks were originally the same, but a dispute arising about two generations previous to the time of the settlement between the ruling chief and his brother, Wahkiacum, the latter seceded, and with his adherents, formed the present horde which continues to go by his name. In this way new tribes or clans are formed and lurking causes of hostility engendered.

The Cathlamets lived opposite to the lower village of the Wahkiacums, and numbered ninety four warriors.

These four tribes, or rather clans, have every appearance of springing from the same origin, resembling each other in person, dress, language and manners. They are rather a diminutive race, generally below five feet five inches, with crooked legs and thick ancles, a deformity caused by their passing so much of their time sitting or squatting upon the calves of their legs and their heels, in the bottom of their canoes; a favorite position, which they retain even when on shore. The women encrease this deformity by wearing tight bandages round the ancles, which prevent the circulation of the blood and cause a swelling of the muscles of the leg.

Neither sex can boast of personal beauty. Their faces are round with small but animated eyes. Their noses are broad and flat at top, and fleshy at the end with large nostrils. They have wide mouths, thick lips and short, irregular and dirty teeth. Indeed good teeth are seldom to be seen among the tribes west of the Rocky Mountains who live chiefly on fish.

In the early stages of their intercourse with white men these savages were but scantily clad. In summer time the men went entirely naked; in the winter and in bad weather, the men wore a small robe, reaching to the middle of the thigh, made of the skins of animals, or of the wool of the mountain sheep. Occasionally they wore a kind of mantle of matting, to keep off the rain; but, having thus protected the back and shoulders, they left the rest of the body naked.

The women wore similar robes, though shorter, not reaching below the waist: beside which they had a kind of petticoat, or fringe reaching from the waist to the knee, formed of the fibres of cedar bark, broken into strands, or a tissue of silk grass twisted and knotted at the ends. This was the usual dress of the women in summer, should the weather be inclement they added a vest of skins similar to the robe.

The men carefully eradicated every vestige of a beard, considering it a great deformity. They looked with disgust at the whiskers and well furnished chins of the white men, and in derision called them Long beards. Both sexes, on the other hand, cherished the hair of the head, which with them is generally black and rather coarse. They allowed it to grow to a great length, and were very proud and careful of it, sometimes wearing it plaited, sometimes wound round the head in fanciful tresses. No greater affront could be offered to them than to cut off their treasured locks.

They had conical hats with narrow rims, neatly woven of bear grass or of the fibres of cedar bark, interwoven with designs of various shapes and colours; sometimes merely squares and triangles, at other times rude representations of canoes with men fishing and harpooning. These hats were nearly water proof and extremely durable.

The favorite ornaments of the men were collars of bears' claws, the proud trophies of hunting exploits; while the women and children wore similar decorations of elks' tusks. An intercourse with the white traders, however, soon effected a change in the toilettes of both sexes. They became fond of arraying themselves in any article of civilized dress which they could procure, and often made a most grotesque appearance. They adapted many articles of finery, also, to their own previous tastes. Both sexes were fond of adorning themselves with bracelets of iron, brass or copper. They were delighted also with blue and white beads, particularly the former, and wore broad tight bands of them round the waist and ancles; large rolls of them round the neck, and pendants of them in the ears. The men, especially, who, in savage life carry a passion for personal decoration farther than the females, did not think their gala equipments complete, unless they had a jewel of haïqua or wampum dangling at the nose. Thus arrayed, their hair besmeared with fish oil and their bodies bedaubed with red clay, they considered themselves irresistible.

When on warlike expeditions they painted their faces and bodies in the most hideous and grotesque manner, according to the universal practice of American Savages. Their arms were bows and arrows, spears and war clubs. Some wore a corslet formed of pieces of hard wood, laced together with bear's grass, so as to form a light coat of mail, pliant to the body; and a kind of casque of cedar bark, leather and bear's grass sufficient to protect the head from an arrow or a war club. A more complete article of defensive armour was a buff jerkin or shirt of great thickness, made of doublings of elk skin, and reaching to the feet, holes being left for the head and arms. This was perfectly arrow proof; add to which, it was often endowed with charmed virtues, by the spells and mystic ceremonials of the medicine man or conjurer.

Of the peculiar custom, prevalent among these people, of flattening the head, we have already spoken. It is one of those instances of human caprice, like the crippling of the feet of females in China, which are quite incomprehensible. This custom prevails principally among the tribes on the sea coast, and about the lower parts of the rivers. How far it extends along the coast we are not able to asertain. Some of the tribes, both north and south of the Columbia, practice it; but they all speak the Chinook language, and probably originated from the same stock. As far as we can learn the remoter tribes, which speak an entirely different language, do not flatten the head. This absurd custom declines, also, in receding from the shores of the Pacific; few traces of it are to be found among the tribes of the Rocky Mountains, and after crossing the mountains it disappears altogether. Those Indians, therefore, about the head waters of the Columbia, and in the solitary mountain regions, who are often called Flatheads, must not be supposed to be characterized by this deformity. It is an appellation often given by the hunters east of the mountain chain, to all the western Indians excepting the Snakes.

The religious belief of these people was extremely limited and confined; or rather, in all probability, their explanations were but little understood by their visitors. They had an idea of a benevolent and omnipotent Spirit, the creator of all things. They represent him as assuming various shapes at pleasure, but generally that of an immense bird. He usually inhabits the sun, but occasionally wings his way through the aerial regions, and sees all that is doing upon earth. Should any thing displease him he vents his wrath in terrific storms and tempests, the lightning being the flashes of his eyes, and the thunder the clapping of his wings. To propitiate his favor they offer to him annual sacrifices of salmon and venison, the first fruits of their fishing and hunting.

Beside this aerial spirit they believe in an inferior one who inhabits the fire, and of whom they are in perpetual dread, as, though he possesses equally the power of good and evil, the evil is apt to preponderate. They endeavor, therefore, to keep him in good humor by frequent offerings. He is supposed also to have great influence with the Winged Spirit, their sovereign protector and benefactor. They implore him, therefore, to act as their intercessor and procure them all desireable things, such as success in fishing and hunting, abundance of game, fleet horses, obedient wives and male children.

These Indians have likewise their priests, or conjurers, or medicine men, who pretend to be in the confidence of the deities, and the expounders and enforcers of their will. Each of these medicine men has his idols carved in wood representing the Spirits of the air and of the fire, under some rude and grotesque form of a horse, a bear, a beaver, or other quadruped, or that of a bird or fish. These idols are hung round with amulets and votive offerings, such as beavers' teeth, and bears' and eagles' claws.

When any chief personage is on his death bed, or dangerously ill, the medicine men are sent for. Each brings with him his idols with which he retires into a corner to hold a consultation. As doctors are prone to disagree, so these medicine men have now and then a violent altercation as to the malady of the patient, or the treatment of it. To settle this they beat their idols soundly against each other; which ever first loses a tooth or a claw is considered as confuted and his votary retires from the field.

Polygamy is not only allowed, but considered honorable, and the greater number of wives a man can maintain, the more important is he in the eyes of the tribe. The first wife, however, takes rank of all the others, and is considered mistress of the house. Still the domestic establishment is liable to jealousies and cabals, and the lord and master has much difficulty in maintaining harmony in his jangling household.

In the manuscript from which we draw many of these particulars, it is stated that he who exceeds his neighbors in the number of his wives, male children and slaves, is elected chief of the village; a title to office which we do not recollect ever before to have met with.

Feuds are frequent among these tribes, but are not very deadly. They have occasionally pitched battles, fought on appointed days, and at specified places, which are generally the banks of a rivulet. The adverse parties post themselves on the opposite sides of the stream, and at such distances that the battles often last a long while before any blood is shed. The number of killed and wounded seldom exceed half a dozen. Should the damage be equal on each side, the war is considered as honorably concluded; should one party lose more than the other, it is entitled to a compensation in slaves or other property, otherwise hostilities are liable to be renewed at a future day. They are much given also to predatory inroads into the territories of their enemies, and sometimes of their friendly neighbors. Should they fall upon a band of inferior force, or upon a village, weakly defended, they act with the ferocity of true poltroons, slaying all the men and carrying off the women and children as slaves. As to the property, it is packed upon horses which they bring with them for the purpose. They are mean and paltry as warriors, and altogether inferior in heroic qualities to the savages of the buffalo plains on the east side of the mountains.

A great portion of their time is passed in revelry, music, dancing and gambling. Their music scarcely deserves the name; the instruments being of the rudest kind. Their singing is harsh and discordant, the songs are chiefly extempore, relating to passing circumstances, the persons present, or any trifling object that strikes the attention of the singer. They have several kinds of dances, some of them lively and pleasing. The women are rarely permitted to dance with the men, but form groups apart, dancing to the same instrument and song.

They have a great passion for play, and a variety of games. To such a pitch of excitement are they sometimes roused, that they gamble away every thing they possess, even to their wives and children. They are notorious thieves, also, and proud of their dexterity. He who is frequently successful, gains much applause and popularity; but the clumsy thief, who is detected in some bungling attempt, is scoffed at and despised, and sometimes severely punished.

Such are a few leading characteristics of the natives in the neighborhood of Astoria. They appear to us inferior in many respects to the tribes east of the mountains, the bold rovers of the prairies; and to partake much of the Esquimaux character; elevated in some degree by a more genial climate and more varied style of living.

The habits of traffic engendered at the Cataracts of the Columbia have had their influence along the coast. The Chinooks and other Indians at the mouth of the river soon proved themselves keen traders, and in their early dealings with the Astorians never hesitated to ask three times what they considered the real value of an article. They were inquisitive, also, in the extreme, and impertinently intrusive; and were prone to indulge in scoffing and ridicule at the expence of the strangers.

In one thing, however, they shewed superior judgment and self command to most of their race; this was, in their abstinence from ardent spirits and the abhorrence and disgust with which they regarded a drunkard. On one occasion a son of Comcomly had been induced to drink freely at the factory, and went home in a state of intoxication, playing all kinds of mad pranks, until he sank into a stupor, in which he remained for two days. The old chieftain repaired to his friend M'Dougall with indignation flaming in his countenance and bitterly reproached him for having permitted his son to degrade himself into a beast and to render himself an object of scorn and laughter to his slaves.

CHAPTER XLI

As the spring opened the little settlement of Astoria was in agitation and prepared to send forth various expeditions. Several important things were to be done. It was necessary to send a supply of goods to the trading post of Mr. David Stuart, established in the preceding autumn on the Oakinagan. The cache, or secret deposit made by Mr. Hunt at the Caldron Linn was likewise to be visited, and the merchandize and other effects left there, to be brought to Astoria. A third object of moment was to send despatches overland to Mr. Astor at New York, informing him of the state of affairs at the settlement, and the fortunes of the several expeditions.

The task of carrying supplies to Oakinagan was assigned to Mr. Robert Stuart, a spirited and enterprizing young man, nephew to the one who had established the post. The cache was to be sought out by two of the clerks named Russell Farnham and Donald M'Gilles, conducted by a guide, and accompanied by eight men, to assist in bringing home the goods.

As to the despatches, they were confided to Mr. John Reed, the clerk, the same who had conducted one of the exploring detachments of Snake River. He was now to trace back his way across the mountains by the same route by which he had come, with no other companions or escort than Ben Jones the Kentucky hunter and two Canadians. As it was still hoped that Mr. Crooks might be in existence, and that Mr. Reed and his party might meet with him in the course of their route, they were charged with a small supply of goods and provisions, to aid that gentleman on his way to Astoria.

When the expedition of Reed was made known, Mr. M'Lellan announced his determination to accompany it. He had long been dissatisfied with the smallness of his interest in the copartnership, and had requested an additional number of shares; his request not being complied with, he resolved to abandon the Company. M'Lellan was a man of a singularly self willed and decided character, with whom persuasion was useless; he was permitted therefore to take his own course without opposition.

As to Reed he set about preparing for his hazardous journey with the zeal of a true Irishman. He had a tin case made, in which the letters and papers addressed to Mr. Astor were carefully soldered up. This case he intended to strap upon his shoulders, so as to bear it about with him, sleeping and waking, in all changes and chances, by land or by water, and never to part with it but with his life!

As the route of these several parties would be the same for nearly four hundred miles up the Columbia, and within that distance would lie through the piratical pass of the rapids and among the freebooting tribes of the river, it was thought adviseable to start about the same time, and to keep together. Accordingly on the 22d of March they all set off, to the number of seventeen men, in two canoes.

And here we cannot but pause to notice the hardihood of these several expeditions, so insignificant in point of force, and severally destined to traverse immense wildernesses, where larger parties had experienced so much danger and distress. When recruits were sought in the preceding year among experienced hunters and voyageurs at Montreal and S' Louis, it was considered dangerous to attempt to cross the Rocky Mountains with less than sixty men; and yet here we find Reed ready to push his way across those barriers with merely three companions. Such is the fearlessness, the insensibility to danger, which men acquire by the habitude of constant risk. The mind like the body becomes callous by exposure.

The little associated band proceeded up the river, under the command of Mr. Robert Stuart, and arrived early in the month of April at the Long Narrows, that notorious plundering place. Here it was necessary to unload the canoes, and to transport both them and their cargoes to the head of the Narrows by land. Their party was too few in number for the purpose. They were obliged, therefore, to seek the assistance of the Cathlasco Indians, who undertook to carry the goods on their horses. Forward then they set, the Indians with their horses well freighted, and the first load convoyed by Reed and five men, well armed; the gallant Irishman striding along at the head, with his tin case of despatches glittering on his back. In passing, however, through a rocky and intricate defile, some of the freebooting vagabonds turned their horses up a narrow path and galloped off, carrying with them two bales of goods, and a number of smaller articles. To follow them was useless; indeed, it was with much ado that the convoy got into port with the residue of the cargoes; for some of the guards were pillaged of their knives and pocket handkerchiefs, and the lustrous tin case of Mr. John Reed was in imminent jeopardy.

Mr. Stuart heard of these depredations, and hastened forward to the relief of the convoy, but could not reach them before dusk, by which time they had arrived at the village of Wish-ram, already noted for its great fishery, and the knavish propensities of its inhabitants. Here they found themselves benighted in a strange place, and surrounded by savages bent on pilfering, if not upon open robbery. Not knowing what active course to take, they remained under arms all night, without closing an eye, and at the very first peep of dawn, when objects were yet scarce visible, every thing was hastily embarked, and, without seeking to recover the stolen effects, they pushed off from shore; "glad to bid adieu," as they said, "to this abominable nest of miscreants."

The worthies of Wish-ram, however, were not disposed to part so easily with their visitors. Their cupidity had been quickened by the plunder which they had already taken, and their confidence increased by the impunity with which their outrage had passed. They resolved, therefore, to take further toll of the travellers, and, if possible, to capture the tin case of despatches; which, shining conspicuously from afar, and being guarded by John Reed with such especial care, must, as they supposed, be "a great medicine."

Accordingly, Mr. Stuart and his comrades had not proceeded far in the canoes, when they beheld the whole rabble of Wish-ram stringing in groups along the bank, whooping and yelling, and gibbering in their wild jargon, and when they landed below the falls, they were surrounded by upwards of four hundred of these river ruffians, armed with bows and arrows, war clubs, and other savage weapons. These now pressed forward, with offers to carry the canoes and effects up the portage. Mr. Stuart declined forwarding the goods, alleging the lateness of the hour; but, to keep them in good humor, informed them that, if they conducted themselves well, their offered services might probably be accepted in the morning; in the meanwhile, he suggested that they might carry up the canoes. They accordingly set off with the two canoes on their shoulders, accompanied by a guard of eight men well armed.

When arrived at the head of the falls, the mischievous spirit of the savages broke out, and they were on the point of destroying the canoes, doubtless with a view to impede the white men from carrying forward their goods, and laying them open to further pilfering. They were with some difficulty prevented from committing this outrage by the interference of an old man, who appeared to have authority among them; and, in consequence of his harangue, the whole of the hostile band, with the exception of about fifty, crossed to the north side of the river, where they lay in wait, ready for further mischief.

In the meantime, Mr. Stuart, who had remained at the foot of the falls with the goods, and who knew that the proffered assistance of the savages was only for the purpose of having an opportunity to plunder, determined, if possible, to steal a march upon them, and defeat their machinations. In the dead of the night, therefore, about one o'clock, the moon shining brightly, he roused his party, and proposed that they should endeavor to transport the goods themselves, above the falls, before the sleeping savages could be aware of their operations. All hands sprang to the work with zeal, and hurried it on in the hope of getting all over before daylight. Mr. Stuart went forward with the first loads, and took his station at the head of the portage, while Mr. Reed and Mr. M'Lellan remained at the foot to forward the remainder.

The day dawned before the transportation was completed. Some of the fifty Indians who had remained on the south side of the river, perceived what was going on, and, feeling themselves too weak for an attack, gave the alarm to those on the opposite side, upwards of a hundred of whom embarked in several large canoes. Two loads of goods yet remained to be brought up. Mr. Stuart despatched some of the people for one of the loads, with a request to Mr. Reed to retain with him as many men as he thought necessary to guard the remaining load, as he suspected hostile intentions on the part of the Indians. Mr. Reed, however, refused to retain any of them, saying that M'Lellan and himself were sufficient to protect the small quantity that remained. The men accordingly departed with the load, while Reed and M'Lellan continued to mount guard over the residue. By this time, a number of the canoes had arrived from the opposite side. As they approached the shore, the unlucky tin box of John Reed, shining afar like the brilliant helmet of Euryalus, caught their eyes. No sooner did the canoes touch the shore, than they leaped forward on the rocks, set up a war whoop, and sprang forward to secure the glittering prize. Mr. M'Lellan, who was at the river bank, advanced to guard the goods, when one of the savages attempted to hoodwink him with his buffalo robe with one hand, and to stab him with the other. M'Lellan sprang back just far enough to avoid the blow, and raising his rifle, shot the ruffian through the heart.

In the meantime, Reed, who with the want of forethought of an Irishman, had neglected to remove the leathern cover from the lock of his rifle, was fumbling at the fastenings, when he received a blow on the head with a war club that laid him senseless on the ground. In a twinkling he was stripped of his rifle and pistols, and the tin box, the cause of all this onslaught, was borne off in triumph.

At this critical juncture, Mr. Stuart, who had heard the war whoop, hastened to the scene of action with Ben Jones, and seven others of the men. When he arrived, Reed was weltering in his blood, and an Indian standing over him and about to despatch him with a tomahawk. Stuart gave the word, when Ben Jones levelled his rifle, and shot the miscreant on the spot. The men then gave a cheer, and charged upon the main body of the savages, who took to instant flight. Reed was now raised from the ground, and borne senseless and bleeding to the upper end of the portage. Preparations were made to launch the canoes and embark in all haste, when it was found that they were too leaky to be put in the water, and that the oars had been left at the foot of the falls. A scene of confusion now ensued. The Indians were whooping and yelling, and running about like fiends. A panic seized upon the men, at being thus suddenly checked, the hearts of some of the Canadians died within them, and two young men actually fainted away. The moment they recovered their senses, Mr. Stuart ordered that they should be deprived of their arms, their under garments taken off, and that a piece of cloth should be tied round their waists, in imitation of a squaw; an Indian punishment for cowardice. Thus equipped, they were stowed away among the goods in one of the canoes. This ludicrous affair excited the mirth of the bolder spirits, even in the midst of their perils, and roused the pride of the wavering. The Indians having crossed back again to the north side, order was restored, some of the hands were sent back for the oars, others set to work to caulk and launch the canoes, and in a little while all were embarked and were continuing their voyage along the southern shore.

No sooner had they departed, than the Indians returned to the scene of action, bore off their two comrades, who had been shot, one of whom was still living, and returned to their village. Here they killed two horses; and drank the hot blood to give fierceness to their courage. They painted and arrayed themselves hideously for battle; performed the dead dance round the slain, and raised the war song of vengeance. Then mounting their horses, to the number of four hundred and fifty men, and brandishing their weapons, they set off along the northern bank of the river, to get ahead of the canoes, lie in wait for them, and take a terrible revenge on the white men.

They succeeded in getting some distance above the canoes without being discovered, and were crossing the river to post themselves on the side along which the white men were coasting, when they were fortunately descried. Mr. Stuart and his companions were immediately on the alert. As they drew near to the place where the savages had crossed, they observed them posted among steep and overhanging rocks, close along which the canoes would have to pass. Finding that the enemy had the advantage of the ground, the whites stopped short when within five hundred yards of them, and discharged and reloaded their pieces. They then made a fire, and dressed the wounds of Mr. Reed, who had received five severe gashes in the head. This being done, they lashed the canoes together, fastened them to a rock at a small distance from the shore, and there awaited the menaced attack.

They had not been long posted in this manner, when they saw a canoe approaching. It contained the war chief of the tribe, and three of his principal warriors. He drew near, and made a long harangue, in which he informed them that they had killed one and wounded another of his nation; that the relations of the slain cried out for vengeance, and he had been compelled to lead them to the fight. Still he wished to spare unnecessary bloodshed; he proposed, therefore, that Mr. Reed, who, he observed, was little better than a dead man, might be given up to be sacrificed to the manes of the deceased warrior. This would appease the fury of his friends; the hatchet would then be buried, and all thenceforward would be friends. The answer was a stern refusal and a defiance, and the war chief saw that the canoes were well prepared for a vigorous defence. He withdrew, therefore, and, returning to his warriors among the rocks held long deliberations. Blood for blood is a principle in Indian equity and Indian honor; but though the inhabitants of Wish-ram were men of war, they were likewise men of traffic, and it was suggested that honor for once might give way to profit. A negotiation was accordingly opened with the white men, and after some diplomacy, the matter was compromised for a blanket to cover the dead, and some tobacco to be smoked by the living. This being granted, the heroes of Wish-ram crossed the river once more, returned to their village to feast upon the horses whose blood they had so vaingloriously drunk, and the travellers pursued their voyage without further molestation.

The tin case, however, containing the important despatches for New York, was irretrievably lost; the very precaution taken by the worthy Hibernian to secure his missives, had, by rendering them conspicuous, produced their robbery. The object of his over-land journey, therefore, being defeated, he gave up the expedition. The whole party repaired with Mr. Robert Stuart to the establishment of Mr. David Stuart, on the Oakinagan River. After remaining here two or three days, they all set out on their return to Astoria, accompanied by Mr. David Stuart. This gentleman had a large quantity of beaver skins at his establishment, but did not think it prudent to take them with him, fearing the levy of "black mail" at the falls.

On their way down, when below the forks of the Columbia, they were hailed one day from the shore in English. Looking around, they descried two wretched men, entirely naked. They pulled to shore; the men came up and made themselves known. They proved to be Mr. Crooks and his faithful follower, John Day.

The reader will recollect, that Mr. Crooks, with Day and four Canadians, had been so reduced by famine and fatigue, that Mr. Hunt was obliged to leave them, in the month of December, on the banks of the Snake River. Their situation was the more critical, as they were in the neighborhood of a band of Shoshonies, whose horses had been forcibly seized by Mr. Hunt's party for provisions. Mr. Crooks remained here twenty days, detained by the extremely reduced state of John Day, who was utterly unable to travel, and whom he would not abandon, as Day had been in his employ on the Missouri, and had always proved himself most faithful. Fortunately the Shoshonies did not offer to molest them. They had never before seen white men, and seemed to entertain some superstitions with regard to them, for, though they would encamp near them in the day time, they would move off with their tents in the night; and finally disappeared, without taking leave.

When Day was sufficiently recovered to travel, they kept feebly on, sustaining themselves as well as they could, until in the month of February, when three of the Canadians, fearful of perishing with want, left Mr. Crooks on a small river, on the road by which Mr. Hunt had passed in quest of Indians. Mr. Crooks followed Mr. Hunt's track in the snow for several days, sleeping as usual in the open air, and suffering all kinds of hardships. At length, coming to a low prairie, he lost every appearance of the "trail," and wandered during the remainder of the winter in the mountains, subsisting sometimes on horse meat, sometimes on beavers and their skins, and a part of the time on roots.

About the last of March, the other Canadian gave out, and was left with a lodge of Shoshonies; but Mr. Crooks and John Day still kept on, and finding the snow sufficiently diminished, undertook, from Indian information, to cross the last mountain ridge. They happily succeeded, and afterwards fell in with the Wallah Wallahs, a tribe of Indians inhabiting the banks of a river of the same name, and reputed as being frank, hospitable and sincere. They proved worthy of the character, for they received the poor wanderers kindly, killed a horse for them to eat, and directed them on their way to the Columbia. They struck the river about the middle of April, and advanced down it one hundred miles, until they came within about twenty miles of the falls.

Here they met with some of the "chivalry" of that noted pass, who received them in a friendly way, and set food before them; but, while they were satisfying their hunger, perfidiously seized their rifles. They then stripped them naked, and drove them off, refusing the entreaties of Mr. Crooks for a flint and steel of which they had robbed him; and threatening his life if he did not instantly depart.

In this forlorn plight, still worse off than before, they renewed their wanderings. They now sought to find their way back to the hospitable Wallah Wallahs, and had advanced eighty miles along the river, when fortunately, on the very morning that they were going to leave the Columbia, and strike inland, the canoes of Mr. Stuart hove in sight.

It is needless to describe the joy of these poor men at once more finding themselves among countrymen and friends, or of the honest and hearty welcome with which they were received by their fellow adventurers. The whole party now continued down the river, passed all the dangerous places without interruption, and arrived safely at Astoria on the 11th of May.

CHAPTER XLII

Comprehensive views—To supply the Russian fur establishment—An agent sent to Russia—Project of an annual ship—The Beaver fitted out—Her equipment and crew—Instructions to the captain—The Sandwich islands—Rumors of the fate of the Tonquin—Precautions on reaching the mouth of the Columbia.

Having traced the fortunes of the two expeditions by sea and land to the mouth of the Columbia, and presented a view of affairs at Astoria, we will return for a moment to the master spirit of the enterprize, who regulated the springs of Astoria, at his residence in New York.

It will be remembered, that a part of the plan of Mr. Astor was to furnish the Russian fur establishment on the north west coast with regular supplies, so as to render it independent of those casual vessels which cut up the trade and supplied the natives with arms. This plan had been countenanced by our own government, and likewise by Count Pahlen, the Russian minister at Washington. As its views, however, were important and extensive, and might eventually affect a wide course of commerce, Mr. Astor was desirous of establishing a complete arrangement on the subject with the Russian American Fur Company, under the sanction of the Russian government. For this purpose, in March, 1811, he despatched a confidential agent to S' Petersburgh, fully empowered to enter into the requisite negotiations. A passage was given to this gentleman by the government of the United States, in the John Adams, one of its armed vessels, bound to a European port.

The next step of Mr. Astor was, to despatch the annual ship contemplated on his general plan. He had as yet heard nothing of the success of the previous expeditions, and had to proceed upon the presumption that every thing had been effected according to his instructions. He accordingly fitted out a fine ship of four hundred and ninety tons, called the Beaver, and freighted her with a valuable cargo destined for the factory, at the mouth of the Columbia, the trade along the coast, and the supply of the Russian establishment. In this ship embarked a reinforcement, consisting of a partner, five clerks, fifteen American laborers, and six Canadian voyageurs. In choosing his agents for his first expedition, Mr. Astor had been obliged to have recourse to British subjects experienced in the Canadian fur trade; henceforth it was his intention, as much as possible, to select Americans, so as to secure an ascendancy of American influence in the management of the company, and to make it decidedly national.

Accordingly, Mr. John Clarke, the partner who took the lead in the present expedition, was a native of the United States, though he had passed much of his life in the north west, having been employed in the fur trade since the age of sixteen. Most of the clerks were young gentlemen of good connections in the American cities, some of whom embarked in the hope of gain, others through the mere spirit of adventure incident to youth.

The instructions given by Mr. Astor to Captain Sowle, the commander of the Beaver, were, in some respects, hypothetical, in consequence of the uncertainty resting upon the previous steps of the enterprize.

He was to touch at the Sandwich islands, enquire about the fortunes of the Tonquin, and whether an establishment had been formed at the mouth of the Columbia. If so, he was to take as many Sandwich islanders as his ship would accommodate, and proceed thither. On arriving at the river, he was to observe great caution, for even if an establishment should have been formed, it might have fallen into hostile hands. He was, therefore, to put in as if by casualty or distress, to give himself out as a coasting trader, and to say nothing about his ship being owned by Mr. Astor, until he had ascertained that every thing was right. In that case, he was to land such part of his cargo as was intended for the establishment, and to proceed to New Archangel with the supplies intended for the Russian post at that place, where he could receive peltries in payment. With these he was to return to Astoria; take in the furs collected there, and, having completed his cargo by trading along the coast, was to proceed to Canton. The captain received the same injunctions that had been given to Captain Thorn of the Tonquin, of great caution and circumspection in his intercourse with the natives, and that he should not permit more than one or two to be on board at a time.

The Beaver sailed from New York on the 10th of October, 1811, and reached the Sandwich islands without any occurrence of moment. Here a rumor was heard of the disastrous fate of the Tonquin. Deep solicitude was felt by every one on board for the fate of both expeditions, by sea and land. Doubts were entertained whether any establishment had been formed at the mouth of the Columbia, or whether any of the company would be found there. After much deliberation, the captain took twelve Sandwich islanders on board, for the service of the factory, should there be one in existence, and proceeded on his voyage.

On the 6th of May he arrived off the mouth of the Columbia, and running as near as possible, fired two signal guns. No answer was returned, nor was there any signal to be descried. Night coming on, the ship stood out to sea, and every heart drooped as the land faded away. On the following morning they again ran in within four miles of the shore, and fired other signal guns, but still without reply. A boat was then despatched, to sound the channel, and attempt an entrance; but returned without success, there being a tremendous swell, and breakers. Signal guns were fired again in the evening, but equally in vain, and once more the ship stood off to sea for the night. The captain now gave up all hope of finding any establishment at the place, and indulged in the most gloomy apprehensions. He feared his predecessors had been massacred before they had reached their place of destination; or if they should have erected a factory, that it had been surprised and destroyed by the natives.

In this moment of doubt and uncertainty, Mr. Clarke announced his determination, in case of the worst, to found an establishment with the present party, and all hands bravely engaged to stand by him in the undertaking. The next morning the ship stood in for the third time, and fired three signal guns, but with little hope of reply. To the great joy of the crew, three distinct guns were heard in answer. The apprehensions of all but Captain Sowle were now at rest. That cautious commander recollected the instructions given him by Mr. Astor, and determined to proceed with great circumspection. He was well aware of Indian treachery and cunning. It was not impossible, he observed, that these cannon might have been fired by the savages themselves. They might have surprised the fort, massacred its inmates; and these signal guns might only be decoys to lure him across the bar, that they might have a chance of cutting him off, and seizing his vessel.

At length a white flag was descried hoisted as a signal on Cape Disappointment. The passengers pointed to it in triumph, but the captain did not yet dismiss his doubts. A beacon fire blazed through the night on the same place, but the captain observed that all these signals might be treacherous.

On the following morning, May 9th, the vessel came to anchor off Cape Disappointment, outside of the bar. Towards noon an Indian canoe was seen making for the ship, and all hands were ordered to be on the alert. A few moments afterwards, a barge was perceived following the canoe. The hopes and fears of those on board of the ship were in tumultuous agitation, as the boat drew nigh that was to let them know the fortunes of the enterprize, and the fate of their predecessors. The captain, who was haunted with the idea of possible treachery, did not suffer his curiosity to get the better of his caution, but ordered a party of his men under arms, to receive the visitors. The canoe came first along side, in which were Comcomly and six Indians; in the barge were M'Dougall, M'Lellan, and eight Canadians. A little conversation with these gentlemen dispelled all the captain's fears, and the Beaver crossing the bar under their pilotage, anchored safely in Baker's bay.

CHAPTER XLIII

Active operations at Astoria—Various expeditions fitted out—Robert Stuart and a party destined for New York—Singular conduct of John Day—His fate—Piratical pass and hazardous portage—Rattlesnakes—Their abhorrence of tobacco—Arrival among the Wallah Wallahs—Purchase of horses—Departure of Stuart and his band for the mountains.

The arrival of the Beaver with a reinforcement and supplies, gave new life and vigor to affairs at Astoria. These were means for extending the operations of the establishment, and founding interior trading posts. Two parties were immediately set on foot to proceed severally under the command of Messrs. M'Kenzie and Clarke, and establish posts above the forks of the Columbia, at points where most rivalry and opposition were apprehended from the North West Company.

A third party, headed by Mr. David Stuart, was to repair with supplies to the post of that gentleman on the Oakinagan. In addition to these expeditions, a fourth was necessary to convey despatches to Mr. Astor, at New York, in place of those unfortunately lost by John Reed. The safe conveyance of these despatches was highly important, as by them Mr. Astor would receive an account of the state of the factory, and regulate his reinforcements and supplies accordingly. The mission was one of peril and hardship, and required a man of nerve and vigor. It was confided to Robert Stuart, who, though he had never been across the mountains, and a very young man, had given proofs of his competency to the task. Four trusty and well-tried men, who had come over land in Mr. Hunt's expedition, were given as his guides and hunters. These were Ben Jones and John Day, the Kentuckians, and André Vallar and Francis Le Clerc, Canadians. Mr. M'Lellan again expressed his determination to take this opportunity of returning to the Atlantic states. In this he was joined by Mr. Crooks, who, notwithstanding all that he had suffered in the dismal journey of the preceding winter, was ready to retrace his steps and brave every danger and hardship, rather than remain at Astoria. This little handful of adventurous men we propose to accompany in its long and perilous peregrinations.

The several parties we have mentioned all set off in company on the 29th of June, under a salute of cannon from the fort. They were to keep together, for mutual protection, through the piratical passes of the river, and to separate, on their different destinations, at the forks of the Columbia. Their number, collectively, was nearly sixty, consisting of partners and clerks, Canadian voyageurs, Sandwich islanders, and American hunters; and they embarked in two barges and ten canoes.

They had scarcely got under way, when John Day, the Kentucky hunter, became restless, and uneasy, and extremely wayward in his deportment. This caused surprise, for in general he was remarked for his cheerful, manly deportment. It was supposed that the recollection of past sufferings might harass his mind in undertaking to retrace the scenes where they had been experienced. As the expedition advanced, however, his agitation increased. He began to talk wildly and incoherently, and to show manifest symptoms of derangement.

Mr. Crooks now informed his companions that in his desolate wanderings through the Snake River country during the preceding winter, in which he had been accompanied by John Day, the poor fellow's wits had been partially unsettled by the sufferings and horrors through which they had passed, and he doubted whether they had ever been restored to perfect sanity. It was still hoped that this agitation of spirit might pass away as they proceeded; but, on the contrary, it grew more and more violent. His comrades endeavored to divert his mind and to draw him into rational conversation, but he only became the more exasperated, uttering wild and incoherent ravings. The sight of any of the natives put him in an absolute fury, and he would heap on them the most opprobrious epithets; recollecting, no doubt, what he had suffered from Indian robbers.

On the evening of the 2d of July he became absolutely frantic, and attempted to destroy himself. Being disarmed, he sank into quietude, and professed the greatest remorse for the crime he had meditated. He then pretended to sleep, and having thus lulled suspicion, suddenly sprang up, just before daylight, seized a pair of loaded pistols, and endeavored to blow out his brains. In his hurry he fired too high, and the balls passed over his head. He was instantly secured, and placed under a guard in one of the boats. How to dispose of him was now the question, as it was impossible to keep him with the expedition. Fortunately Mr. Stuart met with some Indians accustomed to trade with Astoria. These undertook to conduct John Day back to the factory, and deliver him there in safety. It was with the utmost concern that his comrades saw the poor fellow depart; for, independent of his invaluable services as a first rate hunter, his frank and loyal qualities had made him a universal favorite. It may be as well to add that the Indians executed their task faithfully, and landed John Day among his friends at Astoria; but his constitution was completely broken by the hardships he had undergone, and he died within a year.

On the evening of the 6th of July the party arrived at the piratical pass of the river, and encamped at the foot of the first rapid. The next day, before the commencement of the portage, the greatest precautions were taken to guard against lurking treachery, or open attack. The weapons of every man were put in order, and his cartridge box replenished. Each one wore a kind of surcoat made of the skin of the elk, reaching from his neck to his knees, and answering the purpose of a shirt of mail, for it was arrow proof, and could even resist a musket ball at the distance of ninety yards. Thus armed and equipped, they posted their forces in military style. Five of the officers took their stations at each end of the portage, which was between three and four miles in length; a number of men mounted guard at short distances along the heights immediately overlooking the river, while the residue thus protected from surprise, employed themselves below in dragging up the barges and canoes, and carrying up the goods along the narrow margin of the rapids. With these precautions they all passed unmolested. The only accident that happened was the upsetting of one of the canoes, by which some of the goods sunk, and others floated down the stream. The alertness and rapacity of the hordes which infest these rapids, were immediately apparent. They pounced upon the floating merchandize with the keenness of regular wreckers. A bale of goods which landed upon one of the islands was immediately ripped open, one half of its contents divided among the captors, and the other half secreted in a lonely hut in a deep ravine. Mr. Robert Stuart, however, set out in a canoe with five men and an interpreter, ferreted out the wreckers in their retreat, and succeeded in wresting from them their booty.

Similar precautions to those already mentioned, and to a still greater extent, were observed in passing the long narrows, and the falls, where they would be exposed to the depredations of the chivalry of Wish-ram, and its freebooting neighborhood. In fact, they had scarcely set their first watch one night, when an alarm of "Indians!" was given. "To arms!" was the cry, and every man was at his post in an instant. The alarm was explained; a war party of Shoshonies had surprised a canoe of the natives just below the encampment, had murdered four men and two women, and it was apprehended they would attack the camp. The boats and canoes were immediately hauled up, a breastwork was made of them, and the packages, forming three sides of a square, with the river in the rear, and thus the party remained fortified throughout the night.

The dawn, however, dispelled the alarm; the portage was conducted in peace; the vagabond warriors of the vicinity hovered about them while at work, but were kept at a wary distance. They regarded the loads of merchandize with wistful eyes, but seeing the "long beards" so formidable in number, and so well prepared for action, they made no attempt either by open force or sly pilfering to collect their usual toll, but maintained a peaceful demeanor, and were afterwards rewarded for their good conduct with presents of tobacco.

Fifteen days were consumed in ascending from the foot of the first rapid, to the head of the falls, a distance of about eighty miles, but full of all kinds of obstructions. Having happily accomplished these difficult portages, the party, on the 19th of July, arrived at a smoother part of the river, and pursued their way up the stream with greater speed and facility.

They were now in the neighborhood where Mr. Crooks and John Day had been so perfidiously robbed and stripped a few months previously, when confiding in the proffered hospitality of a ruffian band. On landing at night, therefore, a vigilant guard was maintained about the camp. On the following morning a number of Indians made their appearance, and came prowling round the party while at breakfast. To his great delight, Mr. Crooks recognized among them two of the miscreants by whom he had been robbed. They were instantly seized, bound hand and foot, and thrown into one of the canoes. Here they lay in doleful fright, expecting summary execution. Mr. Crooks, however, was not of a revengeful disposition, and agreed to release the culprits as soon as the pillaged property should be restored. Several savages immediately started off in different directions, and before night the rifles of Crooks and Day were produced; several of the smaller articles pilfered from them, however, could not be recovered.

The bands of the culprits were then removed, and they lost no time in taking their departure, still under the influence of abject terror, and scarcely crediting their senses that they had escaped the merited punishment of their offences.

The country on each side of the river now began to assume a different character. The hills, and cliffs, and forests, disappeared; vast sandy plains, scantily clothed here and there with short tufts of grass, parched by the summer sun, stretched far away to the north and south. The river was occasionally obstructed with rocks and rapids, but often there were smooth placid intervals, where the current was gentle, and the boatmen were enabled to lighten their labors with the assistance of the sail.

The natives in this part of the river resided entirely on the northern side. They were hunters, as well as fishermen, and had horses in plenty. Some of these were purchased by the party, as provisions, and killed on the spot, though they occasionally found a difficulty in procuring fuel wherewith to cook them. One of the greatest dangers that beset the travellers in this part of their expedition, was the vast number of rattlesnakes which infested the rocks about the rapids and portages, and on which the men were in danger of treading. They were often found, too, in quantities about the encampments. In one place, a nest of them lay coiled together, basking in the sun. Several guns loaded with shot were discharged at them, and thirty seven killed and wounded. To prevent any unwelcome visits from them in the night, tobacco was occasionally strewed around the tents, a weed for which they have a very proper abhorrence.

On the 28th of July the travellers arrived at the mouth of the Wallah Wallah, a bright, clear stream, about six feet deep, and fifty five yards wide, which flows rapidly over a bed of sand and gravel, and throws itself into the Columbia, a few miles below Lewis River. Here the combined parties that had thus far voyaged together, were to separate, each for its particular destination.

On the banks of the Wallah Wallah lived the hospitable tribe of the same name who had succored Mr. Crooks and John Day in the time of their extremity. No sooner did they hear of the arrival of the party, than they hastened to greet them. They built a great bonfire on the bank of the river, before the camp, and men and women danced round it to the cadence of their songs, in which they sang the praises of the white men, and welcomed them to their country.

On the following day a traffic was commenced, to procure horses for such of the party as intended to proceed by land. The Wallah Wallahs are an equestrian tribe. The equipments of their horses were rude and inconvenient. High saddles, roughly made of deer skin, stuffed with hair, which chafe the horse's back, and leave it raw; wooden stirrups, with a thong of raw hide wrapped round them; and for bridles they have cords of twisted horse hair, which they tie round the under jaw. They are like most Indians, bold, but hard riders, and when on horseback gallop about the most dangerous places, without fear for themselves, or pity for their steeds.

From these people Mr. Stuart purchased twenty horses for his party; some for the saddle, and others to transport the baggage. He was fortunate in procuring a noble animal for his own use, which was praised by the Indians for its great speed and bottom, and a high price set upon it. No people understand better the value of a horse, than these equestrian tribes; and no where is speed a greater requisite, as they frequently engage in the chase of the antelope, one of the fleetest of animals. Even after the Indian who sold this boasted horse to Mr. Stuart had concluded his bargain, he lingered about the animal, seeming loth to part from him, and to be sorry for what he had done.

A day or two were employed by Mr. Stuart in arranging packages and pack saddles, and making other preparations for his long and arduous journey. His party, by the loss of John Day, was now reduced to six, a small number for such an expedition. They were young men, however, full of courage, health, and good spirits, and stimulated, rather than appalled by danger.

On the morning of the 31st of July, all preparations being concluded, Mr. Stuart and his little band mounted their steeds and took a farewell of their fellow travellers, who gave them three hearty cheers as they set out on their dangerous journey. The course they took was to the southeast, towards the fated region of the Snake River. At an immense distance rose a chain of craggy mountains, which they would have to traverse; they were the same among which the travellers had experienced such sufferings from cold during the preceding winter, and from their azure tints, when seen at a distance, had received the name of the Blue Mountains.

CHAPTER XLIV

Route of Mr. Stuart—Dreary wilds—Thirsty travelling—A grove and streamlet—The Blue Mountains—A fertile plain with rivulets—Sulphur spring—Route along Snake River—Rumors of white men—The Snake and his horse—A Snake guide—A midnight decampment—Unexpected meeting with old comrades—Story of trappers' hardships—Salmon falls —A great fishery—Mode of spearing salmon—Arrival at the Caldron Linn—State of the caches—New resolution of the three Kentucky trappers.

In retracing the route which had proved so disastrous to Mr. Hunt's party during the preceding winter, Mr. Stuart had trusted, in the present more favorable season, to find easy travelling and abundant supplies. On these great wastes and wilds, however, each season has its peculiar hardships. The travellers had not proceeded far, before they found themselves among naked and arid hills, with a soil composed of sand and clay, baked and brittle, that to all appearance had never been visited by the dews of heaven.

Not a spring, or pool, or running stream was to be seen; the sunburnt country was seamed and cut up by dry ravines, the beds of winter torrents, serving only to balk the hopes of man and beast, with the sight of dusty channels where water had once poured along in floods.

For a long summer day they continued onward without halting; a burning sky above their heads, a parched desert beneath their feet, with just wind enough to raise the light sand from the knolls, and envelope them in stifling clouds. The sufferings from thirst became intense; a fine young dog, their only companion of the kind, gave out, and expired. Evening drew on without any prospect of relief, and they were almost reduced to despair, when they descried something that looked like a fringe of forest, along the horizon. All were inspired with new hope, for they knew that on these arid wastes, in the neighborhood of trees, there is always water.

They now quickened their pace; the horses seemed to understand their motives, and to partake of their anticipations, for, though before, almost ready to give out, they now required neither whip nor spur. With all their exertions, it was late in the night before they drew near to the trees. As they approached, they heard, with transport, the rippling of a shallow stream. No sooner did the refreshing sound reach the ears of the horses, than the poor animals snuffed the air, rushed forward with ungovernable eagerness, and, plunging their muzzles into the water, drank until they seemed in danger of bursting.

Their riders had but little more discretion, and required repeated draughts to quench their excessive thirst. Their weary march that day had been forty five miles, over a tract that might rival the deserts of Africa for aridity. Indeed, the sufferings of the traveller on these American deserts, is frequently more severe than in the wastes of Africa or Asia, from being less habituated and prepared to cope with them.

On the banks of this blessed stream the travellers encamped for the night; and so great had been their fatigue, and so sound and sweet was their sleep, that it was a late hour the next morning before they awoke. They now recognized the little river to be the Umatalla, the same on the banks of which Mr. Hunt and his followers had arrived after their painful struggle through the Blue Mountains, and experienced such a kind relief in the friendly camp of the Sciatogas.

That range of Blue Mountains now extended in the distance before them; they were the same among which poor Michel Carriere had perished. They form the southeast boundary of the great plains along the Columbia, dividing the waters of its main stream from those of Lewis River. They are, in fact, a part of a long chain, which stretches over a great extent of country, and includes in its links the Snake River Mountains.

The day was somewhat advanced before the travellers left the shady banks of the Umatalla. Their route gradually took them among the Blue Mountains, which assumed the most rugged aspect on a near approach. They were shagged with dense and gloomy forests, and cut up by deep and precipitous ravines, extremely toilsome to the horses. Sometimes the travellers had to follow the course of some brawling stream, with a broken, rocky bed, which the shouldering cliffs and promontories on either side, obliged them frequently to cross and recross. For some miles they struggled forward through these savage and darkly wooded defiles, when all at once the whole landscape changed, as if by magic. The rude mountains and rugged ravines softened into beautiful hills, and intervening meadows, with rivulets winding through fresh herbage, and sparkling and murmuring over gravelly beds, the whole forming a verdant and pastoral scene, which derived additional charms from being locked up in the bosom of such a hard-hearted region.

Emerging from the chain of Blue Mountains, they descended upon a vast plain, almost a dead level, sixty miles in circumference, of excellent soil, with fine streams meandering through it in every direction, their courses marked out in the wide landscape, by serpentine lines of cotton wood trees, and willows, which fringed their banks, and afforded sustenance to great numbers of beavers and otters.

In traversing this plain, they passed, close to the skirts of the hills, a great pool of water, three hundred yards in circumference, fed by a sulphur spring, about ten feet in diameter, boiling up in one corner. The vapor from this pool was extremely noisome, and tainted the air for a considerable distance. The place was much frequented by elk, which were found in considerable numbers in the adjacent mountains, and their horns, shed in the spring time, were strewed in every direction around the pond.

On the 10th of August, they reached the main body of Woodpile creek, the same stream which Mr. Hunt had ascended in the preceding year, shortly after his separation from Mr. Crooks.

On the banks of this stream they saw a herd of nineteen antelopes; a sight so unusual in that part of the country, that at first they doubted the evidence of their senses. They tried by every means to get within shot of them, but they were too shy and fleet, and after alternately bounding to a distance and then stopping to gaze with capricious curiosity at the hunter, they at length scampered out of sight.

On the 12th of August, the travellers arrived on the banks of Snake River, the scene of so many trials and mishaps to all of the present party excepting Mr. Stuart. They struck the river just above the place where it entered the mountains through which Messrs. Hunt and Crooks had vainly endeavored to find a passage. The river was here a rapid stream four hundred yards in width, with high sandy banks and here and there a scanty growth of willow. Up the southern side of the river they now bent their course, intending to visit the caches made by Mr. Hunt at the Caldron Linn.

On the second evening a solitary Snake Indian visited their camp at a late hour and informed them that there was a white man residing at one of the cantonments of his tribe about a day's journey higher up the river. It was immediately concluded that he must be one of the poor fellows, of Mr. Hunt's party, who had given out, exhausted by hunger and fatigue, in the wretched journey of the preceding winter. All present, who had borne a part in the sufferings of that journey, were eager now to press forward and bring relief to a lost comrade. Early the next morning, therefore, they pushed forward with unusual alacrity. For two days, however, did they travel without being able to find any trace of such a straggler.

On the evening of the second day they arrived at a place where a large river came in from the east, which was renowned among all the wandering hordes of the Snake nation for its salmon fishery, that fish being taken in incredible quantities in this neighborhood. Here, therefore, during the fishing season, the Snake Indians resort from far and near, to lay in their stock of salmon, which, with esculent roots, forms the principal food of the inhabitants of these barren regions.

On the bank of a small stream emptying into Snake River at this place, Mr. Stuart found an encampment of Shoshonies. He made the usual inquiry of them concerning the white man of whom he had received intelligence. No such person was dwelling among them, but they said there were white men residing with some of their nation on the opposite side of the river. This was still more animating information. Mr. Crooks now hoped that these might be the men of his party who, disheartened by perils and hardships, had preferred to remain among the Indians. Others thought they might be Mr. Miller and the hunters who had left the main body at Henry's fort, to trap among the mountain streams. Mr. Stuart halted, therefore, in the neighborhood of the Shoshonie lodges and sent an Indian across the river to seek out the white men in question and bring them to his camp.

The travellers passed a restless, miserable night. The place swarmed with myriads of musquitoes, which, with their stings and their music set all sleep at defiance. The morning dawn found them in a feverish irritable mood, and their spleen was completely aroused by the return of the Indian without any intelligence of the white men. They now considered themselves the dupes of Indian falsehoods and resolved to put no more confidence in Snakes. They soon, however, forgot this resolution. In the course of the morning an Indian came gallopping after them. Mr. Stuart waited to receive him. No sooner had he come up than, dismounting and throwing his arms round the neck of Mr. Stuart's horse, he began to kiss and caress the animal, who, on his part, seemed by no means surprized or displeased with his salutation. Mr. Stuart, who valued his horse highly, was somewhat annoyed by these transports: the cause of them was soon explained. The Snake said the horse had belonged to him and been the best in his possession, and that it had been stolen by the Wallah Wallahs. Mr. Stuart was by no means pleased with this recognition of his steed, nor disposed to admit any claim on the part of its ancient owner. In fact it was a noble animal, admirably shaped, of free and generous spirit, graceful in movement and fleet as an antelope. It was his intention if possible, to take the horse to New York, and present him to Mr. Astor.

In the mean time some of the party came up and immediately recognized in the Snake an old friend and ally. He was, in fact, one of the two guides who had conducted Mr. Hunt's party, in the preceding autumn, across Mad River Mountain to Fort Henry, and who subsequently departed with Mr. Miller and his fellow trappers to conduct them to a good trapping ground. The reader may recollect that these two trusty Snakes were engaged by Mr. Hunt to return and take charge of the horses which the party intended to leave at Fort Henry, when they should embark in canoes.

The party now crowded round the Snake and began to question him with eagerness. His replies were somewhat vague, and but partially understood. He told a long story about the horses, from which it appeared that they had been stolen by various wandering bands, and scattered in different directions. The cache too had been plundered, and the saddles and other equipments carried off. His information concerning Mr. Miller and his comrades was not more satisfactory. They had trapped for some time about the upper streams, but had fallen into the hands of a marauding party of Crows, who had robbed them of horses, weapons and every thing.

Further questioning brought forth further intelligence, but all of a disastrous kind. About ten days previously he had met with three other white men, in very miserable plight, having one horse each, and but one rifle among them. They also had been plundered and maltreated by the Crows, those universal freebooters. The Snake endeavored to pronounce the names of these three men, and as far as his imperfect sounds could be understood they were supposed to be three of the party of four hunters, viz. Carson, S' Michel, Detayé and Delaunay, who were detached from Mr. Hunt's party on the 28th of September to trap beaver on the head waters of the Columbia.

In the course of conversation the Indian informed them that the route by which Mr. Hunt had crossed the Rocky Mountains, was very bad and circuitous, and that he knew one much shorter and easier. Mr. Stuart urged him to accompany them as guide, promising to reward him with a pistol with powder and ball, a knife, an awl, some blue beads, a blanket and a looking glass. Such a catalogue of riches was too tempting to be resisted; beside, the poor Snake languished after the prairies; he was tired, he said, of salmon, and longed for buffalo meat, and to have a grand buffalo hunt beyond the mountains. He departed, therefore, with all speed to get his arms and equipments for the journey, promising to rejoin the party the next day. He kept his word, and, as he no longer said any thing to Mr. Stuart on the subject of the pet horse they journeyed very harmoniously together; though now and then the Snake would regard his quondam steed with a wistful eye.

They had not travelled many miles when they came to a great bend of the river. Here the Snake informed them that, by cutting across the hills they would save many miles of distance. The route across however would be a good day's journey. He advised them, therefore, to encamp here for the night and set off early in the morning. They took his advice, though they had come but nine miles that day.

On the following morning they rose bright and early, to ascend the hills. On mustering their little party the guide was missing. They supposed him to be somewhere in the neighborhood and proceeded to collect the horses. The vaunted steed of Mr. Stuart was not to be found. A suspicion flashed upon his mind. Search for the horse of the Snake!— He likewise was gone—the tracks of two horses, one after the other were found, making off from the camp. They appeared as if one horse had been mounted and the other led. They were traced for a few miles above the camp until they both crossed the river. It was plain, the Snake had taken an Indian mode of recovering his horse, having quietly decamped with him in the night.

New vows were made never more to trust in Snakes or any other Indians. It was determined also to maintain hereafter the strictest vigilance over their horses, dividing the night into three watches and one person mounting guard at a time. They resolved also to keep along the river instead of taking the short cut recommended by the fugitive Snake, whom they now set down for a thorough deceiver. The heat of the weather was oppressive, and their horses were at times rendered almost frantic by the stings of the prairie flies. The nights were suffocating, and it was almost impossible to sleep from the swarms of musquitoes.

On the 20th of August they resumed their march, keeping along the prairie parallel to Snake River. The day was sultry and some of the party, being parched with thirst, left the line of march and scrambled down the bank of the river to drink. The bank was overhung with willows, beneath which, to their surprize, they beheld a man fishing. No sooner did he see them than he uttered an exclamation of joy. It proved to be John Hoback, one of their lost comrades. They had scarcely exchanged greetings when three other men came out from among the willows. They were Mr. Joseph Miller, Jacob Rezner, and Robinson, the scalped Kentuckian, the veteran of the Bloody ground.

The reader will perhaps recollect the abrupt and wilful manner in which Mr. Miller threw up his interest as a partner of the Company, and departed from Fort Henry in company with these three trappers and a fourth named Cass. He may likewise recognize in Robinson, Rezner and Hoback, the trio of Kentucky hunters, who had originally been in the service of Mr. Henry, and whom Mr. Hunt found floating down the Missouri, on their way homeward; and prevailed upon, once more to cross the mountains.

The haggard looks and naked condition of these men proved how much they had suffered. After leaving Mr. Hunt's party they had made their way about two hundred miles to the south ward, where they trapped beaver on a river which, according to their account discharged itself into the Ocean to the south of the Columbia, but which we apprehend to be Bear River, a stream emptying itself into Lake Bonneville, an immense body of salt water, west of the Rocky Mountains.

Having collected a considerable quantity of beaver skins, they made them into packs, loaded their horses and steered two hundred miles due east. Here they came upon an encampment of sixty lodges of Arapahayas, an outlawed band of the Arapahoes, and notorious robbers. These fell upon the poor trappers; robbed them of their peltries, most of their clothing, and several of their horses. They were glad to escape with their lives, and without being entirely stripped, and after proceeding about fifty miles further, made their halt for the winter.

Early in the spring they resumed their wayfaring but were unluckily overtaken by the same ruffian horde, who levied still further contributions, and carried off the remainder of their horses excepting two. With these they continued on, suffering the greatest hardships. They still retained rifles and ammunition, but were in a desert country where neither bird nor beast was to be found. Their only chance was to keep along the rivers and subsist by fishing, but at times no fish were to be taken, and then their sufferings were horrible. One of their horses was stolen among the mountains by the Snake Indians; the other, they said, was carried off by Cass who, according to their account, "villanously left them in their extremities." Certain dark doubts and surmises were afterwards circulated concerning the fate of that poor fellow, which, if true, shewed to what a desperate state of famine his comrades had been reduced.

Being now completely unhorsed, Mr. Miller and his three companions wandered on foot for several hundred miles, enduring hunger, thirst and fatigue while traversing the barren wastes which abound beyond the Rocky Mountains. At the time they were discovered by Mr. Stuart's party they were almost famished, and were fishing for a precarious meal.

Had Mr. Stuart made the short cut across the hills, avoiding this bend of the river, or had not some of his party accidentally gone down to the margin of the stream to drink, these poor wanderers might have remained undiscovered, and have perished in the wilderness.

Nothing could exceed their joy in thus meeting with their old comrades, or the heartiness with which they were welcomed. All hands immediately encamped; and the slender stores of the party were ransacked to furnish out a suitable regale.

The next morning they all set out together; Mr. Miller and his comrades being resolved to give up the life of a trapper and accompany Mr. Stuart back to S' Louis.

For several days they kept along the course of Snake River, occasionally making short cuts across hills and promontories where there were bends in the stream. In their way they passed several camps of Shoshonies, from some of whom they procured salmon, but in general they were too wretchedly poor to furnish any thing. It was the wish of Mr. Stuart to purchase horses for the recent recruits to his party but the Indians could not be prevailed upon to part with any, alleging that they had not enough for their own use.

On the 25th of August they reached a great fishing place to which they gave the name of The Salmon falls. Here there is a perpendicular fall of twenty feet on the north side of the river, while on the south side there is a succession of rapids. The salmon are taken here in incredible quantities, as they attempt to shoot the falls. It was now a favorable season, and there were about one hundred lodges of Shoshonies busily engaged killing and drying fish. The salmon begin to leap shortly after sunrise. At this time the Indians swim to the center of the falls where some station themselves on rocks and others stand to their waists in the water, all armed with spears, with which they assail the salmon as they attempt to leap or fall back exhausted. It is an incessant slaughter so great is the throng of the fish.

The construction of the spears thus used is peculiar. The head is a straight piece of elk horn about seven inches long; on the point of which an artificial barb is made fast with twine well gummed. The head is stuck on the end of the shaft; a very long pole of willow to which it is likewise connected by a strong cord a few inches in length. When the spearsman makes a sure blow he often strikes the head of the spear through the body of the fish. It comes off readily, and leaves the salmon struggling with the string through its body, while the pole is still held by the spearsman. Were it not for the precaution of the string, the willow shaft would be snapped by the struggles and the weight of the fish.

Mr. Miller, in the course of his wanderings, had been at these falls, and had seen several thousand salmon taken in the course of one afternoon. He declared that he had seen a salmon leap a distance of about thirty feet from the commencement of the foam at the foot of the fall completely to the top.

Having purchased a good supply of salmon from the fishermen the party resumed their journey and on the twenty ninth arrived at the Caldron Linn; the eventful scene of the preceding autumn. Here the first thing that met their eyes was a memento of the perplexities of that period: the wreck of a canoe lodged between two ledges of rocks. They endeavored to get down to it, but the river banks were too high and precipitous.

They now proceeded to that part of the neighborhood where Mr. Hunt and his party had made the caches, intending to take from them such articles as belonged to Mr. Crooks, M'Lellan and the Canadians. On reaching the spot they found, to their astonishment, six of the caches open and rifled of their contents, excepting a few books which lay scattered about the vicinity. They had the appearance of having been plundered in the course of the summer. There were tracks of wolves in every direction to and from the holes, from which Mr. Stuart concluded that these animals had first been attracted to the place by the smell of the skins contained in the caches, which they had probably torn up, and that their tracks had betrayed the secret to the Indians.

The three remaining caches had not been molested: they contained a few dry goods, some ammunition and a number of beaver traps. From these Mr. Stuart took whatever was requisite for his party; he then deposited within them all his superfluous baggage, and all the books and papers scattered around; the holes were then carefully closed up and all traces of them effaced.

And here we have to record another instance of the indomitable spirit of the western trappers. No sooner had the trio of Kentucky hunters, Robinson, Rezner and Hoback, found that they could once more be fitted out for a campaign of beaver trapping, than they forgot all that they had suffered and determined upon another trial of their fortunes; preferring to take their chance in the wilderness rather than return home ragged and penniless. As to Mr. Miller he declared his curiosity and his desire of travelling through the Indian countries fully satisfied; he adhered to his determination therefore to keep on with the party to S' Louis and to return to the bosom of civilized society.

The three hunters, therefore, Robinson, Rezner and Hoback were furnished, as far as the caches and the means of Mr. Stuart's party afforded, with the requisite munitions and equipments for a "two years' hunt;" but as their fitting out was yet incomplete, they resolved to wait in this neighborhood until Mr. Reed should arrive; whose arrival might soon be expected; as he was to set out for the caches about twenty days after Mr. Stuart parted with him at the Wallah Wallah River.

Mr. Stuart gave in charge to Robinson a letter to Mr. Reed reporting his safe journey thus far, and the state in which he had found the caches. A duplicate of this letter he elevated on a pole and set it up near the place of deposit.

All things being thus arranged Mr. Stuart and his little band, now seven in number, took leave of the three hardy trappers, wishing them all possible success in their lonely and perilous sojourn in the wilderness; and we, in like manner, shall leave them to their fortunes, promising to take them up again at some future page, and to close the story of their persevering and illfated enterprize.

CHAPTER XLV

On the 1st of September Mr. Stuart and his companions resumed their
journey, bending their course eastward, along the course of Snake River.
As they advanced the country opened. The hills which had hemmed in
the river receded on either hand, and great sandy and dusty plains
extended before them. Occasionally there were intervals of pasturage
and the banks of the river were fringed with willows and cotton wood,
so that its course might be traced from the hill tops, winding under an
umbrageous covert through a wide sun burnt landscape. The soil,
however, was generally poor; there was in some places a miserable
growth of wormwood, and a plant called salt weed, resembling penny
royal; but the summer heat had parched the plains, and left but little
pasturage. The game too had disappeared. The hunter looked in vain
over the lifeless landscape; now and then a few antilope might be seen,
but not within reach of the rifle. We forbear to follow the travellers in a
week's wandering over these barren wastes, where they suffered much
from hunger; having to depend upon a few fish from the streams, and
now and then a little dried salmon, or a dog, procured from some forlorn
lodge of Shoshonies.

Tired of these cheerless wastes, they left the banks of Snake River
on the 7th of September, under guidance of Mr. Miller, who, having
acquired some knowledge of the country during his trapping campaign,
undertook to conduct them across the mountains by a better route than
that by Fort Henry, and one more out of the range of the Blackfeet. He
proved, however, but an indifferent guide, and they soon became
bewildered among rugged hills and unknown streams and burnt and
barren prairies.

At length they came to a river on which Mr. Miller had trapped and
to which they gave his name; though, as before observed, we presume
it to be the same called Bear River, which empties itself into Lake
Bonneville. Up this river and its branches they kept for two or three
days, supporting themselves precariously upon fish.

They soon found that they were in a dangerous neighborhood. On
the 12th of September, having encamped early, they sallied forth with
their rods to angle for their supper. On returning they beheld a number
of Indians prowling about their camp, whom, to their infinite disquiet,
they soon perceived to be Upsarokas or Crows.

Their chief came forward with a confident air. He was a dark herculean fellow, full six feet four inches in height, with a mingled air of the ruffian and the rogue. He conducted himself peaceably, however, and despatched some of his people to their camp, which was somewhere in the neighborhood and from whence they returned with a most acceptable supply of buffalo meat. He now signified to Mr. Stuart that he was going to trade with the Snakes who reside on the west base of the mountains below Henry's fort. Here they cultivate a delicate kind of tobacco much esteemed and sought after by the mountain tribes. There was something sinister, however, in the look of this Indian that inspired distrust. By degrees the number of his people encreased, until by midnight, there were twenty one of them about the camp, who began to be impudent and troublesome. The greatest uneasiness was now felt for the safety of the horses and effects, and every one kept vigilant watch throughout the night.

The morning dawned, however, without any unpleasant occurrence, and Mr. Stuart, having purchased all the buffalo meat that the Crows had to spare, prepared to depart. His Indian acquaintance, however, were disposed for further dealings, and, above all, anxious for a supply of gunpowder, for which they offered horses in exchange. Mr. Stuart declined to furnish them with the dangerous commodity. They became more importunate in their solicitations, until they met with a flat refusal.

The gigantic chief now stepped forward, assumed a swelling air, and, slapping himself upon the breast, gave Mr. Stuart to understand that he was a chief of great power and importance. He signified, further, that it was customary for great chiefs when they met, to make each other presents. He requested, therefore, that Mr. Stuart would alight and give him the horse upon which he was mounted. This was a noble animal, of one of the wild races of the prairies, on which Mr. Stuart set great value; he, of course, shook his head at the request of the Crow dignitary. Upon this the latter strode up to him and taking hold of him, moved him backwards and forwards in his saddle as if to make him feel that he was a mere child within his grasp. Mr. Stuart preserved his calmness, and still shook his head. The chief then seized the bridle and gave it a jerk that startled the horse, and nearly brought the rider to the ground. Mr. Stuart instantly drew forth a pistol and presented it at the head of the bully ruffian. In a twinkling his swaggering was at an end, and he dodged behind his horse to escape the expected shot. As his subject Crows gazed on the affray from a little distance, Mr. Stuart ordered his men to level their rifles at them, but not to fire. The whole crew scampered among the bushes, and, throwing themselves upon the ground, vanished from sight.

The chieftain thus left alone, was confounded for an instant, but recovering himself, with true Indian shrewdness burst into a loud laugh, and affected to turn off the whole matter as a piece of pleasantry. Mr. Stuart by no means relished such equivocal joking, but it was not his policy to get into a quarrel; so he joined, with the best grace he could assume, in the merriment of the jocular giant and to console the latter for the refusal of the horse, made him a present of twenty charges of powder. They parted, according to all outward professions, the best friends in the world; it was evident, however, that nothing but the smallness of his own force, and the martial array and alertness of the white men, had prevented the Crow chief from proceeding to open outrage. As it was, his worthy followers, in the course of their brief interview, had contrived to purloin a bag containing almost all the culinary utensils of the party.

The travellers now kept on their way due east, over a chain of hills. The recent rencontre shewed them that they were now in a land of danger, subject to the wide roamings of a predacious tribe; nor in fact had they gone many miles, before they beheld sights calculated to inspire anxiety and alarm. From the summits of some of the loftiest mountains, in different directions, columns of smoke began to rise. These they concluded to be signals made by the runners of the Crow chieftain, to summon the stragglers of his band, so as to pursue them with greater force. Signals of this kind, made by outrunners from one central point, will rouse a wide circuit of the mountains in a wonderfully short space of time; and bring the straggling hunters and warriors to the standard of their chieftain.

To keep as much as possible out of the way of these freebooters Mr. Stuart altered his course to the north, and, quitting the main stream of Miller's River, kept up a large branch that came in from the mountains. Here they encamped after a fatiguing march of twenty five miles. As the night drew on the horses were hobbled, or fettered, and tethered close to the camp; a vigilant watch was maintained until morning, and every one slept with his rifle on his arm.

At sunrise they were again on the march, still keeping to the north. They soon began to ascend the mountains and occasionally had wide prospects over the surrounding country. Not a sign of a Crow was to be seen; but this did not assure them of their security, well knowing the perseverance of these savages in dogging any party they intend to rob, and the stealthy way in which they can conceal their movements, keeping along ravines and defiles. After a mountain scramble of twenty one miles they encamped on the margin of a stream running to the north.

In the evening there was an alarm of Indians, and every one was instantly on the alert. They proved to be three miserable Snakes, who were no sooner informed that a band of Crows was prowling in the neighborhood than they made off with great signs of consternation.

A couple more of weary days and watchful nights brought them to a strong and rapid stream, running due north, which they concluded to be one of the upper branches of Snake River. It was probably the same since called Salt River. They determined to bend their course down this river, as it would take them still further out of the dangerous neighborhood of the Crows. They then would strike upon Mr. Hunt's track of the preceding autumn, and retrace it across the mountains. The attempt to find a better route under guidance of Mr. Miller had cost them a large bend to the south; in resuming Mr. Hunt's track they would at least be sure of their road. They accordingly turned down along the course of this stream, and at the end of three days' journey, came to where it was joined by a larger river, and assumed a more impetuous character, raging and roaring among rocks and precipices. It proved, in fact, to be Mad River, already noted in the expedition of Mr. Hunt. On the banks of this river they encamped on the 18th of September, at an early hour.

Six days had now elapsed since their interview with the Crows; during that time they had come nearly a hundred and fifty miles to the north and west, without seeing any signs of those marauders. They considered themselves therefore beyond the reach of molestation and began to relax in their vigilance, lingering occasionally for part of a day where there was good pasturage. The poor horses needed repose. They had been urged on, by forced marches, over rugged heights, among rocks and fallen timber, or over low swampy valleys, inundated by the labors of the beaver. These industrious animals abounded in all the mountain streams and water courses wherever there were willows for their subsistence. Many of these they had so completely dammed up as to inundate the low grounds, making shallow pools or lakes and extensive quagmires: by which the route of the travellers was often impeded.

On the 19th of September they rose at early dawn; some began to prepare breakfast, and others to arrange the packs preparatory to a march. The horses had been hobbled, but left at large to graze upon the adjacent pastures. Mr. Stuart was on the bank of the river at a short distance from the camp when he heard the alarm cry—"Indians! Indians!—to arms! to arms!"

A mounted Crow gallopped past the camp bearing a red flag. He reined his steed on the summit of a neighboring knoll and waved his flaring banner. A diabolical yell now broke forth on the opposite side of the camp beyond where the horses were grazing, and a small troop of savages came gallopping up whooping and making a terrific clamor.

The horses took fright and dashed across the camp in the direction of the standard bearer, attracted by his waving flag. He instantly put spurs to his steed and scoured off, followed by the panic stricken herd, their fright being encreased by the yells of the savages in their rear.

At the first alarm Mr. Stuart and his comrades had seized their rifles and attempted to cut off the Indians who were pursuing the horses. Their attention was instantly distracted by whoops and yells in an opposite direction. They now apprehended that a reserve party was about to carry off their baggage. They ran to secure it. The reserve party, however, gallopped by, whooping and yelling in triumph and derision. The last of them proved to be their commander, the identical giant joker already mentioned. He was not cast in the stern poetical mould of fashionable Indian heroism, but on the contrary, was grievously given to vulgar jocularity. As he passed Mr. Stuart and his companions he checked his horse, raised himself in the saddle, and clapping his hand on the most insulting part of his body, uttered some jeering words, which, fortunately for their delicacy they could not understand. The rifle of Ben Jones was levelled in an instant, and he was on the point of whizzing a bullet into the target so tauntingly displayed. "Not for your life! not for your life!," exclaimed Mr. Stuart, "you will bring destruction on us all!"

It was hard to restrain honest Ben when the mark was so fair and the insult so foul. "Oh Mr. Stuart," exclaimed he, "only let me have one crack at the infernal rascal and you may keep all the pay that is due to me."

"By heaven, if you fire," cried Mr. Stuart, "I'll blow your brains out."

By this time the Indian was far out of reach and had rejoined his men, and the whole dare devil band, with the captured horses, scuttled off along the defiles, their red flag flaunting over head and the rocks echoing to their whoops and yells and demoniac laughter.

The unhorsed travellers gazed after them in silent mortification and despair; yet Mr. Stuart could not but admire the style and spirit with which the whole exploit had been managed, and pronounced it one of the most daring and intrepid actions he had ever heard of among Indians. The whole number of the Crows did not exceed twenty. In this way a small gang of lurkers will hurry off the cavalry of a large war party, for when once a drove of horses are seized with a panic they become frantic and nothing short of broken necks can stop them.

No one was more annoyed by this unfortunate occurrence than Ben Jones. He declared he would actually have given his whole arrears of pay, amounting to upwards of a year's wages, rather than be balked of such a capital shot. Mr. Stuart, however, represented what might

have been the consequence of so rash an act. Life for life is the
Indian maxim. The whole tribe would have made common cause in
avenging the death of a warrior. The party were but seven dismounted
men, with a wide mountain region to traverse, infested by these people,
and which might all be roused by signal fires. In fact the conduct
of the band of marauders in question shewed the perseverance of
savages when once they have fixed their minds upon a project. These
fellows had evidently been silently and secretly dogging the party
for a week past, and a distance of a hundred and fifty miles, keeping
out of sight by day, lurking about the encampments at night, watching
all their movements, and waiting for a favorable moment when they
should be off their guard. The menace of Mr. Stuart, in their first
interview, to shoot the giant chief with his pistol, and the fright caused
among the warriors by presenting the rifles, had probably added the
stimulus of pique to their usual horse stealing propensities, and in
this mood of mind they would doubtless have followed the party
throughout their whole course over the Rocky Mountains rather than
be disappointed in their scheme.

CHAPTER XLVI

Travellers unhorsed—Pedestrian preparations—Prying spies—Bonfire of baggage—A march on foot—Rafting a river—The wounded elk—Indian trails—Wilful conduct of Mr. M'Lellan—Grand prospect from a mountain—Distant craters of volcanos—Illness of Mr. Crooks.

Few reverses in this changeful world are more complete and disheartening than that of a traveller, suddenly unhorsed, in the midst of the wilderness. Our unfortunate travellers contemplated their situation for a time in perfect dismay. A long long journey over rugged mountains and immeasureable plains, lay before them, which they must painfully perform on foot, and every thing necessary for subsistence or defence, must be carried on their shoulders. Their dismay, however, was but transient, and they immediately set to work, with that prompt expediency produced by the exigencies of the wilderness, to fit themselves for the change in their condition.

Their first attention was to select from their baggage such articles as were indispensable to their journey; to make them up into convenient packs, and to deposite the residue in caches. The whole day was consumed in these occupations: At night they made a scanty meal of their remaining provisions and lay down to sleep with heavy hearts. In the morning they were up and alert at an early hour, and began to prepare their knapsacks for a march, while Ben Jones repaired to an old beaver trap which he had set in the river bank at some little distance from the camp. He was rejoiced to find a middle sized beaver there, sufficient for a morning's meal to his hungry comrades. On his way back with his prize, he observed two heads peering over the edge of an impending cliff several hundred feet high which he supposed to be a couple of wolves. As he continued on he now and then cast his eye up; the heads were still there, looking down with fixed and watchful gaze. A suspicion now flashed across his mind that they might be Indian scouts; and, had they not been far above the reach of his rifle, he would undoubtedly have regaled them with a shot.

On arriving at the camp he directed the attention of his comrades to these aerial observers. The same idea was at first entertained that they were wolves; but their immoveable watchfulness soon satisfied every one that they were Indians. It was concluded that they were watching the movements of the party to discover their place of concealment of such articles as they would be compelled to leave behind. There was no likelihood that the caches would escape the search of such keen eyes and experienced rummagers, and the idea was intolerable

277

that any more booty should fall into their hands. To disappoint them, therefore, the travellers stripped the caches of the articles deposited there, and collecting together every thing that they could not carry away with them, made a bonfire of all that would burn, and threw the rest into the river. There was a forlorn satisfaction in thus balking the Crows by the destruction of their own property; and, having thus gratified their pique they shouldered their packs, about ten o'clock in the morning, and set out on their pedestrian wayfaring.

The route they took was down along the banks of Mad River. This stream makes its way through the defiles of the mountains into the plain below Fort Henry, where it terminates in Snake River. Mr. Stuart was in hopes of meeting with Snake encampments in the plain, where he might procure a couple of horses to transport the baggage. In such case he intended to resume his eastern course across the mountains and endeavor to reach the Cheyenne River before winter. Should he fail, however, of obtaining horses, he would probably be compelled to winter on the Pacific side of the mountains, somewhere on the head waters of the Spanish or Colorado river.

With all the care that had been observed in taking nothing with them that was not absolutely necessary, the poor pedestrians were heavily laden, and their burthens added to the fatigues of their rugged road. They suffered much too from hunger. The trout they caught were too poor to yield much nourishment; their main dependance, therefore, was upon an old beaver trap which they had providentially retained. Whenever they were fortunate enough to entrap a beaver it was cut up immediately and distributed, that each man might carry his share.

After two days of toilsome travel, during which they made but eighteen miles, they stopped on the 21st to build two rafts on which to cross to the north side of the river. On these they embarked, on the following morning, four on one raft, and three on the other, and pushed boldly from shore. Finding the rafts sufficiently firm and steady to withstand the rough and rapid water, they changed their minds and, instead of crossing, ventured to float down with the current. The river was in general very rapid, and from one to two hundred yards in width, winding in every direction through mountains of hard black rock, covered with pines and cedars. The mountains to the east of the river were spurs of the Rocky range, and of great magnitude; those on the west were little better than hills, bleak and barren, or scantily clothed with stunted grass.

Mad River though deserving its name from the impetuosity of its current, was free from rapids and cascades, and flowed on in a single channel between gravel banks, often fringed with cotton wood and dwarf willows in abundance. These gave sustenance to immense quantities of beaver, so that the voyagers found no difficulty in procuring food. Ben Jones, also, killed a fallow deer and a wolverine, and as they were enabled to carry the carcasses on their rafts, their larder was well supplied. Indeed they might have occasionally shot beavers that were swimming in the river as they floated by, but they humanely spared their lives, being in no want of meat at the time.

In this way they kept down the river for three days, drifting with the current and encamping on land at night, when they drew up their rafts on shore. Towards the evening of the third day they came to a little island on which they descried a gang of elk. Ben Jones landed and was fortunate enough to wound one which immediately took to the water, but, being unable to stem the current, drifted above a mile when it was over taken and drawn to shore. As a storm was gathering they now encamped on the margin of the river, where they remained all the next day sheltering themselves as well as they could from the rain and hail and snow, a sharp foretaste of the impending winter. During their encampment they employed themselves in jerking a part of the elk for future supply. In cutting up the carcass they found that the animal had been wounded by hunters, about a week previously, an arrow head and a musket ball remaining in the wounds. In the wilderness every trivial circumstance is a matter of anxious speculation. The Snake Indians have no guns; the elk, therefore, could not have been wounded by one of them. They were on the borders of the country infested by the Blackfeet, who carry fire arms. It was concluded, therefore, that the elk had been hunted by some of that wandering and hostile tribe who, of course, must be in the neighborhood. The idea put an end to the transient solace they had enjoyed in the comparative repose and abundance of the river.

For three days longer they continued to navigate with their rafts. The recent storm had rendered the weather extremely cold. They had now floated down the river about ninety one miles, when finding the mountains on the right diminished to moderate sized hills, they landed and prepared to resume their journey on foot. Accordingly, having spent a day in preparations, making moccasins, and parcelling out their jerked meat, in packs of twenty pounds to each man, they turned their backs upon the river on the 29th of September, and struck off to the north east; keeping along the southern skirt of the mountain on which Henry's fort was situated.

Their march was slow and toilsome; part of the time through an alluvial bottom thickly grown with cotton wood, hawthorn and willows, and part of the time over rough hills. Three antelopes came within shot but they dared not fire at them, lest the report of their rifles should betray them to the Blackfeet. In the course of the day they came upon a large horse track apparently about three weeks old, and in the evening encamped on the banks of a small stream, on a spot which had been the camping place of this same band.

On the following morning they still observed the Indian track, but after a time they came to where it separated in every direction and was lost. This shewed that the band had dispersed in various hunting parties and was, in all probability, still in the neighborhood; it was necessary, therefore, to proceed with the utmost caution. They kept a vigilant eye as they marched, upon every height where a scout might be posted, and scanned the solitary landscape and the distant ravines, to observe any column of smoke; but nothing of the kind was to be seen; all was indescribably stern and lifeless.

Towards evening they came to where there were several hot springs, strongly impregnated with iron and sulphur, and sending up a volume of vapour that tainted the surrounding atmosphere and might be seen at the distance of a couple of miles.

Near to these they encamped in a deep gulley, which afforded some concealment. To their great concern, Mr. Crooks, who had been indisposed for the two preceding days, had a violent fever in the night.

Shortly after day break they resumed their march. On emerging from the glen a consultation was held as to their course. Should they continue round the skirt of the mountain they would be in danger of falling in with the scattered parties of Blackfeet who were probably hunting in the plain. It was thought most adviseable, therefore, to strike directly across the mountain, since the route, though rugged and difficult would be most secure. This council was indignantly derided by M'Lellan as pusillanimous. Hot headed and impatient at all times, he had been rendered irascible by the fatigues of the journey and the condition of his feet, which were chafed and sore. He could not endure the idea of encountering the difficulties of the mountain and swore he would rather face all the Blackfeet in the country. He was over ruled, however, and the party began to ascend the mountain, striving, with the ardour and emulation of young men, who should be first up. M'Lellan who was double the age of some of his companions, soon began to lose breath and fall in the rear. In the distribution of burthens it was his turn to carry the old beaver trap. Piqued and irritated he suddenly came to a halt, swore he would carry it no further, and jerked it half way down the hill. He was offered in place of it a package of dried meat but this he scornfully threw upon the ground. They might carry it, he said, who needed it; for his part, he could provide his daily food with his rifle. He concluded by flinging off from the party and keeping along the skirts of the mountain, leaving those, he said, to climb rocks who were afraid to face Indians. It was in vain that Mr. Stuart represented to him the rashness of his conduct and the dangers to which he exposed himself: he rejected such counsel as craven. It was equally useless to represent the dangers to which he subjected his companions; as he could be discovered at a great distance on these naked plains, and the Indians, seeing him, would know that there must be other white men within reach. M'Lellan turned a deaf ear to every remonstrance and kept on his wilful way.

It seems a strange instance of perverseness in this man thus to fling himself off alone, in a savage region, where solitude itself was dismal, but every encounter with his fellow man full of peril. Such however is the hardness of spirit, and the insensibility to danger that grow upon men in the wilderness. M'Lellan, moreover, was a man of peculiar temperament, ungovernable in his will, of a courage that absolutely knew no fear, and somewhat of a braggart spirit, that took a pride in doing desperate and harebrained things.

Mr. Stuart and his party found the passage of the mountain somewhat difficult on account of the snow, which in many places was of considerable depth though it was now but the 1st of October. They crossed the summit early in the afternoon, and beheld below them a plain about twenty miles wide, bounded on the opposite side by their old acquaintances the Pilot Knobs, those towering mountains which had served Mr. Hunt as land marks in part of his route of the preceding year. Through the intermediate plain wandered a river about fifty yards wide, sometimes gleaming in open day, but oftener running through willowed banks, which marked its serpentine course.

Those of the party who had been across these mountains pointed out much of the bearings of the country to Mr. Stuart. They shewed him in what direction must lie the deserted post called Henry's fort, where they had abandoned their horses and embarked in canoes, and they informed him that the stream which wandered through the plain below them, fell into Henry River, half way between the Fort and the mouth of Mad or Snake River. The character of all this mountain region was decidedly volcanic, and to the north west, between Henry's Fort and the source of the Missouri Mr. Stuart observed several very high peaks covered with snow, from two of which smoke ascended in considerable volumes, apparently from craters in a state of eruption.

On their way down the mountain when they had reached the skirts they descried M'Lellan at a distance in the advance traversing the plain. Whether he saw them or not, he shewed no disposition to rejoin them, but pursued his sullen and solitary way.

After descending into the plain they kept on about six miles until they reached the little river, which was here about knee deep, and richly fringed with willow. Here they encamped for the night.

At this encampment the fever of Mr. Crooks increased to such a degree that it was impossible for him to travel. Some of the men were strenuous for Mr. Stuart to proceed without him, urging the imminent danger they were exposed to by delay in that unknown and barren region, infested by the most treacherous and inveterate of foes. They represented that the season was rapidly advancing; the weather for some days had been extremely cold; the mountains were already almost impassable from snow, and would soon present effectual barriers. Their provisions were exhausted; there was no game to be seen, and they did not dare to use their rifles, through fear of drawing upon them the Blackfeet.

The picture thus presented, was too true to be contradicted, and made a deep impression on the mind of Mr. Stuart; but the idea of abandoning a fellow being, and a comrade, in such a forlorn situation, was too repugnant to his feelings to be admitted for an instant. He represented to the men that the malady of Mr. Crooks could not be of long duration, and that in all probability, he would be able to travel in the course of a few days. It was with great difficulty, however, that he prevailed upon them to abide the event.

CHAPTER XLVII

Ben Jones and a grizzly bear—Rocky heights—Mountain torrents—
Traces of M'Lellan—Volcanic remains—Mineral earths—Peculiar clay
for pottery—Dismal plight of M'Lellan—Starvation—Shocking proposi-
tion of a desperate man—A broken down bull—A ravenous meal—Indian
graves—Hospitable Snakes—A forlorn alliance.

As the travellers were now in a dangerous neighborhood, where the
report of a rifle might bring the savages upon them, they had to
depend upon their old beaver trap for subsistence. The little river
on which they were encamped gave many "beaver signs," and Ben
Jones set off at day break, along the willowed banks, to find a proper
trapping place. As he was making his way among the thickets with
his trap on his shoulder and his rifle in his hand, he heard a crashing
sound, and turning beheld a huge grizzly bear advancing upon him
with a terrific growl. The sturdy Kentuckian was not to be intimidated
by man or monster. Levelling his rifle he pulled the trigger. The bear
was wounded, but not mortally: instead, however, of rushing upon
his assailant, as is generally the case with this kind of bear, he retreated
into the bushes. Jones followed him for some distance, but with
suitable caution, and bruin effected his escape.

As there was every prospect of a detention of some days in this
place, and as the supplies of the beaver trap were too precarious to
be depended upon, it became absolutely necessary to run some risk
of discovery by hunting in the neighborhood. Ben Jones, therefore,
obtained permission to range with his rifle some distance from the camp,
and set off to beat up the river banks in defiance of bear or Blackfeet.

He returned in great spirits in the course of a few hours, having
come upon a gang of elk about six miles off, and killed five. This
was joyful news, and the party immediately moved forward to the
place where he had left the carcasses. They were obliged to support
Mr. Crooks the whole distance, for he was unable to walk. Here they
remained for two or three days, feasting heartily on elk meat, and
drying as much as they would be able to carry away with them.

By the 5th of October some simple prescriptions, together with an
"Indian sweat" had so far benefited Mr. Crooks that he was enabled
to move about; they, therefore, set forward slowly, dividing his pack
and accoutrements among them, and made a creeping day's progress
of eight miles south. Their route for the most part lay through swamps
caused by the industrious labours of the beaver. For this little animal
had dammed up numerous small streams issuing from the Pilot Knob

Mountains, so that the low grounds on their borders were completely inundated. In the course of their march they killed a grizzly bear, with fat on its flanks upwards of three inches in thickness. This was an acceptable addition to their stock of elk meat.

The next day Mr. Crooks was sufficiently recruited in strength to be able to carry his rifle and pistols, and they made a march of seventeen miles, along the borders of the plain.

Their journey daily became more toilsome and their sufferings more severe as they advanced. Keeping up the channel of a river they traversed the rugged summit of the Pilot Knob Mountain, covered with snow nine inches deep. For several days they continued, bending their course as much as possible to the east, over a succession of rocky heights, deep valleys and rapid streams. Sometimes their dizzy path lay along the margin of perpendicular precipices several hundred feet in height, where a single false step might precipitate them into the rocky bed of a torrent which roared below. Not the least part of their weary task was the fording of the numerous windings and branchings of the mountain rivers, all boisterous in their currents and icy cold.

Hunger was added to their other sufferings, and soon became the keenest. The small supply of bear and elk meat which they had been able to carry in addition to their previous burthens, served but for a very short time. In their anxiety to struggle forward they had but little time to hunt, and scarce any game came in their path. For three days they had nothing to eat but a small duck and a few poor trout. They occasionally saw numbers of antelopes and tried every art to get within shot; but the timid animals were more than commonly wild, and after tantalizing the hungry hunters for a time, bounded away beyond all chance of pursuit. At length they were fortunate enough to kill one; it was extremely meagre and yielded but a scanty supply, but on this they subsisted for several days.

On the 11th they encamped on a small stream near the foot of the Spanish River Mountain. Here they met with traces of that wayward and solitary being, M'Lellan, who was still keeping on a head of them through these lonely mountains. He had encamped the night before on this stream; they found the embers of the fire by which he had slept, and the remains of a miserable wolf on which he had supped. It was evident he had suffered, like themselves, the pangs of hunger, though he had fared better at this encampment; for they had not a mouthful to eat.

The next day they rose hungry and alert, and set out with the dawn to climb the mountain, which was steep and difficult. Traces of volcanic operations were to be seen in various directions. There was a species of clay also to be met with out of which the Indians manufacture pots and jars and dishes. It is very fine and light, of an agreeable smell and of a brown colour spotted with yellow, and dissolves readily in the mouth. Vessels manufactured of it are said to impart a pleasant smell and flavour to any liquids. These mountains abound also with mineral earths or chalks of various colours; especially two kinds of ochre, one a pale, the other a bright red, like vermillion; much used by the Indians, in painting their bodies.

About noon the travellers reached the "drains" and brooks that formed the head waters of the river, and later in the day descended to where the main body, a shallow stream about a hundred and sixty yards wide, poured through its mountain valley.

Here the poor famishing wanderers had expected to find buffalo in abundance, and had fed their hungry hopes during their scrambling toil, with the thoughts of roasted ribs, juicy humps, and broiled marrow bones. To their great disappointment the river banks were deserted; a few old tracks shewed where a herd of bulls had some time before passed along, but not a horn nor hump was to be seen in the sterile landscape. A few antelopes looked down upon them from the brow of a crag, but flitted away out of sight at the least approach of the hunter.

In the most starving mood they kept for several miles further along the bank of the river, seeking for "beaver signs." Finding some, they encamped in the vicinity and Ben Jones immediately proceeded to set the trap. They had scarce come to a halt when they perceived a large smoke at some distance to the south west. The sight was hailed with joy for they trusted it might rise from some Indian camp where they could procure something to eat, and the dread of starvation had now overcome even the terror of the Blackfeet. Le Clerc, one of the Canadians, was instantly despatched by Mr. Stuart to reconnoiter; and the travellers sat up till a late hour, watching and listening for his return, hoping he might bring them food. Midnight arrived, but Le Clerc did not make his appearance, and they laid down once more supperless to sleep, comforting themselves with the hopes that their old beaver trap might furnish them with a breakfast.

At day break they hastened with famished eagerness to the trap— they found in it the fore paw of a beaver; the sight of which tantalized their hunger and added to their dejection. They resumed their journey with flagging spirits, but had not gone far when they perceived Le Clerc approaching at a distance. They hastened to meet him in hopes of tidings of good cheer. He had none such to give them; but news of that strange wanderer M'Lellan. The smoke had risen from his encampment, which took fire while he was at a little distance from it fishing.

Le Clerc found him in forlorn condition. His fishing had been unsuccessful. During twelve days that he had been wandering alone
through these savage mountains he had found scarce any thing to
eat. He had been ill, way worn, sick at heart, still he had kept forward,
but now his strength and his stubbornness were exhausted. He expressed his satisfaction at hearing that Mr. Stuart and his party were
near, and said he would wait at his camp for their arrival in hopes
they would give him something to eat, for without food he declared
he should not be able to proceed much further.

When the party reached the place they found the poor fellow
lying on a parcel of withered grass, wasted to a perfect skeleton and
so feeble that he could scarce raise his head or speak. The presence
of his old comrades seemed to revive him; but they had no food to
give him, for they themselves were almost starving. They urged him
to rise and accompany them, but he shook his head. It was all in
vain, he said, there was no prospect of their getting speedy relief,
and without it he should perish by the way. He might as well, therefore, stay and die where he was. At length, after much persuasion,
they got him upon his legs; his rifle and other effects were shared
among them, and he was cheered and aided forward.

In this way they proceeded for seventeen miles over a level plain
of sand, until, seeing a few antelopes in the distance, they encamped
on the margin of a small stream. All now that were capable of the
exertion turned out to hunt for a meal. Their efforts were fruitless and
after dark they returned to their camp famished almost to desperation.

As they were preparing for the third time to lay down to sleep
without a mouthful to eat, Le Clerc, one of the Canadians, gaunt
and wild with hunger, approached Mr. Stuart with his gun in his
hand. "It was all in vain," he said, "to attempt to proceed any further
without food. They had a barren plain before them three or four
days' journey in extent, on which nothing was to be procured. They
must all perish before they could get to the end of it. It was better,
therefore, that one should die to save the rest." He proposed, therefore,
that they should cast lots; adding, as an inducement for Mr. Stuart
to assent to the proposition, that he, as leader of the party, should
be exempted.

Mr. Stuart shuddered at the horrible proposition, and endeavored
to reason with the man, but his words were unavailing. At length,
snatching up his rifle he threatened to shoot him on the spot if he
persisted. The famished wretch dropped on his knees, begged pardon
in the most abject terms, and promised never again to offend him
with such a suggestion.

Quiet being restored to the forlorn encampment, each one sought repose. Mr. Stuart, however, was so exhausted by the agitation of the past scene, acting upon his emaciated frame, that he could scarce crawl to his miserable couch; where notwithstanding his fatigues he passed a sleepless night, revolving upon their dreary situation, and the desperate prospect before them.

Before daylight the next morning they were up and on their way; they had nothing to detain them; no breakfast to prepare and to linger was to perish. They proceeded, however, but slowly, for all were faint and weak. Here and there they passed the sculls and bones of buffaloes, which shewed that those animals must have been hunted here during the past season; the sight of these bones served only to mock their misery. After travelling about nine miles along the plain, they ascended a range of hills, and had scarcely gone two miles further when, to their great joy, they discovered "an old run-down buffalo bull," the laggard probably of some herd that had been hunted and harassed through the mountains. They now all stretched themselves out to encompass and make sure of this solitary animal, for their lives depended upon their success. After considerable trouble and infinite anxiety they at length succeeded in killing him. He was instantly flayed and cut up, and so ravenous was their hunger that they devoured some of the flesh raw. The residue they carried to a brook near by where they encamped, lit a fire, and began to cook.

Mr. Stuart was fearful that in their famished state they would eat to excess and injure themselves. He caused a soup to be made of some of the meat, and that each should take a quantity of it as a prelude to his supper. This may have had a beneficial effect, for though they sat up the greater part of the night, cooking and cramming, no one suffered any inconvenience.

The next morning the feasting was resumed, and about mid day, feeling somewhat recruited and refreshed, they set out on their journey with renovated spirits, shaping their course towards a mountain, the summit of which they saw towering in the east, and near to which they expected to find the head waters of the Missouri.

As they proceeded, they continued to see the skeletons of buffalos scattered about the plain in every direction, which shewed that there had been much hunting here by the Indians in the recent season. Further on they crossed a large Indian trail forming a deep path, about fifteen days old, which went in a north direction. They concluded it to have been made by some numerous band of Crows, who had hunted in this country for the greater part of the summer.

On the following day they forded a stream of considerable magnitude, with banks clothed with pine trees. Among these they found the traces of a large Indian camp which had evidently been the head quarters of a hunting expedition from the great quantities of buffalo bones strewed about the neighborhood. The camp had apparently been abandoned about a month.

In the centre was a singular lodge one hundred and fifty feet in circumference, supported by the trunks of twenty trees about twelve inches in diameter and forty four feet long. Across these were laid branches of pine and willow trees, so as to yield a tolerable shade. At the west end immediately opposite to the door, three bodies lay interred with their feet towards the east. At the head of each grave was a branch of red cedar firmly planted in the ground, at the foot was a large buffalo's scull, painted black. Savage ornaments were suspended in various parts of the edifice and a great number of children's moccasins. From the magnitude of this building, and the time and labour that must have been expended in erecting it, the bodies which it contained were probably those of noted warriors and hunters.

The next day (October 17th) they passed two large tributary streams of the Spanish River. They took their rise in the Wind River Mountains, which ranged along to the east, stupendously high and rugged, composed of vast masses of black rock, almost destitute of wood and covered in many places with snow. This day they saw a few buffalo bulls and some antelopes, but could not kill any; and their stock of provisions began to grow scanty as well as poor.

On the 18th, after crossing a mountain ridge, and traversing a plain, they waded one of the branches of Spanish River, and on ascending its bank, met with about a hundred and thirty Snake Indians. They were friendly in their demeanor, and conducted them to their encampment, which was about three miles distant. It consisted of about forty wigwams, constructed principally of pine branches. The Snakes, like most of their nation, were very poor; the marauding Crows, in their late excursion through the country, had picked this unlucky band to the very bone, carrying off their horses, several of their squaws, and most of their effects. In spite of their poverty, they were hospitable in the extreme, and made the hungry strangers welcome to their cabins. A few trinkets procured from them a supply of buffalo meat, and of leather for moccasins of which the party were greatly in need. The most valuable prize obtained from them, however, was a horse: it was a sorry old animal in truth, but it was the only one that remained to the poor fellows, after the fell swoop of the Crows; yet this they were prevailed upon to part with to their guests for a pistol, an axe, a knife, and a few other trifling articles.

They had doleful stories to tell of the Crows, who were encamped on a river at no great distance to the east, and were in such force that they dared not venture to seek any satisfaction for their outrages or to get back a horse or squaw. They endeavoured to excite the indignation of their visitors by accounts of robberies and murders committed on lonely white hunters and trappers by Crows and Black-feet. Some of these were exaggerations of the outrages, already mentioned, sustained by some of the scattered members of Mr. Hunt's expedition; others were in all probability sheer fabrications, to which the Snakes seem to have been a little prone. Mr. Stuart assured them that the day was not far distant when the whites would make their power felt throughout that country, and take signal vengeance on the perpetrators of these misdeeds. The Snakes expressed great joy at the intelligence and offered their services to aid the righteous cause, brightening at the thoughts of taking the field with such potent allies, and doubtless anticipating their turn at stealing horses and abducting squaws. Their offers of course were accepted; the calumet of peace was produced, and the two forlorn powers smoked eternal friendship between themselves and vengeance upon their common spoilers the Crows.

CHAPTER XLVIII

Spanish River scenery—Trail of Crow Indians—A snow storm—A rousing fire and a buffalo feast—A plain of salt—Climbing a mountain —Volcanic summit—Extinguished crater—Marine shells—Encampment on a prairie—Successful hunting—Good cheer—Romantic scenery— Rocky defile—Foaming rapids—The fiery narrows.

By sunrise on the following morning (October 19th) the travellers had loaded their old horse with buffalo meat, sufficient for five days' provisions, and, taking leave of their new allies, the poor but hospitable Snakes, set forth, in somewhat better spirits; though the increasing cold of the weather, and the sight of the snowy mountains, which they had yet to traverse, were enough to chill their very hearts. The country along this branch of the Spanish River, as far as they could see, was perfectly level, bounded by ranges of lofty mountains both to the east and west. They proceeded about three miles to the south where they came again upon the large trace of Crow Indians which they had crossed four days previously; made no doubt by the same marauding band that had plundered the Snakes; and which, according to the account of the latter, was now encamped on a stream to the eastward. The trail kept on to the south east, and was so well beaten by horse and foot, that they supposed at least a hundred lodges had passed along it. As it formed, therefore, a convenient high way, and ran in a proper direction, they turned into it and determined to keep along it as far as safety would permit; as the Crow encampment must be some distance off, and it was not likely those savages would return upon their steps. They travelled forward, therefore, all that day in the track of their dangerous predecessors, which led them across mountain streams, and along ridges, and through narrow valleys, tending generally towards the south east. The wind blew coldly from the north east, with occasional flurries of snow which made them encamp early, on the sheltered banks of a brook. The two Canadians Vallér and Le Clerc killed a young buffalo bull in the evening which was in good condition and afforded them a plentiful supply of fresh beef. They loaded their spits, therefore, and crammed their camp kettle with meat, and while the wind whistled and the snow whirled around them, huddled around a rousing fire, basked in its warmth and comforted both soul and body with a hearty and invigorating meal. No enjoyments have greater zest than these snatched in the very midst of difficulty and danger; and it is probable the poor way worn and weather-beaten travellers relished these creature comforts the more highly, from the surrounding desolation and the dangerous proximity of the Crows.

The snow which had fallen in the night made it late in the morning before the party loaded their solitary pack horse and resumed their march. They had not gone far before the Crow trace which they were following changed its direction and bore to the north of east. They had already begun to feel themselves on dangerous ground in keeping along it, as they might be descried by some scouts and spies of that race of Ishmaelites, whose predatory life required them to be constantly on the alert. On seeing the trace turn so much to the north, therefore, they abandoned it, and kept on their course to the south east for eighteen miles, through a beautifully undulating country, having the main chain of mountains on the left, and a considerably elevated ridge on the right. Here the mountain ridge which divides Wind River from the head waters of the Columbia and Spanish rivers ends abruptly and, winding to the north of east, becomes the dividing barrier between a branch of the Big Horn and Cheyenne rivers, and those head waters which flow into the Missouri below the Sioux country.

The ridge which lay on the right of the travellers having now become very low, they passed over it and came into a level plain about ten miles in circumference, and encrusted to the depth of a foot or eighteen inches with salt as white as snow. This is furnished by numerous salt springs of limpid water, which are continually welling up, overflowing their borders, and forming beautiful chrystalizations. The Indian tribes of the interior are excessively fond of this salt, and repair to the valley to collect it, but it is held in distaste by the tribes of the sea coast, who will eat nothing that has been cured or seasoned by it.

This evening they encamped on the banks of a small stream in the open prairie. The north east wind was keen and cutting, they had nothing wherewith to make a fire but a scanty growth of sage or wormwood, and were fain to wrap themselves up in their blankets and huddle themselves in their "nests" at an early hour. In the course of the evening Mr. M'Lellan who had now regained his strength, killed a buffalo, but it was some distance from the camp and they postponed supplying themselves from the carcass until the following morning.

The next day (October 21st) the cold continued accompanied by snow. They set forward on their bleak and toilsome way, keeping to the east north east, towards the lofty summit of a mountain which it was necessary for them to cross. Before they reached its base they passed another large trail steering a little to the right of the point of the mountain. This they presumed to have been made by another band of Crows, who had probably been hunting lower down on the Spanish River.

The severity of the weather compelled them to encamp at the end of fifteen miles, on the skirts of the mountain, where they found sufficient dry aspen trees to supply them with fire, but they sought in vain about the neighborhood for a spring or run of water.

At day break they were up and on the march, scrambling up the mountain side for the distance of eight painful miles. From the casual hints given in the travelling memoranda of Mr. Stuart, this mountain would seem to offer a rich field of speculation for the geologist. Here was a plain three miles in diameter, strewed with pumice stones and other volcanic reliques, with a lake in the center, occupying what had probably been the crater. Here were also, in some places, deposits of marine shells, indicating that this mountain crest had at some remote period been below the waves.

After pausing to repose, and to enjoy these grand but savage and awful scenes, they began to descend the eastern side of the mountain. The descent was rugged and romantic, along deep ravines and defiles, over hung with crags and cliffs, among which they beheld numbers of the Ahsahta or Big horn skipping fearlessly from rock to rock. Two of them they succeeded in bringing down with their rifles, as they peered fearlessly from the brow of their airy precipices.

Arrived at the foot of the mountain, the travellers found a rill of water oozing out of the earth, and resembling in look and taste the water of the Missouri. Here they encamped for the night and supped sumptuously upon their mountain mutton, which they found in good condition and extremely well tasted.

The morning was bright and intensely cold. Early in the day they came upon a stream running to the east, between low hills of bluish earth strongly impregnated with copperas. Mr. Stuart supposed this to be one of the head waters of the Missouri, and determined to follow its banks. After a march of twenty six miles, however, he arrived at the summit of a hill, the prospect of which induced him to alter his intention. He beheld in every direction south of east a vast plain bounded only by the horizon through which wandered the stream in question in a south, south east direction. It could not therefore be a branch of the Missouri. He now gave up all idea of taking this stream for his guide, and shaped his course towards a range of mountains in the east about sixty miles distant, near which he hoped to find another stream.

The weather was now so severe, and the hardships of travelling so great, that he resolved to halt for the winter at the first eligible place. That night they had to encamp on the open prairie, near a scanty pool of water, and without any wood to make a fire. The north east wind blew keenly across the naked waste, and they were fain to decamp from their inhospitable bivouac before the dawn.

For two days they kept on in an eastward direction against wintry blasts and occasional snow storms. They suffered also from scarcity of water, having occasionally to use melted snow; this, with the want of pasturage, reduced their old pack horse sadly. They saw many tracks of buffalo, and some few bulls, which however got the wind of them, and scampered off.

On the 26th of October they steered east north east for a wooded ravine in a mountain at a small distance from the base of which, to their great joy, they discovered an abundant stream running between willowed banks. Here they halted for the night, and Ben Jones having luckily trapped a beaver and killed two buffalo bulls, they remained all the next day encamped, feasting and reposing and allowing their jaded horse to rest from his labours.

The little stream on which they were encamped was one of the head waters of the Platte River which flows into the Missouri; it was in fact the northern fork or branch of that river, though this the travellers did not discover until long afterwards. Pursuing the course of this stream for about twenty miles they came to where it forced a passage through a range of high hills, covered with cedars, into an extensive low country affording excellent pasture to numerous herds of buffalo. Here they killed three cows, which were the first they had been able to get, having hitherto had to content themselves with bull beef, which at this season of the year is very poor. The hump meat afforded them a repast fit for an epicure.

Late on the afternoon of the 30th they came to where the stream, now encreased to a considerable size, poured along in a ravine between precipices of red stone two hundred feet in height. For some distance it dashed along over huge masses of rock, with foaming violence as if exasperated by being compressed into so narrow a channel, and at length leaped down a chasm that looked dark and frightful in the gathering twilight.

For a part of the next day the wild river, in its capricious wanderings, led them through a variety of striking scenes. At one time they were upon high plains, like platforms among the mountains, with herds of buffaloes roaming about them; at another among rude rocky defiles, broken into cliffs and precipices, where the black tailed deer bounded off among the crags and the big horn basked on the sunny brow of the precipice.

In the after part of the day they came to another scene surpassing in savage grandeur those already described. They had been travelling for some distance through a pass of the mountains keeping parallel with the river as it roared along, out of sight, through a deep ravine. Sometimes their devious path approached the margin of cliffs below which the river foamed, and boiled and whirled among the masses of rock that had fallen into its channel. As they crept cautiously on, leading their solitary pack horse along these giddy heights, they all at once came to where the river thundered down a succession of precipices, throwing up clouds of spray, and making a prodigious din and uproar. The travellers remained for a time gazing with mingled awe and delight at this furious cataract, to which Mr. Stuart gave, from the colour of the impending rocks, the name of "The fiery narrows."

CHAPTER XLIX

Wintry storms—A halt and council—Cantonment for the winter—Fine hunting country—Game of the mountains and plains—Successful hunting—Mr. Crooks and a grizzly bear—The wigwam—Big horns and black tails—Beef and venison—Good quarters and good cheer—An alarm—An intrusion—Unwelcome guests—Desolation of the larder—Gormandizing exploits of hungry savages—Good quarters abandoned.

The travellers encamped for the night on the banks of the river below the cataract. The night was cold, with partial showers of rain and sleet. The morning dawned gloomily, the skies were sullen and overcast, and threatened further storms; but the little band resumed their journey in defiance of the weather. The encreasing rigour of the season, however, which makes itself felt early in these mountainous regions and on these naked and elevated plains, brought them to a pause, and a serious deliberation, after they had descended about thirty miles further along the course of the river.

All were convinced that it was vain to attempt to accomplish their journey on foot at this inclement season. They had still many hundred miles to traverse before they should reach the main course of the Missouri, and their route would lay over immense prairies, naked and bleak and destitute of fuel. The question then was where to choose their wintering place, and whether or not to proceed further down the river. They had at first imagined it to be one of the head waters, or tributary streams, of the Missouri. Afterwards they had believed it to be the Rapid or Quicourt River, in which opinion they had not come nearer to the truth; they now, however, were persuaded, with equal fallacy, by its inclining somewhat to the north of east, that it was the Cheyenne. If so, by continuing down it much further they must arrive among the Indians from whom the river takes its name. Among these they would be sure to meet some of the Sioux tribe. These would apprize their relatives, the piratical Sioux of the Missouri, of the approach of a band of white traders; so that, in the spring time, they would be likely to be way laid and robbed on their way down the river by some party in ambush upon its banks.

Even should this prove to be the Quicourt, or Rapid, River, it would not be prudent to winter much further down upon its banks, as though they might be out of the range of the Sioux, they would be in the neighborhood of the Poncas, a tribe nearly as dangerous. It was resolved, therefore, since they must winter somewhere on this side of the Missouri, to descend no lower, but to keep up in these solitary regions, where they would be in no danger of molestation.

They were brought the more promptly and unanimously to this decision by coming upon an excellent wintering place, that promised every thing requisite for their comfort. It was on a fine bend of the river, just below where it issued out from among a ridge of mountains, and bent towards the north east. Here was a beautiful low point of land, covered by cotton wood and surrounded by a thick growth of willow; so as to yield both shelter and fuel, as well as materials for building. The river swept by in a strong current, about a hundred and fifty yards wide. To the south east were mountains of moderate height, the nearest about two miles off, but the whole chain ranging to the east, south and south west as far as the eye could reach. Their summits were crowned with extensive tracts of pitch pine chequered with small patches of the quivering aspen. Lower down were thick forests of firs and red cedars, growing out in many places from the very fissures of the rocks. The mountains were broken and precipitous, with huge bluffs protruding from among the forests. Their rocky recesses and beetling cliffs afforded retreats to innumerable flocks of the big horn, while their woody summits and ravines abounded with bears and black tailed deer. These, with the numerous herds of buffalo that ranged the lower grounds along the river, promised the travellers abundant cheer in their winter quarters.

On the second of November, therefore, they pitched their camp for the winter on the woody point, and their first thought was to obtain a supply of provisions. Ben Jones and the two Canadians accordingly sallied forth, accompanied by two others of the party, leaving but one to watch the camp. Their hunting was uncommonly successful. In the course of two days they killed thirty two buffalos, and collected their meat on the margin of a small brook about a mile distant. Fortunately a severe frost froze the river, so that the meat was easily transported to the encampment. On a succeeding day a herd of buffalo came trampling through the woody bottom on the river banks and fifteen more were killed.

It was soon discovered, however, that there was game of a more dangerous nature in the neighborhood. On one occasion Mr. Crooks had wandered about a mile from the camp, and had ascended a small hill commanding a view of the river. He was without his rifle, a rare circumstance, for in these wild regions where one may put up a wild animal or a wild Indian at every turn, it is customary never to stir from the camp fire unarmed. The hill where he stood overlooked the place where the massacre of the buffalo had taken place. As he was looking around on the prospect his eye was caught by an object below moving directly towards him. To his dismay he discovered it to be a grizzly bear with two cubs. There was no tree at hand into which he could climb; to run would only be to provoke pursuit, and he should soon be overtaken. He threw himself on the ground, therefore, and lay motionless watching the movements of the animal with intense anxiety. It continued to advance until at the foot of the hill, when it turned and made into the woods, having probably gorged itself with buffalo flesh. Mr. Crooks made all haste back to the camp, rejoicing at his escape, and determining never to stir out again without his rifle. A few days after this circumstance a grizzly bear was shot in the neighborhood by Mr. Miller.

As the slaughter of so many buffaloes had provided the party with beef for the winter, in case they met with no further supply, they now set to work heart and hand to build a comfortable wigwam. In a little while the woody promontory rang with the unwonted sound of the axe. Some of its lofty trees were laid low, and by the second evening the cabin was complete. It was eight feet wide and eighteen feet long. The walls were six feet high and the whole was covered with buffalo skins. The fire place was in the centre and the smoke found its way out by a hole in the roof.

The hunters were next sent out to procure deer skins for garments, moccasins and other purposes. They made the mountains echo with their rifles and, in the course of two days' hunting, killed twenty eight Big horns and black tailed deer.

The party now revelled in abundance. After all that they had suffered from hunger, cold, fatigue and watchfulness; after all their perils from treacherous and savage men, they exulted in the snugness and security of their isolated cabin, hidden as they thought even from the prying eyes of Indian scouts, and stored with creature comforts; and they looked forward to a winter of peace and quietness; of roasting and boiling, and broiling, and feasting upon venison, and mountain mutton, and bear's meat, and marrow bones and buffalo humps and other hunters' dainties, and of dosing and reposing round their fire, and gossipping over past dangers and adventures, and telling long hunting stories, until spring should return; when they would make canoes of buffalo skins, and float themselves down the river.

From such halcyon dreams they were startled one morning at day break by a savage yelp. They started up and seized their rifles. The yelp was repeated by two or three voices. Cautiously peeping out they beheld, to their dismay, several Indian warriors among the trees, all armed and painted in warlike style; being evidently bent on some hostile purpose.

Miller changed countenance as he regarded them. "We are in trouble," said he, "these are some of the rascally Arapahays that robbed me last year." Not a word was uttered by the rest of the party, but they silently slung their powder horns and ball pouches and prepared for battle. M'Lellan who had taken his gun to pieces the evening before, put it together in all haste. He proposed that they should break out the clay from between the logs, so as to be able to fire upon the enemy.

"Not yet," replied Stuart—"it will not do to shew fear or distrust— we must first hold a parley. Some one must go out and meet them as a friend."

Who was to undertake the task—it was full of peril, as the envoy might be shot down at the threshold.

"The leader of a party," said Miller, "always takes the advance."

"Good!" replied Stuart. "I am ready." He immediately went forth: one of the Canadians followed him; the rest of the party remained in garrison, to keep the savages in check.

Stuart advanced holding his rifle in one hand, and extending the other to the savage that appeared to be the chief. The latter stepped forward and took it: his men followed his example, and all shook hands with Stuart in token of friendship.

They now explained their errand. They were a war party of Arapahay braves. Their village lay on a stream several days' journey to the eastward. It had been attacked and ravaged, during their absence, by a band of Crows who had carried off several of their women and most of their horses. They were in quest of vengeance. For sixteen days they had been tracking the Crows about the mountains, but had not yet come upon them. In the mean time they had met with scarcely any game and were half famished. About two days previously they had heard the report of fire arms among the mountains, and on searching in the direction of the sound, had come to a place where a deer had been killed. They had immediately put themselves upon the track of the hunters and by following it up had arrived at the cabin.

Mr. Stuart now invited the chief and another who appeared to be his lieutenant, into the hut, but made signs that no one else was to enter. The rest halted at the door; others came straggling up, until the whole party, to the number of twenty three, were gathered before the hut. They were armed with bows and arrows, tomahawks and scalping knives and some few with guns. All were painted and dressed for war, and had a wild and fierce appearance. Mr. Miller recognized among them some of the very fellows who had robbed him in the preceding year; and put his comrades upon their guard. Every man stood ready to resist the first act of hostility; the savages however conducted themselves peaceably, and shewed none of that swaggering arrogance which a war party is apt to assume.

On entering the hut the chief and his lieutenant cast a wistful look at the rafters, laden with venison and buffalo meat. Mr. Stuart made a merit of necessity and invited them to help themselves. They did not wait to be pressed. The rafters were soon eased of their burthen: venison and beef were passed out to the crew before the door, and a scene of gormandizing commenced, of which few can have an idea, who have not witnessed the gastronomic powers of an Indian, after an interval of fasting. This was kept up throughout the day; they paused now and then, it is true, for a brief interval, but only to return to the charge with renewed ardor. The chief and the lieutenant surpassed all the rest in the vigor and perseverance of their attacks; as if, from their station they were bound to signalize themselves in all onslaughts. Mr. Stuart kept them well supplied with choice bits, for it was his policy to over feed them and keep them from leaving the hut, where they served as hostages for the good conduct of their followers. Once only, in the course of the day, did the chief sally forth. Mr. Stuart and one of his men accompanied him, armed with their rifles, but without betraying any distrust. The chieftain soon returned and renewed his attack upon the larder. In a word, he and his worthy coadjutor the lieutenant ate until they were both stupified.

Towards evening the Indians made their preparations for the night according to the practice of war parties. Those outside of the hut threw up two breast works, into which they retired at a tolerably early hour and slept like over fed hounds. As to the chief and his lieutenant, they passed the night in the hut; in the course of which they two or three times, got up to eat. The travellers took turns, one at a time, to mount guard until the morning.

Scarce had the day dawned when the gormandizing was renewed by the whole band, and carried on with surprizing vigour until ten o'clock, when all prepared to depart. They had six days' journey yet to make, they said, before they should come up with the Crows, who they understood were encamped on a river to the northward. Their way lay through a hungry country where there was no game; they would, moreover, have but little time to hunt; they, therefore, craved a small supply of provisions for the journey. Mr. Stuart again invited them to help themselves. They did so with keen fore thought, loading themselves with the choicest parts of the meat and leaving the late plenteous larder far gone in a consumption. Their next request was for a supply of ammunition, having guns but no powder and ball. They promised to pay magnificently out of the spoils of their foray. "We are poor now," said they, "and are obliged to go on foot, but we shall soon come back laden with booty, and all mounted on horseback, with scalps hanging at our bridles. We will then give each of you a horse to keep you from being tired on your journey."

"Well," said Mr. Stuart, "when you bring the horses you shall have the ammunition, but not before." The Indians saw by his determined tone that all further entreaty would be unavailing, so they desisted, with a good-humoured laugh, and went off exceedingly well freighted both within and without, promising to be back again in the course of a fortnight.

No sooner were they out of hearing than the luckless travellers held another council. The security of their cabin was at an end, and with it all their dreams of a quiet and cosey winter. They were between two fires. On one side were their old enemies the Crows; on the other side the Arapahays—no less dangerous freebooters. As to the moderation of this war party, they considered it assumed to put them off their guard against some more favorable opportunity for a surprizal. It was determined, therefore, not to await their return, but to abandon, with all speed, this dangerous neighborhood. From the accounts of their recent visitors they were led to believe, though erroneously, that they were upon the Quicourt, or Rapid River. They proposed now to keep along it to its confluence with the Missouri; but, should they be prevented by the rigours of the season from proceeding so far, at least to reach a part of the river where they might be able to construct canoes of greater strength and durability than those of buffalo skins.

Accordingly, on the thirteenth of December they bade adieu, with many a regret, to their comfortable quarters, where, for five weeks, they had been indulging the sweets of repose, of plenty and of fancied security. They were still accompanied by their veteran pack horse; which the Arapahays had omitted to steal, either because they intended to steal him on their return, or because they thought him not worth stealing.

CHAPTER L

Rough wintry travelling—Hills and plains—Snow and ice—Disappearance of game—A vast dreary plain—A second halt for the winter—Another wigwam—New Year's feast—Buffalo humps, tongues and marrow bones—Return of spring—Launch of canoes—Bad navigation—Pedestrian march—Vast prairies—Deserted camps—Pawnee squaws—An Otto Indian—News of war—Voyage down the Platte and the Missouri—Reception at Fort Osage—Arrival at S' Louis.

The interval of comfort and repose which the party had enjoyed in their wigwam, rendered the renewal of their fatigues intolerable for the first two or three days. The snow lay deep and was slightly frozen on the surface, but not sufficiently to bear their weight. Their feet became sore by breaking through the crust, and their limbs weary by floundering on without firm foothold. So exhausted and dispirited were they, that they began to think it would be better to remain and run the risk of being killed by the Indians, than to drag on thus painfully with the probability of perishing by the way. Their miserable horse fared no better than themselves, having for the first day or two no other fodder than the ends of willow twigs and the bark of the cotton wood tree.

They all, however, appeared to gain patience and hardihood as they proceeded, and for fourteen days kept steadily on, making a distance of about three hundred and thirty miles. For some days the range of mountains which had been near to their wigwam, kept parallel to the river at no great distance, but at length subsided into hills. Sometimes they found the river bordered with alluvial bottoms and groves with cotton wood and willows; sometimes the adjacent country was naked and barren. In one place it ran for a considerable distance between rocky hills and promontories covered with cedars and pitch pines, and peopled with the big horn and the mountain deer; at other places it wandered through prairies well stocked with buffalos and antelopes. As they descended the course of the river they began to perceive the ash and white oak here and there among the cotton woods and willows; and at length caught a sight of some wild horses on the distant prairies.

The weather was various; at one time the snow lay deep, then they had a genial day or two, with the mildness and serenity of autumn; then again the frost was so severe that the river was sufficiently frozen to bear them upon the ice.

During the last three days of their fortnight's travel, however, the face of the country changed. The timber gradually diminished, until they could scarcely find fuel sufficient for culinary purposes. The game grew more and more scanty, and finally none were to be seen but a few miserable broken down buffalo bulls, not worth killing. The snow lay fifteen inches deep, and made the travelling grievously painful and toilsome. At length they came to an immense plain, where no vestige of timber was to be seen; nor a single quadruped to enliven the desolate landscape. Here then their hearts failed them and they held another consultation. The width of the river, which was upwards of a mile, its extreme shallowness, the frequency of quick sands, and various other characteristics had at length made them sensible of their errors with respect to it, and they now came to the correct conclusion that they were on the banks of the Platte or Shallow River. What were they to do? Pursue its course to the Missouri? To go on at this season of the year seemed dangerous in the extreme. There was no prospect of obtaining either food or firing. The country was destitute of trees, and though there might be drift wood along the river, it lay too deep beneath the snow for them to find it.

The weather was threatening a change, and a snow storm on these boundless wastes might prove as fatal as a whirlwind of sand on an Arabian desert. After much dreary deliberation, it was at length determined to retrace their three last days' journey, of seventy seven miles, to a place which they had remarked; where there was a sheltering growth of forest trees and a country abundant in game. Here they would once more set up their winter quarters, and await the opening of the navigation to launch themselves in canoes.

Accordingly, on the twenty seventh of December they faced about, retraced their steps and on the thirtieth regained the part of the river in question. Here the alluvial bottom was from one to two miles wide, and thickly covered with a forest of cotton wood trees; while herds of buffalo were scattered about the neighboring prairie, several of which soon fell beneath their rifles.

They encamped on the margin of the river, in a grove where there were trees large enough for canoes. Here they put up a shed for immediate shelter and immediately proceeded to erect a hut. New Year's day dawned when, as yet, but one wall of their cabin was completed; the genial and jovial day, however, was not permitted to pass uncelebrated even by this weather beaten crew of wanderers. All work was suspended except that of roasting and boiling. The choicest parts of the buffalo meat, with tongues and humps and marrow bones, were devoured in quantities that would astonish any one that has not lived among hunters or Indians; and as an extra regale, having no tobacco left, they cut up an old tobacco pouch, still redolent with the potent herb, and smoked it in honour of the day. Thus for a time in present revelry, however uncouth, they forgot all past troubles and all anxieties about the future, and their forlorn wigwam echoed to the sound of gaiety.

The next day they resumed their labors and by the sixth of the month it was complete. They soon killed abundance of buffalo, and again laid in a stock of winter provisions.

The party were more fortunate in this their second cantonment. The winter passed away without any Indian visitors; and the game continued to be plenty in the neighborhood. They felled two large trees and shaped them into canoes; and, as the spring opened, and a thaw of several days' continuance melted the ice in the river, they made every preparation for embarking. On the eighth of March they launched forth in their canoes, but soon found that the river had not depth sufficient even for such slender barks. It expanded into a wide but extremely shallow stream, with many sand bars, and occasionally various channels. They got one of their canoes a few miles down it, with extreme diffi- culty, sometimes wading, and dragging it over the shoals; at length they had to abandon the attempt and to resume their journey on foot, aided by their faithful old pack horse, who had recruited strength during the repose of the winter.

The weather delayed them for a few days, having suddenly become more rigorous than it had been at any time during the winter; but on the twentieth of March they were again on their journey.

In two days they arrived at the vast naked prairie, the wintry aspect of which had caused them, in December, to pause and turn back. It was now clothed in the early verdure of spring, and plentifully stocked with game. Still, when obliged to bivouac on its bare surface, without any shelter, and by a scanty fire of dry buffalo dung, they found the night blasts piercing cold. On one occasion a herd of buffalo, straying near their evening camp, they killed three of them merely for their hides, wherewith to make a shelter for the night.

They continued on for upwards of a hundred miles; with vast prairies extending before them as they advanced; sometimes diversified by undulating hills, but destitute of trees. In one place they saw a gang of sixty five wild horses, but as to the buffalos they seemed absolutely to cover the country. Wild geese abounded, and they passed extensive swamps that were alive with innumerable flocks of water fowl, among which were a few swans, but an endless variety of ducks.

The river continued a winding course to the east northeast, nearly a mile in width, but too shallow to float even an empty canoe.

The country spread out into a vast level plain, bounded by the horizon alone, excepting to the north, where a line of hills seemed like a long promontory stretching into the bosom of the ocean. The dreary sameness of the prairie wastes began to grow extremely irksome. The travellers longed for the sight of a forest, or grove, or single tree to break the level uniformity and began to notice every object that gave reason to hope they were drawing towards the end of this weary wilderness. Thus the occurrence of a particular kind of grass was hailed as a proof that they could not be far from the bottoms of the Missouri; and they were rejoiced at putting up several prairie hens, a kind of grouse seldom found far in the interior. In picking up drift wood for fuel, also, they found on some pieces the mark of an axe, which caused much speculation as to the time when and the persons by whom the trees had been felled. Thus they went on, like sailors at sea, who perceive in every floating weed and wandering bird, harbingers of the wished for land.

By the close of the month the weather became very mild, and, heavily burthened as they were, they found the noon tide temperature uncomfortably warm. On the thirtieth they came to three deserted hunting camps, either of Pawnees or Otoes, about which were buffalo sculls in all directions; and the frames on which the hides had been stretched and cured. They had apparently been occupied the preceding autumn.

For several days they kept patiently on, watching every sign that might give them an idea as to where they were, and how near to the banks of the Missouri. Though there were numerous traces of hunting parties and encampments, they were not of recent date. The country seemed deserted. The only human beings they met with were three Pawnee squaws, in a hut in the midst of a deserted camp. Their people had all gone to the south, in pursuit of the buffalo, and had left these poor women behind, being too sick and infirm to travel.

It is a common practice with the Pawnees and probably with other roving tribes, when departing on a distant expedition, which will not admit of incumbrance or delay, to leave their aged and infirm with a supply of provisions sufficient for a temporary subsistence. When this is exhausted they must perish, though sometimes their sufferings are abridged by hostile prowlers who may visit the deserted camp.

The poor squaws in question expected some such fate at the hands of the white strangers, and though the latter accosted them in the kindest manner, and made them presents of dried buffalo meat, it was impossible to soothe their alarm or get any information from them.

The first land mark by which the travellers were enabled to conjecture their position with any degree of confidence was an island about seventy miles in length, which they presumed to be Grand isle. If so they were within one hundred and forty miles of the Missouri. They kept on, therefore, with renewed spirit, and at the end of three days met with an Otoe Indian, by whom they were confirmed in their conjecture. They learnt at the same time another piece of information, of an uncomfortable nature. According to his account there was war between the United States and England, and in fact it had existed for a whole year, during which time they had been beyond the reach of all knowledge of the affairs of the civilized world.

The Otto conducted the travellers to his village, situated a short distance from the banks of the Platte. Here they were delighted to meet with two white men, Messrs. Doruin and Roi, Indian traders recently from S' Louis. Of these they had a thousand enquiries to make concerning all affairs foreign and domestic, during their year of sepulture in the wilderness; and especially about the events of the existing war.

They now prepared to abandon their weary travel by land, and to embark upon the water. A bargain was made with Mr. Doruin who engaged to furnish them with a canoe and provisions for the voyage in exchange for their venerable and well tried fellow traveller the old Snake horse.

Accordingly in a couple of days, the Indians employed by that gentleman, constructed for them a canoe twenty feet long, four feet wide, and eighteen inches deep. The frame was of poles and willow twigs, on which were stretched five elk and buffalo hides, sewed together with sinews, and the seams payed with unctuous mud. In this they embarked at an early hour of the 16th of April and drifted down ten miles with the stream when the wind being high they encamped and set to work to make oars, which they had not been able to procure at the Indian village.

Once more afloat, they went merrily down the stream and after making thirty five miles emerged into the broad turbid current of the Missouri. Here they were borne along briskly by the rapid stream, though, by the time their fragile bark had floated a couple of hundred miles, its frame began to shew the effects of the voyage. Luckily they came to the deserted wintering place of some hunting party, where they found two old wooden canoes. Taking possession of the largest, they again committed themselves to the current and after dropping down fifty five miles further, arrived safely at Fort Osage.

Here they found Lieutenant Brownson still in command; the officer who had given the expedition a hospitable reception on its way up the river, eighteen months previously. He received this remnant of the party with a cordial welcome, and endeavored in every way to promote their comfort and enjoyment during their sojourn at the fort. The greatest luxury they met with on their return to the abode of civilized man was bread, not having tasted any for nearly a year.

Their stay at Fort Osage was but short; on reembarking they were furnished with an ample supply of provisions by the kindness of Lieutenant Brownson, and performed the rest of their voyage without adverse circumstance. On the 30th of April they arrived in perfect health and fine spirits at S' Louis, having been ten months in performing this perilous expedition from Astoria. Their return caused quite a sensation at the place, bringing the first intelligence of the fortune of Mr. Hunt and his party in their adventurous route across the Rocky Mountains, and of the new establishment on the shores of the Pacific.

CHAPTER LI

Agreement between Mr. Astor and the Russian Fur Company—War between the United States and Great Britain—Instructions to Captain Sowle of the Beaver—Fitting out of the Lark—News of the arrival of Mr. Stuart.

It is now necessary, in linking together the parts of this excursive narrative, that we notice the proceedings of Mr. Astor in support of his great undertaking. His project with respect to the Russian establishments along the north west coast, had been diligently prosecuted. The agent sent by him to St. Petersburgh, to negotiate in his name as president of the American Fur Company, had, under sanction of the Russian government, made a provisional agreement with the Russian Company.

By this agreement, which was ratified by Mr. Astor in 1813, the two companies bound themselves not to interfere with each other's trading and hunting grounds nor to furnish arms and ammunition to the Indians. They were to act in concert, also, against all interlopers, and to succor each other in case of danger. The American company was to have the exclusive right of supplying the Russian posts with goods and necessaries, receiving peltries in payment at stated prices. They were, also, if so requested by the Russian governor, to convey the furs of the Russian Company to Canton, sell them on commission and bring back the proceeds, at such freight as might be agreed on at the time.

This agreement was to continue in operation four years, and to be renewable for a similar term unless some unforeseen contingency should render a modification necessary. It was calculated to be of great service to the infant establishment at Astoria: dispelling the fears of hostile rivalry on the part of the foreign companies in its neighborhood and giving a formidable blow to the irregular trade along the coast. It was also the intention of Mr. Astor to have coasting vessels of his own, at Astoria, of small tonnage and draft of water, fitted for coasting service. These, having a place of shelter and deposit, could ply about the coast in short voyages in favorable weather, and would have vast advantage over chance ships, which must make long voyages, maintain numerous crews, and could only approach the coast at certain seasons of the year. He hoped, therefore, gradually to make Astoria the great emporium of the American fur trade in the Pacific and the nucleus of a powerful American state.

Unfortunately for these sanguine anticipations, before Mr. Astor had ratified the agreement, as above stated, war broke out between the United States and Great Britain. He perceived at once the peril of the case. The harbor of New York would, doubtless, be blockaded and the departure of the annual supply ship in the autumn prevented: or, if she should succeed in getting out to sea, she might be captured on her voyage.

In this emergency he wrote to Captain Sowle, Commander of the Beaver. The letter, which was addressed to him at Canton, directed him to proceed to the Factory at the mouth of the Columbia, with such articles as the establishment might need; and to remain there, subject to the orders of Mr. Hunt, should that gentleman be in command there.

The war continued. No tidings had yet been received from Astoria; the despatches having been delayed by the misadventure of Mr. Reed at the falls of the Columbia, and the unhorsing of Mr. Stuart by the Crows among the mountains. A painful uncertainty, also, prevailed about Mr. Hunt and his party. Nothing had been heard of them since their departure from the Arickara village; Lisa who parted from them there had predicted their destruction; and some of the traders of the North West Company had actually spread a rumor of their having been cut off by the Indians.

It was a hard trial of the courage and the means of an individual, to have to fit out another costly expedition where so much had already been expended, so much uncertainty prevailed, and where the risk of loss was so greatly enhanced that no insurance could be effected.

In spite of all these discouragements, Mr. Astor determined to send another ship to the relief of the settlement. He selected for this purpose a vessel called the Lark, remarkable for her fast sailing. The disordered state of the times, however, caused such delay that February arrived while the vessel was yet lingering in port.

At this juncture Mr. Astor learnt that the North West Company were preparing to send out an armed ship of twenty guns, called the Isaac Todd, to form an establishment at the mouth of the Columbia. These tidings gave him great uneasiness. A considerable proportion of the persons in his employ were Scotchmen and Canadians, and several of them had been in the service of the North West Company. Should Mr. Hunt have failed to arrive at Astoria the whole establishment would be under the control of Mr. M'Dougall, of whose fidelity he had received very disparaging accounts from Captain Thorn. The British government, also, might deem it worth while to send a force against the establishment, having been urged to do so some time previously, by the North West Company.

Under all these circumstances Mr. Astor wrote to Mr. Monroe, then Secretary of State, requesting protection from the government of the United States. He represented the importance of his settlement in a commercial point of view, and the shelter it might afford to the American vessels in those seas. All he asked was that the American government would throw forty or fifty men into the fort at his establishment, which would be sufficient for its defence until he could send reinforcements over land.

He waited in vain for a reply to this letter, the government, no doubt, being engrossed at the time by an overwhelming crowd of affairs. The month of March arrived and the Lark was ordered by Mr. Astor to put to sea. The officer who was to command her shrunk from his engagement, and in the exigency of the moment she was given in charge to Mr. Northrop the Mate. Mr. Nicholas G. Ogden, a gentleman on whose talents and integrity the highest reliance could be placed, sailed as supercargo. The Lark put to sea in the beginning of March 1813.

By this opportunity Mr. Astor wrote to Mr. Hunt, as head of the establishment at the mouth of the Columbia, for he would not allow himself to doubt of his welfare. "I always think you are well," said he, "and that I shall see you again, which heaven, I hope, will grant."

He warned him to be on his guard against any attempt to surprize the post; suggesting the probability of armed hostility on the part of the North West Company: and expressing his indignation at the ungrateful returns made by that association for his frank and open conduct and advantageous overtures. "Were I on the spot," said he, "and had the management of affairs, I would defy them all; but as it is, every thing depends upon you and your friends about you. *Our enterprize is grand and deserves success, and I hope in God it will meet it.* If my object was merely gain of money I should say think whether it is best to save what we can and abandon the place, *but the very idea is like a dagger to my heart.*" This extract is sufficient to shew the spirit and the views which actuated Mr. Astor in this great undertaking.

Week after week, and month after month elapsed, without any thing to dispel the painful incertitude that hung over every part of this enterprize. Though a man of resolute spirit and not easily cast down, the dangers impending over this darling scheme of his ambition had a gradual effect upon the spirits of Mr. Astor. He was sitting one gloomy evening by his window revolving over the loss of the Tonquin, and the fate of her unfortunate crew, and fearing that some equally tragical calamity might have befallen the adventurers across the Mountains, when the evening newspaper was brought to him. The first paragraph that caught his eye announced the arrival of Mr. Stuart and his party at S' Louis, with intelligence that Mr. Hunt and his companions had effected their perilous expedition to the mouth of the Columbia. This was a gleam of sunshine that for a time dispelled every cloud, and he now looked forward with sanguine hope to the accomplishment of all his plans.

CHAPTER LII

The course of our narrative now takes us back to the regions beyond the mountains, to dispose of the parties that set out from Astoria in company with Mr. Robert Stuart, and whom he left on the banks of the Wallah Wallah. Those parties likewise separated from each other shortly after his departure, proceeding to their respective destinations, but agreeing to meet at the mouth of the Wallah Wallah about the beginning of June in the following year, with such peltries as they should have collected in the interim, so as to convoy each other through the dangerous passes of the Columbia.

Mr. David Stuart, one of the partners, proceeded with his men to the post already established by him at the mouth of the Oakinagan; having furnished this with goods and ammunition he proceeded three hundred miles up that river, where he established another post in a good trading neighborhood.

Mr. Clarke, another partner, conducted his little band up Lewis River to the mouth of a small stream coming in from the north, to which the Canadians gave the name of the Pavion. Here he found a village or encampment of forty huts or tents covered with mats and inhabited by *Nez percés* or Pierced nose Indians as they are called by the traders; but Chopunnish, as they are called by themselves. They are a hardy, laborious and somewhat knavish race, who lead a precarious life, fishing and digging roots during the summer and autumn, hunting the deer on snow shoes during the winter, and traversing the Rocky Mountains in the spring to trade for buffalo skins with the hunting tribes of the Missouri. In these migrations they are liable to be way laid and attacked by the Blackfeet and other warlike and predatory tribes, and driven back across the mountains with the loss of their horses, and of many of their comrades.

A life of this unsettled and precarious kind is apt to render men selfish, and such Mr. Clarke found the inhabitants of this village, who were deficient in the usual hospitality of Indians; parting with every thing with extreme reluctance, and shewing no sensibility to any act of kindness. At the time of his arrival they were all occupied in catching

and curing salmon. The men were stout, robust, active and good looking, and the women handsomer than those of the tribes nearer to the
coast.

It was the plan of Mr. Clarke to lay up his boats here and proceed
by land to his place of destination, which was among the Spokan tribe
of Indians about a hundred and fifty miles distant. He accordingly
endeavored to purchase horses for the journey, but in this he had to
contend with the sordid disposition of these people. They asked high
prices for their horses, and were so difficult to deal with that Mr. Clarke
was detained seven days among them before he could procure a sufficient
number. During that time he was annoyed by repeated pilferings, for
which he could get no redress. The chief promised to recover the stolen
articles; but failed to do so, alleging that the thieves belonged to a
distant tribe and had made off with their booty. With this excuse Mr.
Clarke was fain to content himself, though he laid up in his heart a
bitter grudge against the whole Pierced nose race, which it will be
found he took occasion subsequently to gratify in a signal manner.

Having made arrangements for his departure Mr. Clarke laid up his
barge and canoes in a sheltered place on the banks of a small bay over-
grown with shrubs and willows, confiding them to the care of the Nez
percé chief, who on being promised an ample compensation, engaged
to have a guardian eye upon them. Then mounting his steed and putting himself at the head of his little caravan, he shook the dust off his
feet as he turned his back upon this village of rogues and hard dealers.

We shall not follow him minutely in his journey; which lay at times
over steep and rocky hills, and among crags and precipices; at other
times over vast naked and sun burnt plains, abounding with rattlesnakes,
in traversing which both men and horses suffered intolerably from heat
and thirst. The place on which he fixed for a trading post was a fine
point of land at the junction of the Pointed heart and Spokan rivers.
His establishment was intended to compete with a trading post of the
North West Company situated at no great distance, and to rival it in the
trade with the Spokan Indians; as well as with the Cootonais and Flatheads. In this neighborhood we shall leave him for the present.

Mr. M'Kenzie, who conducted the third party from the Wallah
Wallah, navigated for several days up the south branch of the Columbia, named the Camöenum by the natives, but commonly called Lewis
River, in honor of the first explorer. Wandering bands of various tribes
were seen along this river, travelling in various directions: for the
Indians generally are restless roving beings, continually intent on enterprizes of war, traffic and hunting. Some of these people were driving
large gangs of horses, as if to a distant market. Having arrived at the
mouth of the Shahaptan he ascended some distance up that river and

established his trading post upon its banks. This appeared to be a great thoroughfare for the tribes from the neighborhood of the falls of the Columbia, in their expeditions to make war upon the tribes of the Rocky Mountains; to hunt buffalo on the plains beyond, or to traffic for roots and buffalo robes. It was the season of migration, and the Indians from various distant parts were passing and repassing in great numbers.

Mr. M'Kenzie now detached a small band, under the conduct of Mr. John Reed, to visit the caches made by Mr. Hunt at the Caldron Linn, and to bring the contents to his post; as he depended, in some measure, on them for his supplies of goods and ammunition. They had not been gone a week when two Indians arrived of the Pallatapalla tribe, who live upon a river of the same name. These communicated the unwelcome intelligence that the caches had been robbed. They said that some of their tribe had, in the course of the preceding spring, been across the mountains which separated them from Snake River, and had traded horses with the Snakes in exchange for blankets, robes and goods of various descriptions. These articles the Snakes had procured from caches to which they were guided by some white men who resided among them, and who afterwards accompanied them across the Rocky Mountains. This intelligence was extremely perplexing to Mr. M'Kenzie, but the truth of part of it was confirmed by the two Indians, who brought them an English saddle and bridle, which was recognized as having belonged to Mr. Crooks. The perfidy of the white men who revealed the secret of the caches was however perfectly inexplicable. We shall presently account for it, in narrating the expedition of Mr. Reed.

That worthy Hibernian proceeded on his mission with his usual alacrity. His forlorn travels of the preceding winter had made him acquainted with the topography of the country and he reached Snake River without any material difficulty. Here, in an encampment of the natives, he met with six white men, wanderers from the main expedition of Mr. Hunt, who, after having had their respective shares of adventures and mishaps, had fortunately come together at this place.

Three of these men were Turcotte, La Chapelle and Francis Landry; the three Canadian voyageurs who, it may be recollected, had left Mr. Crooks in February in the neighborhood of Snake River, being dismayed by the encreasing hardships of the journey, and fearful of perishing of hunger. They had returned to a Snake encampment, where they passed the residue of the winter.

Early in the spring, being utterly destitute and in great extremity, and having worn out the hospitality of the Snakes, they determined to avail themselves of the buried treasures within their knowledge. They accordingly informed the Snake chieftains that they knew where a great quantity of goods had been left in caches, enough to enrich the whole tribe; and offered to conduct them to the place, on condition of being rewarded with horses and provisions. The chieftains pledged their faith and honor as great men and Snakes, and the three Canadians conducted them to the place of deposit at the Caldron Linn. This is the way that the savages got knowledge of the caches, and not by following the tracks of wolves, as Mr. Stuart had supposed. Never did money diggers turn up a miser's hoard with more eager delight than did the savages lay open the treasures of the caches. Blankets and robes, brass trinkets and blue beads were drawn forth with chuckling exultation, and long strips of scarlet cloth produced yells of extacy.

The rifling of the caches effected a change in the fortunes and deportment of the whole party. The Snakes were better clad and equipped than ever were Snakes before, and the three Canadians, suddenly finding themselves with horse to ride and weapon to wear, were, like beggars on horseback, ready to ride on any wild scamper. An opportunity soon presented. The Snakes determined on a hunting match on the buffalo prairies, to lay in a supply of beef, that they might live in plenty as became men of their improved condition. The three newly mounted cavaliers must fain accompany them. They all traversed the Rocky Mountains in safety, descended to the head waters of the Missouri and made great havoc among the buffalos.

Their hunting camp was full of meat; they were gorging themselves, like true Indians, with present plenty, and drying and jirking great quantities for a winter's supply. In the midst of their revelry and good cheer the camp was surprized by the Blackfeet. Several of the Snakes were slain on the spot; the residue, with their three Canadian allies, fled to the Mountains, stripped of horses, buffalo meat, every thing; and made their way back to the old encampment on Snake River, poorer than ever, but esteeming themselves fortunate in having escaped with their lives. They had not been long there when the Canadians were cheered by the sight of a companion in misfortune, Dubreuil, the poor voyageur who had left Mr. Crooks in March, being too much exhausted to keep on with him.

Not long afterwards three other straggling members of the main expedition made their appearance. These were Carson, St. Michel and Pierre Delaunay, three of the trappers who, in company with Pierre Detayé, had been left among the mountains by Mr. Hunt, to trap beaver, in the preceding month of September. They had departed from the main body well armed and provided, with horses to ride, and horses to carry the peltries they were to collect. They came wandering into the Snake camp as ragged and destitute as their predecessors. It appears that they had finished their trapping and were making their way in the spring to the Missouri when they were met and attacked by a powerful band of the all pervading Crows. They made a desperate resistance and killed seven of the savages, but were overpowered by numbers. Pierre Detayé was slain; the rest were robbed of horses and effects and obliged to turn back, when they fell in with their old companions as already mentioned.

We should observe that at the heels of Pierre Delaunay came draggling an Indian wife whom he had picked up in his wanderings, having grown weary of celibacy among the savages.

The whole seven of this forlorn fraternity of adventurers, thus accidentally congregated on the banks of Snake River, were making arrangements once more to cross the Mountains, when some Indian scouts brought word of the approach of the little band headed by John Reed.

The latter, having heard the several stories of these wanderers, took them all into his party, and set out for the Caldron Linn, to clear out two or three of the caches which had not been revealed to the Indians. At that place he met with Robinson, the Kentucky veteran who, with his two comrades Rezner and Hoback, had remained there when Mr. Stuart went on. This adventurous trio had been trapping higher up the river, but Robinson had come down in a canoe, to await the expected arrival of the party, and obtain horses and equipments. He told Reed the story of the robbery of his party by the Arapahays, but it differed, in some particulars, from the account given by him to Mr. Stuart. In that he had represented Cass as having shamefully deserted his companions in their extremity, carrying off with him a horse: in the one now given he spoke of him as having been killed in the affray with the Arapahays. This discrepancy, of which of course Reed could have had no knowledge at the time, concurred with other circumstances, to occasion afterwards some mysterious speculations and dark surmises as to the real fate of Cass; but as no substantial grounds were ever adduced for them, we forbear to throw any deeper shades into this story of sufferings in the wilderness.

Mr. Reed having gathered the remainder of the goods from the caches, put himself at the head of his party, now augmented by the seven men thus casually picked up and the squaw of Pierre Delaunay, and made his way successfully to M'Kenzie's post on the waters of the Shahaptan.

CHAPTER LIII

Departure of Mr. Hunt in the Beaver—Precautions at the factory—Detachment to the Wollamut—Gloomy apprehensions—Arrival of M'Kenzie—Affairs at the Shahaptan—News of war—Dismay of M'Dougall—Determination to abandon Astoria—Departure of M'Kenzie for the interior—Adventure at the rapids—Visit to the ruffians of Wish-ram—A perilous situation—Meeting with M'Tavish and his party—Arrival at the Shahaptan—Plundered caches—Determination of the wintering partners not to leave the country—Arrival of Clarke among the Nez percés—The affair of the silver goblet—Hanging of an Indian—Arrival of the wintering partners at Astoria.

After the departure of the different detachments, or *brigades,* as they are called by the fur traders, the Beaver prepared for her voyage along the coast and her visit to the Russian establishment at New Archangel, where she was to carry supplies. It had been determined in the council of partners at Astoria, that Mr. Hunt should embark in this vessel, for the purpose of acquainting himself with the coasting trade and of making arrangements with the commander of the Russian post, and that he should be relanded in October, at Astoria, by the Beaver, on her way to the Sandwich islands and Canton.

The Beaver put to sea in the month of August. Her departure, and that of the various brigades, left the fortress of Astoria but slightly garrisoned. This was soon perceived by some of the Indian tribes, and the consequence was increased insolence of deportment and a disposition to hostility. It was now the fishing season, when the tribes from the northern coast drew into the neighborhood of the Columbia. These were warlike and perfidious in their dispositions; and noted for their attempts to surprize trading ships. Among them were numbers of the Neweetees, the ferocious tribe that massacred the crew of the Tonquin.

Great precautions, therefore, were taken at the factory to guard against surprize while these dangerous intruders were in the vicinity. Galleries were constructed inside of the palisades; the bastions were heightened and centinels were posted day and night. Fortunately the Chinooks and other tribes resident in the vicinity manifested the most pacific disposition. Old Comcomly who held sway over them was a shrewd calculator. He was aware of the advantages of having the whites as neighbors and allies, and of the consequence derived to himself and his people from acting as intermediate traders between them and the distant tribes. He had, therefore, by this time become a firm friend of the Astorians, and formed a kind of barrier between them and the hostile intruders from the north.

315

The summer of 1812 passed away without any of the hostilities that had been apprehended; the Neweetees and other dangerous visitors to the neighborhood finished their fishing and returned home, and the inmates of the factory once more felt secure from attack.

It now became necessary to guard against other evils. The season of scarcity arrived, which commences in October and lasts until the end of January. To provide for the support of the garrison the shallop was employed to forage about the shores of the river. A number of the men, also, under the command of some of the clerks, were sent to quarter themselves on the banks of the Wollamut, (the Multnomah of Lewis and Clark) a fine river which disembogues itself into the Columbia about sixty miles above Astoria. The country bordering on this river is finely diversified with prairies and hills and forests of oak, ash, maple and cedar. It abounded at that time with elk and deer, and the streams were well stocked with beaver. Here the party after supplying their own wants, were enabled to pack up quantities of dried meat and send it by canoes to Astoria.

The month of October elapsed without the return of the Beaver: November, December, January passed away, and still nothing was seen or heard of her. Gloomy apprehensions now began to be entertained: she might have been wrecked in the course of her coasting voyage, or surprized, like the Tonquin, by some of the treacherous tribes of the north.

No one indulged more in these apprehensions than M'Dougall, who had now the charge of the establishment. He no longer evinced the bustling confidence and buoyancy which once characterized him. Command seemed to have lost its charms for him; or rather, he gave way to the most abject despondency, decrying the whole enterprize, magnifying every untoward circumstance, and foreboding nothing but evil.

While in this moody state he was surprised, on the 16th of January, by the sudden appearance of M'Kenzie, way worn and weather beaten by a long wintry journey from his post on the Shahaptan, and with a face the very frontispiece for a volume of misfortune. M'Kenzie had been heartily disgusted and disappointed at his post. It was in the midst of the Tushepaws, a powerful and warlike nation, divided into many tribes under different chiefs, who possessed innumerable horses, but, not having turned their attention to beaver trapping had no furs to offer. According to M'Kenzie they were but a "'rascally tribe;" from which we may infer that they were prone to consult their own interests more than comported with the interests of a greedy Indian trader.

Game being scarce, he was obliged to rely for the most part, on horse flesh for subsistence, and the Indians, discovering his necessities, adopted a policy usual in civilized trade, and raised the price of horses to an exorbitant rate, knowing that he and his men must eat or die. In this way the goods he had brought to trade for beaver skins were likely to be bartered for horse flesh, and all the proceeds devoured upon the spot.

He had despatched trappers in various directions, but the country around did not offer more beaver than his own station. In this emergency he began to think of abandoning his unprofitable post; sending his goods to the posts of Clarke and David Stuart who could make a better use of them as they were in a good beaver country, and returning with his party to Astoria, to seek some better destination. With this view he repaired to the post of Mr. Clarke to hold a consultation. While the two partners were in conference in Mr. Clarke's wigwam an unexpected visitor came bustling in upon them. This was Mr. John George M'Tavish, a partner of the North West Company who had charge of the rival trading posts established in that neighborhood. Mr. M'Tavish was the delighted messenger of bad news. He had been to Lake Winnipeg, where he received an express from Canada containing the declaration of war and President Madison's proclamation, which he handed with the most officious complaisance to Messrs. Clarke and M'Kenzie. He moreover told them that he had received a fresh supply of goods from the North West posts on the other side of the Rocky Mountains, and was prepared for vigorous opposition to the establishments of the American company. He capped the climax of this obliging, but belligerent, intelligence by informing them that the armed ship Isaac Todd, was to be at the mouth of the Columbia about the beginning of March, to get possession of the trade of the river, and that he was ordered to join her there at that time.

The receipt of this news determined M'Kenzie. He immediately returned to the Shahaptan; broke up his establishment; deposited his goods in *cache,* and hastened with all his people to Astoria.

The intelligence thus brought completed the dismay of M'Dougall and seemed to produce a complete confusion of mind. He held Council of War with M'Kenzie, at which some of the clerks were present, but of course had no votes. They gave up all hope of maintaining their post at Astoria. The Beaver had probably been lost; they could receive no aid from the United States, as all the ports would be blockaded. From England nothing could be expected but hostility. It was determined, therefore, to abandon the establishment in the course of the following spring and return across the Rocky Mountains.

In pursuance of this resolution they suspended all trade with the natives except for provisions, having already more peltries than they could carry away, and having need of all the goods for the clothing and subsistence of their people during the remainder of their sojourn and on their journey across the Mountains. Their intention of abandoning Astoria was, however, kept secret from the men lest they should at once give up all labour and become restless and insubordinate.

In the mean time M'Kenzie set off for his post at the Shahaptan, to get his goods from the caches and buy horses and provisions with them for the caravan across the mountains. He was charged with despatches from M'Dougall to Messrs. Stuart and Clarke, apprising them of the intended migration, that they might make timely preparations.

M'Kenzie was accompanied by two of the clerks, Mr. John Reed, the Irishman, and Mr. Alfred Seton of New York. They embarked in two canoes manned by seventeen men and ascended the river without any incident of importance until they arrived in the eventful neighborhood of the rapids. They made the portage of the narrows and the falls early in the afternoon and, having partaken of a scanty meal, had now a long evening on their hands.

On the opposite side of the river lay the village of Wish-ram of free-booting renown. Here lived the savages who had robbed and maltreated Reed when bearing his tin box of despatches. It was known that the rifle of which he was despoiled was retained as a trophy at the village. M'Kenzie offered to cross the river and demand the rifle if any one would accompany him. It was a hare brained project, for these villages were noted for the ruffian character of their inhabitants; yet two volunteers promptly stepped forward,—Alfred Seton the clerk, and Joe de la Pierre the cook. The trio soon reached the opposite side of the river. On landing they freshly primed their rifles and pistols. A path winding for about a hundred yards among rocks and crags led to the village. No notice seemed to be taken of their approach. Not a solitary being, man, woman or child greeted them. The very dogs, those noisy pests of an Indian town, kept silence. On entering the village a boy made his appearance and pointed to a house of larger dimensions than the rest. They had to stoop to enter it; as soon as they had passed the threshold, the narrow passage behind them was filled up by a sudden rush of Indians who had before kept out of sight.

M'Kenzie and his companions found themselves in a rude chamber about twenty five feet long and twenty wide. A bright fire was blazing at one end, near which sat the chief, about sixty years old. A large number of Indians wrapped in buffalo robes were squatted in rows, three deep, forming a semi circle round three sides of the room. A single glance around sufficed to shew them the grim and dangerous assemblage into which they had intruded, and that all retreat was cut off by the mass which blocked up the entrance.

The chief pointed to the vacant side of the room opposite to the door, and motioned for them to take their seats. They complied. A dead pause ensued. The grim warriors around sat like statues; each muffled in his robe with his fierce eyes bent on the intruders. The latter felt they were in a perilous predicament.

"Keep your eyes on the chief while I am addressing him," said M'Kenzie to his companions. "Should he give any sign to his band shoot him and make for the door."

M'Kenzie advanced and offered the pipe of peace to the chief, but it was refused. He then made a regular speech, explaining the object of their visit, and proposing to give in exchange for the rifle two blankets, an axe, some beads and tobacco.

When he had done the chief rose; began to address him in a low voice but soon became loud and violent and ended by working himself up into a furious passion. He upbraided the white men for their sordid conduct in passing and repassing through their neighborhood without giving them a blanket or any other article of goods, merely because they had no furs to barter in exchange, and he alluded with menaces of vengeance, to the death of the Indian killed by the whites in the skirmish at the Falls.

Matters were verging to a crisis. It was evident the surrounding savages were only waiting a signal from the chief to spring upon their prey. M'Kenzie and his companions had gradually risen on their feet during the speech and had brought their rifles to a horizontal position, the barrels resting in their left hands; the muzzle of M'Kenzie's piece was within three feet of the speaker's heart. They cocked their rifles; the click of the locks for a moment suffused the dark cheek of the savage and there was a pause. They coolly but promptly advanced to the door; the Indians fell back in awe and suffered them to pass. The sun was just setting as they emerged from this dangerous den. They took the precaution to keep along the tops of the rocks as much as possible on their way back to the canoe, and reached their camp in safety, congratulating themselves on their escape, and feeling no desire to make a second visit to the grim warriors of Wish-ram.

M'Kenzie and his party resumed their journey the next morning. At some distance above the Falls of the Columbia they observed two bark canoes filled with white men coming down the river, to the full chant of a set of Canadian voyageurs. A parley ensued. It was a detachment of North Westers, under the command of Mr. John George M'Tavish, bound, full of song and spirit, to the mouth of the Columbia to await the arrival of the Isaac Todd.

M'Kenzie and M'Tavish came to a halt and landing encamped together for the night. The voyageurs of either party hailed each other as brothers and old "camerades," and they mingled together as if united by one common interest, instead of belonging to rival companies and trading under hostile flags.

In the morning they proceeded on their different ways, in style correspondent to their different fortunes, the one toiling painfully against the stream, the other sweeping down gaily with the current.

M'Kenzie arrived safely at his deserted post on the Shahaptan, but found to his chagrin that his caches had been discovered and rifled by the Indians. Here was a dilemma, for, on the stolen goods he had depended to purchase horses of the Indians. He sent out men in all directions to endeavor to discover the thieves, and despatched Mr. Reed to the posts of Messrs. Clarke and David Stuart with the letters of Mr. M'Dougall.

The resolution announced in these letters, to break up and depart from Astoria, was condemned by both Clarke and Stuart. These two gentlemen had been very successful at their posts and considered it rash and pusillanimous to abandon, on the first difficulty, an enterprize of such great cost and ample promise. They made no arrangements, therefore, for leaving the country but acted with a view to the maintenance of their new and prosperous establishments.

The regular time approached, when the partners of the interior posts were to rendezvous at the mouth of the Wallah Wallah, on their way to Astoria with the peltries they had collected. Mr. Clarke accordingly packed all his furs on twenty eight horses, and leaving a clerk and four men to take charge of the post, departed on the 25th of May with the residue of his force.

On the 30th he arrived at the confluence of the Pavion and Lewis rivers, where he had left his barge and canoes in the guardianship of the old Pierced nose chieftain. That dignitary had acquitted himself more faithfully of his charge than Mr. Clarke had expected, and the canoes were found in very tolerable order. Some repairs were necessary, and, while they were making them, the party encamped close by the village. Having had repeated and vexatious proofs of the pilfering propensities of this tribe during his former visit, Mr. Clarke ordered that a wary eye should be kept upon them.

He was a tall, good looking man, and somewhat given to pomp and circumstance, which made him an object of note in the eyes of the wondering savages. He was stately too in his appointments, and had a silver goblet or drinking cup, out of which he would drink with a magnificent air and then lock it up in a large *garde vin*, which accompanied him in his travels and stood in his tent. This goblet had originally been sent as a present from Mr. Astor to Mr. M'Kay, the partner who had unfortunately been blown up in the Tonquin. As it reached Astoria after the departure of that gentleman it had remained in the possession of Mr. Clarke.

A silver goblet was too glittering a prize not to catch the eye of a Pierced nose. It was like the shining tin case of John Reed. Such a wonder had never been seen in the land before. The Indians talked about it to one another. They marked the care with which it was deposited in the *garde vin,* like a relique in its shrine and concluded that it must be a "Great Medicine." That night Mr. Clarke neglected to lock up his treasure; in the morning the sacred casket was open—the precious relique gone!

Clarke was now outrageous. All the past vexations that he had suffered from this pilfering community rose to mind, and he threatened that unless the goblet was promptly returned, he would hang the thief should he eventually discover him. The day passed away, however, without the restoration of the cup. At night sentinels were secretly posted about the camp. With all their vigilance a Pierced nose contrived to get into the camp unperceived and to load himself with booty; it was only on his retreat that he was discovered and taken.

At daybreak the culprit was brought to trial and promptly convicted. He stood responsible for all the spoliations of the camp; the precious goblet among the number, and Mr. Clarke passed sentence of death upon him.

A gibbet was accordingly constructed of oars: the chief of the village and his people were assembled and the culprit was produced, with his legs and arms pinioned. Clarke then made a harangue. He reminded the tribe of the benefits he had bestowed upon them during his former visit, and the many thefts and other misdeeds which he had overlooked. The prisoner, especially, had always been peculiarly well treated by the white men, but had repeatedly been guilty of pilfering. He was to be punished for his own misdeeds and as a warning to his tribe.

The Indians now gathered round Mr. Clarke and interceded for the culprit. They were willing he should be punished severely but implored that his life might be spared. The companions too of Mr. Clarke considered the sentence too severe and advised him to mitigate it; but he was inexorable. He was not naturally a stern or cruel man; but from his boyhood he had lived in the Indian country among Indian traders, and held the life of a savage extremely cheap. He was, moreover, a firm believer in the doctrine of intimidation.

Farnham, a clerk, a tall "Green mountain boy" from Vermont, who had been robbed of a pistol, acted as executioner. The signal was given and the poor Pierced nose, resisting, struggling and screaming in the most frightful manner, was launched into eternity. The Indians stood round gazing in silence and mute awe, but made no attempt to oppose the execution, nor testified any emotion when it was over. They locked up their feelings within their bosoms until an opportunity should arrive to gratify them with a bloody act of vengeance.

To say nothing of the needless severity of this act, its impolicy was glaringly obvious. Mr. M'Lennon and three men were to return to the post with the horses, their loads having been transferred to the canoes. They would have to pass through a tract of country infested by this tribe, who were all horsemen and hard riders and might pursue them to take vengeance for the death of their comrade. M'Lennon, however, was a resolute fellow and made light of all dangers. He and his three men were present at the execution, and set off as soon as life was extinct in the victim; but, to use the words of one of their comrades, "they did not let the grass grow under the heels of their horses as they clattered out of the Pierced nose country," and were glad to find themselves in safety at the post.

Mr. Clarke and his party embarked about the same time in their canoes and early on the following day reached the mouth of the Wallah Wallah, where they found Messrs. Stuart and M'Kenzie awaiting them; the latter having recovered part of the goods stolen from his cache. Clarke informed them of the signal punishment he had inflicted on the Pierced nose, evidently expecting to excite their admiration by such a hardy act of justice, performed in the very midst of the Indian country, but was mortified at finding it strongly censured as inhuman, unnecessary and likely to provoke hostilities.

The parties thus united formed a squadron of two boats and six canoes with which they performed their voyage in safety down the river, and arrived at Astoria on the 12th of June, bringing with them a valuable stock of peltries.

About ten days previously the brigade which had been quartered on the banks of the Wallamut, had arrived with numerous packs of beaver, the result of a few months' sojourn on that river. These were the first fruits of the enterprize, gathered by men as yet mere strangers in the land; but they were such as to give substantial grounds for sanguine anticipations of profit, when the country should be more completely explored, and the trade established.

CHAPTER LIV

The partners displeased with M'Dougall—Equivocal conduct of that gentleman—Partners agree to abandon Astoria—Sale of goods to M'Tavish—Arrangements for the year—Manifesto signed by the partners—Departure of M'Tavish for the interior.

The partners found Mr. M'Dougall in all the bustle of preparation; having about nine days previously announced at the factory his intention of breaking up the establishment, and fixed upon the 1st of July for the time of departure. Messrs. Stuart and Clarke felt highly displeased at his taking so precipitate a step, without waiting for their concurrence, when he must have known that their arrival could not be far distant.

Indeed the whole conduct of Mr. M'Dougall was such as to awaken strong doubts as to his loyal devotion to the cause. His old sympathies with the North West Company seemed to have revived. He had received M'Tavish and his party with uncalled for hospitality, as though they were friends and allies; instead of being a party of observation: come to reconnoiter the state of affairs at Astoria, and to await the arrival of a hostile ship. Had they been left to themselves they would have been starved off for want of provisions, or driven away by the Chinooks, who only wanted a signal from the factory to treat them as intruders and enemies. M'Dougall, on the contrary, had supplied them from the stores of the garrison, and had gained them the favor of the Indians by treating them as friends.

Having set his mind fixedly on the project of breaking up the establishment at Astoria in the current year, M'Dougall was sorely disappointed at finding that Messrs. Stuart and Clarke had omitted to comply with his request to purchase horses and provisions for the caravan across the Mountains. It was now too late to make the necessary preparations in time for traversing the mountains before winter, and the project had to be postponed.

In the mean time the non arrival of the annual ship, and the apprehensions entertained of the loss of the Beaver and of Mr. Hunt, had their effect upon the minds of Messrs. Stuart and Clarke: and they began to listen to the desponding representations of M'Dougall, seconded by M'Kenzie, who inveighed against their situation as desperate and forlorn; left to shift for themselves or perish upon a barbarous coast; neglected by those who sent them there, and threatened with dangers of every kind. In this way they were brought to consent to the plan of abandoning the country in the ensuing year.

About this time M'Tavish applied at the factory to purchase a small supply of goods wherewith to trade his way back to his post on the upper waters of the Columbia, having waited in vain for the arrival of the Isaac Todd. His request brought on a consultation among the partners. M'Dougall urged that it should be complied with. He furthermore proposed that they should give up to M'Tavish, for a proper consideration, the post on the Spokan and all its dependencies, as they had not sufficient goods on hand to supply that fort themselves, and to keep up a competition with the North West Company in the trade with the neighboring Indians. This last representation has since been proved incorrect. By inventories it appears that their stock in hand for the supply of the interior posts, was superior to that of the North West Company; so that they had nothing to fear from competition.

Through the influence of Messrs. M'Dougall and M'Kenzie this proposition was adopted; and was promptly accepted by M'Tavish. The merchandize sold to him amounted to eight hundred and fifty eight dollars, to be paid for, in the following spring, in horses, or in any other manner most acceptable to the partners at that period.

This agreement being concluded, the partners formed their plans for the year that they would yet have to pass in the country. Their objects were chiefly present subsistence and the purchase of horses for the contemplated journey, though they were likewise to collect as much peltries as their diminished means would command. Accordingly, it was arranged that David Stuart should return to his former post on the Oakinagan, and Mr. Clarke should make his sojourn among the Flatheads; John Reed the sturdy Hibernian was to undertake the Snake River country, accompanied by Pierre Dorion and Pierre Delaunay as hunters, and Francis Landry, Jean Baptiste Turcotte, André La Chapelle and Giles Le Clerc, Canadian voyageurs.

Astoria, however, was the post about which they felt the greatest solicitude, and on which they all more or less depended. The maintenance of this in safety throughout the coming year was, therefore, their grand consideration. Mr. M'Dougall was to continue in command at it, with a party of forty men. They would have to depend chiefly upon the neighboring savages for their subsistence. These, at present, were friendly, but it was to be feared that, when they should discover the exigencies of the post, and its real weakness, they might proceed to hostilities; or at any rate might cease to furnish their usual supplies. It was important therefore to render the place as independent as possible of the surrounding tribes for its support; and it was accordingly resolved that M'Kenzie with four hunters and eight common men should winter in the abundant country of the Wollamut, from whence they might be enabled to furnish a constant supply of provisions to Astoria.

As there was too great a proportion of clerks for the number of privates in the service, the engagements of three of them, Cox, Ross and M'Lennon were surrendered to them, and they immediately enrolled themselves in the service of the North West Company, glad no doubt to escape from what they considered a sinking ship.

Having made all these arrangements the four partners on the first of July signed a formal manifesto, stating the alarming state of their affairs from the non arrival of the annual ship; and the absence and apprehended loss of the Beaver; their want of goods, their despair of receiving any further supply, their ignorance of the coast, and their disappointment as to the interior trade, which they pronounced unequal to the expenses incurred and incompetent to stand against the powerful opposition of the North West Company. And as by the 16th article of the Company's agreement they were authorized to abandon this undertaking and dissolve the concern, if before the period of five years, it should be found unprofitable; they now formally announced their intention to do so on the 1st day of June of the ensuing year, unless, in the interim, they should receive the necessary support and supplies from Mr. Astor or the stockholders, with orders to continue.

This instrument, accompanied by private letters of similar import, was delivered to Mr. M'Tavish who departed on the 5th of July. He engaged to forward the despatches to Mr. Astor by the usual winter express, sent overland by the North West Company.

The manifesto was signed with great reluctance by Messrs. Clarke and D. Stuart, whose experience by no means justified the discouraging account given in it of the internal trade, and who considered the main difficulties of exploring an unknown and savage country, and of ascertaining the best trading and trapping grounds, in a great measure overcome. They were over ruled, however, by the urgent instances of M'Dougall and M'Kenzie, who, having resolved upon abandoning the enterprize, were desirous of making as strong a case as possible to excuse their conduct to Mr. Astor and to the world.

CHAPTER LV

Anxieties of Mr. Astor—Memorial of the North West Company—Tidings of a British naval expedition against Astoria—Mr. Astor applies to Government for protection—The frigate Adams ordered to be fitted out—Bright news from Astoria—Sunshine suddenly overclouded.

While difficulties and disasters had been gathering about the infant settlement of Astoria the mind of its projector at New York was a prey to great anxiety. The Ship Lark despatched by him with supplies for the establishment sailed on the 6th of March 1813. Within a fortnight afterwards he received intelligence which justified all his apprehensions of hostility on the part of the British. The North West Company had made a second memorial to that government, representing Astoria as an American establishment, stating the vast scope of its contemplated operations, magnifying the strength of its fortifications, and expressing their fears that, unless crushed in the bud, it would effect the downfall of their trade.

Influenced by these representations the British government ordered the Frigate Phoebe to be detached as a convoy for the armed ship Isaac Todd, which was ready to sail with men and munitions for forming a new establishment. They were to proceed together to the mouth of the Columbia, capture or destroy whatever American fortress they should find there, and plant the British flag on its ruins.

Informed of these movements, Mr. Astor lost no time in addressing a second letter to the Secretary of State communicating this intelligence and requesting that it might be laid before the president; as no notice, however, had been taken of his previous letter he contented himself with this simple communication, and made no further application for aid.

Awakened now to the danger that menaced the establishment at Astoria, and aware of the importance of protecting this foothold of American commerce and empire on the shores of the Pacific, the government determined to send the frigate Adams, Captain Crane, upon this service. On hearing of this determination Mr. Astor immediately proceeded to fit out a ship called the Enterprize, to sail in company with the Adams, freighted with additional supplies and reinforcements for Astoria.

About the middle of June, while in the midst of these preparations, Mr. Astor received a letter from Mr. R. Stuart dated S' Louis, May 1st, confirming the intelligence already received through the public newspapers, of his safe return, and of the arrival of Mr. Hunt and his party at Astoria and giving the most flattering accounts of the prosperity of the enterprize. So deep had been the anxiety of Mr. Astor, for the success of this great object of his ambition, that this gleam of good news was almost overpowering. "I felt ready," said he, "to fall upon my knees in a transport of gratitude."

At the same time he heard that the Beaver had made good her voyage from New York to the Columbia. This was additional ground of hope for the welfare of the little colony. The post being thus relieved and strengthened with an American at its head, and a ship of war about to sail for its protection, the prospect for the future seemed full of encouragement, and Mr. Astor proceeded with fresh vigour to fit out his merchant ship.

Unfortunately for Astoria, this bright gleam of sunshine was soon overclouded. Just as the Adams had received her complement of men and the two vessels were ready for sea, news came from Commodore Chauncey, commanding on Lake Ontario, that a reinforcement of seamen was wanted in that quarter. The demand was urgent, the crew of the Adams were immediately transferred to that service and the ship was laid up.

This was a most ill timed and discouraging blow, but Mr. Astor would not yet allow himself to pause in his undertaking. He determined to send the Enterprize to sea alone, and let her take the chance of making her unprotected way across the Ocean. Just at this time, however, a British force made its appearance off the Hook; and the port of New York was effectually blockaded. To send a ship to sea under these circumstances would be to expose her to almost certain capture. The Enterprize was therefore unloaded and dismantled, and Mr. Astor was obliged to comfort himself with the hope that the Lark might reach Astoria in safety, and that aided by her supplies, and by the good management of Mr. Hunt and his associates, the little colony might be able to maintain itself until the return of peace.

CHAPTER LVI

Affairs of state at Astoria—M'Dougall proposes for the hand of an Indian princess—Matrimonial embassy to Comcomly—Matrimonial notions among the Chinooks—Settlements and pin money—The bringing home of the bride—A managing father in law—Arrival of Mr. Hunt at Astoria.

We have hitherto had so much to relate of a gloomy and disastrous nature, that it is with a feeling of momentary relief we turn to something of a more pleasing complexion, and record the first, and indeed only nuptials in high life that took place in the infant settlement of Astoria.

M'Dougall, who appears to have been a man of a thousand projects, and of great, though somewhat irregular ambition, suddenly conceived the idea of seeking the hand of one of the native princesses, a daughter of the one eyed potentate Comcomly, who held sway over the fishing tribe of the Chinooks and had long supplied the factory with smelts and sturgeons.

Some accounts give rather a romantic origin to this affair, tracing it to the stormy night, when M'Dougall, in the course of an exploring expedition, was driven by stress of weather, to seek shelter in the royal abode of Comcomly. Then and there he was first struck with the charms of this piscatory princess, as she exerted herself to entertain her father's guest.

The "journal of Astoria," however, which was kept under his own eye, records this union as a high state alliance and great stroke of policy. The factory had to depend, in a great measure, on the Chinooks for provisions. They were at present friendly, but it was to be feared they would prove otherwise should they discover the weakness and the exigencies of the post, and the intention to leave the country. This alliance, therefore, would infallibly rivet Comcomly to the interests of the Astorians and with him the powerful tribe of the Chinooks. Be this as it may, and it is hard to fathom the real policy of governors and princes, M'Dougall despatched two of the clerks as ambassadors extraordinary to wait upon the one eyed chieftain and make overtures for the hand of his daughter.

The Chinooks, though not a very refined nation, have notions of matrimonial arrangements that would not disgrace the most refined sticklers for settlements and pin money. The suitor repairs not to the bower of his mistress, but to her father's lodge and throws down a present at his feet. His wishes are then disclosed by some discreet friend employed

by him for the purpose. If the suitor and his present find favor in the eyes
of the father, he breaks the matter to his daughter and enquires into
the state of her inclinations. Should her answer be favorable the suit
is accepted; and the lover has to make further presents to the father
of horses, canoes and other valuables, according to the beauty and merits
of the bride; looking forward to a return in kind whenever they shall
go to house keeping.

We have more than once had occasion to speak of the shrewdness
of Comcomly, but never was it exerted more adroitly than on this occasion. He was a great friend of M'Dougall and pleased with the idea
of having so distinguished a son in law; but so favorable an opportunity
of benefiting his own fortune was not likely to occur a second time, and
he determined to make the most of it. Accordingly the negotiation was
protracted with true diplomatic skill. Conference after conference was
held with the two ambassadors: Comcomly was extravagant in his
terms; rating the charms of his daughter at the highest price, and indeed
she is represented as having one of the flattest and most aristocratical
heads in the tribe. At length the preliminaries were all happily adjusted.
On the 20th of July, early in the afternoon, a squadron of canoes crossed
over from the village of the Chinooks, bearing the royal family of Comcomly and all his court.

That worthy Sachem landed in princely state arrayed in a bright
blue blanket and red breech clout, with an extra quantity of paint and
feathers, attended by a train of half naked warriors and nobles. A horse
was in waiting to receive the princess, who was mounted behind one
of the clerks, and thus conveyed, coy but compliant to the fortress. Here
she was received with devout, though decent joy by her expecting
bridegroom.

Her bridal adornments, it is true, at first caused some little dismay,
having painted and anointed herself for the occasion according to the
Chinook toilette; by dint, however, of copious ablutions, she was freed
from all adventitious tint and fragrance, and entered into the nuptial
state, the cleanest princess that had ever been known of the somewhat
unctuous tribe of the Chinooks.

From that time forward Comcomly was a daily visitor at the fort, and
was admitted into the most intimate counsels of his son in law. He took
an interest in every thing that was going forward, but was particularly
frequent in his visits to the blacksmith's shop; tasking the labors of
the artificer in iron for every kind of weapon and implement suited to
the savage state, insomuch that the necessary business of the factory
was often postponed to attend to his requisitions.

The honey moon had scarce passed away, and M'Dougall was seated
with his bride in the fortress of Astoria when, about noon of the 20th

of August, Gassacop, the son of Comcomly, hurried into his presence with great agitation and announced a ship at the mouth of the river. The news produced a vast sensation. Was it a ship of peace or war? Was it American or British? Was it the Beaver or the Isaac Todd? M'Dougall hurried to the water side, threw himself into a boat, and ordered the hands to pull with all speed for the mouth of the harbor.

Those in the fort remained watching the entrance of the river, anxious to know whether they were to prepare for greeting a friend or fighting an enemy. At length the ship was descried crossing the bar, and bending her course towards Astoria. Every gaze was fixed upon her in silent scrutiny until the American flag was recognized. A general shout was the first expression of joy, and next a salutation was thundered from the cannon of the fort.

The vessel came to anchor on the opposite side of the river and returned the salute. The boat of Mr. M'Dougall went on board, and was seen returning late in the afternoon. The Astorians watched her with straining eyes to discover who were on board, but the sun went down and the evening closed in before she was sufficiently near. At length she reached the land and Mr. Hunt stepped on shore. He was hailed as one risen from the dead, and his return was a signal for merriment almost equal to that which prevailed at the nuptials of M'Dougall.

We must now explain the cause of this gentleman's long absence, which had given rise to such gloomy and dispiriting surmises.

CHAPTER LVII

Voyage of the Beaver to New Archangel—A Russian governor—Roy-stering rule—The tyranny of the table—Hard drinking bargains—Voy-age to Kamschatka—Seal catching establishment at S' Paul's—Storms at sea—Mr. Hunt left at the Sandwich islands—Transactions of the Beaver at Canton—Return of Mr. Hunt to Astoria.

It will be recollected that the destination of the Beaver when she sailed from Astoria on the 4th of August in 1812, was to proceed northwardly along the Coast to Sheetka or New Archangel, there to dispose of that part of her cargo intended for the supply of the Russian establish-ment at that place, and then to return to Astoria, where it was expected she would arrive in October.

New Archangel is situated in Norfolk Sound, Lat. 57° 2′ N. Long. 135° 50′ W. It was the head quarters of the different colonies of the Russian Fur Company, and the common rendezvous of the American vessels trading along the Coast.

The Beaver met with nothing worthy of particular mention in her voyage and arrived at New Archangel on the nineteenth of August. The place at that time was the residence of Count Baranoff, the governor of the different colonies: a rough, rugged, hospitable, hard drinking old Russian, somewhat of a soldier, somewhat of a trader; above all a boon companion of the old roystering school, with a strong cross of the bear.

Mr. Hunt found this hyperborean veteran ensconced in a fort which crested the whole of a high rocky promontory. It mounted one hundred guns large and small and was impregnable to Indian attack unaided by artillery. Here the old governor lorded it over sixty Russians, who formed the corps of the trading establishment, beside an indefinite number of Indian hunters of the Kodiak tribe, who were continually coming and going, or lounging and loitering about the fort like so many hounds round a sportsman's hunting quarters. Though a loose liver among his guests the governor was a strict disciplinarian among his men; keeping them in perfect subjection and having seven on guard night and day.

Beside the immediate serfs and dependants just mentioned, the old Russian potentate exerted a considerable sway over a numerous and irregular class of maritime traders, who looked to him for aid and munitions, and through whom he may be said to have, in some degree, extended his power along the whole north west coast. These were American captains of vessels engaged in a particular department of

trade. One of these captains would come in a manner empty handed
to New Archangel. Here his ship would be furnished with about fifty
canoes and a hundred Kodiak hunters and fitted out with provisions
and every thing necessary for hunting the sea otter on the Coast of
California, where the Russians have another establishment. The ship
would ply along the Californian coast from place to place, dropping
parties of otter hunters in their canoes, furnishing them only with water,
and leaving them to depend upon their own dexterity for a maintenance.
When a sufficient cargo was collected, she would gather up her canoes
and hunters, and return with them to Archangel; where the Captain
would render in the returns of his voyage and received one half of the
skins for his share.

Over these coasting captains, as we have hinted, the veteran governor
exerted some sort of sway, but it was of a peculiar and characteristic
kind; it was the tyranny of the table. They were obliged to join him
in his "prosnics" or carousals and to drink "potations pottle deep." His
carousals too were not of the most quiet kind, nor were his potations
as mild as nectar. "He is continually," said Mr. Hunt, "giving entertain-
ments by way of parade, and if you do not drink raw rum and boiling
punch as strong as sulphur, he will insult you as soon as he gets
drunk, which is very shortly after sitting down to table."

As to any "temperance captain" who stood fast to his faith and
refused to give up his sobriety he might go elsewhere for a market,
for he stood no chance with the governor. Rarely, however, did any cold
water caitiff of the kind darken the door of old Baranhoff; the coasting
captains knew too well his humour and their own interests; they joined
in his revels, they drank, and sang, and whooped and hiccuped until
they all got "half seas over," and then affairs went on swimmingly.

An awful warning to all "flinchers" occurred shortly before Mr. Hunt's
arrival. A young naval officer had recently been sent out by the Emperor
to take command of one of the Company's vessels. The Governor, as
usual, had him at his "prosnics" and plied him with fiery potations. The
young man stood on the defensive until the old count's ire was completely kindled; he carried his point and made the green horn tipsey,
willy nilly. In proportion as they grew fuddled they grew noisy, they
quarrelled in their cups; the youngster paid old Baranhoff in his own
coin by rating him soundly; in reward for which, when sober, he was
taken the rounds of four pickets, and received seventy nine lashes,
taled out with Russian punctuality of punishment.

Such was the old grizzled bear with whom Mr. Hunt had to do his
business. How he managed to cope with his humours; whether he
pledged him in raw rum and blazing punch and "clinked the can" with
him as they made their bargains, does not appear upon record: we

must infer, however, from his general observations on the absolute sway of this hard drinking potentate, that he had to conform to the customs of his court, and that their business transactions presented a maudlin mixture of punch and peltry.

The greatest annoyance to Mr. Hunt, however, was the delay to which he was subjected, in disposing of the cargo of the ship and getting the requisite returns. With all the Governor's devotion to the bottle he never obfuscated his faculties sufficiently to lose sight of his interest, and is represented by Mr. Hunt as keen, not to say crafty, at a bargain, as the most arrant water drinker. A long time was expended in negotiating with him, and by the time the bargain was concluded the month of October had arrived. To add to the delay he was to be paid for his cargo in seal skins. Now it so happened that there was none of this kind of peltry at the fort of old Baranhoff. It was necessary, therefore, for Mr. Hunt to proceed to a seal catching establishment which the Russian company had at the island of S' Paul, in the Sea of Kamschatka. He accordingly set sail on the 4th of October, after having spent forty five days at New Archangel boosing and bargaining with its roystering commander, and right glad was he to escape from the clutches of this "old man of the sea."

The Beaver arrived at S' Paul's on the 31st of October, by which time, according to arrangement, he ought to have been back at Astoria. The Island of S' Paul's is in Latitude 57° N. longitude 170° or 171° W. Its shores in certain places and at certain seasons are covered with seals, while others are playing about in the water. Of these the Russians take only the small ones, from seven to ten months old, and carefully select the males, giving the females their freedom, that the breed may not be diminished. The islanders, however, kill the large ones for provisions, and for skins wherewith to cover their canoes. They drive them from the shore over the rocks until within a short distance of their habitations, where they kill them. By this means they save themselves the trouble of carrying the skins, and have the flesh at hand. This is thrown in heaps, and when the season for skinning is over, they take out the entrails and make one heap of the blubber. This with drift wood serves for fuel, for the island is entirely destitute of trees. They make another heap of the flesh; which, with the eggs of sea fowls preserved in oil, an occasional sea lion, a few ducks in winter and some wild roots, composes their food.

Mr. Hunt found seven Russians at the island, and one hundred hunters, natives of Oonalaska, with their families. They lived in cabins that looked like caves; being for the most part formed of the jaw bone of a whale, put up as rafters, across which were laid pieces of drift wood covered over with long grass, the skins of large sea animals, and earth;

so as to be quite comfortable in despite of the rigours of the climate though we are told they had as ancient and fish like an odour "as had the quarters of Jonah, when lodged within the whale."

In one of these odoriferous mansions Mr. Hunt occasionally took up his abode that he might be at hand to hasten the loading of the ship. The operation, however, was somewhat slow, for it was necessary to overhaul and inspect every pack to prevent imposition, and the peltries had then to be conveyed in large boats, made of skins, to the ship, which was some little distance from the shore, standing off and on.

One night while Mr. Hunt was on shore, with some others of the crew, there rose a terrible gale. When the day broke the ship was not to be seen. He watched for her with anxious eyes until night but in vain. Day after day of boisterous storms, and howling wintry weather, were passed in watchfulness and solicitude. Nothing was to be seen but a dark and angry sea and a scowling northern sky, and at night he retired within the jaws of the whale and nestled disconsolately among seal skins.

At length on the 13th of November the Beaver made her appearance; much the worse for the stormy conflicts she had sustained in those hyperborean seas. She had been obliged to carry a press of sail in heavy gales, to be able to hold her ground, and had consequently sustained great damage in her canvass and rigging. Mr. Hunt lost no time in hurrying the residue of the cargo on board of her; then bidding adieu to his seal fishing friends and his whale bone habitation, he put forth once more to sea.

He was now for making the best of his way to Astoria, and fortunate would it have been for the interests of that place and the interests of Mr. Astor had he done so; but unluckily a perplexing question rose in his mind. The sails and rigging of the Beaver had been much rent and shattered in the late storm; would she be able to stand the hard gales to be expected in making Columbia River at this season? Was it prudent, also, at this boisterous time of the year to risk the valuable cargo which she now had on board, by crossing and recrossing the dangerous bar of that river? These doubts were probably suggested or enforced by Captain Sowles, who, it has already been seen, was an over cautious, or rather a timid seaman, and they may have had some weight with Mr. Hunt; but there were other considerations which more strongly swayed his mind. The lateness of the season and the unforeseen delays the ship had encountered at New Archangel, and by being obliged to proceed to S' Paul's, had put her so much back in her calculated time, that there was a risk of her arriving so late at Canton, as to come to a bad market, both for the sale of her peltries and the purchase of a return cargo. He considered it to the interest of the Company, therefore, that he should proceed at once to the Sandwich islands; there wait the arrival of the annual vessel from New York, take passage in her to Astoria, and suffer the Beaver to continue on to Canton.

On the other hand, he was urged to the other course by his engagements; by the plan of the voyage marked out for the Beaver by Mr. Astor, by his inclination, and the possibility that the establishment might need his presence, and by the recollection that there must already be a large amount of peltries collected at Astoria, and waiting for the return of the Beaver, to convey them to market.

These conflicting questions perplexed and agitated his mind, and gave rise to much anxious reflection, for he was a conscientious man that seems ever to have aimed at a faithful discharge of his duties, and to have had the interests of his employers earnestly at heart. His decision in the present instance was injudicious and proved unfortunate. It was, to bear away for the Sandwich islands. He persuaded himself that it was matter of necessity and that the distressed condition of the ship left him no other alternative; but we rather suspect he was so persuaded by the representations of the timid Captain. They accordingly stood for the Sandwich islands; arrived at Woahoo, where the ship underwent the necessary repairs and again put to sea on the first of January 1813: leaving Mr. Hunt on the island.

We will follow the Beaver to Canton, as her fortunes in some measure exemplify the evil of commanders of ships acting contrary to orders; and as they form a part of the tissue of cross purposes that marred the great commercial enterprize we have undertaken to record.

The Beaver arrived safe at Canton, where Captain Sowle found the letter of Mr. Astor, giving him information of the war, and directing him to convey the intelligence to Astoria. He wrote a reply dictated either by timidity or obstinacy, in which he declined complying with the orders of Mr. Astor, but said he would wait for the return of peace, and then come home. The other proceedings of Captain Sowles were equally wrong headed and unlucky. He was offered one hundred and fifty thousand dollars for the fur he had taken on board at S' Paul's. The goods for which it had been procured, cost but twenty five thousand dollars in New York. Had he accepted this offer and re-invested the amount in Nankeens, which at that time, in consequence of the interruption to commerce by the war, were at two thirds of their usual price, the whole would have brought three hundred thousand dollars in New York. It is true, the war would have rendered it unsafe to attempt the homeward voyage; but he might have put the goods in store at Canton until after the peace, and have sailed without risk of capture to Astoria; bringing to the partners at that place tidings of the great profits realized on the outward cargo, and the still greater to be expected from the returns. The news of such a brilliant commencement to their undertaking would have counter balanced the gloomy tidings of the war; it would have infused new spirits into them all, and given them courage and constancy to persevere in the enterprize. Captain Sowle, however, refused the offer of one hundred and fifty thousand dollars and stood wavering and chaffering for higher terms. The furs began to fall in value; this only encreased his irresolution; they sunk so much that he feared to sell at all; he borrowed money on Mr. Astor's account at an interest of eighteen per cent, and laid up his ship to await the return of peace.

In the mean while Mr. Hunt soon saw reason to repent the resolution he had adopted in altering the destination of the ship. His stay at the Sandwich islands was prolonged far beyond all expectation. He looked in vain for the annual ship in the spring. Month after month passed by, and still she did not make her appearance. He too proved the danger of departing from orders. Had he returned from S' Paul's to Astoria, all the anxiety and despondency about his fate and about the whole course of the undertaking would have been obviated. The Beaver would have received the furs collected at the factory and taken them to Canton, and great gains instead of great losses would have been the result. The greatest blunder, however, was that committed by Captain Sowles.

At length about the 20th of June, the ship Albatross, Captain Smith, arrived from China, and brought the first tidings of the War to the Sandwich Islands. Mr. Hunt was no longer in doubt and perplexity as to the reason of the non appearance of the annual ship. His first thoughts were for the welfare of Astoria, and, concluding that the inhabitants would probably be in want of provisions, he chartered the Albatross for two thousand dollars, to land him with some supplies at the mouth of the Columbia: where he arrived, as we have seen, on the twentieth of August; after a year's seafaring that might have furnished a chapter in the wanderings of Sindbad.

CHAPTER LVIII

Arrangements among the partners—Mr. Hunt sails in the Albatross—Arrives at the Marquesas—News of the Frigate Phoebe—Mr. Hunt proceeds to the Sandwich Islands—Voyage of the Lark—Her shipwreck—Transactions with the natives of the Sandwich Islands—Conduct of Tamaahmaah.

Mr. Hunt was overwhelmed with surprize when he learnt the resolution taken by the partners to abandon Astoria. He soon found, however, that matters had gone too far, and the minds of his colleagues had become too firmly bent upon the measure to render any opposition of avail. He was beset, too, with the same disparaging accounts of the interior trade, and of the whole concerns and prospects of the Company that had been rendered to Mr. Astor. His own experience had been full of perplexities and discouragements. He had a conscientious anxiety for the interests of Mr. Astor, and, not comprehending the extended views of that gentleman and his habit of operating with great amounts, he had from the first been daunted by the enormous expenses required and had become disheartened by the subsequent losses sustained, which appeared to him to be ruinous in their magnitude. By degrees, therefore, he was brought to acquiesce in the step taken by his colleagues as perhaps adviseable in the exigencies of the case; his only care was to wind up the business with as little further loss as possible to Mr. Astor.

A large stock of valuable furs was collected at the Factory, which it was necessary to get to a market. There were twenty five Sandwich islanders also in the employ of the Company, whom they were bound by express agreement, to restore to their native country. For these purposes a ship was necessary.

The Albatross was bound to the Marquesas and thence to the Sandwich islands. It was resolved that Mr. Hunt should sail in her in quest of a vessel, and should return if possible by the 1st of January, bringing with him a supply of provisions. Should any thing occur, however, to prevent his return, an arrangement was to be proposed to Mr. M'Tavish to transfer such of the men as were so disposed, from the service of the American Fur Company into that of the North West, the latter becoming responsible for the wages due them, on receiving an equivalent in goods from the store house of the Factory. As a means of facilitating the despatch of business Mr. M'Dougall proposed that, in case Mr. Hunt should not return, the whole arrangement with Mr. M'Tavish should be left solely to him. This was assented to; the contingency being considered possible but not probable.

It is proper to note, that, on the first announcement by Mr. M'Dougall of his intention to break up the establishment, three of the clerks, British subjects, had, with his consent, passed into the service of the North West Company, and departed with Mr. M'Tavish for his post in the interior.

Having arranged all these matters during a sojourn of six days at Astoria, Mr. Hunt set sail in the Albatross on the 26th of August, and arrived, without accident at the Marquesas. He had not been there long when Commodore Porter arrived in the Frigate Essex, bringing in a number of stout London whalers as prizes, having made a sweeping cruize in the Pacific. From Commodore Porter he received the alarming intelligence that the British Frigate Phoebe, with a store ship mounted with battering pieces, calculated to attack forts, had arrived at Rio Janeiro, where she had been joined by the Sloops of War Cherub and Racoon, and that they had all sailed in company on the 6th of July for the Pacific, bound, as it was supposed, to Columbia River.

Here then was the death warrant of unfortunate Astoria! The anxious mind of Mr. Hunt was in greater perplexity than ever. He had been eager to extricate the property of Mr. Astor from a failing concern with as little loss as possible; there was now danger that the whole would be swallowed up. How was it to be snatched from the gulph? It was impossible to charter a ship for the purpose now that a British squadron was on its way to the River. He applied to purchase one of the whale ships brought in by Commodore Porter. The Commodore demanded twenty five thousand Dollars for her. The price appeared exorbitant, and no bargain could be made. Mr. Hunt then urged the Commodore to fit out one of his prizes and send her to Astoria, to bring off the property and part of the people, but he declined, "from want of authority." He assured Mr. Hunt, however, that he would endeavor to fall in with the enemy, or, should he hear of their having certainly gone to the Columbia, he would either follow or anticipate them, should his circumstances warrant such a step.

In this tantalizing state of suspense Mr. Hunt was detained at the Marquesas until November 23d when he proceeded in the Albatross to the Sandwich islands. He still cherished a faint hope that, notwithstanding the war, and all other discouraging circumstances, the annual ship might have been sent by Mr. Astor, and might have touched at the islands and proceeded to the Columbia. He knew the pride and interest taken by that gentleman in his great enterprize, and that he would not be deterred by dangers and difficulties from prosecuting it; much less would he leave the infant establishment without succour and support in the time of trouble. In this, we have seen, he did but justice to Mr. Astor, and we must now turn to notice the cause of the non arrival of the vessel which he had despatched with reinforcements and supplies. Her voyage forms another chapter of accidents in this eventful story.

The Lark sailed from New York on the 6th of March 1813, and proceeded prosperously on her voyage until within a few degrees of the Sandwich Islands. Here a gale sprang up that soon blew with tremendous violence. The Lark was a stanch and noble ship and for a time buffetted bravely with the storm. Unluckily, however, she "broached to" and was struck by a heavy sea that hove her on her beam ends. The helm too was knocked to leeward, all command of the vessel was lost, and another mountain wave completely overset her.

Orders were given to cut away the masts. In the hurry and confusion the boats also were unfortunately cut adrift. The wreck then righted, but was a mere hulk, full of water with a heavy sea washing over it and all the hatches off. On mustering the crew one man was missing, who was discovered below in the forecastle, drowned.

In cutting away the masts it had been utterly impossible to observe the necessary precaution of commencing with the lee rigging that being, from the position of the ship, completely under water. The masts and spars, therefore, being linked to the wreck by the shrouds and rigging, remained along side for four days. During all this time, the ship lay rolling in the trough of the sea, the heavy surges breaking over her, and the spars heaving and banging to and fro, bruising the half drowned sailors that clung to the bow sprit and the stumps of the masts. The sufferings of these poor fellows were intolerable. They stood to their waists in water, in imminent peril of being washed off by every surge. In this position they dared not sleep lest they should let go their holds and be swept away. The only dry place on the wreck was the bow sprit. Here they took turns to be tied on, for half an hour at a time, and in this way gained short snatches of sleep.

On the 14th the first mate died at his post and was swept off by the surges. On the 17th two seamen, faint and exhausted, were washed overboard. The next wave threw their bodies back upon the deck, where they remained swashing backward and forward, ghastly objects to the almost perishing survivors. Mr. Ogden the supercargo, who was at the bow sprit, called to the men nearest to the bodies, to fasten them to the wreck; as a last horrible resource in case of being driven to extremity by famine!

On the 17th the gale gradually subsided and the sea became calm. The sailors now crawled feebly about the wreck and began to relieve it from the main incumbrances. The spars were cleared away, the anchors and guns heaved overboard; the spritsail yard was rigged for a jury mast and a mizen topsail set upon it. A sort of stage was made of a few broken spars, on which the crew were raised above the surface of the water, so as to be enabled to keep themselves dry and to sleep comfortably. Still their sufferings from hunger and thirst were great; but there was a Sandwich islander on board, an expert swimmer, who found his way into the cabin and occasionally brought up a few bottles of wine and porter, and at length got into the run and secured a quarter cask of wine. A little raw pork was likewise procured, and dealt out with a sparing hand. The horrors of their situation were increased by the sight of numerous sharks prowling about the wreck, as if waiting for their prey. On the 24th the cook, a black man, died and was cast into the sea, where he was instantly seized on by these ravenous monsters.

They had been several days making slow head way under their scanty sail when, on the 25th, they came in sight of land. It was about fifteen leagues distant and they remained two or three days drifting along in sight of it. On the 28th they descried, to their great transport, a canoe approaching managed by natives. They came along side, and brought a most welcome supply of potatoes. They informed them that the land they had made was one of the Sandwich islands. The second mate and one of the seamen went on shore in the canoe for water and provisions, and to procure aid from the islanders in towing the wreck into a harbour.

Neither of the men returned, nor was any assistance sent from shore. The next day ten or twelve canoes came along side, but roamed round the wreck like so many sharks, and would render no aid in towing her to land.

The sea continued to break over the vessel with such violence that it was impossible to stand at the helm without the assistance of lashings. The crew were now so worn down by famine and thirst that the Captain saw it would be impossible for them to withstand the breaking of the sea when the ship should ground; he deemed the only chance for their lives, therefore, was to get to land in the canoes, and stand ready to receive and protect the wreck when she should drift to shore. Accordingly they all got safe to land, but had scarcely touched the beach when they were surrounded by the natives, who stripped them almost naked. The name of this inhospitable island was Tahoorowa.

In the course of the night the wreck came drifting to the strand, with the surf thundering around her, and shortly afterwards bilged. On the following morning numerous casks of provisions floated on shore. The natives staved them for the sake of the iron hoops but would not allow the crew to help themselves to the contents, nor to go on board of the wreck.

As the crew were in want of every thing, and as it might be a long time before any opportunity occurred for them to get away from these islands: Mr. Ogden, as soon as he could get a chance, made his way to the island of Owyhee, and endeavored to make some arrangement with the King for the relief of his companions in misfortune.

The illustrious Tamaahmaah, as we have shewn on a former occasion, was a shrewd bargainer, and in the present instance proved himself an experienced wrecker. His negotiations with M'Dougall and the other "Eris of the great American Fur Company" had but little effect on present circumstances, and he proceeded to avail himself of their misfortunes. He agreed to furnish the crew with provisions during their stay in his territories, and to return to them all their clothing that could be found, but he stipulated that the wreck should be abandoned to him as a waif cast by fortune on his shores. With these conditions Mr. Ogden was fain to comply. Upon this the great Tamaahmaah deputed his favorite John Young, the tarpawlin governor of Owyhee, to proceed with a number of the royal guards and take possession of the wreck on behalf of the crown. This was done accordingly, and the property and crew were removed to Owyhee. The royal bounty appears to have been but scanty in its dispensations. The crew fared but meagerly, though, on reading the journal of the voyage it is singular to find them, after all the hardships they had suffered, so sensitive about petty inconveniences as to exclaim against the King as a "savage monster" for refusing them a "pot to cook in" and denying Mr. Ogden the use of a knife and fork which had been saved from the wreck.

Such was the unfortunate catastrophe of the Lark; had she reached her destination in safety, affairs at Astoria might have taken a different course. A strange fatality seems to have attended all the expeditions by sea, nor were those by land much less disastrous.

Captain Northrop was still at the Sandwich islands on December 20th when Mr. Hunt arrived. The latter immediately purchased, for ten thousand dollars, a brig called the Pedlar and put Captain Northrop in command of her. They set sail for Astoria on the 22d of January, intending to remove the property from thence as speedily as possible to the Russian settlements on the north west coast, to prevent it from falling into the hands of the British. Such were the orders of Mr. Astor, sent out by the Lark. We will now leave Mr. Hunt on his voyage and return to see what has taken place at Astoria during his absence.

CHAPTER LIX

Arrival of M'Tavish at Astoria—Conduct of his followers—Negotiations of M'Dougall and M'Tavish—Bargain for the transfer of Astoria—Doubts entertained of the loyalty of M'Dougall.

On the second of October, about five weeks after Mr. Hunt had sailed in the Albatross from Astoria, Mr. M'Kenzie set off with two canoes and twelve men for the posts of Messrs. Stuart and Clarke, to apprize them of the new arrangements determined upon in the recent conference of the partners at the factory.

He had not ascended the river a hundred miles when he met a squadron of ten canoes sweeping merrily down under British colours, the Canadian oarsmen as usual in full song.

It was an armament fitted out by M'Tavish, who had with him Mr. J. Stuart, another partner of the North West Company, together with seven clerks and sixty eight men, seventy five souls in all. They had heard of the Frigate Phoebe and the Isaac Todd being on the high seas and were on their way down to await their arrival. In one of the canoes Mr. Clarke came passenger, the alarming intelligence having brought him down from his post on the Spokan. Mr. M'Kenzie immediately determined to return with him to Astoria and veering about, the two parties encamped together for the night. The leaders, of course, observed a due decorum, but some of the subalterns could not restrain their chuckling exultation, boasting that they would soon plant the British standard on the walls of Astoria and drive the Americans out of the country.

In the course of the evening Mr. M'Kenzie had a secret conference with Mr. Clarke in which they agreed to set off privately before day light and get down in time to apprize M'Dougall of the approach of these North Westers. The latter, however, were completely on the alert. Just as M'Kenzie's canoes were about to push off, they were joined by a couple from the North West squadron, in which were M'Tavish with two clerks and eleven men. With these he intended to push forward and make arrangements, leaving the rest of the convoy, in which was a large quantity of furs, to await his orders.

The two parties arrived at Astoria on the 7th of October. The North Westers encamped under the guns of the fort, and displayed the British colours. The young men in the fort, natives of the United States, were on the point of hoisting the American flag, but were forbidden by Mr. M'Dougall. They were astonished at such a prohibition, and were exceedingly galled by the tone and manner assumed by the clerks and retainers of the North West Company, who ruffled about in that swelling and braggart style which grows up among these heroes of the wilderness; they, in fact, considered themselves lords of the ascendant, and regarded the hampered and harassed Astorians as a conquered people.

On the following day M'Dougall convened the clerks and read to them an extract of a letter from his uncle Mr. Angus Shaw, one of the principal partners of the North West Company, announcing the coming of the Phoebe and Isaac Todd "to take and destroy every thing American on the North West Coast."

This intelligence was received without dismay by such of the clerks as were natives of the United States. They had felt indignant at seeing their national flag struck by a Canadian commander, and the British flag flouted as it were in their faces. They had been stung to the quick, also, by the vaunting airs assumed by the North Westers. In this mood of mind they would willingly have nailed their colours to the staff and defied the frigate. She could not come within many miles of the fort, they observed, and any boats she might send could be destroyed by their cannon.

There were cooler and more calculating spirits, however, who had the control of affairs and felt nothing of the patriotic pride and indignation of these youths. The extract of the letter had, apparently, been read by M'Dougall merely to prepare the way for a preconcerted stroke of management On that same day Mr. M'Tavish proposed to purchase the whole stock of goods and furs belonging to the Company, both at Astoria and in the interior, at cost and charges. Mr. M'Dougall undertook to comply; assuming the whole management of the negotiation in virtue of the power vested in him in case of the nonarrival of Mr. Hunt. That power, however, was limited and specific and did not extend to an operation of this nature and extent; no objection, however, was made to his assumption, and he and M'Tavish soon made a preliminary arrangement, perfectly satisfactory to the latter.

Mr. Stuart and the reserve party of North Westers arrived shortly afterwards and encamped with M'Tavish. The former exclaimed loudly against the terms of the arrangement, and insisted upon a reduction of the prices. New negotiations had now to be entered into. The demands of the North Westers were made in a peremptory tone, and they seemed disposed to dictate like conquerors. The Americans looked on with indignation and impatience. They considered M'Dougall as acting if not a perfidious, certainly a craven part. He was continually repairing to the camp to negotiate, instead of keeping within his walls and receiving overtures in his fortress. His case, they observed, was not so desperate as to excuse such crouching. He might in fact hold out for his own terms. The North West party had lost their ammunition; they had no goods to trade with the natives for provisions, and they were so destitute that M'Dougall had absolutely to feed them while he negotiated with them. He, on the contrary, was well lodged and victualed, had sixty men, with arms, ammunition, boats and every thing requisite either for defence or retreat. The party beneath the guns of his fort were at his mercy. Should an enemy appear in the offing, he could pack up the most valuable part of the property and retire to some place of concealment, or make off for the interior.

These considerations, however, had no weight with Mr. M'Dougall, or were overruled by other motives. The terms of sale were lowered by him to the standard fixed by Mr. Stuart, and an agreement executed on the 16th of October, by which the furs and merchandize of all kinds in the country, belonging to Mr. Astor, passed into the possession of the North West Company at about a third of their real value.* A safe passage through the North West posts was guaranteed to such as did not choose to enter into the service of that Company, and the amount of wages due to them was to be deducted from the price paid for Astoria.

The conduct and motives of Mr. M'Dougall throughout the whole of this proceeding have been strongly questioned by the other partners. He has been accused of availing himself of a wrong construction of powers vested in him at his own request, and of sacrificing the interests of Mr. Astor to the North West Company, under the promise or hope of advantage to himself.

He always insisted, however, that he made the best bargain for Mr. Astor that circumstances would permit: the frigate being hourly

---

* Not quite $40,000 were allowed for furs worth upwards of $100,000. Beaver was valued at $2 per skin though worth $5. Land otter at 50 cents though worth $5. Sea otter at $12 worth from $45 to $60 and for several kinds of furs nothing was allowed. Moreover the goods and merchandize for the Indian trade ought to have brought three times the amount for which they were sold.

The following estimate has been made of the articles on hand and the prices:

17,705 lbs. beaver parchment	valued at	$2.00	worth	$5.00
465 old coat beaver	" "	1.66	"	3.50
907 Land otter	" "	.50	"	5.00
68 Sea otter	" "	12.00	" 45 to	60.00
30 " "	" "	5.00	"	25.00

Nothing was allowed for

179 Mink skins	worth each	. . . .	.40
22 Raccoon	" "	. . . .	.40
38 Lynx	" "	. . . .	2.00
18 Fox	" "	. . . .	1.00
106 "	" "	. . . .	1.50
71 Black bear	" "	. . . .	4.00
16 Grizly "	" "	. . . .	10.00

expected, in which case the whole property of that gentleman would be liable to capture; that the return of Mr. Hunt was problematical, the frigate intending to cruise along the coast for two years and clear it of all American vessels. He moreover averred, and M'Tavish corroborated his averment by certificate, that he proposed an arrangement to that gentleman, by which the furs were to be sent to Canton and sold there at Mr. Astor's risk and for his account, but the proposition was not acceded to.

Notwithstanding all his representations, several of the persons present at the transaction, and acquainted with the whole course of the affair, and among the number Mr. M'Kenzie himself, his occasional coadjutor, remained firm in the belief that he had acted a hollow part. Neither did he succeed in exculpating himself to Mr. Astor; that gentleman declaring, in a letter written some time afterwards to Mr. Hunt, that he considered the property virtually given away. "Had our place and our property," he adds, "been fairly captured, I should have preferred it. I should not feel as if I were disgraced."

All these may be unmerited suspicions; but it certainly is a circumstance strongly corroborative of them that Mr. M'Dougall shortly after concluding this agreement, became a member of the North West Company and received a share productive of a handsome income.

CHAPTER LX

Arrival of a strange sail—Agitation at Astoria—Warlike offer of Comcomly—Astoria taken possession of by the British—Indignation of Comcomly at the conduct of his son in law.

On the morning of the 30th of November a sail was descried doubling Cape Disappointment. It came to anchor in Baker's bay, and proved to be a ship of war. Of what nation? was now the anxious enquiry. If English, why did it come alone?—Where was the merchant vessel that was to have accompanied it? If American, what was to become of the newly acquired possessions of the North West Company?

In this dilemma M'Tavish, in all haste, loaded two barges with all the packages of furs bearing the mark of the North West Company, and made off for Tongue point, three miles up the river. There he was to await a preconcerted signal from M'Dougall on ascertaining the character of the ship. If it should prove American, M'Tavish would have a fair start and could bear off his rich cargo to the interior. It is singular that this prompt mode of conveying valuable but easily transportable effects beyond the reach of a hostile ship, should not have suggested itself while the property belonged to Mr. Astor.

In the mean time M'Dougall, who still remained nominal chief at the fort, launched a canoe manned by men recently in the employ of the American Fur Company, and steered for the ship. On the way he instructed his men to pass themselves for Americans or Englishmen, according to the exigencies of the case.

The vessel proved to be the British Sloop of War Racoon, of twenty six guns and one hundred and twenty men, commanded by Captain Black. According to the account of that officer the Frigate Phoebe and the two sloops of war Cherub and Racoon had sailed in convoy of the Isaac Todd from Rio Janeiro. On board of the Phoebe was Mr. John M'Donald, a partner of the North West Company, embarked as passenger; to profit by the anticipated catastrophe at Astoria. The convoy was separated by stress of weather off Cape Horn. The three ships of war came together again at the island of Juan Fernandez, their appointed rendezvous, but waited in vain for the Isaac Todd.

In the mean time intelligence was received of the mischief that Commodore Porter was doing among the British whale ships. Commodore Hillyer immediately set sail in quest of him with the Phoebe and the Cherub, transferring Mr. M'Donald to the Racoon, and ordering that vessel to proceed to the Columbia.

The officers of the Racoon were in high spirits. The agents of the

North West Company, in instigating this expedition, had talked of immense booty to be made by the fortunate captors of Astoria. Mr. M'Donald had kept up the excitement during the voyage, so that not a midshipman but revelled in dreams of ample prize money, nor a lieutenant that would have sold his chance for a thousand pounds. Their disappointment, therefore, may easily be conceived when they learnt that their warlike attack upon Astoria had been forestalled by a snug commercial arrangement; that their anticipated booty had become British property in the regular course of traffic, and that all this had been effected by the very company which had been instrumental in getting them sent on what they now stigmatized as a fool's errand. They felt as if they had been duped and made tools of by a set of shrewd men of traffic, who had employed them to crack the nut, while they carried off the kernel. In a word, M'Dougall found himself so ungraciously received by his countrymen on board of the ship, that he was glad to cut short his visit and return to shore. He was busy at the fort, making preparations for the reception of the captain of the Racoon, when his one eyed Indian father in law made his appearance with a train of Chinook warriors, all painted and equipped in warlike style.

Old Comcomly had beheld with dismay the arrival of a "big war canoe" displaying the British flag. The shrewd old savage had become something of a politician in the course of his daily visits at the fort. He knew of the war existing between the nations, but knew nothing of the arrangement between M'Dougall and M'Tavish. He trembled, therefore, for the power of his white son in law, and the new fledged grandeur of his daughter, and assembled his warriors in all haste. "King George," said he, "has sent this great canoe to destroy the fort and make slaves of all the inhabitants. Shall we suffer it? The Americans are the first white men that have fixed themselves in the land. They have treated us like brothers. Their great chief has taken my daughter to be his squaw; we are therefore as one people."

His warriors all determined to stand by the Americans to the last, and to this effect they came painted and armed for battle. Comcomly made a spirited war speech to his son in law. He offered to kill every one of King George's men that should attempt to land. It was an easy matter. The ship could not approach within six miles of the fort; the crew could only land in boats. The woods reached to the water's edge; in these he and his warriors would conceal themselves and shoot down the enemy as fast as they put foot on shore.

M'Dougall was, doubtless, properly sensible of this parental devotion on the part of his Savage father in law, and perhaps a little rebuked by the game spirit so opposite to his own. He assured Comcomly, however, that his solicitude for the safety of himself and the princess was superfluous; as, though the ship belonged to King George, her crew would not injure the Americans or their Indian allies. He advised him and his warriors, therefore, to lay aside their weapons and war shirts, wash off the paint from their faces and bodies, and appear like clean and civil savages to receive the strangers courteously.

Comcomly was sorely puzzled at this advice, which accorded so little with his Indian notions of receiving a hostile nation; and it was only after repeated and positive assurances of the amicable intentions of the strangers that he was induced to lower his fighting tone. He said something to his warriors explanatory of this singular posture of affairs, and in vindication, perhaps, of the pacific temper of his son in law. They all gave a shrug and an Indian grunt of acquiescence and went off sulkily to their village to lay aside their weapons for the present.

The proper arrangements being made for the reception of Captain Black, that officer caused his ship's boats to be manned, and landed with befitting state at Astoria. From the talk that had been made by the North West Company of the strength of the place, and the armament they had required to assist in its reduction, he expected to find a fortress of some importance. When he beheld nothing but stockades and bastions calculated for defence against naked savages, he felt an emotion of indignant surprize, mingled with something of the ludicrous. "Is this the fort," cried he, "about which I have heard so much talking?— D——n me but I'd batter it down in two hours with a four pounder!"

When he learnt, however, the amount of rich furs that had been passed into the hands of the North Westers, he was outrageous, and insisted that an inventory should be taken of all the property purchased of the Americans "with a view to ulterior measures in England for the recovery of the value from the North West Company."

As he grew cool however he gave over all idea of preferring such a claim, and reconciled himself, as well as he could, to the idea of having been forestalled by his bargaining coadjutors.

On the 12th of December the fate of Astoria was consummated by a regular ceremonial. Captain Black attended by his officers entered the fort: caused the British standard to be erected, broke a bottle of wine and declared in a loud voice that he took possession of the establishment and of the country in the name of his Britannic majesty, changing the name of Astoria to that of Fort George.

The Indian warriors who had offered their services to repel the strangers, were present on this occasion. It was explained to them as being a friendly arrangement and transfer, but they shook their heads grimly and considered it an act of subjugation of their ancient allies. They regretted that they had complied with M'Dougall's wishes in laying aside their arms, and remarked that, however the Americans might conceal the fact they were undoubtedly all slaves: nor could they be persuaded of the contrary until they beheld the Racoon depart without taking away any prisoners.

As to Comcomly he no longer prided himself upon his White son in law, but, whenever he was asked about him shook his head and replied that his daughter had made a mistake, and, instead of getting a great warrior for a husband, had married herself to a squaw.

CHAPTER LXI

Arrival of the Brig Pedlar at Astoria—Breaking up of the establish-
ment—Departure of several of the Company—Tragical story told by
the squaw of Pierre Dorion—Fate of Reed and his companions—
Attempts of Mr. Astor to revive his enterprize—Disappointment—
Concluding observations and reflexions.

Having given the catastrophe at the Fort of Astoria, it remains now but
to gather up a few loose ends of this widely excursive narrative and
conclude. On the 28th of February the Brig Pedlar anchored in Columbia
River. It will be recollected that Mr. Hunt had purchased this vessel
at the Sandwich Islands, to take off the furs collected at the factory,
and to restore the Sandwich islanders to their homes. When that gentleman learnt, however, the precipitate and summary manner in which
the property had been bargained away by Mr. M'Dougall, he expressed
his indignation in the strongest terms, and determined to make an effort
to get back the furs. As soon as his wishes were known in this respect
M'Dougall came to sound him on behalf of the North West Company,
intimating that he had no doubt the peltries might be repurchased at
an advance of 50 per Cent. This overture was not calculated to soothe
the angry feelings of Mr. Hunt, and his indignation was complete when
he discovered that M'Dougall had become a partner of the North West
Company, and had actually been so since the 23d of December. He
had kept his partnership a secret, however; had retained the papers
of the Pacific Fur Company in his possession; and had continued to
act as Mr. Astor's agent, though two of the partners of the other
company, Mr. M'Kenzie and Mr. Clarke, were present. He had moreover
divulged to his new associates all that he knew as to Mr. Astor's plans
and affairs, and had made copies of his business letters for their perusal.

Mr. Hunt now considered the whole conduct of M'Dougall hollow
and collusive. His only thought was, therefore, to get all the papers of
the concern out of his hands and bring the business to a close; for the
interests of Mr. Astor were yet completely at stake, the drafts of the
North West Company in his favor for the purchase money not having
yet been obtained. With some difficulty he succeeded in getting possession of the papers. The bills or drafts were delivered without hesitation. The latter he remitted to Mr. Astor by some of his associates
who were about to cross the continent to New York. This done he
embarked on board the Pedlar, on the third of April, accompanied by
two of the clerks, Mr. Seton and Mr. Halsey, and bade a final adieu
to Astoria.

The next day, April 4th, Messrs. Clarke, M'Kenzie, David Stuart, and such of the Astorians as had not entered into the service of the North West Company, set out to cross the Rocky Mountains. It is not our intention to take the reader another journey across those rugged barriers; but we will step forward with the travellers to a distance on their way, merely to relate their interview with a character already noted in this work.

As the party were proceeding up the Columbia, near the mouth of the Wallah Wallah River, several Indian canoes put off from the shore to overtake them, and a voice called upon them in French, and requested them to stop. They accordingly put to shore, and were joined by those in the canoes. To their surprize they recognized in the person who had hailed them the Indian wife of Pierre Dorion, accompanied by her two children. She had a story to tell involving the fate of several of our unfortunate adventurers.

Mr. John Reed, the Hibernian, it will be remembered, had been detached during the summer to the Snake River. His party consisted of four Canadians, Gilles Le Clerc, Francois Landry, Jean Baptiste Turcot and Andre La Chapelle together with two hunters, Pierre Dorion and Pierre Delaunay; Dorion as usual being accompanied by his wife and children. The objects of this expedition were two fold: to trap beaver, and to search for the three hunters, Robinson, Hoback and Rezner.

In the course of the autumn Reed lost one man, Landry, by death; another one, Pierre Delaunay, who was of a sullen, perverse disposition, left him in a moody fit, and was never heard of afterwards. The number of his party was not, however, reduced by these losses, as the three hunters, Robinson, Hoback and Rezner had joined it.

Reed now built a house on the Snake River, for their winter quarters, which being completed the party set about trapping. Rezner, Le Clerc and Pierre Dorion went about five days' journey from the wintering house, to a part of the country well stocked with beaver. Here they put up a hut and proceeded to trap with great success. While the men were out hunting, Pierre Dorion's wife remained at home to dress the skins and prepare the meals. She was thus employed one evening about the beginning of January, cooking the supper of the hunters, when she heard footsteps, and Le Clerc staggered, pale and bleeding, into the hut. He informed her that a party of savages had surprized them, while at their traps, and had killed Rezner and her husband. He had barely strength left to give this information, when he sank upon the ground.

The poor woman saw that the only chance for life was instant flight, but in this exigency, shewed that presence of mind and force of character for which she had frequently been noted. With great difficulty she caught two of the horses belonging to the party. Then collecting her clothes and a small quantity of beaver meat and dried salmon, she packed them upon one of the horses, and helped the wounded man to mount upon it. On the other horse she mounted with her two children, and hurried away from this dangerous neighborhood, directing her flight to Mr. Reed's establishment. On the third day she descried a number of Indians on horseback proceeding in an easterly direction. She immediately dismounted with her children, and helped Le Clerc likewise to dismount, and all concealed themselves. Fortunately they escaped the sharp eyes of the savages, but had to proceed with the utmost caution. That night they slept without fire or water; she managed to keep her children warm in her arms; but before morning poor Le Clerc died.

With the dawn of day the resolute woman resumed her course, and, on the fourth day reached the house of Mr. Reed. It was deserted, and all around were marks of blood and signs of a ferocious massacre. Not doubting that Mr. Reed and his party had all fallen victims, she turned, in fresh horror, from the spot. For two days she continued hurrying forward, ready to sink for want of food, but more solicitous about her children than herself. At length she reached a range of rocky mountains near the upper part of the Wallah Wallah River. Here she chose a wild lonely ravine, as her place of winter refuge. She had fortunately a buffalo robe and three deer skins; of these and of pine bark and cedar branches she constructed a rude wig wam which she pitched beside a mountain spring. Having no other food she killed the two horses and smoked their flesh. The skins aided to cover her hut. Here she dragged out the winter with no other company than her two children. Towards the middle of March her provisions were nearly exhausted. She therefore packed up the remainder, slung it on her back, and with her helpless little ones set out again on her wanderings. Crossing the ridge of mountains she descended to the banks of the Wallah Wallah and kept along them until she arrived where that river throws itself into the Columbia. She was hospitably received and entertained by the Wallah Wallahs and had been nearly two weeks among them when the two canoes passed.

On being interrogated she could assign no reason for this murderous attack of the savages; it appeared to be perfectly wanton and unprovoked. Some of the Astorians supposed it an act of butchery by a roving band of Blackfeet. Others, however, and with greater probability of correctness, have ascribed it to the tribe of Pierced nose Indians, in revenge for the death of their comrade hanged by order of Mr. Clarke. If so, it shows that these sudden and apparently wanton outbreakings of sanguinary violence on the part of savages, have often some previous, though perhaps remote, provocation.

The narrative of the Indian woman closes the checquered adventures of some of the personages of this motley story; such as the honest Hibernian Reed, and Dorion the hybred interpreter. Turcot and La Chapelle were two of the men who fell off from Mr. Crooks in the course of his wintry journey, and had subsequently such disastrous times among the Indians. We cannot but feel some sympathy with that persevering trio of Kentuckians, Robinson, Rezner, and Hoback; who twice turned back when on their way homeward, and lingered in the wilderness to perish by the hands of savages.

The return parties from Astoria, both by sea and land, experienced on the way as many adventures, vicissitudes and mishaps as the far famed heroes of the Odyssey: they reached their destination at different times, bearing tidings to Mr. Astor of the unfortunate termination of his enterprize. That gentleman, however, was not disposed even yet to give the matter up as lost. On the contrary, his spirit was roused by what he considered ungenerous and unmerited conduct on the part of the North West Company. "After their treatment of me," said he in a letter to Mr. Hunt, "I have no idea of remaining quiet and idle." He determined, therefore, as soon as circumstances would permit, to resume his enterprize.

At the return of peace Astoria with the adjacent country, reverted to the United States by the treaty of Ghent, on the principle of *status ante bellum*, and Captain Biddle was despatched in the Sloop of War Ontario, to take formal repossession. In the winter of 1815 a law was passed by Congress prohibiting all traffic of British traders within the territories of the United States.

The favorable moment seemed now to Mr. Astor to have arrived for the revival of his favorite enterprize, but new difficulties had grown up to impede it. The North West Company were now in complete occupation of the Columbia River and its chief tributary streams, holding the posts which he had established and carrying on a trade throughout the neighboring region in defiance of the prohibitory law of Congress, which in effect was a dead letter beyond the Mountains.

To dispossess them would be an undertaking of almost a belligerent nature; for their agents and retainers were well armed and skilled in the use of weapons, as is usual with Indian traders. The ferocious and bloody contests which had taken place between the rival trading parties of the North West and Hudson's Bay companies, had shewn what might be expected from commercial feuds in the lawless depths of the wilderness. Mr. Astor did not think it adviseable, therefore, to attempt the matter without the protection of the American flag, under which his people might rally in case of need. He accordingly made an informal overture to the President of the United States, Mr. Madison, through Mr. Gallatin, offering to renew his enterprize and to re establish Astoria, provided it would be protected by the American flag and made a military post; stating that the whole force required would not exceed a lieutenant's command. The application, approved and recommended by Mr. Gallatin, one of the most enlightened statesmen of our country, was favorably received, but no step was taken in consequence, the President not being disposed, in all probability, to commit himself by any direct countenance or overt act. Discouraged by this supineness on the part of Government, Mr. Astor did not think fit to renew his overtures in a more formal manner, and the favorable moment for the reoccupation of Astoria was suffered to pass unimproved.

The British trading establishments were thus enabled without molestation to strike deep their roots and extend their ramifications, in despite of the prohibition of Congress, until they had spread themselves over the rich field of enterprize opened by Mr. Astor. The British government soon began to perceive the importance of this region, and to desire to include it within their territorial domains. A question has consequently risen as to the right to the soil, and has become one of the most perplexing now open between the United States and Great Britain. In the first treaty relative to it, under date of October 20th 1818, the question was left unsettled, and it was agreed that the Country on the North West Coast of America, westward of the Rocky Mountains, claimed by either nation, should be open to the inhabitants of both for ten years, for the purposes of trade, with the equal right of navigating all its rivers. When these ten years had expired a subsequent treaty in 1828 extended the arrangement to ten additional years. So the matter stands at present.

On casting back our eyes over the series of events we have recorded, we see no reason to attribute the failure of this great commercial undertaking, to any fault in the scheme, or omission in the execution of it, on the part of the projector. It was a magnificent enterprize; well concerted and carried on without regard to difficulties or expense. A succession of adverse circumstances and cross purposes, however, beset it almost from the outset; some of them in fact arising from neglect of the orders and instructions of Mr. Astor. The first crippling blow was the loss of the Tonquin, which clearly would not have happened, had Mr. Astor's earnest injunctions with regard to the natives been attended to. Had this ship performed her voyage prosperously and revisited Astoria in due time, the trade of the establishment would have taken its pre concerted course, and the spirits of all concerned, been kept up by a confident prospect of success. Her dismal catastrophe struck a chill into every heart, and prepared the way for subsequent despondency.

Another cause of embarrassment and loss was the departure from the plan of Mr. Astor as to the voyage of the Beaver, subsequent to her visiting Astoria. The variation from this plan produced a series of cross purposes disastrous to the establishment, and detained Mr. Hunt absent from his post when his presence there was of vital importance to the enterprize. So essential is it for an agent in any great and complicated undertaking to execute faithfully and to the letter, the part marked out for him by the master mind which has concerted the whole.

The breaking out of the War between the United States and Great Britain multiplied the hazards and embarrassments of the enterprize. The disappointment as to convoy, rendered it difficult to keep up reinforcements and supplies; and the loss of the Lark added to the tissue of misadventures.

That Mr. Astor battled resolutely against every difficulty and pursued his course in defiance of every loss, has been sufficiently shewn. Had he been seconded by suitable agents and properly protected by government, the ultimate failure of his plan might yet have been averted. It was his great misfortune that his agents were not imbued with his own spirit. Some had not capacity sufficient to comprehend the real nature and extent of his scheme; others were alien in feeling and interest, and had been brought up in the service of a rival company. Whatever sympathies they might originally have had with him were impaired if not destroyed by the war. They looked upon his cause as desperate, and only considered how they might make interest to regain a situation under their former employers. The absence of Mr. Hunt, the only real representative of Mr. Astor, at the time of the capitulation with the North West Company, completed the series of cross purposes. Had that gentleman been present, the transfer in all probability would not have taken place.

It is painful at all times to see a grand and beneficial stroke of genius fail of its aim: but we regret the failure of this enterprize in a national point of view; for, had it been crowned with success it would have redounded greatly to the advantage and extension of our commerce. The profits drawn from the country in question by the British Fur Company, though of ample amount, form no criterion by which to judge of the advantages that would have arisen had it been entirely in the hands of citizens of the United States. That company, as has been shown, is limited in the nature and scope of its operations, and can make but little use of the maritime facilities held out by an emporium and a harbor on that coast. In our hands, beside the roving bands of trappers and traders, the country would have been explored and settled by industrious husbandmen; and the fertile valleys bordering its rivers, and shut up among its mountains, would have been made to pour forth their agricultural treasures to contribute to the general wealth.

In respect to commerce, we should have had a line of trading posts from the Mississippi and the Missouri across the Rocky Mountains, forming a high road from the great regions of the west to the shores of the Pacific. We should have had a fortified post and port at the mouth of the Columbia, commanding the trade of that river and its tributaries, and of a wide extent of country and sea coast; carrying on an active and profitable commerce with the Sandwich islands, and a direct and frequent communication with China. In a word, Astoria might have realized the anticipations of Mr. Astor, so well understood and appreciated by Mr. Jefferson, in gradually becoming a commercial empire beyond the Mountains, peopled by "free and independent Americans, and linked with us by ties of blood and interest."

We repeat, therefore, our sincere regret that our government should have neglected the overture of Mr. Astor and suffered the moment to pass by when full possession of this region might have been taken quietly as a matter of course, and a military post established without disputes at Astoria. Our statesmen have become sensible when too late, of the importance of this measure. Bills have repeatedly been brought into Congress for the purpose, but without success, and our rightful possessions on that coast, as well as our trade on the Pacific, have no rallying point protected by the national flag and by a military force.

In the mean time the second period of ten years is fast elapsing. In 1838, the question of title will again come up, and most probably, in the present amicable state of our relations with Great Britain, will be again postponed. Every year, however, the litigated claim is growing in importance. There is no pride so jealous and irritable as the pride of territory. As one wave of emigration after another rolls into the vast regions of the west, and our settlements stretch towards the Rocky Mountains, the eager eyes of our pioneers will pry beyond, and they will become impatient of any barrier or impediment in the way of what they consider a grand outlet of our empire. Should any circumstance, therefore, unfortunately occur to disturb the present harmony of the two nations, this ill-adjusted question, which now lies dormant, may suddenly start up into one of belligerent import, and Astoria become the watchword in a contest for dominion on the shores of the Pacific.

Since the above was written, the question of dominion over the vast territory beyond the Rocky Mountains, which for a time threatened to disturb the peaceful relations with our transatlantic kindred, has been finally settled in a spirit of mutual concession, and the venerable projector whose early enterprise forms the subject of this work had the satisfaction of knowing, ere his eyes closed upon the world, that the flag of his country again waved over "ASTORIA."

APPENDIX

APPENDIX

Draught of a petition to Congress, sent by Mr. Astor in 1812.

To the honorable the Senate and House of Representatives of the United
States, in Congress assembled,

The petition of the American Fur Company respectfully sheweth:

That the trade with the several Indian tribes of North America, has,
for many years past, been almost exclusively carried on by the merchants
of Canada; who, having formed powerful and extensive associations for
that purpose, being aided by British capital, and being encouraged by
the favor and protection of the British government, could not be opposed,
with any prospect of success by individuals of the United States.

That by means of the above trade, thus systematically pursued, not
only the inhabitants of the United States have been deprived of commercial profits and advantages, to which they appear to have just and natural
pretensions, but a great and dangerous influence has been established
over the Indian tribes, difficult to be counteracted, and capable of being
exerted at critical periods, to the great injury and annoyance of our
frontier settlements.

That in order to obtain at least a part of the above trade, and more
particularly that which is within the boundaries of the United States,
your petitioners, in the year 1808, obtained an act of incorporation from
the state of New York, whereby they are enabled, with a competent
capital, to carry on the said trade with the Indians in such manner as
may be conformable to the laws and regulations of the United States, in
relation to such commerce.

That the capital mentioned in the said act, amounting to one million
of dollars, having been duly formed, your petitioners entered with zeal
and alacrity into those large and important arrangements, which were
necessary for, or conducive to, the object of their incorporation; and,
among other things, purchased a great part of the stock in trade, and
trading establishments, of the Michilimackinac Company of Canada.—
Your petitioners also, with the expectation of great public and private
advantage from the use of the said establishments, ordered, during the
spring and summer of 1810, an assortment of goods from England, suitable for the Indian trade; which, in consequence of the President's
proclamation of November of that year, were shipped to Canada instead
of New York, and have been transported, under a very heavy expense,

into the interior of the country. But as they could not legally be brought into the Indian country within the boundaries of the United States, they have been stored on the island of St. Joseph, in Lake Huron, where they now remain.

Your petitioners, with great deference and implicit submission to the wisdom of the national legislature, beg leave to suggest for consideration, whether they have not some claim to national attention and encouragement, from the nature and importance of their undertaking; which, though hazardous and uncertain as it concerns their private emolument, must, at any rate, redound to the public security and advantage. If their undertaking shall appear to be of the description given, they would further suggest to your honorable bodies, that unless they can procure a regular supply for the trade in which they are engaged, it may languish, and be finally abandoned by American citizens; when it will revert to its former channel, with additional, and perhaps with irresistible, power.

Under these circumstances, and upon all those considerations of public policy which will present themselves to your honorable bodies, in connexion with those already mentioned, your petitioners respectfully pray that a law may be passed to enable the President, or any of the heads of departments acting under his authority, to grant permits for the introduction of goods necessary for the supply of the Indians, into the Indian country that is within the boundaries of the United States, under such regulations, and with such restrictions, as may secure the public revenue and promote the public welfare.

And your petitioners shall ever pray, &c.

In witness whereof, the common seal of the American Fur Company is
        hereunto affixed, the   day of March, 1812.

By order of the Corporation.

AN ACT to enable the American Fur Company, and other citizens, to introduce goods necessary for the Indian trade into the territories within the boundaries of the United States.

WHEREAS, the public peace and welfare require that the native Indian tribes, residing within the boundaries of the United States, should receive their necessary supplies under the authority and from the citizens of the United States: Therefore, be it enacted by the Senate and House of Representatives of the United States, in Congress assembled, that it shall be lawful for the President of the United States, or any of the heads of departments, thereunto by him duly authorized, from time to time to grant permits to the American Fur Company, their agents or factors, or any other citizens of the United States engaged in the Indian trade, to introduce into the Indian country, within the boundaries of the United States, such goods, wares, and merchandise, as may be necessary for the said trade, under such regulations and restrictions as the said President or heads of departments may judge proper; any law or regulation to the contrary, in anywise, notwithstanding.

Letter from Mr. Gallatin to Mr. Astor, dated

NEW YORK, *August* 5, 1835.

Dear Sir,—

In compliance with your request, I will state such facts as I recollect, touching the subjects mentioned in your letter of 28th ult. I may be mistaken respecting dates and details, and will only relate general facts, which I well remember.

In conformity with the treaty of 1794 with Great Britain, the citizens and subjects of each country were permitted to trade with the Indians residing in the territories of the other party. The reciprocity was altogether nominal. Since the conquest of Canada, the British had inherited from the French the whole fur trade, through the great lakes and their communications, with all the western Indians, whether residing in the British dominions or the United States. They kept the important western posts on those lakes till about the year 1797. And the defensive Indian war, which the United States had to sustain from 1776 to 1795, had still more alienated the Indians, and secured to the British their exclusive trade, carried through the lakes, wherever the Indians in that quarter lived. No American could, without imminent danger of property and life, carry on that trade, even within the United States, by the way of either Michilimackinac or St. Mary's. And independent of the loss of commerce, Great Britain was enabled to preserve a most dangerous influence over our Indians.

It was under these circumstances that you communicated to our government the prospect you had to be able, and your intention, to purchase one half of the interest of the Canadian Fur Company, engaged in trade by the way of Michilimackinac with our own Indians. You wished to know whether the plan met with the approbation of government, and how far you could rely on its protection and encouragement. This overture was received with great satisfaction by the administration, and Mr. Jefferson, then President, wrote you to that effect. I was also directed, as Secretary of the Treasury, to write to you an official letter to the same purpose. On investigating the subject, it was found that the Executive had no authority to give you any direct aid; and I believe that you received nothing more than an entire approbation of your plan, and general assurances of the protection due to every citizen engaged in lawful and useful pursuits.

You did effect the contemplated purchase, but in what year I do not recollect. Immediately before the war, you represented that a large quantity of merchandise, intended for the Indian trade, and including arms and munitions of war, belonging to that concern of which you owned one half, was deposited at a post on Lake Huron, within the British dominions; that, in order to prevent their ultimately falling into the hands of Indians who might prove hostile, you were desirous to try to have them conveyed into the United States; but that you were prevented by the then existing law of non-intercourse with the British dominions.

The Executive could not annul the provisions of that law. But I was directed to instruct the collectors on the lakes, in case you or your agents should voluntarily bring in and deliver to them any parts of the goods above mentioned, to receive and keep them in their guard, and not to commence prosecutions until further instructions: the intention being then to apply to Congress for an act remitting the forfeiture and penalties. I wrote accordingly, to that effect, to the collectors of Detroit and Michilimackinac.

The attempt to obtain the goods did not, however, succeed; and I cannot say how far the failure injured you. But the war proved fatal to another much more extensive and important enterprise.

Previous to that time, but I also forget the year, you had undertaken to carry on a trade on your own account, though I believe under the New York charter of the American Fur Company, with the Indians west of the Rocky Mountains. This project was also communicated to government, and met, of course, with its full approbation, and best wishes for your success. You carried it on, on the most extensive scale, sending several ships to the mouth of the Columbia River, and a large party by land across the mountains, and finally founding the establishment of Astoria.

This unfortunately fell into the hands of the enemy during the war, from circumstances with which I am but imperfectly acquainted—being then absent on a foreign mission. I returned in September, 1815, and sailed again on a mission to France in June, 1816. During that period I visited Washington twice—in October or November, 1815, and in March, 1816. On one of those two occasions, and I believe on the last, you mentioned to me that you were disposed once more to renew the attempt, and to re-establish Astoria, provided you had the protection of the American flag; for which purpose, a lieutenant's command would be sufficient to you. You requested me to mention this to the President, which I did. Mr. Madison said he would consider the subject, and, although he did not commit himself, I thought that he received the proposal favorably. The message was verbal, and I do not know whether the application was ever renewed in a more formal manner. I sailed soon after for Europe, and was seven years absent. I never had the pleasure, since 1816, to see Mr. Madison, and never heard again any thing concerning the subject in question.

> I remain, dear sir, very respectfully,
> > Your obedient servant,
> > > ALBERT GALLATIN.

JOHN JACOB ASTOR, ESQ.,
> New York.

Notices of the present state of the Fur Trade, chiefly extracted from an article published in Silliman's Journal for January, 1834.

The North West Company did not long enjoy the sway they had acquired over the trading regions of the Columbia. A competition, ruinous in its expenses, which had long existed between them and the Hudson's Bay Company, ended in their downfall and the ruin of most of the partners. The relics of the company became merged in the rival association, and the whole business was conducted under the name of the Hudson's Bay Company.

This coalition took place in 1821. They then abandoned Astoria, and built a large establishment sixty miles up the river, on the right bank, which they called Fort Vancouver. This was in a neighborhood where provisions could be more readily procured, and where there was less danger from molestation by any naval force. The company are said to carry on an active and prosperous trade, and to give great encouragement to settlers. They are extremely jealous, however, of any interference or participation in their trade, and monopolize it from the coast of the Pacific to the mountains, and for a considerable extent north and south. The American traders and trappers who venture across the mountains, instead of enjoying the participation in the trade of the river and its tributaries, that had been stipulated by treaty, are obliged to keep to the south, out of the track of the Hudson's Bay parties.

Mr. Astor has withdrawn entirely from the American Fur Company, as he has, in fact, from active business of every kind. That company is now headed by Mr. Ramsay Crooks; its principal establishment is at Michilimackinac, and it receives its furs from the posts depending on that station, and from those on the Mississippi, Missouri, and Yellow Stone rivers, and the great range of country extending thence to the Rocky Mountains. This company has steamboats in its employ, with which it ascends the rivers, and penetrates to a vast distance into the bosom of those regions formerly so painfully explored in keel-boats and barges, or by weary parties on horseback and on foot. The first irruption of steamboats into the heart of these vast wildernesses is said to have caused the utmost astonishment and affright among their savage inhabitants.

In addition to the main companies already mentioned, minor associations have been formed, which push their way in the most intrepid manner to the remote parts of the far west, and beyond the mountain barriers. One of the most noted of these is Ashley's company, from St. Louis, who trap for themselves, and drive an extensive trade with the Indians. The spirit, enterprize, and hardihood of Ashley, are themes of the highest eulogy in the far west, and his adventures and exploits furnish abundance of frontier stories.

Another company of one hundred and fifty persons from New York, formed in 1831, and headed by Captain Bonneville of the United States army, has pushed its enterprizes into tracts before but little known, and has brought considerable quantities of furs from the region between the Rocky Mountains and the coasts of Monterey and Upper California, on the Buenaventura and Timpanogos rivers.

The fur countries from the Pacific east to the Rocky Mountains, are now occupied (exclusive of private combinations and individual trappers and traders) by the Russians, on the north west from Bhering's Strait to Queen Charlotte's Island in N. Lat. 53°, and by the Hudson's Bay Company thence, south of the Columbia river; while Ashley's company, and that under Captain Bonneville, take the remainder of the region to California. Indeed, the whole compass from the Mississippi to the Pacific Ocean is traversed in every direction. The mountains and forests, from the Arctic Sea to the Gulf of Mexico, are threaded, through every maze, by the hunter. Every river and tributary stream, from the Columbia to the mouth of the Rio del Norte, and from the M'Kenzie to the Colorado of the West, from their head springs to their junction, are searched and trapped for beaver. Almost all the American furs, which do not belong to the Hudson's Bay Company, find their way to New York, and are either distributed thence for home consumption, or sent to foreign markets.

The Hudson's Bay Company ship their furs from their factories of York fort and from Moose river, on Hudson's Bay; their collection from Grand river, &c., they ship from Canada; and the collection from Columbia river goes to London. None of their furs come to the United States, except through the London market.

The export trade of furs from the United States is chiefly to London. Some quantities have been sent to Canton, and some few to Hamburgh; and an increasing export trade in beaver, otter, nutria, and vicunia wool, prepared for the hatter's use, is carried on with Mexico. Some furs are exported from Baltimore, Philadelphia, and Boston; but the principal shipments from the United States are from New York to London, from whence they are sent to Leipsic, a well-known mart for furs, where they are disposed of during the great fair in that city, and distributed to every part of the continent.

The United States import from South America, nutria, vicunia, chinchilla, and a few deer skins; also fur seals from the Lobos islands, off the river Plate. A quantity of beaver, otter, &c., are brought annually from Santa Fé. Dressed furs for edgings, linings, caps, muffs, &c., such as squirrel, genet, fitch skins, and blue rabbit, are received from the north of Europe; also coney and hare's fur; but the largest importations are from London, where is concentrated nearly the whole of the North American fur trade.

Such is the present state of the fur trade, by which it will appear that the extended sway of the Hudson's Bay Company, and its monopoly of the region of which Astoria was the key, has operated to turn the main current of this opulent trade into the coffers of Great Britain, and to render London the emporium instead of New York, as Mr. Astor had intended.

We will subjoin a few observations on the animals sought after in this traffic, extracted from the same intelligent source with the preceding remarks.

Of the fur-bearing animals, "the precious ermine," so called by way of pre-eminence, is found, of the best quality, only in the cold regions of Europe and Asia.* Its fur is of the most perfect whiteness,. except the tip of its tail, which is of a brilliant shining black. With these black tips tacked on the skins, they are beautifully spotted, producing an effect often imitated, but never equalled in other furs. The ermine is of the

---

* An animal called the stoat, a kind of ermine, is said to be found in North America, but very inferior to the European and Asiatic.

genus Mustela, (weasel,) and resembles the common weasel in its form; is from fourteen to sixteen inches from the tip of the nose to the end of the tail. The body is from ten to twelve inches long. It lives in hollow trees, river banks, and especially in beech forests; preys on small birds, is very shy, sleeping during the day, and employing the night in search of food. The fur of the older animals is preferred to the younger. It is taken by snares and traps, and sometimes shot with blunt arrows. Attempts have been made to domesticate it; but it is extremely wild, and has been found untameable.

The sable can scarcely be called second to the ermine. It is a native of northern Europe and Siberia, and is also of the genus Mustela. In Samoieda, Yakutsk, Kamschatka, and Russian Lapland, it is found of the richest quality, and darkest color. In its habits, it resembles the ermine. It preys on small squirrels and birds, sleeps by day, and prowls for food during the night. It is so like the marten in every particular except its size, and the dark shade of its color, that naturalists have not decided whether it is the richest and finest of the marten tribe, or a variety of that species.* It varies in dimensions from eighteen to twenty inches.

The rich dark shades of the sable, and the snowy whiteness of the ermine, the great depth, and the peculiar, almost flowing softness of their skins and fur, have combined to gain them a preference in all countries, and in all ages of the world. In this age, they maintain the same relative estimate in regard to other furs, as when they marked the rank of the proud crusader, and were emblazoned in heraldry: but in most European nations, they are now worn promiscuously by the opulent.

The martens from Northern Asia and the mountains of Kamschatka are much superior to the American, though in every pack of American marten skins there are a certain number which are beautifully shaded, and of a dark brown olive color, of great depth and richness.

Next these in value, for ornament and utility, are the sea otter, the mink, and the fiery fox.

The fiery fox is the bright red of Asia; is more brilliantly colored and of finer fur than any other of the genus. It is highly valued for the splendor of its red color and the fineness of its fur. It is the standard of value on the north eastern coast of Asia.

The sea otter, which was first introduced into commerce in 1725, from the Aleutian and Kurile islands, is an exceedingly fine, soft, close fur, jet black in winter with a silken gloss. The fur of the young animal is

---

* The finest fur and the darkest color are most esteemed; and whether the difference arises from the age of the animal, or from some peculiarity of location, is not known. They do not vary more from the common marten, than the Arabian horse from the shaggy Canadian.

of a beautiful brown color. It is met with in great abundance in Bhering's island, Kamschatka, Aleutian and Fox islands, and is also taken on the opposite coasts of North America. It is sometimes taken with nets, but more frequently with clubs and spears. Their food is principally lobster and other shell fish.

In 1780 furs had become so scarce in Siberia, that the supply was insufficient for the demand in the Asiatic countries. It was at this time that the sea otter was introduced into the markets for China. The skins brought such incredible prices, as to originate immediately several American and British expeditions to the northern islands of the Pacific, to Nootka Sound, and the north west coast of America; but the Russians already had possession of the tract which they now hold, and had arranged a trade for the sea otter with the Koudek tribes. They do not engross the trade, however; the American north west trading ships procure them, all along the coast, from the Indians.

At one period, the fur seals formed no inconsiderable item in the trade. South Georgia, in south latitude 55°, discovered in 1675, was explored by Captain Cook in 1771. The Americans immediately commenced carrying seal skins thence to China, where they obtained the most exorbitant prices. One million two hundred thousand skins have been taken from that island alone, and nearly an equal number from the island of Desolation, since they were first restored for the purposes of commerce.

The discovery of the South Shetlands, 63° south latitude, in 1818, added surprisingly to the trade in fur seals. The number taken from the South Shetlands in 1821 and 1822 amounted to three hundred and twenty thousand. This valuable animal is now almost extinct in all these islands, owing to the exterminating system adopted by the hunters. They are still taken on the Lobos islands, where the provident government of Montevideo restrict the fishery, or hunting, within certain limits, which insures an annual return of the seals. At certain seasons these amphibia, for the purpose of renewing their coat, come up on the dark frowning rocks and precipices, where there is not a trace of vegetation. In the middle of January, the islands are partially cleared of snow, where a few patches of short straggling grass spring up in favorable situations; but the seals do not resort to it for food. They remain on the rocks not less than two months, without any sustenance, when they return much emaciated to the sea.

Bears of various species and colors, many varieties of the fox, the wolf, the beaver, the otter, the marten, the raccoon, the badger, the wolverine, the mink, the lynx, the muskrat, the woodchuck, the rabbit, the hare, and the squirrel, are natives of North America.

The beaver, otter, lynx, fisher, hare, and raccoon, are used principally for hats; while the bears of several varieties furnish an excellent material for sleigh linings, for cavalry caps, and other military equipments. The fur of the black fox is the most valuable of any of the American varieties; and next to that the red, which is exported to China and Smyrna. In China, the red is employed for trimmings, linings, and robes; the latter being variegated, by adding the black fur of the paws, in spots or waves. There are many other varieties of American fox, such as the gray, the white, the cross, the silver, and the dun-colored. The silver fox is a rare animal, a native of the woody country below the falls of the Columbia river. It has a long, thick, deep lead-colored fur, intermingled with long hairs, invariably white at the top, forming a bright lustrous silver gray, esteemed by some more beautiful than any other kind of fox.

The skins of the buffalo, of the Rocky mountain sheep, of various deer, and of the antelope, are included in the fur trade with the Indians and trappers of the north and west.

Fox and seal skins are sent from Greenland to Denmark. The white fur of the arctic fox and polar bear is sometimes found in the packs brought to the traders by the most northern tribes of Indians, but is not particularly valuable. The silver-tipped rabbit is peculiar to England, and is sent thence to Russia and China.

Other furs are employed and valued according to the caprices of fashion, as well in those countries where they are needed for defences against the severity of the seasons, as among the inhabitants of milder climates, who, being of Tartar or Sclavonian descent, are said to inherit an attachment to furred clothing. Such are the inhabitants of Poland, of Southern Russia, of China, of Persia, of Turkey, and all the nations of Gothic origin in the middle and western parts of Europe. Under the burning suns of Syria and Egypt, and the mild climes of Bucharia and Independent Tartary, there is also a constant demand, and a great consumption, where there exists no physical necessity. In our own temperate latitudes, besides their use in the arts, they are in request for ornament and warmth during the winter, and large quantities are annually consumed for both purposes in the United States.

From the foregoing statements, it appears that the fur trade must henceforward decline. The advanced state of geographical science shows that no new countries remain to be explored. In North America, the animals are slowly decreasing, from the persevering efforts and the indiscriminate slaughter practised by the hunters, and by the appropriation to the uses of man of those forests and rivers which have afforded them food and protection. They recede with the aborigines, before the tide of civilization; but a diminished supply will remain in the mountains and uncultivated tracts of this and other countries, if the avidity of the hunter can be restrained within proper limitations.

Height of the Rocky Mountains.

Various estimates have been made of the height of the Rocky Mountains, but it is doubtful whether any have, as yet, done justice to their real altitude, which promises to place them only second to the highest mountains of the known world. Their height has been diminished to the eye by the great elevation of the plains from which they rise. They consist, according to Long, of ridges, knobs, and peaks, variously disposed. The more elevated parts are covered with perpetual snows, which contribute to give them a luminous, and, at a great distance, even a brilliant appearance; whence they derived, among some of the first discoverers, the name of the Shining Mountains.

James's Peak has generally been cited as the highest of the chain; and its elevation above the common level has been ascertained, by a trigonometrical measurement, to be about eight thousand five hundred feet. Mr. Long, however, judged, from the position of the snow near the summits of other peaks and ridges at no great distance from it, that they were much higher. Having heard Professor Renwick, of New York, express an opinion of the altitude of these mountains far beyond what had usually been ascribed to them, we applied to him for the authority on which he grounded his observation, and here subjoin his reply:—

COLUMBIA COLLEGE, NEW YORK, *February* 23, 1836.

Dear Sir,—

In compliance with your request, I have to communicate some facts in relation to the heights of the Rocky Mountains, and the sources whence I obtained the information.

In conversation with Simon M'Gillivray, Esq., a partner of the North West Company, he stated to me his impression, that the mountains in the vicinity of the route pursued by the traders of that company were nearly as high as the Himalayas. He had himself crossed by this route, seen the snowy summits of the peaks, and experienced a degree of cold which required a spirit thermometer to indicate it. His authority for the estimate of the heights was a gentleman who had been employed for several years as surveyor of that company. This conversation occurred about sixteen years since.

A year or two afterwards, I had the pleasure of dining, at Major

Delafield's, with Mr. Thompson, the gentleman referred to by Mr. M'Gillivray. I inquired of him in relation to the circumstances mentioned by Mr. M'Gillivray, and he stated, that, by the joint means of the barometer and trigonometric measurement, he had ascertained the height of one of the peaks to be about twenty-five thousand feet, and there were others of nearly the same height in the vicinity.

I am, dear Sir,

Yours truly,

JAMES RENWICK.

To W. IRVING, Esq.

Suggestions with respect to the Indian tribes, and the protection of our Trade.

In the course of this work, a few general remarks have been hazarded respecting the Indian tribes of the prairies, and the dangers to be apprehended from them in future times to our trade beyond the Rocky Mountains and with the Spanish frontiers. Since writing those remarks, we have met with some excellent observations and suggestions, in manuscript, on the same subject, written by Captain Bonneville, of the United States army, who has lately returned from a long residence among the tribes of the Rocky Mountains. Captain B. approves highly of the plan recently adopted by the United States government for the organization of a regiment of dragoons for the protection of our western frontier, and the trade across the prairies. "No other species of military force," he observes, "is at all competent to cope with these restless and wandering hordes, who require to be opposed with swiftness quite as much as with strength; and the consciousness that a troop, uniting these qualifications, is always on the alert to avenge their outrages upon the settlers and traders, will go very far towards restraining them from the perpetration of those thefts and murders which they have heretofore committed with impunity, whenever stratagem or superiority of force has given them the advantage. Their interest already has done something towards their pacification with our countrymen. From the traders among them, they receive their supplies in the greatest abundance, and upon very equitable terms; and when it is remembered that a very considerable amount of property is yearly distributed among them by the government, as presents, it will readily be perceived that they are greatly dependant upon us for their most valued resources. If, superadded to this inducement, a frequent display of military power be made in their territories, there can be little doubt that the desired security and peace will be speedily afforded to our own people. But the idea of establishing a permanent amity and concord amongst the various east and west tribes themselves, seems to me, if not wholly impracticable, at least infinitely more difficult than many excellent philanthropists have hoped and believed. Those nations which have so lately emigrated from the midst of our settlements to live upon our western borders, and have made some progress in agriculture and the arts of civilization, have, in the property they have acquired, and the protection and aid extended to them, too many advantages to be induced readily to take up arms against us, particularly if they can be brought to the full conviction that their new homes will be permanent and undisturbed; and there is every reason and motive, in policy as well as humanity, for our ameliorating their condition by every means in our power. But the case is far different with regard to the Osages, the Kanzas, the Pawnees, and other roving hordes beyond the frontiers of the settlements. Wild and restless in their character and habits, they are by no means so susceptible of control or civilization; and they are urged by strong, and, to them, irresistible causes in their situation and necessities, to the daily perpetration of violence and fraud. Their permanent subsistence, for example, is derived from the buffalo hunting grounds, which lie a great distance from their towns. Twice a year they are obliged to make long and dangerous expeditions, to procure the necessary provisions for themselves and their families. For this purpose, horses are absolutely requisite, for their own comfort and safety, as well as for the transportation of their food, and their little stock of valuables; and without them they would be reduced, during a great portion of the year, to a state of abject misery and privation. They have no brood mares, nor any trade sufficiently valuable to supply their yearly losses, and endeavor to keep up their stock by stealing horses from the other tribes to the west and south-west. Our own people, and the tribes immediately upon our borders, may indeed be protected from their depredations; and the Kanzas, Osages, Pawnees, and others, may be induced to remain at peace among themselves, so long as they are permitted to pursue the old custom of levying upon the Camanches and other remote nations for their complement of steeds for the warriors, and pack-horses for their transportations to and from the hunting ground. But the instant they are forced to maintain a peaceful and inoffensive demeanor towards the tribes along the Mexican border, and find that every violation of their rights is followed by the avenging arm of our government, the result must be, that, reduced to a wretchedness and want which they can ill brook, and feeling the certainty of punishment for every attempt to ameliorate their condition in the only way they as yet comprehend, they will abandon their unfruitful territory, and remove to the neighborhood of the Mexican lands, and there carry on a vigorous predatory warfare indiscriminately upon the Mexicans and our own people trading or travelling in that quarter.

"The Indians of the prairies are almost innumerable. Their superior horsemanship, which, in my opinion, far exceeds that of any other people on the face of the earth, their daring bravery, their cunning and skill in the warfare of the wilderness, and the astonishing rapidity and secrecy with which they are accustomed to move in their martial expeditions, will always render them most dangerous and vexatious neighbors, when their necessities or their discontents may drive them to hostility with our frontiers. Their mode and principles of warfare will always protect them from final and irretrievable defeat, and secure their families from participating in any blow, however severe, which our retribution might deal out to them.

"The Camanches lay the Mexicans under contribution for horses and mules, which they are always engaged in stealing from them in incredible numbers; and from the Camanches, all the roving tribes of the far west, by a similar exertion of skill and daring, supply themselves in turn. It seems to me, therefore, under all these circumstances, that the apparent futility of any philanthropic schemes for the benefit of these nations, and a regard for our own protection, concur in recommending that we remain satisfied with maintaining peace upon our own immediate borders, and leave the Mexicans and the Camanches, and all the tribes hostile to these last, to settle their differences and difficulties in their own way.

"In order to give full security and protection to our trading parties circulating in all directions through the great prairies, I am under the impression, that a few judicious measures on the part of the government, involving a very limited expense, would be sufficient. And, in attaining this end, which of itself has already become an object of public interest and import, another, of much greater consequence, might be brought about, viz., the securing to the states a most valuable and increasing trade, now carried on by caravans directly to Santa Fé.

"As to the first desideratum: the Indians can only be made to respect the lives and property of the American parties, by rendering them dependant upon us for their supplies; which can alone be done with complete effect by the establishment of a trading post, with resident traders, at some point which will unite a sufficient number of advantages to attract the several tribes to itself, in preference to their present places of resort for that purpose; for it is a well known fact, that the Indians will always protect their trader, and those in whom he is interested, so long as they derive benefits from him. The alternative presented to those at the north, by the residence of the agents of the Hudson's Bay Company amongst them, renders the condition of our people in that quarter less secure; but I think it will appear, at once, upon the most cursory examination, that no such opposition further south could be maintained, so as to weaken the benefits of such an establishment as is here suggested.

"In considering this matter, the first question which presents itself is, where do these tribes now make their exchanges, and obtain their necessary supplies? They resort almost exclusively to the Mexicans, who, themselves, purchase from us whatever the Indians most seek for. In this point of view, therefore, *cæteris paribus*, it would be an easy matter for us to monopolize the whole traffic. All that is wanting is some location more convenient for the natives than that offered by the Mexicans, to give us the undisputed superiority; and the selection of such a point requires but a knowledge of the single fact, that these nations invariably winter upon the head waters of the Arkansas, and there prepare all their buffalo robes for trade. These robes are heavy, and, to the Indian, very difficult of transportation. Nothing but necessity induces them to travel any great distance with such inconvenient baggage. A post, therefore, established upon the head waters of the Arkansas, must infallibly secure an uncontested preference over that of the Mexicans, even at their prices and rates of barter. Then let the dragoons occasionally move about among these people in large parties, impressing them with the proper estimate of our power to protect and to punish, and at once we have complete and assured security for all citizens whose enterprise may lead them beyond the border, and an end to the outrages and depredations which now dog the footsteps of the traveller in the prairies, and arrest and repress the most advantageous commerce. Such a post need not be stronger than fifty men; twenty-five to be employed as hunters, to supply the garrison, and the residue as a defence against any hostility. Situated here upon the good lands of the Arkansas, in the midst of abundance of timber, while it might be kept up at a most inconsiderable expense, such an establishment within ninety miles of Santa Fé or Tous would be more than justified by the other and more important advantage before alluded to, leaving the protection of the traders with the Indian tribes entirely out of the question.

"This great trade, carried on by caravans to Santa Fé, annually loads one hundred wagons with merchandise, which is bartered in the northern provinces of Mexico for cash and for beaver furs. The numerous articles excluded as contraband, and the exorbitant duties laid upon all those that are admitted by the Mexican government, present so many obstacles to commerce, that I am well persuaded, that if a post, such as is here suggested, should be established on the Arkansas, it would become the place of deposite, not only for the present trade, but for one infinitely more extended. Here the Mexicans might purchase their supplies, and might well afford to sell them at prices which would silence all competition from any other quarter.

"These two trades, with the Mexicans and the Indians, centring at this post, would give rise to a large village of traders and laborers, and would undoubtedly be hailed, by all that section of country, as a permanent and invaluable advantage. A few pack-horses would carry all the clothing and ammunition necessary for the post during the first year, and two light field-pieces would be all the artillery required for its defence. Afterwards, all the horses required for the use of the establishment might be purchased from the Mexicans at the low price of ten dollars each; and, at the same time, whatever animals might be needed to supply the losses among the dragoons traversing the neighborhood, could be readily procured. The Upper Missouri Indians can furnish horses, at very cheap rates, to any number of the same troops who might be detailed for the defence of the northern frontier; and, in other respects, a very limited outlay of money would suffice to maintain a post in that section of the country.

"From these considerations, and my own personal observation, I am, therefore, disposed to believe, that two posts established by the government, one at the mouth of the Yellow Stone river, and one on the Arkansas, would completely protect all our people in every section of the great wilderness of the west; while other advantages, at least with regard to one of them, confirm and urge the suggestion. A fort at the mouth of Yellow Stone, garrisoned by fifty men, would be perfectly safe. The establishment might be constructed simply with a view to the stores, stables for the dragoons' horses, and quarters for the regular garrison; the rest being provided with sheds or lodges, erected in the vicinity, for their residence during the winter months."

THE END.

EDITORIAL APPENDIX

*Textual Commentary,
Discussions, and Lists by
Richard D. Rust*

EXPLANATORY NOTES

Much has been written about the context of the Astorian venture. Notable among numerous books and articles on the subject are Philip Ashton Rollins's edition of *The Discovery of the Oregon Trail: Robert Stuart's Narratives of His Overland Trip Eastward from Astoria in 1812–13* (New York: Charles Scribner's Sons, 1935); Edgeley W. Todd's edition of *Astoria* (Norman: University of Oklahoma Press, 1964); Kenneth A. Spaulding's edition of *On the Oregon Trail: Robert Stuart's Journal of Discovery* (Norman: University of Oklahoma Press, 1953); Hiram M. Chittenden's *History of the American Fur Trade of the Far West*, 2 vols. (Stanford, Calif.: Academic Reprints, 1954); and Kenneth W. Porter's *John Jacob Astor: Business Man*, 2 vols. (Cambridge, Mass.: Harvard University Press, 1931). Rollins provides biographical sketches of the Returning Astorians, extensive notes relating to Robert Stuart's narrative, translations of an account of the *Tonquin's* voyage and of Wilson Price Hunt's diary of his overland trip, an appendix describing the Indian tribes mentioned by Stuart, and notes detailing the probable routes of the Overland and Returning Astorians. Todd's notes are likewise full and extensive—reflecting the dozen years he spent on *Astoria* and related concerns. He also provides an ample bibliography, as do Andrew B. Myers and Wayne R. Kime in their dissertations, "Washington Irving, Fur Trade Chronicler: An Analysis of *Astoria* with Notes for a Corrected Edition" (Columbia University, 1964) and "Washington Irving's *Astoria*: A Critical Study" (University of Delaware, 1968). Biographies of four Astorians, Russel Farnham, Robert McClellan, John Day, and Benjamin Jones, are found in Stella M. Drumm's "More About Astorians," *Oregon Historical Quarterly* 24 (1923), 335–60; and a listing of Overland Astorians, with brief biographical sketches, is given by Kenneth W. Porter in "Roll of Overland Astorians, 1810–12," *Oregon Historical Quarterly* 34 (1933), 103–12. Especially valuable for geographical identification has been J. Nielson Barry's heavily annotated copy of *Astoria* in the Manuscript Collection of The New York Public Library. Thus, rather than being a pioneer effort, the following Explanatory Notes bring together important historical and biographical information mainly from available sources; moreover, they identify a number of previously unmentioned persons, places, and allusions.

The Explanatory Notes are in three sections: (1) Astorians whom Irving mentions by name; (2) Indian tribes encountered by the Astorians; and (3) identifications of persons, places, historical events, quotations, books and authors, and the like. The numbers before all notes in section three indicate page and line respectively in the Twayne edition. Chapter numbers, chapter or section titles, epigraphs, author's chapter or section summaries, text quotations, and footnotes are included in the line count. Only running heads are omitted from the count. The quotation from the text, to the left of the bracket, is the matter under discussion.

ASTORIANS

(Irving uses the designations "hunter" and "trapper" interchangeably. For purposes of simplification, therefore, only "hunter" will be used in referring to the functions of the men. Obviously, a voyageur could also become a trapper.)

Aiken (Aitken), Job—Seaman
Astor, John Jacob (1763–1848)—Partner. See Kenneth W. Porter, *John Jacob Astor, Business Man.*
Brugiere, Regis—Hunter
Cannon (Canning), William—Hunter
Carriere, Michael (Michel)—Voyageur
Carson, Alexander—Hunter
Cass, Martin H.—Hunter
Clappine, Antoine—Voyageur
Clarke, John (1781–1852)—Partner
Coles, John—Seaman
Cox, Ross (1793–1853)—Clerk. Cox's account of the expedition is found in his *Adventures on the Columbia River* (New York: J. & J. Harper, 1832).
Crooks, Ramsay (1787–1859)—Partner. After returning east with Stuart in 1812–13, Crooks became involved in several of Astor's fur-trading operations, and in 1834 became president of the American Fur Company.
Day, John (1770?–1820)—Hunter. After the sale of the Pacific Fur Company, Day entered the service of the North West Company.
Delaunay, Pierre—Hunter
Detayé, Pierre—Hunter
Dorion, Pierre—Interpreter and hunter
Dubreuil, Jean Baptiste—Voyageur
Farnham, Russel (1784–1832)—Clerk. Under his portrait at the Missouri Historical Society is the inscription: "Walked from Oregon to St. Petersburg, 1813–1814."

Fox, Ebenezer D.—Seaman

Franchère, Gabriel (1786–1863)—Clerk. He provided a source for *Astoria* in his *Relation d'un voyage à la Côte du Nord-ouest de Amérique Septentrionale, dans les Anneés 1810, 11, 12, 13, et 14* (Montreal: C. B. Pasteur, 1820).

Gardpie (Gardapie), Jean Baptiste—Hunter

Harrington, Samuel—Hunter

Harrington, William—Hunter. He enlisted in order to induce his brother to leave the expedition.

Hoback (Hobaugh), John—Hunter

Hunt, Wilson Price (1783–1842)—Partner. After his Astorian ventures, he went to Missouri where he became a farmer, fur merchant, and postmaster of St. Louis.

Jones, Benjamin (ca. 1784–1835)—Hunter

LaBonte, Louis—Voyageur. An unmentioned voyageur by the same surname was Jean Baptiste LaBonte.

LaChapelle, Andre—Voyageur

Lamazee (George Ramsay)—Interpreter. See the Explanatory Note for 73.3.

Landry, Francis (Francois)—Voyageur

LeClerc, Francis (Francois)—Voyageur. This is the LeClerc who went overland with Robert Stuart's expedition; he is not to be confused with Giles LeClerc who came on the *Tonquin* and who was killed with Reed's party in 1814.

LeClerc, Giles (Gilles)—Voyageur

Lewis, James—Clerk

McDougall, Duncan—Partner. He remained on the Pacific coast until 1817 and died at Lake Winnipeg, date not known.

McGilles (McGillis), Donald—Clerk

McKay, Alexander—Partner. As a member of the North West Company, McKay had been in the Alexander Mackenzie party that crossed the continent in 1793.

McKenzie, Donald (1783–1851)—Partner. Upon the dissolution of Astoria he became a partner in the North West Company.

McLellan, Robert (ca. 1770–1815)—Partner. His service with General "Mad Anthony" Wayne had been from 1790 to 1794 or 1795.

McLennon (McLennan), Donald—Clerk

Martin, John—Seaman

Miller, Joseph—Partner

Montigny, Ovide de—Clerk

Mumford, John M.—Seaman

Northrop, Samuel H.—Captain

Ogden, Nicholas G. (d. 1823)—Partner

Pierre, Joe de la—Cook
Pillet (Pillot), Francis B.—Clerk
Prevost (Provost), Jean Baptiste—Voyageur
Reed, John—Clerk
Rezner (Reznor, Rizner), Jacob—Hunter
Robinson, Edward—Hunter
Rose, Edward—Guide, interpreter, and hunter
Ross, Alexander (1783–1856)—Clerk. He recounts the Astorian expe-
    rience in his *Adventures of the First Settlers on the Oregon or Colum-
    bia River* (London: Smith, Elder & Co., 1849).
St. Michel, Louis—Voyageur and hunter
Seton, Alfred—Clerk. Seton later became a New York merchant; his
    unpublished journal was one of Irving's sources.
Sowle, Cornelius (b. 1781)—Captain
Shonowane, Ignace—Hunter
Stuart, David (1765–1853)—Partner
Stuart, Robert (1785–1848)—Partner. See the extensive biographical
    sketch in Rollins's *Discovery of the Oregon Trail*, pp. xxv-liii, which
    relates Stuart's post-Astorian successes as Astor's agent and as a
    prominent citizen of Detroit.
Thorn, Jonathan—Captain. Cox, Franchère, and Ross all portray a more
    critical view of Thorn than does Irving. Perhaps Irving's milder por-
    trait stems from his having known Thorn in their younger years
    (see *Astoria*, 78.23–27).
Turcotte, Jean Baptiste—Voyageur
Vallée (Vallé, Vallar), André—Voyageur
Weekes, John—Seaman
Weekes, Stephen—Seaman

INDIAN TRIBES

(Information for these notes comes chiefly from Rollins's *Discovery of the
Oregon Trail*; Frederick Webb Hodge's *Handbook of American Indians*,
2 vols. (Washington: Government Printing Office, 1907, 1910); and
John R. Swanton's *The Indian Tribes of North America* (Washington:
Government Printing Office, 1952).

Akai-chies—An extremely poor people, they resided on the Columbia
    River not far from the mouth of the Umatilla River in Oregon.
Arapahoes (Arapahays)—They originally lived in Red River Valley,
    then moved southwest across the Missouri. Of Algonquin linguistic
    stock, they are frequently coupled to the Cheyennes.

Arikaras (Arickaras)—The name means "horns" or "elk." They were agriculturalists of Caddoan linguistic stock and lived along the Missouri River in South and North Dakotas.

Blackfeet—A North Plains tribe of Algonquin linguistic stock; they were bitterly opposed to traders and explorers.

Cathlamahs (Cathlamets)—Chinookan stock; they were located near the mouth of Columbia River.

Cathlascos (Wascos)—The name means "cup," and refers to a cup-shaped rock a short distance from their main village in the neighborhood of The Dalles. They were of Chinookian linguistic stock.

Cheyenne (Sheyenne, Shienne)—Of the Algonquin linguistic family, they were located on the Missouri on the border of North and South Dakota but later moved to the Black Hills.

Chinooks—The name derives from Tsinuk, their Chehalis name; sometimes they were called Flatheads. Located on the north side of Columbia River in the proximity of Fort Astoria, they were noted for friendly dealing with traders.

Chipunnish (Chopunnish)—Another name for Nez Percés or Piercednose Indians.

Clatsops—From the native word meaning "dried salmon"; of Chinookian linguistic stock, they centered about Cape Adams.

Crows (Absarokas, Upsarokas)—These Indians belonged to the Hidatsa sub-stock of the Siouan family and roamed principally in the watershed of the Big Horn River.

Flatheads—See Irving's definition on p. 181. Rollins notes that both Stuart's and Hunt's "Flatheads" were probably Nez Percés.

Klickitats—Active and enterprising traders in the Shahaptian division of the Shapwailutan linguistic family. Irving notes them as living on the north side of Columbia River between The Dalles and Walla Walla River.

Kodiaks—Indians from the area of St. Paul's harbor at the east end of Kodiak Island, Alaska. Before founding Sitka, Count Baranof had a fur-trading establishment at Kodiak.

Mandans—Of Siouan stock, they were situated on the right bank of the Missouri in the vicinity of present-day Bismarck, North Dakota.

Minatarees—Siouan tribe located on the Missouri River between the Heart and Little Missouri rivers.

Neweetees—There is some question as to the exact location of this group of Nootka Indians. Alexander Ross (*Adventures*, p. 165) locates them in "Eyuck Whoola, Newceut Bay." Ross Cox (*Columbia River*, p. 63) says their village of "New Whitty" was "in the vicinity of Nootka." The *Missouri Gazette* account (May 15, 1813; in Chittenden's *History of the American Fur Trade,* II, 909–11) places them on "Woody Point" on Vancouver Island.

Nez Percés (Chopunnish)—These peaceful Indians of Shahaptian linguistic stock inhabited the lower watershed of the Snake River.

Omaha (Maha)—Living in northeastern Nebraska on the Missouri River, these Indians were of Siouan linguistic stock; their name meant "those who went up stream or against the current."

Osages—Of Siouan stock, the Osage Indians in the 1810's were divided into three bands on the Osage River and Vermilion Creek in present-day Kansas.

Ottoes (Otoes)—These Siouan Indians, whose name meant "lovers of sexual pleasure," were located on the lower course of the Platte River.

Pallatapallas (Palouse)—Of Shapwailutan stock, they lived in the valley of the Palouse River in present-day Washington and Idaho.

Pawnees—Of Caddoan linguistic stock, the Pawnees were located on the Platte River and Republican fork of Kansas River.

Sciatogas—The name means "camass eater" (a bulbous liliaceous plant); it applied variously to several tribes of northern Paiutes and also Cayuses. Rollins (p. 355) argues that it is probable that Hunt's and Stuart's "Sciatogas" were in fact Cayuses.

Shoshonies—The Northern Shoshonies were the strongest and most prominent tribe of the upper plateau (eastern Idaho, western Wyoming, northeastern Utah); the Western Shoshonies, of the same Uto-Aztecan family, lived in central and western Idaho, northwestern Utah, and central and northeastern Nevada.

Sioux (Dakota)—"Sioux" is evolved from "Nadowessiwag" (erroneously transcribed as "Nadiousioux") meaning "snakelike ones" or "enemies." Originally located in Minnesota, northwestern Wisconsin, and neighboring parts of Iowa, they later moved to the area of South Dakota. Besides the Dakotas, Irving refers to the "pirates of the Missouri," the Sioux Tetons (probably a contraction of Titonwan, "prairie-dwellers"), who dwelt west of the Missouri River as far back as the Black Hills and as far southwest as the North Platte River; to Tetons Bois-Brulé ("Burnt Thighs"), who lived near the mouths of the White and Teton rivers; to the Tetons Min-Na-Kine-Azzo (Minneconjou, "planter by the water"); and to the Yanktons Ahna (I-hanke-ya-ton-won-ya: "smallest village" or "smallest band"), who occupied the upper valleys of the James and Big Sioux rivers as well as a long stretch of the Missouri valley.

Snakes—See *Astoria,* 181.14–183.5; here referring to Northern Shoshonies.

Spokans—The name perhaps signifies "sun people." Of Salishan linguistic stock, they were located on the Spokane and Little Spokane rivers.

Tus-che-pas—The term may apply to the Kutenai and Nez Percés (Todd, p. 310 n) or to Tushepaws of Salishan linguistic stock (Rollins, p. 326, n. 254).

Wahkiacums—Of Upper Chinookan linguistic stock, the Wahkiacums lived near the confluence of the Elokomin River with the Columbia River in territory adjoining that of the Chinooks.

Walla Wallas (Wallah Wallahs)—The name "Walla Walla" meant "small swift river," and the tribe lived on the Walla Walla River and on both banks of the Columbia at the mouth of the Walla Walla.

Wishrams—The name comes from Wucxam; they were also called Tlakluit. Of Chinookan stock, they resided on the north side of Columbia River in present-day Klickitat County.

NOTES

3.11 age] Irving traveled to Montreal and back in 1803, when he was twenty years old, and again in 1808.

3.25 far west] Irving's tour is recorded in his *Western Journals* and in *A Tour on the Prairies* (1835).

4.15 Pierre M. Irving] Pierre (1803–1876) was later to become Washington Irving's biographer and literary executor.

4.26 Lewis and Clarke] *History of the Expedition under the Command of Captains Lewis and Clark,* ed. Paul Allen, 2 vols. (Philadephia: Bradford and Inskeep, 1814).

4.26 Bradbury] John Bradbury, *Travels in the Interior of America, in the Years 1809, 1810, and 1811* (London: Sherwood, Neely, and Jones, 1817). For an available edition, see Reuben Gold Thwaites, ed., *Early Western Travels, 1748–1846,* 32 vols. (Cleveland: Arthur H. Clark Co., 1904–07), vol. V. Also edited by Thwaites are narratives by Long, Brackenridge, Franchère, and Alexander Ross.

4.26 Breckenridge] Henry Marie Brackenridge, *Journal of a Voyage up the River Missouri* (Baltimore: Coale and Maxwell, 1815).

4.26 Long] Edwin James, comp., *Account of an Expedition from Pittsburg to the Rocky Mountains, Performed in the Years 1819, 1820 ... under the Command of Major Stephen H. Long,* 2 vols. (Philadelphia: H. C. Carey and I. Lea, 1822–23). Long (1784–1864) was a major in the Army topographical engineers; later he was an important figure in railroad engineering.

4.27 Franchere] Gabriel Franchère, *Relation d'un voyage à la Côte du Nord-ouest de l'Amérique Septentrionale, dans les Anneés 1810,*

11, 12, 13, et 14 (Montréal, 1820). See also *Adventure in Astoria, 1810–1814,* trans. and ed. by Hoyt C. Franchère (Norman: University of Oklahoma Press, 1967).

4.27 Ross Cox] *Adventures on the Columbia River . . .* (New York: J. & J. Harper, 1832).

6.25–26 old French writer] Baron Louis Armand de Lahontan (1666–1715)

7.40 La Hontan] *New Voyages to North-America,* 2 vols. (London: H. Bonwicke, et al., 1703), I, 20–21.

8.12 Michilimackinac] This settlement was located on what is now Mackinac Island in Lake Huron just before it joins Lake Michigan.

9.19 bloody affairs] These Indian attacks on British forts were part of Pontiac's Conspiracy in 1763.

11.33 Grand Portage] The fort was built about 1803 where Dog River empties into Lake Superior.

15.16 elder brother] John Henry Astor

19.3 company] The Russian-American Fur Company

19.22 Captain Gray] Robert Gray (1755–1806)

19.37 Vancouver] George Vancouver (1758?–1798)

19.39 Broughton] William Robert Broughton (1762–1821)

19.42 Mount Hood] Named after British Rear Admiral Samuel Hood (1724–1816)

20.10 Captain Jonathan Carver] Carver (1710–1780) was the author of *Travels through the Interior Parts of North America* (Philadelphia, 1796) referred to below.

20.18 Straits of Annian] This mythical strait, associated variously with the Bering Strait and the Columbia River, was supposed to allow ship passage from the Pacific to the Atlantic.

20.27 Richard Whitworth] Whitworth (1734?–1811) was MP for Stafford, 1768–80.

20.39 Sir Alexander MacKenzie] Mackenzie (1764–1820) led the first transcontinental journey to the Pacific Ocean.

21.8 account] *Voyages on the River St. Lawrence and through the Continent of North America to the Frozen and Pacific Oceans* (London, 1801).

21.29 Lewis and Clark] Meriwether Lewis (1774–1809) and William Clark (1770–1838)

22.43 Russian establishment] On Baronof Island near present-day Sitka, Alaska

23.26–34 "I remember . . . self government."] For a full transcription of this letter see Dorothy W. Bridgwater, "John Jacob Astor Relative to His Settlement on Columbia River," *Yale University Library Gazette* 24 (1949), 55–56.

24.6 New Caledonia] British Columbia

25.35 articles of agreement] The full text of these articles is found in Grace Flandrau's *Astor and the Oregon Country* (St. Paul: Great Northern Railway Co., n.d.), pp. 24–35.

25.38–39 Pacific Fur Company] Although later referred to in the text as the American Fur Company, the association under which the Astorians operated was technically the Pacific Fur Company.

27.26 Tripolitan war] Fought against the Barbary States in 1801–05 to end piracy. Thorn's recognition came from gallantry at Tripoli in 1803.

27.35 twelve clerks] Actually there were eleven clerks: Russell Farnham, Gabriel Franchère, James Lewis, William W. Matthews, Donald McGillis, Thomas McKay, Donald McLennon, Ovide de Montigny, Francis B. Pillot (Pillet), Alexander Ross, and William Wallace.

28.5 artizans] They were Job Aitken, rigger and calker; George Bell, cooper; Johann Koaster, carpenter; and Augustus Roussil, blacksmith.

28.7 voyageurs] In his narrative, Franchère lists Antoine Belleau, J. Baptiste Belleau, Louis Bruslé, P. D. Jeremie, Jacques Lafantaisie, Michel Laframboise, Basile Lapensée, Ignace Lapensée, Oliver Roy Lapensée, Joseph Lapierre, Giles Leclerc, Joseph Nadeau, and Benjamin Roussel.

30.14 Lansingburgh] A village located about thirteen miles up the Hudson River from what is now Troy, New York

31.3 that war] War of 1812

31.12 partners] Alexander McKay and probably Duncan McDougall

31.15–16 Mr. Jackson] Francis James Jackson (1770–1814), minister plenipotentiary to Washington, 1809–11.

31.28–29 Commodore Rogers] John Rodgers (1773–1838). British impressment of American citizens, which Commodore Rodgers was empowered to resist, became one of the grounds for the War of 1812. His most significant naval action was the destruction of the British frigate *Guerrière* in August, 1812.

31.32 Captain Hull] Isaac Hull (1773–1843)

35.34 Fly Market] Named for Vlie or Vly (an abbreviation of valley), this was a market in New York City located at the foot of Maiden Lane.

35.34 Covent Garden] London park and market

35.40 elder Stuart] David Stuart (1765–1853)

37.4 Cape de Verds] Cape Verde islands off West Africa

37.5 Patagonia] Barren region in southern Argentina and Chile between the Andes and the Atlantic

37.7 where Robinson Crusoe ... lived] Juan Fernandez Island, off Chile, where Alexander Selkirk was marooned

38.11–12 Port Egmont]   On Saunders Island, one of nearly two hundred islands in the Falklands, about 60° west and 51°20′ south

38.33 "Old Mortality"]   He is the character in Sir Walter Scott's *Old Mortality* who visited graves of Scottish Covenanters to clean and restore them.

41.13–14 Mouna Roa]   Mauna Loa

41.38 Tamaahmaah]   Kamehameha I (1737?–1815)

42.19 visit]   By Kamehameha II and his queen in 1824

42.30 Karakakooa]   Now known as Kealakekua Bay, it is off the southern part of the eastern shore of Hawaii Island.

42.42 Woahoo]   Oahu

42.43 Tocaigh]   Probably Kawaihae on the northeast coast of Hawaii

44.15 bay of Tocaigh]   Now known as Kihola, or Kailua, Bay

44.37 "even . . . days."]   *Othello*, I, iii, 132

44.41 Captain Metcalf]   Simon Metcalfe

45.1 Nootka]   Nootka Sound, Vancouver Island, British Columbia

45.2 son]   Thomas Humphrey Metcalfe

45.4 Mowee]   Maui

46.15–16 better . . . to rule among savages than serve among white men]   Although this is probably a commonplace, it echoes Milton's *Paradise Lost,* I, 263: "Better to reign in Hell than serve in Heaven."

46.40 Waititi]   Earlier Wai-ki-ki; now Honolulu

47.16 Kraimaker]   Also known as Krai Moku and Kalanimoku

49.33 one of the vessels]   The Lark; see Chapter LVIII

51.29 three Canadians]   Basile Lapensée, Ignace Lapensée, Joseph Nadeau

52.35 Mr. Mumford]   John M. Mumford

52.40 Mr. Aiken]   Job Aiken

56.36 Wappatoo]   Tubers of the plant *Sagittaria variabilis* or *Sagittaria latifolia*; somewhat like potatoes.

58.24 Comcomly]   For additional information on Comcomly (1765?–1830), see J. F. Santee, "Comcomly and the Chinooks," *Oregon Historical Quarterly* 33 (1932), 271–78.

59.8–9 "choked in a trap."]   Irving relies here on Ross Cox, *Columbia River*, p. 146.

61.6 Point George]   Now Smith Point, it is the site of the present-day city of Astoria.

65.34 Lewis River]   Snake River

67.18 Mount Coffin]   Near Longview, Washington

67.22 Cowleskee]   Cowlitz River

67.25 ridges of mountains]   The Cascade Range

67.27 Wallamot]   The Willamette River; Lewis and Clark called it the Multnomah River.

68.19 One of these precipices] Rooster Rock or Beacon Rock

68.31 Falls] Celilo Falls

69.9 The Long Narrows] Also named the Dalles or the Great Dalles, it now is called Five Mile Rapids.

69.40 Quamash] Camas; edible liliaceous bulbs

70.20 honest trader] Robert Stuart; see Rollins, *Discovery of the Oregon Trail*, p. 62.

72.31–32 Strait of Juan de Fuca] Between the Olympic Peninsula of Washington and Vancouver Island

73.3 Lamazee] According to J. Neilson Barry in "Astorians Who Became Permanent Settlers," *Washington Historical Quarterly* 24 (1933), 296–301, this man was George Ramsay (the Chinook Indians could not pronounce the letter *R*). Alexander Ross in *Adventures of the First Settlers on the Oregon or Columbia River* (in Thwaites ed., VII, 165) records the Indian's comments on his name: " 'My name is Kasiascall, but the Chinooks and other Indians hereabouts call me Lamazue.' " Written, and then crossed out, in the *Astoria* manuscript is the name Joseachal.

73.7 harbour of Neweetie] In Templar Channel of Clayoquot Sound. (See the note for the Neweetee Indian tribe.)

74.39 officer of the watch] James Thorn, brother of Captain Thorn

75.17 Mr. Lewis] James Lewis. A novel about his experiences is Gilbert W. Gabriel's *I, James Lewis* (Garden City, N. Y., 1935).

87.1 Falstaff] See *Henry IV*, part 1, IV, ii.

92.36 Manuel Lisa] Lisa (1772–1820) in 1807 built Manuel's Fort at the mouth of the Big Horn River and in 1808 helped organize the St. Louis Missouri Fur Company. See Richard E. Oglesby, *Manual Lisa and the Opening of the Missouri Fur Trade* (Norman: University of Oklahoma Press, 1963).

92.41 Mr. Henry] Andrew Henry (ca. 1775–1833). In 1810–11 he led the first group of American trappers to operate west of the Rockies. His fort was at present-day Three Forks, Montana.

95.14 Nodowa] Nodaway River, Iowa

98.24 Fort Mandan] It was located on the north side of the Missouri River between Knife and Heart rivers across from present-day Fort Clark.

99.14 Squaw] Marie d'Aguivoise Dorion; see J. Neilson Barry, "Madame Dorion of the Astorians," *Oregon Historical Quarterly* 30 (1929), 272–78.

99.20 Mr. Nuttall] Thomas Nuttall (1786–1859)

99.22 "Travels in Arkansas"] *Journal of Travels into the Arkansas Territory, October 2, 1818–February 18, 1820* (Philadelphia, 1821).

99.23 "Genera of American Plants"] *The Genera of North American*

Plants, and a Catalogue of the Species, to the Year 1817 (Philadelphia, 1818).

101.1 Charette] Located near present-day Marthasville, Missouri, it was lost through erosion of the river.

101.16 small stream] Charette Creek

101.17 John Colter] For a biography of Colter (ca. 1770–1813), see Burton Harris, *John Colter: His Years in the Rockies* (New York, 1952).

101.38 Potts] John Potts, a private detached from the Lewis and Clark expedition

104.7 trading post] The fort of Manuel Lisa near the mouth of the Big Horn River

104.39 frontier village] Côte sans Dessein, two miles below the mouth of the Osage River

105.12 Fort Osage] Today an oak replica of the fort stands on the site overlooking the Missouri River near Sibley, Missouri.

105.21 Lieutenant Brownson] John Brownson, First Lieutenant

108.11 swivel] A small cannon mounted on a swivel so as to turn horizontally in any desired direction

108.11 howitzers] Short, lightweight pieces of ordnance designed for horizontal firing of shells with small charges

116.21 river S' Peter] Now the Minnesota River

121.17 white man] Toussaint Charbonneau; his wife was Sacagawea

123.9 Quicourt] Niobrara River

123.36 "The Bloody Ground"] The "Dark and Bloody Ground" was the Indian hunting territory in Kentucky, called so because of the fighting there between the Cherokee of Tennessee and the Shawnee of Ohio.

125.3 Arickara town] This was situated on the west bank of the Missouri a few miles above the mouth of Grand River.

129.17 carottes] Cylindrical rolls of tobacco

130.10 Great bend] About forty miles southeast of Pierre, South Dakota

136.21–22 "cattle upon a thousand hills"] Psalms 50:10

137.25–26 fabled fascination of the rattlesnake] Compare this with the belief detailed in Jedidiah Morse's *The American Universal Geography* (Boston: Isaiah Thomas and Ebenezer T. Andrews, 1793), I, 199: Rattlesnakes "are supposed to have the power of fascination, in an eminent degree; and it is generally believed that they charm birds, rabbits, squirrels and other animals, in such a manner as that they lose the power of resistance."

138.7 island] Ashby Island

138.36 interpreter] Most likely this was Joseph Gravelines, the same interpreter who had helped Lewis and Clark.

150.5–7 "In Rama . . . are not."]   Matthew 2:18

151.17–18 "The Great American desert"]   One place Irving would have encountered this concept was in the account of the Stephen H. Long expedition—although the notion was prevalent in the first half of the nineteenth century, thanks to reports by explorers such as Coronado, Pike, and Long.

152.29–32 "A great company . . . goods."]   Ezekial 38:12, 15

152.34 Tucuman]   Province in northwest Argentine republic

156.5 Big River]   Today, Grand River in northern South Dakota

157.40 Warricanne creek]   Probably the present Beaver Creek, the mouth of which is sixty-four miles south of Bismarck, North Dakota

163.25 rocky hills]   Slim Buttes in Harding County, South Dakota

167.8 Vasconcelles]   Simon Vasconcellos (1599–1670) was the author of *Chronica da Companhia de Jesu do Estado do Brasil* (1663) and other works.

167.10 Piratininga]   Near the center of the state of São Paulo, Brazil

167.21 Guayra]   Northeast of Barretos in north São Paulo

167.25 Orellano]   The Amazon River

167.26 Paraguaxo]   Possibly the area around Paraguaçu in southwest Minas Gerais, Brazil

172.11 Missouri]   Little Missouri

173.12 lofty mountain]   Cloud Peak (13,165 feet)

174.43 "towns of the free and generous spirits"]   Compare Irving's notebook quotation of Jones (*Astoria* Appendix 493.18–28).

179.33 little stream]   Apparently the north fork of Crazy Woman Creek

182.24–25 "horse to ride and weapon to wear"]   *King Lear*, III, iv, 137

183.8 stream running north]   No Wood Creek

183.14 Big Horn ridge]   Owl Creek Mountains

183.17 plain]   Valley of Badwater Creek

183.32 One of its peaks]   Gannett Peak (13,785 feet)

184.13–14 head waters of the Columbia]   The Snake River

184.17 stream]   Green or Spanish River

184.23 height]   Union Pass

184.25–26 three mountain peaks]   These are the three Tetons, the Grand Teton being 13,766 feet high.

185.24 mountain]   Possibly Doubletop Peak (11,715 feet), Gros Ventre Range

185.27 one of its little tributaries]   Beaver Creek

187.21 stream]   Hoback River

190.22 after part]   See *Astoria* 313.34–314.8.

190.36 heart of the mountain]   Grand Canyon of the Snake River

195.27 dangerous strait]   Idaho Falls

197.7 fall]   American Falls

198.24 "The Caldron Linn"] Conjecturally at Murtaugh, Idaho, or Milner, Idaho.

208.10 stream] Boise River

209.9–10 two small rivers] Payette and Weiser rivers

209.14 defile] Apparently on Mann Creek

212.25 Le Clerc] Francis LeClerc

213.8 defile] Near Homestead, Oregon

213.43 rivers] Boise, Payette, and Weiser rivers

218.35 stream] Weiser River

220.13–14 three of them] Jean Baptiste Turcotte, André La Chapelle, and Francis Landry

221.27 small stream] Powder River

222.11 beautiful stream] Grande Ronde River

222.43 mountains] Blue Mountains

223.25 stream] Either McKay Creek or Meacham Creek

223.38 river] Umatilla (Umatalla) River

226.5 Ke-koosh] Todd (*Astoria,* p. 313 n) theorizes this is David Thompson, whom the Indians named Koo-Koo-Sint "from a Salish word, *kukusem,* meaning 'star,' thus referring to his astronomical observations."

226.8 Jacquean Finlay] Jacques Raphael Finlay (d. 1828), who built Spokane House

226.34 Lewis, and Clarke rivers] The Snake and Columbia rivers above the confluence of the Snake.

228.20 falls] Celilo Falls east of The Dalles

232.26 deep channel] The Grand Canyon of Snake River, or Hell's Canyon

233.23 stream] Salmon River

237.21–22 great mountain barrier] Cascade Range

242.39 manuscript] Robert Stuart's "Travelling Memoranda"

247.8–9 "glad . . . miscreants."] Quoted from Stuart's "Travelling Memoranda"; see Rollins, *Discovery of the Oregon Trail,* p. 55.

248.24 Euryalus] One of Aeneas's men who was successful in a night raid against the Latins, Euryalus lost his life near daybreak after the enemy spotted his shining helmet.

251.13 small river] Powder River

251.16 low prairie] Grande Ronde Valley

253.15–16 Count Pahlen] Count Frederick Petrovich Pahlen. He had been appointed minister to the U.S. in May, 1809.

253.21 confidential agent] This was Adrian Benjamin Bentzon, who had married Astor's eldest daughter.

254.20 New Archangel] Present-day Sitka, Alaska

257.39 died within a year]   Day actually did not die until eight years later—February 16, 1820.

259.33 natives]   Klickitats

262.38 shallow stream]   Umatilla River

263.38 vast plain]   Grand Ronde Valley

264.1 pool of water]   Hot Lake

264.8–9 Woodpile creek]   Burnt River

265.1 small stream]   Owyhee River

265.38 Mad River Mountain]   Teton Pass

266.23 one much shorter and easier]   South Pass

267.41 Lake Bonneville]   Great Salt Lake

273.28 large branch]   Thomas Fork

273.40 stream running to the north]   A tributary of Salt River

274.6 Salt River]   More probably Gray's River

280.3 small stream]   Moody Creek

280.14 hot springs]   Pincock Springs

281.25 river]   Teton River

284.10 summit]   Teton Pass

284.33 Spanish River Mountain]   Ridge between Hoback and Green rivers

285.10 river]   Green River

286.29–33 "It was all . . . rest."]   Rephrased from Stuart's "Travelling Memoranda"

287.41 stream]   New Fork River

288.16 streams]   Probably Boulder Creek and East Fork

288.24 one of the branches]   East Fork

288.42 river]   Sweetwater River

290.11 snowy mountains]   Wind River Range

290.31 brook]   Big Sandy Creek

291.28 small stream]   Presumably Little Sandy Creek

292.10 lake]   Perhaps Picket Lake

292.37 mountains]   Green Mountains

293.11 stream]   Muddy Creek

293.21 passage]   Muddy Gap

293.27 stream]   North Platte

295.25 Quicourt River]   Niobrara River

296.3 bend]   Bessemer Bend, southwest of present-day Casper, Wyoming

301.22–23 range of mountains]   Northern extremities of the Laramie Mountains

302.30 encamped]   Near present-day Torrington, Wyoming

305.7 Doruin and Roi]   François Doruin (Derouen, Deroin) and Jean Baptiste Antoine Roi

307.9 agent]   Adrian Bentzon, Astor's son-in-law

309.9 Mr. Northrop]   Samuel H. Northrup

309.9 Mr. Nicholas G. Ogden]   He was a brother of Samuel G. Ogden, prominent New York merchant; he became Astor's agent in Canton around 1817.

310.24 small stream]   Palouse River

311.30 Pointed heart and Spokan rivers]   Now known as the Spokane and Little Spokane rivers

311.43 Shahaptan]   Most likely what is today known as Clearwater River

313.14 horse to ride and weapon to wear]   *King Lear*, III, iv, 137

316.10 Wollamut]   Willamette River

320.26–27 Pavion and Lewis rivers]   Palouse and Snake rivers

322.6 post]   Fort Spokane

325.6 four partners]   Duncan McDougall, Donald McKenzie, David Stuart, and John Clarke

325.7 manifesto]   For the full text, see T. C. Elliott, "Sale of Astoria, 1813," *Oregon Historical Quarterly* 33 (1932), 43–50.

326.31 Captain Crane]   William Montgomery Crane (1784–1846)

327.13–14 Commodore Chauncey]   Isaac Chauncey (1772–1840)

327.22 Hook]   Sandy Hook peninsula in east New Jersey

331.9 Sheetka]   Sitka

331.19 Count Baranoff]   Aleksandr Andreevich Baranov (Baronoff, Baranhoff) (1746–1819), founder of Sitka

332.5 establishment]   Fort Ross, just north of San Francisco

332.16 "potations pottle deep."]   *Othello*, III, ii, 56

332.22 "temperance captain"]   This is a captain who might well drink in private aboard ship but who does not drink ashore.

333.16 S' Paul]   In the Pribilof Islands

333.16–17 Sea of Kamschatka]   Bering Sea

333.20 "old man of the sea."]   Subdued and killed by Sinbad

333.40 Oonalaska]   Unalaska; in the Fox group of the Aleutian Islands

336.21 Captain Smith]   William Smith

338.9 Commodore Porter]   David Porter (1780–1843), of whom Irving had written a biographical sketch for the September, 1814, *Analectic Magazine*.

339.15 one man]   Daniel Choss

339.31 14th]   Of August, 1813

339.31 first mate]   Richard Maxey

339.32 two seamen]   Timothy Trowbridge, William Granniss

340.19 second mate]   Henry Merschel

340.35 Tahoorowa]   Maui

342.14 Stuart]   John Stuart (1779–1847)

346.26–27 Captain Black] William Black. See "Captain Black's Report on Taking of Astoria," *Oregon Historical Quarterly* 17 (1916), 147–48.

346.36–37 Commodore Hillyer] Sir James Hillyar (1769–1843)

350.39 two of the clerks] Clerks Russel Farnham and Benjamin Clapp also went with Hunt.

351.29 house on the Snake River] Located at the mouth of Boise River

353.22 Captain Biddle] James Biddle (1783–1848). See "Captain James Biddle's Orders to Command the U.S.S. *Ontario* to Go to Columbia River and Take Possession of the Post and Territory in the Name of the United States," *Oregon Historical Quarterly* 3 (1902), 310–11.

356.8–9 "free ... interest."] For the full text of the letter from which this comes, see the letter dated May 24, 1812, in Dorothy W. Bridgwater's "John Jacob Astor Relative to His Settlement on Columbia River," *Yale University Library Gazette* 24 (1949), 56.

361.31 Michilimackinac or St. Mary's] Straits of Mackinac and Sault Ste. Marie

363.20 *Silliman's Journal*] *American Journal of Science and Arts* (Benjamin Silliman, ed.)

364.20 Ashley's] William Henry Ashley (ca. 1778–1838)

364.26 Captain Bonneville] Benjamin L. E. Bonneville; see Irving's *The Adventures of Captain Bonneville.*

364.30 Buenaventura] Sacramento River; at first it was thought to extend from the main range of the Rocky Mountains to the Pacific Ocean.

364.30 Timpanogos] It was erroneously believed this river drained the Great Salt Lake by flowing into the Pacific north of Buenaventura River (Sacramento River).

364.41 Rio del Norte] Rio Grande River

365.5 York fort] On Hudson Bay at the mouth of Nelson River

365.5 Moose river] Flows through northeast Ontario into James Bay

365.6 Grand river] Ottawa River

365.35 "the precious ermine"] Ermine fur was chiefly worn by royal personages

366.12 Samoieda] This Siberian region on the Ob and Yenisey rivers and their tributaries was the home of the Samoyeds.

367.17 South Georgia] East of Tierra del Fuego; 54°30′ south, 36°30′ west.

367.22 island of Desolation] This is Islas Desolación in the Antarctic at the west end of the Strait of Magellan.

367.24 South Shetlands] Southeast of Cape Horn off the tip of the Antarctic peninsula

367.29 Lobos islands] Off the coast of Uruguay near Punta del Este

369.9 Long] Major Stephen H. Long

369.14 James's Peak] Present-day Pike's Peak (14,110 feet), it was
called James's Peak after Edwin James, botanist on Stephen Long's
expedition (1821), who climbed it.

369.37–370.1 Major Delafield's] Richard Delafield (1798–1873); his
brother, John, was the subject of Irving's chapter "The Wife" in the
Sketch Book.

370.1 Mr. Thompson] David Thompson (1770–1857); see *Astoria,*
65.4–66.13.

These references are from the *Astoria* notebooks in the Appendix:

492.2 Manitoulin Islands] In the northern part of Lake Huron

492.2 Lakes] *Sketches of a Tour to the Lakes* by Thomas L. McKenney (Baltimore: Fielding Lucas, 1827).

492.20 MKennay] Thomas L. McKenney, *Tour to the Lakes.* The
material from "Manitoulin Islands" to "reside there" ("preside there"
in McKenney; 492.2–14 in the T "Notes for Astoria") is from p.
164; "The Oneidas" to "this state." (492.15–19) is from p. 74.

492.21–23 I bade . . . solitude.] McKenney, p. 367.

492.24–493.2 Since . . . mountain.] [Nicholas Biddle], *History of the Expedition under the Command of Captains Lewis and Clark* (Philadelphia: Bradford and Inskeep, 1814), I, 291–92.

493.3–4 "While . . . being:] James Athearn Jones, *Tales of an Indian
Camp,* 3 vols. (London: Henry Colburn and Richard Bentley, 1829),
I, 147.

493.6 Mountains of the Setting Sun] Jones, I, 148.

493.7 Kanzas . . . Sioux] Jones, I, 148.

493.8–12 Very many . . . 2d 180, 117.] Pierre de Charlevoix's *Journal
of a Voyage to North-America,* quoted in Jones, I, 167.

493.13–14 The spirits . . . fear.] Jones, I, 191; "The spirits . . . oak." are
part of a long poem and "The tree toad . . . fear." is a footnote to it.

493.16 "The crest] Jones, I, 192.

493.18–28 The Blackfoot . . . moon.] Jones, I, 245.

493.31–34 The greater . . . Mount[s]] Jones, II, 141.

494.9 Pike] Zebulon Pike (1779–1813), explorer and author of *An
Account of Expeditions to the Sources of the Mississippi, and through
the Western Parts of Louisiana* (Philadelphia, 1810). Pike, Long, and
Carver are all referred to in *Tales of an Indian Camp.*

494.10 Longs 1 Travels] See the Explanatory Note for 4.26 ("Long").

494.11 Carver] See the Explanatory Note for 20.10.

495.17 Canoe river] Snake River

495.34 Long] Edwin James' account of Long's travels to the Rocky
Mountains is readily accessible in *Early Western Travels,* ed. Reuben

Gold Thwaites, vols. XIV–XVII (Cleveland: Arthur H. Clark Co., 1905). The material Irving quotes here and in the subsequent two paragraphs is in volume XV, pp. 238 and 251.

496.21 The Big Horn . . . particulars of it.]   This section is written in another hand.

TEXTUAL COMMENTARY

Thanks to the generosity of a number of persons and institutions mentioned in the Acknowledgments, manuscript for approximately 90 percent of the *Astoria* text has been made available for use in determining Washington Irving's original intentions. This extant manuscript, which was used as printer's copy for the first American edition, thus forms the basis of the present Twayne edition of Washington Irving; where manuscript is lacking the first American edition serves as copy-text—specifically the copy in the library of the University of North Carolina (call no. V917.8/I72a/1836/v.1[2]).[1]

Collation of all the relevant forms of *Astoria*—the manuscript and all printed versions which could have been altered by the author—reveals nearly 650 passages with differences in substantives (that is, words or "meaning") and many times that number of differences in accidentals (punctuation, spelling, capitalization, word division, and paragraphing). The List of Rejected Substantives which follows contains 300 words or phrases considered nonauthorial, and the List of Emendations contains an additional ninety nonauthorial substantives from the first and second American editions. There are an estimated 8,000 differences in accidentals between the manuscript and the first printing from it, due mainly to the house style imposed on Irving's work.

The history of a text is usually a record of increasing corruption. Among examples of this corruption is one found at 199.21–22 in *Astoria*. Writing about the difficulties Wilson P. Hunt's men had along the Snake River, Irving says, "The two parties returned after a weary scramble among savage rocks and precipices." The compositor using the manuscript to set the first edition misread "savage" as "swamp" and then altered the punctuation to fit his misreading: "a weary scramble among swamp, rocks, and precipices." The compositor for the second American edition, setting type from the first edition, "corrected" the passage to read, "a weary scramble among *swamps*, rocks, and precipices" (italics added). Another example of corruption is found at 242.14–15. Irving wrote, "procure them all desireable things." The compositor for the first edition

1. The one exception to this pertains to manuscript portions covering 5.1–13.23, 14.8–32.17, 301.1–314.36, 315.12–320.16, and 320.27–356.20. Although the owner of manuscript covering these segments of text did not permit unrestricted printing of it, he generously allowed the manuscript to be used in determining authoritative substantive variants and in restoring Irving's intentions in some of the accidentals.

set "describable" for "desireable"; the compositor for the second edition, compromising between "describable" and "desirable," the word called for by the context of the passage, set "desirabable.'

A disregard of corruption in the *Astoria* texts leads Kenneth A. Spaulding to take Irving to task unjustly. First, Spaulding criticizes Irving for including details not found in Robert Stuart's manuscript— ignoring Irving's having met and talked with a number of the participants in the Astorian venture, with the express purpose of gaining additional information for his book. Then Spaulding faults Irving for having made a number of changes from the Stuart manuscript: "Some, for example, appear to have been the result of carelessness: the name André Vallée he changed to Andri Vallar, and Doruin became Dornin.... On one occasion Irving changes 'wood-pile-creek' to Woodville Creek, discarding the homely though meaningful name for one that, without actually meaning anything, suggests a better regulated countryside than was to be found west of the Alleghenies."[2] Actually, Irving has the names copied correctly in the *Astoria* manuscript; further, "Woodpile" also appears in the first edition, is misprinted "Woodvile" in the second edition, and is "Woodville" only in Spaulding's article.

Of course Irving's manuscript is not free from error. In altering phrases he sometimes deleted too much or too little; he occasionally repeated words; at times he omitted necessary punctuation marks or included unnecessary ones; he misspelled words; he was careless or indifferent about capitalization; and he introduced errors because of his method of pasting together fragments of earlier drafts in preparing printer's copy.

THE MANUSCRIPT

Portions of the *Astoria* manuscript used in setting type for the first American edition are owned by three institutions and three collateral descendants of Washington Irving. With the exception of one leaf owned by Irving B. Kingsford, Chapters 1–4 are in the possession of Wilmer H. Kingsford; Chapter 5, the University of Virginia Library, Barrett Collection; Chapters 6–13, The New York Public Library (with Irving B. Kingsford owning one leaf from Chapter 6); Chapter 14, divided equally between The New York Public Library and the University of Virginia; Chapter 15, the University of Virginia; Chapter 16, The New York Public Library (8 leaves) and the University of Virginia (17 leaves); Chapters 17–29, The New York Public Library; Chapter 30, the University of

2. K. A. Spaulding, "A Note on *Astoria*: Irving's Use of the Robert Stuart MS," *American Literature* 22 (1950), 154–55.

Virginia; Chapters 33–34, 36–41, and 44–49 are owned by Virginia Johnson; and, with the exception of one leaf owned by Sleepy Hollow Restorations, Chapters 50–61 are owned by Wilmer H. Kingsford. Portions of this manuscript at The New York Public Library and the University of Virginia have been accessible to scholars for some time and are described in H. L. Kleinfield's census of Washington Irving materials.[3] Some of those now in private hands were lost until recently, when a portion covering most of sixteen chapters was found, in the spring of 1968, in a trunk in a chicken house where it had lain for some twenty years.

At least six different kinds of wove paper were used, indicating progressive stages in the writing. The sheets of poorest quality and which also seem to be the oldest bear a HUDSON watermark; they are yellowed with some foxing, are a bit brittle, and have some ink blots. A few leaves of paper brought from England (as indicated by several notes on backs of leaves) have no watermark. Similar paper infrequently bears a B D watermark. One leaf has half a watermark, J WHA / 18. The paper used most often by Irving in writing *Astoria,* and which apparently was used in later stages of the writing, is a fine quality linen which bears a BISSELL & PEASE watermark. And appearing for the first time in MS Chapter L is a green-tinted paper with the watermark H & O.

Irving's general habit in using the paper was to take a sheet $7\frac{15}{16}$" by $9\frac{9}{16}$", fold it on the short axis, tear it at the fold, and write on what would then be equivalent to pages 1 and 3 were the folded sheet a leaflet. Many of the folios are composed of two or more leaves or parts of leaves joined together with glue—with several instances of as many as four sections glued together. Irving's numbering is highly erratic and frequently altered, evidences of his attempts to give continuity and coherence to the Astorians' diverse adventures and anecdotes.

There are three major indications that this manuscript was used as printer's copy: (1) Spike holes made by the compositor after setting type for each leaf are observable in practically all the manuscript leaves. (2) Compositors' stints are indicated by signatures which appear at irregular intervals. These are "Thomas" (nine times), "Whitney" (eight times), "Rose" (six times), "Havil[?]" (once), and "Osgood" (once); also the word "Office" appears twice as an apparent stint mark. And (3) numerous stint brackets occur, keyed to beginnings of printed pages (but in a few instances they are off two or three lines).

Because Irving strove throughout the spring and summer of 1835 to

---

3. This appeared originally in the *Bulletin of the New York Public Library* 68 (1964), 13–32, and is reprinted as a supplement to William R. Langfeld's *Bibliography of Washington Irving* (Port Washington, N.Y., 1968).

improve the style of *Astoria*, and more so because he used sections of rough draft manuscript in putting together part of his printer's copy, there are many alterations in the manuscript. If an alteration throws light on a textual problem, it is included in the Discussions of Adopted Readings section. (See, for example, the note in the DAR for 290.28.) It is a practical impossibility, however, to list the variants in the entire manuscript—which would necessitate over 5,000 printed lines in the Appendix. Instead, a list of pre-copy-text alterations in chapter XXXIII is furnished in the Appendix to illustrate characteristic revisions, and alterations in the remaining chapters are on file at the University of Texas.

Most of the alterations are of the kind expected in a rough draft: rephrased lines, selection of a better word, interlineations, added detail— especially names, dates, distances, and sizes—and correction of errors in spelling, punctuation, tense, and agreement. Because at times Irving was splicing together several drafts of the same subject, there are cancellations of material duplicated elsewhere. Sometimes his alterations reflect the choice of alternatives, as in the following: "... no one ventured to put off to the ship, ⟨which lay at anchor with her loose sails flapping in the wind.⟩ ↑deterred by the effects of the fire arms.↓" (76.18–19).[4] Other alterations were made to avoid stating a fact about which Irving was uncertain: "⟨It was known⟩ ↑We have already mentioned↓ that the North West Company had established ⟨a post or⟩ posts to the west of the Rocky Mountains ⟨as early as the year 1806⟩ in a district called by them New Caledonia" (64.14–16). In one instance, Irving added an authorial comment on mutability: "disappeared⟨.⟩—Such changes ⟨*Paragraph* At this place Mr. Hunt remained for some time to complete his assortment of Indian goods⟩ does the lapse of a handful of years make in this ever changing country" (88.21–22). It should be mentioned here that, while Irving sometimes wrote a new punctuation mark over an old one (as with "disappeared⟨.⟩—" above), he habitually did not extend cancellation lines to include punctuation connected with the canceled material. For example, at 181.21 he first wrote: "in the course of this work: some account of them may be"; then he put a comma after "work" and before the colon and crossed out "some ... be." In this and in parallel instances, uncanceled punctuation clearly belonging to a deleted construction is considered to be canceled and consequently is not noted in the List of Emendations.

There is evidence that the *Astoria* manuscript was read and altered by Pierre M. Irving and perhaps others.[5] Pierre M. Irving's notations

4. The angle brackets enclose canceled material and the arrows indicate interlineations.

5. Pierre M. Irving's role in the production of *Astoria* is discussed in the Introduction.

are of two kinds and may well have been made at different times. He provided factual information to fill in blanks, to supply specific names where Irving had only general categories, or to correct details of distance, number, and so on; and he suggested stylistic changes, writing in his alterations in pencil, which Washington Irving later traced over in ink— giving in effect his seal of approval to it. Inevitably Irving missed—or ignored—a few of the penciled corrections or alterations. These were accepted by the printer for the first American edition, and are accepted in the Twayne edition as having been perused and not rejected by Irving. In the following examples of Pierre Irving's alterations, a single asterisk (*) indicates Pierre M. Irving's notation and a double asterisk (**) represents his alteration traced over by Washington Irving. "Commodore ⟨Hull, then commanding the Frigate Constitution, at anchor at New York⟩** ↑Rogers**, at that time commanding at New York↓" (31.28–29). "[R]emorse from his mind. ⟨See Bradbury—p 63.*⟩" (114.27). "⟨[P]resenting⟩* ↑exhibiting↓**" (125.12). "They set forward . . . , keeping to the east north east, towards ↑the↓** lofty ⟨mountain⟩ ↑summit of ⟨one of the Wind River⟩ ↑a↓ mountains↓** which it was necessary for them to cross. ⟨It was, in fact, ↑one of↓ the ⟨Big Horn ridge⟩↑ a point ⟨Wind⟩ of the Wind ⟨Horn⟩ River mountains↓ which Mr Hunt had traversed ⟨in his journey to the⟩ the year before⟩**" (291.37–39). "[P]recipices of red stone ⟨at least five⟩** ↑two↓** hundred feet in height" (293.29). In the following examples, an X penciled on a leaf refers to a notation in a hand other than Pierre M. Irving's on the back of the preceding leaf: "an occasional sea lion X [In Is not the Sea lion annother name for a Seal?]" (333.37); "January X [Whats the year.]" (351.36); and lined out in the margin: "I think my MS will shew the Lat. to be some degrees further North" (near 331.13).

Irving used only one side of his paper to write the *Astoria* manuscript, but the backs of the leaves occasionally contain some interesting fragments of writing. A few of these fragments are abortive segments of the *Astoria* narrative. One is an expense memorandum. A few contain portions of other narratives; an example is found on the verso of the leaf covering 53.17–29: "—I have since visited his tomb. It is in the vault of an old grey country church, at the end of one of the aisles. / a Gothic window." Three are portions of letters to Irving, and fourteen are segments of letters Irving began and then discarded. Perhaps the most interesting of the latter (on the verso of the MS folio covering 280.14–25) is that dated "New York, March 27th 1836" which says, "My dear Sir,/ I met with Capt Bonneville yesterday morning about to depart for the west."

TEXTS

There are two printed editions of *Astoria* which are authorized—that is, which appeared during Irving's lifetime and were corrected or altered by him. The first (symbolized in the following discussion by 1A) was published by Carey, Lea, & Blanchard (Philadelphia, 1836). It appears in two states,[6] and in an 1841 impression which is like the second state in significant variations. The second edition (hereafter referred to as 2A) is volume VIII of the Author's Revised Edition (ARE) and was published in 1849 by George P. Putnam in New York.[7] Additional impressions of this edition appeared in 1851, 1852, 1853, 1854, 1855, 1856, 1857, 1859, 1860, and 1861.

In an effort to detect all substantive and accidental variants between the manuscript and 1A, xerox copies of The New York Public Library and University of Virginia manuscripts were sight collated against the University of North Carolina 1A, and all the manuscripts themselves were read twice against the UNC 1A. Then the first impression of this first American edition was fully collated twice with the aid of the Hinman collating machine against other copies of the first impression, and machine collated against the 1841 impression.[8] No resettings were found

6. These are discussed in Jacob Blanck's *Bibliography of American Literature* (New Haven: Yale University Press, 1969), V, 43–44, no. 10148. The major differences between the first state and the scond state are that the first has a copyright notice and printer's imprint on the verso of the title page and in vol. 2, p. 239, has the garbled footnote: "*Bra6.db ury. P. 6 / * Breckenridge." Neither of these appear in the second state. The copy used in the Twayne edition for copy-text where manuscript is lacking corresponds to the first state described by Blanck. It comes from the University of North Carolina library, call no. V917.8/I72a/1836/v.1[2], and collates as follows: vol. I, 12° (8$\frac{7}{16}$" x 5$\frac{1}{4}$"): 1–24^6, pp. (1), title page; (2), copyright entry and printer's imprint; (3)–6, Introduction; (vii)–xii, Contents; (13)–285, text; (286)–(288), blank. vol. II, 12° (8$\frac{7}{16}$" x 5$\frac{1}{4}$"): 1–23^6, 24^2; plus: 25^4; folded map; (i), title page; (ii), copyright entry and printer's imprint; (iii)–viii, Contents; (9)–279, text and appendix; (280), blank; 1–6, (7), advertisements; 8, publisher's memorandum regarding books advertised. Flyleafs are lacking because the volumes were rebound by the UNC bindery. Other copies examined are identical to this except in having flyleafs and in measuring 8$\frac{5}{8}$" x 5$\frac{5}{8}$" or 8$\frac{11}{16}$" x 5$\frac{5}{8}$".

7. The University of North Carolina library copy of the 1849 edition, call no. F880/.I715, collates as follows: 12° (7$\frac{7}{16}$" x 5$\frac{1}{16}$"): 1^4 p. (1); preceded by four leaves 1*8 2^4 2*8 3–21^{12} 22^8, pp. flyleaf; (i), edition title page; (ii), blank; map; (iii), title page; (iv), copyright notice and printer's imprint; (v)–viii, Introduction; (1)–12, Contents; (13)–519, text and appendix; (520), blank; flyleaf.

8. The pattern for collation was UNC 1A (V917.8/I72a/1836/v. 1[2]) vs. Duke 1A (Tr.R./817.24/I72A) and vs. U. Alabama 1A (917.8/Ir8a/1836). Also spot readings were made against 1A copies from eight other libraries, including a copy of the second state in the Berg Collection at The New York Public Library. The UNC 1A was read against the copy of the Friends' Free Library, Germantown, 1841 (T/917.8/Ir8$_{1[2]}$).

in the 1A machine collations, and only these significant differences were found between 1A and the 1841 impression: the publisher is changed from Carey, Lea, & Blanchard to Lea & Blanchard. The printer for 1A was Henry W. Rees, Stereotyper, 45 Gold Street, New York and for 1841 was T. K. & P. G. Collins, Printers, Philadelphia. As with the second state of 1A—for which permission could not be obtained for a machine reading—in the 1841 impression there is the signature "1*" at 1:5.31, whereas there is none on the corresponding page in 1A; at 1:217.12 the signature is "1" which in 1A is "19"; the garbled footnote at 2:239.19–20 is omitted; page number "50" in volume II is lacking; and at 2:148.4 the 1A "jirked" is changed to "jerked" (as it appears in the manuscript). Other differences are in accidentals, practically all of which are dropped punctuation at the ends of lines in the 1841 impression, and thus are apparently the result of type batter in printing rather than of deliberate change.

There is no evidence that Irving himself read the proofs of the 1836 English edition of *Astoria*. He was in America at the time of printing, and Richard Bentley's records show that all arrangements for publication were made by Colonel Thomas Aspinwall.[9] Furthermore, a sight reading of the first English edition (UNC 917.8/I72a/1836.2/v.1[2][3]) against the first American edition (UNC 1A) shows that the former was set from the 1A page proofs. The English printers not only adopted much of the 1A house style—and errors—but introduced variants of their own, twenty-seven substantive errors appearing in the first ten chapters alone.

Two sight collations were made of 1A vs. 2A, and machine collations were made of the 1849 impression of 2A vs. the 1852 impression and of the 1852 vs. the 1860.[10] No extensive resettings were found in any of the ARE impressions. The 1849 vs. 1852 machine collation disclosed a change of year on the edition title page and the volume title page, a change from the 1849 "LEAVITT, TROW & Co., / Printers and Stereotypers" to the 1852 "JOHN F. TROW, / Printer and Stereotyper," and a dropped "a" before "fearful risk" at 147.6 in 1852. In addition to changes of publisher's imprint on the edition title page and the volume title page, the 1852 vs. 1860 collation showed these substantive differences: 25.8 "magnates" vs. "magnate"; 98.29 "a low" vs. "low"; 124.19 "then a" vs. "then"; 129 signature number "6*" dropped in 1860; 370.1–2 "Woodpile" vs.

9. The unpublished agreement between Bentley and Aspinwall, dated September 5, 1836, is in the Bentley Papers in the British Museum, LIII, 301–2.

10. The copies sight collated were UNC 1A vs. UNC 917.8/I72a/1852 and vs. UNC F880/.I715[1849]. The machine collations were U. of Miami 1849 (917.8/Ir8a/1849) vs. 1852 UNC (917.8/I72a/1852) and UNC 1852 vs. Oberlin 1860 (817.2/I48.1861/v.8).

"Woodvile"; and 509.15 "relics" vs. "relict." A check of the Western Reserve University copy of the 1855 impression (817.24/A8/Cop.1) shows that the above changes were made after 1855. It should be noted that all the above differences in the text come at the beginnings or ends of lines and represent dropped type or type incorrectly replaced. Moreover, in the later impressions there is a considerable amount of dropped punctuation at ends of lines.

Not fully compared are the numerous foreign language editions of *Astoria*, nor the many ARE editions after Irving's death. In this regard it is unfortunate that Edgeley Todd in his thoroughly researched and annotated edition of *Astoria* (Norman, Oklahoma, 1964) chose for his copy-text an 1868 impression of what is purported by Putnam's to be the Author's Revised Edition but in actuality is an edition reset from the initial ARE. This edition contains further corruptions of text, including substantive differences in ninety-six different passages—one of which involves a dropped line and three of which involve three or more word differences.[11]

TREATMENT OF SUBSTANTIVES

As the accompanying List of Emendations indicates, Irving made numerous revisions in the proofs of the first edition of *Astoria*—as he had done in proofs of earlier works.[12] In preparing the ARE, though, he evidently was satisfied with the 1A text of *Astoria*; therefore, he added a paragraph bringing the history of Astoria up to date (356.33–39) and made only a very few alterations—mostly simplifications such as changing "fought with them" to "fought them" (147.42). Of all the substantive variants between 1A and 2A, only eight have the clear mark of being Irving's, many are indifferent readings, and the majority are inferior and appear to be compositors' misreadings or "improvements." The 2A, more so than the 1A, has many careless typographical errors and dropped words, which make variants in that text suspicious. An additional reason

11. These four variants with footnotes indicating the 1A readings, are at pp. 190, 193, 257, and 389 in the Todd text.

12. For a discussion of Irving's general practice of making alterations in the proofs, see Henry A. Pochmann's Textual Commentary in his edition of *Mahomet and His Successors* (Madison: University of Wisconsin Press, 1970), pp. 595–96. In the twenty extant proof sheets of *Diedrich Knickerbocker's A History of New York*, Irving made no alterations in the accidentals but did change a number of substantives. Some of these revisions were the rewriting of phrases or passages; others were the alterations of words such as "this" to "the," "that" to "which," "troops" to "troop," "about" to "around," "has acquired" to "acquired," "into" to "in," and "was" to "were."

for mistrusting the 2A substantive variants is the appearance of seven inferior or questionable variants in the Appendix where Irving is quoting someone else and would have had no cause for changing a word in the ARE. (See especially 1A "barometer" vs. 2A "barometric" at 370.4 and 1A "repress" vs. 2A "depress" at 373.28.) For their part, the 1A compositors had been more careful, but they still misread or overlooked numerous substantives—as the List of Rejected Substantives indicates. The Twayne editor's problem, then, has been to determine the authorial variants in 1A and 2A and to find and reject substantive variants which are not Irving's.

In cruxes regarding the MS vs. 1A substantive variants, the first editorial procedure was to choose the reading which agreed with Irving's source—in all instances where the source is available—as at 7.11 ("our East India men") and 324.33 ("at").[13] The next procedure was to choose the MS over the 1A variant when the 1A form is obviously a misreading of Irving's MS word. Examples of these, with the 1A misreading italicized, are: time *turn* (7.6), carried *caused* (8.3), wintered *ventured* (65.17), fanciful *faithful* (107.37), incited *invited* (132.2), motives *notions* (133.29), bawling *brawling* (145.35), prepared *proposed* (177.35), eighty *eight* (197.37), avoiding *winding* (226.30), corner *canoe* (242.27), alert *about* (277.21), wistful *wilful* (298.43), interim *interior* (310.16), caves *canoes* (333.41), and flouted *flowed* (343.13). A third step was to accept the reading called for in context, as with the MS and 1A "moping" vs. 2A "smoking" at 164.37 or the MS and 1A "bases" vs. 2A "basis" at 174.2.

Irving's intentions can sometimes be determined from alterations in the manuscript (see, for example, Discussions of Adopted Readings for 272.24 and 290.28–29) or from his general habits of revision such as simplifying constructions and avoiding repetition of the same root word. There are instances, though, in which the variants are indifferent in meaning and in which none of the above-mentioned principles can be applied. In such cases, the later authorial form is given precedence over the earlier one. Following are some instances of this in *Astoria,* with the earlier variant appearing in brackets: [islands] islanders (41.32; see Discussions of Adopted Readings); [in] of (45.20); [deciduous trees] trees of deciduous foliage (66.27); [take a] take (176.33); [for them] to them (187.14); [Columbia] the Columbia (200.29); [about] upon (274.35); [for] to (352.5). In the first example, neither variant is completely satisfactory. In the third, modern taste might prefer the simpler "deciduous trees"; yet one reading is as valid as the other. And one

13. See the Discussions of Adopted Readings for these numbers. For a discussion of Irving's sources and his use of them see the Introduction.

difficulty inherent in the sixth example is that in parallel MS passages, Irving wrote it both "the Columbia" and "Columbia."

TREATMENT OF ACCIDENTALS

The great disparity between the accidentals in Irving's fair-copy holograph of *Astoria* and those in the first edition can be attributed mainly to the printer's house style under which the compositors regularized or "modernized" Irving's forms and imposed on his text a heavier system of pointing. Much can be said for largely retaining Irving's original accidentals, not only because they are clearly authorial, but more so because they constitute a suggestive part of his total expression and therefore affect his texture of writing. As Irving says regarding *The Sketch Book* in a letter of July 28, 1819, to Henry Brevoort:

> I have not discovered an error in the printing, and indeed have felt delighted at my genteel appearance in print. I would observe that the work appears to be a little too *highly pointed*. I don't know whether my manuscript was so, or whether it is the scrupulous precision of the printer. High pointing is apt to injure the fluency of the style if the reader attends to all the stops.[14]

The following parallel texts exemplify the high pointing placed upon *Astoria* by the printer and illustrate how a sentence, according to Edgar Allan Poe, "may be deprived of half its force—its spirit—its point by improper punctuation."[15]

	MS	1A
202.1–4	The loose soil which had been put aside is then brought and rammed down firmly to prevent its caving in, and is frequently sprin- kled with water to destroy the scent.	The loose soil, which had been put aside, is then brought, and rammed down firmly, to prevent its caving in, and is frequently sprin- kled with water, to destroy the scent.
353.28–32	The North West Company were now in complete oc- cupation of the Columbia River and its chief tributary streams, holding the posts	The North-west Company were now in complete oc- cupation of the Columbia river, and its chief tributary streams, holding the posts

14. Quoted in Pierre M. Irving's *The Life and Letters of Washington Irving* (New York, 1865), I, 425.

15. *Marginalia* in *The Complete Works of Edgar Allan Poe* (New York, 1902), XVI, 130.

which he had established   which he had established,
and carrying on a trade   and carrying on a trade
throughout the neighboring   throughout the neighboring
region in defiance of the   region, in defiance of the
prohibitory law of Congress,   prohibitory law of congress,
which in effect was a dead   which, in effect, was a dead
letter beyond the Mountains.   letter, beyond the mountains.

Unfortunately there are in 1A many punctuation variants which not only "injure the fluency of the style" but also create ambiguity and error, as in the following parallel examples:

	MS	1A
65.15–16	[David Thompson] had persisted in crossing the mountains with eight men who remained true to him. [*That is, his eight men were the ones who did not desert on the eastern side of the Rocky Mountains.*]	[David Thompson] had persisted in crossing the mountains with eight men, who remained true to him. [*That is, the men stayed with him after crossing the mountains.*]
125.23–24	The roads, made by the tramp of buffalos for many ages, along the face of the heights looked like so many well travelled high ways.	The roads, made by the tramp of buffaloes for many ages along the face of the heights, looked like so many well travelled highways.
227.29–31	The country in general in the neighborhood of the river was a continual plain, low near the water, but rising gradually.	The country in general, in the neighborhood of the river, was a continual plain, low, near the water, but rising gradually.
235.41–236.1	Occasionally they sink a cord in the river by a heavy weight, with a buoy at the upper end to keep it floating.	Occasionally, they sink a cord in the river by a heavy weight, with a buoy at the upper end, to keep it floating.

Judicious emendation of Irving's accidentals is made in the Twayne edition when necessary to correct meaning, prevent misreading, rectify unintentional errors, or help the reader.[16] No attempt has been made

---

16. No normalizations are made in quoted material or in the Appendix unless it is apparent that the compositors have changed Irving's original styling (as with the substitution of "fifty-three degrees" for "53°" at 364.34).

to "Americanize" his spelling, and consistency per se has not been a goal, even if it were possible. Some of Irving's anomalies are attributable to his sources (such as "e'en" at 7.14 and "thro'" at 23.31) or may have been intentional. For example, Irving writes both "savages" and "Savages," "aboriginals" and "Aboriginals." It is conceivable that he meant the capitalized words to be synonymous with "Indians" and the lowercase forms to have a broader meaning of "primitive persons." It should also be remembered that, while the twentieth-century reader has had "correct" spelling, punctuation, and pronunciation drilled into him from first grade through college, and while Carey, Lea, and Blanchard in 1836 and Putnam in 1849 were concerned that Irving's writing be in the "proper" form, Irving himself was using language from the last of the eighteenth and the first of the nineteenth centuries when the forms of words were still flexible. The word which appears as "extacy" in the MS, "exstacy" in 1A, and "ecstasy" in 2A was, during Irving's youth, spelled also "extasy," "ectasy," "exstasy," "ecstacy," "ecstasie," "extasie," and "exstacie." Certainly then one cannot hold Irving to rigorous twentieth-century standards of spelling. Nor can he fault Irving for having various spellings of proper nouns when his sources varied so widely and were inconsistent in themselves. Nevertheless there is ample evidence in the manuscript and text of *Astoria* that Irving was sensitive to the problem of spelling proper nouns, especially Indian names. He frequently wrote "Maha" and then returned later to add an *O* in front of it; he altered "Concomly" to "Comcomly"; he concerns himself with the Indian name "Wash-ing-guh-sah-ba" for "Blackbird" (112.13); and he mentions the alternate names for Arickara Indians (139.6)) and the Cheyenne River (157.43).

Unless there are compelling reasons to the contrary, variants in proper nouns such as "Chopunnish-Chipunnish" (310.3, 28) or "Sowle-Sowles" (Chap. LVII) are thus allowed to stand when they are found in Irving's sources or are indifferently used by Irving. Where no clear preference is apparent, variants in capitalizations such as "Valley-valley" or "Fur trade-fur trade" are retained. Again, variant spellings such as "grizlygrizzly," "chaunt-chant," and "dependent-dependant" are acceptable when justified by any of the dictionaries that might have been available to Irving in the 1830's or when nineteenth-century usage of the variant is recorded in the *Oxford English Dictionary*.[17]

Variants in accidentals are normalized when Irving's clear preference

17. For a discussion of dictionaries available to Irving, see Pochmann, *Mahomet*, pp. 607–9. In addition to *OED*, the dictionaries consulted most frequently in connection with *Astoria* were *Johnson's Dictionary* (Philadelphia, 1819; Boston, 1829) and *Webster's Dictionary* (New York, 1828).

for one form or another can be established. For instance, manuscript alterations of "Calderon Linn" to "Caldron Linn" and "Chinnook" to "Chinook" call for normalization of the former spellings wherever they are overlooked by Irving. His majority preference is taken into account also, and exceptions such as "whitemen" and "Black feet" are normalized to Irving's preferred "white men" and "Blackfeet." Irving's usual practice combines with the need to prevent misreading as reasons for infrequently adding a comma to complete an intended pair—as at 103.19 ("action,"), 107.15 ("researches,"), 117.42 ("Sioux,"), 138.20 ("difficult,"), and 312.30 ("natives,"). Many emendations have to do with filling in punctuation where Irving unintentionally neglected it, particularly at the ends of lines or at the edge of the page, at altered matter, and at interlineations or when splicing together portions of MS. It is as though the appearance of the interlined word or phrase on the page seemed to be sufficient to set it off or that the position at the end of the line had the quality of a pause—as in poetry—which could at times take the place of a comma or semicolon. Then again, Irving's frequent carelessness or indifference in his accidentals created errors which necessitate emendation.[18] The 1A compositors were usually alert to these problems and supplied the needed punctuation. Of course where the MS serves as copy-text, variants in the 1A accidentals are not considered authoritative but are regarded merely as precedents for emendation.

Irving's capitalization also presents editorial problems. As Nathalia Wright points out in her General Introduction to Irving's journals,[19] his whimsical and indiscriminate use of capital and lowercase letters is complicated by certain capital and lowercase letters being indistinguishable in their MS forms. This applies especially to letters such as *a, c, m, n, o, r, s,* and *w* which begin the words in *Astoria* most often in question: "autumn," "winter," "spring," "summer," "north," "west," "south," "army," "navy," "continent," "country," "creole," "savages," "mountains," and "river." Irving's variations in capitalizations are allowed to stand when they are indifferently used (as with "bay" and "Bay" in a place name or "government" and "Government"), when Irving capitalized a word to emphasize it as a name (such as "Rangers of the woods" or "Freemen"), or when he capitalized certain words of Hawaiian or Indian extraction (such as "Quamash," "Kihei," and "Wappatto"). On the other hand, capital or lowercase letters that are clearly exceptions from Irving's usual practice are normalized. Thus the infrequent "Elk" and "Buffalo" are

18. For discussions of Irving's idiosyncracies in accidentals, see Pochmann pp. 573, 580–81, 603ff.

19. In *Journals and Notebooks, Volume I, 1803–1806* (Madison: University of Wisconsin Press, 1969), p. xxi.

emended to the lowercase form in which they usually appear in the text. No emendations are made silently.

In many instances it is impossible to distinguish between a superscript *c* and a single quotation mark in names such as "M'Kay." Furthermore, Irving frequently indicated the ᶜ or ' by a flourish, such as in "M 'Dougall." As in 1A, then, the Twayne *Astoria* normalizes all instances of Mc, M', and M to M', but notes them. On the other hand, superscript letters (usually in connection with abbreviations) are lowered to the line, and underscorings of superscripts, infrequently and inconsistently used by Irving, are disregarded as mannerisms of no import beyond indicating an abbreviation, according to the method explained in *Journals and Notebooks*, I, xxiii.

Word division as it appears in the MS is often as difficult to ascertain as capitalization. Sometimes Irving ran together words that normally would be separated such as "ofthe" and "onehundred." Less frequently, words are separated that are intended to be one word such as "dis charging" (113.20) and "inso much" (162.7). His usual practice was to separate words that were subsequently hyphenated in 1A and in many cases are one word today. Normalization of compounds is made only when Irving's practice elsewhere in *Astoria* shows a strong majority preference. Lists of Irving's practices in the manuscripts for *A Tour on the Prairies*, *Goldsmith*, and *Mahomet* have also served as guides in emendation.

Although Irving's text is faithfully and critically rendered, Twayne Publishers is responsible for the so-called appurtenances of the text— that is, such typographical details as the precise arrangement of the title and half-title pages and other preliminary matter, pagination and lineation, footnote symbols, and the typography of chapter titles, running heads, table of contents, synoptic chapter headings, and footnotes. No separate emendations are made in the table of contents, since it is understood to duplicate the synoptic chapter headings. Except for the details just enumerated, then, the Introduction, the Textual Commentary, and the accompanying Discussions of Adopted Readings, together with the Lists of Emendations, of Rejected Substantives, and of End-of-Line Hyphenations, are designed to provide the reader with all the data needed to reconstruct the copy-text and to follow the steps by which the Twayne text of *Astoria* was established. Beyond this, the assembled evidence is designed not only to enable the reader so minded to examine and consider the bases on which all editorial decisions were made but to reconsider them, if he chooses, and in the process to see the relationships that exist among the several texts, ranging from Irving's manuscript to the present edition.

DISCUSSIONS OF ADOPTED READINGS

In these discussions of decisions to emend or not to emend, the symbols to designate texts used in the Textual Commentary are again employed:

MS	Manuscript used as printer's copy for the first American edition of *Astoria* (1836)
1A	First American edition published by Carey, Lea & Blanchard
2A	Second American edition printed by Putnam's in 1849 as vol. VIII of the Author's Revised Edition
SJ	"On the Fur Tade, and Fur-bearing Animals" in *American Journal of Science and Art* [*Silliman's Journal*] 25 (January, 1834), 311–29, from which Irving quoted part of his Appendix
T	Twayne edition

The page and line figures are keyed in each case to a word or words in the text to which the discussion or comment refers. A bracket separates the key word or words from the comment that follows. Brief comments are also to be found in the List of Emendations and the List of Rejected Substantives.

5.27   continents] If this is not simply the 1A compositor's misreading of Irving's MS configuration of "continents" as "countries," it may be a memorial slip making the construction parallel with that in which "countries" appears at 5.18. There is a certain logic to the MS "continents," since Irving begins the chapter speaking of the Americas.

5.30   colonization] This is most likely a compositor's misreading, since Irving says "Their effect on colonization" in the synoptic heading and he speaks at the end of *Astoria* of Astor's enterprise opening the way to future colonization.

5.33   object] The compositor apparently wanted an agreement with "metals," although Irving intended "object" to signify "objective" rather than "objects of search."

6.11   on] The change of MS "upon" to 1A "on" tends to simplification—a mark of Irving's revisions in the 1A proof. Other examples of simplification are the change of MS "off of" to 1A "off" at 31.28 and the change of MS and 1A "but who" to 2A "who" at 95.37.

6.13 year's] First and last, Irving was notoriously lax in his use of apostrophes. In *Astoria* he rarely used apostrophes for possessives in the MS but apparently left it to the printer to include them.

7.11 our East India men] The difference here between the MS "our East India men" and the 1A "an East Indiaman" stems from a compositor's misreading of "our" as "an." The MS reading is further justified by the plural in Irving's source, Baron Louis Armand Lahontan's *New Voyages to North-America* (London: H. Bonwicke, et al., 1703), and by the parallel with "pirates."

7.34 licences] The MS "licenses" is emended in accord with Irving's otherwise consistent spelling of the word. Irving's preference in spelling is likewise the guide for emending the MS forms "inquire" to "enquire" (44.34), "Nodowa" to "Nodawa" (95.14, 107.10), "backwoodmen" to "backwoodsmen" (92.15), "Clark('s)" to "Clarke('s)" (310.3, 323.34), and "recconnoitre" to "reconnoiter" (323.18).

9.24 with] Irving's slip in writing "with" twice was erroneously set as "with much" by the 1A compositor.

10.18 lake] Irving might have written "lakes" in the MS because he was thinking of the Great Slave Lake and the Lesser Slave Lake, both reachable from Lake Athabasca; or, he might have felt that the force of the sentence with its multiple listing of lakes called for "lakes" at the end. Since Irving had not mentioned the Lesser Slave Lake, though, the 1A reading "lake" is preferable because "the great Slave lake" refers, properly, to only one lake.

10.42 Scotland,] The 1A comma is preferred here to its absence in the MS, because it helps clarify the deferred reference of "characterised."

11.1 climates] Among the reasons for rejecting the 1A variant "climate" in favor of the MS "climates" is the accumulation of compositors' errors in number. Additional 1A variants rejected as errors in number are "frontier" (14.31 "frontiers") and "frontiers" (160.37 "frontier"). In the latter the compositor may have mistaken the comma after "frontier" for an *s.*

11.38 unceremonious] Changes of this nature (MS "*san façon*" to 1A "unceremonious") in which there is no possibility of a misreading or memorial error on the part of the compositor are almost always made by Irving. Here it is likely he translated "*san façon*" (more properly "*sans façon*") because it was isolated as the only foreign language adjective in *Astoria.*

12.37 kinds] There is no justification for the MS idiom "kind" in any dictionary consulted: Johnson's (Philadelphia, 1819; Boston, 1829), Walker's (London, 1824), Webster's (New York, 1828), and *OED.*

14.31 frontiers] See the note for 11.1.

15.23 ship,] The MS "ship" is lacking a needed comma, perhaps be-

cause the word comes at the end of the line in the manuscript—a
position that sometimes provided for Irving a pause equivalent to a
comma. Some other examples are at 49.26 ("ignorance") and 68.12
("gulls"), which unquestionably require commas.

16.26   trade] The MS and 1A noun "trade" (vs. the 2A verb "trade")
is used again as a noun at 16.28 and 24.11.

20.35   government,] The addition in the MS of "and" following "government" calls for the 1A change of a semicolon to a comma.

21.15   as] "As" remains capitalized in the MS, because it was the
beginning of a sentence before Irving revised it.

21.22   companies] Irving's use of a capital for the common noun "companies" seems to be an oversight, because he had become accustomed
to writing "North West Company."

30.36   hard, lie hard,] The MS reading "live hard—lie hard—sleep hard,
eat dogs!" creates an inconsistent sequence. The 1A commas are
adopted, therefore, to aid the reader.

31.1   voyage.] In the MS Irving deleted "for" after "voyage;" and
altered "it" to "It" but neglected to alter the punctuation.

31.22   individual$_\Lambda$] Irving revised the MS by deleting "on his" after
"individual" but neglected to strike the now superfluous comma.

31.28   off] See the note for 6.11.

31.28   harbour,] A large space after "harbour" in the MS suggests
that Irving intended a pause, supplied in 1A by a comma. Likewise,
gaps serving as pauses have been supplied with commas at 41.14
("Roa,"), 86.27 ("stationed,") and 217.39 ("him,").

31.35   embarcation,] Irving probably felt a need for a pause in this
sentence but put it after "instruction" in the MS rather than "embarcation," where it more properly belongs.

31.38   on] Irving first wrote "opinions as to aims" and then canceled
"to aims" but neglected to cancel "as" also.

32.13   natives] One of the hallmarks of Irving's alterations in *Astoria*
is his use of synonyms to avoid repetition of the same word. This
variation of 1A "natives" for MS "Indians" is a typical example.
Similarly, Irving has substituted 1A "nautical" for MS "tarpawlin"
(44.29), "enlisted" for "engaged" (48.25, 88.26), "proper" for "true"
(96.15), and "could" for "would" (110.10). In 2A he has substituted
"cantonments" for MS and 1A "encampments" (264.28).

33.38   importance,] Before the MS was altered, it read "importance
and dignity" so that originally no comma was needed after "importance."

34.21   bystanders] The MS "bye standers" is not sanctioned by Johnson,
Webster, or *OED*. In a rejected leaf of *Astoria* covering this same
material, Irving wrote the word "bystanders."

34.33 night cap] In the MS, "night caps" is altered to "night cap," presumably to be in agreement with "beard," "visage," and "eye." The 1A compositor erroneously retained "nightcaps."

35.27 delicacies," said he, "they] The MS indicates that Irving began to narrate the following two sentences in his own words and then decided to give them in the words of the captain, but he neglected to add quotation marks.

36.30 purpose] The 2A "purposes" rather than "purpose" is an example of the 2A compositors' frequent carelessness regarding plurals. Rejected elsewhere as 2A compositors' errors are "canoes" (102.19 "canoe"), "boats" (137.40 "boat"), "preparations" (177.31 "preparation"), and "visits" (321.27 "visit").

37.29 seemed] The 1A "seemed" for the MS "were" is definitely Irving's change in proof, made, no doubt, because Irving was cautious about the facts in his account and did not want to indicate certainty where it did not exist.

37.39 stood] Irving probably changed the MS "had stood" to "stood" for purposes of simplification and to make "stood" parallel with "made." As is pointed out in the Textual Commentary p. 403, n. 12, this is one of the kinds of changes Irving made in the proof sheets of A *History of New York*.

38.35 she] Irving probably changed "it" to "she" to clarify the antecedent reference to the ship.

38.37 island] In using "island" generically rather than as part of a name, Irving practically always uses lowercase—as, for example, at 38.15, 29, 32.

41.10 Owyhee] The MS spelling "Owhyhee" here and at 42.30 are acceptable variants found in possible source books; but since these are the only exceptions out of eleven occurrences of the word, they are normalized to the 1A form.

41.14 Roa,] See the note for 31.28 ("harbour,").

41.32 islanders] Whether to accept the MS and 1A "islands" or the 2A "islanders" appears to present a problem, for at 42.24–25 Irving speaks of "intercourse between these islands and [Astoria]"; yet in this passage, "islanders" is preferable as being related to the first sentence of the paragraph in which the islanders had occasional intercourse with white men. The intercourse might well be between islands, but islands could hardly be said to have sight of each other. Also "islanders" provides the only proper antecedent for "them" in the following sentence.

44.29 nautical] See the note for 32.13.

44.34 enquire] See the note for 7.34.

45.18 by] Irving originally wrote "by the chieftain Tamaahmaah" but then neglected to cancel "the" along with "chieftain."

45.24 of March,] "Of" is added before "March" to conform to Irving's usual practice. For the same reason, at 184.8 "of" is added before "September."

46.4 savages, too,] The 1A commas are accepted here to retain the sense of "too" as meaning "moreover."

46.38 cocoa nut] This is the only MS occurrence of "coco nut"; at 42.36 and 46.43 it is spelled in the MS "cocoa nut."

47.5 ceremonious] Since "ceremonious" is more correct than the MS "ceremonial" as applied to "visiting," the alteration appears to be authorial.

48.25 enlisted] See the note for 32.13.

50.14–15 altercations$_\wedge$ ... humours,] Irving probably intended, as was his usual practice in constructions such as this, to put the comma after "humours" rather than "altercations," as in 1A.

51.4 mischievous] In addition to "mischivious," Irving spelled this word "meschevous" and "mischevious," which were not considered acceptable variants during the nineteenth century.

51.27 Fox,] "The chief mate" is interlined, but Irving neglected to supply commas to set off the added appositive. In like manner, at 206.43 interlined matter in the MS following "hares" requires a comma; again, at 240.12–13 interlined "reaching ... thigh" in the MS calls for commas after "robe" and "thigh."

52.14 river] The MS form "river mouth" (vs. 1A "river's mouth") is analogous to "river bed" or "mountain top."

53.21 its reflux] In the MS Irving first wrote "the" but then crossed it out and interlined "its," apparently to avoid repeating "tide." He neglected, however, to cross out the now unnecessary "of the tide." Therefore, Irving intended neither the MS "its reflux of the tide" nor the 1A "the reflux of the tide."

56.22 cape] Irving began to write "Cape Disappointment" but then altered it to "this cape" without, however, changing C to lower case.

59.19 a day] There are two reasons for rejecting the 2A reading of "the day": the 2A compositors elsewhere showed carelessness in getting the correct articles; moreover, since McDougall and Stuart stayed with the Indians into the next day, it is not exactly correct to say "the" day.

59.26 April 7th] Although both MS and 1A read "March 7th," April is confirmed as the correct month in 58.13 and 61.11.

61.7 gentlemen,] A canceled word after "gentlemen" in the MS probably obscured the need for a comma here.

61.26 musketry] The MS reading "musquetry" is not found in Johnson or Webster; OED gives no example of it later than 1796.

61.34   the embryo] Irving neglected to cancel "the place" along with "which was to be" which followed in the MS. *OED* gives no example of "embrio" later than 1792, and Irving spelled the word "embryo" at 63.24.

64.37   Stuart,] Irving occasionally omitted the comma after the apposition, but the 1A comma is accepted here, as in a few other recorded instances, as one of an intended pair and to facilitate reading.

66.5   accompanied by] In the MS Irving neglected to write "accompanied" before "by," an idiom employed similarly at 245.22, 250.30, 318.9, and especially 324.27. Trying to correct the anomaly, the 1A compositor omitted "by" and added a comma after "voyageurs."

67.2   or other] Although the 2A variants are often suspect, the 2A "or other" for MS and 1A "or" seems to be a valid change and one Irving would have made to indicate that a rock could also be an eminence.

67.15   sunset] MS "sun set" is normalized to "sunset," the form in which the word appears in the MS at 84.15 and 144.25; furthermore, "sunrise" in this passage is one word.

67.37   Columbia: a] Left as it is in the MS, the material beginning "a lovely meadow" is a sentence fragment. Irving's usual practice calls for a colon before "a."

67.40   Wallámot] The word "Wollámot" in the footnote is emended to agree with "Wallamot" in the text. Later in *Astoria*, however, Irving's variant spellings "Wollamut" and "Wallamut" are accepted.

70.13   active,] Irving's MS alterations of interlining "hardy and" and deleting "race" after "active" call for a comma after "active."

71.10   enameled] As it appears in the MS, "enameled" could very possibly be misread for "ornamented." A parallel use of "enameled" appears at 136.18.

72.23   four-pounders] The 1A hyphen is adopted because it facilitates reading.

74.11   by Shewish,] The addition of "Shewish" in the 1A proof is another example of Irving's search for precision and detail right up to the final copy.

75.4   seven] "Some" in 1A is an easily understood compositorial misreading of the MS "seven." For another reference to "seven" see 75.42. It might be noted in passing that the account of the Tonquin disaster in the *Missouri Gazette* of May 15, 1813, mentions the seven men.

78.5   headstrong] This ends MS p. 4, with the "headstrong &c" in the MS apparently referring back to MS p. 18, the first half of which was not used for the final printed copy. That part of p. 18 as well as all of the unused p. 17 appear in the Appendix.

78.39   foresee." He indulged, however,] The 1A punctuation is called

for because of a cancellation in the MS after "foresee," and the interlineation of "however." "Indulges" was changed to "indulged" and
"seeks" to "sought" to make the tense agree with the rest of the
paragraph.

84.8   the dance] Since the 2A compositors made errors in regard to
articles elsewhere, one may suppose that they slipped when they set
"the song and dance"; for Irving evidently considered the song and
the dance as separate entities and not necessarily joined as in the
2A reading. Other 2A articles rejected are "the" at 89.13 (MS and
1A "a"), "the" at 162.13 in "the trees" (MS and 1A "trees"), and
"the" at 355.33 in "the citizens" (MS and 1A "citizens").

85.9   Blackfeet] "Blackfeet" appears both as one word and as two
words in the MS, although at 124.33 it is hyphenated at the end of
the line, indicating that, at that place at least, Irving definitely wanted
it to be one word. Since there is some doubt that two words are intended, plus the fact that more occurrences than not are clearly one
word, all occurrences of "Blackfeet" or "Blackfoot" are so rendered—
especially 90.11, 121.22, and 271.28.

86.27   stationed,] See the note for 31.28 ("harbour,").

87.35   Here were voyageurs frolicking] Earlier Irving had written
"Here were to be seen" before "voyageurs," but then canceled that
phrase without resupplying a verb for the sentence. The 1A reading
"Here voyageurs frolicked" probably was made by the compositor to
create a sentence out of Irving's fragment "Voyageurs frolicking. . . ."
One problem with the 1A emendation, though, is that "fiddling . . . ,
buying," etc., become examples of how the voyageurs "frolicked away
their wages." This may be true in regard to "buying" but is not
equally applicable to "fiddling" or to "parading." The T emendation
simply takes the first two words from a previously canceled phrase in
order to create a sentence, and then lets the rest stand untouched,
thus rendering what appears to have been Irving's intent.

88.26   enlisted] See the note for 32.13.

88.32   any] Irving originally wrote "any thing they," and then canceled
"they" but neglected to cancel "thing."

89.5   regales$_\wedge$ . . . outfits,] Irving originally wrote "amount, they began
to hint that they" and then deleted "they . . . they," marked a caret
over the comma after "amount," and interlined "and squandered . . .
began to." These alterations possibly caused Irving to misplace the
comma after "regales" rather than "outfits," the latter word having
the same syntactical place as "amount" had in the earlier MS version.

89.13   for a] See the note for 84.8.

89.22   "voyageurs$_\wedge$] Irving first wrote " 'voyageurs' in the New Company." Then he interlined "a" above canceled "the" and interlined

"that was to eclipse the North West." This explains the MS form
" 'voyageurs.' "

89.33   Crooks, . . . man, a native] In the MS, "Mr. Ramsay Crooks" is
interlined. The "a" before "native" may well have been added in 1A
to make that phrase parallel with the preceding one.

90.30   Mackinaw; in] Alterations in the MS call for a stronger pause
than the MS comma after "Mackinaw." Irving had originally written,
"Mackinaw, for there   was a propensity . . ." and then canceled the
phrase after "Mackinaw," substituting for it "in . . . propensity."

90.39   yelps] It is likely that the 2A compositor considered 1A "yelps"
an error for "yells." Yet Irving uses the word elsewhere, most notably
at 13.6–7 where he speaks of "Indian yelps and yellings."

92.15   backwoodsmen] See the note for 7.34.

92.38   made] It is possible that Irving made this change from pluperfect
to past tense (MS "had made" to 1A "made") in order to indicate
that Lisa's acquainting himself with the tribes was not necessarily of
a piece with his ascension almost to the source of the Missouri.

92.41   Arickara] Irving had great difficulty with this name, spelling it
variously "Ricara," "Rikara," "Rickara," "Aricara," "Arikara," and
"Arickara." This eventually led him to allude to his struggle with
the word when he speaks (139.6–7) of the "village of the Ricaras,
Arickaras or Ricarees, for the name is thus variously written." Irving's
final preference was "Arickara," which will be used throughout. In
the MS, especially in Chapter XX ff., he altered or canceled the following in perference to "Arickara": "Arikara," "Rikara," "Aricara," and
"Ricara." There is also one instance of his discarding "Rickara" in
favor of another form. The following MS forms have been normalized:
"Ricara(s)": 127.10, 129.26, 130.32, 132.28, 31, 42, 134.4, 139.29, 140.7,
145.12, 17; "Rikara(s)": 136.5, 12, 137.33, 138.2, 7, 143.3; "Arikara":
138.29; "Rickaras": 136.4, 138.39; and "Aricara": 154.6.

93.1   *No paragraph* This] Although Irving's MS began the new paragraph here, his or the printer's decision to begin it at 93.4 instead
attaches the sentence "This . . . voyageurs." to the preceding paragraph
where it more properly belongs, and rightly allows "All these circumstances" to apply to all the preceding details rather than merely the
number and character of the men in Lisa's employ.

94.15   another∧] In the MS Irving interlined "was" after "another,"
but neglected to delete the now unnecessary comma.

94.17   barge; the] The 1A form "barge; the" follows Irving's usual
punctuation in a series such as this better than does the MS "barge:
The"; also, Irving changed the nature of his initial sentence by interlining "was" after "other."

95.14   Nodawa] See the note for 7.34.

95.36–37   Virginia, who] See the note for 6.11.

96.15   proper] See the note for 32.13.

96.19   1811] The MS "1810" is incorrect. Hunt started his journey in 1810 (see 86.1), but at this point in his travels the correct year is 1811.

98.30   Lisa∧] The deletion in the MS of an appositional phrase following "Lisa," eliminates the need for a comma.

100.43   March] The correct month is March rather than January, as is clear in Irving's source, John Bradbury, *Travels in the Interior of America* . . . (London: Sherwood, Neely, and Jones, 1817), pp. 11, 15–16.

101.15   were] Irving probably changed MS "was" to 1A "were" to agree with "they were" in line 16.

102.19   canoe] See the note for 36.30.

107.39   at] MS "at" was probably misread as "of" by the 1A compositor.

110.10   could] See the note for 32.13.

110.18   a charge] The 1A phrase "a charge" is preferred to the 2A "charge" as parallel with "a single."

113.31   to] The 1A "of" rather than the MS "to" was possibly a memorial slip or an anticipation of "capable of love."

119.1   on] Irving originally wrote "of" (which was erroneously set by the 1A compositor) and then interlined "on" to take its place.

120.17   23d] The 2A reading "23d" rather than the MS "22d" is confirmed in John Bradbury's *Travels in the Interior of America,* Irving's source for this passage.

120.28   other perils] The 2A "other perils" is more logical than the MS and 1A "perils," since the Sioux Tetons definitely are a peril, too.

123.31   voyagers] The MS "voyageurs" is an error here, since the hunters can be "voyagers" but clearly are not in the category of the Canadian "voyageurs."

125.5   the] In setting "his," the 1A compositor evidently neglected to see that, while Irving originally had "his," he then wrote "the" over the top of it.

128.36   statues.] In the MS a deleted "the" follows "statues:" and thus in the altered construction a period is in order.

130.38   thoughtless∧] Irving changed the MS "Indian hostilities are incessantly provoked by the individual outrages of idle, thoughtless, or mischevious white men" to "outrages . . . men" which no longer requires a comma after "thoughtless."

131.38   was] Evidently Irving changed MS "were" to 1A "was" in order to provide agreement with "file."

132.40   June] Bradbury, whom Irving is following here, correctly names the month as June—as does Irving at 137.31.

133.12 left him] In setting "left" rather than "left him" the 1A compositor evidently misread "whom" for "when," an error which necessitated canceling "him."

133.25 gallantly] Perhaps the 1A "gently" was erroneously supplied because of similarity of sounds. Certainly the MS "gallantly" much better fits the description of Lisa's party, which had "strained every nerve" to overtake Hunt's party.

136.4 Left] Irving clearly intends "Left handed" to be a proper noun and capitalizes the name at 138.31, 142.6, 20, and 143.13.

137.40 boat] See the note for 36.30.

138.18 Arickaras] That the 1A plural rather than the MS singular was intended is indicated by Irving's rejected MS forms, "Ricaras" and "Arikaras."

138.33 who] The 1A compositor probably misread Irving's colon preceding "who" for a semicolon and altered "who" to "he" for grammatical correctness. It should be noted that Irving canceled "he was called" and interlined in its place, "who was known by the name of."

138.38 frontier,] The semicolon after "frontier" in the MS belongs to a rejected construction.

139.20 canoes,] Irving interlined "each" after "canoes," but he overlooked adding a comma.

139.26 rivers] The MS "rivers" rather than the 1A "the rivers" is correct, since Irving was making a generalization here and had no specific rivers in mind.

139.34 heard.] The MS and 1A semicolon after "heard" is incorrect, since Irving begins the next clause with a capitalized "This," indicating his intention of beginning a new sentence.

140.4–5 negotiation$_\wedge$] "Negociation" is normalized to "negotiation" to agree with the form which in every other instance is used in the MS. The removal of a comma from the MS and 1A form is called for by the interlineation of "had arranged," which followed Irving's cancellation of "It had been arranged by" and interlineation in its place of "Seeing . . . Lisa,".

140.21 between] The MS "between" seems more appropriate than the 1A "between the," since no mention has been made yet of cabins.

142.6 friendship] The MS "friend ship" is split at the end of a line. At a parallel end-of-line compound, however, "friendship" is hyphenated (141.37), and in another instance (141.30) it is one word.

143.31 were] The MS "were" as opposed to the 1A "are" is logical here, with the first two sentences of the paragraph dealing with Indians in general (and thus the present tense) and the last two pertaining to the Arickaras (whose actions described here took place in the past).

144.3 a] Irving first wrote "an honorable service"; then he deleted "honorable service" and added "species of service" neglecting to change "an" to "a."

146.28 expeditions] The 1A plural "expeditions" is more logical than the MS "expedition," since "several parties" are involved.

147.1 Cheyenne] At 147.11, Irving originally wrote "Chayenne" and then altered it to "Cheyenne," thus indicating his preference.

148.38 trophies] In the MS "the" following "trophies," is deleted; hence the comma becomes superfluous.

155.17 prairies] Since "prairies" comes at a place where pieces of MS are glued together, it could be a misreading as "plains" or perhaps a memorial error from the earlier "plains," line 14. A parallel with "lower prairies" is found in "elevated prairies," 155.26.

156.32 prairie,] Irving originally wrote "prairie." and then interlined after it "a sight." Since Irving provided no punctuation to replace the period, a comma is accepted in accord with Irving's usual practice.

159.8 thirty-six] The 1A form "thirty-six," for which MS is lacking here, is emended to follow Irving's usual form in compound numbers.

160.23 barter∧] The deletion in the MS of "so[me]" after "barter," obviates the need for a comma.

160.37 frontier] See the note for 11.1.

162.13 trees] See the note for 84.8.

167.12 had] The tense of MS "has" is changed in 1A to agree with "was found" in line 13. What Irving probably had in mind originally was agreement with "describes" and "compares" of the preceding sentence.

170.21 rifle,] The 1A comma is accepted as one of an intended pair to clarify the reference of "it" to "tree."

173.2 along] "Along" is a better word for the context, meaning "in a line with the length" as contrasted with "near to in place" for "about." The usage compares with that at 295.16. Also Irving may have made the change to avoid using "about" twice in the same sentence.

173.21 forty] The MS variant "forty" (as opposed to the 1A "fifty") is verified in the translation of Wilson P. Hunt's journal in Phillip Ashton Rollins' edition of *The Discovery of the Oregon Trail: Robert Stuart's Narratives* ... (New York: Charles Scribner's Sons, 1935), pp. 282–84.

173.35 early] Since this is not a likely misreading, the substitution of 1A "early" for MS "earliest" probably represents Irving's making the reference less exact.

174.14 sometimes of] Since "sometimes" is slightly blurred in the MS and the word that follows it is deleted, the 1A compositor probably thought that "sometimes" was to be deleted also.

174.41   is] Irving first wrote "Here also are the Towns of the" and then neglected to cancel "are" along with "the Towns of the."

177.16   galled] The 1A version "galled" vs. the MS "their galled" avoids an imprecise reference in which "their" may possibly refer to "Crows."

177.31   preparation] See the note for 36.30.

178.7   companion,] The 1A comma after "companion," is retained to clarify the reference to "companion."

178.25   mountain] The 1A singular is required to be in accord with "it" in the next clause.

184.8   14th of] See the note for 45.24.

184.19   on] The MS "On" originally began a sentence. The 1A compositor correctly changed it to "on."

187.21   them] The 1A "them" was substituted for MS "him" probably to agree with "their" in line 22.

189.12   had hitherto] The 1A compositor in setting "had" evidently missed Irving's interlined "hitherto."

190.18   hearts∧] The necessity of a comma is removed by the deletion after "hearts" of "though to an unpractised mind, their individual courses into the bosom of the wilderness seem as hazardous as."

191.8   Robinson,] A deleted "and" follows "Robinson" in the MS. Irving neglected to substitute a comma.

191.24   sleet.] While deleting a clause following "sleet;" in the MS, Irving neglected to alter the punctuation.

192.3   departure] The appearance of "departure" in the MS led the compositor to read "separation."

193.11   Company] Irving almost always capitalizes "Company" when it is a proper noun.

194.37   pea green] The 1A "pea-green" is emended to conform to Irving's usual practice; also he wrote "pea green" in his "Memd for Astoria."

195.43–196.1   never before] Technically, the 2A construction "never been" makes the passage incorrect, since part of the river (behind them) had been navigated by white men (themselves).

196.13   wide-wandering] In this page of material for which MS is lacking, there are the hyphenated compounds: "wide-wandering," "pains-taking," "quiet-loving," and "all-pervading" [*end of line hyphenation*]. Irving's usual practice was to separate possible compound words such as "death denouncing," "hard riding," "horse stealing," "way laying," and "wild looking"; yet he also wrote "allpervading" and "neverfailing." Consequently, the 1A hyphenations here are retained, since it cannot be clearly determined whether Irving wrote these particular compounds as one word or two words.

199.5   Devil's Scuttle Hole] Although the MS reads "devils Scuttle hole," in an earlier cancellation Irving wrote it "The Devi" and at 203.10 he wrote it as here emended.

200.6   day] The MS "days" is Irving's slip. Hunt, Irving's source, says they returned the next day.

200.10   them;] An interlineation in the MS of "the . . . unnavigable" calls for the 1A semicolon.

201.43   dry grass, bark,] For MS "dry grass" vs. 1A "dried grass" compare 201.40. The omission in 1A of "bark" is probably to be explained as compositor's eye-skip.

205.14   November] That the month is November rather than October is confirmed at 197.40 and 207.3.

206.40   sometimes] Irving's deletion in the MS of "made of" after "were" in line 39 makes the MS "of" after "sometimes" unnecessary.

206.43   hares,] See the note for 51.27.

207.36   prairie] Although Irving used both singular and plural forms of this word, the MS "prairie" here agrees with "prairie" earlier (206.9). Moreover, Wilson Price Hunt uses the singular in the diary that undoubtedly was Irving's main source for this passage.

207.40   of some of] Evidently the 1A compositor set only "of" rather than "of some of" because his eye skipped from one "of" to the other. Hunt records that "several Canadians had begun to drink their urine" and thus confirms the MS "some."

212.22   Gardepie] The name appears correctly as "Gardepie" rather than "Sardepie" at 162.32 and is confirmed in Kenneth W. Porter's "Roll of Overland Astorians," *Oregon Historical Quarterly* 34 (1933), 107.

216.30   river,] In altering the sentence in the 1A proof, Irving neglected to change the semicolon to a comma.

217.39   him,] See the note for 31.28 ("harbour,").

220.5   unknown] The 1A "lonesome" for the MS "unknown" is probably a compositorial misreading, since the MS configuration of "unknown" looks something like "lonesome."

223.9   for four] Hunt confirms that the travelers saw no sun from the second to the sixth.

225.4   or] The MS and 1A "nor" probably resulted from Irving's anticipation of "nor" in the next clause. The word is emended to conform to Irving's usual practice and to be grammatically correct.

226.31   great bend] In the MS the word "great" is so poorly formed that it is only with considerable difficulty that one can make it out. The compositor undoubtedly could not decipher it and just skipped over it. The context clearly indicates that Irving intended "great bend."

228.20 first day] Since the house style of the 1A printer called for putting dates into numerical form, "day" in the MS reading "first day" would have been out of place—which explains the 1A reading "first."

228.22 Long] Irving altered "narrows" to "Narrows" but neglected to capitalize "long" as he had at 69.9, 33.

229.39 *Chapter X, 69.29–70.33] Irving placed an asterisk after "work" at 229.8 but neglected to include the footnote called for—which obviously is a reference to the location of the earlier mention of Wish-ram.

236.31 serviceberries] The MS "service berries" is altered to accord with the form of Irving's other "-berries" compounds.

240.4 round∧] Since "with" is interlined in place of "their eyes," the semicolon after the MS "round" no longer applies.

240.12–13 robe, . . . thigh,] See the note for 51.27.

246.35 vagabonds] "Vagabonds" (MS and 1A) and "vagrants" (2A) are similar in meaning as well as appearance, and it is possible that the 2A compositor was simply careless here. For a parallel use of "free-booting" coupled with "vagabonds" see 258.26, 36.

250.5 the fight] The 1A variant "the fight," meaning "the battle," better fits the context than the 2A "fight."

253.5 on] The more idiomatic "on" (as opposed to 1A "at") agrees with the synopsis in the 1A table of contents.

256.27 André] Robert Stuart throughout the "Travelling Memoranda" spells the name "André Vallée." In setting "Andri" the 1A compositor probably misread Irving's accented é for an i.

258.19 captors] It is likely that Irving wrote "captors" in the MS (which is lacking for this page) and it was misread as "captives." At any rate, the 1A "captives" is obviously incorrect here—and was emended in the 1868 edition of Astoria.

263.15 Michel] In the absence of MS, the 1A reading "Michael" is emended to agree with Irving's spelling of "Michel" in the MS at 220.18 (which was also set erroneously as "Michael" by the 1A compositor).

264.8 10th] Although the 1A (with MS lacking) reads "20th," the date is the 10th in Stuart, Irving's source. Possibly Irving's 1 was misread for a 2.

264.28 cantonments] See the note for 32.13.

265.32 in] It is possible that Irving considered "every" unnecessary in the MS and 1A construction "in every," and deleted it in 2A.

267.26 Mr. Joseph] Irving usually distinguishes the partners from the other men by calling them "Mr." Presumably the 1A compositor omitted "Mr." from the MS "Mr Joseph Miller" to make the names in the series more alike.

270.14–15 had . . . found] The compositor misread "had" as "did" and then changed the tense of the verb to agree with "did." In doing so he also overlooked that the past tense is preferable as agreeing with the following verb, "forgot."

271.2 travellers] The MS reads "Bewildered travelling," but 271.29–30 ("they soon became bewildered") shows that 1A "travellers" is more appropriate here.

271.15 a] Since Irving has a comma after "wormwood," the 2A "a plant" is syntactically better than the MS and 1A "of a plant" and probably represents Irving's revision for the Putnam edition.

272.24 Stuart] The context here clearly calls for "Stuart" rather than "Crooks"; moreover, at 272.29 Irving first wrote "Crooks" and then canceled it to write "Stuart."

273.14 now kept] The compositor may have assumed that "now" was redundant; but if "kept" in the MS "now kept" has the force of "continued to travel," then "now" helps provide a transition from the scene dealing with the Crow chieftain. Also, earlier they had been traveling "eastward" (271.7) but now are traveling "due east."

274.36 the river] The MS and 1A version "the river" more so than the 2A "a river" properly refers back to Mad River (see 274.16).

277.9 long long] The compositor, who set simply "long," undoubtedly thought Irving had made a mistake in writing "long long." However the two words appear in the middle of a sentence, whereas Irving's other double words usually appear on split lines, at the bottom of one page and the top of the next, or next to alterations. Moreover, a phrase out of an old song, "There's a long long trail a'winding," suggests the legitimacy of the double usage.

277.24 camp.] Deleted matter follows in the MS, but Irving failed to substitute a period for the comma.

283.15 a terrific] The "a" is added in conformity with Irving's usual practice, as at 170.37, 198.18, and 274.43.

283.38 swamps] The 1A plural seems more appropriate here as related to "streams." Also the word appears as "swamps" in Stuart, Irving's source.

285.7 pale,] After the MS "pale" there is a deleted "and," but Irving failed to supply a comma.

285.41 none such] In the MS and 1A construction "none such" (as opposed to 2A "none"), "such" places a proper emphasis on tidings of "good cheer" as opposed to tidings concerning M'Lellan.

289.9 felt] Not only is the MS "felt" manifestly superior to the 1A "to be felt" in this context, it is also the kind of simplified verbal construction that Irving preferred.

290.28–29   tending] Irving first wrote that the party traveled in the Crow track which "led them across mountain streams, and along ridges, and ⟨across⟩ through narrow valleys, all the while tending towards the ⟨East⟩ south east." Then he qualified his statement by canceling "the while" (meaning to cancel "all the while") and interlining "generally." His clear intention is that "tending" refers back to "party" rather than to "streams," "ridges," and "valleys."

291.38   mountain] The MS plural remains uncorrected after an earlier cancellation. Irving had first written "summit of one of the Wind River mountains" and then canceled "one ... River" and interlined "a."

293.3   direction∧] Following "direction;" in the MS, Irving wrote and then canceled, "suffering much from the harsh winds and nipped by the wintry blasts;". With this deletion, the punctuation after "direction" seems no longer needed.

297.27   scouts,] After MS "scouts;" Irving has deleted "& in their ample store of creature comforts"; the 1A punctuation is therefore more appropriate.

298.21   absence,] A comma is called for by the interlineation of "during ... absence."

299.24   lieutenant,] Irving originally wrote, "The chief and his lieutenant passed the night. ..." His revision requires the comma that he neglected to add.

302.17   wastes∧] The cancellation in the MS of "it" before "might" calls for the removal of the comma after "wastes."

302.35–36   suspended∧] Irving had originally written: "suspended; the spits and camp," but neither the MS semicolon nor the 1A comma are necessary in the revised construction.

302.36   parts of] The omission of "parts" before "of" in "the choicest of the buffalo meat" was probably Irving's oversight. For a parallel construction see 299.36.

302.37   tongues∧ ... bones,] It appears that Irving felt a need for a comma after his details but erroneously put it after "tongues" rather than "bones."

307.36   Pacific∧] In the MS Irving first ended the sentence with "Pacific." but then added the rest of the sentence as it now stands.

308.18   the means] In the MS "the" is interlined in the margin where the compositor apparently missed it.

310.3   Clarke's] See the note for 7.34.

310.28   hardy] In an earlier MS version Irving had begun to write "hardy" and then canceled it in favor of "sordid." Since the 1A variant "hardy" is not a likely misreading of the MS "sordid," it seems probable that Irving changed his mind again. Certainly "hardy" better fits the nature of the tribe.

311.43 Shahaptan] Although the MS spelling here is "Shahaptin," the word elsewhere (315.4 and 316.32) appears as "Shahaptan."

312.43 caches] Irving considers "cache" to be plural in the phrase "in *cache*" at 317.30. Since the MS and 1A "cache" in this passage lacks italicization, the 2A "caches" is necessary, as in 313.5.

313.36 who,] In the MS "had been dela[yed]" is canceled after "who"; thus the 1A comma is in order.

314.22 Arapahays] Irving makes a distinction between Arapahays and Arapahoes at 268.3 and has a special use of "Arapahays" again at 297.42, 298.19–20, and 300.11. Thus the MS "Arapahoes" is emended to 1A "Arapahays."

315.10 Nez percés] The 1A (MS is lacking) has incorrectly "Nezperce's." The name appears as "Nez Percés" in the Contents.

316.38 M'Kenzie] A canceled "account" follows "MKenzies" in the MS.

318.37 Indians] The MS reads "Indians in" because Irving forgot to cancel "in" along with other matter.

318.39 assemblage] Although "assemblage" and "assembly" are nearly the same in meaning, the MS and 1A "assemblage" is preferred, because it refers to a less formal gathering of persons and because in 1A "assemblage" appears on two lines and was probably read hastily by the 2A compositor as "assembly."

319.40 M'Kenzie] To be correct, the 2A version "Mr. M'Kenzie" would have to read "Messrs. M'Kenzie and M'Tavish. . . ."

320.3–4 correspondent] The 1A compositor probably modernized Irving a bit with his substitution of "corresponding" for the MS "correspondent." According to *OED* it was not until the nineteenth century that "corresponding" began superseding "correspondent" when the word meant "answering to something else in the way of mutual adaptation or fitness."

321.27 visit] See the note for 36.30.

323.18 reconnoiter] See the note for 7.34.

323.34 and they] The 1A "They" substituted for MS "and they" is suspected as a compositorial "improvement," because there are a number of other instances in which the compositor has broken Irving's longer sentences into two parts.

324.33 at] Possibly the compositor misread the MS "at" as "of." Certainly a document of the official proceedings of Astoria which formed one of Irving's sources for this passage says, "Mr. Duncan McDougall shall continue at this place as usual with a party consisting of Forty. . . ." (See T. C. Elliott, "Sale of Astoria, 1813," *Oregon Historical Quarterly* 30 [March, 1932], 45.)

324.41 hunters and eight common] Irving's slip "hundles[?]" was correctly read "hunters" by the compositor. The resolution from which Irving drew this (see Elliott, "Sale of Astoria," p. 45) says, "Mr. Donald McKenzie shall go and winter in the Wallameet or thereabout, with four hunters and eight men."

326.19 which was] In the MS Irving canceled "was provided" after "which" and neglected to restore "was."

329.9 exerted] The MS incorrectly reads "shewn exerted" because Irving interlined "exerted" but neglected to cancel "shewn."

329.24 feathers,] The 1A comma is necessary to help clarify the ambiguous reference of "attended."

331.35 dependants∧] The MS comma after "dependants" belongs to an earlier construction in the MS.

332.22 captain] Irving's usual practice was not to capitalize "captain" when used in a generic sense.

336.15–16 Astoria, ... fate∧] Although the MS has a comma after "fate" and none after "Astoria," Irving's usual practice would have been to place the comma after "Astoria" rather than "fate."

336.30 Sindbad] Elsewhere in the MS the name appears as "Sindbad." Here it is altered by another hand to "Sinbad."

338.9 Commodore Porter] Irving's intention to say "Commodore Porter" rather than just "Porter" is indicated by the canceled phrase "While sojourning there Commodore" which was replaced by the phrase "He had not been there long when." Moreover, at this first introduction of Porter in the narrative it was necessary to identify him as "Commodore Porter."

338.26 exorbitant,] Following "exhorbitant;" in the MS is the deleted matter, "Mr Hunt could not think of subjecting the."

338.37 might] In the MS after "he might" Irving deleted "have some tidings of her at."

340.17 natives] Irving was probably responsible for this logical change from MS "the natives" to 1A "natives," since up to that point in the narrative Hawaiian natives had not been mentioned.

341.4 on] In the MS Irving neglected to cancel "in" after he interlined "on a."

345.2 capture; that] The MS and 1A "capture. That" is emended to follow Irving's usual practice of avoiding sentence fragments.

346.7 Of] Irving's intention here is unclear. The MS reads: "war. ⟨The Astorians were now⟩ but of What nation?" with an ink blot covering the *b* in "but."

346.11 M'Tavish,] The 1A comma is necessary, because in the MS Irving first wrote "M'Tavish embarked" and then canceled "embarked" after "M'Tavish."

348.34 erected] There is a slight possibility that the 1A compositor erred in reading MS "hoisted" as "erected." However, the latter is at least as satisfying in the context as "hoisted" and probably represents an authorial alteration in proof.

351.9 Wallah Wallah] In the MS vol. II, chap. XIV.21, Irving has changed "Walla Wallah" to "Wallah Wallah," a clear indication of his preference.

352.19–20 rocky mountains near] In the MS Irving is careful to make a clear capital *R* for "Rocky Mountains." In this passage the *r* is clearly lowercase. Misconstruing Irving's intent, the compositor capitalized "Rocky" and added "the" before it.

352.37 Others] In the MS Irving canceled material before "others" but neglected to capitalize the *O*.

354.8 Government] Given the 1A compositors' habits of rendering "government" lowercase in each instance, it is understandable that the person setting this passage would add an article to clarify the meaning. However, "Government" as it appears in the MS carries here a meaning parallel with "Congress" in line 13 below.

355.28 view; for, had] It was a frequent 1A compositorial habit to divide Irving's sentences in two or to fuse two sentences into one. However in this case the addition in 1A of "for" to emphasize the logical connection of the two parts might well be Irving's. An additional clue to this being an authorial revision is that it comes at the beginning of a lengthy revision.

355.33 citizens] See the note for 84.8.

361.33 our] This appears as "our own" in *The Writings of Albert Gallatin,* ed. Henry Adams (Philadelphia, 1879), II, 503–5. Other substantive differences between Irving's and Adams' versions of the Gallatin letter are as follows: 361.34 these] 1A; those, *Writings of Gallatin;* 362.26 accordingly] 1A; accordingly by duplicate, *Writings of Gallatin;* 362.28–30 The ... enterprise.] 1A; *No paragraph* The letters were sent, one copy by a War Department express going to General Hull's army, then on its march to Detroit, and the duplicates given to you to be forwarded as you might think proper.

I was informed, either by the collector of Detroit or by yourself, and, as I believe, by both, that Michilimackinac was taken by the Indians before the letter directed to the collector had reached him, and that either the attempt was made too late or that your agents had failed in carrying it into effect. (*Writings of Gallatin.*)

363.2 those] The 1A "those" as opposed to the 2A "these" and the 1A "very" (363.14) as opposed to the 2A "most" are confirmed in *The Writings of Albert Gallatin,* ed. Henry Adams (Philadelphia, 1879), II, 505.

364.31   countries$_\wedge$ ... Pacific$_\wedge$] This emendation of accidentals follows
Irving's usual practice and agrees with the article "On the Fur Trade,
and Fur-bearing Animals," *American Journal of Science and Art* 25
(January, 1834), 311–29. The material in 1A from 363.22 to 364.24 was
paraphrased from this article; that from 364.25–30 was added by
Irving; and that from 364.31 to the end was quoted directly except
in the few instances noted in the List of Emendations and in the
following discussion.

364.31–369.2 The following substantive difference between this section
of the Appendix and the article in *Silliman's Journal* (SJ) from which
it was quoted are considered to be Irving's and therefore are not
emended.

    364.35   while] 1A; from which SJ

    364.37   California] 1A; the coast of California SJ

    365.25   trade.] 1A; trade."* SJ. In SJ there is a footnote reference
           to "Aikin on Furs" here. Other footnotes which Irving did
           not include are to sentences or paragraphs ending at 366.35,
           367.23, 38, 368.13, 17, 21.

    366.37   Aleutian] 1A; the Aleutian SJ

    368.19   is] 1A; are SJ

365.12   with] In this context, "with" makes more sense than "in" as
regards export trade with Mexico.

365.26–34   These two paragraphs were added by Irving. In SJ there
is no break between the material in line 25 and that in line 35.

370.4   barometer] "Barometric" is obviously wrong, because it was
not measurements that were taken; also "barometric" calls for removal
of "the" preceding it. Furthermore, in *The Rocky Mountains* (Philadelphia: Carey, Lea, and Blanchard, 1837), I, 246, Washington Irving
uses the phrase "of the barometer and trigonometric measurement" in
referring to the Renwick letter.

LIST OF EMENDATIONS

In this list of changes in the copy-text, the following symbols are used to designate the sources of the readings:

MS   Manuscript used as printer's copy for the first American edition of *Astoria* (1836)

1A   First American edition published by Carey, Lea, & Blanchard

2A   Second American edition, printed by Putnam's in 1849 as volume VIII of the Author's Revised Edition

SJ   "On the Fur Trade, and Fur-bearing Animals" in *American Journal of Science and Art* [*Silliman's Journal*] 25 (January, 1834), 311–29, from which Irving quoted part of his Appendix

T   Twayne edition

The numbers before each note indicate the page and line. Chapter numbers, chapter or section titles, epigraphs, author's chapter or section summaries, texts, quotations, and footnotes are included in the line count. Only running heads and line-spaces added by the printer to separate running heads from the text are omitted from the count.

These notes identify all emendations of the copy-text. The reading to the left of the bracket is the portion of the text under consideration or discussion and represents an accepted reading that differs from the copy-text. The source of the reading is identified by symbol after the bracket. In all cases where a difference between the MS and 1A is not specifically noted, the two are to be presumed identical; the same holds true for the 1A and 2A.

The reading after the semicolon is the rejected reading of the copy-text and any other text in which that reading appears. If other alternatives are also available, or if further explanatory comment is needed, the editorial remarks follow in italics.

The swung (wavy) dash ∼ represents the same word, words, or characters that appear before the bracket, and is used in recording punctuation variants; the caret ∧ indicates that a mark of punctuation is omitted. T signifies that a decision to emend or not to emend has been made on the authority of the editor of *Astoria* in the Twayne edition. Some of these editorial decisions are explained among the Discussions of Adopted Readings, which include decisions to emend as well as some decisions not to emend. Discussion is identified by an asterisk *. Brief notes in the List of Emendations itself are italicized.

A number of errors or omissions calling for emendations are attributable to certain aspects of Irving's holograph or to the physical makeup of the manuscript leaves. (See the Textual Commentary pp. 399–400.) Occurring most frequently is Irving's neglect to place a needed punctuation mark after a word which came at the end of the line in the manuscript—perhaps because that position provided a pause equivalent to a comma or sometimes a period. This cause for emendation is signified in the List of Emendations by *End of line*. *Edge of page* signifies that needed punctuation is lacking because Irving wrote to the edge of the MS page. Some errors occur at places in the manuscript where Irving spliced together segments of manuscript leaves. Errors or lapses in punctuation are also frequently associated with the *interlineation* of words or phrases in the manuscript.

3.4	North West] T; North-West 1A. *Emended here and at 256.14, 363.22 and 369.28–29 (where MS is also lacking) to conform to the consistent MS spelling.*
3.12	Sindbads] T; Sinbads 1A. *Emended to Irving's MS spelling.*
3.19	enterprizes] T; enterprises 1A. *Irving's consistent MS spelling* enterprize(s) *is accepted here and in the following instances in which MS is lacking:* 3.33, 39, 4.7, 18, 35, 192.31, 193.1, 7, 208.39, 253.9, 254.9, 255.35, 320.16, *and* 364.22, 27.
4.14	commonplace] T; common-place 1A. *Emended to Irving's usual MS form.*
5.1	CHAPTER I] T; Chap 1. MS; CHAPTER I. 1A. *All chapter numbers are normalized to the T form. The MS forms appear in parentheses as follows:* I (Chap 1), II (Chap 2), III (Chap 3), IV (*Chap 4*), V (Chap 5), VI (Chap 6), VII (Chap 7), VIII (Chap 8.), IX (Chap. 9), X (Chap 10.), XI (Chap 11.), XII (Chap. 12.), XIII (Chap 13;), XIV (Chap 14.), XV (Chap 15), XVI–XVIII [*MS lacking*], XIX (Chap. 19), XX (Chap [XX *added later in pencil*]), XXI (Chap A/21), XXII (B / 22), XXIII (C[23 *added later in another hand*]), XXIV [*MS lacking*], XXV (E Chap 25 [*Irving's 24 is canceled and substituted in another hand by* 25]), XXVI (F Chap. 26 [26 *substituted for Irving's* 25]), XXVII (Chap G / 27 [27 *is in another hand, as is* 28

below]), XXVIII (H / 28), XXIX (I), XXX [*MS lacking*], XXXI (Chap. 1.), XXXII [*MS lacking*], XXXIII (Chap 3), XXXIV (Chapr 4), XXXV and XXXVI [*MS lacking*], XXXVII (Chap 7), XXXVIII (Chap. 8), XXXIX (Chap. 9), XL (Chap 10.), XLI (Chap), XLII to XLIV [*MS lacking*], XLV (Chap.) XLVI (Chap. /34 [34 *in left corner, as are numbers* 35–49]), XLVII (Chap / 35), XLVIII (Chap. / 36), XLIX (37), L (Chap L/38), LI (Chap/39), LII (40), LIII (41), LIV (42), LV (43), LVI (44), LVII (65), LVIII (46), LIX (47), LX (48), LXI Chap XXXI [XXXI *added in another hand*] / 49).

5.2   Gold] T; gold MS. *The first word in each phrase in the synoptic headings for which there is no manuscript is normalized to the T form at 33.2–8, 92.2–9, 123.2–7, 159.2–5, 186.2–4, 194.2–5, 212.2–6, 216.2–10, 253.2–6, 256.2–7, 262.2–9, and 315.2–11. The following MS words in the synoptic headings are altered to capitals according to Irving's overall intention and to the T form; page and line numbers appear in parentheses:* Their (5.3), Trading (5.6), Origin (5.8), A (5.9), North West . . . North West . . . North West (5.10–11), Wassailing (5.12), Attempts (14.2), His . . . His (14.4), Arrival (27.5), Their (41.2), His . . . His . . . Views (41.3), Royal (41.4), Description . . . Gaieties . . . Chronicler (41.4–5), A . . . A . . . Grand . . . Close A (41.7–8), Grievances (41.9), Bars (50.4), Disasters (50.4), Burial (50.5), Their . . . Their (56.2), Bold (56.3), Influence (56.6), Their (61.2), The (61.3), Reconnoitering (64.2), An (64.3), Expedition (64.4), The (64.5), An (80.2), Launching (80.3), Festivities (80.4), Pious (85.4), Picture (85.5), Inefficacy (85.7), His (85.8), His warning (85.8), Parting (85.9), Family . . . Cross(97.4), Renegadoes . . . Perplexities (97.4–5), Departure (97.7), Conjugal (97.7), Troubles (97.10), Appearance (107.2), Desertion (107.5), Feudal (107.7), Pirates (116.3), Desertions (116.5), Departure (116.5), Meeting (116.6), Expedient (116.8), Dangers (130.4), Feasting (130.6), A (130.7), Herds . . . Their (136.2), Duties (143.3), Their (143.4), Love (143.4), An . . . A (143.5), Return . . . An (143.6), Fresh . . . Return (143.6–7), Triumphal (143.8), Meetings (143.8), Meeting . . . Festivities (143.9–10),

Parched (151.2), His (151.5), Purity (155.2), Vulgar
. . . Suggestions (155.3–4), Trade . . . Character (155.5),
Three (162.3), Uneasiness . . . A (162.4), New . . . Return (162.5), Haunts . . . Their (166.2), Hidden
(166.4), Impassable (166.5), Distant (166.7), Tracks
. . . Dangerous (166.8), Adventures (166.9), Rough
(172.2), Game . . . A (172.3), Height (172.5), Various
(172.6), Towns (172.7), Visit (176.2), Presents
(176.3), Bargaining (176.4), Perplexities (176.5),
Their (181.3), Alteration (181.4), Preparations
(189.2), An . . . A (189.3), Their (189.4), Confirmed
(189.4), Arrival . . . Detachment (189.5–6), Discouraging . . . Disastrous (199.2), Caches (199.3), Unsuccessful . . . Further (199.4), The (199.5), Dreary (204.2),
Distribution (204.3), Rugged (204.4), Wild . . . Alarm
(204.4), Intercourse . . . Horse (204.6), Value . . . Sufferings . . . A (204.6–7), Snow . . . A . . . A (204.9–10),
A (221.3), A wintry (221.4), Grassy . . . A . . . Joy
(221.6), Dangers . . . Habits (221.7), Fate . . . The . . .
Tidings (221.7–8), Tidings (221.10), Roguery . . .
Their (229.2) Tidings . . . Thieves (229.3), A . . . Embarcation . . . Arrival (229.4), A . . . Old . . . Adventures
(229.4–5), Rejoicing (229.6), A . . . The (235.2), The
. . . Its . . . Vast (235.3), Sturgeon . . . The (235.4), Nature (235.5), A . . . Animals (235.6), Reptiles . . . Mildness . . . Soil (235.6–7), Their (239.2), Causes . . . Their
. . . Their (239.3), Armour . . . Mode (239.4), Extent
. . . Religious (239.5), The . . . Petty (239.6–7), Music
. . . Thieving . . . Keen (239.7–8), Intrusive . . . Abhorrence (239.8), Anecdote (239.9), Scanty . . . Bewildered (271.2), Prowling . . . A . . . A (271.2–3), Smoke
. . . An . . . An (271.4), A . . . A . . . A . . . (271.5), Pedestrian . . . Prying . . . Bonfire (277.2), A . . . Rafting
. . . The (277.3), Wilful . . . Grand (277.4), Distant . . .
Illness (277.5), Traces . . . Mineral . . . Peculiar (283.3),
Dismal (283.4), A . . . A . . . Hospitable . . . A (283.5–6),
Trail . . . A . . . A (290.2), A . . . Climbing (290.3), Volcanic . . . Extinguished . . Marine (290.4), Encampment . . . Successful . . . Good . . . Romantic . . . Rocky
. . . Foaming . . . The (290.4–6), A . . . Cantonment . . .
Game . . . Successful . . . The . . . Big . . . Beef . . .
Good . . . An . . . An . . . Unwelcome . . . Desolation
. . . Gormandizing . . . Good (295.2–7), Hills . . . Snow

... Disappearance ... A ... A ... Another (301.2–4), Return ... Launch ... Bad ... Pedestrian ... Vast ... Deserted ... An ... News ... Voyage ... Reception ... Arrival (301.5–8), Departure ... Their ... ... Thievish ... Laying ... Bands ... Adventures (310.2–7), Equivocal ... Partners ... Sale ... Arrangements ... Manifesto ... Departure (323.2–5), Memorial ... Tidings ... Bright (326.2–5), Matrimonial ... Matrimonial ... Settlements ... The ... A ... Arrival (328.3–5), A ... Roystering ... The ... Hard ... Voyage (331.2–3), Return (331.6), News ... Her ... Transactions (337.3–5), Conduct ... Negotiations ... Bargain ... Doubts (342.2–4), Breaking ... Departure ... Tragical ... Fate ... Attempts ... Disappointment (350.2–5).

5.2   and] 1A; & MS. And *is substituted for* & *again at* 5.20 (and the), 7.18, 32, 10.2, 66.5, 69.41, 76.9, 78.10 (and capture), 92.21 (and the), 108.18 (and the), 112.1, 114.4, 116.6, 119.23, 126.26, 127.28, 130.19, 134.6, 137.5, 142.7, 158.7 (chase and), 166.2, 168.32, 172.7, 173.12, 176.27, 189.6, 229.5, 236.32 (and wild), 301.26, 41, 303.7, 307.3, 307.31, 308.1, 310.4, 325.2, 332.34, 344.32, 350.26, 39 (and Mr.), *and* 351.10 (and requested).

5.3   Ottawa] 1A; Ottowa MS. *Normalized to Irving's usual form also at* 6.32

5.9   Privations] T; privations 1A; privation MS. *Compare* 11.2.

5.10–11   West ... West ... West] T; west ... west ... west   MS

5.20   Frenchman] 1A; French man MS

5.27   savage] 1A; Savage MS

5.31   which gave early] 1A; which early MS

5.35   Lawrence,] 1A; ∼; MS

5.40   commodities] 1A; comodities MS

6.2   settlements,] 1A; ∼∧ MS

*6.11   on] 1A; upon MS

*6.13   year's] 1A; years MS. *For the reader's convenience, apostrophes are added to make possessives in this and the following*: hunters' (12.38, 119.8, 297.31), beavers' (12.38), Astor's (16.7, 18.5, 40.14, 58.12, 336.7, 345.7, 350.25, 27, 354.35), Jefferson's (23.39, 102.3), Carver's (18.3), MacKenzie's (18.4), Clarke's (18.4, 317.12), Gray's (19.40, 66.18), summer's (30.16, 174.7), Captain's (34.22, 35.9, 36.11, 39.17, 40.12, 50.26), ship's

(35.25, 62.33, 75.17, 77.11, 21, 190.20, 348.15), moment's (38.1), harbour's (39.27), owner's (39.34),
Young's (45.15), monarch's (47.37), Tamaahmaah's
(49.23), boat's (50.5, 105.32), Comcomly's (56.7),
Baker's (57.40, 239.18, 346.6), year's (59.10, 99.43,
164.16, 236.22, 275.42, 336.29), Vancouver's (64.5, 67.34,
73.7), Stuart's (81.16, 265.23, 268.25, 270.24), men's
(86.24), Anne's (86.31), cocks' (89.27, 90.20), sutler's
(90.37), Hunt's (93.18, 97.22, 107.10, 111.27, 112.15,
133.19, 134.18, 217.15, 233.34, 264.30, 265.37, 266.19,
267.37, 274.11, 289.5, 332.29), Company's (98.26),
hunter's (101.4, 172.3, 173.3), morning's (107.36),
Hudson's (21.21, 24.16, 353.37), M'Lellan's (116.4),
days' (125.43, 173.5, 189.34, 190.31, 200.18, 210.8
[*MS lacking*], 224.19, 231.15, 274.13, 286.31, 290.8,
297.21, 298.20 [*MS lacking*], 299.29 [*MS lacking*],
302.19, 303.10, 351.31), man's (132.25, 167.21), Dorion's (134.43, 216.16), basilisk's (141.29), fortnight's
(147.24, 301.38), mother's (150.2), Lisa's (153.14,
154.10, 21), day's (163.17, 206.22, 220.21, 223.34,
264.28, 266.38, 283.37), bull's (167.15), afternoon's
(168.32), Day's (170.39, 171.2, 13), Henry's (189.5,
191.15, 199.13, 200.35, 265.10, 272.8, 279.39), bird's
(190.35), winter's (197.23), M'Kenzie's (202.32, 319.23,
342.30), Devil's (199.5, 203.10, 232.11), Dog's (204.8),
river's (205.33), Reed's (207.6, 352.6), Crooks' (219.33),
Year's (222.34, 38, 301.4, 302.32), dog's (222.39,
233.43), night's (223.34, 224.29), wolf's (226.40),
aborigines' (229.7), months' (231.24, 322.31), bears'
(240.37, 242.23), elks' (240.39), bear's (241.15, 16,
297.30), beavers' (242.33), eagles' (242.24), trappers'
(262.6 [*MS lacking*]), years' (270.26), week's (271.20),
Miller's (273.28), morning's (277.25), buffalo's
(288.11), children's (288.12), other's (307.14), miser's
(313.7), Madison's (317.18), speaker's (319.24),
father's (328.39), blacksmith's (329.38), gentleman's
(330.23), Paul's (331.4, 333.21, 23, 334.39, 335.32,
336.15), sportsman's (331.31), count's (332.33). Governor's (333.7), fool's (347.11), George's (347.35),
water's (347.37), M'Dougall's (348.42), lieutenant's
(354.2).

6.24   kettles] 1A; Kettles MS. Kettle(s) *is normalized also at*
        207.25, 217.8, 222.19, 224.14, 225.16, *and* 209.34.

6.28	prohibited,] 1A; ~; MS. *The MS semicolon confuses the modification.*
6.28	consequence] 1A; consequents MS
6.34	*Coureurs des bois*] T; *Coureurs des Bois* MS. *Normalized to Irving's usual form.*
7.4–5	down the] 1A; down to the MS. *Parallel with* up the *at* 6.32.
7.18	civilization] 1A; Civilization MS
7.19	whom] 1A; which MS
*7.34	licences] T; licenses MS.
7.36	merchants] 1A; Merchants MS
7.40	La Hontan] 1A; Hontan MS
7.41–42	undertaken.] 1A; ~∧ MS. *Periods are added at the end of sentences here and at* 12.18, 17.5, 18.16, 26.14, 29, 29.5, 32.14, 17, 35.6, 12, 19, 36.10, 22, 37.38, 38.10, 16, 39.4, 43, 40.2, 41.22, 33, 42.6, 28, 44.37, 46.10, 46.43, 48.22, 49.9, 50.5, 51.19, 52.16, 18, 53.30, 57.11, 30, 61.10, 36, 64.22, 35, 67.40, 68.14, 69.15, 71.24, 72.3, 82.3, 83.40, 89.23 (West.), 93.39, 94.31, 97.31, 98.29, 104.36, 109.12, 120.6, 123.10, 36, 125.21, 33, 141.7, 170.3, 29, 173.10, 179.31, 183.5, 13, 183.37, 197.36, 198.6, 201.11, 30, 204.34, 39, 207.16, 213.7 [*MS lacking*], 221.19, 26, 222.24, 225.23, 229.26, 35, 231.14, 238.6, 245.28, 246.29, 255.23 [*MS lacking*], 257.8 [*MS lacking*], 265.16, 267.17, 35, 269.7, 271.31, 272.15, 282.2, 283.24, 284.40, 294.11, 296.24, 301.8, 302.1, 304.18, 307.5, 40, 309.11, 310.8, 41, 311.6, 312.27, 313.33, 315.31, 316.17, 317.20, 321.6, 323.5, 326.34, 328.6, 329.41, 330.6, 331.6, 333.22, 334.16, 337.19, 40, 338.35, 343.18, 346.24.
8.12	Michilimackinac] 1A; Michilimakinac MS
8.29	Indians] 1A; Indian's MS. *The apostrophe is deleted here and in the following when it is used to make plurals:* M'Tavishes (11.16), North Westers (14.18), Arrieros (28.15), winters (42.12), taboos (61.3), Omahas (111.23), Upsarokas (153.19), buffalos (303.34), bottoms (304.5), cabins (333.40), Eris (341.7).
8.32	New York,] 1A; ~ ~; MS
8.33	bois,] 1A; bois; MS
8.38	lion's] 1A; Lions MS
8.41	residue] 1A; Residue MS
9.1	*Coureurs des bois*] T; Coureurs des Bois MS

9.3	Hudson's] T; Hudson MS. *Emended to Irving's preference again at 181.37.*
9.3	II∧] T; II. MS
9.8	alleged] 1A; alledged MS. Alledg(e, ed, ing) *is altered in the MS to* alleg(e, ed, ing) *at 98.42 and 311.13 and is emended in T also at 116.25 and 269.2.*
9.12	*Coureurs des bois∧*] T; "Coureurs des bois," MS; *coureurs des bois∧* 1A
9.17	traders,] 1A; ~∧ MS
*9.24	with] T; with with MS; with much 1A
*10.18	lake] 1A; lakes MS
*10.42	Scotland,] 1A; ~∧ MS
11.10	commercial] 1A; Commercial MS
11.12	pleasures,] 1A; ~∧ MS. *End of line omission of punctuation in MS.*
11.27	gorgeous] 1A; gorgious MS
*11.38	unceremonious] 1A; *san façon* MS
12.7–8	battered and hardened by hard living and hard service, and whose garments and equipments were all the worse for wear] 1A; sharpened and hardened by the northern blasts, and whose garments and equipments were all the worse for hard service MS
12.11	sovereigns] 1A; sovreigns MS. Sovereign(s) *is corrected also at* 14.20, 42.16, 45.20, 46.19, 47.19, 62.9, 112.20, 138.42, *and* 242.13.
*12.37	kinds] 1A; kind MS. *Corrected also at 33.26 and 88.3.*
12.38	buffalo] T; Buffalo MS. Buffalo(s, es) *is emended to the lowercase form also at* 122.16, 126.14, 177.15, 180.1, 184.20, 207.1, 287.15, 34, 293.7, 13, 296.27, 302.28, 37, 312.5.
13.11–12	when, as yet a stripling] 1A; when, a stripling MS
13.13	ascendant] 1A; Ascendant MS
13.18	oblivion;—] 1A; oblivion∧ MS.
13.19	feudal] 1A; Feudal MS
14.18	to push] 1A; push MS
14.21	pirogues] T; pirorgues MS; perogues 1A
15.10	Heidelberg] 1A; Heidel berg MS. *End of line omission of hyphenation in MS.*
15.17	Mr.] 1A; Mr∧ MS. *A period is added after* Mr. *and* Messrs. *in every occurrence for which there is manuscript.*
*15.23	ship,] 1A; ~∧ MS

16.5   country] 1A; Country MS. *Normalized also at* 17.30, 51.19, *and* 96.9.
16.12   5$_\wedge$] 1A; 5. MS
16.17   United States] 1A; united states MS
16.38   A.] 1A; A$_\wedge$ MS
16.41   "I'll] 1A; Ill MS
17.4   citizens,] 1A; ~$_\wedge$ MS. *End of line.*
17.22   1811$_\wedge$] T; 1811. MS
18.2–3   enterprizes] T; Enterprizes MS
18.4   expedition] 1A; Expedition MS
18.12   watery] 1A; watry MS. *Corrected again at* 59.35.
18.14   discoverer,] 1A; ~$_\wedge$ MS. *End of line.*
18.29   summer ... autumn] 1A; Summer ... Autumn MS. *In accordance with Irving's practice of giving seasons lowercase forms the majority of the time,* autumn *is normalized here and again at* 62.32, 109.37, 245.11, *and* 351.24.
19.6   sovereignty] 1A; sovreignty MS. *Corrected also at* 58.26.
19.12   which,] 1A; ~$_\wedge$ MS. *End of line.*
19.22   Captain] 1A; Capt. MS. Capt *and* Capt. *are expanded to* Captain *according to Irving's majority preference and as in 1A at* 19.35, 40, 27.2, 44.41, 61.8, 63.31, 73.6, 21, 30, 74.39, 78.16, 307.3, 308.4, 35, 334.34, 335.25, 30, 336.3, 20, 21, 341.28, 30, *and* 353.22.
19.24   46° 19'] 1A; 46.19 MS. *Normalized to Irving's preferred form.*
19.25   breakers,] 1A; ~$_\wedge$ MS
20.3   the] 1A; The MS
20.3   River] T; river MS. *Normalized to Irving's majority intentions also at* 27.12, 92.10, 94.16, 104.9, 107.3, 124.4, 183.25, 229.6, 263.18, 20, 271.24, 273.28, 274.5, 16, 278.41, 290.2, 291.43, 295.35, 310.24, 311.38, 351.9, *and* 353.29.
*20.35   government,] 1A; ~; MS
20.40   52° 20' 48"] 1A; 52.20.48" MS
20.41   Travels] 1A; travels MS
20.41   Introd. p. iii. ... 1796.] 1A; P$_\wedge$ III. ... 1796$_\wedge$ MS
21.2   52° 30'] 1A; 52.30 MS
21.6   Lat. 49°] T; Lat$_\wedge$ 49. MS; lat. 49' 1A
21.14   48°] T; 48 MS; 48' 1A
*21.15   as] 1A; As MS
*21.22   companies] T; Company MS, 1A
21.22   charter,] 1A; ~$_\wedge$ MS

21.24	coalesce] 1A; coalese MS
21.29	1804,] 1A; ~ᴧ MS
21.30	Whitworth] 1A; Wentworth MS. *Cf.* Whitworth *at* 20.27.
22.4	mouth] 1A; Mouth MS. *Normalized also at* 66.12, 227.4 *and* 228.2.
22.6	Columbia,] 1A; ~ᴧ MS. *The phrase following* Columbia *is interlined.*
22.10	trade, atᴧ] 1A; tradeᴧ at, MS
22.17	Canton,] 1A; ~ᴧ MS
23.15	fact,] 1A; ~ᴧ MS
23.22	period,] 1A; ~ᴧ MS
24.16	Bay] 1A; bay MS
24.30	evils, . . . Indians,] 1A; ~ᴧ . . . ~ᴧ MS. Both . . . Indians *is interlined in the MS.*
24.37	they] 1A; they had MS
24.43	key] 1A; Key MS
25.6	Astor,] 2A; ~ᴧ MS, 1A
27.4	songsᴧ] 1A; ~, MS
27.18	burthen, . . . guns,] 1A; ~ᴧ . . . ~ᴧ MS. *Commas prevent a misreading.*
27.20	board] 1A; bord MS
27.30	M'Kay, M'Dougall] T; McKay, McDougall MS; M'Kay, M'Dougal 1A. *In this and in the following instances, what appears in the MS to be* Mc *as in* McKay *is normalized to Irving's dominant form* M': 27.30, 31, 38.36, 40.5, 14, 44.18, 59.33, 60.1, 62.13, 65.37, 80.10, 37, 85.33, 116.3, 116.38, 202.31, 232.12 (M'Kenzie), 244.9, 310.6, 319.7, 21, 23, 37, 40, 324.15, 41, 325.30 (M'-Dougall), 329.10, 330.5, 22, 341.6, 342.30, 344.19, 345.11, 347.40, 350.29, 351.1. *What appears to be* M *is normalized to* M' *at:* 34.18, 37.34 (M'Kay), 58.11, 62.5, 32, 63.36, 65.41, 72.16, 73.18, 74.14, 18, 28, 80.20, 85.2, 116.4 (M'Lellan's), 117.1, 118.7, 128.32 (M'Lellan), 130.19, 140.13 (M'Kenzie), 200.38, 202.32, 226.1, 312.7, 20, 316.38, 317.20, 318.7, 320.12, 41, 323.2, 6, 13, 22, 35, 36, 324.14, 330.15, 338.1, 342.3 (M'Tavish), 342.4, 342.39, 346.20, 347.3, 347.24 (M'Dougall), 348.42, 350.14.
28.5	ship] 1A; Ship MS. *Normalized also at* 60.9, 62.28, *and* 336.21.
28.17	water;] 1A; ~ᴧ MS
28.18	batteaux] 1A; batteaus MS
28.21	labyrinth] 1A; labarynth MS

28.30–31   *Coureurs des bois*] T; Coureurs des bois MS
28.40   variegated] 1A; variagated MS
28.40   knife,] 1A; ~∧ MS. *End of line.*
30.1   steamboat] 1A; steam boat MS. *Emended also at* 94.23.
30.15   it] 1A; in MS
*30.36   hard, lie hard,] 1A, ~–~– MS
*31.1   voyage.] 1A; ~; MS
*31.22   individual∧] 1A; ~, MS
*31.28   off] 1A; off of MS
*31.28   harbour,] T; harbor, 1A; harbour∧ MS
*31.35   embarcation,] T; embarkation, 1A; embarcation∧ MS
31.36   instruction∧] 1A; ~, MS
31.38   recommended] 1A; reccommended MS. *Corrected also
                at* 267.13 *and* 354.3.
*31.38   on] 1A; as on MS
31.42   favorable] 1A; favourable MS
32.11   recommend] 1A; reccommend MS
*32.13   natives] 1A; Indians MS
33.5   Quarter deck] T; quarterdeck 1A
33.6   wild goose chase] T; wildgoosechase 1A. *See* 38.6 *for
                the MS form.*
33.13   God] 1A; god MS
33.16   at the] 1A; at the at the MS
33.20   discipline] 1A; dicipline MS. *This word is spelled cor-
                rectly at* 27.27 *and corrected at* 34.9, 97.7, 100.9, 105.35,
                107.38, *and* 165.16.
33.28   braggadocios,] 1A; braggodocios MS
*33.38   importance,] 1A; ~∧ MS
34.10   o'clock] 1A; Oclock MS. Oclock *has been emended to
                *o'clock *again at* 34.10, 52.6, 84.19, 131.28, 139.9, 140.12,
                184.20, *and* 278.7
34.11   was immediately] 1A; immediately was immediately MS
34.12   dignities] 1A; dignaties MS
34.14   M'Dougall] T; M'Dougal 1A, MS. *Irving almost always
                spelled this name correctly with two l's. It is corrected
                also at* 63.36, 255.40 (*MS lacking*), 308.34, 315.5 (*MS
                lacking*), *and* 328.2.
34.17   Thorn] 1A; Thorne MS
34.18   seized] 1A; siezed MS. Seize (s, d) *is corrected also at*
                39.15, 50.30, 54.4, 64.19, 75.39, 80.19, 98.25, 102.16, 31,
                110.25, 119.33, 121.3, 128.16, 153.29, 216.36, 249.6,
                272.34, 275.6, 38, 297.36, *and* 340.11.
*34.21   bystanders] T; bye standers MS; by-standers 1A

35.22	keenness] 1A; keeness MS
*35.27	delicacies," said he, "they] 1A; ~ₐₐ ~~ₐ ₐ~ MS
35.30	these," . . . "are] 1A; ~,ₐ . . . ₐ~ MS
35.31	'eat dogs.' "] 1A; "eat dogsₐₐ" MS
35.35	top."] 1A; top.ₐ MS
35.40	Stuart] 1A; Stewart MS. *Corrected also at 36.4.*
36.21	ₐin] 1A; "in MS
36.28	singing,] 1A; ~ₐ MS. *End of line.*
36.29	groupes,] T; groupesₐ MS; groups, 1A. *End of line.*
*37.29	seemed] 1A; were MS
37.35	occasion] 1A; occassion MS
*37.39	stood] 1A; had stood MS
38.4	reconnoitered] T; recconnoitered MS; reconnoitred 1A. Reconnoiter (s, ed, ing) *is corrected to the single* c *form also at* 62.24, 64.2, 23, 65.29, 137.27, 156.33, 181.16, 186.19 *and* 285.30.
38.5	and,] 1A; andₐ MS
38.19	north west] T; north-west 1A. MS *lacking; the text is emended to Irving's habitual practice here and at* 38.19 *and* 367.11, 14.
38.20	Captain] T; captain 1A. MS *is lacking; emended to Irving's preference.*
38.21	holyday] T; holiday 1A. *Emended to Irving's MS spelling.*
*38.35	she] 2A; it MS, 1A
*38.37	island] 1A; Island MS
39.19	disastrous] 1A; disasterous MS
39.26	he,] 1A; heₐ MS
39.38	however,] 1A; ~ₐ MS. *End of line.*
40.16–17	"and . . . minutes,"] 1A; ₐ~ . . . ~,ₐ MS
40.17–18	"they . . . children."] 1A; ₐ~ . . . ~·ₐ MS
40.21	careered] 1A; carreered MS. Career (ed, ing) *is corrected also at* 113.8, 143.17, 176.34, 186.22, *and* 190.35.
40.22	February,] 1A; ~; MS.
41.4	Karakakooa—] T; ~ₐ MS. *End of line.*
41.7	residence—] 1A; ~ₐ MS. *End of line.*
*41.10	Owyhee] 1A; Owhyhee MS. *Emended also at* 42.30.
*41.14	Roa,] 1A; ~ₐ MS
41.27	white men] 1A; whitemen MS. *Normalized to Irving's usual practice here and at* 60.13, 80.19, 115.3, 118.10, 177.30, 178.2, *and* 265.18.
*41.32	islanders] 2A; islands MS, 1A
41.32	therefore,] 1A; ~ₐ MS. *End of line.*
42.38	succeeded] 1A; suceeded MS

42.43   at the] 1A; at some at the MS
43.38   passengers,] 1A; ~∧ MS. *End of line.*
44.18   M'Kay,] 1A; ~∧ MS
*44.29   nautical] 1A; tarpawlin MS
*44.34   enquire] T; inquire MS, 1A
45.12   guns;] 1A; ~, MS
45.14   ship,] 1A; ~∧ MS. *End of line.*
45.15   account,] 1A; ~∧ MS. *End of line.*
*45.18   by] 1A; by the MS
45.20   of] 2A; in MS, 1A
*45.24   of March,] T; March∧ MS
*46.4   savages, too,] 1A; ~∧ ~∧ MS
46.15–16   to∧ rule] 1A; to, rule MS
46.18   that] 1A; than MS
46.32   Woahoo,] 1A; ~∧ MS. *In the MS the island of Woahoo
                   is interlined.*
*46.38   cocoa nut] T; coco nut MS; cocoa-nut 1A.
*47.5   ceremonious] 1A; ceremonial MS
48.4   that the] 1A; the MS
*48.25   enlisted] 1A; engaged MS
48.31–32   Englishmen] 1A; englishmen MS
48.41   Well,"] 1A; Well,∧ MS
48.41   also." 1A; also.∧ MS
49.7   written] 1A; written by him MS
49.15   &c.] 1A; &c∧ MS. *Periods are added also at* 49.23, 26.
49.26   ignorance,] 1A; ~∧ MS. *End of line.*
49.31–33   a grasping, trafficking savage; as shrewd and sordid in
                   his dealings as a white man] 1A; the hardest of pork
                   dealers MS
*50.14–15   altercations∧ . . . humours,] T; ~, . . . ∧ MS; ~∧ . . .hu-
                   mors, 1A
50.31   conceived] 1A; concieved MS. *Corrected again at* 101.25.
*51.4   mischievous] 1A; mischivious MS. *Corrected here and
                   at* 63.27 *and* 130.38 (*MS* mischevious), *and* 153.15
                   (*MS* meschevous).
*51.27   Fox,] 1A; ~∧ MS
51.28   Martin,] 1A; ~∧ MS
52.22   ship,] T; ~∧ MS, 1A. *End of line.*
52.34   breakers,] 1A; ~∧ MS
52.35   mate, . . . despatched∧] 1A; ~∧ . . . ~, MS
52.40   Aiken, . . . mariner∧] T; ~∧ . . . ~, MS; ~, . . . ~, 1A
53.5   away,] 1A; ~∧ MS. *End of line.*

*53.21	its reflux] T; its reflux of the tide MS; the reflux of the tide 1A
54.6	keel] 1A; Keel MS
54.17	exercise;] 1A; ∼∧ MS. *End of line.*
54.24	surf,] 1A; ∼∧ MS. With . . . surf *is interlined.*
54.30	hours,] T; ∼∧ MS, 1A. *End of line.*
55.9	they] 1A; the islanders MS
56.5	David] 1A; D MS. D *is expanded to* David *again at* 81.16, 320.11, *and* 351.1.
*56.22	cape] 1A; Cape MS
56.27	Chinooks] 1A; Chinnooks MS. Chinook(s) *is spelled with one* n *in all its other occurrences in the* MS *except at* 241.30 *and* 243.39, *where it is also normalized.*
56.35	salmon] 1A; Salmon MS. *Normalized also at* 59.25, 69.11, 34, 70.5, 206.28, 207.5, 235.4, 264.42, *and* 269.7.
57.30	brethren] 1A; bretheren MS
58.26	its] 1A; his MS
58.34	Mountains] T; mountains MS, 1A. *Normalized also at* 82.31, 83.15, 88.38, 97.18, 104.34, 121.23, 124.26, 166.20 [MS *lacking*], 169.28, 174.25, 177.41, 185.25, 191.24, 195.15 [MS *lacking*], 229.6, 241.34, 246.18, 261.9 [MS *lacking*], 263.12, 14, 20, 23, 37 [MS *lacking*], 268.25, 306.4, 310.31, 313.19, 355.42, *and* 356.26.
59.5	pain.] 1A; ∼; MS
*59.26	April 7th,] T; March 7th∧ MS; March 7th, 1A
59.28	high.] 1A; ∼, MS
59.28	Comcomly] 1A; Concomly MS. *Corrected also at* 59.37.
60.4	work,] 1A; ∼∧ MS
*61.7	gentlemen,] 1A; ∼∧ MS
61.10	sporting] 1A; Sporting MS
61.16	Point] T; point MS, 1A
61.17	for the] 1A; for the for the MS
61.18	estuary,] 1A; ∼∧ MS. *End of line.*
*61.26	musketry] 1A; musquetry MS
*61.34	the embryo] 1A; the place the embrio MS
61.38	barter,] 1A; ∼; MS
62.11	ragamuffins] 1A; raggamuffins MS
62.14	and enjoy his] 1A; and MS
63.6	objects] 1A; interests MS
63.7	for] 1A; in MS
63.10	to] 1A; to find MS
63.12	mind,] 1A; ∼∧ MS
63.34	invariably] 1A; altogether MS

64.10	factory] 1A; Factory MS
64.20	forestall] 1A; forstall MS
64.30	north] 1A; North MS
*64.37	Stuart,] 1A; ~∧ MS
65.9–10	stepped on shore,] 1A; landed∧ MS
65.22	the Columbia] 1A; Columbia MS
*66.5	accompanied by] T; by MS; *omitted* 1A
66.15	Point, a long,] 1A; ~∧ ~ ~∧ MS
66.16	Opposite] 1A; Oposite MS
66.27	trees of deciduous foliage,] 1A; deciduous trees∧ MS
66.36	sepulture] 1A; Sepulture MS
*67.2	or other] 2A; or MS, 1A
*67.15	sunset] 1A; sun set MS
67.25	southeast] 1A; south East MS
67.25	parallel] 1A; parrallel MS. Parallel(s) *is corrected also at* 109.29, 139.7, 173.29, 237.28, 239.16, 267.19, 293.43, *and* 301.23.
67.26	east and west] 1A; East and West MS
67.27	Wallamot,*] 1A; Wallamot,∧ MS
*67.37	Columbia: a] T; ~. A MS; ~; a 1A
67.39	Hood,] 1A; ~∧ MS. Mount Hood *is interlined in the* MS.
*67.40	Wallámot] 1A; Wollámot MS
68.3	Astoria;] T; ~, MS; ~. 1A
68.5	hundred tons] 1A; hundred MS
68.12	gulls,] 1A; ~∧ MS. *End of line.*
68.31–32	are situated about one hundred and eighty miles above the mouth of the river] 1A; commences about [*blank*] miles from its mouth MS
68.35	a half] 1A; half MS
68.40	some distance in] 1A; half an hour with MS
69.3	a half] 1A; half MS
69.10	spring] 1A; Spring MS. *Normalized also at* 107.2 *and* 313.43.
69.35	were] 1A; was MS
69.41	Clark. V. II. P.] T; Clark V∧ II. P∧ MS; Clarke, vol. ii. p. 1A
*70.13	active,] 1A; ~∧ MS
70.26	saucy,] 1A; ~∧ MS
70.30	Wish-ram] 1A; Wish∧ram MS
70.36	pointing] 1A; pointing him MS
71.14	fertile,] 1A; ~∧ MS. *End of line.*
71.20	Stuart] 1A; D Stuart MS.

72.13	sturgeon] 1A; Sturgeon MS. *Normalized also at* 72.33 *and* 235.38.
72.15	south] 1A; South MS. *Normalized also at* 185.20.
72.19	haste, 1A; ~∧ MS
*72.23	four-pounders] 1A; four pounders MS
72.25	ensconced] 2A; they ensconced MS, 1A
73.31	wily] 1A; wiley MS
73.35	plain,] 1A; ~∧ MS
73.39	moreover,] 1A; ~∧ MS
*74.11	by Shewish,] 1A; by MS
74.19	Captain] T; captain MS, 1A. Captain *is capitalized in lines* 15 *and* 21.
74.30	demeanor] 1A; demeanour MS. *Emended to Irving's preference also at* 78.28.
74.36	succeeded,] 1A; ~∧ MS. *End of line.*
75.4	weigh] 1A; wiegh MS
75.19	companionway] 1A; hatch way MS
75.23	Thorn] 1A; Thorne MS
75.24	as a] 2A; as MS, 1A
75.26	singled] 1A; had singled MS
76.23	reconnoiter] T; recconnoiitre MS; reconnoitre 1A. Reconnoiter *is regularized to the form found elsewhere in* "*Astoria.*"
76.30–31	for Mr. Lewis, after inviting them,] 1A; the very individual who had invited them∧ MS
77.17	ship,] 1A; ~∧ MS. *End of line.*
77.28	extremity,] 1A; ~; MS
77.43	sacrificed] 1A; sacraficed MS
78.1–3	Some time after their death, the interpreter, who had remained a kind of prisoner at large, effected his escape and brought the tragical tidings to Astoria.] 1A; *omitted* MS
*78.5	headstrong] 1A; headstrong &c MS
78.26	manly,] 1A; ~∧ MS. *End of line.*
78.29	expedition, however,] 1A; expedition MS
78.29	shewed] T; shewd MS; showed 1A
78.32	recollect] 1A; reccollect MS. Recollect (ed, ing, ion) *is corrected also at* 104.23, 122.6, 134.15, 232.4, 265.40, 267.28, 312.34, 331.7, 335.6, *and* 350.9.
78.33	grievous] 1A; grievious MS
*78.39	foresee." He indulged, however,] 1A; foresee," he indulges however MS
78.40	sought] 1A; seeks MS

78.41   same evening] 1A; evening that he received the intelli-
                 gence MS
78.42   disastrous] 1A; disasterous MS
79.2   "Would] T; ∧Would MS; "would 1A
80.18   conceived] 1A; concieved MS. *Corrected also at* 101.25.
80.23   Tonquin,] 1A; ∼; MS
80.24   white] 1A; White MS
81.5   eminence,] 1A; ∼∧ MS
81.24   prepared∧] 1A; ∼, MS
81.35   fur company] 1A; Fur Company MS
82.8–9   complexion] 1A; complexions MS
82.12   ammunition∧] 1A; ∼, MS
82.16   would be] 1A; was MS
82.22   territories.] 1A; ∼: MS
82.32   hunting] 1A; hunding MS
82.38   Christianity] 1A; christianity MS
82.39   colonists] 1A; Colonists MS
83.5   the dormant] 1A; their dormant MS
83.21   80°] T; 80 MS; eighty degrees 1A
83.30   winters] 1A; Winters MS
84.4   by any adversities] 1A; under any circumstances MS
84.10   sunrise] 1A; sun rise MS. *This is one word in the MS at*
                 67.14, 269.11, *and* 290.7, *and is emended also at*
                 273.33.
84.20   1812∧] 1A; ∼. MS
85.2   P.] 1A; P∧ MS
*85.9   Blackfeet] 1A; Black feet MS
85.19   Trenton,] 1A; ∼∧ MS
85.37   strategy] 1A; stratagy MS
86.3   voyageurs] 1A; Voyageurs MS. Voyageur(s) *is normal-*
                 ized at 86.6, 92.21, 93.8, 95.3, 224.27, *and* 324.29.
86.14   ammunition,] 1A; ∼∧ MS. *End of line.*
86.15   board] 2A; board of MS, 1A
*86.27   stationed,] 1A; ∼∧ MS
87.28   voyageurs,] 1A; ∼∧ MS
*87.35   Here were voyageurs frolicking] T; Voyageurs frolick-
                 ing MS; Here voyageurs frolicked 1A
88.10   stigmatized] 1A; stygmatized MS
88.12   in general] 1A; generally MS
*88.26   enlisted] 1A; engaged MS
88.30   seem] 1A; seemed MS
*88.32   any] 1A; any thing MS

88.33–34   him . . . him . . . his ear] 1A; them . . . them . . . their ears
             MS
*89.5   regales_∧ . . . outfits,] 1A; ~, . . . ~_∧ MS
*89.22   "voyageurs_∧] 1A; "~" MS
89.27   tails. Thus] 1A; tails, thus MS
*89.33   Crooks, . . . man, a native] 1A; ~_∧ . . . man, native MS
90.15   it was determined] 1A; determined MS
90.16   sixty] 1A; Sixty MS
90.19   of such] 1A; such MS. *The 1A reading parallels* of a
             crew *above.*
90.21   sailors,] 1A ~_∧ MS. *Like sailors is interlined in the MS.*
90.22   carouse.] 1A; ~; MS
90.24   feast,] 1A; feast_∧ MS. *End of line.*
*90.30   Mackinaw; in] T; Mackinaw, in MS; Mackinaw. In 1A
90.38   fiddles,] 1A; fiddles; MS
91.1   hug,] 1A; hug; MS
92.2   S'] T; St. 1A. *MS is lacking here; the form is normalized
             to Irving's consistent practice also at 92.9 and 253.21.*
92.7   Nodawa] T; Nodowa 1A
92.11   time,] 1A; ~_∧ MS
92.14   colonists] 1A; Colonists MS
*92.15   backwoodsmen] T; backwoodmen MS, 1A
92.16   prairies;] 1A; ~_∧ MS. *End of line.*
92.34   Company,] T; ~_∧ MS; ~; 1A
92.37   of bold] 1A; bold MS
*92.38   made] 1A; had made MS
*92.41   Arickara] T; Aricara MS, 1A
*93.1   *No paragraph* This] 1A; *Paragraph* This MS
93.4   *Paragraph* All] 1A; *No paragraph* All MS
93.7   singing,] 1A; ~_∧ MS. *End of line.*
93.8   Canadian voyageurs] 1A; voyageurs MS
93.10   belt,] 1A; ~_∧ MS. *End of line.*
93.14   colonists;] 1A; ~, MS
*94.15   another_∧] 1A; ~, MS
*94.17   barge; the] 1A; barge: The MS
94.25–26   stream; the] T; ~, ~ MS; ~. The 1A
94.37   had,] 1A; ~_∧ MS
*95.14   Nodawa] T; Nodowa MS, 1A. *Emended also at* 107.10.
95.16   and,] 1A; ~_∧ MS. *End of line.*
*95.36–37   Virginia, who] 2A; Virginia, but who MS, 1A
95.40   open,] 1A; ~_∧ MS
*96.15   proper] 1A; true MS
*96.19   1811] T; 1810 MS, 1A

96.20–21   one hundred] 1A; onehundred MS
96.21   Nodawa.] T; ∼, MS, Nodowa. 1A
97.3   Dorion,] 1A; Dorion∧ MS
97.8   Boon,] 1A; ∼∧ MS
97.11   turkey] 1A; Turkey MS
97.14   that] 1A; this MS
97.16   harassed] 1A; harrassed MS. Harass(ed, ing) *is cor-
                rected also at 111.34, 158.4, 181.29, 257.5, 287.16, *and*
                343.4.
98.1   and] 1A; and and MS
98.4   squaw] 1A; Squaw MS
98.4–5   of whom] 1A; of of whom MS
98.15   Dorion,] 1A; ∼∧ MS
*98.30   Lisa∧] 1A; Lisa, MS
98.35–36   to stand] 1A; stand MS
99.10   backs] T; back MS, 1A. *Emended to agree in num-*
                ber with they.
99.13   refused] 1A; and refused MS
99.21   Englishman] 1A; englishman MS
99.22   "Travels in Arkansas,"] 1A; ∧Travels in Arkansas,∧ MS
99.23   "Genera] 1A; ∧∼ MS
99.23   Plants."] 1A; plants.∧ MS
99.35   Charles,] 1A; ∼∧ MS
99.40   There seemed little dependance to be placed upon the
                promises] 1A; It seemed a desperate hazard to have
                to confide to the fidelity MS
99.43   shoulder,] 1A; ∼∧ MS. A *deleted* and *follows* shoulder.
100.27   month] 1A; Month MS
100.29   branches;] T; ∼, MS; ∼. 1A
*100.43   day, March 17th] T; day∧ Jan 17 MS; day, January
                17th 1A
101.13   backwoodsmen] T; backwodsmen MS; backwoodmen
                1A
*101.15   were] 1A; was MS
101.26   their warriors] 1A; them MS
101.27   Captain Lewis, while attempting to steal horses] 1A;
                Mr. Lewis MS
102.16   canoe,] 1A; ∼∧ MS
102.24   himself,] 1A; ∼∧ MS. *End of line.*
102.38   prairie] 1A; Prairie MS. Prairie(s) *is normalized also at*
                102.43, 145.37, 155.2, *and* 162.2.
102.43   Missouri;] 1A; ∼, MS
103.14   from his] 1A; from MS

103.17	yards,] 1A; ~; MS
103.19	action,] 1A; ~∧ MS
103.23	companion,] 1A; ~∧ MS
103.43	departed,] 1A; ~; MS
104.32	Pacific] 1A; pacific MS
104.37	on] 1A; one on MS
104.38	21st of] 1A; 21st MS
105.1	Saukees] T; Saukee tribes MS; Sawkees 1A
105.4	river;] 1A; ~, MS
105.17	met on] 1A; met MS
106.1	having shown any refractory symptoms] 1A; being possessed with any refractory disposition MS
106.19	ignorant] 1A; the upturned eyes of ignorant MS
107.4	parties—] 1A; ~, MS
107.5	creek—] 1A; ~∧ MS. *End of line.*
107.15	researches,] 1A; ~∧ MS
107.18	rocks,] T; rocks; MS; rock, 1A
107.28	ground,] 2A; ground∧ MS, 1A
108.11	howitzers.] 1A; howitzers the rest were smaller. MS
108.25	Nebraska or Platte] 1A; Platte MS
108.32	ascent,] 1A; ~; MS
108.34	Nebraska] 1A; Platte MS. *This same variant occurs at 108.41 and 109.13.*
109.16	not] 1A; not to be MS
109.33	basking] 1A; basking themselves MS
*110.10	could] 1A; would MS
110.11	throughout] 1A; during MS
110.12	since,] T; ~∧ MS, 1A. *End of line.*
110.37	that may] 1A; that MS
111.18	Omaha] 1A; Maha MS. *Omaha(s) is emended to Irving's preferred form again at 113.10, 13, 114.32, and 121.28.*
111.19	appearance,] 1A; ~∧ MS. *End of line.*
112.5	is] 1A; seemed MS
112.5	is] 1A; was MS
112.6–7	in these parts seems little better than a prolonged] 1A; seemed little better than a prolonged escape from a violent MS
112.8	is] 1A; was MS
112.8	feudal] 1A; the feudal MS
112.22	side,] 1A; ~; MS
112.23	would order] 1A; ordered MS
112.25–26	would soon be] 1A; was soon MS
112.26–27	skins. No] 1A; skins; not MS

112.38–39   supernatural] 1A; super natural MS. *End of line.*
113.4   being;] 1A; ~ₐ MS
113.8   career] 1A; carreer MS
113.31   terrific] 1A; terriffic MS: *Corrected also at* 114.29, 123.18,
             169.22, 170.37, 198.18, 203.6, 242.4, *and* 274.43.
114.6   story] 1A; Story MS
114.36   from] 1A; off of MS
115.24   foodₐ] 1A; ~, MS
115.26   disuse] 1A; dis use MS
116.2   Rumors] 1A; Alarming rumors MS
116.28   over] 1A; to MS
116.29   manner,] 1A; ~ₐ MS
116.30   and at] 1A; and MS
117.12   them,] 1A; ~ₐ MS
117.17   augmented;] 1A; ~, MS
117.26   massacred;] 1A; ~, MS
117.42   Sioux,] 1A; ~ₐ MS
118.17   Indians] 1A; Indian MS. *See* 116.12.
118.32   mutiny,] 1A; ~; MS
119.9   banks,] 1A; ~; MS
119.29   the] 1A; their MS
119.43   useless] 1A; worthless MS
*120.17   23d] 2A; 22d MS, 1A
120.21   enemy's] 1A; enemies MS
*120.28   other perils] 2A; perils MS, 1A
120.35–36   the savage, if hostile in his intents,] 1A; if hostile in his
             intents the savage MS
121.10   appearing] 1A; which appeared MS
121.19   Lisa,] 1A; ~ₐ MS. *End of line.*
121.31   stream,] 1A; ~ₐ MS. *End of line.*
121.32   was] 1A; was was MS
123.10   *L'Eau qui court*] T; L'Eau qui court MS; *l'Eau Qui
             Court* 1A
123.21   Omaha] 2A; Maha MS, 1A
*123.31   voyagers] 1A; voyageurs MS
123.33   Rezner] T; Rizner MS, 1A. *In the other six instances
             this name is spelled* Rezner.
124.13   backwoodsmen] T; backwodsmen MS; backwoodmen 1A
124.36   Captain] 1A; Mr MS
125.19   elk] 1A; Elk MS. *Normalized also at* 126.28, 225.15,
             227.13, 241.19, 279.11, 283.28, 284.4, *and* 284.21.
126.7   without trees] 1A; with scarce a tree to be seen MS
126.9   impart] 1A; give MS

126.15–16   wandering tribes] 1A; tribes of the prairies MS
126.18   danger,] 1A; ∼∧ MS. *End of line.*
126.19   the boundless waste] 1A; those boundless wastes MS.
                   Compare 126.6.
126.25   broad,] 1A; ∼∧ MS. Tranquil *is interlined.*
126.30   exclamations∧ ... stern,] 1A; exclamations, ... stern∧ MS
126.30   *Sioux!" ... Sioux!"*] 1A; ∼!∧ ... ∼!∧ MS
126.42   horseback] 1A; horse back MS. *Elsewhere in the MS*
                   horseback is one word, except at 299.42 where it is
                   emended.
127.19   horseback] 1A; horsback MS
127.26   war,] 1A; ∼∧ MS. *End of line.*
127.30   river∧] 1A; ∼, MS. *A deleted that follows river, in the MS.*
128.12–13   brother! ... oarsman.] 1A; ∼∧ ... ∼! MS
128.20   this,] 1A; ∼∧ MS. At ... this *is interlined.*
*128.36   statues.] 1A; ∼: MS
128.42   porphyry] 1A; porphery MS
130.9   1st] 1A; 1. MS
130.11   peninsula,] 1A; ∼∧ MS. *In the MS the neck of is*
                   interlined.
*130.38   thoughtless∧] 1A; ∼, MS
131.5   history of] 1A; history MS
131.5   which in general is] 1A; that is in general, MS
131.5   some] 1A; the MS
131.6   a] 1A; the MS
*131.38   was] 1A; were MS
132.7   that some] 1A; some MS
132.28   Minatarees] T; Minnetarees MS, 1A
132.31   return to] 1A; return MS
132.32   ammunition] 1A; amunition MS
*132.40   June] T; July MS, 1A
133.3   something] 1A; some thing MS
133.12   manoeuvred] 1A; manouvreed MS
133.15   village;] 1A; ∼, MS
133.22–23   him; ... further, therefore,] 1A; him, so, ... further, MS
134.3   his] 1A; the superior speed of his MS
134.3   them] 1A; them behind MS
134.20   June] T; July MS. *See the discussion for 132.40.*
134.34   under the] 1A; under MS
135.7–8   acted as moderator, endeavoring to prevent a general
                   melée; ... brawl, however,] 1A; had as much as he
                   could do to keep the belligerent parties from a general
                   melee, when ... brawl an MS

136.3	Day,] T; Day$_\wedge$ MS; Day— 1A. *End of line.*
*136.4	Left] T; left MS; Lefthanded 1A.
136.8	Eyes, an Arickara] 1A; Eyes$_\wedge$ a Rikara MS
136.20–21	descriptions] 1A; discriptions MS
137.20	frightened] 1A; frightned MS
*138.18	Arickaras] 1A; Rikara MS
138.20	difficult,] 1A; $\sim_\wedge$ MS
138.32	a ferocious looking savage] 1A; *omitted* MS
138.34	of a gigantic frame] 1A; gigantic in frame and ferocious in aspect MS
*138.38	frontier,] 1A; $\sim$; MS
138.40	chiefs.] 1A; $\sim_\wedge$ MS
*139.20	canoes,] 1A; $\sim_\wedge$ MS
139.24	Indians] 1A; indians MS. Indian(s) *is normalized also at* 235.11, 275.36, *and* 304.42.
*139.34	heard.] T; $\sim$; MS, 1A
*140.4–5	negotiation$_\wedge$] T; negociation, MS, 1A
140.13	by] 1A; with MS
140.22	palisades] 1A; pallisades MS
140.30	ships,] 1A; $\sim_\wedge$ MS
140.37	while] 1A; while while MS
140.39	himself] 1A; himself on his hands
141.13	Arickaras] 1A; Rcaras MS
141.31	own party.] 1A; own. MS
141.38	manifested for me, doing] 1A; treated me, and do MS
*142.6	friendship] 1A; friend ship MS
142.9	expressed] 1A; he expressed MS
143.4	gossipping—] T; $\sim_\wedge$ MS [*end of line*]; gossiping— 1A
143.6	of a] 1A; of a of a MS
143.17	careering] 1A; carreering MS. Career(ing) *is corrected also at* 176.34, 186.22, *and* 190.35.
143.28	are] 1A; is MS
143.32	prairies;] 1A; $\sim$, MS
143.38	Sioux,] 1A; $\sim_\wedge$ MS
144.2	created,] 1A; $\sim_\wedge$ MS
*144.3	a] 1A; an MS
144.12	guests,] 1A; $\sim_\wedge$ MS
144.37	leisure] 1A; liesure MS
145.9	woman] 1A; womans MS
145.16	game,] 1A; $\sim_\wedge$ MS
146.6	let] 1A; broke MS
146.10–11	neighborhood,] 1A; $\sim_\wedge$ MS. *End of line.*
146.12	therefore,] 1A; $\sim_\wedge$ MS. *End of line.*

146.24	continued] 1A; kept up MS
*146.28	expeditions] 1A; expedition MS
146.28	news was] 1A; was MS
146.34	and were] 1A; and MS
*147.1	Cheyenne] 1A; Chayenne MS
147.29	day break,] T; day break∧ MS; daybreak, 1A. *End of line in the MS.*
147.31	neighborhood,] 1A; ~; MS
147.34	The] 1A; The The MS
147.40	were] 1A; were a MS
147.42	fought] 2A; fought with MS, 1A
148.9	toilettes] T; toilette MS; toilets 1A
148.20	is] 1A; are MS
148.20	fox's skin] T; foxes skin MS; fox-skin 1A
148.31	busied in] 2A; busied MS, 1A
*148.38	trophies] 1A; ~, MS
148.39	ornaments] 2A; ornament MS, 1A
148.43	dog,] 1A; ~∧ MS
149.12	clubs;] T; ~, MS, 1A
149.22	procession,] 1A; ~∧ MS. *End of line.*
151.18	treeless] 1A; tree less MS
151.24	no food either] 1A; neither food MS
151.26	the deer] 2A; deer MS, 1A
151.26	parts,] 1A; ~∧ MS. *End of line.*
151.33–34	impassable,] 1A; ~; MS
152.17	Far West] T; far west 1A. *MS is lacking; the emendation follows Irving's MS practice and is repeated at 152.40.*
152.28	north,] T; north; 1A. *MS is lacking.*
153.30	Kentuckyan,] T; Kentuckyan∧ MS [*end of line*]; Kentuckian, 1A
153.39	Missouri—one] 1A; Missouri. One MS. *The MS version leaves a fragment.*
154.9	on a] 1A; on their MS
154.24	shores] 1A; banks of the shores MS
154.25	perish with hunger] 1A; perish MS
155.12	plains∧] 1A; ~, MS
155.40	keep on] 1A; keep MS
156.6	ribald] 1A; ribbald MS
156.10	musical] 1A; euphonious MS
156.19	an object] 2A; a task MS, 1A
*156.32	prairie,] T; prairie. MS; prairie; 1A
157.8	for] 1A; of MS

157.8	statuary;] 1A; ~, MS
157.21	horses,] 1A; ~∧ MS
157.30	horseman] 1A; horse man MS
157.42	Hills] T; hills MS, 1A. Hills *is capitalized according to Irving's usual practice here and at* 166.16, 166.24 *[MS lacking], and* 169.28.
158.17	places,] 1A; ~; MS
158.20–29	this . . . solved?] 1A; such, it would seem from tradition, and from various signs of former population in places now silent and deserted, had been the case before the advent of the white men. MS
*159.8	thirty six] T; thirty-six 1A
159.25–26	designing,] 1A; ~∧ MS. *End of line.*
160.11	where] 1A; and where MS
160.14	mountains,] 1A; ~∧ MS. *End of line.*
160.16	told,] 1A; ~∧ MS
*160.23	barter∧] 1A; ~, MS
160.29	With these] 1A; With MS
161.8	interpreter,] 1A; ~∧ MS. *End of line.*
161.17	and] 1A; and to keep MS
162.32	hunters,] 1A; ~∧ MS
162.35	party,] 1A; ~∧ MS
163.3	elapsed,] 1A; ~∧ MS. *End of line.*
163.9	and∧] 1A; and, MS
163.30	cook only] 1A; only cook MS
164.10	Crows,] 1A; ~∧ MS. *End of line.*
164.15	brethren] 1A; bretheren MS
164.23	sullen,] 1A; ~∧ MS
164.25	13th] 1A; 13 MS
164.30	current,] 1A; ~; MS
165.3–4	ridden . . . had almost . . . become] 1A; thus ridden . . . almost . . . became MS
166.16	forms] 1A; form MS
166.18	Little] 1A; little MS
167.8	Vasconcelles,] T; ~∧ MS, 1A. *End of line in MS.*
167.9	Jesuit] 1A; jesuit MS
*167.12	had] 1A; has MS
167.27	endeavoring] 1A; in endeavoring MS
167.39	than] 1A; rather than MS
167.39	commonplace] T; common place MS
168.11	black,] 1A; ~∧ MS. *End of line.*
168.12	from] 1A; from from MS
168.17	excepting∧] 1A; ~, MS

168.21	therefore,] 1A; ~∧ MS
168.43	Horn] 1A; horn MS. *Normalized also at* 172.13.
169.19	but is] 1A; though MS
169.38	bear,] 1A; ~∧ MS. *End of line.*
170.5	at] 1A; by MS
170.5	had joined] 1A; joined MS
170.12	goods] 1A; good MS
*170.21	rifle,] 1A; ~∧ MS
170.37	legs∧] 1A; legs, MS
170.40	be quiet!] 1A; ~ ~∧ MS. *Compare* 171.4.
171.8	was too] 1A; too MS
171.11	dismayed] 1A; desmayed MS. *Corrected also at* 312.35.
171.14	boy,] 1A; ~∧ MS
172.6	mountains—] 1A; ~∧ MS. *End of line.*
172.8	spirits—] 1A; ~∧ MS. *End of line.*
172.23	weather,] 1A; ~∧ MS
172.24–25	a great] 2A; great MS, 1A
*173.2	along] 2A; about MS, 1A
173.3	the buffaloes were] 1A; there was buffalo MS
173.19	discernible] 1A; discernable MS. *Corrected also at* 238.4.
*173.35	early] 1A; earliest MS
174.8–9	Such . . . extending] 1A; In fact a vast region extends MS
174.26	bare,] 1A; ~∧ MS. *End of line.*
174.28	valleys] 1A; vallies MS. Vallies *is emended here and at* 210.24, 223.39 *and* 237.28 *to Irving's usual spelling,* valleys.
*174.41	is] 1A; are is MS
175.3	by] 1A; to MS
175.11	streams,] 1A; ~∧ MS. *End of line.*
176.33	take] 2A; take a MS, 1A
176.34–35	and dashing] 1A; dashing MS
*177.16	galled] 1A; their galled MS
177.17	also∧] T; also, MS, 1A
*178.7	companion,] 1A; ~∧ MS
178.13	supplied] 1A; stocked MS
*178.25	mountain] 1A; mountains MS
179.8	as,] 1A; as∧ MS. *End of line.*
181.9	brooks,] 1A; ~; MS
181.16	who] 1A; and who MS
181.37	Hudson's] 1A; Hudson MS
182.3	grounds,] 1A; ~; MS
182.22	Diggers] T; diggers MS, 1A. *Originally* Root diggers.

183.3   which] 1A; which a MS
183.15, 22   west] 1A; West MS. *Normalized also at* 184.43, 185.24,
                         220.10, 229.16, 235.7, *and* 267.42.
183.29   resembling] 1A; as if of MS
*184.8   14th of] T; 14th MS, 1A
*184.19   on] 1A; On MS
184.21   led] 2A; lead MS, 1A
184.31   transparency] 1A; transparancy MS
184.37   they had been] 1A; they MS
185.1   California] 2A; Calafornia MS, 1A
185.11   kind,] 1A; ~∧ MS. *In the MS of* . . . flavor, *is interlined.*
185.17   strawberry] 1A; straw berry MS. *Normalized to Irving's
                         usual practice.*
186.28   mounted,] 1A; ~∧ MS
187.10   them,] ~∧ MS. *Edge of page.*
187.14   to them] 2A; for them MS, 1A
*187.21   them] 1A; him MS
189.6   Robinson,] 1A; ~∧ MS. *End of line.*
189.10   doubtful] 1A; doubtful the MS
189.20   change] 1A; changes MS
190.6   Michel,] 1A; ~∧ MS. *End of line.*
*190.18   hearts∧] T; ~, MS, 1A
190.28   information,] 1A; ~∧ MS. *Edge of page.*
191.4–5   a smaller] 1A; an inferior MS
*191.8   Robinson,] 1A; ~∧ MS
*191.24   sleet.] 1A; ~; MS
191.39   8th of] 2A; 8th MS, 1A
192.11   country,] 1A; ~∧ MS
*193.11   Company] T; company 1A
193.27   seventy seven] T; ~-~ 1A [*MS lacking*]
194.14   Diggers] 2A; diggers 1A [*MS lacking*]
194.28   Snakes,] T; ~, 1A [*MS lacking*]
*194.37   pea green] T; pea-green 1A [*MS lacking*]
195.1   cotton wood] T; ~-~ 1A [*MS lacking*]. *Emended also
                         at* 196.11–12.
196.41   visitors] 2A; visiters 1A [*MS lacking*]. *Emended to Irv-
                         ing's MS form again at* 210.5, 247.11, *and* 255.38.
197.24   of] 1A; the MS
197.27   him, and] 1A; him. He MS
197.41   became] 2A; become MS, 1A
198.19   in] 1A; to MS
199.3   Caches,] T; caches∧ MS; caches, 1A. *End of line in the
                         MS.*

ᵘ199.5	Devil's Scuttle Hole] 1A; devils Scuttle hole MS
199.7	Caldron] 1A; Calderon MS. *This has been corrected elsewhere in the MS to* Caldron *and in T is emended again at* 200.31, 202.30, 231.36, *and* 269.34.
199.10	fraternity,] 1A; ∼ₐ MS
*200.6	day] 1A; days MS
*200.10	them;] 1A; ∼. MS
200.14	a white] 1A; white MS
200.29	the Columbia] 2A; Columbia MS, 1A
200.36	horses] 1A; Horses MS
200.42	expeditions,] 1A; ∼ₐ MS. *Edge of page.*
201.10	description] 1A; discription MS
201.29	beneath it,] 1A; ∼∼ₐ MS
201.38	stream,] 1A; ∼ₐ MS. *End of line.*
202.8	spot] 1A; place MS
202.13	morning,] 1A; ∼; MS
202.16	merchandize] 2A; provisions or merchandize MS, 1A
202.22	to be] 1A; was MS
202.26	step,] 1A; ∼ₐ MS
202.27	winter] 1A; Winter MS. *Normalized also at* 353.23.
203.2	and] 1A; or MS
204.17	Beside,] T; Besideₐ MS; Besides, 1A. Beside *is interlined.*
204.31	tracts] 1A; tracks MS
204.39	obtain] 1A; procure MS
205.4	distributed,] 1A; ∼; MS
*205.14	November] T; October MS, 1A
206.5	occasions,] 1A; ∼ₐ MS. *End of line.*
206.11	as] 1A; As MS. As *in the MS formerly began a sentence.*
206.14	frightened] 1A; frightned MS
*206.40	sometimes] 1A; sometimes of MS
*206.43	hares,] T; haresₐ MS; horses, 1A
207.33	use,] 1A; ∼ₐ MS
207.34	knife] 1A; Knife MS. Knife *or* knives *is normalized also at* 224.43, 230.22, *and* 341.22
207.34	hour,] 1A; ∼ₐ MS
208.28	half breed] T; ∼-∼ 1A [*MS lacking*]. *Emended to Irving's MS form again at* 214.35 *and* 216.18.
210.5	probably,] T; ∼ₐ 1A [*MS lacking*]
210.21	black tailed] T; ∼-∼ 1A [*MS lacking*]
210.23	twenty eight] T; ∼-∼ 1A [*MS lacking*]
212.7	seventy two] T; ∼-∼ 1A [*MS lacking*]
212.38	twenty four] T; ∼-∼ 1A [*MS lacking*]
213.20	met] 2A; met with 1A [*MS lacking*]

214.15   night;] 2A; ∼, 1A
216.13   exhausted by] 2A; starved with 1A
216.29   Having seen] 1A; They had seen MS
*216.30   river,] T; river; MS, 1A
216.30   subsequently come out from among the mountains] 1A;
                    come out from the mountains since MS
216.34   an alarm] 2A; alarm MS, 1A
217.13   ready,] 1A; ∼ₐ MS
*217.39   him,] 1A; ∼ₐ MS
218.1   excepting] 1A; but MS
218.12   Dubreuil,] 1A; ∼ₐ MS
218.20   the part of the savages] 1A; their part MS
218.35   east] 1A; East MS. *Normalized also at 287.32, 291.6,*
                    292.37, 295.27, and 303.38.
219.11   shall . . . shall] 1A; will . . . will MS
220.7   December] 1A; Dec MS
220.16   river,] 1A; ∼ₐ MS
220.26   enragée] 1A; enragee MS
221.14   Crooks,] 1A; ∼ₐ MS
221.15   jaded,] 1A; ∼ₐ MS
221.21   the poor Canadian, Carriere] 1A; a poor Canadian named
                    Carrier MS
221.32   29th,] 1A; ∼ₐ MS
221.35   squawₐ] 1A; ∼, MS
222.5   Bonté,] 2A; ∼ₐ MS, 1A
222.12   here,] 1A; ∼ₐ MS. *Edge of page.*
222.17   eagerness] 1A; hungry eagerness MS
223.2   deceived] 1A; decieved MS
223.6–7   trees. They were] 1A; trees, MS
223.8   sank] 1A; sinking MS
223.37   stragglers.] 1A; ∼; MS. *Deleted matter follows.*
224.18   the] 1A; The MS
224.20   descended] 1A; descened MS
224.20   who] 1A; which MS
224.20   M'Lellan] 1A; M'Clellan MS. *Elsewhere in the MS the*
                    name appears as M'Lellan.
*225.4   or] T; nor MS, 1A
225.21   straggler,] 2A; ∼ₐ MS, 1A
225.29   Indians] 1A; Indian MS
225.30   tracks for] 1A; for MS
225.42   M'Lellan,] 1A; ∼ₐ MS
226.8   West] T; west MS, 1A

226.15	general, lived] 1A; general$_\wedge$ lives MS. Before *in line* 16 *calls for the past tense.*
226.28	computation,] 1A; $\sim_\wedge$ MS
226.34	branches,] 1A; $\sim_\wedge$ MS. *End of line.*
227.11	fish$_\wedge$] 1A; $\sim$, MS
*228.22	Long] T; long MS, 1A
229.22	gable] T; gabel MS, 1A
*229.39	*Chapter X, 69.29–70.33.] T; *omitted* MS, 1A
231.40	felicitations,] 1A; $\sim_\wedge$ MS
232.41	condition,] 1A; $\sim_\wedge$ MS
233.4	a more] 2A; more MS, 1A
235.13	times$_\wedge$] 1A; $\sim$, MS
235.28	shoals,] 1A; $\sim$; MS
235.32	constitute] 1A; form MS
236.30	raspberries] 1A; Raspberries MS
*236.31	serviceberries] 1A; service berries MS
236.42	fibres,] 1A; fibres of this vine MS
237.7	ducks] 1A; Ducks MS
237.8	eagles, vultures, crows] 1A; Eagles, Vultures, Crows MS
237.12	black,] 1A; $\sim_\wedge$ MS
237.15	as] 1A; with MS
237.24	prevalent] 1A; that prevail MS
237.25	are but] 1A; but MS. Are *was inadvertently canceled by Irving.*
237.26	countries] 1A; Countries MS
237.33	March,] 1A; $\sim_\wedge$ MS
239.7	Music,] T; music$_\wedge$ MS; music, 1A. *Edge of page.*
239.38	inches,] 1A; $\sim_\wedge$ MS. *End of line.*
*240.4	round$_\wedge$] T; $\sim$; MS; $\sim$, 1A
*240.12–13	robe, ... thigh,] 1A; $\sim_\wedge$ ... $\sim_\wedge$ MS
240.26	sexes,] 1A; $\sim_\wedge$ MS
240.33	of the] 1A; the MS
241.5	men,] 1A; $\sim_\wedge$ MS
241.30	Chinook] 1A; Chinnook MS
241.34	of] 1A; about MS
242.2	aerial] 1A; Aerial MS
242.6	sacrifices] 1A; sacrafices MS
242.25	ill,] 1A; $\sim_\wedge$ MS. *End of line.*
242.27	doctors] 1A; Doctors MS
244.3	race;] 1A; $\sim$, MS
245.30	might] 1A; might still MS
245.35	interest] 1A; share MS
246.21	danger,] 1A; $\sim_\wedge$ MS. *Edge of page.*

246.25	Stuart,] 1A; ~∧ MS
246.26	Narrows,] 1A; ~∧ MS. *Edge of page.*
247.26	good humor] T; ~-~ 1A [*MS lacking*]
248.25	war whoop] T; ~-~ 1A [*MS lacking*]. *For Irving's practice, see 121.6 and 146.6. Emended also at 248.37.*
248.38	others∧] 2A; ~, 1A [*MS lacking*]
249.36	which∧] T; ~, 1A [*MS lacking*]
250.1	war chief] T; ~-~ 1A [*MS lacking*]. *Emended to Irving's usual form again at 250.11.*
250.6	bloodshed;] T; ~, 1A [*MS lacking*]
250.31	gentleman∧] 2A; ~, 1A [*MS lacking*]
251.24	Wallah Wallahs] T; ~-~, 1A. *Emended to Irving's MS form here and at 251.39, 256.5, and 260.18–19.*
*253.5	on] T; at 1A [*MS lacking*]
253.12	north west] T; ~-~ 1A. *Emended to Irving's MS form also at 254.2.*
253.28	effected] T; affected 1A [*MS lacking*]
254.38	off] 2A; off of 1A
255.24	Cape] T; cape 1A. *Emended to Irving's preference also at 255.30.*
255.40	M'Dougall] T; M'Dougal 1A. *Emended also at 315.5.*
256.19	was] T; were 1A
*256.27	André] T; Andri 1A [*MS lacking*]
257.35	frank and] 2A; frank 1A
258.1	cartridge box] T; ~-~ 1A [*MS lacking*]
258.16	merchandize] T; merchandise 1A [*MS lacking*]. *In "Astoria" Irving consistently spells this word with a z. It is emended also at 258.38 and 344.12 in the body of the text where MS is lacking.*
*258.19	captors] T; captives 1A [*MS lacking*]
259.43	thirty seven] T; ~-~ 1A
260.5–6	fifty five] T; ~-~ 1A
260.35	concluded] 2A; conclued 1A
260.43	preparations] 2A; preparation 1A. *See 260.38 above.*
262.14	proceeded] T; proceded 1A [*MS lacking*]
263.3	forty five] T; ~-~ 1A
*263.15	Michel] T; Michael 1A
263.41	cotton wood] T; ~-~ 1A
*264.8	10th] T; 20th 1A [*MS lacking*]
264.24	course,] 1A; ~∧ MS. Intending *is interlined.*
*264.28	cantonments] 2A; encampments MS, 1A
264.42	esculent] 1A; esculant MS
265.6	information] 1A; tidings MS

265.17	aroused by] 1A; aroused MS. By *was erroneously canceled in the MS.*
265.21	an] 1A; they an MS. *Irving forgot to cancel* they.
265.24	part,] 1A; ~∧ MS
265.29	Stuart] 1A; Crooks MS
*265.32	in] 2A; in every MS, 1A
265.38	autumn,] 1A; ~∧ MS. *Edge of page.*
266.18	viz.] 1A; ~∧ MS
266.28	prairies;] 1A; ~, MS
266.33	journeyed] 1A; journeyd MS
268.16	Indians;] 1A; ~, MS
269.13	spears,] 1A; ~; MS. *A splice in the MS follows.*
269.20	by] 1A; with by MS. *Irving neglected to cancel* with.
269.27	wanderings,] 1A; ~∧ MS. *Edge of page.*
270.1	about the vicinity] 1A; in every direction MS
*271.2	travellers] 1A; travelling MS
271.6	of September] 1A; September MS
*271.15	a] 2A; of a MS, 1A
271.25	7th of] 1A; 7th MS
271.34	called] 1A; river called MS
272.20	Stuart] 1A; Stewart MS
*272.24	Stuart] T; Crooks MS, 1A
272.29	prairies] 1A; praries MS
272.39	Crows] 1A; crows MS
273.10	men,] 1A; ~∧ MS
274.5	was] 1A; is MS
274.11	south;] 1A; ~, MS
274.19	Crows;] T; ~∧ MS; ~, 1A. *End of line in the MS.*
274.24	horses] 1A; animals MS
274.33	On] 1A; The travellers now indulged their jaded horses with part of a days repose in a meadow on the borders of Mad river. On MS
274.35	upon] 2A; about MS, 1A
275.3	off,] 1A; ~∧ MS. *End of line.*
275.15	grievously] 1A; grieviously MS
275.22	all!"] 1A; all!." MS
275.24	Stuart,"] 1A; ~∧∧ MS. *End of line.*
275.27	I'll] 1A; Ill MS
275.33	despair;] 1A; ~∧ MS. *Edge of page.*
275.38	drove] 1A; herd MS
276.12	in] 1A; in at MS
277.12	dismay,] 1A; ~∧ MS. *Edge of page.*
277.20	heavy hearts] 1A; a heavy heart MS

*277.24	camp.] 1A; ∼, MS
278.4	made] 1A; they made MS
278.39	magnitude;] 1A; ∼, MS
279.16–17	the rain] 2A; rain MS, 1A
279.20	previously,] 1A; ∼∧ MS
279.23	guns;] 1A; ∼, MS
279.25	Blackfeet,] 1A; ∼; MS
279.26–27	some of that wandering and hostile tribe who, of course,] 1A; them. If so some of that wandering and hostile tribe MS
279.40	toilsome;] 1A; ∼∧ MS. *End of line.*
281.2	afraid] 1A; affraid MS
281.14	men] 1A; a man MS
281.16	no] 2A; not MS, 1A
281.30	Henry's] 1A; Henry MS. *Emended again at line 35.*
281.35	north west] T; North West MS; north-west 1A
*283.15	a terrific] T; terriffic MS; terrific 1A
283.16	the trigger] T; trigger MS, 1A
283.20	caution,] 1A; ∼∧ MS. With . . . and *is interlined.*
283.26	bear] 1A; Bear MS. *Normalized also at 284.21.*
283.28	and] 1A; of which he had MS
283.34	*Paragraph* By] 1A; *No paragraph* By MS
283.37	accoutrements] 1A; acoutrements MS
*283.38	swamps] 1A; swamp MS
284.42	steep] 1A; steep steep MS
285.6	mineral] 1A; metalic MS
*285.7	pale,] 1A; ∼∧ MS
285.12	wide,] 1A; ∼∧ MS. The main . . . wide *is interlined.*
285.15	toil] 1A; ascent MS
285.30	Canadians,] 1A; ∼∧ MS. *End of line.*
286.2	he had] 1A; had MS
286.16	their] 1A; there MS
286.33	rest."] 1A; ∼.∧ MS
286.43	encampment,] 1A; ∼∧ MS. A *canceled* and *follows.*
288.21	antelopes,] 1A; ∼∧ MS. *End of line.*
289.4–5	outrages, . . . mentioned,] T; ∼∧ . . . ∼∧ MS; ∼∧ . . . ∼, 1A. Already mentioned *is interlined in the MS.*
290.8	days'] 2A; days days MS; day's 1A
290.19	latter,] 1A; ∼∧ MS
290.20	eastward] 1A; Eastward MS
*290.28–29	tending] T; all tending MS, 1A
290.30	which] 1A; that MS
291.16	north of east] 1A; North of East MS

291.17	Cheyenne] 1A; cheyenne MS
291.33	killed] 1A; had killed MS
*291.38	mountain] 1A; mountains MS
292.21	mountain,] 1A; ~ ∧ MS. *End of line.*
292.35	now gave] 1A; gave now MS
*293.3	direction ∧] T; ~; MS
293.5	water,] 1A; ~ ∧ MS. *End of line.*
293.6	pasturage,] 1A; ~ ∧ MS
293.9	east north east] T; East north east MS; east-north-east 1A
293.10–11	which, . . . joy,] 1A; ~ ∧ . . . ~ ∧ MS. *Irving interlined* to . . . joy.
293.12	night,] 1A; ~ ∧ MS. *End of line.*
293.25	bull] 1A; Bull MS
293.37	them;] 1A; ~, MS
295.10–11	overcast,] 1A; ~; MS
295.24	streams,] 1A; ~ ∧ MS
295.25	be the] 2A; be MS, 1A
295.35	be the] 1A; be MS
296.17	recesses ∧] T; ~, MS
296.20	river,] 1A; ~ ∧ MS
297.2–3	therefore,] 1A; ~ ∧ MS. *Edge of page.*
*297.27	scouts,] 1A; ~; MS
297.29	venison] 1A; Venison MS
298.4	fire] 1A; fire and MS
298.10	threshold.] 1A; ~." MS
*298.21	absence,] T; ~ ∧ MS
298.34	three,] 1A; ~ ∧ MS
299.16	his] 2A; the MS, 1A
*299.24	lieutenant,] 1A; ~ ∧ MS
299.29	o'clock,] 1A; ~; MS
299.33	would,] T; ~ ∧ MS
299.38	ammunition] T; amunition MS, 1A
299.40	"and] 1A; ∧ ~ MS
*302.17	wastes ∧] T; ~; MS
*302.35–36	suspended,] 1A; ~; MS
*302.36	parts of] T; of MS, 1A
*302.37	tongues ∧ . . . bones,] T; ~, . . . ~ ∧ MS
303.1	wigwam ∧] 1A; ~, MS
303.13–14	but extremely shallow stream] 1A; stream, but extremely shallow MS
303.23	prairie,] 1A; ~ ∧ MS. Naked prairie *is interlined.*
304.30	for a] 2A; for MS, 1A

305.17   long, ... wide,] 1A; $\sim_\wedge$ ... $\sim_\wedge$ MS. Four feet wide *is interlined.*

305.21   16th] 1A; 16 MS

306.1   months in] 2A; months MS, 1A

*307.36   Pacific$_\wedge$] T; $\sim$. MS; $\sim$, 1A

309.10   placed,] 1A; $\sim_\wedge$ MS

310.3   Oakinagan] 1A; Oakanagan MS. *Elsewhere in the MS it is spelled* Oakinagan.

*310.3   Clarke's] 1A; Clarks MS

310.6   Indians—] 1A; $\sim_\wedge$ MS. *Edge of page.*

310.18   partners] 2A; parties MS, 1A

310.24   stream] 1A; streams MS

310.27   Pierced] 1A; pierced MS. *Emended here and at* 311.16 *and* 322.21 *in accord with Irving's dominant practice.*

*310.28   hardy] 1A; sordid MS

311.20   confiding] 1A; and confided MS

311.21   on] 1A; on of MS

311.21   engaged] 1A; promised MS

311.23   off] 2A; off of MS, 1A

311.38   tribes$_\wedge$] 1A; $\sim_\wedge$ MS

*311.43   Shahaptan] 1A; Shahaptin MS

312.2   the neighborhood] 1A; neighborhood MS

312.8   caches] 1A; Caches MS. *Emended also at* 318.5.

312.12   communicated] 1A; gave them MS

312.14   had,] 1A; $\sim_\wedge$ MS. *The following phrase is interlined.*

312.26   Hibernian] 1A; hibernian MS. *Normalized also at* 324.26 *and* 351.16.

312.30   natives,] 1A; $\sim_\wedge$ MS

*312.43   caches] 2A; cache MS, 1A

313.8   robes,] T; $\sim$; MS

313.35   Carson,] 1A; $\sim_\wedge$ MS

*313.36   who,] 1A; $\sim_\wedge$ MS

313.37   Detayé] 1A; Detayè MS. *The name is spelled* Detayé *at* 190.6, 9, *and* 314.3.

314.11   Mountains,] T; Mountains; MS; mountains, 1A

314.14   wanderers,] 1A; $\sim_\wedge$ MS

314.15–17   to clear ... Indians.] 1A; to glean such things as might remain in the caches. MS

*314.22   Arapahays] 1A; Arapahoes MS

314.27   Arapahays] 1A; Arrapahoes MS

*315.10   Nez percés] T; Nezperce's 1A [*MS lacking*]

315.22   fortress] 2A; little fortress MS, 1A

315.29   that] 1A; that had MS

316.22	Tonquin,] 1A; $\sim_\wedge$ MS
316.24	than] T; that MS, 1A
316.35	Tushepaws,] 1A; $\sim_\wedge$ MS
*316.38	M'Kenzie] 1A; MKenzies MS
317.1	exorbitant] 1A; exhorbitant MS. *Emended also at* 338.26.
317.10–11	With this view] 1A; For this purpose MS
317.17	where he received] 1A; received MS
317.19	with] 1A; with with MS
317.36	blockaded.] 1A; $\sim$; MS
317.40	this] 2A; the MS, 1A
318.10	Irishman,] 1A; $\sim_\wedge$ MS
318.28	man,] T; $\sim_\wedge$ MS, 1A. *End of line.*
318.36	chief] 1A; cheif MS
*318.37	Indians] 1A; Indians in MS
319.4	"Keep . . . him,"] 1A; $_\wedge\sim$ . . . $\sim_{,\wedge}$ MS
319.10	axe,] 1A; $\sim_\wedge$ MS
319.15	goods] 1A; good MS
319.22	to] 2A; to to MS, 1A
319.31	themselves on their escape,] 1A; themselves MS
319.38	bound,] 1A; $\sim_\wedge$ MS
320.11–12	Mr. M'Dougall] T; M'Dougall MS; Mr. M'Dougal 1A
320.16	pusillanimous] T; pusilannimous MS; pusilanimous 1A
320.21	Wallah Wallah] T; $\sim$-$\sim$ 1A [*MS lacking*]
320.23	twenty eight] T; $\sim$-$\sim$ 1A [*MS lacking*]
320.27	rivers] 1A; river MS
320.31	making them] T; making MS
321.13	was] 2A; were MS, 1A
322.10	and made] 1A; that made MS
322.12	comrades,] 1A; $\sim_\wedge$ MS
322.18	they] 1A; he MS
322.18	them] 1A; him MS
322.21	excite . . . by] 1A; win . . . at MS
322.30	had arrived] 1A; arrived MS
323.7	previously$_\wedge$] 1A; $\sim$, MS
323.14	as to] 2A; of MS, 1A
*323.18	reconnoiter] T; recconnoitre MS; reconnoitre 1A
323.34	Clarke] 1A; Clark MS
323.36	inveighed] 1A; invieghed MS
323.38	dangers] 1A; dangers and perplexities MS
324.5	it] 1A; his request MS
324.5	furthermore$_\wedge$] 1A; $\sim$, MS
324.17	following] 1A; succeeding MS
324.20	that they] 1A; that MS

324.30   Astoria,] 1A; ~∧ MS
324.39   to render] 1A; to take every precaution to render MS
°324.41   hunters and eight common] T; hundles[?] and eight
              men MS; hunters, and eight common 1A
325.2   privates] 1A; common men MS
325.14   Company's] T; Companies MS; company's 1A
325.25   D.] 1A; D∧ MS
326.2   Memorial] T; memorial 1A; machinations MS
326.14   operations,] 1A; ~∧ MS. *End of line.*
°326.19   which was] 1A; which MS
326.22   its ruins] 1A; the ruins of Astoria MS
326.30   Pacific,] 1A; ~∧ MS
326.31   Crane,] 1A; ~∧ MS. *Compare* 336.21.
326.36   R.] 1A; R∧ MS
327.6–7   being thus relieved and strengthened] 1A; strengthened
              from these two sources; MS
327.12   complement] 2A; compliment MS, 1A
327.28–29   maintain itself] 1A; keep up a lingering existence MS
328.2   Affairs] 1A; Delicate affairs MS
328.11–14   Astoria.... a] 1A; Astoria. This was a match between
              McDougall the great Eri of the American Fur Com-
              pany and an Indian princess, MS
328.18–23   Some ... guest.] 1A; The reader may reccollect that the
              susceptible heart of McDougall, which was said to
              be alive to indiscriminate impressions from the gentler
              sex of every caste and complexion, was peculiarly
              touched by the charms of this piscatory princess, dur-
              ing a nights lodging in her fathers palace, when weath-
              er bound on his first exploring expedition about the
              mouth of the Columbia. MS
328.24   Astoria,] 1A; ~∧ MS
°329.9   exerted] 1A; shewn exerted MS
329.14   Conference] 1A; Conferences MS
329.17   represented as having] 1A; said to have had MS
329.19   afternoon,] 1A; ~∧ MS
329.19–20   crossed over] 2A; crossed MS, 1A
°329.24   feathers,] 1A; ~∧ MS
329.29–33   *Paragraph* Her ... state,] 1A; *No paragraph* She had
              nothing but her native charms for a dowry; however,
              M Dougall consoled himself with the old adage "one
              can have nothing of the cat but her skin," and though
              in the present instance the skin was none of the
              fairest; yet by copious ablutions and scrapings it was

cleared from all the paint and fish oil with which it had been enamelled and anointed for the occasion, and she came to the arms of the uxorious McDougall MS

329.31	toilette] T; toilet 1A [*MS lacking*]. *Usual MS form.*
329.34	unctuous] 1A; unctious MS
329.42	and] 1A; and the politic and enamoured MS
330.1	Comcomly,] 1A; ~∧ MS
330.5	hurried to the water side] 1A; tore himself from his bride MS
330.7	watching] 1A; straining their eyes towards MS
331.3	tyranny] 1A; tyrrany MS. *Corrected also at* 332.15.
331.5	islands] 1A; island MS
331.11	and then] 1A; and MS
331.13	Sound,] 1A; ~∧ MS
331.14	50'] 1A; 50. MS
331.24	this] 1A; this old MS
*331.35	dependants∧] 1A; ~, MS
331.37	maritime] 1A; maratime MS
332.2	ship would be] 1A; ships was MS
332.8	dexterity] 1A; dextexity MS
332.11	would render] 1A; rendered MS
*332.22	captain] 1A; Captain MS. Captain(s) *is emended to a lowercase form also at* 332.26 *and* 347.17.
332.37	he] 1A; he he MS
332.40	do his] 1A; do MS
333.13	it so] 1A; so it MS
333.21	31st] 1A; 31″ MS
333.31	of] 1A; from MS
334.2	ancient] 1A; antient MS
334.26	place∧] T; ~, MS
334.42	He considered it] 1A; It seemed MS
335.22	evil] 1A; evils MS
*336.15–16	Astoria, . . . fate∧] T; ~∧ . . . ~, MS
*336.30	Sindbad] T; Sinbad MS, 1A
*338.9	Commodore Porter] T; Porter MS, 1A
338.15	that they] 1A; they MS
*338.26	exorbitant,] 1A; exhorbitant: MS
*338.37	and might] 1A; and he might MS
339.4	1813,] 1A; 1813. MS
339.10	leeward] 1A; leward MS
339.31	*Paragraph* On] 1A; *No paragraph* On MS
339.36	sprit,] 1A; ~∧ MS

340.4   swimmer] 1A; diver MS
340.8   were] 1A; was MS
*340.17   natives] 1A; the natives MS
*341.4   on] 1A; in on MS
341.7   Fur] 1A; fur MS
341.24–26   Such . . . course.] 1A; Such was the fate of the Lark;
               furnishing another chapter in this singular series of
               misfortunes and cross purposes. Had she reached her
               destination in safety the fortunes of Astoria might
               have been different. MS
341.31   of January] T; January MS
342.14   J.] 1A; J$_\wedge$ MS
342.14   Stuart, . . . Company,] 1A; $\sim_\wedge$ . . . $\sim_\wedge$ MS
342.23   chuckling] 1A; swaggering MS
342.26   secret] 1A; private MS
343.1   swelling] 1A; swaggering MS
343.2–3   wilderness; they, in fact,] 1A; wilderness, who MS
343.13   quick,] 1A; $\sim_\wedge$ MS
343.14   Westers] T; westers MS, 1A
343.19   spirits,] 1A; $\sim_\wedge$ MS. *The MS formerly read* spirits at
               work.
343.21   apparently,] 1A; $\sim_\wedge$ MS. *End of line.*
343.41   observed,] 1A; $\sim_\wedge$ MS
343.43   West] T; west MS, 1A
344.1   they were] 2A; were MS, 1A
344.12   furs and merchandize] T; property and establishments
               MS; furs and merchandise 1A
344.13   Astor,] 1A; $\sim_\wedge$ MS
344.28 2_\wedge$] T; $2. MS
344.28   though worth] 1A; worth MS
344.29 12_\wedge$] T; $12. MS
344.29 60_\wedge$] T; 60. MS
344.32   prices:] T; $\sim_\wedge$ MS; $\sim$:– 1A
344.33   lbs.] 1A; $\sim_\wedge$ MS
344.33   valued at $2.00] T; $2 MS; valued at $2,00 1A. *In the*
               following list of prices, Irving used a decimal point
               in only one number, 1.66. Instead of 3.50 he wrote 3½
               and instead of 1.50 (344.43) he wrote 1½. Irving's
               numbers are emended for the reader's convenience
               according to the pattern in 1A, with periods instead
               of commas being used to mark decimal points. These
               numbers follow, with the manuscript form in paren-
               theses: 5.00 (5), 3.50 (3½), .50 (50), 5.00 (5), 12.00

(12), 60.00 (60), 5.00 (5), 25.00 (25), .40 (40 cents each), .40 ("), 2.00 ($2), 1.00 (1), 1.50 (1½), 4.00 (4), 10.00 (10.). *Added according to the system in* 1A *are the ditto marks under* valued at, worth, *and* worth each.

344.37	30 " "] 1A; 30 . . . MS
344.43	106 "] 1A; 106$_\wedge$ MS
*345.2	capture; that] T; ~. That MS, 1A
345.2	problematical,] T; ~$_\wedge$ MS. *Edge of page.*
345.4	vessels] 1A; Vessels MS
345.5	certificate,] 1A; ~$_\wedge$ MS
345.13	Astor; that] 1A; ~. That MS. *See 345.2 above.*
345.16–17	"been . . . disgraced."] 1A; $_\wedge$~ . . . ~·$_\wedge$ MS
346.2	strange sail] 1A; Strange Sail MS
*346.7	Of] 1A; but of MS
*346.11	M'Tavish,] 1A; ~$_\wedge$ MS
346.29	Janeiro.] 1A; ~, MS. *A splice follows.*
347.26	and assembled] 1A; and, assemblying MS
347.27	"King George," . . . "has] 1A; $_\wedge$~~,$_\wedge$ . . . $_\wedge$~ MS
347.28	it?] 1A; it. MS
348.2	the] 1A; either the MS
348.3–4	wash . . . appear] 1A; to wash . . . to appear MS
348.5	courteously] 1A; as friends MS
348.18	required] 1A; craved MS
348.30	reconciled] 1A; recconciled MS
*348.34	erected] 1A; hoisted MS
348.40	being a] 1A; a MS
350.3	Company–] T; Company$_\wedge$ MS; company– 1A. *End of line in the MS.*
350.20	feelings] 1A; feeling MS
350.22	December.] 1A; ~, MS. *Canceled matter follows in the MS.*
350.26	Clarke,] 1A; ~$_\wedge$ MS
350.32	the drafts] 1A; The drafts MS
350.39	Halsey,] 1A; ~$_\wedge$ MS
351.1	4th,] 1A; 4th$_\wedge$ MS
351.1	M'Kenzie,] 1A; ~$_\wedge$ MS
351.6–7	relate their . . . noted] 1A; relate an occurrence which closes the fortunes of one of the persons occasionally noticed MS
*351.9	Wallah Wallah] T; Walla Wallah MS; Wallah-Wallah 1A. *Emended again at 352.20, 30 and 352.32 (Wallah Wallahs).*

351.14–15   of our unfortunate adventurers.] 1A; persons in the employ of the Company. MS
351.18   Canadians,] 1A; ~∧ MS
351.18   Clerc] 1A; clerc MS
351.23   Rezner] 1A; Reznor MS. Rezner *is by far the dominant form in the MS. Emended also at 351.28, 30, 39.*
351.25   sullen,] 1A; ~∧ MS. *End of line.*
351.27   not,] 1A; ~∧ MS. *End of line.*
351.28   had] 1A; had now MS
351.31   wintering] 1A; Wintering MS
351.34   hunting,] 1A; ~∧ MS. *Emended to avoid ambiguity.*
351.37   staggered,] 1A; ~∧ MS
352.5   to] 2A; for MS, 1A
352.6   descried] 1A; discried MS
*352.37   Others] T; others MS, 1A
352.38   have ascribed] 1A; ascribed MS
352.40–42   If ... provocation.] 1A; *omitted* MS
353.1–8   of this ... savages.] 1A; who have figured in the course of this motley story, and shews the perils of a hunters life in the wilderness. Reed and Dorion have been frequently and particularly mentioned. Turcot and La Chapelle were two of the men who abandoned Mr Crooks in the course of his wintry journey and had afterwards such disastrous times among the Indians. Robinson, Rezner and Hoback were the trio of Kentucky hunters, who twice turned back when on their way home, and lingered in the wilderness to perish. MS
353.11   Odyssey] 1A; Odessy MS
354.4   country] 1A; Country MS
355.18   company] 1A; Company MS
355.24   Company,] 1A; ~∧ MS
*355.28   view; for, had] 1A; view. Had MS
355.29   greatly to the advantage] 1A; to the great advantage MS
355.29–356.5   The profits ... China.] 1A; We should have had a line of trading posts from the Mississippi and the Missouri, across the Rocky Mountains, forming a high road from the great regions of the West to the shores of the Pacific and thence to the East Indies. We should have had a fortified post and port at the mouth of the Columbia, commanding the trade of that river and its tributaries, and of a wide extent of country and sea coast; as well as carrying on an active and profit-

able commerce with the Sandwich Islands.

The profits drawn from the Country by the British fur Company, though of ample amount, form no criterion by which to judge of the advantages that would have arisen had it been entirely in the hands of citizens of the United States. That company, as has been shewn, is limited in the nature and scope of its trade, and can make but little use of the maritime facilities held out by an emporium and a harbor on that coast. In our hands, the country would have been explored and settled by industrious husbandmen; and the fertile valleys bordering its rivers and shut up among its mountains, would have been made to pour forth their agricultural treasures to contribute to the general wealth. MS

356.6	understood] 1A; under stood MS. *Elsewhere this is one word.*
356.19	second] 1A; Second MS
356.31	belligerent] T; belligerant 1A [*MS lacking*]
356.33–39	Since . . . "ASTORIA."] 2A; *omitted* MS, 1A. *This paragraph was added in the Author's Revised Edition.*
359.4	Congress] 2A; congress 1A. Congress *is emended to Irving's usual capitalization again at* 361.1 *and* 362.25.
359.35	President's] 2A; president's 1A
360.3	Lake] 2A; lake 1A. *Emended to Irving's preference again at* 362.14.
360.20	President] 2A; president 1A. *Emended to Irving's usual form again at* 361.2, 9, 362.3, *and* 363.6.
362.4	Secretary] Gallatin; secretary 1A
362.4	Treasury] Gallatin; treasury 1A
362.6	Executive] 2A; executive 1A. *Emended also at* 362.20.
362.34	Mountains] 2A; mountains 1A. *Normalized to Irving's usual form also at* 364.10, 29, 31, 369.4–5, 13, 26, *and* 370.15–16, 20.
*364.31	countries$_\wedge$ . . . Pacific$_\wedge$] SJ; $\sim$, . . . $\sim$, 1A
364.33	Russians, . . . north west$_\wedge$] SJ; $\sim$; . . . $\sim$-$\sim$, 1A
364.34	Island in N. Lat. 53°] SJ; $\sim$, in north latitude fifty-three degrees 1A. *This agrees with Irving's usual practice.*
365.7	Columbia river] SJ; Columbia 1A
*365.12	with] SJ; in 1A
366.1, 11	Mustela] SJ; mustela 1A
366.35	north eastern] T; North Eastern SJ; north-eastern 1A
367.5	shell fish] SJ; shell-fish 1A

367.17   55°] SJ; fifty-five degrees 1A
367.24   63°] SJ; sixty-three degrees 1A
369.2   hunter] 2A; vunter 1A
373.39   of] T; or 1A

LIST OF REJECTED SUBSTANTIVES

This list provides a historical record of substantive variants in the authorized texts that appeared during Irving's lifetime, but that were not adopted for the text of *Astoria* in the Twayne edition. The following symbols are used to designate the sources of the readings:

MS	Manuscript used as printer's copy for the first American edition of *Astoria* (1836)
1A	First American edition published by Carey, Lea, & Blanchard
2A	Second American edition, printed by Putnam's in 1849 as volume VIII of the Author's Revised Edition (New York, 1848–51)
T	Twayne edition

The numbers before each note indicate the page and line. Chapter numbers, chapter or section titles, epigraphs, author's chapter or section summaries, texts, quotations, and footnotes are included in the line count. Only running heads and rules added by the printer to separate running heads from the text are omitted from the count.

These notes identify all 1A or 2A substantives not accepted in the Twayne edition. The reading to the left of the bracket represents the accepted reading, with the source of the reading identified by symbol after the bracket. The reading after the semicolon is the rejected reading. Brief explanatory comments, if needed, follow in italics. Readings requiring lengthier discussions are identified by an asterisk*, and the editorial decisions are explained in the Discussions of Adopted Readings.

3.11	the imagination] 1A; imagination 2A
*5.27	continents] MS; countries 1A
*5.30	colonization] MS; civilization 1A
*5.33	object] MS; objects 1A
7.6	time] MS; turn 1A. *This is obviously a compositor's misreading.*
*7.11	our East India men] MS; an East Indiaman 1A
8.3	carried] MS; caused 1A
8.22	those] MS; these 1A

*9.24	with avidity] T; with with avidity MS; with much avidity 1A
10.32	from] MS; from a 1A
*11.1	climates] MS; climate 1A
12.38	buffalo] T; Buffalo MS; buffalo's 1A; buffaloes' 2A
13.13	then] MS, 1A; the 2A
13.14	their] MS, 1A; the 2A
14.2	Attempts] T; attempts MS; attempt 1A
*14.31	frontiers] MS; frontier 1A
15.8	but be] MS, 1A; be but 2A
15.42	upward] MS, 1A; upwards 2A
16.24	sides] MS; side 1A. *Compare* frontiers *at* 14.31.
*16.26	trade] MS, 1A; a trade 2A
16.32	wider] MS; wide 1A
17.37	British] MS, 1A; the British 2A
19.19	We now come] MS, 1A; We come now 2A
20.4	its] MS, 1A; the 2A
21.43	national] MS; maternal 1A
22.26	on casual voyages] MS; or casual voyagers 1A
22.37	Still] MS; Yet still 1A. *Irving canceled* Yet *in the MS.*
24.16	port] MS; post 1A
28.39	leggings] MS; legging 1A; leggins 2A
30.14	on] MS; in 1A
*34.33	night cap] MS; nightcaps 1A
35.39	moods] MS; mood 1A
36.20	voyage] MS, 1A; voyages 2A
*36.30	purpose] MS, 1A; purposes 2A
37.19	techy] MS; touchy 1A
42.27	these] MS; their 1A
47.32	on] MS; in 1A
48.27–28	subsequently] MS; afterwards 1A. Afterwards *is canceled in the MS.*
49.21	sitting] MS, 2A; setting 1A
50.19	suspicions] MS; suspicious 1A
*52.14	river] MS; river's 1A
57.9	sits] MS; sets 1A
*59.19	a day] MS, 1A; the ~ 2A
63.25	avowed] MS; averred 1A
63.36	proven] MS, 1A; proved 2A
64.5	sepulchres] MS; sepulchre 1A
65.17	wintered] MS; ventured 1A
67.21	rise on] MS; ~ in 1A
68.13	with] MS, 1A; and 2A

69.39	visited] MS, 1A; visit 2A
*71.10	enameled] MS; ornamented 1A
73.4–5	languages] MS, 1A; language 2A
73.22–23	out his wares upon the] MS, 1A; his wares upon 2A
*75.4	seven] MS; some 1A
77.9	were] MS; was 1A
77.41	these] MS; those 1A
80.4	forests] MS; forest 1A
81.1	least act of] MS, 1A; least 2A
81.42	lapse] MS, 1A; relapse 2A
82.8	the Indians] MS, 1A; Indians 2A
*84.8	the dance] MS, 1A; dance 2A
84.20	Year's] T; Years MS; year 1A
85.18	already been] MS; been already 1A
85.23	amiable] MS, 1A; amicable 2A
86.6	vices] MS; vice 1A
*89.13	for a] MS, 1A; ~ the 2A
90.28	pursers] MS; purses 1A
*90.39	yelps] MS, 1A; yells 2A
90.41	difficulty that] MS; difficulty 1A
92.29	farther] MS; further 1A
98.23	this] MS, 1A; his 2A
*102.19	canoe] MS, 1A; canoes 2A
102.34	and to] MS; to 1A
103.7	run] MS; ran 1A
103.10	faster] MS, 1A; fastest 2A
103.20	to hurl] MS, 1A; hurl 2A
103.31	where] MS; whose 1A
104.17	on] MS; in 1A
107.18	rocks] MS; rock 1A
107.37	fanciful] MS; faithful 1A
*107.39	at] MS; of 1A
*110.18	a charge] MS, 1A; charge 2A
111.14	another.*] MS; another. 1A
111.42	*Bradbury. P. 66.] MS; *omitted* 1A
113.19	by his] MS, 1A; by 2A
*113.31	to] MS; of 1A
113.42	Poncas] MS; Ponca 1A
114.32	prairies] MS, 1A; prairie 2A
117.7	their] MS; these 1A
*119.1	on] MS; of 1A
120.26	ran] MS, 2A; run 1A
123.1	XVIII] T; XVI 1A

123.19   in] MS, 2A; on 1A
124.36   him] MS; them 1A
*125.5   the] MS; his 1A
127.12   these] MS; those 1A
127.25   the passage] MS, 1A; their ∼ 2A
128.5   to the] MS, 1A; to 2A
132.2   incited] MS, 2A; invited 1A
133.12   when] MS; whom 1A
*133.12   left him] MS; left 1A
*133.25   gallantly] MS; gently 1A
133.29   motives] MS; notions 1A
133.30   writings] MS; writing 1A
137.13   like a] MS; like 1A
*137.40   boat] MS, 1A; boats 2A
*138.33   who] MS; he 1A
*139.26   rivers] MS; the rivers 1A
*140.21   between] MS; between the 1A
141.42   *Breckenridge.] MS; *omitted* 1A
142.18   these] MS; them 1A
143.8   relatives] MS; relations 1A
*143.31   were] MS; are 1A
145.35   bawling] MS; brawling 1A
146.10   hunters] MS, 2A; hunter 1A
146.19   fatted] MS; fattened 1A
146.36   relatives] MS; relations 1A
147.8   observant] MS, 1A; observing 2A
148.13   gay] MS, 1A; gray 2A. *The usage is similar to that in line* 16.
*155.17   prairies] MS; plains 1A
155.26   the more] MS, 1A; more 2A
157.33   these] MS; those 1A
160.7   narrative] MS; narration 1A
160.10   Horn] MS; Horse 1A
*160.37   frontier] MS; frontiers 1A
161.4   associated] MS; and associated 1A
161.15   thought] MS, 1A; though 2A
*162.13   trees] MS, 1A; the trees 2A
162.22   peaceable] MS, 1A; peaceful 2A
162.24   unusually] MS, 1A; usually 2A
163.1   these] MS; those 1A
163.36   discernible] T; discernable MS; discoverable 1A
164.13   constraint] MS, 1A; restraint 2A
164.37   moping] MS, 1A; smoking 2A

165.5	once] MS; ever 1A
166.36–37	significancy] MS; significance 1A
168.28	hope] MS, 1A; hopes 2A
169.26	prairies] MS, 1A; prairie 2A
*173.21	forty] MS; fifty 1A
174.2	bases] MS, 1A; basis 2A
*174.14	sometimes of] MS; of 1A
174.33	Hills] MS; hills 1A; Hill 2A
177.25	whom] MS; who 1A
*177.31	preparation] MS, 1A; preparations 2A
177.35	prepared] MS; proposed 1A
179.32	fairly out] MS, 2A; ~ ought 1A
182.6	subjected] MS, 1A; subject 2A
183.33	the Rocky] MS; the the Rocky 1A
184.18	passed through] MS, 1A; passed 2A
186.10	in] 1A; on 2A
187.26	towards] MS; toward 1A
187.27	contributions] MS; contribution 1A
*189.12	had hitherto] MS; had 1A
189.34	proceed for] MS; proceed 1A
*192.3	departure] MS; separation 1A
*195.43–196.1	never before] 1A; never 2A
197.37	eighty] MS, 1A; eight 2A
199.21	savage] MS; swamp 1A; swamps 2A
200.38	four] MS; five 1A. *It is also* four *in Hunt.*
*201.43	dry grass, bark,] MS; dried grass 1A
202.23	their] MS; this 1A
205.35	hollows] MS; hollow 1A. *Compare* 232.32.
206.3	into] MS; in 1A
206.37	parts] MS, 1A; part 2A
206.43	except hares] MS; excepting horses 1A
*207.36	prairie] MS; prairies 1A
*207.40	of some of] MS; of 1A
208.6	streak] MS; streaks 1A
*212.22	Gardepie] T; Sardepie 1A
217.12	over] MS; on 1A
217.40	fires] MS, 1A; fire 2A
*220.5	unknown] MS; lonesome 1A
221.16	baggage] MS; luggage 1A
221.32	this] MS; the 1A
221.33	continual] MS; continued 1A
*223.9	for four] MS; for 1A
223.34	night's] T; nights MS; night 1A. *Cf.* 224.29.

223.40   joyful] MS; jovial 1A
226.30   avoiding] MS, 2A; winding 1A
*226.31   great bend] MS; bend 1A
226.35   was here] MS; was 1A. *In the MS,* here *is partially* blotted.
227.15   dog] MS, 1A; dog's 2A
*228.20   first day] MS; first 1A
230.5   large] MS, 2A; larger 1A
231.42   camerades] MS; comrades 1A
236.11   the seine] MS; seine 1A
237.2   elk,] MS; *omitted* 1A. *Irving wrote* elk, *in the margin of the MS.*
237.19   in the] MS; on the 1A
239.3   for] MS; of 1A
240.1   this] MS; the 1A
241.15, 16   bear's] T; bears MS; bear 1A
242.10   preponderate] MS; predominate 1A
242.14   intercessor] MS; interpreter 1A
242.14   desireable] MS; describable 1A; desirabable 2A
242.22   a bird] MS, 1A; bird 2A. *The 1A form is correct in context.*
242.23   bears' and] T; bears and MS; bear's and and 1A
242.27   corner] MS; canoe 1A
244.11   slaves] MS; slave 1A
*246.35   vagabonds] MS, 1A; vagrants 2A
*250.5   the fight] 1A; fight 2A
257.3   remarked] 1A; remarkable 2A
264.20   Hunt] MS; Stuart 1A
*267.26   Mr. Joseph] T; Mr Joseph MS; Joseph 1A
268.32   in] MS; on 1A
269.1   recruits to] MS, 1A; ~ of 2A. *In the context, the 1A version is more correct.*
269.9   were] MS, 2A; where 1A
269.22   readily] MS; easily 1A
*270.14–15   had ... found] MS; did ... find 1A
272.5   and from] MS; from 1A
*273.14   now kept] MS; kept 1A
274.29   these] MS; them 1A
*274.36   the river] MS, 1A; a river 2A
276.10   encampments] MS; encampment 1A
*277.9   long long] MS; long 1A
277.21   alert] MS; about 1A
279.2   voyagers] MS; voyageurs 1A

281.6	these] MS; those 1A
281.17	harebrained] MS; hairbrained 1A
281.18	passage] MS; passages 1A
284.24	came in] MS, 1A; in 2A
284.43	operations] MS, 1A; eruptions 2A
*285.41	none such] MS, 1A; none 2A
286.18	where he] MS, 1A; where 2A
287.10	those] MS, 1A; these 2A
*289.9	felt] MS; to be felt 1A
290.16	trace] MS; trail 1A
292.4	run] MS; rill 1A
292.36	this] MS; the 1A
293.39	on] MS; in 1A
295.4	Big horns] MS; bighorn 1A
295.17	vain] MS, 1A; in vain 2A
297.5	when] MS, 2A; where 1A
297.36	yelp] MS, 1A; yell 2A. *See the discussion for* 90.39.
297.37	yelp] MS, 1A; yell 2A
298.43	wistful] MS, 2A; wilful 1A
301.28	cedars] MS; cedar 1A
301.32	cotton woods and willows] MS; cottonwood and willow 1A
*308.18	the means] MS; means 1A
309.16	attempt] MS; attempts 1A
310.16	interim] MS; interior 1A
316.12	this MS; the 1A
317.22–23	establishments] MS, 1A; establishment 2A
318.1	Their] MS; This 1A
318.15	their] MS, 2A; the their 1A
318.21	hare brained] MS; hair-brained 1A
318.35	about] MS; of about 1A. Of *is canceled in the MS.*
*318.39	assemblage] MS, 1A; assembly 2A
*319.40	M'Kenzie] MS, 1A; Mr. M'Kenzie 2A
319.42	camerades] MS; comrades 1A. *Cf.* 231.42.
*320.3–4	correspondent] MS; corresponding 1A
*321.27	visit] MS, 1A; visits 2A
323.15	seemed] MS, 1A; seem 2A
*323.34	and they] MS; They 1A
324.8	fort MS; post 1A
324.11	that] MS, 2A; that that 1A
*324.33	at] MS; of 1A
324.40	of the] MS, 1A; of 2A
325.2	Cox] MS; Ross Cox 1A. *In the MS Ross is canceled.*

326.25	that it] MS; it 1A. *In the MS* that *is smeared and easy to miss.*
327.16	were] MS; was 1A
331.35	Beside the] MS; ~ those 1A. *In the MS Irving has altered* those *to* the.
332.11	received] MS; receive 1A
332.21	sitting] MS, 2A; setting 1A
332.41	humours] MS; humor 1A
332.42	him] MS, 1A; himself 2A
333.7	devotion] MS; devotions 1A
333.10–11	expended in] MS; expended 1A
333.38	composes] MS, 1A; compose 2A
333.41	caves] MS; canoes 1A
336.2	spirits] MS; spirit 1A
339.27	holds] MS; hold 1A
340.11	where] MS; when 1A
340.40	nor] MS; or 1A
341.36	absence.] MS, *second state of* 1A, 2A; absence./ *Bra6.db ury. P.6/ * Breckenridge. *First state of* 1A
342.15	seven] MS; some 1A
342.31	were] MS; was 1A
343.13	flouted] MS; flowed 1A
343.23	that] MS, 1A; the 2A
344.41	38] MS, 1A; 28 2A
346.10	possessions] MS; possession 1A
346.29	was Mr.] T; was Mr MS; Mr. 1A. Was *is blurred in the* MS.
347.1	this] MS; the 1A
347.8	snug] MS, 1A; sung 2A
347.27	this] MS; his 1A
350.5	revive] MS; renew 1A. *Cf.* 353.27.
350.14	Mr. M'Dougall] T; Mr M Dougall MS; Mr. M'Dougal 1A; M'Dougal 2A
352.15	around] MS, 1A; round 2A
352.15	ferocious] MS; furious 1A
*352.19–20	rocky mountains near] MS; the Rocky mountains, near 1A
352.38	Pierced nose] MS; Pierced-nose 1A; Pierced-nosed 2A
*354.8	Government] MS; the government 1A
*355.33	citizens] 1A; the citizens 2A
356.14	disputes] MS; dispute 1A
*363.2	those] 1A; these 2A
363.14	very] 1A; most 2A
364.33	on] 1A; and on 2A

367.22   purposes] 1A; purpose 2A
*370.4   barometer] 1A; barometric 2A
373.28   repress] 1A; depress 2A
373.35   advantage] 1A; advantages 2A

LIST OF COMPOUND WORDS
HYPHENATED
AT END OF LINE

List I includes compound and possible compound words that are hyphenated at the end of the line in the copy-text (*Astoria* MS, or 1A where MS is lacking). In deciding whether these words should be printed in the T text as hyphenated, one word, or two words, the editor has made his decision first on the use of each compound word elsewhere in the copy-text; or second, when the word does not appear elsewhere in the copy-text, on Irving's practice in other writings of this period; or finally, if the word does not appear in Irving's other writings of the period, on contemporary American usage. Each word is listed in its editorially accepted form after the page and line numbers of its appearance in the T text.

List II presents compounds, or possible compounds, that are hyphenated at the end of the line in the T text. They are listed in the form in which they would have appeared in the T text had they come in midline.

LIST I

8.25	canoemen	157.1	overjoyed
9.9	bloodshed	177.30	white men
9.28	outbid	181.29	Blackfeet
10.13	warehouses	183.10	strawberries
11.24	goldsmiths	193.16	without
31.12	Scotchmen	196.13	wide-wandering
37.22	landsmen	196.21	all-pervading
42.21	serio-comic	196.37	bottle-green
44.39	boyhood	209.4	westward
53.43	overwhelmed	210.23	northward
61.7	gentlemen	210.28	chokecherries
68.28	Strawberry	236.31	cranberries
70.1	fishermen	245.15	overland
95.36	backwoods	254.2	north west
124.33	Blackfeet	259.31	boatmen
144.43	quidnuncs	259.39	rattlesnakes
156.6	commonplace	264.8	Woodpile

269.21	spearsman	364.13	horseback
296.39	overlooked	369.6	North West
303.1	wigwam	372.3	warfare
310.34	Blackfeet	372.8	warfare
320.21	Wallah Wallah	374.10	field-pieces
336.29	seafaring		

LIST II

29.20	steersman	230.5	northward
82.22	forethought	237.11	rattlesnake
95.9	boatsongs	272.11	midnight
100.37	superabundant	311.19	overgrown
123.2	woodman	325.28	overcome
179.14	horseback	327.14	seamen
215.4	frost-bitten	337.4	shipwreck

PRE-COPY-TEXT ALTERATIONS
IN CHAPTER XXXIII

As is mentioned in the Textual Commentary, the following list of alterations is an example of the kinds of alterations Irving made in a regular
MS chapter. Erasures and significant cancellations are included in angle
brackets ⟨ ⟩. Interlineations are indicated by arrows↑↓. Editorial explanations are italicized within square brackets and doubtful readings
are followed by a question mark in brackets. When one or more letters
are canceled or written over, the substitution appears immediately
after the canceled matter, without an intervening space: for example,
"th⟨is⟩ese." Cancellations which are identical with the substitution,
canceled fragments of letters which are illegible, mere slips of the
pen, and meaningless false starts are not reproduced.

199.10	of their ⟨class[?]⟩
199.13	distance ⟨that the canoes had come, since⟩ ⟨they had come⟩ ⟨they had ↑come↓ floated down this⟩
199.18	was ⟨further⟩
199.21	among ⟨wil[?]⟩
199.22	very ⟨discou⟩
199.23	along ⟨this⟩
199.25	⟨by the⟩ in
199.27	⟨and⟩ sometimes
199.33	↑however,↓
199.35	be ⟨launched with some chance⟩
199.37	⟨Six of the⟩ ⟨f⟩ Four
199.39	⟨fourt⟩ sixteen
200.1	↑scouting↓
200.6–7	⟨lost⟩ ↑swept away↓
200.10–11	them⟨,⟩. ⟨This disastrous experiment put an end to all hope of navigating the river any further.⟩ ↑the . . . unnavigable.↓
200.14	[*Back of MS p. 4 which ends at* route]: the river still further down than the previous parties had gone; and at the same time to endeavor to find some Indian village or encampment ↑where they might obtain a supply of↓ where horses↑ ⟨and⟩ provisions, and↓ might be procured, should it be found

200.16	th⟨is⟩ese
200.17	repeated ⟨losses⟩
200.21	last ⟨consideration⟩
200.24	⟨led by⟩ headed by
200.24	⟨Each ⟨par⟩ detachment was to shift for itself and shape its course according to circumstances.⟩ Should
200.25–26	↓within a reasonable distance↑
200.31	Linn, ⟨in these [*or* those]⟩
200.35	↓should↑ reach⟨ed⟩
200.36	⟨would⟩ ↑hoped to↓
200.37	⟨for the⟩ to the
200.38	↑composed↓ ⟨consisting⟩
201.1	⟨a woman and⟩ ⟨besi⟩ ⟨together with⟩ ↑beside↓
201.2	⟨Trappers were sent out⟩ There
201.3	but ⟨a number of⟩ beavers were ↑occasionally↓
201.6	with ⟨the⟩
201.7	⟨As it⟩ Mr Hunt
201.9	themselves ⟨a⟩ ⟨previous[?]⟩
201.10	a ⟨word or two⟩
201.12	hunters ⟨in the wilderness⟩
201.14	and ⟨was in⟩ ⟨used by⟩
201.15	the ⟨expedient which it⟩
201.17	hordes ⟨of savages⟩
201.23	⟨spot⟩ ↑bank of clay↓
201.24	⟨upon, the grass and bushes in the vicinity are covered with⟩ ↑upon↓ blankets, ⟨↑and↓⟩ ⟨horse⟩ ↑saddle↓ cloths, ⟨and other⟩ ⟨to prevent their being⟩ ⟨marked as⟩
201.28–29	↑with . . . beneath it↓
201.30	⟨impure mixture with other soil, or from⟩ ↑any↓
201.35	⟨and⟩ in which
201.38	⟨so⟩ earth
201.41–42	⟨provisions and merchandize are⟩ ↑property intended to be hidden is↓
201.42	⟨more[?] grass⟩ a hide
201.43	⟨heaped⟩ thrown in ⟨until⟩
202.2–3	⟨in the⟩ ⟨until nearly level with the surrounding surface. To prevent it from caving in, and to destroy t⟩ ↑to prevent its caving in,↓
202.5	⟨tear up the ground⟩ root
202.6	⟨replaced⟩ ↑again fitted in↓
202.8	⟨positions⟩ ↑places↓
202.12	⟨gathered⟩ gleaned

202.15   sufficient ⟨to⟩
202.17–18   ⟨Mr Hunt was obliged⟩ ↑Mr Hunt found it ⟨it would be⟩
                  necessary↓
202.30   ⟨They· now⟩ their
202.33   they ⟨looked f⟩
202.33   in ⟨making its⟩
202.39   was ⟨not[?]⟩ also
202.41   ⟨↑At the end↓⟩ At length
203.2   Indians ⟨to⟩
203.4   walls. ⟨A linger⟩ ⟨Here⟩ ⟨dis[?] he⟩ ⟨dismayed by⟩
203.6   up⟨:⟩. ⟨t⟩The

OWNERSHIP OR LOCATION

OF

EXTANT ASTORIA MANUSCRIPT

In the chart below, these symbols will be used to indicate the location or ownership of various portions of the *Astoria* manuscript:

WK	Wilmer H. Kingsford
IK	Irving B. Kingsford
J	Owned by Virginia Johnson and at John Howell—Books in San Francisco
N	The New York Public Library, Manuscript Division
V	The University of Virginia, Barrett Collection
SHR	Sleepy Hollow Restorations, Tarrytown, New York

5.1	("Chap")–13.23 ("they")	WK
14.1	("Chap")–14.7 ("Company.")	IK
14.8	("The success")–32.17 ("them.")	WK
33.9	("On")–38.18 ("latter")	V
38.30	("in")–40.23 ("horizon.")	V
41.1	("Chap")–42.22 ("style")	N
42.23	("It")–42.40 ("snow.")	IK
42.41	("The")–91.6 ("September.")	N
92.10	("S' Louis")–94.26 ("the")	N
94.26	("force")–112.38 ("the")	V
112.38	("Blackbird")–113.15 ("inhabitants")	N
113.15	("and burnt")–113.26 ("fact")	V
113.26	("did")—113.35 ("fury,")	N
113.35	("and")–114.4 ("Omahas.")	V
114.5	("This")–122.19 ("trader")	N
123.8	("It")–152.5 ("that a")	N
152.41	("dangers")–158.29 ("solved?")	N
159.14	("Their")–185.37 ("country.")	N
186.13	("of")–187.30 ("the")	V
189.2	("A *consultation*")–192.29 ("post,")	J
197.1	("Shortly")–208.15 ("lodges")	J
216.24	("Mr")–242.32 ("field")	J
243.36	("elevated")–244.11 ("slaves.")	J

245.8   ("As")–246.30 ('Indians,")   J
264.14 ("bounding")–282.5 ("Mr")   J
283.1   ("Chap")–288.22 ("poor")   J
288.35 ("moccasins")–300.28 ("stealing.")   J
301.1   ("Chap.")–314.36 ("Shahaptan.")   WK
315.12 ("After")–320.16 ("the")   WK
320.16 ("first")–320.27 ("at the")   SHR
320.27 ("confluence")–356.20 ("will")   WK

PARTS OF PRINTED EDITIONS
USED AS COPY-TEXT

For the following segments of the Twayne *Astoria* no manuscript has been found; consequently, the editions closest to the missing manuscript serve as copy-text. The specific copies are as follows: for the first American edition, University of North Carolina Library copy number V917.8/- I72a/1836/v.1[2]; for the second American edition, which provides only the last paragraph in the Twayne *Astoria* (356.33–39), UNC Library copy number F880/.I715.

3.1   ("INTRODUCTION")–4.38 ("history.")
33.1   ("CHAPTER")–33.8 ("Owyhee")
38.18 ("was")–38.30 ("inscriptions,")
92.1   ("CHAPTER")–92.9 ("S' Louis")
123.1 ("CHAPTER")–123.7 ("making")
152.5 ("great")–152.40 ("in the")
159.1 ("CHAPTER")–159.13 ("litter.")
186.1 ("CHAPTER")–186.13 ("picture")
187.30 ("men")–188.17 ("ONE")
192.29 ("or")–196.43 ("prizes.")
208.15 ("but")–216.24 ("starvation.")
242.33 ("Polygamy")–243.36 ("character;")
245.1 ("CHAPTER")–245.7 ("Astoria.")
246.30 ("who")–264.14 ("alternately")
282.5 ("Stuart")–282.21 ("event.")
288.23 ("On")–288.35 ("for")
315.1 ("CHAPTER")–315.11 ("Astoria.")
356.20 ("again")–356.32 ("Pacific.")
356.33 ("Since")–356.39 ("'ASTORIA.'") [*From* Author's Revised Edition]
359.1 ("APPENDIX")–374.30 ("months.'")

SEGMENTS OF MANUSCRIPT
NOT INCLUDED
IN THE COPY-TEXT

In the following genetic transcriptions of material not used as printer's copy, these editorial symbols are used:

[*italic*]   Editorial explanations
⟨ ⟩   Restorations of canceled matter
[?]   A doubtful word
↑ ↓   Interlinear insertions, above or below the line

[*Unused MS p. 4/4 essentially covering material from 34.14 to 34.23*]: occasion, he was ⟨a small but⟩ ↑an↓ active, ⟨and⟩ ↑valiant,↓ vainglorious, irritable little man, and elevated, in his own opinion, by ⟨the⟩ being the proxy of Mr Astor. High words ensued between him and the Captain, in the course of which the latter threw out a threat of putting the partners in irons should they prove refractory. ⟨Upon this M Dougall sna⟩ ⟨took⟩ ↑The pride of the doughty M'Dougall took fire at the menace,— he snatched↓ down a pistol and swore to be the death of the Captain should he ever offer such an indignity. It was some time before the irritated parties could be pacified by the interference of the bystanders. Such was the beginning of discord ⟨between the Captain and the partners.⟩ ↑in the Cabin.↓

The clerks, too, were regarded by the Captain with supreme contempt. Some of them

[*Unused MS material from part of MS p. 16, all of MS p. 17, and part of MS p. 18—covering material from 77.13 to 78.5*]:

They proved to be the four gallant survivors who had made such ⟨gallant⟩ desperate defence from the cabin. The interpreter gathered from them some of the particulars communicated in his narrative. ⟨After having beaten off the savages they had attempted to escape in the night in the ships pinnace, in hopes of getting back to Astoria. Lewis was too severely wounded to accompany⟩

After the savages had been beaten off Lewis advised ⟨these⟩ his companions to slip the cable and endeavour to get to sea. ⟨The wind, however,⟩ ⟨They⟩ Why they did not take his advice does not clearly appear, it is supposed that the wind set too strongly into the bay. As soon as it was dark they attempted to escape in one of the ships boats, hoping to be able to get back to Astoria. ⟨The⟩ Being unable to weather a point of land they had put to shore, ⟨and⟩ where, exhausted by fatigue and watching they had fallen into a sound sleep, and in that state had been surprized by the savages. Lewis had refused to accompany them, ⟨being⟩ despairing of their success or of his own recovery, and determining to terminate his life by a signal act of vengeance. For this purpose he had decoyed as many savages as possible on board of the ship and set fire to the powder magazine. It is said that on the voyage out he had repeatedly expressed a presentiment that he should die by his own hands; thinking it highly probable that he should ⟨have⟩ contacts with the natives and being resolved to commit suicide rather than be made a prisoner.

As to the four unfortunate captives, they were put to death with all the tortures of savage cruelty ⟨and rage[?]⟩. The interpreter alone was spared and sometime afterwards effected his escape and brought the tragical tidings to Astoria. ⟨It must⟩ Such was the melancholy fate of the Tonquin, of her brave, but headstrong

[*This unused page covers material from* 189.8 *to* 189.18]:
Vol 2).
Chap.

On the banks of Mad River Mr Hunt held a consultation with his associates as to their future progress. The aspect of the river inspired him with doubt⟨;⟩. ⟨it might abound with⟩ The hunters who had guided him thus far knew nothing of ⟨the character of the river,⟩ ↑its character,↓ how far it might be navigable for canoes & what rocks and shoals and rapids might obstruct it, rendering the navigation tedious and hazardous, if not impracticable. Should they then cast themselves ⟨lose,⟩ ↑loose, therefore,↓ in fragile barks upon this wild, impetuous and unknown river, or continue their more sure, though weary course by land?

NOTES FOR ASTORIA / *1835*

Manitoulin Islands (Lakes[)] once peopled by the Amicways who were descend[d] from the great Beaver a mythological personage of distinction. Manitoulin signifies the residence of Manitoes or Spirits[.] Impressions probably made by *mirage* or looming[.] ⟨These changes attributed to genii or Spirits⟩ We saw a variety of forms given by mirage—castle would appear with ruins—suddenly all would vanish—sometimes a promontory stretching for miles—apparently above the surface of the lake.

These changes which the children of nature could not comprehend were attributed to genii or Spirits and the places where they were most frequently witnessed were considered as being inhabited by manitoes—"It is to these islands made thus strangely various by the mists and vapours & the light, that the indians go to perform their mysterious rites or to pacify the spirits which reside there.

The Oneidas & their confederates were once a powerful people[.] The oneidas had been traced as far back as the S'Lawrence & are said to have once occupied the country in the neighborhood of Montreal; but forced southward by their enemies the Adirondacks[.] I believe they finally settled in the lake country in this state.

MKennay

———

I bade perhaps a final farewell to Lake Superior, and its billowy and changeful surface; its moonlight scenery; its broken and barren shores its grand Sablés; its pictured rocks; its islands and its solitude.

Since our arrival at the falls we have repeatedly heard a strange noise coming from the mountains in a direction a little to the north of west. It is heard at different periods of the day & night, sometimes when the air is perfectly still & without a cloud & consists of one stroke only, or of five or six in quick succession. It is loud & resembles precisely the sound of a 6 pound piece of ordnance at the distance of three miles. The Minnetarees frequently mentioned this noise like thunder, which they said the mountains made; but we paid no attention to it, believing it to have been some superstition or perhaps a falsehood. The watermen also of the party say that the Pawnees & ⟨Rickaras⟩ Ricaras give the same account of a noise heard in the Black mountains to the westward of them. The solution of the mystery given by the philosophy of the watermen is, that it is occasioned by the bursting of the rich mines of silver contained in the bosom of the mountain.

Lewis & Clark V.1.P292

"While the nation of the Ottoes had their hunting grounds in the shade of the Mountains of the great being:

Mountains of the Setting Sun

Kanzas, Pawnees, Omawhaws, Poncas, Sioux

Very many of the Western Indians believe that the Supreme being has his residence in the Rocky mountains; & some of them make him the sun

Charlevoix ⟨II.180⟩
2d 180, 117.

The spirits that watch by night in the air or chirp in the hollow oak.——
  The tree toad is an object that impresses the Indian with great fear.
Tales of Ind Camp
"The crest of the world (I.E. The Rocky Mount^s)

Lake Timpanogos—The salt lake west of Rocky Mount^s

The Blackfoot believes that the people of his tribe when released from the load of flesh come to a steep mountain, up whose huge projecting sides they have to scramble. After many moons of unwearied labor, tired & exhausted, they reach the top, from which they behold the land of the dead. They see stretched out before them an extensive plain, interspersed with new tents, pitched by the sides of beautiful streams, the banks of which resound with the humming of bees & the music of birds, & are shaded from the summer sun by the ever blooming tree with great white flowers. Some of the tents are pitched upon hills[,] some in valleys, some to meet the whispering breezes of the month of Buds and some the strengthening winds of the Harvest moon.

V 1. 247.

⟨R⟩ Plateau lying between Rocky Mts & Pacific—(a mistake.)

The greater part of the Indians of the Western Continent believe themselves descended from or colonies of the Lenni Lenapes ↑delawares↓ & hence give that tribe the epithet "Grandfather." Several of the tribes have a tradition that they came from beyond the Rocky Mount^s

T. Ind C. V 2. 141

The Mississippi reckoning from the source of the Missouri, its true head
has a course of 4,300 miles. 3,900 of which is navigable for boats.

It has been estimated that the basin of this river has an area of
1 300,000 square miles & that the whole amt of boat navigation afforded
by the river system of which it is the main trunk is nearly 40,000 miles.

Qu. What kind of looking fellow was the Crow chief at the foot of Big
Horn mount[s]?—How dressed?— Did any particular scene take place at
the encampt.

Pike
Longs 1 Travels
Carver

ASTORIA
1835
MEMD; FOR ASTORIA

Everything on a larger scale[—] talk of distances—regions of which we
knew nothing—our city—the casual discoverer[?]—what we inhabited
is a mere nucleus[?]

Jones & Carson? Enquire about the circumstance of meeting with
them—Their previous adventures.

Sickness in the camp on the Big River (5 days after leaving Rikares)[.]
What was the nature of the sickness. How was the weather on the
prairies? did they suffer from flies—musquitoes &c.

Edward Rose & his plans.

In the course of the march after first seeting the Big Horn, ↑mountain↓
they must be kept in sight.

Get a description of the two Crows who visited their camp at the
foot of the Big Horn mountain

The Crow camp—Their tents?

Ship Enterprize. dispatched by Mr Astor in 1809 on a preparatory
or recconnoitering voyage to the NW coast. Returned in 1813. just
on the ⟨eve of a⟩ day before the declaration of war. At that time an

English vessel of war lay off Sandy Hook, overhauling ⟨great[?]⟩ enemy[?] vessels & giving great annoyance to merchts. Mr Barclay ↑British consul,↓ sent to the commander informing him that ⟨he⟩ as ⟨a⟩ the serious & delicate question of peace or war was before congress & the public mind in an excited state his conduct might cause [?] irritation. The commander accordingly ⟨he[?]⟩ ⟨Mr[?]⟩ made[?] sail. As he was going off to search[?] the enterprize Hailed her & asked whence[?] from[?] to [unrecovered]—permitted her to proceed. Shortly after wards the Enterprize spoke a pilot boat, who gave the intelligence ⟨of the⟩ rec^d at NYork that morning from Washington that War was declared—A narrow ⟨[unrecovered]⟩ escape. The cargo of the Enterprize was between 3 and 400,000 Dollars

White Bear

Spanish River?

The Trappers who separated on Mad River to go in couples—What is their mode of hunting & living?

In going down Canoe river—How did they encamp at night? Get a description of their mode of sheltering themselves—disposing of their canoes. Keeping watch &c

Qu. Water ↑of Canoe River↓ light pea green—was it transparent—like glass—How do the beaver build ⟨along⟩ ↑on↓ the Canoe River?—along the banks?

Qu. Particulars of the wreck of the canoe and loss of Clappin?—Character & anecdotes of Clappin.

Qu. Breaking up of Expedition at Caldron Linn. On what terms did parties set out

Arrival of Hunt & party at Astoria—how were they rec^d What condition were they in.

Qu? Carson S'Michel Pierre Delaunay & Pierre Detayé—What became of the latter?

Stuart when robbed of his horses by the Crows had about 2000 miles to haul on foot. "1500 thro' a country wholly unknown as their route lay considerably to the S of that of Lewis & Clarke"

Long. v.1. P. 466

As we approached the mountains we felt, or fancied, a very manifest change in the character of the weather & the temperature of the air. Morng⁵ and evg⁵ were usually calm, & the heat more oppressive than in the middle of the day. Early in the forenoon a light & refreshing breeze often sprung up, blowing from the West or S.W. which again subsided on the approach of night. ⟨We were⟩ ⟨induced⟩ This phenomenon was so often observed that we were induced to attribute it to the operation of the same local cause which, in the neighborhood of the sea, produces a diurnal change in the winds, which blow alternately to and from the shore. The R. Mount⁵ may be considered as forming the shore of that sea of sand, which is traversed by the Platte, & extends northward to the Missouri, above the great bend.

Long. 1. P. 476/7

The rarefication of the air over this great plain, by the reverberation of the suns rays during the day, causes an ascend⁵ current, which is supplied by the rushing down of the condensed air from the mount⁵— ⟨Th⟩ though the sun's rays in the middle of the day were scorching & extremely afflictive to our eyes, the temperature of the air as indicated by the thermometer, had hitherto rarely exceeded 80° Fah.

Idem. 1. 477.

The Big Horn, Ibex & Mountain sheep——are they the same?

Had the party any difficulty with the Crows they first met.

An account of the killing of the first grizzly bear.

Separation of Miller. Crooks' object in returning from Caldron Linn to Henry Fort.

Crooks' meeting with Reed & McKenzie in the Snake River Mts.

The attack upon the Snakes to obtain horses—particulars of it.

Qu. About the affair of Crooks and M Lellan with the Sioux Tetons. Was it one or two years previous to the expedition of Mr Hunt—Was Mr Miller with them—What were the particulars

INDEX

Aiken (Aitken), Job, 52, 53, 54
Akai-chi Indians, 226, 380n.
American Fur Company, 17, 60, 64, 307, 337, 359, 360-62, 364
Annian, Straits of, 20, 384n.
Arapaho (Arapahay) Indians, 268, 298f., 380n.
Arikara (Arickara) Indians, 127, 129, 132, 138, 143, 147, 381n.
Ashley, William Henry, 364, 393n.
Astor, John Jacob, ix, xf., 3, 15-16, 21f., 30f., 253f., 256, 307f., 326, 327, 337, 355, 361, 364, 378n.
Astoria, Fort, 23, 72, 81, 231, 235f., 243, 245, 256, 324, 327, 338, 348, 353, 365

Baker's Bay, 56, 58, 62, 239, 255, 346
Baranoff (Baranov, Baranhoff), Count Aleksandr Andreevich, 331f., 392n.
Beaver, 253, 254, 256, 308, 315, 316, 323, 325, 327, 330, 331, 354
Bering Sea (Sea of Kamschatka), 333
Biddle, Captain James, 353, 393n.
Biddle, Nicholas, 394n., 492-93
Big Horn Mountains, 168, 183
Big Horn River, 160
Big Man (Arikara chief), 138, 143
Big River, 156, 163
Black, Captain William, 346, 393n.
Blackbird (Omaha chief), 112f.
Blackfeet Indians, 90, 101, 153, 279, 280, 381n.
Black Hills, 146, 151, 157, 166, 168, 169, 174
"Bloody Ground, The," 23, 128, 388n.
Blue Mountains, 261, 263
Bonneville, Captain Benjamin L. E., xiii, 364, 370
Bonneville, Lake, *see* Great Salt Lake
Boone (Boon), Daniel, 101
Brackenridge (Breckenridge), Henry Marie, 4, 135, 137, 154, 383n.
Bradbury, John, 4, 107, 119-21, 125, 135, 154, 383n.
Brevoort, Henry, Jr., ix
British Columbia (New Caledonia), 24
Broughton, Lieutenant William Robert, 19, 67, 384n.
Brownson, Lieutenant John, 105, 305

Brugiere, Regis, 81-82
Burnt River (Woodpile Creek), 264

Caldron Linn, 198, 245, 390n.
Cannon (Canning), William, 170
Canton, China, 19, 22, 254, 307, 315, 365
Cape Disappointment, 52, 53, 56, 61, 239, 255, 346
Cape de Verd Islands, 37
Cape Horn, 40, 346
Carriere, Michael (Michel), 220, 221, 224-25
Carson, Alexander, 119, 130, 162, 190, 266
Carver, Captain Jonathan, 20, 384n.
Cass, Martin H., 192, 268, 314
Cathlamah (Cathlamet) Indians, 56f., 239f., 381n.
Cathlasco Indians, 246, 381n.
Celilo Falls, *see* Falls of the Columbia
Chauncey, Commodore Isaac, 327, 392n.
Cheyenne (Sheyenne, Shienne) Indians, 147, 157-58, 381n.
Cheyenne River, 147, 157, 166, 278, 291, 295
Chinook Indians, 56f., 239f., 315, 328f., 381n.
Chipunnish (Chopunnish) Indians, *see* Nez Percé Indians
Clappine, Antoine, 198, 199
Clark (Clarke), William, 4, 21, 65, 383n., 384n.
Clarke, John, 254, 255, 256, 310f., 317, 320f., 324, 325, 342, 350-51, 378n.
Clatsop Indians, 56f., 239f., 381n.
Coffin, Mount, 67, 386n.
Coles, John, 52, 54
Colter, John, 101-104, 388n.
Columbia River, ix, 51, 56, 226, 229, 236, 362
Comanche (Camanche) Indians, 153
Comcomly, 58f., 62, 239, 315, 328, 329, 347, 348-49, 386n.
Cook, Captain James, 18, 41, 44
Cootonai Indians, 311
Coureurs des Bois, 7-9, 27
Cowlitz (Cowleskee) River, 67
Cox, Ross, 4, 325, 378n., 384n.